Praise for *Sea of Eden*
Winner of the National Critics Award, 2014

'Andrés Ibáñez is an extraordinary novelist. *Sea of Eden* is outlandish, un-expected, unusual… [this] masterpiece situates the author comfortably alongside Roberto Bolaño.'

ABC Cultural

'A work of great experience and enlightenment, unique not only in the landscape of recent Spanish literature but, I would argue, across our entire literary history. Pure literary magic, of the kind we encounter only in the work of great talents.'

Revista de Libros

'A literary wonder of unbridled fantasy and imagination.'

Diario de Lecturas

'An excellent and entertaining novel… A story of feeling and passion in which love, friendship, eroticism, hatred, suspicion, pleasure and pain are always present, not to mention humour.'

Babelia

'A book that will fill many hours with pleasurable, entertaining, philo-sophical reading.'

El Placer de la Lectura

'One of the most necessary, ambitious and, yes, fun novels published in Spanish (or, indeed, in any language) in the past few decades.'

Notodo.com

SEA
OF
EDEN

ANDRÉS IBÁÑEZ

Translated by Sophie Hughes

ONEWORLD

A Oneworld Book

First published in the United Kingdom, Ireland and Australia
by Oneworld Publications, 2023

ISBN 978-1-78607-920-6
eISBN 978-1-78607-921-3

Printed and bound in Great Britain by Clays Ltd, Elcograf S.p.A

GOBIERNO
DE ESPAÑA

MINISTERIO
DE CULTURA
Y DEPORTE

This work has been published with a subsidy
from the Ministry of Culture and Sport of Spain

Oneworld Publications
10 Bloomsbury Street
London WC1B 3SR
England

MIX
Paper from
responsible sources
FSC
www.fsc.org   FSC® C018072

For Mariajo

1

Our plane goes down

M*any would later maintain that* they'd spotted the island from the air a few minutes before we crashed. That would mean from an altitude of around ten thousand metres, although it's possible the plane had already been descending for some time. I don't know. I didn't see it. The fact is that at some point during our flight, somewhere over the middle of the Pacific Ocean – by my calculations, somewhere around the 170th meridian – the plane's electrical systems failed. We passengers knew straight away something was wrong. Our video screens cut out, as did the LED lights you see dotted around planes, and the air vents stopped pumping out their streams of ice-cold air. The people using the bathroom started banging on the doors, finding themselves suddenly trapped in the dark. It was like nothing we'd ever experienced before: not only was the cabin suddenly plunged into darkness, but everyone's electrical devices had stopped working too, including people's laptops, mobile phones and games consoles. None of these things were too serious, of course, but the problem was the aircraft's navigation system had also cut out. All of a sudden, the plane – a Boeing 747 with almost four hundred passengers on board – was a rock hurtling through the air, propelled solely by its own weight.

I remember how quickly it all happened, and how little time it took us to realise that something was terribly wrong. The flight attendants were running up and down the aisles and bellowing at each other from opposite ends of the plane. Neither the loudspeakers nor the intercom were working, which meant the cockpit door had to be opened for the co-pilot to call out instructions to the flight staff. The news spread through the plane like wildfire, from the seats in First Class on the upper floor, down through Business Class and then right to the Economy seats in the tail end. *The electrics have failed! The engines have stopped! If the system failure isn't resolved in a few minutes, we'll have to make an emergency landing on the water.*

I'd never actually believed that a jet could land on the sea. I'd always thought that those instructions they give on what to do in the event of landing on water were either fantastically delusional or there to reassure us. I'd never heard of a plane having technical problems and successfully landing in the middle of the ocean. I'd always imagined that the most likely outcome was that the plane would smash into the waves and sink to the bottom of the sea with all its passengers on board. I've since looked it up (I wanted to know if what happened to us had ever happened anywhere else in the world; or, to put it another way, if what happened to us had actually happened), and, sure enough, I discovered that there have been very few occasions where commercial aircraft, huge airliners, have had to land on the sea, and that the majority of those cases ended in tragedy. With one well-known exception: the emergency landing of the US Airways Airbus A320 on the Hudson River in 2009. This was a special case for three reasons: first, because the jet had just taken off from La Guardia airport and was therefore still travelling fairly slowly, at a low altitude; second, because a river is a particularly flat and calm body of water; and third, because within five minutes of landing, the plane was surrounded by rescue boats. But not even this success story went entirely to plan: the rubber rafts inflated, but most of the passengers couldn't reach one and so climbed out onto the aircraft's wings where they piled on top of one another, the water creeping up their legs and the plane rapidly sinking as the rescue boats rushed to save them. Many of the passengers hadn't put on their life jackets. If they had been in the middle of the sea, help wouldn't have reached them anything like as fast and they would all have drowned.

And yet, when I heard that we were going to have to ditch the plane, I didn't feel scared exactly. More like excited, nervous. There was the sea below us. You could see it from the windows. The only thing we had to do was descend towards that blue surface and touch down on it.

The flight attendants were standing in the aisles, calling for calm, telling us to fasten our seatbelts and not to leave our seats. We were experiencing 'technical difficulties', they told us. The passengers bombarded them with questions. One man even got to his feet and demanded to speak directly with the captain. But beyond this chaos, the thing I most remember is the silence. It's not that the travellers had fallen quiet; plenty of people were talking, some were screaming. I mean the silence of the machines. The sheer horror of hearing a machine fall silent when you know that your life depends on it! Both the jet engines and the air vents were completely quiet. I'd never fully appreciated how noisy planes are until that moment. Even from the isolation of the cabin, the engine's racket is deafening.

Around me, my fellow passengers were screaming and wailing. Some were praying. Several times the wind tipped the plane upwards before letting it fall again. It was a truly awful sensation just to free-fall, with no engines to propel us, no landing gear, no protection whatsoever; only the increasing, terrifying certainty of what awaited us below. A raging world of wind and waves. A blue abyss lit only by the glow of floating jellyfish. The young woman next to me was so petrified that she'd turned completely white. 'I'm scared,' she whispered. It was the first thing she'd said to me throughout the whole flight. I had a couple on my left – a man and woman of colour. The man had undone his seatbelt, and from the way he was sitting, he seemed about to bolt off down the aisle. One of the flight attendants marched up to him and chided: 'If you don't put your seatbelt on and stay in your seat, you are going to die.' I think it was only then, in that moment, that I began to realise the gravity of the situation. 'What?' the man asked. He was tall and well built, and dressed in an elegant blue suit with gold cufflinks in his shirtsleeves. His name was Ngwane. His wife was Omotola. They were Nigerians, and worked in the film industry back home. Obviously I found all this out later. 'When the plane hits the water, the impact will be terrible,' the flight attendant explained to Ngwane with glacial composure.

'If you don't have your seatbelt on, you'll come flying out of your seat and smash your skull.' I looked at the flight attendant's badge. She was called Eileen.

'Eileen,' I said, 'have you ever had to land on water before?'

She turned and looked at me blankly, then checked I had my seatbelt on and said: 'Put your hands on the seat in front and rest your forehead on them.'

'Eileen,' I repeated, 'have you ever seen anything like this?'

'Nobody's ever seen anything like this,' she snapped. 'But we've been trained for every eventuality.' And I could see that she was truly terrified, far more so than the others.

Parents put their children's life jackets on them. Several women were crying. You could hear prayers being spoken in different languages, offered up to a host of different gods. In that moment, all the names for God sounded the same; they all sounded like the name of a dog in the distance, a grey dog who turned back and looked on, vaguely surprised by what he had done. The young woman next to me was so pale I thought she was going to faint.

'Please, please, please,' she murmured.

'What's your name?' I asked her. 'Look at me,' I said. 'What's your name?'

'Swayla,' she said. 'Swayla Sanders.'

'I'm John,' I told her. 'John Barbarin.'

'John,' she said, 'are we going to die?'

Some planes, I later discovered, have a backup emergency system that kicks in when the electrics fail. Small turbines that unfold in the wings and work as a kind of air-activated propeller to generate electricity from wind. Really well thought through, cheap and environmentally friendly, you might say. And you would be right. But the problem with our plane wasn't mechanical, as I've explained, and even though the turbines did open and the propellers did begin to turn at full pelt, absolutely no electricity was produced. All my knowledge of these technical details came from Luigi Campanella, the Italian engineer.

At the precise moment it hit the water, the plane was moving at around four hundred kilometres per hour, which, as any aeronautic aficionado will tell you, is one hell of a speed to touch down at, even in normal circumstances. The collision was so violent I was knocked out cold. What's more, the plane entered the sea at a slight angle. The first things to touch the water were the left-hand engines; two immense cylinders that caused a tremendous blow the second they clipped the sea's surface, and then, as the wing sank into the water and snapped off, broke the fuselage into three pieces.

At four hundred kilometres per hour, the water's surface is rock solid. I remember having seen our own cross-like shadow from the window, advancing at breakneck speed across the sea. It felt like that shadow was moving much faster than the plane itself, and that any minute it might pull away from us and speed off into the distance. In fact, it was getting closer and closer. It was coming to meet us. At a certain point, we had drawn too close even to see it.

I felt a violent jolt, and then fell into a kind of bottomless pit, a gentle, silent drop down into the night. I don't know how long I was out for. A few minutes, I imagine, although it felt like an eternity.

2

We reach the island

The first thing I saw on opening my eyes was a large, triangular strip of clear blue sky and a heron with long white wings gliding smoothly across it. I was very disoriented, and couldn't work out what was happening or where I was, but I had the vague impression that neither the sky nor the bird were where they were supposed to be. My head was muddled: wasn't I a bird? Hadn't I just been travelling in a bird? Was I, in fact, that very bird I was seeing? Around me everyone was screaming. It was blisteringly hot in the plane, like the inside of a preheated oven. Even worse was the pernicious, stifling humidity. In those first moments of confusion, I attributed the heat to the accident, and hoped, somewhat ridiculously, that the temperature would begin to cool down now that the plane had ditched into the sea.

And cutting through that heat, the screams. As I came back to my senses, the screaming became gradually clearer. They were screams in different languages: English, Spanish, Hindi and French. But what really struck me were all the different timbres and pitches of anguish and pain. The howls of the wounded, the shrieks of those whose bodies had been smashed to pieces, or who'd turned in their seat to find their loved one dead beside them. There were also people screaming and wailing in a state of absolute hysteria. I looked down at my body. A bright red Samsonite suitcase had fallen from somewhere and burst open, emptying its contents all over me. A few objects had landed on my ribs, others on my face, leaving me covered in cuts and bruises. The suitcase must have belonged to a rabbi because it contained, among countless other items, Torah scrolls with their dark blue velvet covers, two brass-tipped wooden handles (one of which had smacked me in the chin) and silver, bell-shaped decorative rimonim, along with a brass Hanukkah menorah.

I couldn't work out where all that stuff had come from, and how such chaos could have broken out in a matter of mere seconds. At least I was in one piece. I wasn't injured. I touched my head, my body and legs. A few bruises, a bump caused by one of the gold jars, a cut on my chin, perhaps from one of the little bells on the rimonim. With trembling fingers I removed the rest of the items from my lap and tried to unfasten my seatbelt. It took a while because I was shaking so hard; it was as if my brain couldn't connect properly to my nerves and muscles. I looked around. Ngwane, the man who had been sitting on my left, was now in a strange position on the floor in the aisle: head down with his legs up on the arm and backrest of one of the seats so that his patent leather shoes were pointing up towards the sky. Omotola, his wife, wouldn't stop crying for help. I looked to my right. Swayla was completely still, her head slumped. I shook her on the shoulder, then lifted her head and said her name aloud several times. She didn't look hurt. She opened her eyes. I asked her if she was okay. She didn't understand. She looked about her like a crazed animal. Meanwhile, the chaos around us was mounting as the passengers began getting to their feet to evacuate the plane.

'Swayla,' I said, 'are you able to stand? Can you walk? We have to get out of here.'

Standing up turned out to be no easy task, because the plane tilted slightly to the left. Seats had smashed right into one another, and in some sections entire overhead compartments had come away from the body of the plane, injuring and in some instances killing passengers. Some seats had also become dislodged, and the metal bars that had once held them down were now lethal weapons, and had gored some passengers and dismembered others. But something else had happened too. Like I said before (and this was the reason for the fraction of sky blue I'd seen when I opened my eyes), the impact on the fuselage as it landed had been so violent that the body of the plane had broken into three. One of the fractures was just a few metres along from where I was sitting. The plane's body had snapped open on the left-hand side, but not entirely split off, leaving a gaping hole around five metres long at its widest part. When I sat up in my chair, holding onto the back of the seat in front for balance, I saw that through the hole not only could you see the sky, but also the calm sea and, a couple of hundred metres in the distance, the horizon, a beach with coconut trees. We had somehow managed to land on the sea, and we were close to the coast.

My first priority was to help the man who'd fallen into the aisle to my left. 'Please,' his wife was screaming, 'please, help me.' There was a man sitting in the seat right in front of me. He seemed very tall, had a shaved head and was around fifty-five. I think the suitcase of Jewish curios that had landed on top of me had also hit him on the way down because he had a gash on the crown of his head. I realised, though, that he was conscious, and clearly distressed, looking wide-eyed from left to right. What I didn't understand was why he stayed in his seat without even trying to get out of it.

'Give me a hand,' I said, prodding him on the shoulder. He might have been conscious, but he was also in a state of severe shock. 'You and I are going to pick this man here off the floor.'

'Believe me, I'd like to!' he said, his voice loud and unwavering.

'Are you hurt?' I asked.

'No, no, I'm fine,' he said. 'I'm not hurt.'

'So *help me* pick up this man,' I said. 'That way we can clear the aisle for the others.'

The man obstructing the aisle, Ngwane, had fallen directly beside the man in front, who without so much as moving in his chair, began to tug on one of Ngwane's arms. It would have made far more sense to get up and take Ngwane under both arms and sit him up. It was pretty clear from his posture that Ngwane was dead. What I was trying to do was to place his body in one of the window seats to leave the aisle free and allow other passengers to get off. The feeble contribution of the man in front was of little help to me. I couldn't understand what he was doing.

'Get up!' I shouted. 'I can't do a thing if you just sit there!'

'I can't get up,' he said, clearly very agitated. He turned around to face me. I'll never forget those blue eyes. When I close my own eyes to fall asleep there they are, watching me, scrutinising me, each of them containing their own azure world.

I assumed he was trapped, so I stepped over the man on the floor in the aisle to see if I could help him. But the bald man was comfortably seated in his place and there was nothing, at least as far as I could tell, stopping him from getting up. A backlog of passengers was beginning to form in the aisle. Someone else helped me to pick the dead man off the floor, and together we were able to lift him into one of the seats by the wing, bending his legs and leaving him in the fetal position. I was shocked by just how easily a man that sturdy and stylish could have died. The dead man's wife tried to help us too, all the while wailing and calling out her husband's name: Ngwane, Ngwane, Ngwane. But Ngwane was dead. He died in exactly the way the flight attendant had told him he would, flying out of his seat on impact and crushing his neck.

I walked towards the opening in the plane, taking care not to be dragged down by the hysterical passengers elbowing their way through to get there, many of them carrying their luggage. The fuselage was ripped almost completely open at one point, revealing a complete cross-section of the plane's main body, like a cutaway diagram. Above was the main cabin where the passengers travelled, with its three seating classes; and then there was the hold below, which was rapidly filling up with seawater. At that point I thought we were done for. If the fuselage had remained in one piece the plane could have floated for a while, but as it was, water was rushing into the plane like a river. Any minute now the cabin would be completely submerged and we'd all be drowned. And after we'd landed right by a coast!

Some passengers jumped into the water and began to swim away, but were dragged under by the force of the water rushing into the plane. Some of them grabbed onto the fuselage. You could see that those who jumped in with their luggage were being hauled under with it, but even then some of them wouldn't give up their belongings. And despite this chaos, passengers continued to jump into the water from both ends of the plane. Not everyone was wearing a life jacket, and plenty of people leapt in without even looking to see who was in the water beneath them, which meant that those who'd already jumped ran the risk of having someone fall on top of them if they didn't swim away from the plane straight away. On top of this, we were all fully dressed, and not exactly in lightweight clothes. Those who plunged into the water wearing trousers and sweaters were quickly weighed down by their sopping clothes. Most of the passengers still on board had put on their life jackets, and plenty had inflated them, making them even less mobile. But how do you convince someone who doesn't know how to swim not to inflate their life jacket before jumping into the water?

A flight attendant appeared on the other side of the break in the plane. It was the same woman from before: Eileen. She was around thirty-five and had lipstick and dark eyeshadow on.

'We have to open the doors to release the rafts!' she shouted. And then, looking at me, she added: 'You! Look for men!'

'There's no time!' I said. 'The plane's going to sink!'

'We've already touched the bottom,' Eileen said. 'It's not going to sink and it's not going to fill up with water. Do you understand?'

'It's not going to sink?'

'No.'

'Are you sure?'

'What's your name?'

'John Barbarin. John.'

'My name's Eileen Stevens. You have to open the emergency door to release the raft. Then look for more men and organise the evacuation. Have you got that, John?'

'Yes, Eileen.'

I don't know what it was about her, or her voice, that made me trust her. I turned around and worked out that the emergency door was five rows behind me. But I needed help, and next thing I heard myself shouting at the top of my voice: 'I need help! Anyone who's not looking after some-one, stay where you are, don't move.'

'It's going to explode!' a woman next to me screamed. 'We have to get out or we'll all die!'

'The plane isn't going to sink and it's not going to explode,' I heard Eileen shout. 'You need to remain calm.'

A man came striding up the aisle behind Eileen and shoved past her. She lost her balance and fell into the water. She tried to get back on the plane but it proved impossible because the people diving into the water were scrambling and clinging onto her, and in the end she was forced to swim off in the direction of the beach. The man who had pushed her, a blond-haired, athletic-looking thirty-something, was holding a tennis racket in its case. Our eyes met for a second before he jumped into the water. For a split second he seemed startled, as if I'd caught him in some devious act. Then he smirked and winked at me. And just before leaping into the sea with his racket, he said something I'll never forget:

'Sayonara!'

It was Jimmy Bruëll.

Water was fast beginning to fill up the cabin. I thought our chances of opening the doors and releasing the rafts were getting worse by the min-ute, but I knew that we'd have to find a way if we were to save as many people as possible. To this day I don't know how or why I was able to think so clearly and act with such composure. Why didn't I become hysterical like everyone else?

The bald man was still sitting in his seat, unmoving. I grabbed him by the shoulder and shouted at him to get up and help me. He stared at me with his blue eyes, so pale I felt I might look straight through them. He began to get up, supporting his long muscular arms on the arm-rests. At this point I realised he really was very tall, considerably taller than me. I asked him his name, and he told me it was Wade Erickson. And then something extraordinary happened: for the first time, some-one *smiled* on board the plane wreck. First I saw him looking at me with his eyes wide open in astonishment, a look I couldn't quite decipher. And then I saw his smile. A smile of intense happiness, I'd say almost of peace.

'Let's go,' I said. 'We have to get the door open.'

I clambered across rows of seats, stepping on lifeless bodies and arm-rests, and Wade took the aisle, moving slowly with that same wide grin on his face. Despite his gargantuan height (he was practically a giant) and the logjam down the aisle, he was able to catch up with me. When we reached the emergency door I pulled hard on the bright red handle and a large inflatable orange raft immediately burst forth in front of us.

'We've already hit the seabed,' I told him. 'The plane won't sink.'

'Are you sure?' Wade asked me.

'You can see the rocks right there,' I said. 'It can't be more than four metres deep.'

Wade poked his head out of the open door.

'You get on the raft, take it to the shore and come back,' Wade said. 'I'll stay here and get all this in order.'

'There's a raft!' the passengers were shouting.

'You need to keep calm,' I shouted back. 'We're going to do a series of trips. The children and injured first. You,' I said, gripping a young man by the arm, 'stay here and help Wade.'

'Okay, man,' he said in heavily accented English. 'But in that case my girlfriend's getting on the raft.'

His girlfriend was standing behind him, a dark-skinned girl with long hair. She didn't want to jump onto the raft, but she had little choice, be-cause the people behind were pushing her. We recruited one more man of around forty who agreed to stand in the doorway next to Wade and the younger guy to oversee the boarding of the raft. We quickly introduced ourselves and shook hands. The older man told us his name was Joseph Langdon, the young one was called Christian and, as I later found out, he was Chilean. Our most pressing task was to stop people from leaping onto the raft and pulling on one another, and to make sure the raft didn't get overloaded and capsize, leaving the injured passengers to drown. Then there was the added problem of those who had already inflated their life jackets. They took up so much space that between them they blocked the way, and I even saw people having little scraps. Slowly but surely, the raft filled up. I jumped in last. We wanted to make absolutely sure that the raft came back to the plane after its first trip, which meant one of us had to go with it. The raft was kitted out with two pairs of oars, and we were able to row to the coast with relative ease. You could already see some figures on the beach, the first travellers arriving there after having swum the distance separating the plane from terra firma. We picked up more swimmers along the way, although a few unpleasant scenes ensued when we had to stop more people getting onto the raft, which was already carrying far more than the safe number of passengers, and whose sides were sinking hazardously into the water. I also spotted Eileen, who was swimming towards the beach.

'Eileen!' I shouted.

She looked at me and gave me a thumbs-up. I wondered how she was able to swim with her uniform on, with that jacket and pencil skirt. Even the little cap was still perched on her head, fixed with pins.

The colour of the water was unlike anything I'd seen before. Not blue, not green, but a perfect combination of the two. It was radiant turquoise, a colour so exquisite I thought it was the most beautiful thing I'd ever laid my eyes on; the colour of a peacock's train transformed into the living skin of the sea. Staring into the water, the turquoise colour morphed into a rich green that glimmered with flecks of gold, lilac and pink. It was supernaturally clear, so that even from some five metres up, you could see the rectangular shadow of our raft on the sandy bed, as well as the concentric lines made by the oars as they entered the water. A shoal of black and white fish moved as one below us, joined soon after by a large pink creature that flapped its fins gently as it swam on alone. About a hundred metres ahead it was shallow enough to stand, so the swimmers could do the last part walking along the ocean floor. I wasn't responsible for any of the four oars on the raft, which left me free to take in everything around me. The sun was burning my arms and face, but after being stuck on the plane, it felt glorious to be out in the open, breathing in big gulps of sea air. Marine birds were flying above us screeching their desolate, mournful cries. I spotted frigates, gulls, cormorants and herons, and in the distance a pelican soaring just above the surface of the water.

I turned around and contemplated the plane that had just crashed down to earth. It was a strange and terrifying scene. The plane, or rather its remains, its corpse, appeared lodged in the sea, a shining white body that looked totally out of place in the middle of the deserted tropical setting in that forgotten corner of the world. Only two of its three broken parts were visible, separated by the gaping crack that had opened up just a few metres ahead of my seat. The right wing, facing out to the open sea, was still intact, pointing up to the sky and with its two jets also where they should be. But the left wing had disappeared. I guessed it had sunk somewhere between the main body of the plane and the coast, perhaps just beneath us, although that didn't turn out to be the case. Hitting the water's surface it had ripped completely off and flown hundreds of metres away. It was the impact of that violent blow that had had a kind of levering effect on the steel, which bent and ripped off as if it were paper. The third chunk of plane, the tail end, was nowhere to be seen. In fact, a good part of the back end was missing, and with it the passengers who had been seated there. To the east, the coastline cut off the view of the sea beyond, and I imagined that the tail must be somewhere over there, on the other side of the headland of the bay where we had fallen. Once severed from the rest of the plane, the tail must have filled with water and sunk in a matter of minutes.

I turned back to take a closer look at the coast. We were still far from the shore but the water was at waist height, meaning that those swimming could now comfortably wade. I spotted a fish nearby, and it seemed to observe me blankly. Its tameness suggested that it had never encountered a fisherman. It was a strange shape, which reminded me of the coelacanths I'd seen as a child in a Willy Ley book about fantastical animals: large scales, fleshy lobes at the base of its fins and a rounded tail like a fan emerging from its body.

It didn't take us long to get to the beach, where many of the survivors were already standing on the sand, staring back at the plane, and protecting themselves from the fierce tropical sun under the shade of the coconut trees. The beach was about two kilometres end to end and fairly wide; the bright sand was made up of pulverised mollusc shells, and was so pale, almost white, that it hurt your eyes. Behind the ample stretch of sand began the jungle: first coconut palms dotted here and there, and then the thick tropical vegetation above which, a little to the west, you could make out the outline of the mountains that glowed indigo in the distance. I was surprised to see those mountains, and wondered whether behind them there might be more even taller peaks, hidden in the clouds. It was an island, without a doubt, but it felt like a very big one. I asked myself which it might be, given that west of Hawaii, with the exception of a few atolls that barely peep out of the water, there is virtually no land until you reach the Maloelap or Wotje Atolls, or the Marshall Islands. But we weren't in the Marshalls, and less likely still in Polynesia. We couldn't have got that far. According to my calculations (based on the moving map on my screen on the plane, which I always watch obsessively during long-haul flights), we had to be around one thousand four hundred kilometres south-east of Hawaii, in an all but uninhabited part of the ocean. What's more, the little land there was in that part of the world – for example, the Johnston Atoll, a speck of territory barely three kilometres long in the middle of the Pacific – was coral, not volcanic like the island we'd landed up on.

When we got to the beach, I jumped out of the raft into the water to help carry off the injured, the children and elderly passengers. That was the moment I first set foot on the island. We hauled the raft onto the shore and I walked a few metres until I was under the shade of the coconut trees. The place was strangely still. You could hear the gentle rushing of the waves, the whistle of the wind, the distant caws of marine birds, but that was it. It was like the silence of paradise, or perhaps the silence that exists in the land of the dead.

3

We rescue the injured

We *were all convinced that* the helicopters wouldn't take long to show up, and that within a few short hours we would be receiving medical assistance, if not already safely on some cargo ship on our way to be repatriated. However, the hours passed and no rescue materialised. Our devices were now working normally again, but our mobile phones had no signal, so were all but useless. The radios weren't picking up any signal either; just static, which was bizarre, given that long-wave radio programmes can be heard in outer space. It gave us the feeling of having ended up in the most remote, isolated place on earth.

And yet, a Boeing 747 loaded with passengers can't be that easily overlooked. International air traffic control and radars in plenty of countries would know our exact position. Having lost radio contact with the aircraft, and worse still, its signal on their radars, they would have guessed that something terrible had happened and immediately raised the alarm. But hours passed and nobody came.

I made plenty of runs with the raft back and forth between the plane and the coast. We tried opening the other emergency doors to release the remaining rafts, but to no avail. They'd been rendered useless by the crash, so we had to make do with just one. By now it was clear that the plane wasn't going to sink. It perched motionless among the rich coral reefs in waters six or seven metres deep.

Slowly but surely, we transported all of the surviving passengers to the beach. Moving the wounded was hardest of all. Anguished, imploring voices could be heard coming from all over the plane. Wade, Joseph and

Christian had recruited some more passengers to help pull everyone who was still alive out of the debris, in some cases with terrible injuries or impaled by chunks of steel. I noticed that Joseph had taken charge of the situation, and it occurred to me that he might be a doctor.

'Surgeon,' he replied when I asked him. 'Saint Vincent Hospital, Los Angeles. Harvard medical school.'

'I found another doctor on the beach,' I told him. 'A woman.'

He asked me what kind of a doctor she was and I told him I didn't know. Then he said, perfectly seriously, that he hoped she wasn't a psychiatrist, and I felt a sudden burst of affection for this man who, in the middle of the chaos, was cool enough to crack a joke. He said we had to find as many medical supplies as we could. We looked for the plane's first aid kits and loaded them onto the raft. There were still lots of passengers waiting to be transported to dry land, but by now it was clear that the plane was stable and that there was no immediate danger of it sinking. In successive trips we got all the wounded to the shore. Joseph stayed on land to see to the most urgent cases, and he instructed me to bring all the clothes, blankets, material and paper napkins I could find, as well as belts, which is how I wound up undoing and removing trousers and skirts from dead bodies. Later, I saw that Joseph used the belts to make tourniquets and secure broken bones. It never would have occurred to me that a belt could have so many uses. We set about moving the wounded under the shade of the coconut trees, lying or sitting them directly on the sand. There were a fair number of serious injuries. Joseph told me that many of the survivors would have internal bleeding and would almost certainly die. Others might survive if we were rescued and they received medical assistance soon. In any event, Joseph went on, the number of fatalities was growing by the hour.

Since then, I've thought many times about how Joseph could tell, just by glancing at the injured in those first moments, who was going to die over the course of the following hour. He must have been able to tell who would hold out for five or six hours, or for two or three days, who would die in peace, in a gentle stupor, and which poor souls were destined to suffer horrific pain and die with screams of agony.

By this point, we all saw Joseph as a kind of saviour, a gift from above. He had boundless energy and unflagging ingenuity in his use of the rudimentary tools at his disposal. He had black scraggly hair, squinty eyes and a friendly face. You could tell that he was used to seeing death and soothing patients on a daily basis, able to remain calm when faced with the most difficult situation. Even so, the lack of equipment and painkillers exasperated him.

The other doctor on the beach was Roberta, a forty-something Canadian with a prematurely lined face. She was a paediatrician and didn't have much surgical experience, but it was reassuring to know that there were at least two doctors among us. Three, if you counted Roberta's husband, an elegant and distinguished gentleman called Bentley, who was indeed a psychiatrist. But even he was able to admit that he knew very little about general medicine, let alone surgery. If we became depressed, or started hearing voices in our head, or if we thought we saw faces spying on us from behind the trees then he might be able to help us. If only we'd known. Two pairs of glasses hung from a string around his neck, and he had a third pair of rose-tinted sunglasses, all of which, God knows how, he'd had the presence of mind to bring off the plane with him. He'd also managed to save his pipe, a packet of tobacco and his *Herald Tribune.* At the time it seemed completely ridiculous that he should have brought his newspaper with him in the raft, but within a matter of hours I'd learnt just how many purposes a newspaper can have when you're lacking the most basic commodities.

The plane's passengers held a few surprises. To my astonishment, a group of Spaniards had been travelling on the plane. More surprising still, I knew several of them, but had missed them as I rushed to board the plane last minute in Los Angeles.

And there was my old friend Ignacio! How many years had it been since I'd seen him? Fourteen, at least. I couldn't believe my eyes when I spotted him leaning out of the plane door waiting for the raft to pick him up. Was that really Ignacio Recalde, my old partner in crime from the Conservatory days? And was that Idoya next to him? When they spotted me, their faces, like mine, collapsed in utter shock and disbelief.

'Juan Barbarín!' Ignacio shouted. 'What on earth are you doing here?'

We lowered as many of the wounded as we could into the life raft and then Ignacio and Idoya jumped in. On the way to the beach they told me they had been travelling to India as part of a 'spiritual journey'.

'What kind of spiritual journey?' I asked, distracted by Idoya's beauty. She was about thirty now, and still wore her hair in plaits and had the same rosy blush to her cheeks she had at twenty, when I was secretly in love with her. Ignacio told me they were on their way to Rishikesh to visit Swami Kailashananda's ashram. Swami Kailashananda was Julián's guru.

'Julián?' I asked. 'Julián Fuentes?'

'Yes,' he said, adding that Julián had also been on our flight. Plus Matilde, and a few others I knew. Pedro, Eulalia and Joaquín, Cristina's cousin. So we were all there, the old crew! Cristina herself might even be there, I thought, given that most of them knew her, and one of them was family. I couldn't get my head around the reappearance of these ghosts from my past, but the circumstances were so extraordinary that nothing could shock me any more.

It took me by surprise to hear those words again, words I thought belonged to my past: *ashram*, *swami*, and Rishikesh, the Yoga Capital of the World, located on the Ganges in the foothills of the Himalayas. They brought back memories of years gone by, when we were all young and Cristina and I were a couple.

Ignacio seemed content, a strange kind of contentedness that almost troubled me as we rowed, in turns, towards the shore, me throwing furtive glances at Idoya, who seemed totally calm about the whole situation, leaning on the edge of the inflatable life raft like someone enjoying their holidays, squinting her eyes while she gazed at the island.

'It's been a long journey,' he said. 'First we travelled to Mexico and spent a month there. Then New York for two weeks. Then Los Angeles to take a course. And it was there we decided to come to India. This flight was so cheap. Global Orbit flights are so cheap...'

'Right, and look what you get,' I said, pointing to the plane wreck.

'None of this is Global Orbit's fault,' one of the other passengers piped up in Spanish, but with a strong accent I couldn't quite place. 'This was no technical fault.'

'Ah, no?' Ignacio asked. 'So what was it then?'

'An electromagnetic problem,' the man said. 'All the electrical equipment went off. Nothing to do with the plane.'

We sat there in silence. The man apologised for having butted in. I told him no problem, that we were all upset and on edge. With my perfect American manners I introduced myself, as did he: Luigi Campanella, an engineer from Milan.

'What kind of engineer?' I asked.

'The engine-building kind,' he said. 'Car and lorry engines.'

He was about seventy, with a thick head of blond white hair, black-framed glasses, a hook nose and a reddish, leathery face scored with deep lines. He was small and jumpy and I wanted to like him.

I turned around to look at Idoya and caught her staring at me. She smiled and asked me how I was and why I had been on my way to India. I explained that the University of Calcutta had invited me to give a two-week composition workshop. The usual questions followed, their sole purpose being to find out whether or not I was a famous composer. I reeled off words like Oakland and Rhode Island, and mentioned my Quartet No. 3, which had been premiered in the New York Public Library by the Emerson String Quartet no less. It was my greatest accomplishment to date. Ignacio was impressed to hear that the Emerson Quartet had played my music. But we had more pressing concerns just then than our professional achievements or tender looks from old girlfriends.

The job of rescuing the injured and transferring them onto the life raft was becoming increasingly difficult. Joseph was needed on land, and between us we barely had a clue about how to lift or move those suffering bodies. On top of that, the volunteers didn't generally last long. The heat inside the plane was unbearable, barely tempered by the occasional breeze that entered through the open tail and the gaping section in the middle of the fuselage. It was especially hard rescuing the First Class passengers, whom we had to bring down the spiral staircase. We helped a Swiss couple, who we practically carried in our arms to the raft only to discover that they didn't have a scratch on them (they were the Kunzes, who I'll come to later), and a forty-something attractive blonde woman whose face was familiar. She wasn't hurt, but she was frozen with panic.

4

Joseph Langdon. The aftermath of the crash

Most of the wounded died instantly from contusions of their vital organs, including severe brain injuries. Many were crushed to death by seats or cases that fell from the overhead lockers. Others were knocked unconscious. In the absence of oxygenated blood, the brain starts sending signals, powerful at first, to cause the heart to react, but it can't, and the signals to the lungs and heart become weaker and weaker and then you have to begin cardiac massage to revive the victim and prevent cardiac arrest. This has to be done immediately, because after three minutes without oxygen, the damage to the brain starts to become irreversible. In other cases, the unconscious person might stay alive for thirty or forty minutes, although they'll die if they don't regain consciousness. It's not easy to tell a dead person from an unconscious one. Roberta came back to the plane with a stethoscope to assess the unmoving victims and try to pick up any trace of a heartbeat.

We saved some lives, but many we believed we'd saved in those first moments went on to die in the following hours or days. In many cases they had bleeding lesions and open fractures. Airplane seats are no more than chunks of steel bolted to the fuselage. In a crash, they become lethal weapons that can shatter a femur or tibia, pierce a spine, break a thoracic cavity puncturing a lung, or embed themselves in the stomach. If we're talking about lesions in either the upper or lower limbs the most crucial thing is to stop the bleeding with a tourniquet. If there's someone there with some common sense, or the injured person gets seen by medics quickly, their life can be saved. When a vessel bursts, masses of blood platelets rush to the ruptured area to seal it. The human body is well designed and has an awe-some capacity for self-healing. I found out then that plenty of haemor-rhages can be stopped in a matter of minutes by simply covering and compressing the wound. Joseph explained to us (and I can still hear his calming, constant and insistent voice amidst the screams and moans) that if major arteries were damaged, the passenger would inevitably bleed to death, but if the bleeding wasn't too severe and we applied pressure to the wound, they might just reach the coast alive.

Although many people needed immediate attention, we simply couldn't help them all inside the plane. Instead, we had to transfer them to dry land, and often the journey over was slower than we would have liked. Many died on that raft, the dark blood of the victims mixing with the seawater to gradually stain the rubber deck red.

Some people were in urgent need of surgery, but Joseph didn't have the means to operate to an acceptable standard. And, as you'll come to see, not even when we found anaesthetics could he fully put his patients to sleep, the result being some of the most chilling scenes I've ever seen. Scenes befitting a butcher's shop. Medieval horrors. In an operating theatre, an anaesthetist not only puts the patient to sleep, but also administers pain relief and muscle relaxants. In the precarious situation in which we found ourselves, Joseph did what he could, and in many cases performed the seemingly impossible. Approximately a quarter of the plane crash survi-vors died in the days that followed.

5

Holidays

The hours passed and nobody appeared in the sky or out at sea. Almost all of the passengers had taken refuge under the many coconut palms that lined the beach. Together they formed a considerable patch of shade, further cooled by the sea breezes – the trade winds we'd all studied as children in school. Joseph recruited a team of helpers to assist him with the sick. He had a knack for making people do what he said; he only had to ask someone to do something, and they would obey him. Swayla was one such impromptu nurse, but turned white on seeing the things Joseph had to do – cutting and stitching fresh wounds, stemming streams of blood by holding a handful of Kleenex to the wound, and using belts, sticks and cables to make arm splints – and the doctor ordered her to leave on realising she couldn't stand the sight of blood. For some reason, the women seemed more willing to fulfil that role than the men. An American lady who must have been about eighty offered to help. Her name was Jean Jani and she was from Ohio. Other volunteers followed: Sophie Leverkuhn, the wife of the famous architect from Los Angeles; Josephine Winslow, an underwater systems analyst from Sydney with absolutely no medical experience; Ruth Sweelinck, a Canadian feminist science-fiction author; my old friend Idoya; and Violeta Lubetzki, an Argentinian woman who claimed to have been a nurse in her youth and was now a specialist in Tarot and the Occult.

'If you know something I don't,' Joseph said to her, 'a touch of magic wouldn't go amiss.'

He was charming, even in the midst of a crisis.

So these were our valiant nurses, none of whom, apart from Violeta, had any medical training.

For his part, Wade gathered a group of three men and two women and they set off eastwards to find the tail end of the plane and make themselves known to the other survivors, if indeed there were any. They came back about an hour and a half later. They'd walked a fair few kilometres along the coast and seen no trace of the missing section of the plane. It couldn't possibly be further out. The Boeing couldn't have travelled more than two kilometres after hitting the water, and they'd walked nearly five along the coast. So we guessed the tail must have sunk into the sea, taking all the poor wretches inside with it. If there had been survivors, some at least would have made it to the shore. This news further saddened and shocked us. Of the four hundred passengers flying on the Boeing, only about a hundred and twenty had survived.

I decided not to go near Joseph's makeshift hospital. A person knows their own limits, and I can't stand gaping wounds or blood. Besides, I realised all of a sudden that I was exhausted. Exhausted and thirsty – thirstier than I'd ever been in my life. And I wasn't the only one. The raft, which seemed to have fallen under Wade's control, had just set off in the direction of the aircraft on a mission to retrieve, among other things, all the drinks left on board. I'd had the chance to drink on my expeditions back and forth to the plane, but the castaways on the beach – losing fluids faster than a running tap – had gone for hours without drinking a drop. Above all, I remember the children's wails. They were crying from thirst, fear and exhaustion. They'd soon start crying out of hunger too.

The next raft trips were to bring back any luggage left on the plane, which is how we ended up with such a curious assortment of objects on the beach: a wheelchair, which, as far as we could tell, didn't belong to any of the survivors; some golf clubs, also seemingly ownerless; and a hunting rifle, a Lazzeroni, still in its wooden case. That belonged to Stephan Kunze, the Swiss millionaire. Some people went back to the plane looking for their things, even diving down into the submerged holds to see what they could find, possessed by a spirit not at all unlike that of ancient (or indeed modern-day) looters. It's true that this looting was at least in part justifiable – we could make use of just about anything those suitcases might contain, starting with the medicine. Really, we needed everything we could get our hands on: clothing to make bandages, drinks, food, cleaning and hygiene products. But I did get the feeling that not everyone who went on these expeditions had entirely honourable intentions. Even I, who doesn't have a thieving bone in my body, did think for a split second about the jewels, diamonds, bracelets and designer watches.

I sat on the sand to rest in the shade of the palm trees, took off my jacket and shirt and left them folded on top of my shoes. I was wearing, I must confess, a ridiculous egg-yellow suit, a white shirt with cufflinks, a small spinach green necktie and a Stetson hat I'd bought years earlier through one of those ads you find in the margins of the *New Yorker*. One of my absurd Aschenbach-style suits which, at least I thought, lent me a sophisticated European air and impressed the ladies of Oakland; a stupid sahib's garb, which was already a little over the top for the Rhode Island summers, and here, in the tropics, looked preposterous. Looking back, I can't for the life of me think what possessed me to wear it, and I seem to remember that once I removed that suit in exchange for some lighter clothing, I didn't put it on again. I'm not even sure what happened to it.

Framed by the slender trunks of the palm trees, our tragedy suddenly looked like a scene from a beach holiday. There were a fair number of castaways talking calmly in groups or wandering around, chatting about sport or India's tourist attractions, where they'd been heading when we crashed. Some were perusing maps or travel guides – *Fodor's*, the *Michelin*, *Lonely Planet* – using suitcases as stools. Christian and Sheila, the two young Chileans, went past me as they strolled along the water's edge. They'd retrieved their wetsuits and surfboards and were headed to the mouth of the bay looking for big surf on the open sea. A fair number of people were swimming in the wonderfully clear and tranquil green waters of the bay, some in swimsuits, others in their underwear. I saw Swayla, too, who was going down to the water dressed in a scanty orange bikini that showed off the svelte, bony, golden quality of her beauty. It was like watching Eve taking her first steps in the original Eden.

6

Wade has some strange ideas

The hours passed and nobody came to our rescue. The sky was still bare, the waters deserted, the telephones without signal and radios mute. From what we could tell, we'd ended up in a part of the world unreached even by GPS signals. Such a place, we told ourselves, couldn't exist. I had heard of an area in the Sonoran Desert where you couldn't pick up satellite signals, but I've always thought that was more myth or metaphor than fact. Luigi, the Italian engineer, said that the plane's radio had to work, and that we could use it to call for help. Another expedition set off for the plane to give it a go, again without success. The electrical equipment on the plane was working now, but they couldn't get anything but static from the radio. You could neither receive nor emit anything. The report from those who came back from the plane, including Luigi, left us even more bewildered. They also confirmed that everyone left in the cabin had died.

And with that news, night drew in – our first night on the island. I had never seen a sunset in the tropics, and it seemed to me that what happened between the sky and sea at that hour had something supernatural, no, something truly spiritual about it. It's a difficult sensation to explain. Night fell, but nobody even contemplated sleeping. In the tropics it gets dark early, but we were still convinced we'd soon be rescued.

However, the creeping sense of doubt, the feeling that something deeply strange and disturbing was going on, became more pronounced as night fell. We ate from the supplies we'd found on the plane, hundreds and hundreds of trays of food loaded with mountains of fruit salads, bread rolls, chicken curry, vegetable pasta, fillet steak with mustard sauce, apple pie, flavoured yoghurts and several more of the kinds of delicacies they serve on planes. I ate with my old friends Eulalia, Julián, Matilde, Joaquín and the others, reminiscing about the past, the old days in Madrid when Cristina and I were a couple and Julián was my best friend. And yet, the situation was so strange that our conversation didn't flow naturally, and again and again we fell back to talking about the crash, about how bizarre it all was, about our own take on the experience, and about how lucky we were to have survived. Some of the other people from their group came to let them know that Dharma, their spiritual advisor, was going to start a meditation session in a few minutes. My friends invited me to join them, assuring me that I would enjoy meeting Dharma. I made my excuses, claiming to be tired and adding that I'd never practised any kind of meditation and wouldn't know what to do.

They looked at me with wide, frightening smiles. They spoke to me in cloying tones, their eyes full of love and kindness, and I told myself that these people couldn't possibly be my friends. No, these were extra-terrestrial beings who had somehow invaded my friends' bodies. Even my old buddy Ignacio had gone all 'Eastern' and seemed to be searching, in amidst the chaos and horror, for an elusive peace. They assured me I'd have no trouble following their master's instructions, and again insisted – the women above all – that I join them. I graciously declined the offer.

I went then to look for Wade and Joseph to discuss our situation. I found them also sitting on the beach around a little fire which can't have been lit to warm them up given that it was still stiflingly hot. Swayla was with them, still in her orange bikini. Among the rest I noticed a chunky, Hispanic-looking lad with long curly hair and a thin patchy beard. I call him a 'lad', although he must have been about thirty-five. There was something about the defenceless look in his eyes and mouth – pursed permanently in distress – which made him look youthful, childish even. He was one of those people who everyone trusts and likes. His name was Santiago Reina, but he introduced himself as Jack. Jack Reina.

'We need to get organised,' Wade said. 'There are a hell of a lot of people here, and we don't know who they all are. I've seen some of them lifting bracelets and watches off dead bodies. We've no idea who we can and can't trust. We have to set up some means of organisation and surveillance. Especially for the most vulnerable, the youngest and elderly.'

'Any minute now they'll be here to rescue us,' Joseph said. He had heavy dark rings under his eyes and looked exhausted. 'This won't go on much longer.'

He was smoking a cigarette. I later learnt it was the first he'd smoked in five years.

'I think you're wrong, Joseph,' Wade said, looking straight into the surgeon's big blue eyes. 'I don't think things are as you think they are.'

'Is that right?' Joseph said, throwing Wade a jaded, sceptical look. 'So how are they, then?'

'I don't think anyone's coming to rescue us,' Wade said, looking up at the stars. 'I just don't think they are. That's all.'

'Dude, the radars clearly mark our position,' Jack Reina began. 'The only weird thing is that no one's showed up yet. Let's say the signal was lost when the power went, they could still easily gauge the plane's point of impact. They're not just going to leave us here.'

Wade shook his head, smiling. And once again I found myself captivated by that smile. What was behind it? It was unmistakably a smile of happiness, of fulfilment, joy, relief and trust. But why was Wade so happy? His face glowed red in the firelight. Deep lines ran vertically from his eyes across his cheeks, on both sides of his mouth, dividing his chin in two. In the light of the flames, his eyes seemed paler and more intensely blue than ever. On the bonfire, the thick palm roots burnt red, giving off little sparks that flashed like the eyes of a serpent.

'I think Wade knows something,' I said. 'Or he thinks he knows something.'

'What is it you know, Wade?' Joseph asked, a hint of tired irritation in his voice. 'What makes you say they aren't coming to rescue us?'

'Because *we haven't been in an accident*,' Wade said, raising his eyebrows. 'This was no accident at all.'

'I'm sorry?' I said. 'Would you care to explain that one to us?'

'I think it's self-explanatory, John,' Wade said, and then he added, as if quoting from familiar song lyrics, *'All the mysteries will be revealed / for you, my friend, as well as for me...* And now, gentlemen, I think it's time to get some rest.'

When he stood up I was once again taken aback by his imposing stature. He was still wearing the same clothes as earlier, khaki trousers and shirt, but he'd now acquired a black leather rucksack, a thick belt with a metal flask hanging from it and a sizeable knife inside a rubber sheath. He was also donning a pair of chunky, military-style boots that I hadn't noticed before. When I first saw him on the plane he only had socks on his feet. It's true that plenty of people take their shoes off on planes, but on seeing those boots I had the distinct impression they weren't his. He left, marching stiffly into the shadows.

'It takes all sorts,' Joseph said, smiling weakly. *'We haven't been in an accident.'*

I said we were probably all in a state of shock, and that nothing we might think or say that night should be taken too seriously. We stayed there for a while chatting, but tiredness soon got the better of me. Swayla had fallen asleep on Santiago's round, inviting shoulder, and now it was time for me to retire. I looked for a quiet spot, laid one of the blankets we'd brought from the plane on the ground and instantly fell asleep.

7

We empty the plane. A scream

I *remember the unpleasant feeling of* waking up the following morning and discovering that I was asleep on the ground, still in my clothes from the day before, my skin itching and stinging from the sand and sea salt. Around me, people were still sleeping, stretched out in strange positions. Others were wandering about. Santiago Reina had caught a crab and was showing it to a group of children who screamed when it threatened them with its long pincers. Among the children I recognised Sebastian and Carl, the Leverkuhn kids, and also the Indian girl who was now laughing uncontrollably (in fact, she was always laughing). It sounded as if her name was Syra.

The mood was a strange mixture of bewilderment, fear and tropical relaxation. A few people were reading guide books on India or swimming in the sea, while others sat crying in each other's arms. Two young Mormons, whose names were Robert Frost and Robert Kelly, went from group to group spreading their evangelical message, handing out copies of the *Book of Mormon* and asking the castaways if they wouldn't like to live for the rest of eternity with their loved ones, and in death transform into the gods of some far-off world. They were wearing black trousers and white, long-sleeved shirts – the excessively formal clothes of most Mormons. Some people sent them on their way. Others seemed grateful for such an out-of-context exchange, and began quizzing the pair about polygamy.

I recognised the attractive woman with blonde hair and long legs from First Class, the one whose face had been familiar the day before. It was Nicollette Sheridan, the actress from those Martini ads from the eighties, back when I was very young. Nicollette Sheridan, who left such an indelible mark on my generation. In one of the ads she's dressed in a vest and miniskirt, skating along the streets holding a tray with a bottle of Martini on it – a bottle that by some miracle stays in place even as Nicollette skates into an elevator, gently swaying her hips, and the doors close. In another she walks along a tropical beach, very similar to the one on which we found ourselves, in a white bikini, and finds a television half-buried in the sand. The waves roll back and forth over the telly. Against all odds, it's working, and on the screen you can see sparkling images of bottles of Martini Rosso. But I'd also seen her in *Knots Landing*, a TV series in which she played the role of Paige Matheson, and in *Noises Off* by Peter Bogdanovich, where she spent the entire film in her underwear. The Mormons also approached her to chat. I asked myself why it is that almost all actors from the big screen seem small and vulnerable to us when we see them in real life. I watched as Nicollette Sheridan roared with laughter with the two Mormons, and how they laughed back. I told myself to pluck up the courage to speak to her, that I'd never forgive myself if I didn't. I came up with a couple of different approaches and tried to work out which might go down better: pretending I didn't know who she was, or playing the old unconditional admirer card.

Wade had been off in the jungle and was now back with two enormous branches of bananas, a little green on the outside but delicious inside. He chopped up the branches with his big fixed blade knife, handing out bunches to the castaways like some sort of wild god of abundance. There was still a lot of food from the plane for breakfast, but the milk, for example, was rancid, and the rest of it starting to turn. I'll never forget the croissants and scones and Danish pastries from the First Class breakfasts, or the melted butter and the small containers holding a prism of cherry or peach jelly. We didn't know it then, but that really was to be our last civilised meal.

It wasn't at all pleasant being without any personal hygiene facilities. When you had to go, you simply squatted hiding in the jungle among the trees, which began right there by the beach. There were so many of us at times it was hard to avoid company, and you had to whistle or politely let them know that 'the facilities were in use'. I was forced to do my business there a couple of times, after breakfast (my body's preferred hour). I only had to go a few metres inland to find myself completely immersed in the thickest, lushest vegetation I'd ever seen – thick vines that hung from the trees, themselves tall like gothic pillars; twisted roots emerging out of the earth; great big leaves like green elephant ears – and to be completely hidden from view. But that jungle frightened me, and the two occasions I took refuge in its green labyrinth to relieve my bowels I had the distinct feeling I was being watched by invisible eyes among the leaves. I even thought I heard voices and whispers around me. Both times I responded aloud, asking if anyone was there, because I was sure I had heard whispers. But I told myself surely they were insects or birds, leaves rustling, or who knows what fear-induced figment of my imagination.

And so began our second day on the island. We continued looking up at the sky and out to sea, waiting for the rescuers who still hadn't appeared. I walked towards the hospital area and came across Joseph, Josephine Winslow and Sophie Leverkuhn (the architect's wife) looking after the casualties, some of whom hadn't slept at all and looked wretched. Josephine explained that seven of those who'd been worst injured had died in the night, and Joseph told me, between us, that at least one of the casualties left had to be operated on in the next few hours or he too would die. By this stage the young man had managed no more than moans and wails, and they didn't even know if he spoke English. They'd established from his passport that he was a Japanese kid called Noboru Endo (like the novelist), and had been born in 1977. Noboru had a metal bar impaled in his stomach. That's how they'd found him on the plane, and that's how they'd transported him to land. Joseph said that for now it was better not to try to remove the bar, or he would start to haemorrhage and it would be impossible to save him. It seemed strange to me that they left him there with that awful chunk of metal in his stomach, but Joseph did no more than administer analgesics to alleviate his pain. I couldn't understand how he was able to make all those critical decisions with such conviction, but I didn't doubt for a second that he knew what he was doing.

I called for volunteers to come with me to the plane, and we climbed aboard the life raft with the intention of bringing as much equipment as possible back to dry land. This time we were looking for anything that might be of use in the hospital: cutting and sewing implements, bandages, cotton, gauze or some kind of alternative, and finally, morphine and alcohol. It seemed highly unlikely that we'd find morphine on the plane (unless we happened to have a drug trafficker in our midst), but, as Joseph had told me, a simple craft knife and sewing needle sterilised in a fire were enough to stitch wounds and perform certain emergency treatments. We were also hoping to dive down into the holds and see what we could salvage from there.

Jimmy Bruëll joined the group when I called for volunteers who were strong swimmers. He had some diving goggles that he'd found, God knows where, and which turned out to be useful for getting into the inundated holds. At that moment in time, to me he was just the guy who'd shoved a woman into the water in order to get out of the plane himself; the guy who'd winked at me with his 'sayonara'. In other words, a despicable low life. But I didn't think I had the authority to tell him not to come with us. I also had my eye on his goggles. I didn't know then that Jimmy was a swindler, a seducer, a con artist and an out-and-out opportunist, or that one of his strong suits was always having what other people wanted or desired. Later I found out that he'd taken the goggles off Syra, the young Indian girl from the Spanish group, trading them for a shell he'd found on the beach. From what I gathered, Syra received a serious earful from her mother for letting herself be tricked like that. But if Bruëll made a living out of seducing and robbing rich women, what chance did a twelve-year-old girl have?

When we reached the plane I was surprised to see whole flocks of birds perched on the fuselage: seagulls, cormorants, and something that looked like a buzzard or vulture. Several more circled around the remains of our own great fallen bird. It only clicked what was going on once we entered the plane and smelt the stench of the corpses. It still wasn't completely unbearable, but it was more than noticeable. I asked myself what we were going to do with all those dead bodies. To bury them all would have been shattering, impossible even, given that we didn't have the tools to dig graves on the island. Nor could we throw them into the sea, because the waves would have washed them onto the beach. In any case, in that moment we still thought we would be rescued soon. We didn't think it would fall to us to deal with the corpses, but rather to our rescuers, whoever they turned out to be.

I thought about what a stroke of luck it was that the corpses had remained above the water. Had they sunk, they would have become fish food, or even attracted schools of sharks. We were lucky too in that the carrion birds, who'd no doubt caught a whiff of their next meal, were almost all too big and cumbersome to get inside the cabin. All the same, we had to shoo away some gulls and frigates who'd found their way in, and were already attacking the corpses closest to the open air. They went straight for the most tender parts. I was horrified to see a seagull savagely pecking at the eyes of a dead girl. I screamed at the ravenous bird and threw a shoe I found lying around at it, but I knew that the moment I moved away it would come back.

We managed to salvage several cases from the hold. We also took a few of the rubber nets that had been keeping the baggage in place, thinking that they might be of use to us. As far as the containers were concerned, obviously we couldn't carry them up to the surface. Two had been smashed against the rocks and their cargo scattered across the reefs and seabed. We were lucky, because at least one of them was almost entirely full of boxes of packaged food. There were tins of condensed milk and jars of chocolate spread, different kinds of jam, tins of crabmeat and tuna, pickled quails' eggs and beef stew, as well as ravioli in marinara sauce, red caviar, peaches and pineapple in syrup, and other such delicacies. Retrieving all this food from the bottom of the sea tested our divers to the limit. Some of the boxes were so heavy we had to tie them to wires and haul them up from above. As well as these provisions, we unearthed a few useless items, including a racing bike and a cello in its case. But we also came across a box packed with syringes prefilled with sedatives like the ones zoologists use to put large mammals to sleep when they have to be vaccinated or given medical treatment. Joseph's eyes lit up when he saw those boxes full of blue vials, and they grew even brighter when he read what they contained. They were cartridges of a hundred milligrams of ketamine and tiletamine with zolazepam. We also found two Shark air rifles for firing tranquiliser darts, which led us to think a group of zoologists or vets must have been travelling to work on wildlife reserves in India, though no one among the survivors ever made sense of those medicines or weapons. In any case, Joseph told us that ketamine and tiletamine combined with zolazepam could be and was often used as an anaesthetic for humans, which meant that, for now at least, they'd overcome the problem of pain. As for the air rifles, they remained under the watchful eye of Wade, who for some reason had become something like the group's military commander. I guessed that Wade was a military man, probably ex-Marine.

We found more weapons and a small collection of barber's blades, which could be used as scalpels by Joseph, along with the accompanying leather sharpening belt and grinding stone. Wade examined the blades and announced they were from Mexico (sure enough, two of them had been made in Michoacán in the state of Morelia, and another in Mexico City, although the others were Japanese) and that those weapons were banned in several American states.

'Legal in Texas, Pennsylvania and Boston, banned in Connecticut and New York,' he explained to us with that mysterious smile that never left his face.

I took the opportunity to ask him where he was from, and he replied: 'From all over, from here and there, like the birds.' But he added that he'd been living in Farber, Connecticut for years.

'Far, far away, in the West,' he said, looking up, as if the sky were the West.

What a way with words Wade had. He spoke like a poet. There was something that possessed him, a kind of light, a kind of force. I asked him, too, what he did for a living and he answered: 'This and that, my friend, depending on the season, heading upstream like a salmon, downstream like a tree trunk, scaling the snowy peaks with the caribou and flocking back down with the thrush...'

But Wade's story is of particular interest, and I'll go into it in more detail later.

The second day on the island was unremarkable. I ate with my old friends, Julián, Matilde, Ignacio, Idoya and Joaquín, the cousin of Cristina, whose presence hovered over us like one of those invisible dinner guests in ghost stories. I wondered what she was doing, where she was living, if she'd gone back to Spain, if she was married, if she had kids... I was dying to ask all these things, but something, some strange impulse or force, stopped me.

A force! How often we use that term and how little we understand by it. A force! There truly are forces that move us, that drive us to do this or that, and even silence us. What other explanation could there be for the fact that as I talked to Joaquín I didn't ask a single question about Cristina, when we'd spent almost our entire childhood with her and her brothers?

'And you, Joaquín,' I asked, 'how did you end up with this lot? How did you meet Ignacio and Julián?'

'There's no easy answer to either of those questions,' he said with that little chuckle of his. 'I believe that there is Something that unites those of us who are looking for the same thing. Like whatever brought us all together on this island, right?'

I realised it was impossible to get any kind of sensible answer out of this bunch of New Age hippies, and I told Joaquín that what had brought us together on that island was chance, plain and simple. The sum of multiple actions, coincidences and circumstances.

'You really believe that?' Joaquín asked me. 'You believe our life is the sum of a set of coincidences and circumstances without any meaning whatsoever?'

'Of course,' I said. 'Any "meaning" it has is of our own making.'

My old friends looked at me in pity, as if I was missing something blatantly obvious. As if I'd been left behind. As if, since the moment we'd lost contact years earlier (many years earlier in the case of Joaquín, whom I hadn't seen since I was around fourteen), they had carried on evolving and developing internally and I'd remained at a standstill, stagnating. It dawned on me then that all of their humility was feigned, and that really they all felt superior in their 'spirituality'. My God, I said to myself, how had all that mystic crap – which I identified with California and the Vermont hippies – carried all the way across to Spain? And how could it have got such a hold of my old friends, who were all atheist lefties back in the day?

It seemed that Mother Nature had decided to throw us a bone the day we arrived, for early that afternoon it began to rain. From then on it rained every day, normally in the middle of the afternoon; torrential rains that lasted a couple of hours, after which the sun would make a spectacular reappearance. Some people, and in particular the parents of small children, now began to build small thatched gazebos with palm leaves; shanties or favelas propped up with any material they could get their hands on.

As for the castaways, they really were a curious and motley bunch. Stephan and Brigitta Kunze, for example, travelled with an assistant-cum-manservant – a prematurely bald young man who went by the somewhat grand name of Udo. Udo was responsible for all the husband's affairs, and was accompanied by a secretary-cum-maid – Di Di – who took care of Brigitta. She was quite the friendly young lady and reminded me of the gamekeeper's wife in Jean Renoir's *The Rules of the Game.* I would later learn that Udo and Di Di were married, although she was unfaithful with just about every man who crossed her path.

The Kunzes were Swiss millionaires who, as they explained to us, spent a good part of the year travelling, seeing the world, hunting and making philanthropic visits and donations, given that their first-born, Herbert Emile, had now taken over the running of the family businesses in Zürich. They were very religious, and quickly made good friends with Tudelli, a priest who turned out to be no less than a bishop of the Los Angeles archdiocese of the American Catholic Church. They called him

Monsignor, and kissed his limp, ring-adorned hand in deference. I found
Tudelli decidedly unpleasant. He must have been about sixty, and was one
of those consumed priests, the sort Francisco de Zurbarán would paint; a
steely cold glint in his eyes and the voice of a lyrical bird. Neither his
black-rim glasses nor his sanctimonious smirk ever left his face. As soon as
he found out that I was Spanish, he looked at me with fake friendliness, as
if he saw me as a potential sidekick or ally. Of course, in his eyes and in
the eyes of the Kunzes, my friends were all misguided: the Spanish set (to
which I didn't actually belong but was clearly connected) were travelling
with an Indian Swami. Then there was Wade, our very own commando.
No one, however, could compete with Swayla, the bikini-clad nymph
whose flagrant nudity was deemed scandalous by the religious cohort.
There was one other priest, a man in his thirties called Septimus Hansa.
He was Austrian with a carnal, guileless face who'd been living in Mexico
for years and belonged to the Legionaries of Christ. The Kunzes rubbed
along well with him too.

All of them, the Kunzes, Tudelli and Hansa, were impeccably behaved
and sweetly spoken. They talked among themselves in German, Latin, and
in English with a Swiss accent. As night fell on our second day, they organised a mass led by Bishop Tudelli and the young Hansa, and to which all
of the castaways were invited. It attracted quite a crowd. Even those of us
who weren't religious joined in, I suppose because we all saw it as a kind
of celebration of our survival, a thanksgiving rite. But there was certainly
something exciting about celebrating mass among the palm trees on a deserted beach to the steady rush of white waves, no pews, no cardinal purple, no chalices or crosses – no paraphernalia whatsoever. I looked on
from a distance, positioning myself at the back of the congregation, not
wanting to avoid participating altogether (I didn't want to be rude) but not
especially keen to get involved either. I have always respectfully abhorred
the Catholic Church, and never been much of a believer or a churchgoer,
but I tried to convince myself that what we were celebrating wasn't exactly
a religious act, but rather a ceremony of union, friendship and comfort
between the lost.

I spotted Wade in one of the front rows, kneeling down in the sand and looking very devout, which surprised me. Joseph had excused himself to go and see to his patients. The Indian Swami leading my group of yogi friends was also there, kneeling down and getting up in line with the celebrant's instructions. There was a woman next to him who I thought was his assistant or disciple, but who turned out to be his wife: the Swami was in fact married, and wasn't really a Swami. It was beyond me why he was taking part in a ceremony from another religion, but my friends later enlightened me, explaining that in yoga God is adored in any form, and that in an ashram it wouldn't be strange to find images of the Buddha, Christ, Francis of Assisi or Kabir. I asked them if I could adore God in the form of Johann Sebastian Bach or, better still, in the figure of Nicollette Sheridan in a white bikini. But the joke was lost on them, for no one apart from Ignacio knew who Nicollette Sheridan was.

The mass under the palm trees wasn't an entirely selfless act on Tudelli's part, however. During his homily, the bishop spoke of the extraordinary circumstances in which we found ourselves, and said that in moments of extreme privation and need we would have to be organised and come together. He proposed none other than Stephan Kunze as the natural leader of our group: a highly regarded businessman throughout Europe, he explained, in addition to being a father of eight and grandfather of nineteen, well used to tackling difficult situations and also commanding much larger and more diverse groups than even our own. Tudelli also spoke of the casualties, paid respects to the dead and mentioned the need to uphold 'human dignity' (those were his exact words), courtesy and mutual respect in the extraordinary circumstances in which we found ourselves, paying special attention to the weakest among us – by which he meant the women, children and elderly. He asked, for instance, in his birdlike voice which seemed to try to compete with the shrieks of the gulls and frigates flying overhead, for us all to adhere to a respectfully modest dress code, and told us that the public acts of nudity and blatant defiance of decent customs thus far witnessed could not be tolerated, and that despite the extraordinary circumstances in which we found ourselves we must defend Christian discretion and rigorously respect the universal rules (to him, at least, they seemed universal) of community. I presumed he must have been referring to the survivors who had swum in their underwear, some topless, and even (in the case of Christian and Sheila when they removed their wetsuits) stark naked.

I stopped listening, turned my back on the group and strolled along the shore to be alone for a while and watch the sunset in peace. I noticed that Swayla had also edged away from the group and was walking towards the sand. When she reached the water, she took off her white shorts and orange bikini top and dived into the sea; an overt act of defiance against Tudelli's preaching, given that everyone attending mass could now clearly see her topless chest. I waved at her and she waved back, standing in water up to her waist. Her breasts were almost non-existent, but that made her no less attractive to me.

I carried on towards the other end of the beach, where I came across Santiago Reina, the heavyset Hispanic lad. He was sitting on the wet sand letting the smooth waves wash over him and soak his trousers before they rolled back out again. He sank his hands into the water then let the trickles of violet and pink clay slop through his chubby fingers.

'So you're not a fan of Catholic priests' voices either?' he asked, a little melancholy. 'Brings back bad memories for you too, right?'

I asked him if he spoke Spanish and he told me he did, that his parents were Puerto Rican. We spoke for a moment in Spanish, but he had been born in the States, in Jersey City, New Jersey, and his Spanish wasn't fluent, so we soon switched back to English. After a little while we both fell silent, spellbound by the sight of the sunset.

'It's beautiful,' he said, pointing at the supernatural lights of the tropical nightfall, the orange clouds, the green light hovering above the sea.

'Yes,' I said. 'What a shame we won't have long to enjoy it.'

'Why not?'

'Because any minute now we'll be rescued.'

'No, man, you're wrong,' he said, deadly seriously. 'We're not going to be rescued.'

'What'd you mean?'

'Nobody's coming to rescue us,' he said. 'We're not getting out of here. This is it, man.'

'What makes you say that?'

Santiago seemed stuck for an answer. He was a tall, solidly built boy, but he gave me the impression that intellectually speaking he was no more than a child. A big, scared child full of secrets and mysteries, not so different from the rest of us.

'Look, Juan,' he said in Spanish, 'I might not believe in God, but I'm not stupid either. I know that this is a punishment. We're being punished.'

'What are you talking about?' I asked.

'Tell me something. Do you know anyone who doesn't deserve to be punished? I know I deserve it, and you know you do too. I'm no church-goer, you understand. I don't go in for that mumbo-jumbo. But I do believe in punishment. Punishment follows us all our lives, but it's not God who doles it out, man. If there's a God, he doesn't know a thing about me and he isn't watching. It's not some kind of just punishment, you understand. It's *the* punishment, the burden we were born with. And it starts the day we're born. It's eternal. We deserve it, but the person punishing us isn't out to improve us or make us pay for whatever it was we did, and that's why it just keeps going. It lasts for as long as we walk the earth. It follows us every day of our lives. And in the end it catches up with us. You see? We can run and hide, run and escape far, far away. Run and run and put up barriers, but the day comes when it catches up with us. And when it does it's like a dog who's caught a rat. It doesn't let go.'

Next thing we knew, a strange thing happened to make us both jump out of our skin. We heard a tremendous scream coming from the interior of the island. It sounded like an animal wailing in agony. It lasted about five seconds, then there was a pause, and then it came back. I don't know why I had the feeling it was coming from far away. Very far, kilometres away, although you could hear it perfectly clearly. We noticed how everyone who'd been following the mass had turned in the direction of that sound. Flocks of birds had flown off into the jungle.

'What was that?' I asked. 'Did you hear that?'

'Course I heard it, man,' Santiago said.

'What was it?' I asked again.

'I don't know, man,' Santiago said, looking at me in dismay. 'A little taster of what awaits us, I guess.'

8

The children. I meet Rosana

The next day I was woken by the sound of a violin playing the beginning of Johann Sebastian Bach's Partita No. 3 in E major, BWV 1006. It was Sebastian, the Leverkuhns' eldest son. He was only twelve years old but played with a technical brilliance beyond his years, and had perfect control over the phrasing and style. Sophie Leverkuhn was listening to him, kneeling on the sand; she was wearing a fairly grubby shirt (which presumably she hadn't changed since the night before) and some khaki shorts. Her eyes were puffy and red and I supposed she'd hardly slept a wink. Nights in the hospital were horrendous.

I admired the attention and seriousness with which Sophie listened to her child, matched only by the seriousness and dedication with which he played. There seemed to me something at once beautiful and terrible about their relationship, the root of all great artistic careers and all great personal downfall. It was clear that Sebastian wasn't playing for her, but for Bach, for the music, for himself. And yet, at the same time, that rush of warm music was devoured by the loving ears of his self-sacrificing mother.

Sebastian and Sophie were surrounded by a crowd of onlookers who listened with the astonishment that music so often provokes, even in people who don't like or understand it. The other children, Syra, Carl, Branford, Adele and Estelle, also sat in a circle nearby and listened with rapt attention.

Sebastian finished playing and lowered his bow. Everyone clapped, but Sophie immediately began to point out what he needed to work on next time. I imagine she was simply parroting the remarks she'd heard the boy's teacher make. She corrected some of his bowing, rather well in fact, which surprised me because I knew that she didn't have any musical training or play an instrument. She also told him he was too *espressivo* in a few passages, and that he'd overdone the *ritardando*, which I'd found exquisite and richly musical. For me, Sophie's observations had the echo of the old Conservatory professor who clips away at the performance as one might a rose bush or bonsai tree, reducing it to a stiff, hard stem.

I admired Sophie, but she intimidated me. Her evident intelligence set her apart from others, but at the same time she radiated a sort of social grace which ensured she could slot effortlessly into any situation. She could talk to anyone, treated everyone with kindness, gently challenged others when she disagreed with them. She'd been the editor of a major *Harper's Bazaar*-style magazine (perhaps even *Harper's Bazaar* itself), but unlike many of the have-it-all mothers I'd encountered in the US, she'd given up her career to look after her children. She'd grown accustomed to living in the shadow of her celebrated husband, who had made his name designing mansions for millionaires living in the hills and valleys around Los Angeles. She was tall and statuesque, blonde and beaming. But there was something about her smile that looked as if it had been awkwardly stuck to her face for decoration, rather than a genuine expression of happiness or warmth. It gave her face a hard appearance; uncompromising and harsh.

Sophie then turned to Carl, her youngest son, and asked him to multiply a three-digit number by another three-digit number. Carl gave the answer in a flash. I thought it was a joke. Surely it was impossible for a ten-year-old boy to solve a sum that difficult without even having to work it out. One of the onlookers, who was still lingering after Sebastian's performance, had some battery left on his mobile phone. He did the multiplication on the calculator and confirmed that the answer was indeed correct. This inspired even more exclamations of admiration than Sebastian's musical prowess. They all began asking Carl impossible arithmetic problems and the boy answered, apparently unfazed, taking barely a second to work out the solution. They quizzed him on prime numbers, shouting out an

absurdly high number before asking him for the next prime number. And
he always knew the answer.

'You've got two child geniuses,' I told Sophie. 'Sebastian plays very
well. He's going to be a great violinist.'

'Technically, Carl is the only "genius",' she said, without taking her
eyes off her sons, staring at them with avid, insatiable pride. 'He's got an
IQ of 163. Higher than Einstein.'

But the other children wanted to play, especially Syra, the little girl
who was only a few weeks Sebastian's senior. She was standing next to
him, watching the scene unfold with her arms crossed and a big grin
across her face. She had long spindly legs which were ever so slightly
knock-kneed. She scampered off and then reappeared out of nowhere to
jump on Carl – who was still calling out sums and solving equations –
sending him tumbling, with a gentle thump, onto the sand. She was a light
little thing, with barely any strength in her wrists, but she was quite a bit
taller than Carl and had caught him by surprise. She pinned his arms and
legs down on the sand and said that was enough with all his stupid numbers and sums. Carl screamed hysterically, humiliated at having been
floored by a girl, convinced that everyone watching the scene was laughing
at him.

'I'm going to kill you, Syra!' he shouted.

Just then, Syra's mother showed up. She was a Spanish lady about the
same age as me, and was with the group of meditators travelling with the
Indian guru. I think I may have mentioned her already. She was a little
shorter than me, and with her petite form, her plump, bow-shaped lips
painted geranium red, and her dark, auburn hair cascading over her shoulders, she was undeniably beautiful. She wore prescription glasses, the
aqueous lenses making her small cross-eyes appear enormous and seduc-
tively dark. She was wearing a white shirt knotted casually at the waist,
and khaki pedal-pushers. Her name was Rosana.

'Syra!' she snapped. 'What the hell do you think you're doing?'

I was taken aback by this outburst, and wondered what could have
happened earlier for Rosana to be quite so furious with her daughter.

I noticed how the girl immediately cowered, and then hung her head slightly. In a matter of seconds the smile on her face had disappeared, to be replaced by a look of intense annoyance. She lowered her eyelids and let her mouth droop.

'This child. Jesus Christ, she tries my patience,' her adoptive mother said. 'What were you doing, Syra? Answer me when I talk to you!'

'They were just playing,' Sophie said.

'Answer me!' Rosana repeated to the child. 'Look at me properly. Are you deaf or something?'

'It's nothing,' I said. 'They were only playing.'

Sophie looked at her with her big, turquoise eyes and a vague smile that I found impossible to read. It was her fake smile, the smile that seemed to say: *if I could kill you, I would.* Aside from her one interjection, she'd observed the outburst impassively, glaring at Rosana as if sizing her up. She didn't say anything, but I know that Rosana felt judged by Sophie and that she'd taken a visceral dislike to the perfect, blue-eyed blonde.

I think that was the first time Rosana and Sophie came face to face, and from that moment on they secretly despised one another. They were both formidable mothers, but this one similarity only served to highlight the otherwise vast differences between them.

'We're cracking coconuts,' Rosana told me. 'Can I tempt you with a coconut, Juan Barbarín?'

Oh, there it was. We'd only just met, but already she'd picked up the universal habit of calling me by my full name. I told her she could tempt me with anything drinkable, and we walked in the direction of the Spanish group who were spending their energies on the endeavour of cracking rock-hard coconuts.

It was Wade who showed us how to do it: with a fat knife and in such a way that we didn't waste the precious liquid as the shell broke to pieces.

Rosana and I strolled along the beach chatting and getting to know one another. She told me that she had set the wheels of Syra's adoption in motion when she was still married, and went through the long bureaucratic process together with her husband. Then he'd fallen in love with

another woman and eventually walked out after a long-drawn-out period
of indecision and short-lived make-ups. The moment to go and collect
Syra from the Mother Teresa orphanage in Calcutta had come at the end
of this long, agonising separation. Back then, Syra was but a photograph
that the nuns had sent Rosana: a small, brown-skinned, two-year-old girl
with beautiful, startled eyes. But the photo was living proof of the real
existence of a human being, a little girl who lived and breathed and cried.
And who was waiting for her.

Rosana went to India with a friend to collect the girl and take her back
to Madrid. What followed was gentle hell for both of them, and went on for
several years. Syra arrived plagued with illnesses and eating and sleeping
problems. In the orphanage the children were always surrounded by other
children and they slept with the light on in packed cribs. It's not that they
were poorly looked-after, she explained: the orphanage was clean and the
carers and nuns kind, efficient people, but the overcrowding and subsequent spread of disease were inevitable. Syra had had tuberculosis and scabies, and although she was now cured of both, the scabies had left her with
the habit of scratching herself at all hours. She also had problems with her
intestinal flora and skin, and she'd suffered horribly as a result of some
parasites in her eyes. She had a permanent hacking cough – the kind the
doctors called 'unproductive' – which stemmed from unhealed wounds in
her throat. Syra also had attention problems in school, initially as a result of
her poor vision, which her teachers and mother were late in identifying,
and then because of her strong tendency to introversion and the trouble she
had expressing herself verbally. Syra had a babyish temperament, was shy
and mysterious and deeply insecure. She liked animals and very young children: anything that was alive but didn't talk. When she felt relaxed she
would laugh uncontrollably, flitting between giggles and that dry, unproductive cough of hers. She was very thin and particularly tall for her age,
although early development like that could also be an indication that she
would soon stop growing and end up a short teenager. Short and lean with
long glossy hair and East Asian facial features. Yes, she looked more East
Asian than Indian. She'd been born in the foothills of the Himalayas, in

Darjeeling, and was actually of Tibetan ethnicity. The funny thing was that she looked quite like Rosana, who had a round face and almond eyes, and very even, subtle features. It's also possible that the curious similarity between mother and daughter had developed gradually over years of cohabitation, each mimicking the other's gestures unconsciously.

We reached the far end of the beach, then scaled the rocks and headed into the jungle for four hundred metres before clambering back down onto the next beach, where we sat in the shade of the coconut trees and stared out to sea.

'What could be taking them so long? Why haven't they come for us yet?' Rosana wondered aloud.

'I don't know. But it can't be much longer,' I said.

'I suppose in the end we've been lucky,' she said. 'We've survived.'

'Yes.'

'It's as if we'd been given a second chance.'

'Yes.'

'As if we were in limbo between one life and another,' she said. 'That's how I feel.'

'In limbo between two lives?'

'Yes. As if this island weren't really a place in the world, but an interim world of its own. A parenthesis.'

'Some people are saying they don't think anyone's coming to rescue us.'

'What?'

'I've heard more than one person say it. Wade, Santiago Reina...'

'What do they mean no one's coming to rescue us?'

'They think we've landed in a strange place. A place of no return.'

'I don't understand a word you're saying,' Rosana said. 'What are you talking about, Juan Barbarín?'

'I don't know,' I said.

'When I get home I'm going to make some serious changes to my life.'

'Is that so?'

'Yes. I see everything clearly. Now that I've stopped, now that I've come off the treadmill I can see it all so clearly.'

'What do you do for a living?'

'I work for a multinational. I'm the big boss. A super-executive, Juan Barbarín.'

'Well, well.'

'I earn a shitload of money.'

'Will you marry me?' I said.

She laughed.

'Sure,' she replied.

'Sure?'

'Why not?'

We fell silent. From this beach, the sea looked different. How strange. Wasn't it the same sea as on the other beach – the same sand, identical palm trees? The music in the air seemed different, as if on this beach certain things were possible that on the other one weren't. Why do our senses play tricks on us like that? We're slaves to our feelings.

'I want to spend more time doing yoga and meditation. I want to devote more time to my daughter and my allotment, to my friends and to listening to Mozart.'

'What about love?'

'Love? I've given up on love.'

I kept quiet. What could I say? Hadn't I also given up on love? Impossible, abandoned, hopeless love.

And yet, I found myself saying: 'We're not old enough to have given up on love.'

'No,' she said, 'but what if love's given up on you?'

There were more children on the plane. It'll become clear later why I keep going back to the subject of children and why I describe them in such detail. Basically, the children were important on the island. Or rather, they were important to the island.

There was Branford, the five-year-old son of a New Zealand couple, Bruce and Gloria Griffin, who were scriptwriters for CBS in Los Angeles. He was a sweet kid, and reminded me of Dennis the Menace – both because of his looks and his trousers, which were constantly falling down.

He spent most of his time combing the beach for shells, winkles and dead crabs, which he'd then shove in his pockets.

There were two little girls, Adele and Estelle, who were seven and eight years old respectively and the daughters of a pair of Australian diplomats, Henry and Diffy McCullough. They went around dressed in matching short white dresses, two perfect little ladies in the middle of the jungle. They were very shy and could always be found together somewhere near their parents. We'd later learn that Adele was autistic and had learnt to talk very late. The two sisters had developed a language of their own, which sounded like bird calls and made the pair seem mysterious and poetic.

And there was Seymour, the youngest among us. He was just two months old, the son of a girl called Lizzy, a platinum blonde waitress at a diner in Sausalito who hadn't finished high school. Apparently Seymour had a brain tumour and Lizzy was taking him to India to be seen at an Ayurvedic hospital in Madras. All the waiters at the diner had chipped in their tips for the week to help her raise the airfare.

It didn't take long for Lizzy's story to get around, not least because the group – especially the women – buzzed around the new mum to help with the baby. We were all in a sorry situation, but Lizzy's was particularly dramatic: there with a baby she had to breastfeed every two or three hours, with no nappies, changes of clothes or fresh water to clean him. Seymour often cried through the night. Lizzy was exhausted and stressed. She didn't have much milk and the baby wailed in hunger. She had fashioned him a makeshift crib, or rather nest, out of palm leaves, twigs, and blankets and pillows from the plane, but she soon learnt that this crib wouldn't protect her baby from animals. On one occasion, as Seymour slept soundly after a feed, Lizzy decided to go for a quick dip in the sea a few metres away, but she'd barely stepped foot in the water when she felt a terrible premonition which made her race back to the baby's crib. There, running rings around the crib, was a dark-skinned lizard, almost two metres long, its slim pink tongue slipping in and out of its mouth. She managed to startle the lizard by shouting at it and throwing sand in its eyes, and it trudged off, but from then on Lizzy wouldn't let Seymour out of her sight for a second.

Sophie Leverkuhn, Josephine and the other women in the group helped her look after him, as did a young, friendly lad called George who spent the day chatting with her, helping her to change the baby and carrying him in his arms when they took strolls.

Whatever George's intentions were, Seymour's story and the reason behind Lizzy's trip to India with her baby had quickly spread through our small community. When he met her, Joseph took Lizzy aside to tell her that it didn't make any sense to leave Los Angeles, which boasted some of the best hospitals in the world, to take her son to a Third World country where he'd receive treatment that relied on old traditions – oils, massages and tree bark.

'I think you should let Lizzy make her own decisions,' Wade said to Joseph, very gently and still with that smile on his face.

'People should be informed before making any decision, Wade,' Joseph replied. 'I think in medical matters I am a reasonably trustworthy source of information.'

'They told me my baby boy was gonna die,' Lizzy said through gritted teeth. 'That's what they said to me.'

'No one should say that kind of thing,' George said. 'No one should just dash someone's hopes like that.'

Somebody, one of the women, asked Lizzy about the boy's father, and she said that the boy didn't have a father, that her son was all hers, that the two of them had always been alone, and that's how they'd stay – they were just fine on their own. Then she picked up Seymour and together with George they took off along the beach. George was much taller than her, a gentle-looking fellow. I didn't know what he did for a living, but I imagined him working in a shop – a stationer or copy shop maybe – but definitely engaged in some sort of easy and hassle-free activity where he could be nice to clients, helping them out and flashing them his impersonal smile.

9

We find the aerial

Wade *pointed out that we* urgently needed to find fresh water and asked for volunteers to go with him to look. I volunteered, and we were also joined by Christian and Sheila, Gwen Heller, Santiago Reina, Joaquín, and lastly Xóchitl, a Mexican girl from the Latin American contingent among us. Xóchitl had a sort of tragic Mexican beauty – intense and disturbing – and I think Joaquín was into her. We were certainly a motley old crew. I was surprised that Santiago, who was considerably overweight, had put himself forward to spend the whole day walking. As for Gwen, I think it was the first time I'd laid eyes on her. She must have been around thirty and was dressed like an explorer, with a leaf-green shirt, khaki shorts and chunky boots. We learnt that Gwen was a biologist and worked in San Diego Zoo where she was in charge of the young litters and newborns.

My principal motive for joining the expedition wasn't to woo Gwen but to get to the bottom of those murmurs and voices in the bushes; the ones I'd heard every time I'd gone to relieve myself. And yet, now that we were together as a group I couldn't hear anything besides the squawking birds and the sound of us swatting mosquitoes against our own skin. The murmuring and rustling I thought I'd heard among the leaves on my solo trips into the bush had disappeared.

The vegetation was very thick, but luck would have it that we found a machete lodged into the branch of a tree. God knows how many years it had been there. It was very old and rusty, and Wade said in all likelihood a Japanese soldier had wedged it there during the Second World War. It took him a good while to dislodge the machete, but when at last it came free, he held it up in the air. I thought of Arthur's sword stuck inside the anvil – Wade had just secured himself the title of King of the Island. I told him as much and he looked at me with that strange smile on his face, as if I'd touched a sensitive subject.

Half an hour later we came across a fresh water stream and all of us crouched down to drink from cupped hands. Wade opened his rucksack and took out a metal camping mug, which he handed to us solemnly. Only after each of us had quenched our thirst did he drink himself. There was something of the hero about him, especially over those first few days; something of the knight at the round table, the old king, magnanimous, powerful, kind, inscrutable. He seemed perfectly at home in that godforsaken place. He moved effortlessly around the island, climbing trees, forecasting the rains, cutting up fruit and drawing it to his mouth. On top of all this, he always seemed to know what it was we should do. Given his age, I wondered whether he might have been in Vietnam, and if it was there, in South Asia, where he'd learnt to navigate and survive in the jungle. I imagined him as the type to fall for the tropics. And yet, there was nothing dark or morbid about him. No, it wasn't death or impunity or even the night that he loved about the jungle, but rather its fluidity, its permanent state of rapture, its contagious humidity. He told us we'd keep heading inland for another hour to try to find a high point from which to see the surrounding landscape before heading back to the stream and follow it to its mouth. It was there, he said, where the stream opened out into the sea, where we should set up our camp. It seemed entirely logical, but I doubt such an idea would have ever occurred to me.

We carried on hiking in the direction of the hills. Along the way we didn't come across a single decent-sized animal – our main hope for finding sustenance on the island – most likely because our presence scared them off. Huge trees loomed above us, species new to me with thick trunks and branches covered in vines that hung down to the ground. In the canopy we spotted long-tailed monkeys peering at us – to me at least it seemed they were – but not daring to come closer. They were capuchin monkeys, with pale, ghostly faces. Back then I didn't think monkeys were edible, nor would it have occurred to me to eat a creature with a face and hands. We also saw an enormous pink and white cockatoo soaring beneath the crowns of the trees, as beautiful as an angel. We emerged from the wooded area on a higher patch where the vegetation was sparser – a kind of plateau where the trees were more spread out and from where we could see several green hills in the near distance. Sheila let out a cry when we spotted at the top of one of the hills what was unequivocally a radio aerial. I think that in that moment we thought we were saved, that at last our ordeal was over.

It took us almost an hour to get to the top of the hill where the aerial was. It was much taller than it had looked from below, a formidable metallic construction fixed with long steel cables suspended thirty metres above the summit, and set on top of a concrete platform on which we also found a kind of bunker and several abandoned buildings. It didn't take us long to work out that the place was deserted and that it had been years since the aerial had operated.

We scoured the buildings for clues, for pointers. It turned out the radio station was useless without an electric generator, although the equipment all seemed to be in good condition. There were a few rooms with bunk beds, and also a kitchen full of cooking utensils and a larder brimming with supplies, although all the cans were out of date. There was a lounge with some furniture: a sofa, a small table, some games (a chess set, another of backgammon, and Scrabble) and a magazine rack with an issue of *Playboy* dated from July 1957, and whose pin-up was none other than Jean Jani, a stunning long-haired brunette. The photos of her in a swimsuit reminded me of photos of my mother on the beach in the late fifties.

Joaquín, Cristina's cousin, was going through the other rooms with Xóchitl. I could hear them giggling like a pair of teenagers messing around on a school trip. I'd known Joaquín since we were kids but had hardly seen him over the previous years, and the only news I did hear of him came via other people. I'd got it into my head that he'd become something of an 'oddball', and that despite his scientific background (he'd studied

Chemistry) he was now into extra-terrestrials and spiritual energies. I also knew he had a thing for beautiful, problematic women, and that he'd had a few turbulent and difficult relationships. I was fond of him, but also wary of his peculiarities. For reasons that will become clear later on, I didn't want to have anything to do with Buddhists, spirituals, vegetarians or wackos who stare up at the sky on the lookout for moving lights. People who are wholeheartedly convinced of something, and who abide by their own inner laws, whatever they might be, have always made me profoundly uneasy. And yet, Joaquín didn't seem dogmatic or inflexible. Instead, he reminded me of a playful imp craving adventure, craving spectacles.

Xóchitl laughed as they roamed about the place together unsealing metal boxes and forcing open cupboards. She was a tall, slim girl with very dark skin, a great mop of black hair, an Aztec nose and lips, and huge melancholy black eyes. They found a sort of glass ring in one of the cupboards and Joaquín said it was the ring of power and slipped it onto Xóchitl's finger. I don't think she was the slightest bit interested in his fantasy game.

I heard Joaquín calling me and I went inside to see what was going on. They were in the back room, which was full of stacked-up furniture.

'Take a look at this,' Joaquín said, pointing at the wall. The serious, even fearful look on his face took me by surprise. I think it was the first time I'd seen a look like that in his eyes.

It was then that I saw the writing daubed on the wall. I could make out the words:

NOTHING IS WHAT IT SEEMS

THIS IS NOT AN ISLAND

MAY GOD HAVE MERCY ON US

A shudder ran through me. I couldn't figure out what those words really meant, but nor did I intend to hang around to try. I walked out and called Wade over to read it. Joaquín insisted the message had been written recently, and was directed at us.

'Come on, guys,' Xóchitl said, 'we're the only ones on this island. Someone, for whatever reason, must have written it aeons ago.'

'What it's telling us,' Joaquín cut in, 'is that we mustn't believe everything we see. It's warning us, and in the most direct way.'

'You like mysteries, don't you, Joaquín?' Xóchitl said to him with a sad smile. 'Didn't you know there are no mysteries in the world?'

Wade didn't say a word. He frowned, stroked his chin with his right hand and stared intently at the words written on the wall. We left him there, leaning on his rifle as if it were a staff, reading and re-reading the sign as if it contained a message he alone was meant to unlock.

It was time to be heading back. We grabbed a couple of pots, spoons and knives – to us the most useful utensils – and some boxes of Swedish matches – of which we'd found an endless supply and which didn't look to have been damaged by the humidity – and we set off back to the stream. It fed into a second stream, and then another, and became even wider. Now it was a full-blown river, almost twenty metres wide. It occurred to me then that it was unusual for an island to have such a big river.

Banana plants the height of a man and laden with purplish, reddish, green and yellow fruits appeared like daubs of pure green among the mysterious shade of the taller trees. There were breadfruits, with their enormous yellow-green fruits hanging from the branches. Gwen also pointed out yam plants on the banks of that spectacular river. It felt like we'd arrived in the land of abundance. We headed eastwards back to our camp along the coast. We were only five kilometres from our beach, although our trek inland and obeying the whims of the stream (not having reckoned on the uphill climb to the radio tower) had taken us almost all day.

I remember the feeling of euphoria on arriving back; euphoria born of sheer exhaustion, but also of the feeling of having accomplished a feat, a great deed even. I have never had the slightest interest in physical exercise or exploits, but on the island I felt different. Something new had been born in me, a taste for risk, the need to size myself up against the world – and against my old self. And it wasn't only that physical feeling – that boldness (that's how it felt then) to explore a strange island rife with potential dangers – but also the feeling of doing something that wasn't only good and vital for me, but good and vital for others. I felt a desire to help and to serve others like I'd never felt before. I thought about how, any minute now, the rescue crew would finally show up and get us out of there. And I realised it saddened me to think of our adventure coming to an end.

10

We abandon the bodies

I went looking for the mature lady whose name, as far as I could remember, was Jean Jani, and found her in the hospital looking after patients. I asked her if she was the same Jean Jani who'd been a pin-up for *Playboy* many years ago and, to my great surprise, she laughed and told me that it was indeed her, adding that there was no way I could recognise her. I showed her the magazine we'd found. There she was on the front cover, sprawled across the deck of a yacht, dressed only in a red jacket with its zip open so as to suggest a mere hint of a breast.

'Well, well, it just keeps resurfacing,' she said, smiling. 'A few years ago my daughter found a copy – she found out I'd been a pin-up. Nobody knew a thing! When they discovered my secret they were as proud as anything. I thought that was all good and buried, but there you go – nothing stays in the past forever. Everything bobs back up to the surface eventually.'

I told her I thought it an extraordinary coincidence us finding that magazine there, but she didn't seem surprised. *Playboy* is a popular magazine – you can find a copy just about anywhere.

I ran into Rosana, who had just come out of the sea and was drying her long thick hair with a towel. There, partially hidden among the palm trees and bromeliads, in the dense jungle setting that reminded me of Rousseau's *The Snake Charmer*, although it must be said that Rosana's skin against the dark leaves and the pink, tubular flowers was in stark contrast to the almost black skin of the snake charmer in the painting. I thought she'd hidden in the shrubs to get undressed, but she didn't have a change of clothes on her. I spoke to her for a while, telling her about our adventure inland and the river we'd found. I noticed she was looking at me in a new way and grinning. Nor was she wearing her glasses. I asked about them and she congratulated me on my powers of observation. Apparently I was the first person all day to spot that she wasn't wearing them. She explained that since we'd washed up on the island she'd noticed something strange going on with her glasses, as if she no longer needed lenses. At first she'd thought that her gradation had got worse, even though her eye problem wasn't degenerative and she had no reason to expect her sight to deteriorate. But when she took off her glasses she realised that in fact the opposite had happened – she could now see without them.

'And?' I asked.

'My eyes are cured,' she said. 'Don't ask me how, but I can see perfectly.'

'How long have you been wearing them?'

'Since I was four!' Rosana said. 'I've always had weak eyes. When I was a little girl they patched one eye so the other didn't become lazy. I was cross-eyed, seriously cross-eyed, with terrible eyesight. I've worn glasses my whole life!'

'And so…?'

'What do I know, Juan? Now I can see fucking perfectly.'

'But this is really odd, isn't it?'

'Completely baffling.'

Rosana wrapped the towel around her head like a turban, one of those tricks it seems all women know how to do, and which I'm always in awe of. Next she slipped on a pair of sandals to go walking along the beach. We were alone there, surrounded by the palm trees and delicious breeze. I told her it was the first time I'd seen her without lipstick on, to which she responded by walking up to me, raising herself on tiptoes and kissing me on the lips. It was a fleeting, possibly friendly peck, but not so fleeting that I didn't detect a soft, strange intimacy to the contact of her small, compact lips. Her mouth was still cold from her dip, but all the same I felt the warmth of her blood. I don't know why she kissed me out of the blue like

that. Perhaps for no other reason than that she felt happy. I didn't know
what to make of that kiss, but I enjoyed it.

A big meeting for all the castaways was called as evening fell. For the
first time, and by the light of a great fire, we jointly confronted the unbelievable situation in which we found ourselves. Wade told everyone about
our discovery. He explained that five or so kilometres westwards along the
beach, the river we'd found fed into the sea – an ideal place for us to settle.
However, many of the castaways, especially those under the influence of
the Kunzes and Bishop Tudelli, voted against leaving 'our' beach. It won't
be long before help arrives, they argued, and if we disappear from the
beach, our rescuers will assume we're all dead at the bottom of the ocean.
Their reasoning was sound enough, but the problem they raised had a
simple solution: set up a lookout post on the beach near the site of the
crash to receive our hypothetical rescuers.

Joseph restated our basic priorities: to find water, bury the bodies still
left on the plane, build shelters against the constant rain and organise
ourselves into groups to find food. He insisted that if we wanted to stay
alive and well until help arrived, we would have to get organised and work
together in teams.

We also disagreed over whether it was necessary to recover and bury
the bodies still on the plane. In the end, we decided that we had neither
the means nor the time to transport almost two hundred already decom-
posing bodies to the coast and dig them all graves. Nobody who hasn't
tried can imagine just how difficult it is to dig a grave in the hard earth
without the appropriate tools. Jimmy Bruëll resolved the matter elegantly
by asking for a show of volunteers to go to the plane and collect the reek-
ing bodies, battle with the birds that would swoop down on us, carry the
bodies to the island and then spend three or four days digging graves in
the ground until we'd managed to inter them all. Only three or four hands
went up, so the problem resolved itself. Bishop Tudelli railed against
Bruëll, arguing that to leave the bodies to rot in the open air and be devoured by scavengers wasn't Christian.

'So you go back to the plane, bro,' Jimmy replied. 'No one's stopping you!'

'Have you no feelings?' Tudelli asked. 'No compassion?'

'I'm just saying I've got zero intention of doing it myself,' Jimmy said. 'Let the dead bury their own dead. Ain't that what the Good Book says?'

Tudelli was gawping at him, clearly taken aback. I'm sure he wasn't used to being spoken to like that. And yet, even so, he went on smiling.

'This is a Man of the Cloth you're speaking to!' Kunze said to Jimmy, clearly furious. 'Show some respect!'

Kunze, the Swiss millionaire, was well into his seventies, but something about him commanded absolute respect. He oozed power, wealth and authority.

Jimmy turned and flashed him an extraordinarily warm, friendly look, although his blue eyes glistened with an almost frightening violence and contempt.

It was one of those impossible exchanges: the millionaire chatting with the crook.

'Your mate Puccini can be a Man of the Cloth, the Dalai Lama, Grand Pasha or the Sith Lord himself back where he's from,' Jimmy said, 'but on this island we're all equal.'

'You, sir, are a barbarian!' Kunze cried.

'You can call me Conan,' Jimmy said with a wink.

11

I meet Carlos

We *relocated to the estuary* we'd found the previous day and began building huts on its wide banks, but set back from the fresh water to avoid being plagued by mosquitoes. The river didn't flow directly into the sea, but rather into a lagoon of still, crystalline water, which rose and fell softly with the tide, and which was to become the children's preferred playground. That shallow oval of turquoise water was as still as a swimming pool and had generous white shores.

On our side of the lagoon there was a cluster of coconut trees, and on the other, downwind, a grove of vast plants with dark crowns whose medicinal smell wafted across the waters carried on the trade winds. According to Dr Masoud, a retired judge from Lucknow, they were camphor trees, which in India are considered bad luck and whose leaves are lethal to birds and can poison river water, rendering it unsafe for drinking. Luckily they were downwind and set apart from our settlement. In any case, Dr Masoud seemed to have a sort of love affair with those intensely perfumed trees, because he built himself a little boat and an oar to row across the lagoon and visit the camphor trees. He would collect any fallen branches still in good shape and use them to make little carvings of animals that he'd later hand out to the children. He was a master at those carvings, and had a huge repertoire. He gave me a penguin and a dolphin.

The toughest part of our move was transporting the wounded, some of whom were severely deteriorating because of the unhygienic conditions. Their sores and cuts would become infested with maggots and Joseph had to open them up again to clean and disinfect them. The patients shrieked

like the gulls. Joseph wanted to save the anaesthetic for any potential surgical interventions, and the regular analgesics sometimes weren't strong
enough. On the island I became more aware than I'd ever been of the reality of human pain.

Once we'd finished moving the sick and our few belongings to the
banks of the river, we began constructing our huts. It was on that afternoon that I met a seventy-something Brazilian, an exceptionally skilled
woodworker who offered to help me build my thatched shelter, no doubt
moved by my own ham-fisted attempts. A few days later I discovered he
hadn't even built a hut for himself and that despite spending all day helping others put up their roofs and walls, he slept on the sand, out in the
open. I was quite astounded by his generosity. We stuck to English mainly,
but every now and then the man would speak to me in very slow and deliberate Portuguese, which I could understand. And through those Portuguese words I got a sense of the full scale of that man's heart – as sweet
and tranquil as the green river that flowed a little way beyond us. I told
him there were people who needed his help more than I did: people with
children, the sick and elderly, and he told me that he'd give me some basic
instructions so that I could finish it off myself and then – better still – help
others. In very few words, and sometimes with none at all – he wasn't what
you'd call a talker – he would show me how to cut canes and tie them together to form a frame, and then how to fold the palm leaves and weave
them through the frame to form more or less waterproof sheets. He had an
axe, a chisel and a hand plane; carpentry tools that he used to cut trees
and branches, stripping the bark from them, polishing them and transforming them into pieces that somehow, miraculously, fitted together. He
taught me how to plait rope with plant fibres, and how to make firm knots
that wouldn't come undone.

'Now you know a little, you can help the sick,' he said.

I asked him what his name was and he introduced himself as Carlos.
We shook hands. He had grey hair, was small but very muscly, with large
carpenter's hands that ended in pink palms and long sausage fingers. He
worked conscientiously, never hurriedly, and always with a smile on his

face. He would measure up, take a look, check, then measure again. I asked him where he was from and he told me he was born in Belo Horizonte, in the state of Minas Gerais, but that he'd been living in the United States for over thirty years. I guessed he was a carpenter, or a cabinet-maker, but, as was becoming the norm on the island, I was wrong.

12

I join the meditators

We *built a small settlement* which we called 'the village', on the edge of a river we called 'the river', close to a beach we called 'our beach', as opposed to 'airplane beach', where we'd spent the first few days.

By now a ghost, a constant presence, had settled in among us. It was hunger. We soon realised we would have to devote almost all of our energies to finding food. If not, we'd either die or start eating each other.

For the first few days it was the fishermen who had the most success among us. The sea became our main food source. There was a Korean, a businessman called Mr Lee who had grown up on an island where most of the inhabitants lived off the sea, and he boasted an entire repertoire of fishing techniques. He could make cages out of reeds to trap lobsters and fish. He knew how to fish with rods, with nets, with harpoons. He knew where the fish hid under the sand, and where you could unearth clams by sinking your feet down to the water's depths near the shore. Led by Mr Lee, the fishermen cobbled together harpoons and went to airplane beach, where the water was calm and shallow, to catch octopuses. Later we would pulp the cephalopods' flesh with rocks to soften it, then boil it and cut it into slices. A delicious meal, but how many octopuses do you have to catch a day to feed that many people? Others collected crabs and sea urchins or looked for oysters among the rocks. They were mouth-wateringly good, but had to be rationed to make sure we didn't finish them all in a couple of days. Others simply threw fishing lines with handmade hooks and waited patiently for the fish to bite; fish that we'd later bake on hot rocks, or fry in their own oil. I didn't recognise the fish we caught in those waters. Some of them were like red seabream; others reminded me of the 'San Pedro' you get in Mallorca. The rest were new to me. The big, harmonious fish I'd admired on my original boat journey to the island and that looked like coelacanths turned out to be particularly delicious and easy to catch. They didn't flee human company and seemed to swim voluntarily into the traps we put out. Someone recalled how the Buddha Shakyamuni, in one of his previous incarnations, had been a fish that willingly threw himself into the fishermen's nets, offering himself up as food, and this gave us the idea of calling them Buddha fish.

Gwen explained to me that, despite appearances, tropical jungle actually offers the least nutriment of all kinds of forests. While there were lots of edible species in the forests surrounding the village, there would never be quite enough fruit and vegetables to feed a population as big as ours. There were abundant coconuts, perhaps our main source of vitamins, together with the squeezed bitter limes that grew on the wild lime trees on the same beach. But we soon finished all the bananas on the nearest plants and the breadfruits that grew along those banks that had seemed indescribably rich to us at first. After that we struggled to find other fruit trees. Jung Fei Ye and his wife, Pei Pei Je, a Chinese couple from Singapore, found some that we Europeans hadn't even recognised as fruit: tamarind, for example, which grew in tall, tangled ferns bursting with pink flowers; dragon fruit, an extraordinary prickly pink pod with long green spikes; and also durian, a typical Singaporean fruit, a kind of enormous spiky nut, much bigger than a coconut, inside of which the hungry scavenger will find something akin to two preserved yellow livers, foul-looking and -smelling, but actually rather tasty.

The hunters were less lucky, despite having two rifles, two shotguns and plenty of ammunition at their disposal. Several different hunting groups were formed, but for some reason the animals always got away. The hunters smeared their faces with mud and avoided wearing loud colours or perfume, deodorant or mosquito repellent, which would alert the animals to their presence from miles away. But even so, they only ever managed to hit a couple of birds, a lizard or the odd capuchin monkey, which, although we were ravenous, none of us could bring ourselves to eat.

On the third or fourth day, the hunters had an unexpected encounter. We hadn't really imagined there might be dangerous animals on the island, but that afternoon the hunters came back to the village with tales of having been attacked by a pack of giant wolves. I remembered the wolves from *The Jungle Book*, and how strange it had always seemed to me to find wolves – animals I associated with the snow or the north – in the middle of the Indian jungle (although the 'jungle' in that book perhaps wasn't the dense tropical forest I had imagined back then). A hunter, Bill Higgins, had been bitten by one of these wolves. Bill must have been almost six foot five, was a divorce lawyer in Los Angeles and had lost his wife in some sort of accident. He was in a terrible state, covered in blood and deathly pale. He'd lost three fingers from his right hand, and his right arm, the one he'd used to defend himself from the animal's fangs before the others had been able to pull him off, was completely maimed. We'd set up a kind of hospital in the coolest, breeziest part of the village, a wide, open space protected from the rain with several beds and a rudimentary operating table. It was there that Joseph assessed Bill Higgins and there where, a few days later, he would have to amputate the man's arm from the elbow down. Bill Higgins's story shook us all to the core.

Gwen had been part of that particular hunting expedition and had seen the wolves. I spoke to her at the end of the day, and found her profoundly disturbed by what had gone on in the jungle.

'It's one thing to come across capuchin monkeys on an island in the Pacific, and quite another to find giant wolves,' she told me. 'Those were Canadian wolves, Juan Barbarín. With thick coats of fur. Animals genetically adapted to live in the boreal regions. But most unbelievable of all was the size of them. They were like horses. Wolves that size simply don't exist, not anywhere on the planet. Siberian wolves are enormous, and it's said there are wolves in the Taiga that can weigh up to a hundred kilos. And then there are always deluded hunters with overactive imaginations who say they've caught wolves of, like, one hundred and fifty kilos. But the wolves we saw today must have weighed between two hundred and two hundred and fifty kilos. They were immense, Juan Barbarín. It's not possible. It's simply not possible.'

'So how do you explain it?'

'I don't know,' she said. 'I can't explain it.'

I remember we spoke about the other strange things that happened on the island and I asked her if she too heard voices in the undergrowth when she went into the jungle alone. She told me she did, that we all heard them.

'But no one talks about it,' I said.

'They're scared they'll be branded lunatics.'

'Sometimes I think they're talking to me,' I said. 'I don't just hear voices: I hear voices talking *to* me, saying my name.'

'Your name?'

'Yes.'

'That is weird,' she said. 'I never hear them that clearly.'

'It's a sign of schizophrenia,' I said. 'Isn't that right? Hearing voices in your head?'

'But they're not in your head.'

'No, because you can hear them too.'

'That's right, I can hear them too.'

'If we all hear them, then I'm not crazy,' I said.

'Either that, or we all are.'

'Or we all are.'

'I don't think you're crazy, Juan Barbarín.'

'When you go into the jungle in a group you don't hear them. You have to be alone for them to start.'

'That's right.'

There were several campfires going around the village, and the delicious aroma of baked fish wafted over to where we were sitting. Gwen had been busy with other things and she hadn't built a hut yet, so I invited her to come and sleep in mine after supper. I told her I had no ulterior motives; that I was simply offering her shelter from the rain. She said thanks, but that she felt more comfortable sleeping next to another woman. I don't know what face I must have pulled, because she took me by the hand and told me straight out that she liked me but that now wasn't the time to be starting something.

In fact, even though my offer had been genuinely innocent, that night I did feel quite sexually frustrated. Perhaps it was the heat, the humidity, or the promiscuity our life as castaways seemed to impose. That evening we ate baked fish and biscuits with jam, dragon fruit – which our Chinese friends ate sprinkled with lime juice – and a little bit of durian, sliced and fried like crisps. I saw Swayla, wearing – as ever – her spectacular bikini. She was eating next to Jimmy Bruëll; the two of them seemed to have hit it off. After supper, I went up to the Spanish group to speak to Rosana. I found them all sitting in a circle, getting ready to start a group meditation with their Indian guru. Rosana spotted me straight away and made signs at me to join them. I've never been attracted by Eastern ideas or practices, and the word 'meditation' stirs up memories I'd rather forget (painful memories that pierce like stakes right through my heart). Despite my scepticism I was still attracted to Rosana, so after a moment's hesitation I joined the circle and sat at her side.

I was in for a surprise. The guru wasn't Indian at all. I'd always seen him from afar and had never got a proper look at his face. I'm sorry to admit that I hadn't looked at him as an individual, but rather as the representative of a type. He was wearing a yellow shirt covered in Sanskrit words, a string of rudraksha prayer beads and a pair of white trousers. But on closer inspection, he was none other than Carlos, the Brazilian I'd been working with that very afternoon and who had helped me build my hut. The man radiated a sense of peace and kindness that had penetrated me to the very core. So Carlos wasn't a carpenter or cabinetmaker, nor did he work in a studio or woodshed, as I'd assumed. Carlos was Dharma Mittra. I settled down to listen to his instructions during the meditation session, but I couldn't concentrate. He spoke of a rose in the centre of one's chest, and that rose had twelve petals that were like twelve rooms, and there was a winding path that led from one to the other until it reached the central room, which was completely empty. And in the central

room burnt the flame of a single candle. I was so tired my eyelids began
to droop. Or perhaps I was dreaming already? Perhaps I dreamt the rose
with twelve chambers and the central chamber like a niche in an ancient
wall made of dark stone where the flame of the unknown I burns? In the
end I fell asleep in that position, fast asleep, snoring, and Rosana had to
tap my shoulder to wake me up. I'm not sure how long I was asleep for,
perhaps only a couple of minutes, but I truly did have an extraordinary
dream.

I dreamt I was a bird, a bit like a peacock, with a blue body and a long
golden tail. Perhaps it was more like the tail of a pheasant, made out of
little sparkles and jewels, electric circuits and iridescent condensers. I was
a bird, but at the same time the bird was a kind of spaceship, a vessel of
the skies, and I was inside the bird's head, in a control room full of wheels
and gold helms from which I controlled the flight's progress. The belly of
the bird was full of unborn babies that smelt intensely of green apples.
Children with their eyes closed and wrapped in tight-fitting white, embroidered fabric, the way indigenous people tend to swaddle their babes to
soothe them. And the bird flew over immense landscapes of factories, in-
dustrial towers topped with great flames and black ponds like ink reflecting those flames. And there were football pitches with floodlights between
the black ponds, and motorways lit up by avenues of streetlamps that vanished into the night, curving gently to the left and right through residen-
tial areas of white bungalows, whose windows glowed orange under the
black crowns of giant ceiba trees. And our mission, the bird's mission, was
to go around casting the children into the world so that they could be
born. They were stored in the belly of the bird, which was like the hold of
a ship or a plane, a vast, long room with chandeliers, oval mirrors hanging
at an angle and walls lined with pink diamond-print damask, and whose
floor opened up like two lips of an enormous vulva to release – just as a
mushroom releases its spore into the nothingness – the lightly swaddled
babies, who then fell like shining dots on the landscape of factories, motorways, ponds, football pitches and illuminated bungalows. And the great
bird that was in fact me, its voice, like a whisper in the pink damask belly

that was my belly full of babies yet to be born, said each time: 'Be born…
you must be born… go, the time has come to be born…'

Rosana nudged me gently and I woke to see her smiling eyes and violet
lips. She told me the meditation was over, and brought her face up to mine,
closed her eyes and kissed me on the lips. I wasn't sure if this was something people tended to do at the end of a session – kiss the person next to
them on the lips – but I didn't see anyone else doing it, so I guessed that
she was saying to me 'I'm yours, if you want me'. No, there was no reason
to interpret that second kiss as a friendly peck. We chatted for a while and
kissed a couple more times on the lips, and finally I invited her to sleep
with me in my hut. She gave me an almost patronising look and told me
no, thanks very much, that she'd sleep with her daughter. For as long as
those kisses had lasted, I'd forgotten what women – or maybe just Spanish
women – can be like.

13

Noboru dies. The blue column

I *think we all heard Bill* Higgins's sobs when Joseph told him what had to be done. He wasn't crying in pain, because we still had plenty of anaesthetic, but out of fear and desperation. The wolf that attacked him, or rather the wolf's fangs, had ripped his arm in such a way that there was no way it would heal. It had to come off. If not, Joseph explained, it would turn gangrenous. He'd be dead within a week. The barber's straight razors they'd found on the plane had become part of Joseph's surgical kit, but to cut through the bone he had to borrow a saw from Carlos, my kind carpenter pal from Belo Horizonte. I went to see Bill Higgins a couple of times after the operation. I'll never forget the look in his eyes.

Everyone has a limit, a limit to how much wretchedness they can bear, a limit to their hope. Once that limit has been crossed, the person is left undone, reduced to nothing. This is one of the things I learnt on the island. I also learnt that nobody can know what their limit is going to be in any given situation until they are forced to confront it. Sometimes you reach it quickly. Sometimes a person shows great courage and true heroism in the face of adversity. Sometimes they'll stand as firm as a baobab; at others they're but a reed in the wind. In Bill Higgins's case, the amputation of his right arm was too much for him. I could see it in his eyes, in the fear and helplessness in his stare after the operation. The wolves hadn't only ripped his arm to shreds; they'd torn apart his soul. He was utterly consumed by fear. His hair had turned grey. He'd grown old. He was already dead.

One of those we'd brought over to the village on our makeshift stretcher was Noboru, the Japanese kid with the same name as the famous author of *Michio the Cat, Diary of an Ancient Shadow* and *Korb in the Planet of Unfaithful Women*. I call him 'kid' but he was in his late thirties. He'd suffered horrific internal injuries. There was nothing Joseph could do to save him.

I didn't want to go near Joseph's hospital, where he and Roberta looked after the wounded in inhuman conditions, assisted by Sophie and Jean Jani. Sometimes they were forced to stem the flow of blood with their bare hands, looking on powerlessly as the sick died one by one, unable to do a thing about it. I did feel I ought to do something to help those suffering, though, and the afternoon after we'd moved to the river I went looking for Noboru to chat with him for a while. He was the only Japanese man among us and seemed particularly solitary. As Santiago and I carried him over to the hospital on a stretcher, he told us that he couldn't bear how much exposure to the sun there was on the island, couldn't stand the feeling of being permanently unprotected in such an open, seemingly limitless natural space. I asked him if he suffered from agoraphobia and he said he'd never thought about it before, but that prior to travelling to the US, he'd spent three years shut up in his room in the city of Yokohama, without once venturing outside. He told us he was a *hikikomori*. The word was new to me, but he explained that it described people who locked themselves up in their rooms, sleeping all day and staying up all night glued to their computers. I had a sneaking suspicion there was a story behind these revelations that I wouldn't mind hearing. I spent the next couple of days asking around until I finally managed to find someone who was willing to give up their sunglasses. It was Jimmy Bruëll who gave them to me in the end, in exchange for my Stetson hat. I took them to Noboru to relieve him, if only a little, of his photophobia. But when I got to the hospital, he was nowhere to be found. One of the assistants looked at me with pale blue eyes, her jaw clamped tightly shut with the effort of holding herself together. She told me they didn't expect Noboru to make it through the night and that they'd put him in the shade of the palm trees by the lagoon to rest.

Noboru was suffering terribly and had a fever. Joseph gave him painkillers to relieve his agony, which went on day after day. I secretly hoped that Joseph was wrong, and that after a while Noboru would recover. But of course, it didn't work out like that.

I found him by the lagoon, lying against the trunk of a palm tree. He looked terrible, his face ashen and his eyes already unfocused and vacant. He was running a high fever and every now and then became delirious and unaware of where he was, just as Joseph had warned me. But he did recognise me. I think my being there comforted him, but he didn't even have the energy to smile. I handed him the sunglasses, but had to put them on him myself.

'How are you doing?' I asked.

'This is it,' he said. 'I know it is. No one's said anything to me, but I know that this is the end.'

He died practically in my arms, the poor kid. Josephine came and felt for his non-existent pulse. We moved Noboru's body to the hospital hut and laid him out on one of the beds, first placing a canvas sheet over the palm leaves, which we would later use as a shroud to wrap up the body. Joseph confirmed the cause of death was a generalised infection in the intestinal cavity. We decided to bury him that same afternoon. There was no point in delaying. Decomposition set in quickly on the island, and in a few hours' time Noboru's body would begin to give off a stench that would only attract insects and other animals.

But we didn't end up burying Noboru's body. Christian, Santiago and I spent the rest of the day digging a deep grave in a spot some two hundred metres from the village. When it was ready, we wrapped the corpse in the white sheet and laid him on the ground, next to his grave. Out of all the castaways, I was the one who had spoken to Noboru most and knew him best, so it was left to me to offer up a few words. Very few. I said goodbye to Noboru. I bid him peaceful rest, or to reach the place one should reach when one dies, if such a place exists. That was enough. The ritual had been honoured.

Then something happened. A storm broke inland and lightning bolts came crashing down, flashing in the near distance. But it didn't feel like a real storm. It wasn't raining. Nor were there any dark clouds. You could hear the rumble of thunder and the flare of the lightning in the distance, towards the south, but above us the sky remained clear and not a drop of water fell. Those of us at Noboru's funeral looked up at the sky apprehensively. I think we all felt that we wanted to get the ceremony over and done with and return to the huts before the heavens opened.

And then that scream again, the terrifying howl we'd heard a few days earlier coming from somewhere further inland. It felt like this time it was closer, as if some creature in the jungle was circling us ever more tightly. Something immense and terrifying. Something magnificent and sublime. When I thought about it, when I imagined it, anxiously turning my eyes towards the source of that howl, I almost felt a quiver of happiness. At last, something was coming! At last, something was about to happen! Even if it were bad, terrible even, it didn't matter. Santiago and Christian were both standing inside the grave, ready to receive Noboru's body and lower it down. The grave was the proverbial six feet deep, which meant their heads just about reached ground level. Both of them had turned to look in the direction of the lightning flashes and thunder. The horrendous wailing returned. A howl of pain and fear that seemed to stem from the earth's very core.

'Look!' Santiago shouted, pointing upwards.

Bolts of lightning were raining down. Bright, golden rays landing all over the ground. They were coming from above, but there were still no clouds in the sky. They pelted down in hard, straight lines.

But these weren't normal lightning bolts. Within their midst, we could make out an immense blue column some two hundred metres tall. I don't know what it was or where it could have come from; it might have risen up out of the ground or descended on us from the jungle for all I knew, but I'd never seen anything like it. It looked like a tornado, except that it remained stock still, suspended above the forest canopy. There was another scream, but this time it came not out of the forest, but from the sky. A scream of lacerating pain and utter desperation.

Those golden rays of lightning also struck the sand between the trees, scorching leaves and burning branches that fell to the ground in flames.

Almost everyone fled, terrified. A few of us stayed put, though. I can't quite say why, but my guess is that we were frozen in fear, and simply had no idea what to do. One of the bolts struck Christian, who was violently illuminated, shrouded in a white and golden glare. I thought it had killed him but he was unharmed, although the fierce golden light didn't fade. Another bolt of lightning fell near Wade, who jumped back, and a third struck Noboru's corpse. And then a fourth, and a fifth: three bolts through the inert body of Noboru wrapped in his makeshift shroud next to his open grave. The cloth was lightly singed, and one edge caught fire before fizzling out again. At that moment, the lightning stopped, and the blue column simply disappeared into thin air. The thunder, lightning, flashes and wild wailing were gone.

We were all screaming. Christian was screaming. Santiago screamed as he struggled to get out of the grave. Wade was screaming. As was I. Sheila ran screaming towards Christian, jumped into the grave and wrapped her arms around him. He was still shrouded in a kind of golden glow, but wasn't hot to the touch.

That's when I noticed Noboru's body moving. Joseph and Tudelli noticed it too. At first I assumed that the electric shocks from those three bolts of lightning had caused some sort of muscular spasm. But that wasn't the case. Joseph pulled the sheet aside to see what was going on, and revealed Noboru flailing his arms and legs about and turning his head from side to side. Then he fell still, opened his eyes and sat up, there on the sand, in apparent tranquillity. He let out a hacking cough and opened his eyes. The wide, staring eyes of a dead man, I thought. But he wasn't dead. Or rather, he was no longer dead. He looked at us questioningly, but didn't seem to recognise us. I knelt down beside him.

'Noboru!' I shouted. 'Noboru, you're alive!'

'Yes,' he said, as if that were stating the obvious.

'But you were dead,' I spluttered. 'You died.'

'I died?' he said, looking about himself in confusion and spotting the open grave dug in the earth beside him.

'You died,' I said once more. 'You were dead.'

'I was dead?'

Joseph took his wrist and felt for a pulse. He stared at Noboru with a look of alarm and fear. Wade came and joined us, but his eyes betrayed neither alarm nor fear. I looked at him and he winked. He was smiling. Smiling again. But why? What did he know that the rest of us didn't?

From there, Noboru recovered quickly. A couple of days later he began eating solids, walking and even cracking jokes. His peritonitis symptoms, even the scar from his wound, had vanished completely.

Several different versions of events went around. Tudelli spoke of a miracle. And he wasn't the only one. The esoteric bunch – Christian and Sheila, Violeta Lubetzki, my New Age friends – were all prepared to believe (or rather wanted to believe) that what had happened was a miracle. Joseph swore blind that there was no question that Noboru had died a few hours before he came back to life, although some questioned his diagnosis and guessed that the doctor, perhaps because he was overworked, had been too quick to declare that Noboru's heart had stopped beating. Joseph told us Noboru had shown all the symptoms of having died, not only the lack of a heartbeat. He had stopped breathing, his body temperature had dropped, and two and a half hours after his death rigor mortis had set in.

Others brought up the great column of light, the wails from the heavens, the lightning and the three rays that had rained down and struck Noboru's inert body. There weren't that many of us who'd witnessed these phenomena, and not all of us had seen the same thing: some had seen the column of blue light, others a kind of cloud suspended over the jungle, others a blue giant walking through the trees. Most, though, had seen nothing at all, and this confused and absurd version of the story fell into oblivion.

And yet, there was still the matter of those rays and their effect. As far as I'd seen – or at least as far as I thought I'd seen – they appeared to have fallen not from the clouds, but from the top of that extraordinary blue column that had sprung up and towered over us. Their effect on Christian was plain to see: he was now permanently shrouded in a faint golden glow, which became more pronounced at night. Their effect on Noboru had been even more spectacular.

Joseph looked confused and miserable in the wake of the Noboru episode. It was as if something inside him had broken. Out of all of us it was he who was best prepared to accept the reality of death, so it makes sense that he was the least prepared to face the scandal of resurrection.

Human beings don't understand transitions. They don't need them. They adapt to change immediately, forget what things were like before and accept how things are now as if they'd always been that way. Noboru made a full recovery and began to build himself a hut and enjoy as normal a life as the rest of us castaways had. When all's said and done, he'd only been dead a couple of hours. According to the man himself, during those hours he'd dreamt a lot, and the experience had allowed him to see that the afterlife was similar to a dream. I asked him what exactly he'd dreamt about, if the dreams had been good or bad, but he told me he wasn't ready to talk about any of that yet. He assured me that he would tell me his dreams one day, though, those visions he'd had when he was dead.

Joseph and I chatted about Noboru's case more than once, and the good doctor told me that while inexplicable and illogical cases abound in medicine, he simply couldn't find an explanation for what had happened. He also told me he didn't believe in miracles, but that what had happened to Noboru was the closest thing he'd ever seen to one. There are certain plants which, when eaten, can produce a deathly stillness, and insect and fish bites that can make it look as if a person has died. But even if something like that could explain the resurrection, Noboru's abdominal cavity had been critically infected. How could that have simply disappeared? How could there not be a single trace of the wound?

I told him about Noboru's dreams when he was dead, and he told me that this wasn't possible either. When the heart stops, the blood flow stops reaching the brain, and if there's no blood circulating in the brain, it simply can't function. The dead don't dream, he told me. I said that perhaps dreams don't depend solely on the brain, or that perhaps it's true what people say, that we don't dream with our brains.

'No,' he said, 'no, John. With all due respect, that's nonsense. There can be no consciousness when the brain shuts down. Consciousness is a function of the brain.'

'Nor can the dead come back to life,' I said.

'Well,' he said, 'you've got me there.'

14

The Third Reich

The Latin Americans had a board game called The Third Reich. It belonged to a Chilean called – or, perhaps more accurately, who made us call him – Roberto B., and whom I found profoundly irritating. I don't know quite what caused me to feel such an aversion to him. Maybe it was his style, that typical Latin American look from the eighties: scruffy hair, round-frame, faux-intellectual glasses (he was, apparently, a writer), three days' worth of stubble, a cigarette always hanging out of the corner of his mouth, and a polo-neck jumper which he never took off, despite the god-awful heat on the island. It was a slightly forlorn look that seemed intended to say 'I'm the salt of the earth and at the same time tremendously interesting'. It grated on me, too, that he made us call him Roberto B. Why the 'B'? What was he hiding beneath that 'B'?

The Third Reich was played on a large board about a metre by seventy, printed with a geopolitical map of Europe divided into small hexagons. You could play individually or in teams: one team formed the Axis and the other the Allies, although it was also possible to divide the players up into Germany, the USSR, Britain, Italy, etc. It was a compulsive and extremely complicated game that involved hundreds of hexagonal pieces that represented the soldiers and each country's resources (tanks, air force, artillery, supplies, etc.); certain world leaders and key figures (there was a piece for Hitler, Goebbels, Churchill, Stalin, etc.); two packs of cards, one red and one blue; dice of different shapes and colours, some the traditional cube shape and others tetrahedron, octahedron and icosahedron; more pieces, hexagonal or otherwise, representing I'm not sure what exactly; and lastly the instructions, which came in the form of a little booklet – very well thumbed – which the players were constantly passing around and consulting. Apparently, part of the appeal of The Third Reich was that you could make up your own rules ('openings' and 'solutions' they called them), which you could later send in to one of the specialist magazines (*Wargames, Black Sun Zone, Battle Ground*). Once reviewed and evaluated by the game's creators, your new rules could potentially end up in the official manual, which was updated and reissued twice a year. Roberto B. would spend hours and hours playing The Third Reich with Christian, Sheila and Óscar Panero – a Mexican, also a writer, with a little goatee. At other times he played one-on-one with Óscar Panero, in whom he'd managed to inspire a deep fascination in the Second World War that rivalled his own.

Roberto B. was a novelist and poet. Óscar Panero, a poet and essayist. Óscar's girlfriend was also a writer, poet and novelist. She was called Brenda Esquivias Ponce. Xóchitl was part of the group too. Roberto, Óscar and Xóchitl went back years. They'd been travelling to India together. Xóchitl wasn't a writer; she was a sociologist.

Brenda Esquivias, Óscar Panero's girlfriend, was a petite young woman with brown skin and long black hair who spent all day reading Chekhov (she had a collection of his stories in Spanish) and had written a novel called *Suffering Servant* about the lives of six young women living in Ciudad Juárez, in the northern Mexican state of Chihuahua. All six of these women were friends from secondary school and were part of Ciudad Juárez's upper middle class. In the novel, the girls spend their free time popping over the border to El Paso to visit the gringos' fabulous hotels, the gringos' fabulous swimming pools, and the gringos' fabulous malls to buy underwear, shoes and dresses, until one of them disappears for a fortnight and they eventually find her body savagely mutilated and abandoned in a plastic bag on a rubbish dump in the outskirts of the city. And this was the crux of the story: that the murderers had targeted the daughter of one of the city's bourgeoisie.

Apparently, the novel, which Brenda had written by hand on a large pad of graph paper with a lime green cover, was finished, but she read and

edited it obsessively. She swam in the river every second she could, and
when she did so she covered herself with a top like something out of the
nineteenth century, never using a swimsuit or bikini. In my head I invented a reason for this: her body was covered in scars she didn't want
anyone to see. When she wasn't swimming, or collecting tubers, coconuts
or breadfruits, or reading her Mexican copy of Chekhov, she spent every
available second editing her novel. Roberto B. was obsessed with *Suffering
Servant* and spent his days trying to convince Brenda to let him read it, but
she refused, and so he would ask her things about the Chihuahuan Desert
and Ciudad Juárez, where Brenda had endured a terrible adolescence, the
very thought of which was enough to make her eyes shine like metal and
her tone change.

One of her sisters, Brenda told us that evening, had been assaulted and
raped twice before the family decided to leave Ciudad Juárez for Mexico
City, which is where she'd met Óscar. The three sisters had all received
threats or perceived some kind of danger. In Mexico, she went on, this
feeling permeates your life as a woman, you get used to living in fear, and
to living in a kind of hyper-alert state that makes you grow a third eye at
the back of your head. And with this third eye you can see behind you into
the dark spots, the passageways, the alleys; see the jicama and amaranth
sellers, the taco stands, the houses where they sell tamales as evening sets
in, the groups of men drinking beer on street corners. For women in Mexico, fear is something so habitual that it becomes ingrained in their reality,
and they live like that year on year, going out for a smoothie with their
girlfriends or cocktails in the Radisson hotel, to the movies, to friends'
houses to study, to the library, university, the theatre, to watch the sunset
from the mountains (in groups, in cars, and with men, of course). And the
fear was there all the time, even if you were in a group, in cars, and with
men. The fear was there even if they had fancy cars and double-barrel
names and knew that the police wouldn't give them any trouble because of
their big cars and double-barrel names. But the attackers always knew
whom to target, and that's why they went for Lucrecia; twice they went for
her sister Lucrecia (one of those times on Noche Triste, near the Plaza de

Armas); that's why they went for Lucrecia and not her other sister Bernadina, because Lucrecia was made out of grass, and Bernadina cast out of
metal. And Brenda, well, Brenda was cut from stone, and those fucking
bastards had only to see her shadow projected onto a wall at dusk to know
that. Those men were born to recognise an easy target in the same way
coyotes can spot the weakest ram, the one who'll be intimidated, the one
who won't fight back, or the way sharks can smell blood from miles away,
or mosquitoes know which skin is the thinnest.

Roberto B. listened to her engrossed, although he played down his
fascination with a condescending smirk. But he didn't stop asking her
questions, all kinds of things about the north of Mexico: what the light
was like in Ciudad Juárez at night; if the streets were lined with tall dark
eucalyptus trees, and if the streetlights filtered through them. He asked
about the bars and *boîtes* in Ciudad Juárez, and he asked her if there were
big, ominous nightclubs in the middle of the desert. He asked if there
were swimming pools in Ciudad Juárez, and whether she used to frequent
them, and how the boys would look at the girls at the swimming pools,
and how the girls would look at the boys, and what colour the water was,
whether it was blue, or green, or grey, and if there was dust on the bum-
pers of the cars and on the agave plants, and what colour the dust on the
agave was, whether it was russet or white, yellow or brown, ochre or ash
grey. He asked her which kind of tobacco they smoked there, which brand
of tequila and beer they drank, and which brand of condoms they sold in
the pharmacies and what colour the condoms were. He asked if there were
ravines or rocky terrains, and whether nopales grew there, and if she'd
ever seen one of the city's rubbish dumps, those extraordinary rubbish
dumps you come across in so much of Latin America, where you find
enormous birds of prey with huge brown wings, ribbons of thick, dark
smoke rising from fires that never go out, and children caked in dirt, their
faces black from the muck and misery they endure there among the mountains of rubbish, like giant spiders with bright eyes.

'And what's so "amazing" about all that?' Brenda asked him, before
adding that there were no swimming pools in Ciudad Juárez, that there

was no water, or trees, or parks, that nothing he was imagining really existed there, that Ciudad Juárez was a living hell full of pawn shops, taco stands, waste grounds and endless streets of single-storey buildings surrounded by metal fences, with one solitary palm tree growing patiently in the front yard and peeling walls and abandoned dogs, and that everything there was obliterated by the sun, pounded down to the ground, flattened, singed, destroyed, as if the city were no more than a heap of old, fragmented bones, and then there was the Rio Bravo, and the bridges that led to the north, to gringo paradise (bridges surrounded by barbed wire fences), and then Roberto B. asked her if she'd ever been to one of the ranches around there, and she answered asking him if he was nuts, that it was precisely on the Chihuahuan Desert ranches that the narcos hid out and made all the snuff movies, and where they had their sick, twisted parties, fucked-up parties where they went deer hunting.

'For actual deer?' I asked, and she explained that the deer were the women, women whom they released naked into the desert. The narcos would give them an hour or two head start before hunting them down like animals; sometimes they gave them boots so they could run faster, get further, but they always caught up with them in the end. Normally they buried them there, in some ditch, but some of the men were so fucked in the head they took them home, like a hunter might take home their kill, and apparently some of these ranchers kept rooms with stuffed jaguar and African buffalo heads mounted on the walls, and alongside them stuffed human heads: a 'doe'. Some of their prey went missing for days. And according to those hunters, that's when things became interesting because – to give an idea of the level of sophistication of their sense of humour – their prey 'were almost as intelligent as human beings'.

Desert ranches in the middle of nowhere that looked abandoned, only coming to life when they threw parties, at which point the black Peregrino four-by-fours would come rolling in out of the desert dust, great tank-like cars with blacked-out windows driven by men in dark glasses; parties that went on for days... By the end, there was always some girl from a nearby textile factory who ended up in a plastic bag, strangled with her own bra, her belly covered in bruises. And upper-class people were mixed up in this whole sordid business too, politicians, people with money, people with the power to halt the police investigations as, gradually, one by one, the women fell. The police would investigate, but no one was ever arrested.

'Brenda, oh, Brenda, why won't you let me read your novel?' Roberto B. would ask, over and over again.

But she refused.

'It's not finished,' she would say. 'Not yet.'

And this only made Roberto B. obsess even more. Those were Roberto B.'s obsessions: the Third Reich game; Brenda Esquivias Ponce's novel; and Sheila. Beautiful, beguiling Sheila: he spent days flirting with her, right in front of her boyfriend's eyes.

Jesus, he was irritating. There was something slow, graceful, almost peaceful about Roberto B. A sort of idleness, a lack of urgency, an almost divine indifference. The fact that he was impervious or indifferent to the heat irritated me. His seventies, lefty liberal look irritated me. The almost insolent profile of his chin irritated me. His pale cheeks irritated me. The watery, tender look in his blue eyes irritated me, because he had those sweet fuck-me eyes that drive women crazy. The way he held his cigarette between his fingers as if it were a kind of sacred artefact with supernatural powers, and the way he squinted as he took a drag – both these details irritated me. I was irritated by his self-confidence, and again by the fact that I found him so interesting, so captivating, when there was nothing really about him to merit my fascination. But he would reel off anecdotes about Santiago in Chile, or Mexico City, where he'd spent his teenage years and youth, or about Los Angeles, and I'd sit listening to him and praying inside for him not to stop, for him to carry on talking. And one day he spoke about the Third Reich, and the Second World War, and the meaning of the world and the mysteries of evil, whose one terrible, terrifying mystery, he said, was that it wasn't any mystery at all, because the world holds no mysteries, no key, there is no secret rose, as Yeats would have us believe. And then he'd be off preaching about Milton's rose, not that he'd actually read Milton (I don't think he read English, and definitely not Milton's English), but he had read Borges, lots of him, including Borges's poem 'A Rose and Milton'. In that poem, he explained, the rose isn't a symbol of the world but just another object in it. As he spoke, he squinted his eyes to stop the smoke from his cigarette going into them. I listened, both transfixed and furious at myself, like a dog raging against the hand that feeds it because it's so full of fury that it wants to bite that hand clean off. But it can't, and, worst of all, it knows that it can't. He said it was Borges's best poem, a truly important poem, a poem to snap you out of your dreaming, because the world is uncontainable, unaccountable, impossible to define. There is only world, he said, only world, world and more world; objects, beds, milk, semen, rain, eucalyptus, the shadow of rain on the bedsheets and the shadow of rain on the thighs of the girl we're making love to in a cheap hotel, and the hairs on her groin – the most beautiful thing in existence, the hairs on her groin, black on white, like black words on a white page – and neon signs above abandoned hotels and motels, and coyotes with glistening eyes roaming the desert night, and buried bodies, and trains and trucks carrying wood, and trucks loaded with pigs on their way to the slaughterhouse, and trucks loaded with girls on their way to the brothels in the north, and fear and rage, and bars at the border and murdered dogs and crucified dogs and blue drunken nights and violet drunken nights, and girls and more girls and women, pregnant women who scream in labour, and men dreaming alone, and men lurking down dark alleys, and married men who meet up in hotels to fuck and don't even tell each other their name, and sleeping children, and children on their way to school, and army barracks, and a young recruit who resembles Benito Juárez and looks at the pale-legged girls who look back at him and they all dream; and there is the sea and the desert, and there are desires and dreams, poems and books, telephone conversations; there is showering and writing at night, or at any time really, but above all at night, after making love, in the clarity the night brings after sex and after a cool shower after sex, and what absolutely categorically doesn't exist is a secret rose, Roberto B. said. What absolutely categorically doesn't exist is a secret rose, unless we're talking

about the one between a young woman's thighs. That's the only secret
rose, Roberto B. said. As Empedocles understood. As Courbet understood. The Origin of the World. The world's rose. Aphrodite's mother of
pearl shell. As Chiron the centaur, in Rubén Darío's poem, understood.
The rose, the conch, the cunt. The world's triumphant rose.

'Roberto, get a grip, man,' Christian said to him, staring fixedly at the
Third Reich board. 'Your Rommel's going down, you know?'

'No chance,' Roberto B. replied, taking a drag on his cigarette. 'I've got
Rommel in a hooker joint in Tripoli fucked out of his skull. An Argentinian hooker by the name of Sibila just got her knees dirty, if you catch my
drift, and left him as limp as a boiled corncob. The girl doesn't know she's
just sucked the dick of the Desert Fox, and he doesn't know he's just been
serviced by a daughter of Israel.'

'Keep your nasty shit to yourselves,' Brenda said, screwing up her nose.

'Get a grip, Roberto,' Christian repeated.

'That's the best thing about playing The Third Reich with Bobby B.,'
Óscar said. 'After a while it's like you're not watching the board any more,
but some kind of animated movie.'

I left them to it and went for a walk along the beach, because my eyes
were full of the world's splendour as Roberto B. had described it between
drags on his cigarette. The splendour, and misery, the noise and glory of
the world.

My soul was filled with gladiators, sunlight, the world's din, just like in
the Nabokov story I'd read years earlier. I felt overcome with emotion, and
I didn't know where that emotion stemmed from. Perhaps from the island,
from the intense feeling of solitude. Perhaps it came from what Roberto B.
had said about Milton's rose and Yeats's secret rose: that there is no centre,
no explanation, no key to the world. Perhaps it came from his rhapsodic
description of the world and what it was. Rain, sadness, love, coyotes
crossing the desert. I was filled with a very dark feeling of wonder.

Could it really be, I found myself wondering again, that we had come
to this island to be born?

15

My relationship with Roberto B.

A *few days later, I came* across Roberto B. as I was doing my laundry. We tended to wash our clothes on the edge of the river, as I'd watched others do in Spanish villages as a boy. He called me Johnny, and in turn I called him Bobby B. because I knew it grated on him. He washed his clothes, a little shoddily it seemed to me, without removing his cigarette from his mouth. I asked him about his books, which apparently were published in Spain, where he'd also lived. He told me he'd been a night watchman on a campsite on the Costa Brava, among other casual jobs and trips he'd made here and there with a rucksack on his back, living off ham baguettes and sleeping in youth hostels or with girls he met along the way, visiting writer friends' houses and crashing on their sofas. He was, he told me, a bit of a connoisseur when it came to sofas. He lived on other people's sofas. He was a sofa writer, he told me. There, where it all happens, where you can hear everything, where you can find out about everything. Living at the intersection of things, the intersection of day and night, of the living room and the bedroom, because it's precisely at the intersection where the interesting stuff happens, the intersections of the body, the city and the house. I'm not sure how, but from there we got on to women.

'It's been like one long orgy since we washed up here,' he said. 'I'll almost be sad when they come and take us off this goddamn island.'

'Why's that?'

'Because of the women, man,' he said.

'The women, right…' I replied, still not quite catching his drift.

'I'm not sure what the deal is with this place, but ever since we got here it's been a different woman each night, man. The island gets them going.'

'Wow,' I said. 'As many as that?'

He listed them off: Swayla, Sophie Leverkuhn, Idoya, Rosana, an American girl whose name I can't remember, an Australian woman whose name I never found out, Mrs Lee (the best of the lot, he told me, despite the cross around her neck), Brenda and Sheila, although with those two it hadn't gone further than a bit of a fumble. I was lost for words.

'Rosana?' I asked.

'You have no idea. We wore each other out! Spanish girls are so passionate.'

Slightly illogically, I went straight to talk to Rosana. I found her in her hut, tidying up and putting Syra's clothes away in a suitcase. She was wearing a pair of white shorts and a lacy bra. God, she drove me crazy. She had voluptuous rolls of fat at her waistline, like one of Rubens's Venuses, but the skin on her back was smooth and rosy, with the marble-like gleam of someone who works out a lot. What might it be, in her case? Pilates, aerobics, workouts, paddle ball?

'Knock, knock,' I said.

She turned around, and didn't attempt to cover herself up.

'I'll come back, you're not dressed.'

'There's no need,' she said, nonchalantly repositioning one of her straps. 'I'm just so hot.'

The elastic left thick red marks on the soft skin on her shoulders. Her lips were painted cherry red. There were tiny beads of sweat on her forehead and top lip.

'I just wanted to ask you something. I'm not sure what you'll think of me afterwards, but I don't care, because I have to ask you anyway. Did you sleep with Roberto B.?'

'Who's Roberto B.?' she asked, her beautiful black eyes opening wide. They had seemed so enormous under her glasses, but were now small and intense. I described him in quite careful detail and she told me she'd only ever spoken to him briefly, but that in any case it was none of my business.

'You're right,' I said. 'It's none of my business.'

'Of course I haven't slept with Roberto B.,' she said. 'Why do you ask?'

'Because he's going around saying you did and how passionate Spanish women are.'

'Well, well,' she said. 'I don't believe it. Juan Barbarín, are you jealous?'

'No, merely curious.'

'Curious about why he'd go around saying that, right?' she said. She had an amused, almost affectionate look on her face, although I knew those sentiments weren't directed towards me.

'Anyway, why were you talking about me?' she said, adjusting her other bra strap and staring me straight in the eyes as if butter wouldn't melt in her mouth. The white of the garment against the dewy pink of her skin was as striking as the flame of a fire, and she took a few steps towards me, coming dangerously close, clearly fully aware of the effect she had on me.

'We weren't talking about you. We were talking about something else, and then Roberto B. said… Oh, listen, it doesn't matter. Forget it.' I walked out of her hut, but no sooner had I left than I turned around and went straight back in again. She had knelt down in front of the suitcase, and saw me come back in. I knelt down beside her. She looked at me with one eyebrow raised, clearly amused. I began to stroke her dark, wavy hair and she knelt there, accepting my caresses. Her neck was sweaty and burning. Her whole body was dripping in sweat, just like mine, just like all of ours. I moved in to kiss her on the lips. We kissed for a while but although she didn't pull away, she didn't really reciprocate either. She kissed timorously and discreetly, refusing to separate her lips or offer me her tongue. It was like kissing a statue.

'I really like you,' I told her.

'I like you too,' she said.

'So?'

'So,' she said, placing five fingers – the nails painted violet – on my chest and gently pushing me away, 'be patient. Don't mess it up.'

The wolves came to the village that night. Word spread that they were angry and looking for revenge for the wolf our lot had killed a few days earlier. I was woken up by screaming, and then ran out of my hut as fast as I could and spotted Wade with a torch going into the jungle and shouting. I don't know when he'd made that torch, but there were more of them, and more men wielding them. Their silhouettes in the orange light of the flames broke the pitch blackness of the trees. I heard the sound of women screaming and the unmistakable wail of baby Seymour.

'The wolves,' they cried, 'the wolves have come!'

I didn't dare go into the undergrowth unarmed and without a torch, and I was ashamed of my own fear. But the thought of Bill Higgins's arm came to me and I felt my very bladder quiver. The sound of shots could be heard coming from the trees. I spotted the Leverkuhns and their children, who'd been woken by the shouts and screams. The men returned from the forest a while later with their torches, and not long after that followed Wade. He seemed shaken, and for the first time since arriving on the island he wasn't smiling, although he hadn't lost his heroic, almost superhuman aura. They asked him if it was the wolves and he answered that he thought so, that he'd seen the wolves' eyes glinting in the darkness, but that the torches had frightened them off.

'We have to build fires every night,' he said. 'And the children should all sleep together in a well-protected area. Wolves always target the weakest prey.'

It was then that he noticed some of the children were there, listening to him. I saw his blue eyes open wide in the knowledge that adrenalin and his nerves had got the better of him. The last thing he'd wanted to do was scare the children, or for terror to spread among the castaways. Sebastian Leverkuhn looked at him, pale-faced and serious, but it was his brother Carl who spoke.

'Mr Erickson,' the boy said with a surprising level of composure. 'Don't worry about the wolves. The wolves don't want to harm the children.'

'And how do you know that?' Wade asked, the smile returning to his face.

'Wolves are friends of children,' Carl said. 'It's the adults they don't like. And besides, those creatures tonight weren't real wolves.'

'Weren't real?' Wade asked. 'What are you talking about?'

'Wade, he's a little boy,' Joseph said. He'd been among the torchbearers. 'Don't listen to him as if he were an oracle.'

'No, wait, Joseph,' Wade said raising a finger in the air. 'Bear with me... let the boy tell us what he knows.'

'He doesn't *know* anything, Wade,' Joseph said. 'He's ten years old.'

'They were fake wolves,' Carl said. And then, pointing all around him with his finger, he added, 'Everything on this island is fake.'

'What do you... what do you mean?' Wade asked.

Sophie spoke up then, saying that it was very late and the children needed to rest, and the group gradually dispersed. There were still several campfires burning here and there, and I guess the vision of the fire calmed me down. I saw Rosana in the distance and gave her a wave, which she returned. It was the same old story, the tale of old Sir John Barbarin. I'd only been on the island a week or so, and already there were too many women in my life. And yet at the same time, there were really none at all.

And another thing. A new emotion had begun to grow inside of me on the island. The annoyance I felt at Roberto B. had now turned into genuine hatred. I hated him because he'd taken me for a ride. I hated him because he'd laughed at my expense and made a fool of me. I suddenly realised why Roberto B. was invincible playing The Third Reich; why it was impossible to hold back his advancing armies. Brenda, Óscar, Christian and Sheila together couldn't beat him. And the reason was: Roberto B. cheated. This was the only possible explanation. He did it at night, when everyone was asleep and the board was left on the special table they'd built to play on. It was impossible to remember the exact position of hundreds of pieces on hundreds of hexagons. On one of those nights I watched him creep stealthily towards the board and switch pieces, both adding and removing them. I can't say for sure that that's what he was doing, but the more I think about it in retrospect, the more certain I am. I saw him sitting in front of the board, in the pitch darkness, a darkness so impenetrable it was impossible to see the pieces or hexagons, although I think I remember he had a flashlight and that he turned it off as I walked towards him. He told me he couldn't sleep, and I replied that it was impossible to sleep in that infernal heat. He told me he was thinking over the following day's moves and I asked him how he could see the board in the dark.

'When you've been playing for long enough,' he said, 'you develop a kind of connection with the board. Sometimes,' he went on, 'I think I could play with my eyes closed. It's when you can start to play intuitively that the game gets interesting.' And I hated him, and didn't want to carry on talking to him, but Roberto B. fascinated me and I couldn't walk away.

'I've always looked for that thing you call the Secret Rose,' I said.

'I know,' he replied.

Then he offered me a cigarette and told me it was one of his last, and I accepted his offer even though I'm not a smoker, and I smoked alongside him without inhaling.

'I know,' he said again. 'You can see it in your eyes. But, you know, some of us were born with no faith, no hope and very little charity.'

'But knowing that there is no Secret Rose,' I said, 'isn't that the same as knowing the meaning of the world? Knowing that the world is meaning-less? Isn't that the Secret Rose?'

'I do believe in the Secret Rose,' he said after a moment's pause, which he spent aggressively scratching his right ankle, the mosquitoes' favourite spot. 'I think it exists, but in a place we can't reach.'

'Perhaps it's on this island. Maybe we've come to this island to be born.'

'You mean, maybe we've come to this island to die,' he said. 'I don't know why I have the feeling we're never getting out of here, that we're all going to rot here, that we're already in our own cemetery.'

That's what Roberto B. said, that sometimes he felt like we were in a cemetery. That our island of flowers and palm trees and birds was, in fact, a graveyard.

16

Santiago uncovers a traitor

We set up a lookout post on airplane beach to greet our hypothetical rescuers. The shifts were six hours long, and were always taken in pairs to avoid anyone being left on their own and nodding off. At night, the guards kept a campfire burning. Santiago Reina was in charge of organising the shifts. To help him, he had a list of all the passengers' names that someone had found in one of the flight attendants' lockers on the plane. And it was thanks to this list that he made a truly strange discovery.

That night he gathered together Joseph, Wade, Christian and me in his hut to tell us what it was he'd found out. He spoke very quietly, as if someone were listening in. He seemed terrified, excessively so given the circumstances, I couldn't help thinking. In his hand he held the list of passengers. He'd spent days glued to that list, reading and re-reading it from top to bottom, back to front. Now he'd lit a candle to see by, even though we were running low on candles and tried to use them only when strictly necessary. The one Santiago was holding barely illuminated the tired, crumpled pieces of paper and our haggard faces, gleaming with sweat. We were always sweating on the island, day or night.

'Guys,' he whispered, 'there's no one by the name of George on the list of passengers.'

'What do you mean?' Joseph asked.

'I mean, man, that George wasn't on the plane!'

'George the gentle giant who wouldn't hurt a fly and who spends all day with Lizzy and her baby helping her bath him?'

'Yes, that George! He's not on the list,' he repeated, showing us the pieces of paper and moving them into the candlelight so we could read the names for ourselves.

'Look, I'm sure there's an explanation,' I said. 'Names often appear wrong on plane tickets. If it's a long name, they shorten it.'

'He's called George,' Santiago said. 'And on this list of almost four hundred people there isn't a single George, nor anyone called G. or any name remotely like George. I've looked it over so many times I can practically recite it, guys. I think George was already on the island when we got here, and when we showed up he decided to pass himself off as one of us. He infiltrated our little society.'

'George looks like he wouldn't say boo to a goose,' I said. 'He's just a kind, friendly guy.'

'He's faking it,' Santiago said. 'I'm sure of it. It's all an act.'

'Does anyone remember seeing George on the plane, or at Los Angeles airport?' Wade asked.

All five of us fell silent.

'There has to be a rational explanation,' Joseph repeated. 'Let's go and talk to him.'

'Whoa there,' Santiago said. He'd clearly given a lot of thought to the matter and had it all planned out. 'We can't go and talk to him just like that. We have to think about what we're going to say first. It's possible he's anticipated this eventuality and has his story prepared. We need a plan.'

'But I don't understand why you're so frightened by the possibility that he was already on the island,' I said.

'Something really weird is going on here,' Santiago said. 'I think this George has a plan. What worries me isn't so much that George was already on the island, but that in all likelihood he's not alone. Do you see what I'm getting at?'

And that is how terror struck the island: by the light of a candle burning on the floor of a hut. I noticed then that Santiago's hands were shaking, and that he was totally and utterly terrified.

'The only explanation is that they're a group,' Santiago said. 'There are other people on the island. They've been watching us since we got here.'

'You're insane,' I said.

'Don't call me insane,' Jack said, glaring at me. 'Don't you ever call me insane again.'

'I'm sorry, Santiago.'

'It's all right. Just don't do it again.'

'I didn't mean to offend you, man.'

We decided to talk to George first thing the next day. I slept well, and the next morning ate breakfast with my Spanish friends and Rosana and Syra, cracking the same old jokes about whether we wanted our coffee strong or weak, with full-fat or skimmed milk, and then I spotted Santiago and Joseph coming towards us, making signs at me with their eyes. I got up and joined them. We picked up Wade, who was emerging from the jungle with two birds tied at his waist, and went to find George.

He was washing his clothes in the laundry area, surrounded by women and joking around with them. He was the embodiment of the roguish lad. We told him we wanted a word, took him aside and then headed to Santiago's hut. George said he hadn't finished his laundry, that he didn't want to leave his clothes there by the river. He tried to get away but we didn't let him. Santiago came straight out with what was obviously a well-rehearsed trump card. He told him that we knew he hadn't been on our plane and that he was already on the island when we fell from the sky. George's reaction was the strangest part of all.

He was outraged. He said the whole theory was laughable. We told him that we'd been asking around and that nobody recalled having seen him either on the plane or before boarding. We told him his name wasn't on the list of passengers.

Anyone innocent would have demanded to see the passenger list, or would have given an explanation for why his name, or at least his first name 'George', wasn't on it. But George didn't do any of that. He didn't make the least attempt to see the list of passengers, which Santiago still had. He said, tersely, that it wasn't his fault they'd made a mistake and missed his name off the list. He said our accusations were absurd, that we were crazy and paranoid. Santiago asked him his surname and he said it was Payne. There was one passenger on the list by the name of Payne, a certain Olga Payne, who clearly hadn't survived. Santiago asked him where he lived, and George told him he worked in a paint shop in Hollywood and that he lived with a room-mate called Irving who was a construction engineer and played the tuba. Santiago asked him how he'd arrived on the island. He asked him what he'd been on his way to India for. He asked him over and again. I was amazed by that great clumsy lad, who spoke like someone who hadn't finished school but possessed a mental clarity and shrewdness that was beyond the rest of us. He asked George which seat he'd been in on the plane, to which George responded that he couldn't remember. But then this wasn't so unusual: I wasn't sure I could recall my own seat number by then. There are people without a head for numbers, just as there are people without a head for names.

George said we were crazy, and that he didn't have to put up with our nonsense. We let him go. What else could we do? We couldn't hold him there. We had no proof he'd done anything, nor was there any real reason to leave him there tied up, which in retrospect is what we should have done.

So George stormed off and went straight to Lizzy's hut. Lizzy herself was in the lagoon area, where the children played. She was sitting in the shade, finishing breastfeeding Seymour. When George showed up, Lizzy asked him to watch the baby for a few minutes while she took a dip. Seymour stopped feeding, she covered herself up and handed the baby to George. The little thing was well fed and calm, still awake but heavy-eyed, sated and happy. The moment Lizzy turned her back, George took off with the baby boy in his arms and disappeared into the jungle. Nobody saw him. Nobody was able to say, later on, in which direction he'd gone.

It took us a long time to clock that George and Seymour were missing. When she found that they weren't where she'd left them, Lizzy assumed George had gone back to the village to change the baby, perhaps, or lay him in his cot. So she'd gone looking for him first in her hut, then George's.

She thought perhaps that Seymour might have had wind and colic and that George had taken him for a walk. She looked for him further upriver; she looked for him on the beach. Finally, she began to worry. When we learnt that it had been a couple of hours since anyone had seen George and that he'd disappeared with Seymour, the penny dropped for Santiago, Wade, Joseph and me.

We organised search parties. We spent the day trekking through the jungle in several directions. We tried to be rational and to think where George might have fled to. We told ourselves that a man carrying a baby in his arms can't get too far very quickly, and that if we all joined in the search, we would find him eventually. But we didn't.

17

Fear

Terror set in among us.
Some imagined that George was a castaway who'd been on the island for some time, and that his long period of isolation had slowly sapped his mental faculties. 'Ben Gunn,' I would say. 'George is Ben Gunn, that character from *Treasure Island* who frightened the life out of me as a kid.' We figured that George had been living in a cave somewhere where he could take shelter from the constant rains in the island's interior. On seeing our plane fall from the sky and discovering the beach full of castaways it must have occurred to him – God knows why – to pass himself off as one of us, abandon his shelter and come and live in our settlement.

Another possibility, just as Jack Reina had imagined it, was that it wasn't a desert island at all, and that there was a group of men living further inland. We couldn't imagine what those hypothetical men might want with an unweaned baby, but there was no other decent explanation.

In our heads we visualised a band of criminals – pirates of the kind that still exist in the South Seas, perhaps – watching us for days with all kinds of sick and twisted plans in store: to kill us, or force us to work for them, blackmail us to release Seymour, rape our women, use us as fodder. Might that be the reason George ran off with the baby? Had he taken Seymour to stew and eat him? I remembered having read tales long before of people who'd been driven mad by hunger in Siberia, China and Manchuria. I also remembered having read another story about the famines in China during Mao's 'Great Leap Forward', when the authorities robbed the peasants' grain and kept it in silos, and about how many of those peasants who were starving to death had begun to eat little girls (little boys have always been more highly regarded in China, and all over for that matter), and I also remembered a phrase from a terrible book, or perhaps it was a report from Amnesty International, that said: 'a newborn baby girl would only last two days'. By which they meant that a couple of days later the family would be starving again and would have to go looking for another little girl.

It was from this time on that I joined the circle of meditators each evening. The sessions tended to last an hour and a half, and I struggled to stay awake for that long.

According to Dharma Mittra's teachings, one's breathing, posture, physical fitness, as well as healthy vital organs and well-functioning glands, were all directly related to one's spiritual health and to one's mood. I was surprised to hear that 'spiritual' wisdom depended so heavily on the proper functioning of the organs. Many of the mental exercises we did in preparation for meditation had to do, as my good friend the Brazilian carpenter explained, with stimulation of the pituitary gland or the pineal gland, as well as the stimulation of the nervous system and undeveloped areas of the brain. The breathing exercises were often complicated and I would get lost trying to keep up, although Rosana and my friends, Julián and Matilde, helped me out. Yes, I was interested. Yes, I was intrigued. It intrigued me to discover, for example, the effect that certain breathing rhythms can have on your spirits or on your clarity of thought, topics I promised myself I'd look into further when I had time and occasion to do so, because that clarity of vision and hearing could be useful tools for an artist.

But most appealing of all to me was the moment we began the journey of introspection and entered into the world of interior images. Dharma explained time and again that the whole idea of meditation was to go beyond; to reach a place with no thoughts; to make the mind stop completely. It was at this point that true meditation began, he told us. But in order for the mind to relax, yogis practised voluntarily creating interior images (in line with tantric techniques) that in turn helped them to channel their psychic energy in the desired direction and to learn to control the mind. Once one has gained this control then it is possible, with time, to achieve a fleeting instant of total pause or interruption of the mind, and it was at this moment that true meditation could begin.

'Only when the mind stops,' Dharma explained, 'can the spirit descend and reveal itself.'

Four days after Seymour's abduction there was another wolf attack, this time at night. A second child disappeared. I didn't see them, or maybe I did: shadows of huge great dogs darting between the trees and our huts. But I certainly heard them. I think we all heard their baying and harrowing yowls. Kunze came out with his Lazzeroni and fired several shots without managing to injure a single wolf. In the middle of this commotion, nobody noticed that young Branford, the Griffins' boy, had disappeared. His parents didn't clock that he'd gone until the following morning, when they went to wake him up and discovered that somebody had gone to the trouble of padding out the sheets with clothes so that it looked like the boy was still sleeping there. I remember Gloria's screams when she realised her son wasn't there in his little bed. They were like the screams of an injured animal, a creature in agony.

Branford was five years old and was a fairly solitary kid. In my memory he was always sulking and dishevelled. He had the kind of unruly blond hair that always found a way to become matted in clumps. I also remember he had a strong personality, and you could already sense what kind of man he would become. It's like that with some kids: you can look at them and know exactly what they'll be like at forty. Branford spent a lot of time among the rocks on the shore looking for small marine animals, starfish and crabs, and he had a blue glass bottle where he kept the tiny white snails he found on the beach. Oddly enough, that bottle had also disappeared. It was as if his abductor, or abductors, knew how important that bottle was to Branford, or as if the boy had found a moment to take it with him. So why hadn't he screamed? Why had he gone with his abductors?

My God, it was strange. The wolf attacks, the disappearance of the boy, and above all the atrocious, sinister doll under the sheets. It all seemed perfectly planned and ruthlessly executed. I found myself asking if it might be true that the wolves weren't wolves at all, just like young Carl said. But we'd seen and heard them on several occasions by then, and some of our lot had got a good look at them in the jungle in the full light of day and described them in detail, among them Gwen, a wildlife biologist. And then, of course, one of them had ripped off Billy Higgins's arm. No, the wolves were real, there was no doubt about it, and George and his lot had taken advantage of their attack on the village to snatch little Branford in the midst of the mayhem. I wondered whether they might even have been the ones to deliberately provoke the beasts.

By that point we were under no illusions that George was acting alone. We imagined a handful of others, a group of four of five desperate, savage men living somewhere in the interior, castaways washed up on the island years ago and driven mad by isolation and hunger.

We headed back out in search of the abducted children. And we searched for days, but once again we found no trace of them.

There was something deeply weird in all this to me. It's true that we looked for the children for days, but why did we decide to call off the search? How could their parents consent to us stopping the search? It's true that we looked high and low, but the island was big, and the children could have been taken very far away, somewhere deep in the island's interior. Why did it take us so long to head inland?

18

Fear sets in

Bruce and Gloria, Branford's parents, had a complete breakdown after their son's disappearance. I can't even begin to imagine what they must have been going through, knowing that some mentally unstable person, or a group of mentally unstable people, had taken their son who knows where, and to do who knows what with him. The torment of their fear and imaginations was beyond my comprehension. And how can you stop your imagination? Sometimes, during our meditation sessions, I would envision children skewered on a spit and roasting on a fire surrounded by a group of ruthless, drooling men, and I'd have to open my eyes to erase the horrendous images from my mind. During that time, I frequently thanked God that I didn't have any children of my own, and I told myself I'd never have them. The sheer terror and responsibility of procreating have always seemed unbearable to me.

Gloria blamed Bruce for Branford's disappearance and abandoned the family hut to shack up with Jimmy Bruëll. A stranger reaction I can't imagine. Instead of clutching to her husband in her anguish, Gloria now spent her nights drinking beer and vodka with Jimmy and letting him fuck her. I guess humiliation is easier to stand than dread.

We were all outraged by Jimmy's behaviour and by how he took advantage of the couple's breakdown and of Gloria's deranged state. We had a word with him, and Jimmy told Gloria he didn't want her in his hut any more. But Gloria refused to go back to her husband. She tried it on with Joseph. She tried it on with me. Finally, Omotola, the Nigerian woman, took her under her wing. I suspect the pain of their respective losses united them. They hardly ever spoke; at least I never heard them talking. But if nothing else, Gloria had calmed down a little.

After the night of Branford's disappearance we began putting all the children to bed together in Rosana and Syra's hut, right in the middle of the village, and took turns guarding them. Nothing happened that night, or the next. But on the third day, at some point over the course of the day (we couldn't watch them 24/7, or keep them cooped up in a cage day and night), Adele and Estelle, the little sisters who spent their time nattering like squirrels and playing indecipherable games, disappeared. All it took was a brief moment of distraction on the part of their parents, Henry and Diffy (short for Daffodil, I think) McCullough. Perhaps they overslept and the girls left the hut and were snatched while playing further upriver. Henry McCullough was an Australian diplomat who'd been the embassy's commercial attaché in various posts in Africa and South Asia. His wife Diffy was tall, majestic and beautiful. We all saw her crying silently. We saw them fighting and we saw them praying. We saw Henry, a burly, imperious-looking man, scouring the jungle with the search parties as he clutched his gun – a gun, incidentally, that his wife claimed he didn't even know how to use. The groups went looking for Adele and Estelle just as they'd gone looking for Branford before them, and Seymour before him, and they didn't find a thing. And now there were four children missing, and the feeling of fear and despondency among the group was mounting. I'm not sure if it was around this time that we began to refer to George and those who were with him in the interior as the Insiders.

The Leverkuhns were never seen apart now, and they took turns at night to stay awake. As for Rosana and Syra, they weren't getting on any better. Syra kept on escaping and doing the odd little things that so amused her: taking objects and hiding them or 'rearranging' them so that someone might go mad looking for their sunglasses, or their watch, or their diary, or the book they were reading, or the trousers they'd hung out to dry, only to find them later somewhere completely unexpected: at the top of a tamarind tree or down on the bed of the crystalline river. And she was constantly disappearing, toying with her mother who would be terrified that her daughter, too, had been abducted, and enjoying this small act of revenge. Rosana would spend all day calling out to Syra in her shrill, piercing voice, and whenever this happened I found I didn't even want to see Rosana, because it pained me to hear the things she would say to Syra and to watch how her rage got the better of her as she dissolved into a total meltdown.

Subjected as she was to the constant criticism and unrelenting control of her mother, Syra had developed her own twisted and indirect forms of rebellion. She chewed the torn skin around her fingernails until they were red raw, a habit that drove her mother out of her mind (although Rosana admitted to me that she'd had exactly the same bad habit as a child). Syra also scratched her mosquito bites until they turned into cuts, and finally sores that never healed. Rosana would chase after her daughter to stop her from scratching. She would cut the girl's nails, file them down and wrap them in plasters as she chided her. But Syra still found ways to carry on scratching, making herself bleed, letting the sores heal over and then picking at the scabs, enjoying the delicious sting, the delicious pain. Sometimes Syra would hide from Rosana to avoid being seen scratching, but the habit was so deep-rooted that she'd end up doing it in plain sight of Rosana, who would catch her at it and lose it all over again.

Once, without saying a word to her mother, but assuring the others she had her permission, Syra joined a group of castaways who were heading to airplane beach to collect coconuts. Rosana spent the whole morning looking for her, completely hysterical, and just when she'd convinced herself that the mystery abductors had taken her daughter too, up popped Syra, beaming away as she clasped Josephine's hand alongside Óscar and Brenda, Udo and Di Di, all wielding bags full of coconuts. Rosana blew a fuse.

'You walked off?' Rosana screamed hysterically as she saw Syra arrive hand in hand with Josephine. 'You walked off without saying a word to Mummy? Answer me!'

'I told you I was going,' Syra said meekly.

'Didn't you tell your mother you were coming with us?' Josephine asked Syra in what little broken Spanish she had. 'You told us a fib?'

'I don't know,' Syra said, looking down and pouting.

'You stupid child!' Rosana shouted, striding towards her daughter and grabbing her by the arm. 'Do you know how scared Mummy's been? Don't you know how to listen to instructions?' She was so furious she was twisting the girl's arm. Unsure what to do with her rage, she yanked Syra hard by the arm. 'I'm going to tie you up with a rope. You'll be punished for this. You're not getting out of it. You haven't seen the half of what I'm capable of!'

'You're hurting me!' Syra said, still in her meek voice.

I was close to the girl and I looked her in the eyes. And she looked back at me from under her dark locks and she smiled. My God, it scared the life out of me, that smile. Her face was twisted in pain under Rosana's vice-like grip, and yet the girl was smiling at me, as if trying to make me party to her secret. Several people from the village had approached us on hearing the shouts, among them Sophie Leverkuhn and the young Chinese couple from Singapore, Jung Fei Ye and his wife Pei Pei Je.

'That's enough!' Sophie shouted. 'Let the girl go!'

'Keep out of this,' Rosana snapped back. 'She's my daughter!'

She was so incensed she could barely find the words in English.

Sophie drew herself up to her full height, towering over Rosana. She was bigger and stronger than her, and cut an imposing figure next to her petite adversary.

'No!' she said. 'You will not touch that girl. I won't have it. Day after day I've watched how you treat your daughter and I can't bear it a second longer. And I'm not the only one! We've discussed it among ourselves and you simply cannot go on treating her this way.'

'The Spanish lady is right,' Pei Pei Je said out of nowhere. 'This girl behaves very badly.'

'"This girl" is subjected to abuse,' Sophie said. 'She's terrorised! That's why she does the things she does.'

'She does not obey her mother,' Pei Pei went on, with a cold glint in her eyes. 'Children must obey their parents. And she does not. Children must do as they are told!'

'At least someone's on my side,' Rosana said, clearly on the brink of tears.

'This girl ought to be lashed,' Pei Pei said. 'That way she will learn to do as her elders say.'

19

We call an assembly

That night was the second of our general assemblies including all the castaways. The most skilled fire makers among us lit a campfire on the riverbank so that we could see one another's faces, but even then, the forest shadows seemed to engulf us. Small creatures, birds, little reptiles and sprightly primates peeped out and observed us warily from the undergrowth, using the vines and branches to get closer to that human assembly. I won't relate everything that was said there, but instead will give a general overview.

Sophie brought up the need to establish some sort of code of conduct. She made reference to *Lord of the Flies* which I think went over many people's heads (I have to confess that I've never read the book, although I know the story and saw Peter Brook's film adaptation), and said that we had to make an effort to carry on behaving as civilised human beings and not buckle under the pressure of the extreme situation in which we found ourselves. Everyone agreed with her, although the interpretation of her words couldn't have been more varied. For Jung Fei Ye and his wife, as well as for Tudelli, Hansa, the Lees and the Kunzes, this meant establishing a far stricter code in order to check anyone who didn't behave properly, and 'nip it in the bud'.

Pei Pei formally proposed some sort of punishment for Syra. That child, she told us, behaved very badly, didn't do as she was told, and must be lashed with a rattan cane in front of everyone. That way she'd learn the importance of discipline once and for all. It would do her good, she went on. It would be the best thing for her.

'That's what they did to you, is it, baby girl?' Jimmy Bruëll began. 'That's how you learnt the importance of discipline?'

'My husband could have you whining in agony on the floor in a milli-second,' Pei Pei responded calmly. 'I ask you, don't provoke him.'

'Please,' Jung Fei Ye said, 'speak to my wife with respect.'

'I'm all for respect,' Jimmy said. 'What I don't like is administering it with whippings. Or was it with Ben Wa balls? I'm a bit lost.'

I can't be certain Jung Fei Ye got Jimmy's racist joke. But I'm con-vinced a man like him would know exactly what Ben Wa balls are, espe-cially coming from Singapore, which despite its moralistic laws is a well-known den of vice. Perhaps he didn't hear him, or perhaps to him Jimmy was nothing but a hillbilly whose insults didn't merit a response.

'Corporal punishment is absolutely out of the question,' Joseph inter-vened. 'We're not barbarians, and we're not going to turn into barbar-ians.'

'You're calling me a barbarian?' Jung Fei Ye said. 'The North Ameri-cans once again schooling the rest of us in values? *I'm* the barbarian? I haven't thrown napalm on children, or atomic bombs on cities. I haven't had Black slaves or massacred any Indians. *I'm* the barbarian?'

'All right, folks, everyone calm down,' Wade said, standing up and moving towards the fire with his arms up. 'I think we're all missing the real point here. We're all worked up and scared, and fear and nerves are the worst possible guides.'

'So what is "the real point", Mr Erickson?' Stephan Kunze asked. 'In your opinion, what is this important point we're all missing?'

Kunze spoke very softly and didn't make the slightest effort to raise his voice, but despite this, when he spoke, the group stopped their muttering. I've never understood how certain people wield that kind of gravitas, nor where it comes from. The Kunzes could usually be found sitting in blue seats taken from the plane and which their 'assistants' were constantly moving from here to there. Tudelli had one to himself too.

'Do tell us, Mr Erickson,' Kunze continued, 'what is this important point? Because as far as I can see, we're coming apart at the seams: our little society is falling apart and it needs leadership. Moral leadership first and foremost.'

'What we're forgetting,' Wade said, 'is that nothing that happens on this island happens by chance. There's a reason we're all here. Everything that happens on this island happens for a reason. Even the terrible and inexplicable things that happen, the things that terrify and baffle us, happen for a reason.'

'It's all God's will,' Hansa said.

'I don't know if it's God's will,' Wade said, 'I don't know if God has a will, or if God exists, or if he does exist whether he's all that bothered about us. I'm not even sure God knows this place exists. It may be that this is a place God has forgotten. And maybe, just maybe, in spite of everything, that is our great fortune – the fortune of being in a place where God can't see us. I'm not a wise man. There are wiser, more intelligent, more cultured men than me here. We've got doctors, psychiatrists, bankers, bishops, architects, professors. I'm a nobody. But ever since I landed on this island I've been someone. I'm someone who knows that his life isn't a drop of water that gets sucked down the drain when someone pulls the bath plug. Because I'm here. Because I'm standing on my two legs here and alive. Because I survived, like all of you. We've been handed a second chance at life. We can't waste it. We all know that this is no ordinary place. Extraordinary things happen here. We've experienced them. We experience it every day. Miracles happen in this place. *This* is what we should be talking about. Not punishing children. Not punitive laws. We should be talking about the miracles, and we should be giving thanks and trying to make sense of it. We have to leave behind our need for revenge. I've always wanted revenge. I think ever since I was twelve, maybe even younger, I've always felt fear, and hate, and resentment, and I've wanted to take my revenge. I've lived under the permanent weight of having to be the person I didn't want to be, or who I could never become. But the moment I arrived on this island all of that disappeared. My desire for revenge disappeared. I forgive everyone who's ever hurt me. I forgive everyone who's ever hurt me because now they can't touch me. Nor can my own guilt touch me; I'm freeing myself from my guilt too. I forgive everyone who's ever hurt me and also those people I hurt. I forgive myself. I accept who I am. I embrace myself. I welcome myself. I'm so much more than I was, and I'm capable of so much more than I used to be. Nothing can touch me because now I know who I am. And I know it thanks to this island.'

'You're insane, Erickson,' Kunze said. 'I don't want to hear another word.'

'Well, Kunze,' Wade replied good-humouredly, 'I'm not sure how you're going to shut me up. The truth is you can't.'

'Anyone would think you were happy to be here,' Kunze said. 'Happy! You think you're on some kind of mission. You're a maniac.'

Tempers began to fray, and here and there voices spoke up to defend Wade, others to take Kunze's side. Some had questions for Wade, and others shouted that we were getting off the point. And then, through this cacophony, we heard the sound of a violin. It was Sebastian Leverkuhn, who had taken out his instrument and begun to play.

He played the Largo from Bach's Sonata for Solo Violin No. 3. I'm not sure what prompted him to start playing, or if the idea to pick up his violin had been his own or his mother's, although I do know Sebastian didn't need anyone to tell him what to do.

When Sebastian began playing, everything changed. I can't explain exactly how it changed, or what the others heard in that moment, or even what it meant to them. The meeting began to disperse. A few women broke down in tears. The Kunzes and Tudelli carried on speaking feverishly among themselves, still sitting in their ridiculous reclining seats. But mainly I remember all those people embracing, and my own burning desire to do the same. I don't think this had to do with Sebastian's playing, although I suppose it's possible it was the music, which went on playing and seemed to me quite the most beautiful and strange music I'd ever heard. And it didn't sound like music; this was nothing like the familiar German music of the Reformation written by some man with a quill by candlelight. It didn't sound like music. I don't know what it was, but it wasn't music.

I looked for Gwen and found her hugging Joseph, who had his eyes closed and was whispering in her ear. I looked for Swayla and found her hugging Santiago Reina, sort of buried in his enormous, doughy chest. I looked for Idoya and found her hugging Ignacio. I looked for Sheila and found her hugging Christian. I looked for Nicollette Sheridan and found her hugging Jean Jani. I looked for Rosana and found her hugging her daughter, stroking her long black hair. I looked at Syra's face to see what her eyes were doing and noticed she was distracted, watching everything around her – the lights from the fire, the reflections in the river, the capuchin monkeys, which in turn were watching the scene from the tops of branches. The look in her eyes was unfathomable, but it also seemed to me that the little girl was thinking about something else, something unconnected to the suffering, the remorse, or her mother's tough love. When she spotted me there next to them, she smiled.

20

We see a flying saucer

I was awoken the next day by Sheila's ecstatic cries. I stood up from my bed of leaves and ran towards the lagoon. There were several others down there, all looking up at an enormous, dazzlingly white flying saucer hovering in the sky. Its shadow was visible on the surface of the sea where it met the coastline.

Christian was convinced there was an underground base of flying saucers somewhere inland, almost certainly accessible via the crater of the central volcano (a volcano that, as far as our knowledge of the island's topography stretched at that point, didn't even exist). He, Sheila and Joaquín – who were growing increasingly excited – speculated that extra-terrestrial beings living on the island had heard we were lost and distressed, and had sent one of their space probes to give us a message of reassurance. The truth was, they went on, the extra-terrestrials had struggled to understand us. It had taken them days to finally interpret our confused and contradictory psychological states, since our minds are too fast, too volatile for them. But at last they'd understood that we were lost and in need of help. Wade was also looking up at the sky. Sophie was there too, as well as Rosana and my Spanish friends, the Latin Americans, the Indians. Tudelli was frowning up at the flying saucer looking displeased, as if our rivals had suddenly come down from on high. Robert Frost and Robert Kelly scurried around telling everyone that flying saucers were part of the beliefs of the religion announced by Joseph Smith and were nothing less than ships inhabited by angels who came from other planets to spread the gospel of Latter-day Saints among the world.

Joseph Langdon was there too, watching the scene unfold with his arms crossed. Our eyes met and I sauntered towards him. Santiago Reina was also there, eating peach jam directly from the jar, scratching himself absent-mindedly, as we had all taken to doing by then, and frowning at the flying saucer. It was undeniably beautiful. It was perfectly round and gleaming white, made out of who knows what strange material. A splendid, awe-inspiring white. Hovering completely still in the middle of the sky, its oval shadow darkening the sea below.

'The sacred cow,' Santiago said to us, now sinking his fingers into the jam jar. 'What on earth is up with these guys?'

'They're desperate,' Joseph said. 'They need something to hold onto.'

'But come on,' I said to Joaquín and the Chileans. 'You guys do realise it's a cloud, right?'

Joaquín glared at me, almost pouting with disgust.

'It's not a cloud, Johnny!' Sheila said, talking to me as if I were a complete imbecile. 'It just *looks* like a cloud, that's all. It's a classic camouflage.'

'Have you ever seen a cloud that shape?' Joaquín protested.

'The truth is I've seen plenty of photos of clouds like that,' Joseph said. 'I'm not saying they're common, but they're not all that rare, especially in the tropics.'

'They're called altocumulus,' Gwen said. 'And they don't only appear in the tropics. You find them all over the planet. These altocumulus are called lenticulars, because they look like round lenses stacked one on top of the other. Shadows cast by the sun's rays give the impression of very well-defined volume.'

'Here come the rationalists, smashing any glimmer of romance,' Joaquín muttered between his teeth. 'Dashing all hope...'

'But, Joaquín,' I said, 'why do you want to believe in something that's not real? What good can come of that?'

People from all the various groups of castaways were arguing over whether what we were seeing was a flying saucer or a cloud. Next thing we knew, the cloud began to move. There was nothing unusual about that in and of itself. What was truly bizarre was the speed at which this cloud

– if indeed it was a cloud – was moving. Its shadow raced across us, then the beach, and then loomed over the lagoon before continuing upriver, heading inland into the jungle, and then, even faster, darting in a straight line towards the mountains. I turned to look at Joseph, who was standing behind me. In his eyes was the same look of bemused confusion that I was feeling.

'We don't need any more signals or signs,' Wade said. 'It's time for us to move inland.'

'Move inland?' Santiago said with a look of desolation, his eyes still fixed on the cloud as it moved further and further away. 'Why the hell would we want to do that? Move inland so that we're easier prey for the wolves?'

'And what if someone comes to rescue us in the meantime?' Joseph asked.

Wade stared down at the ground, still not having wiped that smile from his face, and for a split second I had the feeling he was looking down at the ground all the way up from the cloud. Or that he himself was the cloud. I don't know how to explain it.

'Joe,' he said, still smiling, and I think it was the first time I'd heard him call Joseph that. 'Why do you have so much trouble getting your head around the idea that *no one is coming to rescue us?*'

'Because it's absurd,' Joseph said.

'Yeah, it's absurd. More than absurd, it ought to be impossible,' Wade said, now talking much slower. 'But that ought to give you the key. If they could rescue us, they already would have. The fact is that *they can't.*'

'Why not, man?' Santiago said. 'What are you talking about?'

'I hardly know myself, Jack. I really don't. I only know that no one can save us but ourselves.'

'Come off it, Wade,' Joseph said.

'It's entirely possible that the weird cloud is just a cloud,' Wade said. 'Gwen's right. Lenticular altocumulus, regularly mistaken for flying saucers. But we're no castaways.'

'So what are we?' Joseph asked.

'We're settlers. In fact, we're not even that yet. We're pioneers. That's why we have to go west. As our fathers did before us, and their fathers before them.'

He pointed inland with his knife.

'We have to head in there, doc,' he said with his wide grin and those unforgettable bright blue eyes. 'To look for those missing kids. To find those kids.'

21

Someone comes down from the jungle

A *group soon formed, consisting of* Wade, Santiago, Joseph, Christian, Sheila, Gwen and yours truly, Juan Barbarín, half-dead, but nonetheless ready and willing. We planned to leave late that morning, as soon as we'd kitted ourselves out with weapons and supplies. I think we were all afraid. Wade was going around like some kind of Marvel superhero, but even he seemed a little afraid. He reminded me of Captain Forest, the one-eyed commando who swung on implausible vines across the azure rivers of Korea. I remember my reservations when the time came to join the expedition, but despite everything, there was something inside of me that wanted to go. Somebody who craved the danger, the fear, the adventure. It was the new Juan Barbarín, the one that had emerged on the island.

But then something else happened which further delayed our departure. A coincidence, you might say, if you still believed in such things as coincidences on our island.

Someone came down from the jungle.

They'd spent days walking to our beach. A woman, or what was left of a woman, possessed by that inexplicable force we sometimes call 'the survival instinct' which makes us capable of impossible physical feats. I'm not one hundred per cent certain who spotted her first. She was naked, and had emerged, from amidst the trees, almost at the limit of her strengths. She had very long black hair that fell down her back. It was filthy and tangled, as if she'd been rolling around in a bog. It might have been one of the cricketers who first noticed her – Dr Sutteesh, a young professor of English Literature at the University of Calcutta, bat in hand, ready to receive a bowl. Stumbling towards them, the woman looked like a monster, one of the living dead. She was covered in cuts, scratches and burns. From her ankles to her shoulders her skin was smeared with streaks of dry blood, grazes and welts. Her left breast had been cut off, and the barbaric scar from where shreds of the skin had been stitched up was still tender. The cricketers stopped in their tracks, overcome by panic. On seeing them, the woman held out her hand as if asking for help. Then she simply collapsed to the sand, incapable of taking another step. But she didn't say anything, not a word. Nor did she call out or scream. She couldn't, because her lips were sewn together with some kind of plant fibre, thin but as strong as a fishing line. The cricketers discovered this final, macabre detail when they bent down to pick her up off the floor and carry her to the village. There was no blood on her lips, which meant the wounds from the stitches had already healed. But how had she survived with her lips sealed, unable to eat or drink anything?

A small crowd gathered around the woman who'd emerged from the jungle. When Dr Sutteesh, Dr Masoud and the others carried her to the hut, we called the hospital for Joseph to see to her. The doctor asked us all to leave, and only Josephine and Sophie, his regular nurses, stayed to help him clean and examine the woman. But I knew that face. Even with her face disfigured by agony and exposure to the elements, I recognised the woman. It was Eileen, the flight attendant.

Eileen, of course. How could I not have noticed that she, out of all the passengers, had disappeared without a trace? The last time I'd seen her was from the life raft – she had been swimming towards the beach, still in her uniform and with her little blue cap pinned to her hair. We made some sort of sign to one another, as far as I remember – a wave, or a thumbs-up. A smile, maybe. And then she'd been wiped from my mind.

The first thing Joseph did was unstitch her lips. That punishment, if indeed it had been a form of punishment, had been done with a very fine needle and great skill. It was hard to tell how long she'd been in that state. It would have been possible to poke a straw between the stitches to allow her to drink, but how long had she gone without food? Whatever the answer, she didn't seem malnourished, so it seemed unlikely she'd spent more than a few days in that wretched state. Wherever she'd been, and however much she'd suffered, her captors had kept her well fed.

My friend Julián claimed that her mouth hadn't been sewn up as a punishment, but rather as a message. A pretty easy one to deduce at that: 'Don't talk. Keep the secret safe.' At that point we still believed the island's messages were easy to decipher.

Sophie and Josephine washed Eileen's body and then began treating her wounds, most of which she seemed to have obtained as she made her way, naked, through the jungle, perhaps running from her captors or hiding in the undergrowth, dragging herself along the ground so as not to be seen. Other wounds were more mysterious, and seemed to have been caused by a knife or sharp object cutting parallel lines across her buttocks and on the backs of her thighs. She had small burn marks all over her body – on her torso, her back and thighs – as if someone had applied scorching wires to her skin. Her wrists and ankles, too, were red raw, as if she'd been tied up tightly with coarse, scratchy ropes. As for the horrendous scar on her chest, Joseph confirmed it was recent. They'd cut one breast clean off and then sewed the skin, pulling it from here and there in flaps folded one on top of the other. Whoever had done this to her, Joseph told us, appeared to have some surgical experience, because the wound was well closed and seemed to be healing well, with no seeping or infection. Later, when he came to give us an update on Eileen's condition, he also shared with us some technical details about mastectomies, details I'd rather not have heard, and which made me never want to see another breast in my life. What wasn't possible, he told us, was knowing exactly how they'd performed the operation: whether Eileen's captors had had access to anaesthetic, or if she'd been conscious during the dreadful procedure. Nor was it clear why they'd do such a thing. As a punishment? A warning? As part of some strange, primitive ritual? The whole thing was incomprehensible.

Apart from this, Eileen was in reasonably good health. As far as it was possible to tell, Joseph told us, bar the dehydration and exhaustion, she was clinically well, and it looked like she would make a swift physical recovery. The problem was that she wasn't talking. Nor did she seem to recognise us or understand where we were. Her gaze was completely and utterly blank.

At Joseph's request, I went to talk to her. I was the only one out of all the passengers, it seemed, who remembered her name and had shared a few words with her. When I went into the hut I found her lying on one of the straw beds. They'd fed her some smoked fish, a bit of durian and some chocolate biscuits from the dwindling supplies left from the plane, all of which she'd hungrily gobbled up. She'd also drunk some water and coconut water. She must have been exhausted, but despite everything she was still awake. I called her by her name, but she didn't seem to react.

'Eileen,' I said. 'Do you remember me? From the plane. Do you remember?'

She looked at me blankly.

'Do you understand me?' I asked. 'Do you understand what I'm saying to you?'

Still no movement. She was staring at me, but didn't seem to compute that I was a person. We called Bentley, the psychiatrist, so he could assess her, and he confirmed what we already knew: that she must be in a state of shock from the appalling experiences she'd been through. But he also said, after the assessment, that Eileen had been heavily drugged. He said we must wait for the effects of the drugs to wear off before we could evaluate her real situation.

We tried to establish the facts. From what we could tell, someone had abducted Eileen the second she'd set foot on the island, carrying her off to the interior where they'd tied her by the feet and hands and abused and tortured her for weeks. It made me shudder to think that the island's occupants, wherever they were, had spotted us so soon, and what's more that they'd been so close that they could have abducted any one of us as little as an hour after we came ashore.

It became clear to us all that George wasn't alone on the island; that there was a well-organised group inland somewhere, and that they, whoever they were, were capable of the most heinous atrocities. Were they educated Westerners like George, these islanders? Or a bunch of criminals? Or pirates, perhaps? We drove ourselves mad trying to picture who they might be, and how many, and above all what reason they could possibly have for abducting one of ours to torture and mutilate her, sewing her lips together. This wasn't the behaviour of your average villain, but rather of brutes who lived completely cut off from civilisation on that island. The very idea seemed ludicrous; after all, there's no such thing as a society that exists in true isolation from the rest of the world any more. Farewell, beautiful tribes of yore. Adieu, solitary footprint in the sand. Or at least, that's what we thought then. An island inhabited by people from the Stone Age who practised cannibal rituals and mutilations. Was it possible? Gwen Heller swore that it was, and that in Indonesia alone there were several thousands of nameless islands (thousands!) which no one had set foot on. Ernst-Maria Hovorka, an Austrian Professor Emeritus of Anthropology at UCLA (and a friend and ex-patient of Bentley), claimed that cannibalism had ended in the Pacific in the thirties, but that there were indeed still some totally isolated populations on the planet, in particular in the Amazon.

'More than a hundred or so left in the Amazon,' Hovorka confirmed. 'Communities of between one hundred and three hundred individuals in most cases, and often we don't know what name these indigenous peoples use to refer to themselves, or the language they speak.'

'It's a message, man,' Christian said. 'A message.'

'What's a message?' Roberto B. asked, engrossed in a game of The Third Reich with Óscar Panero.

'The lips stitched together, man. It means: "Keep your mouth shut. Don't say a thing."'

The Allies had just invaded Sicily, just as the bears had once famously done, coming down from the mountains. The Allies had also invaded Holland and recovered Stalingrad, although the Axis forces, in an unplanned and quite inspired move, had invaded Iceland and were now heading into uninhabited Greenland with the ostensible intention of invading the Arctic Ocean and arriving at the North Pole. But what was there of tactical interest in the North Pole?

'It's possible the sewn-up mouth is a message,' Roberto B. said, never taking his eyes off the board where the Second World War was being played out for the umpteenth time. 'But it doesn't mean what you think, man. It doesn't mean: "Don't talk, keep schtum." The thing is that the woman's body is the island. She's not a person any more; she's the island. The sealed mouth means: "The island is sealed." The real message is: "Don't come any further inland." Don't you think, Óscar?'

'It's possible,' Óscar Panero said, staring perplexed at the advance of the German forces across vast and desolate expanses of snow and remote glaciers.

'I ought to take a peep at those stitched-up lips with my own eyes,' Roberto B. said with a sigh. 'I ought to get up right now and go and see them for myself.'

'God, you're morbid,' Brenda said.

'Yeah, I'm morbid,' Roberto B. said. 'But that's not why I'm going. Or it's not the only reason. Mainly I'm going because I'm a novelist. You are too – don't you want to come and see a sewn-up mouth? You'll never have the opportunity to see something like this again. It's sick. Properly sick.'

Despite everything he said, Roberto B. remained firmly planted in his chair staring at the pieces of The Third Reich and trying to find the way to break up the blockade that the Russians, British and Americans had put up against the Axis troops.

'I don't get this thing about wanting to see it *because you're a novelist,*' Óscar said. 'As if you had to see everything in person.'

'No one can just make things up out of nothing,' Roberto B. said. 'There's a passage in *The Notebooks of Malte Laurids Brigge*... Have you read it? You can't make up a thing... when it talks about the man they're going to stab in the heart with a needle...'

'What are you talking about?' Óscar interjected. 'That's what the imagination is for.'

'That's your mistake right there,' Roberto B. said, finally moving a piece and assassinating Charles de Gaulle. With a single roll of the dice, Roberto B. pulled off what the assassin in *The Day of the Jackal* never could. But it wasn't clear what kind of mistake he was referring to. 'The imagination doesn't just make things up from nothing. The imagination isn't there to invent, my friend.'

'Charles de Gaulle,' Óscar muttered under his breath. 'The old bastard.'

'You can't invent anything. Not a thing. That's what Malte says, and we should take his word for it. "No, no, there's nothing that we can imagine, not even the smallest thing in the world. It's because everything is made up of so many individual details that are unforeseeable."'

'Where did you read that? In Francisco Ayala's translation?'

'No, it's an Argentinian edition,' said Roberto B., who probably only knew isolated passages from *Malte* and wasn't even aware of the existence of Francisco Ayala's translation.

The birds were singing in the forest, the children swimming in the lagoon, the waves were breaking on the beach, and the intellectuals were chatting away in the shade of a breadfruit tree. They rambled on and on about what it was and what it wasn't, about what should and shouldn't be done, about versions and translations, and books and theories on reality and the imagination. How pointless all their talk was. How bleak, and how pointless. And all the while a mutilated and abused human body was squirming in pain on a bed of dry grass.

It was astonishing to see how life went on, indifferent and almost jolly, all around us.

I looked for Rosana and found her shouting at her daughter for having ripped the dress she was wearing climbing a tree. She was telling her, quite rightly, that we had to look after the clothes we had, because they were few and far between and there was no way of mending or replacing the ruined items. But why was she so furious? Why such rage, such rancour? And what did any of that matter compared to what had happened

to Eileen? I looked for Gwen, and found her with Wade and the Kunzes
going over the guns and ammunition we had left and discussing the possibility of teaching those who didn't know how to shoot to do so. This
conversation didn't exactly float my boat either. Now I didn't know who
to turn or talk to. I realised I was longing for female company – simply
the voice and presence of a woman. I spotted Swayla gazing at me from
behind a cloud of white smoke from the smouldering embers smoking
the fish. There she stood on the other side of this hazy veil, which then
floated across the river's green waters in wispy trails. I waved at her and
she waved back.

I went looking for my old friends, fearing that I'd find them sitting in
yet another meditation circle. But Dharma, their teacher, was busy sculpt-
ing a piece of wood with a chisel and hammer, and Eva, his wife, was
washing white clothes on the rocks next to the river. They were almost
never together, and I'd never seen them talking to one another. I don't
even think they slept in the same bed. They were only ever together for
meditation or during yoga sessions, where the pair of them performed the
most extraordinary contortions. I found Ignacio, Idoya, Pedro, Eulalia,
Julián and Matilde sitting in Julián and Matilde's hut. I asked to join
them. 'Of course,' they said. 'Juan Barbarín, where would you like to sit?
We still haven't had a chance to catch up. And there's so much to catch up
on. We still haven't spoken, or barely, about how strange it is that we've
all ended up here together. But what are you up to? Where do you live?
Why so mysterious?'

I told them, in all honesty, that I didn't know.

They were drinking tea and chatting about Eileen, speculating as to
what had happened. It was the topic on everyone's lips, and nobody wanted
to talk about anything else. I also ventured a hypothesis, rejecting the
theory that there were uncontacted peoples on the island, although admittedly my opinion changed so frequently that, in another moment, I might
have argued the exact opposite. I looked for theories I only half believed
in (that there were no more unexplored islands in our globalised world),
and almost managed to convince myself. The others rejected my theories,

one after another after another. I counterattacked. I'd almost forgotten the curious pleasure of these Spanish conversations where everyone defends contrary views and systematically refutes the other's ideas, no matter how sensible or coherent they might be.

A group of women, among them Nicollette Sheridan, Brenda Esquivias, Omotola, Gloria Griffin and Lizzy, approached the hut, and Brenda told us they'd had the idea of going along together to see Eileen and enveloping her in female company, in feminine warmth and affection, in their maternal force as mothers and sisters, wives and daughters. She told us they wanted to make her feel safe and protected in a female environment, and that any of the women who wanted to join them could do so. Idoya, Eulalia and Matilde stood up, and we men were left alone.

I took my leave as well and watched as they walked towards the very edge of the village, to the hospital. They called out politely at the canvas door, and Joseph came out with his hands and forearms all soapy and a white towel thrown over his shoulder.

Eileen was stretched out motionless on one of the grass beds, her eyes staring into the void. They'd tended her wounds, put her in a light floral dressing gown and laid her down on one of the makeshift beds to sleep, but her eyes remained open. She had so many cuts and bruises it can't have been easy to find a comfortable position to put her in, although she didn't appear to be in any pain at all. The women stepped inside the covered hut, and surrounded Eileen, embraced her. Gently, they touched her mutilated lips. Nicollette Sheridan discreetly opened Eileen's dressing gown, and on seeing the pleated mash of stitched and twisted skin that was her left breast – a horrendous fleshy rose next to her right breast, which was white, full and maternal – some of the women broke down in tears. Sophie and Josephine immediately threw out those who were crying. The rest of them cradled Eileen, talking to her in soothing voices. Nicollette Sheridan sang an English nursery rhyme. Idoya would tell me later that it was then that Eileen turned to look at Nicollette, to stare at her mouth. And tears welled up in her eyes. It seemed she was waking up, regaining consciousness. Who knows, maybe that song stirred some memory in her.

Eileen opened her mouth.

'They don't want us to go further into the island,' she said. 'It's their island, and they don't want us on it. They don't want us on their island.'

'Who are "they", sweetheart?' Nicollette asked.

'The ones living on the island, further inland,' Eileen said. 'There are so many of them, and they have weapons, lots of weapons, and they don't want us to go any further into their island.'

'But how many do you mean?' Rosana asked. 'Lots? How many?'

'Lots. I don't know exactly. They have weapons, and they run the island. There are men, and also some women. They run this place, and they don't want us to go further in.'

'But who are they? What do they want?'

'I don't know. I don't know who they are. I don't know them,' Eileen said, falling in and out of consciousness. 'I didn't recognise them. I'd never seen them before. They did things to me. Lots of things. I screamed. They didn't want me to scream. They told me I couldn't talk. "You can't talk on the island. You can't talk on the island," they kept saying.'

'But who *are* they? Where do they live?'

'I don't know. Far from here. Very far from here. Very far. They run the island, and they don't want us to go further in.'

She repeated the same lines over and over again, and gradually fell asleep.

22

We learn how to shoot

W*e set off two days* after Eileen reappeared, leaving at the crack of dawn to make the most of the coolest hours of daylight. The group was made up of Wade, Joseph, Christian and Sheila, Gwen, Santiago, Joseph and me, and we were armed with the Weatherby Magnum rifle, the Remington 870, the Beretta 8000 and the Smith & Wesson Centennial 442 revolver. Wade had the shotgun, Joseph the rifle, Sheila the Smith & Wesson, and Gwen the pistol, a semiautomatic with a fifteen-round magazine. We had left the rest of the guns in the village so that those left behind could defend themselves in case of an attack. We'd understood from the message Eileen had relayed to us that if we stayed within the limits of our small kingdom on the coast and by the mouth of the river, our mysterious aggressors wouldn't hurt us. And yet, in light of Eileen's abduction, the disappearance of the children and the wolf attacks, it was pretty clear that we weren't entirely safe on the coast, despite the sinister warning.

While not all of us on our expedition were carrying guns, those of us who had never used one had been taught how to shoot the previous day. Swayla had deserted the group the second the guns came out. Christian and Sheila seemed unsure at first, but everything changed when Stephan Kunze, our shooting instructor, put a beautiful Smith & Wesson Centennial 442 – with its swing-out stainless-steel cylinder – into Sheila's hands, telling her that that gun was a favourite among the ladies and that she should try it for size, like she might try on a diamond necklace, just to see how she liked it, just to see how she felt holding it. Sheila told him that bourgeois values weren't of the least interest to her, and that she detested diamonds.

'Nobody *detests* diamonds!' Kunze said, with a loud guffaw.

Then he asked her (imploring her to answer honestly) if she felt more or less attractive holding the gun in her hands. And after this he asked Christian if he found his girlfriend more or less attractive. Christian was enthralled. I think the vision of his girlfriend in her bikini wielding a Smith & Wesson was giving him an erection. He didn't say a word.

'Guns are like expensive underwear,' Kunze continued. 'Worn close to the skin, hidden from sight, and not for parading about. But they say something about us, about the way we see ourselves, and they protect us – they make us feel more secure. They have that dual quality of intimacy and exhibition, like that bikini you're wearing, which covers a lot less than it reveals. That bikini screams: "Here I am, I'm not afraid of my body, and I know my allure. Look by all means, fantasise if you like, but this body belongs to just one person. Or to no one." Your gun says the same thing. "I belong to no one. I belong only to myself."'

'I thought you deemed this bikini immoral,' Sheila said, staring fixedly at him. 'I wouldn't have imagined you'd like it.'

'If you were my wife,' Kunze said, 'I wouldn't let you wear it, if that's what you mean.'

Kunze had the ability to shoot you the most ruthless daggers with his eyes while from his lips came pure warmth and cordiality.

'You think I'm immodest, do you?' Sheila went on, the pistol still in her hand.

'Your entire generation is immodest,' Kunze said cheerfully. 'It's not just you. It's not personal. You lot don't know the value of things, or the power of your instincts. You don't know the meaning of desire, or love, or respect, or value. You think I'm a mad old fool? Give it a few years. This isn't playschool: it's a battlefield. Nobody has chosen to be here. Now this is a firearm, and it's in your hand not because you're seeking violence or revenge, or because you're afraid. You cannot give a gun to a madman, or a coward, or a child. You don't give a gun to someone quaking in fear, but to someone who knows how to control themselves. When you have a gun in your hand, you know your actions count and that they can have consequences. And you accept that responsibility because you've learnt to be the boss of yourself. That's what having a gun means. So hold out your arms, grip the gun firmly and aim. Now release the safety and pull the trigger.'

Joaquín wouldn't back down, despite Kunze's lecture. He insisted he still wanted to come with us on the expedition, but refused to carry a weapon. He said he didn't believe in violence or 'an eye for an eye'.

'In which case you can't come, son,' Wade said. 'We just can't take the risk.'

Joaquín was furious, furious about the manner in which the pro-arms and pro-war brigade had managed to convince the feebler and more feeling among us. He looked to me for support, but I no longer knew what to think. I've always been more of a thinker than a man of action. I'm an artist, an intellectual, a professor (in that order, I hope). My life has been all music, concerts, books, equable university routine, tedious university routine. But Joaquín's justifications now seemed weak to me all of a sudden. They were my justifications too, the same ones I'd always defended and which I continued to defend. But I thought about Roberto B. and Óscar Panero staring at their board game, lost, hypnotised by a fake war when all around them a real one was raging. I thought about Hovorka and his Puebloan Indians, about Bentley and his meerschaum pipe and three pairs of glasses, about Violeta and her constellations, about Rosana and her meditation, about Robert Kelly and Robert Frost and their shirts emblazoned with Mormon teachings, about Brenda and her dog-eared volume of Chekhov stories, and I told myself that all of that made less and less sense. Culture, beauty, reflection, spirituality, escaping from the world, the fear of being muddied in life's mire: what was all of this compared to action, science, reality? I thought about Gwen Heller and how she studied animals and plants. She was capable of seeing their beauty, but she also saw their function, while the rest of us – so delicate, so sensitive – only saw a subjective beauty based on a complicated system of symbols. Joaquín was looking at me imploringly as if to say: 'Say something: you speak English, you're a man of the world, a cultured European, you're no fanatic.' But I no longer knew what to say or think. Now I found myself asking if I hadn't been wrong all this time, if a life of science and action wasn't actually far more mysterious and stimulating than a life of reflection and art.

'Joaquín,' Xóchitl spoke up. 'We need guns in this world. Were you born yesterday or what?'

'You may well need them in Mexico,' Joaquín said, 'but maybe that's because everyone else has them.'

'And it's different in Europe, is it?' Xóchitl asked, with what seemed to me genuine curiosity.

'I think it is. In Europe it's different,' Joaquín said.

'Well, aren't you the lucky ones.'

As for the rest of them, Santiago said he didn't want to lay a finger on a gun because he was ham-fisted, and scared that if he picked up a rifle he'd only end up blowing off one of his feet or hurting someone else. But when he actually held one of the hunting rifles – probably a Remington – in his arms, it was love at first sight. Christian took the other revolver, and I think he and Sheila suddenly felt like Luke Skywalker and Princess Leia, or Brad Pitt and Angelina Jolie, shoulder to shoulder, young, handsome – and armed.

At the tail end of the morning, just when we were about to stop for lunch, Joseph showed up at our shooting range. We were all surprised that he wanted to join us, but according to him there was no one in the hospital that Roberta couldn't care for, and Eileen was recovering nicely. He knew how to fire a gun because he was a hunter, or had been in his youth. Finally, I too decided to take part in the group. There was barely any time left to show me how to use a gun, but I'd been there for everyone else's training, so they gave me the green light. I think they probably accepted me because of the high status I'd somehow managed to gain in our small society; because I'd managed the plane evacuation, taken part in the initial expedition for water, and perhaps, more generally, because they liked me.

We spent the rest of the day packing our bags. Bottles of water, food (smoked fish, coconut flesh, durian, roasted breadfruit, papayas, four tins of condensed milk and another four jars of Nutella, delicacies rationed protectively), appropriate footwear, a basic first aid kit, boxes of bullets, matches and gas to light fires, a small canvas to protect us from the rain through the night, two torches and two twenty-metre lengths of rope in case we had to climb or descend any mountainsides or steep terrain. The compass was useless on the island; the needle pointed all over the place depending on the spot you were standing in. Wade supervised as we packed our clothes, and instructed us to avoid pale colours, red, yellow and white. In fact, we were only allowed to wear green, brown or grey. Wade also advised us to wear full-length trousers if we didn't want to end up covered in scratches and bites.

We would be gone for eight days: four there and four back. We predicted that in four days we'd reach the mountains inland and be able to get a general idea of the place. The main objective of our mission was to find the children and bring them back to the village. The second objective, to find out who lived on the island and what the hell was going on there.

It was agreed that Kunze would stay behind to take charge of defending the village in our absence. This was Wade's idea, I imagine because he wanted to win Kunze over and because he saw the importance of us remaining united. The plan was settled.

23

I meet Cristina

One spring *afternoon in the* early seventies (I must have been eleven), my parents and I went to Pozuelo to meet some new friends. Juan Villar, an old chum of my father, had just returned to Spain with his family after a few years living in England, where he'd been a professor at the University of Leeds and, if I remember correctly, Birmingham. He and my father hadn't seen each other for years. I'm not sure exactly how they met. I imagine in England when my father was studying at Fircroft College in Birmingham.

Juan Villar was a theoretical physicist for whom my father had boundless admiration because he understood the Theory of Relativity, a feat of mental gymnastics that few could master and which, according to my father, made him nothing short of a genius. In England he'd married a woman called Marianne and the couple had two children roughly my age: a girl a year or two younger than me, and a boy a year younger than her. They now lived in Pozuelo, where they had rented a vast, modernist-style holiday home which reminded me of photos of Frank Lloyd Wright's buildings that I'd seen in old issues of *Life* magazine lying around our house. It was surrounded by a huge garden: almost half a hectare of perfectly cut lawn with rose beds bursting with yellow and white flowers (Marianne didn't like the red ones), a few birch trees and a small vegetable patch where Juan Villar grew lettuces, green beans, tomatoes and pumpkins.

When we arrived, the children weren't there. The adults explained they weren't back from fencing class yet. I was surprised that the Villars' children went off to Madrid to learn to play with swords – most kids learn that without anyone having to teach them, after all – but I was also sure there was nothing run-of-the-mill about that family. The children were delayed (we learnt later that Patricia, the neighbour who'd gone to pick them up, had got a flat tyre on the motorway), and I had nothing to do at that grown-up reunion. Not that it mattered, because I was busy looking at Marianne, the woman of the house. I quite literally couldn't take my eyes off her. Marianne, I think, was twenty-nine at the time, eighteen or so years my senior, and she was six months pregnant.

She was very tall and very blonde, swathed in that warm, healthy glow that radiates off pregnant women. She was the most beautiful woman I'd ever seen. Her cheeks were flushed and her eyes moist, shining with a mysterious sadness, and these delicate feminine traits left such an impression on me that even today I can't quite understand it. Eleven-year-old boys don't usually take the slightest interest in pregnant women of her age. What's more, up until that afternoon I hadn't shown any signs of early sexual development. I remember how I couldn't take my eyes off Marianne's sumptuous breasts, the way they rested gently on her prominent, round belly. She was wearing one of those wide, flimsy maternity dresses which only accentuated the roundness of her curves, and a spotty beige cardigan which she could only just do up with one button. I stared at Marianne so intensely that she didn't stop smiling at me and dishing me up more portions of cake and ice cream. I was too shy to refuse it, ate the lot and nearly made myself sick.

In order to take my eyes off Marianne, perhaps, and not just sit there ogling her, I turned my attention to Juan Villar's music collection. I'd never seen so many records. Back then, my parents owned about twenty or twenty-five records, and they were avid music lovers. But Villar had hundreds, maybe even thousands; an entire wall stacked with records. I was amazed to find all of Wagner's operas, which I'd just begun to listen to, all of Verdi's operas, all of Beethoven's sonatas, and sleeves and sleeves of Hayden quartets, Schubert arias, Bach cantatas and Hugo

Wolf song cycles. There were also plenty of records from composers I'd never heard of like Havergal Brian, Vagn Holmboe, Erich Wolfgang Korngold, Sir Granville Bantock, and then other names I was completely obsessed with and who I read about avidly but whose music I'd never had the chance to hear, like Hans Pfitzner, Anton Bruckner or Gustav Mahler. Juan Villar was something of a specialist in British composers, late symphonists and the neoromantics (in time I too would become a late symphonist and neoromantic) and he took great pleasure in telling us about such rare gems as Vagn Holmboe's *Requiem for Nietzsche*, or Martinů's *The Epic of Gilgamesh*. He was shocked to learn that we'd never heard of Anton Bruckner, who was one of his favourite composers. He asked me what I wanted to listen to, but I was so stunned I couldn't pick. Villar then pulled out the sleeve containing Bruckner's Eighth Symphony, the version by Klemperer with the Philharmonic Orchestra, and played the Adagio.

Anton Bruckner was far from a popular composer in Spain at that time. My music history books dismissed him as a crackpot, and there's no denying that he was something of an eccentric. His symphonies were criticised for being too long, poorly orchestrated and lacking in 'spirit', that curious musical concept which I'd also seen applied to Wagner's *Parsifal*. Bruckner, so my music history books told me, was a religious composer, a kind of child saint, a big kid who had been mistaken in choosing the symphony as a vehicle to express his musical message: evangelical and abstract, not worldly and epic, as befitted a true symphonist. 'Bruckner's music,' it said in one of my favourite books, K.B. Sandved's *The World of Music*, 'enjoyed substantial success from 1880, but today opinion is divided as to its quality. In general, its melodic richness is recognised, as are its lively rhythms and the dexterity with which Bruckner weaves one with another. But many critics find its form vague, its expression pompous and its ideas lacking in dramatic quality.' In *The Great Composers of the Romantic Period*, one of the books from my childhood library, Adolfo Salazar speaks, referring to Bruckner, of the 'contrived and barren extensions that his terrible dead weight brought to the post-Beethoven symphony', of the 'shapeless, echolalic ramblings'... His works were rarely performed and barely recorded.

I've always been a loner. I was an only child, a solitary boy obsessed with music and books. Since Cristina and I split up, after I left for the States, I've always lived alone. My house in Oakland is the house of a loner. Well do Oakland's elms know my shadow as evening falls. Sometimes I go several days without seeing a soul but Ballard, my trusty Labrador. I've always been drawn to solitary types and lonely wanderers, be they Rousseau's, Whitman's, Wordsworth's, Adalbert Stifter's or even Caspar David Friedrich's, who also seemed to have the ability to reach glorious heights and float above the clouds. Anton Bruckner was another solitary man, a lonely wanderer who roamed the streets of Vienna counting the windows of the houses and trying not to step on the cracks in the pavement. He was single and plagued by nervous tics. He suffered from arithmomania, a disorder that compels you to count everything you see – windows, suit buttons, trees along the street. He was an angelic man. As far as we know he was never with a woman. He spent his life falling in love with young, unsophisticated women whom he would ask to marry him when they had only just met, only to be perpetually rejected until he was an old man with grey hair. And even then he carried on falling in love and declaring his honourable intentions towards the daughters of friends, the pretty young things he'd meet on his daily strolls through the outskirts of Vienna, and his housemaids. 'Why, Herr Bruckner,' one of them says to him, 'you're an old man!' An old, lonely man. A lonely man who strolls beneath the lime trees daydreaming about the Emperor.

The Emperor, too, must have been a lonely man. But I never was much of a fan of that Emperor, because when Bruckner dedicated his Eighth Symphony – the most beautiful music ever written – to him, he chose to go off hunting deer and bison instead of to the opening performance. The fool!

Solus Rex. A chess problem.

Solus Barbarinus.

We only listened to a few minutes of that astonishing music, but for me it was enough. At the tender age of eleven, I knew already that I'd found my path and destiny. Then the Villar children arrived home in the neighbour's car and the house was filled with voices and laughter. And there, in my life – my wretched life – appeared the crowning touch of magic for that afternoon. It was Cristina.

24

I enter the Meadow

Is it possible to fall in love at the age of eleven? I've felt it. I know it's possible. But I didn't only fall hopelessly and irrevocably in love with Cristina that day. It's hard to explain, but at the same time as I fell in love with Cristina, I'd also fallen for her mother, the mesmerising, aristocratic Marianne. It goes without saying that what I felt for these women, mother and daughter, were very different emotions. One was an eagle, the other a dove. I loved Cristina and revered Marianne. What would tie me to Cristina all those years was simple love, while my dreams of Marianne over those wild, disconsolate years were complex lust-fuelled fantasies. Or perhaps it was the other way around? I don't know and never will, because it's not in my nature to hold the spirit above the flesh, nor do I know how to distinguish between the two.

Cristina was very different from her mother. She had dark hair, a pretty chestnut colour which sometimes looked black, and she had inherited more of her father's looks than Marianne's. She was certainly lovely, fine-looking, but she didn't have Marianne's majestic air or her frame, her Valkyrie- or Venus-like stature as she rose from the sea. Marianne was a beauty; Cristina was merely pretty. Marianne was Venus; Cristina was a fairy. And I'm not only talking about how mother and daughter were back then, when Cristina was a little girl barely nine years of age, but about later: Cristina at eighteen, at twenty-two, at twenty-five. She would never grow to be as tall as her mother, and she was positively short compared to the two towering figures of her brothers Edgar and Ian. Cristina didn't possess her mother's physical exuberance, but she did have something Marianne lacked altogether, which was an immense sweetness and an incredibly kind heart.

We went out to play in the garden. The Villar kids had a rather exotic pet at that time. When I saw it, standing on its four paws in the middle of the garden, I thought it was a puppy. But there was something very strange indeed about that puppy. Its head was too big, its snout too square, and its little paws too short, ending in three webbed toes which didn't look anything like a dog's paws. It was covered in a thick coat of reddish hair and had small pointy ears. The children called it Trixie, and they'd taught it to sit. They'd also put a blue collar on it with a dicky bow that made it look faintly ridiculous. Who puts a bow tie on an animal? 'Sit, Trixie,' they'd say, and the strange dog-that-wasn't-a-dog would sit. Then it would dash around the lawn, and Cristina and her brother Edgar would run after it. I watched as Trixie darted across the allotment, cantering like a miniature horse, then ran around a swimming pool filled with rainwater and dead leaves, behind the vegetable patch, and finally disappeared through a hole in the hedge of cypresses.

'Come on!' Cristina shouted to me. 'Come on, let's follow Trixie!'

I watched her and her brother slip into the hole in the hedge and disappear from sight. I was a shy city kid, and what they were doing seemed intolerably reckless. Shouldn't we tell their parents we were leaving the garden? I followed them in spite of myself and slipped through the hole in the hedge, grazing my knees on the hard ground and the scratchy cypresses (I was a good deal bigger than both of them). What choice did I have? I didn't want to come off as a scaredy-cat. And besides, I was on my friends' patch, and I figured that if they went through the hole, I should do the same.

The next-door garden was abandoned and completely overrun with parasitic plants. I'm not sure exactly when we started to call it 'the Meadow', nor who invented the name. I suppose it's possible that Cristina and her brother had been calling it that for some time. It was completely covered in thick, wild grass that nobody ever mowed or tended, so the name wasn't completely unjustified. Whatever the reason, the garden next to the Villars' place was always the Meadow to us.

It was split on two levels by a stone step that ran the whole width of the garden. On the upper level stood a little house in ruins, its walls entirely buried under honeysuckle, and on either side of the house grew two huge trees, one very dark and the other very pale. God knows how, but Trixie had managed to jump up the stone step that divided the garden into two levels (the stone step was almost a metre high, and there was no way that short-legged chubby little creature could have jumped that high) and was running along the upper section. My friends ran after Trixie, trying to catch her. The animal hid in the dilapidated house, but my friends didn't want to go inside and they called her from the front door.

'Why don't you just go in?' I asked, perplexed, once I'd caught up with them. If they could escape from home, climb through the hedge and trespass on private property, what was the big deal about going inside a derelict house?

'It's haunted,' Cristina told me. 'We're not going in there.'

'And your puppy?' I asked.

'What puppy?'

'Trixie,' I said.

The two siblings burst out laughing.

'Trixie isn't a dog,' Edgar told me. 'She's a capybara.'

'A capybara? What's a capybara?'

'It's like a rabbit. It's like a giant rabbit, only with shorter ears and no tail. It's a rodent that lives in the rivers of South America,' Cristina added. 'She needs damp conditions. The pool in the garden's for her. If she doesn't stay wet, she gets sick and dies.'

That night I couldn't sleep for all the excitement, images and information. When tiredness finally got the better of me, I slipped into one of those dreams that turns out to contain yet more dreams, a maze of feverish slumber that leaves you anxious and exhausted. I drifted in and out of dreams and then I found myself in an unpleasant limbo between wakefulness and unconsciousness, as if I were under anaesthetic. Marianne appeared in my dreams. So too did Bruckner's music and the image of Bruckner that I knew so well, looking very dignified with his little bow tie, his nigh-on invisible moustache and his tiny bird-like head; Cristina running through the grass in the Meadow in a short blue dress that revealed her svelte, pale legs; the capybara, stock-still in the middle of the damp, shiny grass; the Meadow beyond the haunted house split on two levels, with the stretched stalks of the fennel plants swaying in the breeze.

And all of it mixed and merged into a single creature in an extraordinary, sacred place. Marianne's breasts, the firm skin over her slightly swollen and rose-blushed cheekbones, her smile when she saw me smiling at her, another offer of cherry pie and vanilla ice cream, Bruckner's portrait, Bruckner's bow tie transmuted into Trixie's bow tie, Trixie transformed into Bruckner in a black-and-white photo, her bright eyes taking the place of Bruckner's tired, melancholy eyes, the Meadow as Marianne's great, glowing, alarmingly naked maternal body (naked all but for her feminine curves, which were covered and transformed by spindle trees, beds of wild fennel and flowing rivers of honeysuckle creeping up the walls), Cristina's face floating like a cloud above the dense garden of wild plants, her tender eyes, her fairy voice, her soft calves, her surprising agility, the music of the Adagio from the Eighth Symphony floating between her legs just like the Meadow's wild grass. And everything merged together, and everything was one and the same. The Adagio from the Eighth Symphony was the Meadow, and the Meadow was Cristina, and the capybara was a messenger from the other side, like the hound that guards the gates to the underworld. The garden of the abandoned house was the Adagio and it was impossible to get out of there. We tried without success. We ran from one side to the other, from one hedge to the other, from one melody to the other, from a tuba chorale to a polyphonic passage on strings. Me, Cristina, her brother, the capybara with its bow tie and a fourth presence I never got a clear look at all bounded up the stone step to the house in ruins, and it was impossible to get out of there. And the music played on, enveloping us in musical arcs, musical paths in the air, paths that were lost among the sounds, open windows between the sounds through which we could just about glimpse other lands from the world of sounds, sights from the very backs of our minds. Then Marianne's breasts morphed into two round capybara heads, and Bruckner and Cristina melded into one single prodigious creature with Bruckner's bird head and Cristina's short dress and slim legs, and it hovered above the grass in the Meadow leaving a trace of light in the air.

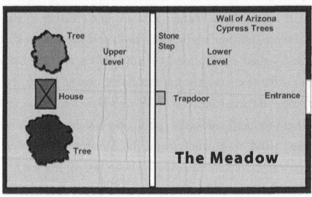

The Villars' Garden

25

I become jealous

From then on, our two families began to see each other regularly. We almost always went to the Villars' place in Pozuelo to spend the afternoon, although once or twice they came to us in Madrid. But I preferred it in Pozuelo because there we would play with Cristina's friends who lived over the road, the children of a very famous composer from that time, Dionisio Recalde. That's how I met Ignacio Recalde and his sister Yvonne. My parents said that Recalde belonged to Opus Dei and that Villar fostered their friendship as much as he did because he wanted friends in high places. I didn't know what Opus Dei was, but I was amazed at my parents' capacity to be constant killjoys and find fault in everyone. Every time we left Pozuelo, they would spend hours criticising and nit-picking everything the Villars and the Recaldes said and did (the three families often got together): the way they raised their children; the fact that Patricia, Recalde's wife, drove a Simca 1000 and chain-smoked; the way they had the children eat at the kitchen table as if they were the hired help; the fact that they sent them to private school, the Langlam, an 'Anglo-Spanish' academy where my father had been an English teacher a few years earlier; and that Marianne and Patricia belonged to a tennis club and played in white miniskirts and visors. As far as my parents were concerned, everything they did was wrong. Everything irritated them. They called the Villars snobs, said that the Recaldes had only got to where they were thanks to Franco's regime, and that Juan Villar was a social climber. What a pair, my parents. They were at war with the whole world. Perhaps that's why I came out so easy-going, so soft, so compliant. A man with no personality at all. Charming, maybe even seductive at times, but destined always to play a supporting role.

Every now and then on our trips to Pozuelo we'd find Joaquín at the house, Cristina's only cousin based in Madrid. He was an olive-skinned, lanky kid, the same age as Cristina, and the son of one of Juan Villar's cousins. I remember him as a shy, pensive boy who wore thick glasses and kept his hands permanently thrust in his pockets. He had a younger brother who was always off playing with Cristina's brother Edgar.

Ignacio, the Recaldes' eldest son, was my age and went around saying that Cristina was his girlfriend and that he was going to marry her when they grew up. This generated a permanent state of rivalry between the two of us. It made me sick to think that he lived in the house opposite Cristina's and got to see her every day, while I could only enjoy my sweet love's company during our brief visits to Pozuelo, which never lasted as long as I wanted them to, were never enough. It was Yvonne who told me one day about how her brother and Cristina used to escape to the garden with the abandoned house to kiss on the lips. My eyes must have popped out of my head. She swore she'd seen them with her own eyes, and not just once or twice, but lots of times. Those words came crashing down on me like the embers of a burning building. Kissing on the lips! How could they do such a thing? Emboldened by seeing the effect of her words, Yvonne then told me that not only did they run off to the Meadow to kiss, but that they also sometimes took off all their clothes and lay down next to one another.

'Naked?' I asked, flabbergasted.

'Yup.'

'And then?'

'Then nothing.'

'But what do they do?'

'They look at each other.'

'Look at each other?'

'They look each other in the eyes and kiss on the mouth.'

'Naked?'

'Yes, naked.'

'I don't believe you,' I said.

'I swear!' Yvonne said.

'You've seen them with your own eyes?' I asked, shaking.

'Yes. Whenever I see them escaping to the abandoned house, I tag along behind and spy on them. They're there in the Meadow and my brother takes off all Cristina's clothes, and she lets him. And then he takes all his clothes off.'

'But why do they get naked?' I asked, inconsolable. 'What for?'

'Because they're in love,' Yvonne said. 'Don't you know that people in love like to be naked when they're together?'

'I don't believe you,' I said. 'You're making it up. If Ignacio tried to take off Cristina's clothes she'd punch him on the nose. This is ridiculous! I know lots of people in love, and they're never naked. And anyway, Cristina isn't in love with Ignacio.'

'Fine. I don't care if you believe me or not.'

'Swear on it.'

'I swear,' Yvonne said.

'Swear on God, and that all your family die if you're lying.'

'Swearing on God is a sin,' Yvonne said.

'You don't want to swear on God because you're lying.'

'No, I won't do it because it's a mortal sin.'

Of course I see now that Yvonne was in love with me, and was just trying to lure me away from Cristina, but her made-up stories only made me more jealous and obsessed with my little fairy. Despite my protestations, I know that Cristina and Ignacio liked each other and that sometimes they kissed, because Ignacio was a real ladykiller and knew how to speak to women and break down their defences. He was also taller and better-looking than me. One day I saw them crossing the street holding hands and staring at each other all gooey eyed. When they spotted me standing by the back door leading out to Cristina's garden, they jumped apart, clearly caught unawares.

Another day, in the Meadow, Ignacio told Cristina that she had to choose between the two of us and decide once and for all which of us was her boyfriend. She said she chose us both, then kissed us both on the mouth: first Ignacio, then me. These were the games we played as children. I think she enjoyed making me jealous, because years later she admitted she'd never been the slightest bit interested in Ignacio, and that really it was me she'd liked. But I think she did carry a torch for him, and that that flame went on burning for years.

26

My encounter with Marianne.
The Villars return to England

Two years passed. Cristina was beautiful, and her body was becoming more womanly. My penis had grown too and a line of dark fuzz appeared on my top lip. Cristina no longer let me kiss her as I had when we were children and we would escape to the garden of the house in ruins, the garden we called the Meadow. As far as I know, she'd stopped letting Ignacio kiss her by then. The house next door was sold and the new owners cleared the garden of all the weeds and began to reconstruct the dilapidated house. It was the family of Juan Luis Panur, the poet. Of course, Villar was pleased as punch when he found out his new neighbour was an important poet. 'A regime poet at that,' my parents said. 'And ex-Falangist. Villar's got all sides covered.' The capybara died, probably because it didn't use the pool enough, or maybe because it wasn't suited to Madrid's climate.

Marianne was about thirty-two by this time, and was approaching that stage of golden plenitude that women seem to enter in their third decade, and which, in some cases, goes on well into the fourth. She wore expensive outfits which must have been made by English designers, because those floral patterns, that lace, those sheer, tight-fitting, bust-enhancing garments didn't look like anything I'd ever seen before. I always remember her as being immaculately made up, her face powdered, her lips either painted deep ruby red or simply slick with cacao and gloss (like her daughter, she suffered from chronically dry lips) and her eyes with a thin, neat line of kohl. She had oily, mousy blonde hair, which was always cut just above the shoulders and perfectly groomed in two blocks on either side of her face, normally decorated with a ribbon or a thick hairband above her forehead. Her skin was firm, and she had that ruddy complexion so common among the British. She had prominent cheekbones and eyes that always seemed a little puffy and pink, as if she'd just been crying, and her bottom lip was permanently curled down in disappointment. That look of disappointment didn't escape my attention, and it troubled me. Was it a hangover from the past? Was that habit inherited from a childhood spent with her jaw clenched (as so many English childhoods are, Cristina would later tell me) and was it possible that it no longer reflected her daily reality? She always seemed sad. And more than sad, disappointed. And more than disappointed, bored.

Something happened one day. I can't recall the reasons why, but my parents had left me at the Villars' house that afternoon. Juan Villar wasn't in, and we were being looked after by Jeanne, a young Irish woman the Villars had hired to nanny the three children, and in particular Ian, the youngest. The Recalde boys weren't in either, so Cristina and I decided to entertain the younger ones with a game of volleyball, and later badminton, at the net that Villar had put up in the garden. I heard Marianne tell Jeanne in English that she was going to have a bath and that Jeanne should give us kids an afternoon snack. By this time the baby was about two and would waddle around the house like a wind-up doll, grabbing everything in sight and sticking his chubby fingers into every dark nook and cranny.

While it's true I did hear Marianne's high-pitched, defeated voice telling the nanny she was going to take a bath, what happened next was a genuine accident on my part. I'm not even sure I really understood Marianne's words; I didn't know much English back then, and I'd overheard it said from inside the house, in another room, between the hallway and the kitchen, or perhaps between the kitchen and the utility room. What happened was that at some point I went into the house to get something from Cristina's room. It was a boomerang we sometimes played with. A genuine Australian boomerang that Juan Villar had bought in Sydney for the kids,

which really did come back if you threw it properly, and which we hoped
would keep the younger ones entertained.

Passing in front of Cristina's parents' room, I caught a glimpse of Marianne through the half-opened door. It was a fleeting look, and not pre-
meditated. I was simply walking down the hallway and the door was ajar
and my eyes just fell naturally towards the open crack. She knew I was
inside the house. She knew perfectly well that I might walk in on her, and
yet in spite of this she hadn't taken the trouble of closing the door. I suppose it was a mere oversight. She had her back to me, looking at herself in
her dresser mirror. She was in the nude, and her golden body seemed to
glow in the room's olive-green tones. The only thing covering her was a
white bra, its elastic back clipped just beneath her shoulder blades and the
straps lightly digging into the soft skin on her shoulders. But I saw her full
figure reflected in her oval dresser mirror. She'd had three children, and
her body was a miracle. Two curling f's like the holes on a cello appeared
in the lowest scoop of her paper-white back. Her buttocks were full and
pale, even paler where her bikini had left a tan line, which marked out the
forbidden zone with a mere difference in shade. I was paralysed. Our eyes
met in the mirror. We looked at each other for a moment without saying a
word. Any other person would have mumbled some excuse and bolted out
of there, but I didn't move from my spot. I thought about smiling, but I
couldn't smile. My bones ached and my skin had turned to cardboard.
Sometimes, when this memory comes to mind, I get the feeling that that
instant – it can't have lasted more than an instant – still isn't over, and that
we're both still there, trapped in that moment, gazing at one another in the
mirror in silence. Then she did something I wasn't expecting. She turned
around, exactly as she was, making no attempt to cover herself. She looked
at me with a serious unsmiling expression, perhaps running a few things
over in her mind.

How old must I have been then? I guess thirteen, maybe even fourteen. I've never been very good with times, or dates, or what came before
and what after. I've never been able to say 'this was in 1983' unless I happen to have some external and unequivocal reference to tie the event to a

specific date. But if Ian, Cristina's little brother, was at least two, I must have been fourteen. Marianne turned around, looked me straight in the eyes and took a few steps towards the half-open door. It looked like she was moving in to close it, but I was wrong. She stopped still in the middle of the room, her arms hanging down either side of her body, and looked at me solemnly. For a second I thought she was angry, but what she was really doing was allowing me to look at her body while simultaneously watching the effect it had on me. And the effect was devastating. I wouldn't have even recognised that body in front of me – that beautiful body – as belonging to a woman, because it looked nothing like anything I'd seen until then. I felt it as a pure smack of reality, a sudden revelation of the meaning of everything: the reason we exist, the reason we suffer and are born and kill and hate and love and desire one another. Beauty, violence, light, blood, reality, love, dreams, battles, suffering. All of this her body offered me, and more besides. A naked woman. The first naked woman. Her golden, slim legs like a long stem supporting the cup of her body, a V-shaped cup, out of which bloomed like a stalk on a rosebush this siren with her arms down at her sides and her symmetrical breasts still hidden in their white lace casing; her slightly raised chin and green eyes and thick head of golden hair, her head cocked slightly to the right, as if that hair were made of a heavy material – gold or marble – and she struggled to keep it upright; the pink triangle of her belly and her intensely and movingly white loins, tender and vulnerable, which ran all the way around to trace, then complete, the pale tan line I'd already seen on her buttocks; and her groin, covered in a thick triangle of dark hair which – now that I laid my eyes on it, and despite having always been hidden, or perhaps precisely because it had always been protectively hidden – looked like the centre of her body, the core of her entire person, the true revelation of who she was, the explanation, at last. Reality.

She smiled almost imperceptibly. Then, to my utter amazement, I realised that not only was she not angry, she was inviting me into her room. Without saying a word, without moving a muscle. And now I saw that the door wasn't going to be closed on me, but rather opened to me, that I was

being admitted. I walked with difficulty, my knees trembling, then gently
pushed the door open and entered the Villars' bedroom. It was a large
room, with a long horizontal window facing out onto the garden and an
enormous bed covered by a leaf-green quilt. On each bedside table stood
a porcelain lamp with a lampshade, and on one of them there was a Har-
old Robbins novel face down and some reading glasses. That's how I discovered that Marianne Wilson, Mrs Villar, used reading glasses. Neither
of us said a thing. She walked towards the door, closed it and slid the bolt
across. Her buttocks quivered as she moved. Her bikini line moved pleasingly on the pinkish skin of her hips. I'd seen the bikini itself many times
before when Marianne sunbathed in the garden. It was yellow and had
high-waisted bottoms, as was the fashion at the time. She drew the curtains shut. Then, very slowly and deliberately, she turned back to face me,
took off her bra and let it run down her arms until it fell to her feet. A
shudder ran through me on seeing that white garment fall like a big white
feather onto the pale green carpet. I thought, who knows why, of the fairy
tale in which the swan casts off its wings and transforms into a woman.
Marianne's toenails were painted a nude colour. She had large, perfect
breasts with flesh-coloured nipples. In those days women didn't tend to
remove their pubic hair, not even when they wore swimsuits, a detail I'd
noted all the times I'd watched Marianne sunbathing in the garden in her
yellow bikini, although it must be said that the vision of those fine little
brown curls sprouting out between her thighs had never provoked in me
any special excitement. Marianne's pubis was covered in an uneven, fine
patch of brownish blonde hair, through which I could make out the folds
of her vulva, which reminded me of the genitals of the one or two girls I'd
happened to see naked as a boy. A silvery caesarean scar ran up her stomach vertically, the crosses from the stitches painfully visible. Marianne
took me by the hand and led me to the bed. I remember how her hands
felt; large, skilful hands that knew what they were doing and were in control. I remember the heat from those hands as she stroked my face and
undressed me. I remember the heat from her body, her soft tenderness, the
feel of her hair as it brushed against my skin.

I can't say how long our petting went on for, but I do know that it would be impossible to measure what went on between me and Marianne that afternoon with a clock. I felt completely and utterly engulfed by her, as if her body were both on top of and behind me, enveloping me, entangling me. She guided me wordlessly, because I was so dumbfounded I couldn't do anything. Nor did I know what to do. The touch of her wet mouth on my neck made me feel faint. The heat radiating from her body. The inconceivable softness of her breasts, her belly, her groin. I had always imagined the female body to be firm, perhaps thinking of the marble perfection of classical nudes or stone statues. The softness with which she touched me. The feeling of her tongue in my mouth, of her hand on my crotch, of her mouth around the head of my penis. The naturalness with which she kissed and licked me, as if it were something normal, something she did every day. Her green, cat-like eyes, and the way she looked at me and smiled at me as she ran her thick, bovine tongue around my penis. It wasn't love, but like love it was mysterious and profound and delirious. Never before had I felt in front of me, around me, an expression of such intense, radiant and stirring power. It seemed to me that she wasn't really a woman, but rather a long line of women, something akin to the caryatids on a temple, which surrounded and supported the one true woman, immense like a firmament poised over me. She was the very force of feminine love, the feminine force of the earth, the scent of the mother and sister, the girlfriend and wife. I may have been a man physically, but mentally I was still a boy. She gave a gentle laugh and held me against her soft, snug breasts, and I felt as though I were drowning in the sea, a warm summer sea, a translucent and velvety sea. I told her I loved her, that I'd loved her for years. I was captivated by the pale, pink abundance of her breasts, in one of which her heart boomed like a great clock inside a church.

She lay back on the bed, moved me on top of her, took my penis and slowly guided it inside her. She was so smooth I didn't even notice: I whispered in her ear that I wanted to enter her, and she laughed gently at me that I already was. The sensation was as tantalising, as distant as a dream. It was a total revelation. I was convinced that penetration must be painful for the man, when you consider the hypersensitivity of the tip, and I wasn't prepared to be received and swathed in this smoothness. It was the first time I'd been with a woman and I had no way of knowing if what was happening between us was an insignificant, botched affair, or an intense and wildly passionate sexual encounter. Looking back now, I think it was a bit of both. I wanted to kiss her on the lips, but now I was inside her she rejected my mouth. When it was all over, she gave me a gentle kiss on the lips and then got up, picked her bra off the floor and began to put it on. My desire for her in that moment was unbearable, and I would've killed to have her come back to bed, but she told me that what had happened wouldn't ever happen again. I tried on a few other occasions to catch a word with her in private, but in her eyes, in her polite, glacial smile, something I can only describe as a brick wall always blocked my way.

It never did happen again, and perhaps for that reason the idea of a kid and an older lady making love in the middle of the afternoon with the muffled sound of voices and birdsong filtering through the drawn curtains became an obsession, a myth. I felt an insatiable desire; the feeling of a physical and emotional need impossible to satisfy. The knowledge of a secret circle of love, a world glowing with beauty and pleasure to which few are admitted: The World of the Beautiful Women. The Gynaeceum of the Rose-Women. The Harem of Desiring Men and Desiring Women. The heaven of sexual love.

I now know that Marianne already knew on that fateful afternoon when she took me to bed that the family was returning to England. It wasn't just boredom or the thrill that made her open her door that afternoon, but the feeling of impunity spurred by the knowledge that we would soon part ways, probably forever.

Villar had received a job offer he couldn't refuse from the University of Oxford. A few months later, the Villars moved back to England, and I lost Cristina for the first time.

27

We set off on our expedition

W*e left at dawn, when* the jungle was still choked with mist. Thick curls of mist between the taro leaves (which we called 'elephant ears') and the pale trunks of the coconut trees. Wispy threads of mist between the deliquescent ficus roots and the elongated leaves of the *Cordyline fruticosa*, or 'good luck plants', that grew all over the island. It was a clear day, although to the east some ominous storm clouds were beginning to darken the sky. Almost everyone in the village was asleep when we set off, silent like ancient warriors, along the riverbank.

Wade, good old Wade, was back to his heroic self. You could tell he was in his element diving headfirst into the unknown with a rucksack on his back and a shotgun over his shoulder. He looked at us all with a warm smile that twinkled with beauty and hope. My God, there was so much hope in his eyes. His smile lit up his unusually symmetrical features, lined with deep creases like the face of an idol. When this happened, the deep blue of his eyes looked more intense than ever. He reminded me of Marlon Brando's Walter Kurtz in *Apocalypse Now*, only an inverse Kurtz. Not damned, but blessed. Not corrupted by evil, but mysteriously liberated from his heavy load and torment. I had the feeling that this sense of liberation was directly connected to his arrival on the island.

Before setting off, we huddled in a circle holding hands and Wade said a prayer. A short and strange prayer, because it wasn't directed to the Christian God, but to some anonymous, blind or indifferent force. I still ask myself today if Wade spent hours refining those words or if they simply spilled spontaneously from his mouth.

'Fate strikes all men, but we have been handed a destiny. Let us be worthy of our destiny. And let our destiny be worthy of us.'

We set off and were soon engulfed by the vegetation.

The jungle seemed to have kept back small pockets of night among the plants. I tried to listen out for those whispering voices, but they never came out when you were in a group. And that's why I held back, to see whether the noises would return if I were alone. At this point we still weren't completely sure what had happened to Eileen, because she hadn't fully recovered her powers of speech. If I had known then what she had to say, I wouldn't have taken such risks. Because the truth was she hadn't been kidnapped, at least not at first: it was the voices that had lured her into the jungle. The moment she came ashore she had gone into the bushes to relieve herself and it was there that she heard the voices. Following them, she had ventured further and further into the jungle, and there, once she was deep enough in, they'd snatched her.

It was the coolest time of day when we left, and we made good progress, taking turns using the machete to clear the way, although the humidity made the plants heavy and hard to cut through. The insects were drowsy at that time of day, and moving through the jungle I could see the pleasant side of the excursion, of our country hike. Then the sun came up and the forest came alive. The birds, bugs and monkeys began to buzz, squawk, hoot and howl. The jungle awoke. Even I, who had always loved the idea of the jungle, began to feel an aversion, then an abhorrence and fear for that motley tangle of plants. They wound their way around one another, strangling themselves and their neighbours, mutually depriving each other of food and life. Voluptuous creepers snaked up and down tree trunks like a boa constrictor might coil around a ram. Parasitic epiphytes grew by feeding off the sap of other trees. Dropsical roots fought underground searching out the damp earth and sweet nourishment, tying themselves up in knots. Looking at the forest now I saw neither its poetry nor its beauty, but a merciless battle, a silent war between fertility and putrefaction.

The rains came early that day. We tried to protect ourselves from them, cutting leaves from the 'elephant ears' with our knives and machetes, which we then held over our heads by their thick stalks as if they were umbrellas. We crossed a stream and then a river, which must have been our river, flanked magnificently by palm trees, and then we began to climb the natural paths carved out by the water on the craggy hillside. They were deep trenches with rock bases half covered by plants that formed a roof so dense that sometimes it felt like we were walking in the darkness, although the absence of undergrowth on the ground meant crossing the clearing was relatively quick and easy. The monumental trunks of acacia koas and pervasive paper mulberries towered over us, their roots sometimes crossing from one side of the trench we were climbing to the other, obstructing our way. The higher we got, the fewer and further apart the trees became. I'd only ever come across these species in the tales I'd read as a boy of Jack London on the South Seas. Palmito trees, palm trees, giant bamboos and tree ferns grew all over, and ficus too, with their liquid, labyrinthine roots which intermingled with everything they came across. Every now and then we passed under the outline of an almost-dead tree in the middle of the jungle. They looked like ashen skeletons, their branches overrun with giant bats that slept hanging upside down. They were vile, red-eyed creatures with huge fangs which, when caught unawares, had the nasty habit of opening their bowels, releasing a load of foul-smelling excrement in order to travel a little lighter. For this reason, whenever we walked underneath one of those trees we moved as silently as ghosts.

We trekked for hours up that deep trench, the ground beneath us sloping ever more steeply, until it became full of water and mud and we had to abandon it. Once back up at the surface we came across two noni trees, one of which was laden with a yellowish fruit that we plundered despite its unpleasant smell, so pungent that we called it 'cheese fruit'. Wade ate some right there and then, having first sliced them in half with his knife to check for worms and larvae. Wade never stopped eating. Whenever we paused for a break, he would have a snack or start chewing on something.

After a while the sun came out again. The pitter-patter of the rain died away and back came the screeches and caws of the birds and monkeys. We stopped to eat lunch in a clearing, and I think it was because we were all so miserable and exhausted that we avoided eye contact with one another. I remembered how on our first trip, when we'd found the abandoned aerial, we'd managed to get back out of the jungle relatively quickly, but it was clear the island's topography was completely unpredictable and full of surprises. I remember now obsessing over whether to abort and head back to the village. If only I had.

By early afternoon we'd managed to leave the densest jungle behind us. Now we were walking on relatively open terrain with barely any undergrowth and fewer and fewer trees. There were still acacias here and there, and a type of conifer that reminded me of Mediterranean pines, although they lacked the uniform elegance of the latter. It felt to me like we were very high up. I thought we'd already reached the mountains. But that wasn't the case. In fact, we were on a raised plateau from which we could see the mountains in the distance arranged in blue, purple, umber ranges, stacked one on top of the other like piles of multicoloured rugs. One or two of the valleys were completely covered in mist. The highest peaks of the main volcano were hidden by a permanent canopy of cloud. I felt like I was living a great adventure.

We descended the plateau and crossed the swampy, malarial mosquito-infested valley until the path led us upwards again and we found ourselves back on the plateau. I thought I spied a man standing beside a tree watching us, but it turned out to be the stump of another tree charred by lightning. We decided to sing. Joseph perked things up with a little bluegrass (he was originally from Kentucky) and sang 'Roll in My Sweet Baby's Arms' by Flatt & Scruggs and 'Shenandoah', which I'd only ever heard in Thomas Hampson's operatic rendition. He followed up with 'Blue Moon of Kentucky' by Bill Monroe. He sang in the high-pitched nasal voice typical of a bluegrass singer, and with the confidence of a professional.

Gwen snapped, telling him that was enough and could we all cut it out. I'd already noticed that she wasn't singing along with the rest of us. I'd just figured that she was one of those people who don't like singing, or don't have a good ear. Gwen said we were out of our minds, that in the wild sound travels fast and that now everyone and everything would know our whereabouts for miles around. So that put an end to our impromptu sing-along.

From the flies buzzing around us, the stench, and the several dozen crows, gulls and other birds of prey circling overhead, we knew we were near a dead animal. I suppose the most logical thing would have been to switch route to avoid coming into contact with the unpleasant spectacle, but Gwen, backed by Wade and Joseph, insisted on finding out what it was. She headed straight to the spot where the carrion was – a dark red mass completely surrounded by wings and beaks – and began to shoo away the birds with the butt of her rifle. Wade and Joseph joined in. The birds resisted abandoning their precious feast and some fought back with their ferocious beaks wide open. Soon, they'd all gone, although several soared above our heads and others perched on the ground a few metres away waiting for us to leave.

We were standing over the remains of a human corpse. Despite the putrid stench, it can't have been there for more than a few days. The birds had pecked it savagely, riddling the flesh with cuts and disfiguring the whole body. The face was almost entirely pecked off: the animals had removed the eyes and devoured the lips, exposing the dental plate, which was now fixed in a sinister smile. It was the body of a young man. Joseph leant in to examine him more closely, turning the body from side to side and prodding him all over. It was a horrendous scene. The body had a blackish tinge to it, a sort of deep, dusty red. The muscles and white tendons were clearly visible, folded over the bone like something out of an anatomy textbook. Not a single vestige of skin remained, and where his hands and feet, guts and sexual organs would once have been, there were only gaping holes. I assumed it was the animals that had eaten all the innards. But how could a handful of birds peck away all the insides and leave the corpse's abdomen so spotlessly clean? How had they managed to cut into the thick joints at the wrists and ankles?

'This man has been flayed, but not by animals,' Joseph pronounced once he'd examined the body.

'What's that supposed to mean?' Wade asked. 'You mean *someone* ripped this guy's skin off?'

'Without a shadow of a doubt,' Joseph said, rolling the body onto its front so he could inspect the back and buttocks before turning it over again. I couldn't understand how he could bear to touch that lump of rotting flesh. 'Animals don't rip the skin off their prey to eat them,' he went on. 'Someone has stripped this body from head to toe. This was clearly slow, painstaking work; a professional taxidermist would be proud. There's not a single inch of skin or scalp left on the corpse. They flayed him with true artistry, making incisions around the eyes and slicing clean off anything that might get in the way of their work.'

'The animals ate the hands and feet, man,' Santiago said, ghostly pale and seemingly on the brink of tears. 'Why are you saying they were cut?'

'The animals? That's unlikely,' Joseph said, still bent over the body. 'It looks like they pulled off the skin using a lateral incision the length of his body before carefully peeling it from the flesh in two whole pieces. Then they gutted him. In that order.'

He showed us the marks left by the scalpel on the side of the body, from the head to the ankles, on both sides. Then Joseph stood up and started looking around. None of us understood what he was after. A few minutes later he was back, but now holding two severed hands in his own. They were an unhealthy yellow, as if they'd been soaked in sulphur, and the nails were black. In fact, they looked fake, like those severed hands they sell at Halloween.

'I found them hidden among the ferns. The feet are there too. I haven't found his genitals. Some capuchin monkey is probably eating them for breakfast as we speak.'

'I'm going to be sick,' Sheila muttered under her breath. She'd gone deathly pale. She took a couple of steps back, leant on the trunk of a pine tree and began projectile-vomiting. I tried not to look at her, knowing that if I did, I'd be sick too.

'There's something I just don't get,' Wade said. He was crouching down beside the corpse, gazing at it absorbed. 'How can you be sure they killed him then skinned him in that order? Isn't it possible… isn't it possible they did this *while he was still alive?'*

'There's no way of knowing for sure,' Joseph said, after thinking it over for a moment. 'They could have. It's possible he was conscious for some of the flaying, or indeed the whole process.'

'Fuck, man, don't say that shit,' said Santiago, as white as snow and now looking distinctly faint. 'Fuck…'

'What do you think we're looking at here?' Wade asked Joseph, searching carefully for the right words. 'An execution? A crime? Torture? A ritual? Cannibalism?'

Joseph shook his head and repeated that he didn't know, that he didn't know what he was looking at, that he didn't know how to read it. He said he was just a surgeon at the Saint Vincent Hospital in Los Angeles, and that he couldn't get his head around what this was. He said that if it was torture, it was the cruellest, most savage torture imaginable. 'Worse than torture. A particularly cruel form of execution,' he said, 'the kind of thing you read about people practising in medieval times, or in the most isolated societies on the planet.

'I hope for his sake they killed him *before* they flayed him,' he said, fumbling for a cigarette in his pockets only to find an empty packet which he rummaged through in vain.

Gwen knelt down beside the body and began to analyse it. She told us Joseph was right and that who or whatever had done it was no animal. She said it looked to her like they had skinned him alive, because whoever did it hadn't wanted to kill him or torture him so much as take his skin, and all animals' skin is more lustrous and pliable if you rip it off while the animal is still alive, just as coat makers do with foxes and sables. On hearing her words, I felt a shiver run through my perineum, a particularly sensitive area of my body, and the hairs on my neck and back stood on end.

I don't think I'd ever felt such visceral terror before. I was struggling to breathe, and could feel my stomach churning as sparks flashed before my eyes. It was a feeling of fear, but also of powerlessness, an army of ants crawling all over my body, the feeling of being exposed and somehow naked, and also a terrible sense of pity and sympathy towards the victim. Fear that they'd do the same thing to me, and pity towards the poor soul who'd suffered those horrors. But my compassion and pity for the other's pain was the most unbearable part.

Santiago declared that there was no way in hell he was going to let them do the same thing to him, and announced that we should go straight back to the village. Wade told him to calm down and Santiago became even more furious. He started to swear, which wasn't like him, and shouted that he was sick to death of these kiddy-snatching, woman-torturing, people-skinning, prehistoric, cannibal sons of bitches. He was in such shock and so livid that the words streamed out of his mouth in a torrent, and despite everything, what he said struck us as comical. Several of us, especially Wade, Joseph and I, couldn't contain our laughter.

'Jack's right,' Gwen piped up suddenly. 'It's madness to head further into unknown territory with so few weapons and without knowing exactly what we're facing. We have to turn around.'

She was very calm and spoke slowly and deliberately, almost as if she were giving a university lecture. In fact, her tone reminded me of some of my colleagues from Rosley College.

Wade said it wasn't true that we were any safer in the village, and that the 'savages', or whoever it was that inhabited the island, had already ventured as far as the beach on several different occasions, snatching Eileen and the children from right under our noses. We weren't safe anywhere, he said. Our only chance of surviving in that place was to gather all the intel we could.

'Intel, intelligence,' he said, and once again I was struck by his military lexicon and the fluency with which he used it.

We went back and forth, not listening to one another's arguments. Sheila was as terrified as Santiago and seconded the motion to go back, but if Sheila went back then Christian would go with her, and our numbers and weapons would be severely reduced. I said that we had to overcome our fear and think about the children and about what they could be going through as we spoke, and to remember that we were the only chance they had. In the end, having taken a moment to calm down, we decided we'd all keep going.

Yes, I think that if we all decided to keep going at that point, it was because of the words spoken by old Juan Barbarín. Given everything that happened afterwards, I wish I'd kept quiet. Someone once said that all heroes are fools. They were probably right.

By late afternoon we found ourselves at the edge of a steep drop, a rocky peak that opened out into the nothingness. We decided to spend the night there and leave the climb down until the morning. The view was impressive. Below us was a wide valley, an immense, fecund flood plain, fringed on both sides by trees. A river ran along the bottom of the valley, etching broad meandering lines through the jungle tapestry that covered the whole basin.

Wade used the binoculars to take a closer look at the valley. Next thing I saw him duck down and crouch behind the tall grass as if trying to hide from someone. I crawled over to him on all fours. He passed me the binoculars and pointed out where I should focus them. He told me to look for the nearest waterfall then follow the line directly below that point down to the bottom of the valley. It took me a while to spot them, because their skin was the same colour as the leaves or the shadows beneath the trees. But eventually, I made out a group of some fifteen semi-naked men and women bearing spears, bows and arrows. They walked in a line through the trees on the valley floor, and from what I could see they were wearing loincloths and had feathers on their heads and chokers around their necks. Their skin seemed to be covered in marks or tattoos of some sort. A shiver of terror ran through me upon seeing them. But the most chilling thing of all was that there were several children with them. I saw a child of about five and was left in no doubt that it was Branford. Trailing behind him were two little girls dressed in white: Adele and Estelle. I thought I saw one of them carrying something in her hand. A teddy bear perhaps. I couldn't tell if the children were tied at the wrists. There was no sign of Seymour, and I shuddered as it occurred to me that they might have eaten him already. Nor was there any sign of George. Wade and I took turns using the binoculars to watch the row of cannibals as they darted through the vegetation. We tried to count them, but it wasn't easy. Aside from the three children, I counted fourteen. Wade, seventeen. Then they vanished and we lost sight of them. We told the others, who then attempted, without luck, to find them through the binoculars. Night was falling and the light fading. The sheer sides of the mountains turned a radiant emerald green, but the valley itself was already bathed in shadow.

28

We see the blue man

The sun had been up for some time when I stirred. We lit a small fire to make coffee, adding dollops of delicious condensed milk, and cut noni fruit in half to check for parasites before chewing its white, seed-packed flesh without enthusiasm.

We were just putting away our breakfast things when we noticed that an electrical storm had broken in the distance. The mountains inland were always covered with thick clouds. This was a fairly familiar phenomenon – I'd seen it many times before on other islands and other mountains. Lightning flashes lit up those grey and purple clouds, and bolts came crashing down in vertical lines just like those we'd seen during Noboru's burial.

Then something truly bizarre happened. I'm not sure exactly where it came from, or how it got there. I was busy eating the last of my breakfast when the whoops and cries of my fellow adventurers made me look up and follow their gaze down towards the valley. And then I saw it. Or rather, I saw *something*, but what exactly it was is still not entirely clear to me. A giant man was striding through the valley. He was stark naked and sky blue in colour. I couldn't say how far he was from us – three or four kilometres maybe. The lightning bolts we'd seen weren't coming from the storm up in the mountains, nor from any mysterious and inexplicable blue column, but rather from the giant creature's brow. Every now and then he would turn and stare at a point in the distance, fire a ray from his forehead, and then carry on walking. It dawned on me then that this colossus was the blue column we'd seen during Noboru's burial. We took out the binoculars to get a better look; none of us could understand quite what we were looking at. It wasn't a puppet, nor did it appear to be a machine. It seemed to be made out of sky-blue light, but at the same time it appeared to be solid, opaque. Given how far away it was from us and how high it towered over the trees, which barely reached its ankles, we estimated it must have been three hundred metres tall. It was completely hairless and entirely naked. Its eyes were open, but we couldn't see any trace of a pupil or iris. Between its eyebrows sat a perfectly drawn third eye, and it seemed to be this that was shooting out the electrifying bolts of lightning.

It was such an altogether ridiculous, impossible, surreal vision that we made no attempt to hide. Would it be able to make out our tiny figures from so far away? We watched as it lumbered through the valley, rays of light shooting out of its forehead and landing here and there on different spots in the surrounding vegetation. At one point, it stopped and looked in our direction. I don't know if it could see us. I don't know if it was looking at us. But just then something terrifying happened. The giant let out a cry, an atrocious screech; a mixture between a trumpet, a roar, cawing and human shrieking, so disconcertingly intense it seemed to penetrate and alter the deepest recesses of your mind. I'm not sure how long it lasted. Perhaps only a second or two.

The blue giant didn't cry out again. Instead, he turned to his left and slowly walked off in the direction of one of the valleys to the right of the open plain where we saw him disappear off behind the craggy ridge until the peaks eclipsed his perfect, dome-shaped head.

We were utterly bewildered, but the vision of the blue man – and I have no idea why – boosted morale among us. Suddenly, we were all laughing.

Joseph then speculated whether perhaps it was a kind of projection.

'And what kind of projection might that be, doc?' Wade asked cheerily. 'I haven't seen a cinema projector lying around anywhere.'

Joseph said he was thinking more along the lines of a hologram, given that the figure we'd seen was three-dimensional. Exactly where these enor-

mous hologram projectors capable of creating perfect images were remained
to be seen. Santiago said the blue man was just like Doctor Manhattan. Scandalised by our total ignorance of who this doctor was, Santiago explained
that he was a character from *Watchmen*, the iconic work by Alan Moore and
Dave Gibbons which revolutionised superhero comics in the late eighties. He
said the blue man was the spitting image, with just one difference: Doctor
Manhattan, who could destroy by merely raising a finger and who used this
ability to strike down Vietcong fighters, didn't have a third eye painted on his
forehead, but rather the structure of a hydrogen atom.

We set off again. The cliff edge turned out to be too steep to climb
down on foot, so we had to skirt around it. We walked westward until the
slope levelled out considerably, and then descended the craggy wall using
the climbing ropes we'd brought with us, until we finally reached the valley floor. We found ourselves surrounded by the most beautiful and mysterious tropical jungle I'd ever seen. We could never have imagined such
beauty looking down on the valley from above.

We reached the bank of the river that ran through the valley and re-
filled our bottles and calabashes. We thought about following its course,
but the undergrowth was especially dense along the banks. I looked at
that chocolate-coloured river and felt as if I were looking at the River of
Paradise. But, as I said, all the rivers on that island had this effect on me.
Truth be told, there were plenty of occasions during my time on the island
when I felt like I was in paradise.

We set off up the valley in the same direction we'd seen the crowd of
strangers and the blue man take. It was a forest of giants: more acacias and
ficus with their trunks covered in a carpet of moss. Vines, *Freycinetia ar-
borea* and hanging roots from the ficus or banyans hung in the air, and the
floor was carpeted in a thick, almost impenetrable fabric of ferns. The
bush was so unmanageable that we even considered building a canoe and
rowing upriver, but we didn't have the tools to fell a tree, let alone to carve
a canoe out of the trunk. So we had no choice but to carry on using the
machete. It pelted it down with rain for almost the entire day and we were
drenched from head to toe. We stopped for lunch and fixed the canvas

sheet between the gargantuan roots of a ficus, which were growing into undulating metre-tall walls and thus provided a small, tent-like shelter. We stank like wild animals and joked about it. After we ate we were overcome by exhaustion. Gwen put her arm around my waist, rested her head on my shoulder and drifted off to sleep. I could feel the fullness of her right breast pressed into my body, the warmth of her cheeks and mouth on my neck, and the smell of her breath and skin.

It stopped raining, the clouds scattered and the sun began to shine down on the forest. People began to climb out of our makeshift tent, but Gwen was still asleep next to me and I closed my eyes and pretended to be sleeping too. Santiago said he was going for a dip in the river, and the idea caught on. They left me and Gwen in peace, believing us to be asleep. When they'd all left, I brushed my lips against Gwen's and she stirred. Our faces were touching and her breast was still pressed against my arm. She shifted position and pulled back a little, apologising for having fallen asleep. A second later we were kissing, her tongue hungrily entering my mouth. I unbuttoned her shirt and kissed her breasts, pulling down the cups of her bra and licking her hard, dark nipples, and she touched my penis through my trousers with a mixture of daring and timidity that drove me wild. But we didn't make love. We were both filthy and sweaty and we decided to join our fellow trekkers to have a swim down by the river. The powerful water, the colour of milky tea, was only two hundred metres away, but when we reached the wide sandy banks of the shore our friends were nowhere to be seen, so we took our clothes off (she fell about laughing at how I hid my erection) and swam in the river like Adam and Eve themselves must have done in the Euphrates before they were cast out of the Garden of Eden. With the water up to our necks, we stared into the forest and kept seeing animals and human faces among the leaves. They swam in and out of sight, appeared briefly then disappeared, metamorphosed and transformed. I thought about Gwen's flushed breasts and dark nipples and about her dark pubis submerged under the water, invisible. And I thought about how unattainable even the woman right by one's side can be.

When we got back to our temporary camp, the others were already there and I caught several knowing looks: from Wade, who seemed indifferent, and from Joseph, in whom I thought I noted a forced smile. It occurred to me that perhaps Joseph was also attracted to Gwen, but of course I know now that I was wrong: Joseph already had a love interest on the island by then.

We wanted to reach the area where the giant blue man had been, but having got all the way to one end of the valley, there wasn't a single sign of his tracks, nor, indeed, was there any trace of a hologram projector. We could, however, now see the effect of his rays. We came across several trees burnt to cinders in the middle of the forest, sort of open pockets in the canopy, and almost perfectly round bald spots on the floor where all of the plants and vegetation had been reduced to embers. In two of these bald spots we found charred human remains; a single corpse in one, and two in another. Both were still warm. They were almost unrecognisable, though we could tell that they were male.

At last we reached the mountains. We passed through an area where there were rocks floating in mid-air: small stones, sometimes just shingle hovering thirty or fifty centimetres above ground, others as high as fifteen metres. It was a sight to behold.

Wade climbed a tree to try to orient himself in the maze of valleys and sierras in which we found ourselves, and also to try to spot any smoke trails that might indicate where our enemies could be found. But either they didn't light fires, or they knew how to diffuse the smoke so as not to be located. Christian, Sheila and Joseph also climbed the tree, joining Wade. It didn't seem too difficult to get up there, but I was so exhausted I chose to stay down on the ground.

You could see a lot up there, apparently. Another wide, forested flood plain, perhaps the continuation of the huge valley we'd spent the day crossing, and where we'd seen the blue man. But our friends had spotted something else in the valley beyond. A motorway. A stretch of viaduct supported by reinforced concrete pillars which came to a sudden stop in the middle of the valley.

We all had a chance to see the motorway when we got to the next valley. It was a formidable feat of engineering: two parallel stretches of road supported by sixty-metre-high reinforced pillars, an unimaginably complex piece of structural engineering in that cut-off, godforsaken place. So who had built it? The Japanese during the Second World War? But, why would they want a motorway through the mountain? If they'd needed communication channels, wouldn't they have just built a coastal road? From our position it was hard to know if construction work had been interrupted at the place where it came to a sudden stop, or if it had been blown up with dynamite or bombed from above.

We climbed down into the valley and the motorway disappeared from sight, engulfed by the trees. We didn't see it again until an hour or so later when it peeped back out from the tops of the giant forest canopy. My God, it was strange to see that titanic man-made construction towering over nature's own handiwork. What desolate beauty there was in that concrete, now yellowed from the constant rains. I've always thought reinforced concrete has a great melancholy and majestic beauty about it. The closer we got, the more lugubrious that motorway seemed, lost out there in the middle of the jungle. But its dark beauty profoundly moved me. There is as much wonder to be found in the hideous and dilapidated, the macabre and useless, as there is in the delicate and lovely.

We climbed the slope to reach the carriageway. When we got to the top and finally set foot on the asphalt, we were almost drunk on euphoria. We walked along that road suspended over the valley until the point at which it stopped dead, leaving a sixty-metre sheer drop. Everything looked different from up there. We were above the forest canopy now, looking down on the valley from a man-made, albeit abandoned and weather-beaten construction. It was hard to tell how old it was, but something told me it couldn't be as old as we'd first thought. I checked out the metal barriers on either side, looking for inscriptions, series numbers or anything else that might reveal its nationality or year of construction, and I found, on one of the horizontal beams, something like a plaque covered in dust and mud. I rubbed it clean, revealing a round insignia containing the letters 'SIAR' and an image of a lion and a goat seated on either side of a table. It was the first time I'd ever seen that image and it took me a moment to work out what it depicted, because it was still partly encrusted with mud. The lion and the goat were sitting on benches to the left and right of a table, on top of which you could make out a chess set. We later learnt that that design, the SIAR insignia, was a faithful copy of an illustration from an ancient Egyptian papyrus. The others began scouring the barriers along different points, and soon found similar symbols. We also found serial numbers that didn't tell us anything, although many of them ended in 75, which led us to believe that was the year of construction. As for the SIAR, nobody had the slightest clue what those initials might stand for. We all tried coming up with our own solutions to the riddle, with varying degrees of success. Of course, nobody came up with the correct answer: Skinner Institute for Anthropological Research. That is, the official name for the overseers of hell.

Then, in the vain hope that the motorway carried on indefinitely through the mountains and across the island, we retraced our steps and entered the tunnel that led into the mountainside. But just a few hundred metres in, the tunnel was blocked off by a barrage of earth, rocks and rubble, as if the mountain had literally collapsed into itself.

It was pitch black inside, but we could see thanks to the glow that Christian was still giving off. He was beginning to be able to control his luminescence and knew now how to make it brighter or dimmer at will, concentrating on certain images or emotions. According to him, the source of that light was in the region of the solar plexus, and by concentrating on that general area he could increase the glow to the brightness of a seventy-watt light bulb. He gave us a demonstration, thanks to which we were able to make out the dam of earth, rubble and roots blocking the tunnel.

We went back out into the open and explored the other tunnel. It was the same story: we could only get a couple of hundred metres inside the mountain before it was blocked by earth and rubble. So we headed back to the first tunnel and set ourselves up to sleep there for the night.

We unpacked our rucksacks and rolled out our bed mats ten metres or so from the mouth of the tunnel, just far enough to protect us from the rain, but close enough so as not to be too far into the tunnel. It was nice being under a roof and on a smooth floor without rocks, roots and spines, but the darkness soon began to frighten and unnerve me. A completely irrational and uncontrollable fear. I tried telling myself that we were much safer in there than out in the open. But fear doesn't respond to reason. The pitch darkness that spread throughout the mountain cave gave me the same feeling of vertigo that I get when swimming in deep water.

We discussed the possibility of moving our village to those tunnels. There was more than enough room for everyone. On the one hand, we'd solve the terrible problem of the rains and have a proper roof over our heads, but on the other, we'd be lost in the heart of the island, in the middle of the mountains. Would it be worth it? We were two days' walk from the coast, so moving there would be tantamount to settling on the island definitively and giving up any hope of being rescued. And then there was the minor detail of the armed and angry islanders, whose settlement was clearly not too far away. Having weighed up the pros and cons, we all agreed that moving into those tunnels wasn't such a good idea.

It was dusk, and we had nothing to do. We didn't want to light a fire for fear of being discovered, so we ate in the dark. Night fell, as if someone had drawn the curtains suddenly. It was always like that on the island. The twilight hours were unforgettable but short-lived. Suddenly, we could only make out the outlines of things. Then the rain came lashing down again. Santiago yelled that he was sick of the rain, that he couldn't bear it any more. Perhaps to calm him down, Wade replied that within a month the rainy season should be over, and that the rains would soon stop coming down with such force. It was a strange attempt at reassurance! Santiago snapped back that if he had to spend another month on that island he'd go mad, or die of desperation and misery. He said he couldn't hack another week in that filthy hole and that on more than one occasion it had occurred to him to throw himself off a cliff into the sea and be done with it all.

Wade looked at him with a tired smile on his face. Gwen asked Santiago what he had been doing on our Global Orbit flight to India.

'You don't want to know,' he answered.

'Actually, I'd like very much to know,' Gwen went on.

'Why?'

'To get to know you. We've spent over a month sleeping ten metres apart and I don't know the first thing about you.'

Santiago seemed to be on the verge of tears.

'I was following a girl,' he said. 'A girl I was really into. That's why I was going to India.'

'I see,' Gwen said.

'She was working for Mother Teresa's orphanage. She liked working with kids. She'd wanted to go to India for ages, since she was a little girl. I'm not sure why. I'm not sure what they told her in school, or if she saw a documentary or something, but anyway, she'd always wanted to go to India to work with orphans or with sick and starving kids. I don't see what's so special about India. There are millions of orphans all over. Even in the States she could have had all the sick, needy orphans she wanted. Or in Guatemala, or Dominican Republic. You don't have to go to India, right? At the end of the day, a sick starving kid is a sick starving kid, what does the colour of their skin matter, or whether they speak English or Indian or Spanish? Do you catch my drift? Why this obsession with going to India? I don't give a shit about India. I've already got India right back in New Jersey. I've got India right there in my neighbourhood, in my house. I've got my own India going on right inside of me, man.'

We fell silent and sat watching the rain.

That night, once everyone was asleep, I went looking for Gwen. Once I'd finally found her, I lay down beside her and began stroking her cheek and lips. She was asleep, but woke up straight away. She whispered my name and I said: 'Yes, it's me.' And they were the only words we spoke.

29

What I saw inside the tunnel

When I opened my eyes, the dawn light was flooding the entrance to the tunnel. At first, I didn't understand where I was. Then I saw Gwen's face next to me. It seemed immense, now that she didn't have glasses on. Immense and very beautiful: her features, all so deeply relaxed, gave the impression of absolute peace.

I walked out of the tunnel, stretching and loosening my muscles, and looked out over the dawn landscape. The mountains on the other side of the valley prevented me from seeing the sun's show as it rose, but even so, the view was spectacular. The jungle was still smothered in mist, a thick, milky mist out of which poked the tallest, vine-laden crowns, like imaginary caravels floating over the sea. The dual carriageway, which went across the valley curving to the left, was also floating above the mist, and the pillars supporting it disappeared inside the hazy swirls. Flocks of big white birds flew from tree to tree. And then I did something I hadn't done for a long time. I began singing to myself.

In fact, I wasn't quite singing, but I wasn't humming either. It was something I did a lot as a child, attempting to recreate the musical sounds of different instruments. I began to sing the opening tune from Bruckner's Eighth Symphony. I remembered the movement fairly well and could sing a decent chunk of it without making a mistake, pulling off a passable imitation of the strings, horns and woodwinds.

Then, out of nowhere, I heard a sound behind me inside the tunnel. I stopped singing at once and spun around. Something was moving among my friends' slumbering bodies. I was frightened, thinking at first that it was a giant rat. It was sniffing Wade's rucksack where lots of our supplies were stored. But although it did look vaguely like a rat, it was actually far bigger than any I'd ever seen, and it didn't have a tail. Not only this, but it was covered in a coat of long, thick dark brown hair. It was a capybara.

It wasn't completely inconceivable that on an island on the Pacific where there were packs of Canadian wolves and tribes of capuchin monkeys there were also capybaras, those giant South American rodents. But there was something special about this capybara that caught my attention and almost made me cry out. It had a blue collar around its neck and a small bow tie, exactly the same as the ones Trixie, Cristina's capybara, used to wear. In fact, I was quite sure that this was Cristina's capybara. I was scared and disgusted by that animal; the same emotions it had first provoked in me as a child. All the same, I approached it. It seemed very interested in Wade's bag, which it was sniffing and nuzzling with its horrible square, hairy snout. But when I went up to it, it became startled and took off. And you'd be surprised at the speed at which an adult capybara can run, despite its chubby body and ridiculous stubby legs. I ran after it until we were both buried in the darkness of the tunnel, but the sun's rays were starting to reach deeper into it now, and I had no trouble seeing the dark figure of the capybara running about ahead of me. Eventually we reached the section where a pile of earth and rubble blocked the tunnel and I watched as the animal scuttled up that mound and disappeared. I followed it. In fact, the earth and rubble didn't block the tunnel completely, and at the top there was a narrow hole you could just about squeeze through to reach the other side. I squeezed through it and began to descend the mound of earth and rubble on the other side. At the bottom, in the distance, I could see the tunnel's other exit, a semicircle of light in the middle of the darkness. Once my feet were back on the asphalt, having stumbled and tumbled my way over the bumps in the earth and rubble, I began walking briskly in the direction of the light. I'd gone a fair distance when I spotted the capybara a few hundred metres ahead of me, already approaching the tunnel exit. When it heard my footsteps and saw me appear out from the shadows, it started running again. I followed it, also running. It left the other mouth of the tunnel and I watched it disappear off to the left.

The motorway only went on for ten or fifteen more metres after the tunnel. Then it turned into a mud track. Now that I was on the other side of the mountain there was something else that took me by surprise: the air there was crisp, almost chilly, and a shiver of pleasure ran through me. It had been so long since I'd felt the caress of cold air! I assumed that the coolness was owing to the fact that the morning sun didn't reach that other side of the mountain. The tunnel opened out onto a wide, open pasture, bordered by a dense thicket hedge. It didn't make any sense: why would they build a stretch of motorway crossing the valley and a long, costly tunnel through the mountain, only to abandon the construction and let the road recede again into forest? I watched the capybara shoot across the grass and disappear into a thicket. Which is where I went too.

In fact, it wasn't so much a thicket as a dense wall of plants. Had it not been completely absurd, I would have said that it was a thick hedge of cypress trees exactly like those I'd known as a child in Pozuelo, and which they planted to separate the villas. I managed to wrestle my way through, covering my feet and arms in scratches in the process. I had to find out what the hell that impossible creature from my childhood recollections, the depths of my memory, was doing there. Next thing I knew, I was on the other side: in the Meadow. The same Meadow from my childhood. The Meadow where I'd played so many times with Cristina and Ignacio.

I stopped dead in my tracks and looked left and right. My body was there, but my mind couldn't make sense of what I saw before me.

Down at the back on the upper level was a stone house in ruins with a tall tree on either side, one pale-coloured and the other dark. The capybara was nowhere to be seen. I walked towards the stone step and touched it with both hands. It was made of the same blocks of limestone that I remembered so well. I couldn't understand what was going on. A hallucination, maybe? A dream? Had it been staged there to confuse me, to drive me insane? Had someone really gone to the trouble of setting all of that up there in the middle of the island, an exact replica of my childhood Meadow? What was all of this? Some big practical joke?

'A joke, Juan Barbarín. We stitched you up.' But who? Who could possibly know about my Meadow? And above all, why would anyone care about it?

I jumped up onto the upper level and walked towards the derelict house. The roof had fallen in and there was a window on either side of the front door; exactly the same as the house in our Meadow on Calle de los Olmos. I pushed open the door and went inside.

The space was divided into three rooms. The one on the left was empty. In the one on the right there was an old writing desk with a drawer and slim legs. I tried to open the drawer but it was stuck. In the central room, also empty, I noticed something painted on the wall. It was an oriental-style representation of a human body and the seven centres of energy according to tantric texts. If there was one thing I was certain of, it's that there was never any image of that kind in the house in *our* Meadow.

I studied it carefully. It seemed to have been painted a long time ago and was faded. There were seven lotus flowers painted onto the body: one on the base of the torso, another above the genitals, one on the navel region, one on the sternum, two more on the throat and between the eyebrows, and lastly, at the top of the head. They were painted in rainbow colours: poppy red, calendula orange, mango yellow, emerald green, seagreen turquoise, indigo blue and petunia violet, the lowest flower starting in red. The figure was painted in a pale sky blue, and above its head, sort of floating in mid-air, was an eighth flower, painted white. It was a little different from the rest because it wasn't a lotus flower, but rather a rose – a white rose.

I left the house and walked around it searching for signs, clues, keys. I studied the darker tree, a Spanish fir, and then the paler one, which was a beech. It was perfectly clear that these two trees didn't belong here, among the island's vegetation. Nor did the cypresses surrounding the Meadow or the wild grasses growing inside it, among which I spotted cool climate species like clover, dandelions, fennel, mullein and even the odd daisy.

Unsure what to do, I sat on the stone step that divided the Meadow in two. I don't know, maybe I was waiting for something. 'But what kind of something?' you might say. Something, or someone. The arrival of something. The approach of Someone.

The white cloud shaped like a flying saucer had reappeared in the sky. It was moving slowly, seemingly carried on the wind, and floated in my direction until it stopped just above my head. But it no longer looked like a flying saucer. It looked like the corolla of a white rose. I suppose it was the angle I was looking at it. I watched as that great white rose descended towards me until it was just a couple of hundred metres above the garden. But now it was clear it wasn't a cloud; a cloud couldn't be this close. I didn't know what it was, nor was I brave enough to look up and risk finding out.

A white rose was floating above me.

30

A lone man roams the streets

A *man is strolling along the* street. He's tall and dressed in simple but well-made attire: a pair of loose-fitting trousers, a dark cropped jacket belonging to no particular fashion, a peasant's smock. It's spring, and the lime trees along the avenue are in bloom. The fences around the houses are covered in red, pink, yellow and white roses. He has the stately, distant air of an elderly man, although he's not, in fact, elderly. He is tall, well built and has a tiny round head, minuscule in fact, with a beak-like nose. His head is shaven, although when he comes closer, walking very slowly under the shade of the lime trees, we can see that he's not bald. He just has very, very short hair. Pale blond hair that's greying, making it almost invisible. His fine moustache, too, which runs in a thin line over his top lip, is barely visible. The city is Linz. The year, 18… something. The man roams the streets and eventually leaves the city to walk among the fields, just like Adalbert Stifter's characters, whose fate always seemed to be to walk the endless footpaths and streets of Austria, either consumed by some nameless sorrow or motivated by some divine joy.

The man walks among the fields and comes to the edge of a stream, where he watches the fishermen spread out along the grassy banks trying to catch pike, carp and trout. The man counts the fishermen. He counts the number of trees he sees along both sides of the path: elms, limes and chestnuts. He takes a path and disappears into the forest. It's harder to count here. He walks briskly through the trees. He has to walk, because walking is how he does his best thinking. No, that's not true: he does his best thinking when he's playing the organ. But walking and playing the organ are, for him at least, comparable activities. He has spent the whole day playing the organ: as many hours as the liturgical demands of the church allow him to play. He always plays the organ when he has an important decision to make, or a thorny problem to solve. He's not a bad pianist either, although his instrument is really the organ. He sits on the stool, opens the stops he wants to use, rests his feet on the pedalboard, places his hands on the double keyboard and starts playing, perhaps a Bach chorale or one of the old master's preludes or fugues. But his real passion is improvisation. He's a virtuoso in the art of improvisation, a skill that's in decline nowadays. His ability to ad-lib fugues with multiple voices, his harmonic and contrapuntal skill as an improviser, is already provoking the sorts of admiration usually reserved for great feats from bygone eras. Yes, perhaps he is the last great organ improviser. Things are a little different among the pianists of the time; for some years yet there will still be virtuosos who are composer-performers and who have a considerable gift for improvisation, albeit another kind of improvisation: more rhapsodic and fantastic, like those befitting Liszt's fantasies on operatic themes, or Chopin's melismatic inventions. Yes, perhaps he is the only European organist capable of sitting at the organ and improvising, from nothing, a four-voice fugue from a symphony based on the fugal theme, a theme that someone had just whistled to him, and which nobody had ever heard before.

He walks through the woods until he can go no further, because he loves nature almost as much as he loves the sound of the organ; almost as much as he loves God, who sends him such misfortune, all shrouded in blessings. He is flushed from his stroll. He sits down against an oak and removes a large colourful handkerchief from his jacket pocket, which he uses to fan himself. He contemplates the thousands of leaves surrounding him, cut-out oak leaves all with different light shining through them. He counts them. He counts and counts, unable to stop, until he gets to 777. Unable to stop. He doesn't know why he has to count everything he sees; he doesn't know what deep thirst is quenched by that desire to count, but for him this passion for numbers is related to music, to long walks, to the organ, to God, and to solitude. He also obsessively counts the bars of his scores: organ scores, choral scores, orchestral scores.

Solitude. A lone man strolls beneath the branches of the trees in May. He has no friends. In his will, he has stated that he doesn't want to be buried beside anyone. Even in the next life, he wants to be alone. He wants his body to be immersed in stone, in a raised tomb in a church. He has never been loved. He will never marry, despite his countless attempts to do so. 'Nobody wants me,' he thinks, crestfallen. He doesn't know how to be around others. He doesn't know how to be around women. When he sees a girl he likes, he approaches her with a small posy of flowers and asks her sweetly and with great respect: 'Would you do me the honour of marrying me?' They look at him and see nothing but an old fool.

He is a victim of his complexes, fears and obsessions. He is in no way a simple, happy man. He's a simple and tremendously unhappy man, and that unhappiness makes the simplicity of his soul even stranger than the tortured and sophisticated types so typical of his times. He is a child of the *Vormärz*, of the Austrian peasant tradition, respectful of institutions, happily at the orders of the Emperor. The great mountain, the Emperor, the organ and God are his undying sources of inspiration. He writes letters abounding in old-fashioned expressions. He talks like a village schoolmaster, in terms belonging to the dialect and archaic, outmoded words. His father was exactly that: the village schoolmaster. It was from him he learnt to play the violin and organ, secondary occupations for the schoolmaster of Austrian mountain villages and towns. From his father he learnt the importance of submission, the pleasure of singing in a choir, and to obey one's superiors. He also inherited his father's excessive respect for titles and diplomas. Nobody has studied as much or for as many years as him. At twenty, thirty, forty he has remained a willing student, always obedient and well disciplined. Working against the myth of the 'genius composer', he has spent the best part of his life studying harmony, improvisation, the organ, counterpoint – practically self-taught, though passing obligingly from teacher to teacher until he had achieved every possible title and couldn't study any more. He no longer studies, for the simple fact that he knows more than all the teachers in the country, towards whom, in spite of all, he continues to show enormous respect and devotion. He is simple of character, but in the complex and tortured world of the end of the nineteenth century, this bumpkin simplicity can no longer be understood as an idyllic hangover from medieval times. No, it's something far stranger. They are right, those people who see – in his out-of-place character, his ability to repeatedly invite ridicule, his inability to establish normal social relationships with either men or women, be they inferiors or superiors, colleagues or admirers – a form of neurosis. His neurosis isn't megalomania or paranoia or schizophrenia. His neurosis isn't Strauss's desire to please, or Mahler's inner turmoil, or Zemlinsky's inferiority complex. While it's true, to a degree, that he does suffer from each of these conditions, it's also true that he is no love-struck teen, no tortured aesthete, no romantic *bon vivant*.

His particular form of neurosis doesn't have a name. It is the result, first and foremost, of a painful achronism. He is not to be confused with an anachronistic man: it isn't that he belongs to another time, but rather that he doesn't belong to *any* time. He lives outside of time. He's not old-fashioned. His clothes aren't exactly outmoded. For some time and right up until his death, he orders his smocks and trousers from a tailor from Saint Florian, the Augustinian monastery where he grew up and became an organist. He doesn't dress in a frock coat like an old-fashioned fellow; he dresses like a man for whom history simply doesn't exist. His music isn't the slightest bit reactionary: on the contrary, it's astoundingly original. But why such insistence on the chorales, motets and the baroque? He's not reactionary, but he does seem anchored in luminous antiquity. His symphonies sound like religious music, and are reminiscent of the vast spaces of gothic cathedrals. His problem is achronism: he is neither ancient nor modern, neither reactionary nor revolutionary. He has decided to live as if history didn't exist. He is an *individual*, an idiot. His tastes and inclinations don't come from anywhere in particular. He is drawn to remote lands like Russia, Mexico, the North Pole. He wants to travel far, far away. He tries the United States, but his requests are refused in Philadelphia and Cincinnati. He is a profoundly solitary man, openly devoted to the art of being himself, possessed by incredibly powerful internal forces that separate him, time and again, from the normal course of life. Forces that determine the narrative movement of his symphonies, which don't relate and describe external life, but rather *life within the soul*, the hidden battles that take place in the very depths of a human being.

There are plenty of strange things about him. His passion for death, for corpses, for human remains. At social gatherings, if he happens upon a medic, he bombards him with questions about death and the different conditions that obsess him. He's not a hypochondriac; he's a necrophile. After the death of his maestro Johann Baptist Weiss, who had given him his first lessons in harmony and the organ, he put in several requests to the ecclesiastic authorities to acquire his skull. He wanted to have the skull of that beloved and admired man with him in his room more than anything. To have it close by, perhaps on his desk, or in an armoire, lovingly wrapped in a plush shroud. What for? To touch it? To stare at the hollow eyes and frozen smile? When they moved the bodies of Schubert and Beethoven to be rehomed in more worthy tombs than those that were bequeathed to them in their own times, he asked permission to look at those venerated bones. In this case it is amorous fetishism, the intense admiration (which, according to Franz Werfel, can easily take on an erotic hint) that makes him want to see those modest remains which are, in reality, fairly insignificant. After all, when it comes down to it, what is one of Beethoven's tibias or Schubert's patella? But his obsession went even further: in 1881, when they revealed to the public the charred bodies from the fire at Vienna's Ringtheater, he was one of the first to queue up to see those men, women and children, now deformed black dolls. Perhaps on seeing those charred bodies he prophesied an age in which millions would perish in a similar way, although not as a result of accidental fires. Perhaps he prophesied the phosphorous bombs, the crematoriums at Auschwitz, the bombs that blitzed London and Dresden, the bodies burnt to a crisp in Hiroshima. For better or worse, most human beings tend to look inside themselves for equilibrium, for some kind of balance, but his intense spirituality, his eternal celibacy, his desperate solitude seem, by contrast, to crave contact with the most earthly and mortal part of man: the silent friendship of a corpse. The desire for elevation tends to be offset by displays of intense prosaicism or of an attraction towards the vulgar or obscene. Perhaps his obsession with seeing corpses was a symbolic substitute for an unspeakable desire to see naked bodies.

When he roams the streets, children chase after him and laugh. He takes out his large colourful handkerchief, like a clown at a fair, and fans himself like a peculiar butterfly. He looks like a Roman Caesar with his great shaven head. When he's invited for lunch, he never knows how to use the cutlery and he snaps the fish bones with his hands. The guests' children stare at him and laugh despite the stern glares from their parents. When he meets up with friends or colleagues to have a drink or celebrate after a concert, he never gets the jokes. He eats and drinks too much. He eats like a peasant, one platter after the other. On one occasion, he tipped the director Hans Richter after a rehearsal, and told him to drink a few bock to his health. Richter hung the thaler on his watch chain and carried it with him always. One of his biographers said that there never existed a man quite as brilliant and quite so lacking in talent as he. 'Talent excites the masses, while genius sates the soul,' this hagiographer wrote with subtle intelligence.

It's curious, for example, that the greatest improviser of his time had difficulties sight-reading, a skill within the reach of countless mere mechanical talents. He had genius, but no talent. Sight-reading means immersing yourself in the work of another, and this is precisely what he doesn't know how to do. This devout Christian, this humble servant of God, doesn't know how to put himself in another's shoes. He is like a child; children live in their own world, unaware of the wider universe around them. Perhaps that's the reason he is always rejected by women. They sense, or so say his biographers, that he will never be a partner who stands at their side, that he'll always be somewhere else, in some remote fantasy land, as if his walks took place on the other side of the earth, across pathways and landscapes from another, distinct reality. They sense that they will always be alone with him. But then, why his obsession to marry? Why was he always going after very young, very simple girls? Was he, deep down, a voluptuary? Did he desire physical intimacy with a young woman, or rather was he looking for a kind of spiritual daughter? Or perhaps all he wanted was a housekeeper who smelt good and was pleasing to the eye? Maybe he longed for a warm companion at his side, the kind dog- or cat-owners enjoy? Only one woman accepted his proposal of marriage, Ida Buhz, a young girl who worked as a hotel maid. But as soon as it became clear that she would never abandon her Lutheran faith to convert to Catholicism, the engagement was called off: he would never marry a Protestant.

In 1887, after the resounding failure of his Eighth Symphony, he suffered a nervous breakdown. Now we see him on his way home, retracing his steps through the woods, through the fields. Back along the streets of Vienna, but now with his eyes fixed on the ground. What is he doing? He's counting the paving stones in the pavement. He can't stop counting. He wants to know the exact number of paving stones between the gates of the city and his front door. On passing one of the numerous churches adorning the city, he interrupts his count and becomes engrossed in a new, even more complex one. He needs to know the exact number of gargoyles inside or on this church. The exact number of windows and pilasters. He circles the church, completely absorbed, counting. He makes a mistake. He goes back to the beginning and starts again. He never stops thinking about suicide. It's not just the failure of his Eighth Symphony, his biggest work to date, but also his failure to believe that his great champion and friend Hermann Levy didn't rate the Eighth and even went so far as to publish his negative opinions through another mutual friend, Joseph Schalk.

He wallows in despair. All of the symptoms of his neurosis come back to haunt him. The doctor recommends a period of repose in Bad Kreuzen, the sanatorium where in fact he had spent some time in his twenties. He mustn't touch the piano or organ. He mustn't compose. He mustn't work. As on the first occasion, he is prescribed cold baths, a healthy diet, walks and rest. His doctor in Bad Kreuzen goes by the name of Fadinger. He mustn't study, he tells his patient, or do any work of any kind. They rifle through his room, his table and trunk, looking for that dreaded ruled paper. He is tremendously agitated, his nerves are shot, and all because of the lack of recognition of his work. He has an enormous inferiority complex. He cannot be a true loner, given how much he craves other people's opinions. It is a new kind of neurosis. In the sanatorium garden, he scandalises the women by counting the buttons on their dresses. This well-built man with his bird-like head cannot take his eyes off the striking widow Moser. It looks like he's admiring her bust in a most unseemly way, but in fact he's just counting her buttons. 'Oh, please, Herr Bruckner,' she pleads. And she sends him off to count the flowers, trees and dandelions.

And that is how, one afternoon, he receives a visitor. He is sitting in a wicker chair enjoying the cool afternoon breeze with its whiff of elder trees and wilting roses, when a stranger approaches him, mumbling his name deferentially and asking permission to take the seat beside him.

'Of course, of course,' he mutters, ever obsequious, modest and eager to please. 'Do we know one another?'

The stranger replies that in Vienna everybody knows of him: the master composer, the famous organist, the incomparable improviser, professor and choirmaster. He isn't sure whether to believe him. He feels flattered. He feels faintly disconcerted. The stranger talks to him about his passion for numbers. He smiles bitterly.

'Oh, yes,' he says. 'The doctors call it "arithmomania". At first I thought it was merely a harmless pastime, but apparently it is far more dangerous than that,' he tells him.

'Dangerous how?' the stranger asks.

He tells the stranger about Pythagoras, about numbers being the ultimate reality of things. The visitor asks him the key question: whether he would be able to compose music from numbers. He feels uneasy. Professor Fadinger has told him he mustn't work under any circumstances; he's even forbidden him from keeping scores or manuscript paper in his room. No music at all. The stranger introduces himself. He is Count Balasz, a

Hungarian nobleman who served the Emperor in his youth and who now devotes his time, he explains, to the study of truth.

'With the greatest respect, honourable sir,' he tells Count Balasz, 'I urge you not to forget that the truth can only be found in Our Lord God and in Jesus Christ, his Son and Our Redeemer.'

Count Balasz smiles softly. 'Sir, indeed, you are quite right, but have you never considered that he who we call God is in fact an entity composed of numbers?'

Count Balasz isn't a resident at the sanatorium: he visits frequently because his wife, Princess Wilarda Philarda, a tall, dark and distinctly moustached woman, was sectioned after a nervous breakdown and several suicide attempts. She is kept company by their daughter, Miss Delphine, a very beautiful girl who spends all day writing letters and, when she thinks no one is looking, talking to an invisible companion, probably male from the way she giggles and blushes, and from her coquettish gestures. He has caught her doing this on several occasions. He has walked in on her sitting in an empty room and talking animatedly with someone, and he's seen her on the path lined with alders along the river, leaning against a tree trunk and embracing someone who wasn't there, lifting up her skirt to touch herself between her thighs. Is Miss Delphine truly sick? Or is her illness just the latest craze among young people her age? Is she mad, or just a romantic teen? He is moved by her youth and the translucency of her skin. He is moved by the supernatural beauty of her thighs, the only ones he'll ever see in his life, the most intimate part of a woman. He thinks about confessing his love to her and asking for her hand, but he would never dare to imagine marrying into nobility. All the women he proposes to are from humble backgrounds.

Count Balasz comes back a few days later, and the pair continue their discussion about music, numbers and the mystery of the universe. They take a turn in the park. His eyes become lost in the vision of the building's façade.

'How many windows are there on that façade?' the Count asks out of the blue.

And he, without a moment's hesitation, gives the precise number. The Count talks to him about the Fibonacci sequence, about the mystery of Pi, about squaring the circle, but he soon realises he can barely follow him. He's not one of those intellectuals accustomed to discussing abstract themes; he knows nothing of mathematics and, what's more, isn't remotely interested in the subject. His fondness for numbers isn't profound or cultured, Count Balasz discovers: it's simply a mania. But Balasz also knows that he is a genius, and that geniuses have their own problem-solving methods. Geniuses are allowed to take shortcuts – shortcuts earned at the sake of sanity, but shortcuts all the same.

'Master Composer,' Balasz says, 'I, too, am a Catholic, like you. I revere Our Lord Jesus Christ and am the most humble servant of the Good Shepherd. But it is clear that God is far removed from us, and that he does not speak to us in a language we understand. God does not come before us to give advice; nor does he write us consoling letters in his best German. In days gone by he did, at least that's what the sacred texts say. But maestro, sir, tell me, when do you feel the presence and reality of God most powerfully?'

'Oh, humbly, Your Reverence,' he says, always overly ceremonious and prone to mixing up his titles and forms of address in his obsequious desire to show respect, 'when I'm playing the organ, and on my walks in the countryside.'

'The language of music and the language of the world, do you see, sir?' the Count replies. 'God doesn't have languages through which to communicate directly with us because of the difference in our respective natures. That's why God has designed different languages: one is nature, which surrounds us on all sides, the language of the moon and the sun, of the force of the sea and storms, of the constant rebirth of the trees and flowers. That is the most elemental language, and it is within all of our reach. The other language is the language of music. We all feel that it puts us in touch with something bigger than ourselves. Everyone, even atheists. But what do these languages have in common? Both those who study music and those who study nature all end up talking about the same thing:

numbers. Numbers, sir, are the true language of God. Thanks to them we are able to understand all mysteries: the mundane and the human; those of growth and generation; of decay and decadence; of form and of growth. Thanks to numbers we can understand all of the processes that govern our world. Our very souls are governed by numbers. Mathematical laws govern the shifts in our passions, the fall of kings, revolutions and battles, rejections and affection. History, the stars and all the conditions that plague us throughout our lives are all but a consequence of mathematical laws. Everything is governed by numbers because everything is governed by Divine Providence. And to say that everything is governed by numbers is the same as saying that everything is governed by music. The ancients knew this well, sir. It is we who have forgotten it. Oh, yes, how much we've forgotten! Orpheus knew it, as did Pythagoras, his disciple, and from them Plato learnt the same. Dante knew it, and Goethe, the last wise man from antiquity and the first of the modern age.'

But he has already fallen into a daze. He is flattered by the attentions of this wise, sophisticated man; he's not used to being treated as an equal by great men, but at the same time he doesn't know what to do with this information, nor how he's supposed to react to it. So he reacts in the only way he knows how.

'Consider me humbly at your service, Your Eminent Reverence,' he says. 'How might this humble servant of Our Lord be of help to you?'

The Count smiles inside.

'Herr Bruckner,' he says, 'we need you. We're looking for something, a sacred place, and we have no way of finding it.'

'We?' he asks, taken aback and imagining secret societies. Imagining conspiracies.

Count Balasz introduces himself as a member of a society founded in the nineteenth century by Christian Rosenkreutz, whose body remains pure. He has seen it with his own eyes: the sweet smile of their founder, the hands crossed over his chest, and held in them a white rose, also pure. He feels uneasy. Fears the Devil's work. He fears it as a country dweller fears anything that isn't the Holy Cross.

'But we worship the Cross. We're Christians, Herr Bruckner. The Holy Apostolic Church has never had a word to say against us. We're not heretics. We're men of science, Herr Bruckner. We search for God in other ways. And we know that there is a place in the world, a holy place, but we don't know how to reach it. We would like you to help us.'

'Me?' he says, shocked, light-headed, on the brink of another nervous breakdown. 'Why me? I don't know anything, Your Eminence. I don't know anything. If it's an erudite composer you're looking for, why not ask Herr Liszt, or Herr Wagner? They are the true luminaries of our age.'

'We already have,' Balasz tells him. 'We're travelling the world in our search, treading many paths, knocking on many doors. We're searching, Herr Bruckner, for the place of the resurrection. We know, from certain ancient writings, that somewhere in the world there exists a garden where it's possible to meet Our Saviour. They call it The Garden of the White Rose, because he who enters that place and has purified himself sufficiently can look up and find above him in the air the corolla of a spiritual rose. This rose comes down over one's head in the form of a sanctified halo and carries God's blessing. He who receives the light of the White Rose transforms inside; he sees all the darkness within him turned to light and all his impurities burn away, transubstantiated. He who is thus touched can start a new life. Being touched by the rose means dying and being reborn. The old self dies and a new creature is born. It is the Saviour born in the bosom of our hearts. It is Christ born inside of us. He who is thus touched becomes wisdom and light, and from then on his is a life of servitude towards others. He acquires new powers. He can rise above all of humankind's present limitations, like an eagle soaring above the clouds.

'No, Herr Bruckner, I'm not talking about anything "mystical", not in the normal sense of the word. What I mean is that everything in this world exists not only in a three-dimensional space, but in many other dimensions. According to our calculations, the product of years of exhaustive work, there are as many as ten dimensions. Which means that we are existing now, right here and now, in ways that our reason cannot fathom. When we talk about the soul, visions, ghosts, sylphs, intuition, premonitions, we're actually referring to those dimensions that form part of our reality and are unknown to us. Dreams and art are also connected to these dimensions. What we call "the imagination" and life's startling coincidences – which we don't tend to notice because we're not paying attention – are really just another kind of mathematics, Herr Bruckner. Sir Isaac Newton's laws of physics are wrong. That is: they're incomplete. They are, in relation to the reality of the ten dimensions, like the sketch of a flower in relation to the flower itself.

'But let me tell you about the tenth dimension, Herr Bruckner, which is the most important of the ten. It is very small. It is like a grain of sand in the middle of the universe. It's like an infinitesimal dot. But inside this infinitesimal dot is *everything*. We call this tenth dimension the White Rose.

'Many people have been touched by the White Rose, perhaps at some point during their childhood, perhaps because they were lucky enough to stumble across the garden by accident, perhaps for their work or the purity of their heart. I think, Herr Bruckner, that you are one of these people.'

'Me?' he says again, and he asks his extraordinary friend what makes him think as much.

'Oh, it's very simple,' Balasz replies, still smiling. 'One only has to hear your music, Herr Bruckner. One only has to listen to your music to know that you have been there. And this is why we want you to explain to us where this place is, Herr Bruckner. And in return we'll offer you anything you desire.'

'I don't desire anything,' he lies.

'Oh, but all men desire something,' the Count replies. 'Tell me your heart's greatest desire. However big or small, it doesn't matter. Tell me what it is you desire more than anything else in the world.'

Bruckner takes a deep breath. He daren't confess the truth. He doesn't name his desire. He thinks he'll disappoint his friend, the great philosopher, alchemist, mystic and mathematician. He admires him so much that he doesn't ask for the thing he really desires, which is for Hanslick, the Viennese music critic, to stop picking on him. That is his desire. But he doesn't say anything; he's too embarrassed to talk about Hanslick to this cultured and elegant man, and his small silence forms part of the great silence of the world. And the silence of the world engulfs them both, just like the breeze coming off the mountains. And time goes by. Ships cross the seas. The clouds' shadows sweep across the wheat fields. The years weather the oaks and stain the statues green. Then Bruckner dies. Then Count Balasz dies. Then Miss Delphine dies, having had the secret love child of an anonymous father. Time passes. The elms grow green again. The storks return to the bell towers. The black elder trees come into flower. The peasants cut down branches to stack the wood on their horses' backs, and they shoo away the flies. As night falls, Grandma Liese boils leaves to make a tea. Autumn comes and Grandpa collects berries to make liquor. The trees' heartwood hides the secret to all things, the mystery, the deep, terrifying silence. Nobody knows it, but inside the elder tree an old lady tells stories in her dreams. And inside one of these dreams is where we live.

31

Our encounter with the islanders

When I *arrived back with* my friends, having retraced my steps through the tunnel, I found them already packing up our things and getting ready to set off. I almost got the impression they were about to leave without me.

'Juan Barbarín!' Sheila screamed. 'Where the hell have you been?'

'We were beginning to think you'd been abducted,' Joseph said. 'Where were you, mate?'

'The tunnel isn't completely blocked,' I said, pointing into the darkness. 'You can get through the other side.'

I was about to tell them about my discovery, but I got the feeling that they weren't in the least bit interested. Something had got them extremely worked up. They took me by the arm and pulled me to the edge of the tunnel. In the distance, to the east, you could make out a column of black smoke. Wade said it couldn't have been more than an hour and a half away and that it was our chance to locate the 'savages'. Perhaps our only chance.

We gathered all of our gear and weapons and left the tunnel and the strip of motorway cutting through the valley, the last vestiges of anything man-made in a place otherwise completely abandoned to nature. We climbed down the mountainside and back into the bush, heading in the direction of the smoke. The vegetation in those high valleys wasn't as dense as the jungle we'd left behind so we made better progress, but were also left more exposed to the enemy. It took us about an hour to get to their settlement, a ring of huts; or rather, one large ring-shaped hut covered by a single long roof, with a big open area in the middle and just one entrance. We watched all of this from a distance through our binoculars. A fire was burning in the middle of the settlement, and there, sitting on the ground close to the fire, were the missing children, Branford, Adele and Estelle. They were tied to a pole with a loose rope that allowed them to move a little bit – just as you might tie up an animal. They barely moved and appeared to be on their own. We hesitated, thrown by how little activity there was in the settlement. There wasn't another soul there; it looked like they had had left the children tied up and just disappeared.

Our rescue mission was simple: enter the settlement, release the children and take them back with us. If anyone attacked us, we would shoot them. That was our best strategy. We debated possible plans of action for half an hour or so. Joseph suggested we wait until nightfall, but we weren't entirely convinced that our strategy would work better in the pitch dark than in the plain light of day. We didn't know the terrain and were probably less vulnerable during the day when our guns gave us a clear advantage. And what's more, the three children were together and in clear view. What would we do if they took them off and separated them?

We were tremendously twitchy and nervous. I don't think any of us felt ready for the task ahead. Wade, Joseph and Gwen were the most composed. Gwen, in particular, seemed inexplicably calm. Our eyes had met several times and I'd looked for the embers of our lovemaking from the night before in her gaze, but she clearly didn't want anyone to know and avoided my gaze. We edged in towards the settlement. Joseph and Wade were up in front, then came Sheila, Christian and I, and then Santiago and Gwen. The guns were in the hands of Wade (a hunting rifle), Joseph (a pistol), Santiago (a shotgun) and Gwen (the revolver). Sheila, Christian and I, all of us wielding knives, were to cut the ropes and release the children. We didn't know what kind of state we'd find them in, so we decided that Sheila would take Branford in her arms and Christian and I would pick up one of the girls each, so that we could get out of there as quickly as possible.

We made our way towards the circle of deserted huts, crouching and hiding in the scrub, and then entered the settlement. The entrance was

quite big, about six or seven metres wide, but it was clear that it turned
the settlement into a trap: easy to defend with a handful of men; easy to
shut off and transform into a trap from which it would be impossible to
escape. The huts were really one connecting roof, a framework of thick
tree trunks tied with reed and, as far as I could make out, makeshift
hemp ropes. They were held up by a series of crosspieces and pairs of
giant bamboos with red wooden rafters, perhaps sandalwood, all expertly cut and fastened with more reeds and rope. The beams and rafters,
also made of green bamboo, supported a cover made out of tree bark,
palm and yucca leaves. Beneath this cosy roof the cannibals enjoyed protection from the rain and sun, although the communal living conditions
were anything but private. I supposed that in a society as remote as this
one, incest was inevitable and that the children were brought up commu-
nally. Impossible as it seems, all these things went through my mind as we
entered the settlement.

In the middle of the central circle we saw a few rush mats, some clay
tools, a pile of rotten mangos covered in bugs and flies, and several calabashes for collecting water with crude triangular drawings carved into
them. The children were still sitting on the floor, close to the fire, completely still. All three were tied to a painted white and red peg about two
metres tall and with a small animal skull perched on top – the skull of a
reptile, perhaps, or a large snake. We crept towards them. Their stillness
was strange and unnatural. For a moment I thought they might be dead,
and that they'd been killed and left behind by their captors, propped up
by small rods and canes hidden under their clothes to look like they were
in a seated position when really they were already emaciated, nothing but
carcasses, shells, devoured by ants. But there was another explanation for
their stillness, as we learnt when we got close enough to whisper their
names at them. What we were looking at were three dolls that had been
dressed in the abducted children's clothes and propped up with their legs
crossed and heads bowed. Wade pushed one of the fake girls with his foot,
and the doll flopped sideways onto the ground. The head was in fact a
green coconut which they'd whitewashed and covered with a kind of

blonde wig, no doubt made out of the hair that grows at the top of papyrus plants in ponds and which is a bit like the fibrous hair that covers corn. The white lace dress was stuffed with straw. I pushed the little figure of Branford with my foot, and it too collapsed to the ground.

'It's a trap,' Wade said out of nowhere, looking around. 'They've set a snare for us.'

But it was too late. There was no time to get out of there. Suddenly, we found ourselves surrounded by some thirty heavily armed strangers clutching spears, bows and arrows, slings and darts. I was surprised, though, that they didn't seem especially threatening and weren't brandishing their weapons, or aiming their bows or darts at us. Instinctively we drew in towards one another until we were standing back to back, primed to shoot at the first sign of attack. I heard the click of safeties being unlocked.

'Don't shoot,' Wade said. 'We can still get out of here alive.'

Gwen hadn't joined the rest of us, and was standing apart from the group. Then I watched as she did something I was completely unprepared for. She cocked the revolver, then raised it to Wade's temple.

'Drop all your weapons,' she said. 'Now. Throw them on the ground.'

'Gwen, what are you doing?' Wade said, trying to swivel his eyes to look at her. 'What the fuck are you doing?'

'None of them are loaded,' Gwen said. 'I mean, you needn't bother trying to shoot.'

I was struggling to compute what was going on. The situation was so bizarre that I wondered if the whole thing was some kind of joke.

'And yours, Gwen?' Joseph said. 'Is yours loaded?'

Gwen raised her arm and fired a shot in the air before returning the barrel to Wade's right temple. The noise from the shot sent a shockwave through me. A handful of birds flew from the surrounding trees, cawing. There was also a dog barking somewhere.

'What are you doing, Gwen?' Wade repeated, standing completely still and his neck tense to the touch of the warm barrel against his temple. 'Who the fuck are you? What is this?'

'Put your weapons on the ground,' Gwen repeated. 'We don't have all day.'

We all did as she said, placing the two rifles, the pistol, the blades and knife on the ground. Gwen made a sign at Wade with the tip of her shoe and Wade bent down slowly, lifted his trouser leg and removed a knife from a sheath tied to his calf, letting it drop to the floor. A few of the armed islanders came forward to pick up our weapons. Then we saw George standing behind them, among them. I hadn't spotted him at first, and I'm not sure where he came from, but he must have been hiding with the others in the huts. He was still in the same clothes he'd been wearing when he'd been with us: a cotton t-shirt, faded jeans and trainers. He looked the same, too, but now I saw him as a completely different person to the kid I'd met a few days before: the friendly, unassuming guy who would spend his days helping Lizzy look after her baby. Something in his eyes, his gestures, his gait, had changed. I was taken aback by his dramatic showmanship, because now I saw a distant, almost childlike expression in him, which he'd never shown before. His round, child's eyes and rosy, innocent lips made me think of the mugshot of a petty criminal. Gwen told us all to get down on our knees and put our hands on our heads. She, too, had changed. I was taken aback by how effortlessly she handled the gun, with the confidence you might expect from organised criminals or the armed forces, although I was still convinced that she was a woman of the sciences. She didn't look like a petty villain or a crook. She gave the appearance of being a cultured woman, a professional, someone who worked in a specialised field.

And yet, something in her had changed. But when? On the island, or before? It wasn't unthinkable that she'd known how to shoot since she was a little girl and that she'd always been in contact with rifles and shotguns. But going out to shoot glass bottles or even killing the odd deer isn't the same as ruthlessly unlocking the safety catch of a revolver and aiming it at someone's head. They took our rucksacks, calabashes and everything else we were carrying, including a fair amount of ammunition. George paced around us with his hands on his hips. It was a pose that would have made another man look masculine and superior, but in his case it merely added to his soft, effeminate air. It was clear that he was in charge, but he didn't give me the impression of being the boss. Nothing in his looks or demeanour implied that he was a leader.

'What shall we do with them?' Gwen asked, still holding the gun to Wade's head.

'I don't know. Fuck,' George said. 'I don't know what to do with them. I wish Abraham was here.'

'They were prepared to massacre us,' Gwen said. 'They were prepared to shoot us. These people are completely and utterly insane.'

'*We're* insane?' Santiago said under his breath. 'Fuck me, man...'

'Who the fuck are you?' Joseph asked. 'Who the fuck are you? What's wrong with you?'

'Quiet!' Gwen said, pointing the gun at Joseph's face. 'Not another word! Keep your mouth shut! I don't want to hear a word from any of you! The first one to speak gets shot!'

The whole scene was so extraordinary that I think we were all paralysed with shock. Now there were more guns being pointed at us, by six or seven of the strangers. At last Gwen uncocked her own and lowered it.

'You weren't on the plane either, were you, Gwen?' Wade said to her, his eyes narrowed into two slits. 'You sneaked in among us and studied all our habits. What for? We're castaways. You know this damn well. We're not here out of choice. We were in a plane crash.'

'I've told you not to speak!' Gwen replied. 'I don't want to hear another word from you!'

'We want the kids,' Wade went on. 'We want to know what's happened to the baby, to Seymour.'

Then George pulled what looked like an ocarina flute from his pocket and began to play. He played well, a sad, exotic tune; a single melody that repeated itself over and again. This went on for a long time. We looked at each other, not knowing what to do. There we were, all of us on our knees on the ground, our hands on our heads, just like we'd seen so many times on the news when they show footage of Colombian guerrillas or some

African revolution. I couldn't understand why he played for so long. He wasn't playing for us, clearly, but nor was it for the sake of mere distraction. I guessed the sound of the ocarina was a kind of signal, a call, but it wasn't particularly loud. In fact, it was probably inaudible just on the other side of the huts.

All around us, the settlement seemed to have come to life. It looked as if the men and women were gathering their things to leave. I could hear their talking and laughter, and the tone of their voices was familiar. Then I heard someone say in perfect English: 'Holy cow!' It was at this point that I realised we were being duped. The settlement, the outfits, the spears, darts, slings, bows and arrows, the loincloths, necklaces, the stake in the ground with the skull at the top – it was all part of an elaborate performance. I gazed, open-mouthed, at the scene as these phony 'savages' took off their feather headdresses and their seashell necklaces and put on jeans and t-shirts. I watched two of them carry what I thought was a giant wolf, which, on closer inspection, turned out to be nothing more than a puppet with yellow glass eyes. There went our packs of vicious, bloodthirsty Canadian wolves. And there and then the message someone had written on a wall of one of the outhouses we'd found next to the aerial came back to me: nothing is what it seems.

'It's no use with this lot,' Gwen said to George. 'I've been with them longer than you and I'm telling you I don't know what to do with them. They're absolute animals. There's no stopping them.'

'Did you see the flayed body today?' George asked.

'I led them straight there,' Gwen replied. 'It only made them angrier. There was no way of holding them back.'

'And the flight attendant? Did they see her?'

'Of course they saw her. She came at just the right time.'

'And she passed on the message?'

'Yes. She took her time before talking, but eventually she did.'

'Who would you say are the ringleaders?' George asked.

'Erickson and Langdon,' Gwen said, pointing to Wade and Joseph. George nodded, as if agreeing with her. 'But there are lots of leaders.

Different kinds. I've never come across such a bunch of maniacs. Although Erickson is the worst. He's by far the most dangerous.'

'Okay,' George said.

He stood with his hands on his hips and looked at us one by one, as if searching for the right words to say. I was sure then that he wasn't the big boss. A minor one, perhaps one who'd only been given that position for want of anyone with better leadership qualities. He spoke with a firm voice, and his threats rang out as clear as gunshots in the morning silence, but it was obvious, at least to me, that the conviction with which he spoke wasn't genuine. It seemed to come from something much bigger, much more complex.

'I want you to listen, and listen carefully,' he said, his eyes suddenly lit up by that smile which I had always put down to friendliness, but which now seemed forced and sinister. 'And I don't want any of you to speak. I don't want to hear your voices. My voice is the only one that's going to be heard here. Mine and Carmen's, got it?' he said, turning to his associate and touching her hand, a gesture that didn't escape either my or Wade's notice. 'You know her as Gwen. Okay, mine and Gwen's voice. That's it. You lot, shut it: rule number one.

'The first thing you should know is that we don't have permission to kill you. In fact, we don't want to kill or even hurt you. I hope that's understood. But you can't carry on behaving as you have been. There are rules here, and they are there to be followed. Whoever doesn't obey the rules, dies. Got it?

'We still don't know your reasons for coming here. But we don't want you here. This island already has a keeper, and *we* are that keeper. This is *our* island, and you're not welcome here. I think that's pretty easy to understand. Nobody invited you here, did they? No,' he said, raising his hand on seeing Santiago about to speak. 'You're here to listen and to obey. Anyone who doesn't obey us gets a bullet in the head. I think I'm explaining myself clearly.

'You're going to go back to your beach, the one you call your village, and you're going to stay there. If we see you again in any other part of the island, we'll shoot you. For now you can stay where you are at the mouth of the river, but you can't come inland, or move further along the coast. If you come back into the interior of our island, we'll find you faster than you can say Jack Robinson, and shoot you like wild game.

'You've already killed one of ours. Ron left home one morning and never came back. We haven't touched any of yours. You've killed one of ours, so we'd have every right to retaliate by killing one of yours. But we're not going to. We're not vindictive. It's true we did a bit of work on the air hostess. It's true. But we had to. We're not barbarians. We didn't do it for fun. We had to do a bit of damage to work out what the hell was going on. They were exceptional circumstances. It's only pain. Pain is merely physical. We didn't do anything to her that she won't be able to recover from. Wounds heal. In a couple of weeks she'll be right as rain.'

'They don't believe you,' Gwen said, raising one hand to her heart. George looked at Gwen's chest, not understanding at first.

'Oh, right,' he said. 'We had to operate on her. She had breast cancer. We located the tumour and removed it. I hope this shows you we're not savages. We're good people.'

'How could you know she had a tumour?' Joseph said. 'Where and how did you operate on her?'

'Shut up,' George said. 'If any of you says another word we'll gag you all. Is that what you want?'

He snatched Gwen's gun from her hand and pointed it at us, proceeding from one person to the next, as if deciding who to shoot.

'And Billy Higgins?' I said.

'You want me to shoot you in the leg?' George shouted. 'Are you deaf? Or don't you understand English?'

'Billy Higgins was a slip-up,' Gwen said, avoiding my eyes. 'But what were they supposed to do? You were shooting at them! We made a pack of giant wolves to scare you and keep you there on your beach, but nothing's gruesome enough for you people. You went out hunting wolves! I mean, fuck! Billy Higgins lost an arm, but you lot bumped off Ron.'

'Who is Ron, man?' Santiago asked under his breath.

'This conversation is over,' George said harshly. 'The next person to open their mouth gets a bullet in the leg, understood?'

We all fell silent. Gwen and George took a few steps back and began to confer. Gwen pointed at the sky as if describing something, while George nodded in agreement. The sun beating down on us was unbearable; I was dying of thirst. But we didn't move. We didn't dare look one another in the eyes. There were seven or eight fake 'savages' surrounding us, all armed with rifles. Not one of them had said a word.

'Talk to Gwen,' Wade whispered to me. He was directly on my right and didn't even move his lips as he spoke.

'What?'

'Talk to her about last night.'

'What are you talking about?'

'Last night, John. You slept together, right?'

Last night. Yesterday. Our skinny-dip in the river. Her rosy breasts looking at me. Her tongue in my mouth. Her thighs wrapped around me. Me inside her.

'Why?' I asked.

'Do it,' Wade said. 'She slept with you. It might get her in trouble with her lot.'

'He said he's going to shoot us.'

'Nobody's going to shoot anybody,' Wade snapped back.

'So your real name's Carmen, is it?' I called out. Gwen and George were so engrossed in their conversation that they didn't hear me at first. 'Carmen,' I repeated. 'Explain to me what went on last night.'

She turned to look at me as if she didn't know what I was talking about.

'Why did you sleep with me?'

On hearing this, George's eyes popped out. I'm not sure if he was amused or scandalised by my revelation, but his arms went back on his hips, and once again he seemed to me strangely effete. Gwen snatched the revolver from his hand, walked over to where I stood, cocked the gun and shot me in my left foot. The bullet entered – shattering bones and ripping apart tendons – and pierced my foot just at the height of my metatarsal. I fell to the floor, writhing in pain and squealing like a pig. It felt as though someone had cut off my foot, as if they were burning it. The pain was so unbearable I fainted.

32

Cristina returns

I*'ll tell you about our* reunion. Five years passed. One day my father told me that Juan Villar was coming back to Europe with his family. Or rather, that they were already back. They'd been in Madrid for a week, which, to my teenage brain at least, meant that Marianne had been getting undressed and slipping into bed every night for the last week in my very own city. The news burst like sunlight onto the dining room table, onto a dish of spaghetti Bolognese, the smell of which mingled with that of the recently planted geraniums in the beds on the terrace. I didn't know where to look, whether to be worried or to just smile. Those two smells – the spaghetti Bolognese and the flowers with raked-up soil – seemed to endow the scene with a special, unfathomable intensity.

The Villars were back. They no longer lived in Pozuelo, but on Príncipe de Vergara, close to Plaza de la República Dominicana, just a few bus stops away from my house. They were going to call us to meet up one day, 'as soon as they'd settled in'. And yet, there was no reason for me to wait for that hypothetical meeting between the two families. I could call Cristina whenever I wanted. The idea that this was possible – that I could pick up the phone, dial her number and speak to her – seemed exotic and exciting to me. I wondered what she would be like now. She must have changed a lot, both physically and as a person. But the days and weeks passed and I didn't call her. The last time I'd seen Cristina, I'd been about fourteen and she perhaps thirteen. We were two children, and now we were nearly adults. Was there any point in us seeing each other again? What if we no longer had anything in common?

Ignacio and I had also grown apart a little over the years, although we had both studied music at the Conservatorio de Madrid and bumped into one another now and then in the corridors of the old opera building, or in Monje or the Alabardero Tavern where we'd share a beer or two. Ignacio had a girlfriend by this point, a violinist called Silvana, blonde and two years his elder. Her mother was Italian, and Ignacio was sleeping with them both. He told me this because he was suffering. He said that Susanna, Silvana's mother, had seduced him three years earlier, when he was still a virgin, and that he couldn't see any way of breaking off their relationship. If Silvana found out she'd be devastated, he told me, but who could resist sleeping with a married woman, horny as hell and with that much experience – a woman also at the height of her beauty? Oh, Ignacio, if only you knew. I was dying to tell him, but kept my secret to myself.

I told him Cristina was back, and he seemed vaguely interested, but it's possible he was just being polite. Ignacio lived in the present. He wasn't the nostalgic type, or perhaps it was just that his nostalgia never lasted long.

Looking back on it now, the whole thing seems completely ridiculous, but the truth is that around that time Ignacio and I were semi-rivals in terms of our music and aesthetic motivations. He was 'modern' and I, according to him, was a 'reactionary romantic'. For him, music began with Schönberg's *Pierrot Lunaire*; for me it ended with Schönberg's *Gurrelieder*. To my mind, Anton Webern was the Devil himself; to Ignacio he was God. I endorsed tonality, which for him was abhorrent. 'You like *pretty* music,' he'd say bitingly. 'You like *nice* sounds.' For me, he stood for ugliness, tedium and avant-garde snobbery; he wasn't so much an artist as an art theorist.

And then, one day, I called her. It was a sunny, late summer's day, that magical time in Madrid when everything is turquoise and gold and dogs still run around happily on the streets. It must have been a Saturday morning, because I didn't have class, or perhaps class hadn't started yet. I worried Marianne would be the one to answer the phone, but it was Cristina. She said 'Hello' in English, out of habit.

'Hi, Cristina,' I said, doing my best to sound natural. 'It's Juan Barbarín.'

'I know who it is,' she replied cheerfully.

Her voice was the same as ever, but there was a new musicality about it. It seemed to me an extraordinarily kind, warm and feminine voice. A voice that sounded like mint sprigs and rhubarb crumble, like trains crossing Europe, and acrobatics in indoor swimming pools and on trampolines. Above all, there was so much joy in her response. There was no way that this joy was the result of my call alone, and I imagined I'd caught her off guard in the middle of a family gathering or hanging out with her friends.

I had thought of asking something like 'Do you remember me?' or 'I hope you remember me', or even saying something as pitiful as 'It's your old childhood friend' but the only thing that came out of my mouth was:

'Shall we go for a walk?'

How strange to come out with those words after five years of silence. But she didn't seem to find the suggestion in the least unusual.

'Yes, great idea!' she said. 'But I can't right now. Tomorrow?'

She later admitted that she'd had absolutely nothing to do that afternoon, that she'd spent hours lying on her bed brushing her hair and hurting herself as a punishment for having been so stupid. So we met up the following day in Parque de Berlín, on the corner of Ramón and Cajal and Príncipe de Vergara.

Cristina had grown. She was no longer a little girl. And yet, to me there was still something childlike about her. By which I mean that I was surprised on seeing her how little she'd changed. She was taller, of course, now a seventeen-year-old young woman. She had pale skin and black hair and very red cheeks and lips, like Snow White. She was exceptionally beautiful. But there was still something of the girl from before in her, something childish, naïve and fragile. I'd imagined that her childish air would fade with time and that really she was already a fully fledged woman. But I was wrong. The years had passed and she'd remained a girl, and would remain one until she was thirty.

We entered Parque de Berlín and strolled beneath the chestnut and bay trees, and the conversation flowed naturally. It was as if we'd never lost contact, although in reality we were two strangers who barely knew the first thing about each other. I talked a lot, and later she told me she'd let me go on like that on purpose, because she knew I needed to talk and impress her with my words, because men always need to expound long and florid observations on existence to get a woman's attention.

Our legs eventually grew tired, and we sat down on the grass and were quiet for a while. It wasn't for a lack of things to talk about, but rather a kind of oversaturation of feelings and emotions. It was growing dark, and the glow-worms were beginning to burn among the trees. She said she'd always thought that glow-worms were actually fairies. And that's how, as early as that first afternoon, I discovered her obsession with the world of the little people. People of the *Sídhe*, dwellers of the Land, little balls of light that dance in among the leaves. I asked her why she was interested in all that stuff, and she said that in Spain we didn't really get what fairies were. She told me that fairies weren't silly beings with colourful wings, but a complex, ambiguous race made up of all different creatures, some luminous and others dark, some good-natured and others cruel and ruthless. The one thing fairies never were was gentle and sweet, because these were purely human traits, whatever you might think after watching the fairy in *Pinocchio*, or Tinker Bell in *Peter Pan*. She tried to explain to me that fairies were actually mischievous, uninhibited, rebellious, wild, scary, exceedingly beautiful and full of a strength garnered from the forces of nature.

She told me that in England 'fairy' meant the same as the Spanish '*duende*', a concept that leans closer towards all that is occult and mysterious, all that lies beyond the rational realm, and she told me about the Morrígan and the banshees, about female fairies and male fairies and child fairies and old fairies, and about the king and queen of the fairies, and then she spoke to me about curses, retributions and revenge. She also told me about hurley, which is a ball game that fairies like to play in dells, and about the penchant the dwellers of the Land had for checked waistcoats, red skirts, and gold and pearl trinkets. I told her fairies made me hungry and that we should go and grab something to eat. She seemed keen on the idea. Yes, keen is probably the word, a keenness that almost disconcerted me. She told me she always trusted people who made firm decisions about food, and that food was very important to her. This remark surprised me, not least in the context of her erudite treatise on the world of the Beings from the Land, as I've since grown used to calling them (the Land is always the Land of Yesteryear, the Land of Summer, the Land Without Death or Forgetting, that is, the Land of the Blackthorn and the Oak, the Land of Wind in the Alder Trees, the Land Below, the Land of the Fairies). She asked me where I planned to take her, and I suddenly felt a huge weight of responsibility. I suggested a fancy restaurant close by, but neither of us had the money. She said I was crazy and that any old bar would do. We went to Rocky's, sat down and ordered a few different tapas plates. I don't remember exactly what we ate, maybe king prawns and a slice of tortilla. Everything seemed delicious to her. I ordered a beer and she a grape juice. I asked her if grape juice was a fairy drink. She looked at me with a smile on her face and asked if drinking beer made me feel important. I told her I rarely felt important, and this seemed to surprise her.

'Why not?' she asked.

'Why would I feel important?' I said. 'I haven't done anything important, and I don't think I will do anything important in my life.'

'How do you know?' she asked, staring at me with her big dark eyes.

'Because it's not me,' I said. 'I'm like a cat, you know? I like lazing in the sun. Funny goodness!' I said, putting on my best *Asterix in Britain* English accent. 'Just lazing in the sun.'

'You didn't used to be like that, Juan Barbarín,' she said.

'Would you like to go back to Calle de los Olmos to your old house?' I asked, in an attempt to change the subject.

'I've thought about it,' she said. 'But I wouldn't know how to get there by myself.'

That weekend we took the bus from Moncloa and disembarked ages away from Calle de los Olmos. We didn't recognise a thing. Pozuelo had changed in those five years; there were fewer open green spaces than before. The hill was filling up with villas and urban developments.

A long walk and several unintended detours later, we arrived at last at the bottom of Calle de los Olmos and the house where the Villars had lived. But it was occupied by other tenants now, and we couldn't get in to have a snoop. We approached the house in front where the Recaldes had once lived, and which was also now occupied by a new family. The lady of the house watched us suspiciously from the kitchen window where we'd spent so many afternoons drinking glasses of milk and eating ginger biscuits that Patricia, Ignacio's mother, baked, using a recipe that Marianne had given her. Then we went over to the house next door to the Villars', to the once abandoned property where the Meadow was, and which, to our great surprise, was still uninhabited. We found out later that the Panurs, the poet's family, had left when their father died and that the children had fought over the inheritance. We jumped the fence and crossed the garden where we'd played as children, but we couldn't find a way into the Meadow. And this was the strangest thing, because the pair of us had been in that Meadow hundreds of times. We both remembered exactly where it had been and what it was like – a large rectangle of grass split into two levels by a stone step, with a small crumbling building with a tree on either side on the upper level. But the Meadow didn't appear to be there; we searched and searched but it wasn't there. Having gone around and searched the grounds several times, we remembered that at some point the owners had done some work on the property and changed the layout of the garden. In truth, though, the whole place looked pretty neglected, as if no one had done anything with it for years. At some point the limestone step must have been removed, the ground levelled with diggers, the little house on the upper level knocked down, and the two trees felled and their stumps uprooted by a tractor. Would someone really go to all this trouble and then just leave the property to fall into disrepair and fill up with weeds again? I noticed Cristina was looking around as if searching for something.

'Do you remember Trixie?' she asked.

'That god-awful rat,' I said, exaggerating my disgust. 'I never understood how you could touch that thing with your bare hands.'

'She was very sweet. Like a little puppy. And she wasn't a rat.'

'She was a chinchilla.'

'A capybara.'

'They're related.'

'Don't take the mickey.'

'Funny goodness, don't take the biscuit!' I said, copying her English.

'Why do you keep saying "funny goodness" anyway? What does that even mean?' she asked, her big dark eyes somehow yearning for the past, in the middle of the shrubs of the abandoned garden, tall mock-orange bushes swaying in the early-autumn breeze, both of us lost in time, lost in the wind whipping up the leaves with the flowers, mingling dreams with days, children with adults. There, right in that moment, something began. A wind, a crossing, a long and beautiful crossing.

'Isn't that something you English say, as in *bondad graciosa?*' I asked her, reaching out my arm and touching her shiny hair.

'*Bondad graciosa?*' she said. 'Funny goodness? The English don't say that.'

'Well, I don't know,' I said. 'According to *Asterix* you say it.'

'Oh!' she said. 'You mean "goodness gracious"! Is that it? Goodness gracious!'

She burst out laughing. I moved towards her, put my arms around her waist and kissed her. I thought she'd push me away or simply not return my kiss, but she didn't. We kissed for a while, and when I pulled my face away from hers I saw a shining tear track running down her cheek.

'Why are you crying?' I asked.

She shrugged her shoulders and lowered her gaze, and we kissed again. She opened her mouth and offered me her tongue, and I was taken aback by how passionate her kiss was. I would have preferred, in fact, for her to open it less. I felt like she was a big, strong, dark animal that wanted to devour me. But it's true that I hadn't had much practice in the art of kissing back then. I'd kissed maybe four girls, but never like that. There was no doubt that of the two of us, Cristina had more experience than I had and was the one in control of the situation. Later she would tell me that she'd had a couple of boyfriends in England, nothing serious, summer flings involving lazy afternoons together, smooches under the oak trees, lots of plucked daisies, unbuttoned blouses and fumbles under skirts. She was still a virgin, and I never got to the bottom of how far she'd gone with those boyfriends of hers, or how far she'd let them go, although the very thought of it would give me the most delicious invidious shivers in the months and years to come.

How marvellous women are, and what a way they have of surprising us. Their daring, their imagination, their realism. They always have one over on us. They are always just out of reach, like our reflection in a river. They are always the decision makers. Always opening, always closing.

But I could feel her sweet-smelling skin, the warmth of her face against mine, the sweet, burning touch of her lips, wet against my own, and all the tremulous, disturbing fullness of her body in my arms. I felt the reality of her tongue in my mouth and my tongue in hers. The mysticism of the kiss, under whose spell men and women fall, and enter one another, and please one another, and transubstantiate; her taste, the taste of her saliva and her breath, the moment when flesh becomes spirit and the spirit flesh, and everything in the middle of the abandoned garden, with the mock-orange shrubs swaying around us and the clouds racing above our heads in the frayed fluid of time, in the years to come and in the sexual passion to come.

'I adore you, my sweet Cristina,' I whispered into her ear.

'I've always loved you, all these years,' she said.

'So why didn't you write?'

'Because I thought I was a silly little girl and that you weren't interested in me. Anyway, it was you who stopped writing.'

'I've loved you all this time too. But I imagined I'd never see you again.'

'I thought the same,' she said. 'But I always thought I'd come back to Spain when I was older.'

'Come back? Why?'

'Because I'm Spanish,' she said. 'I don't like England. I don't like the people there. And because you were here.'

'But we barely know each other,' I said.

We were still locked in our embrace and kissed gently between replies. I could feel her trembling in my arms.

'Don't be silly, of course we know each other,' she said, her eyes welling up with tears.

'You're so beautiful.'

'And you're so handsome,' Cristina said. 'And tall. You didn't used to be so tall.'

'You see? We don't know each other.'

'Do you really love me?' she asked.

'I've always loved you.'

I remember the first time we were fully naked together, side by side, on my teenage loner's bed, on my worn, golden bedspread, one afternoon when my parents were out. We had no intention of making love, because she wasn't ready yet. I don't think she really wanted to see me naked, or to undress in front of me. A warm, coppery light filled the room with the secret peacefulness of that March afternoon. Inevitably, I compared Cristina's naked body to that of her mother, and I asked myself if what I was looking for in Cristina wasn't in fact to be with Marianne again. But luckily for both of us, Cristina didn't physically resemble her mother in the least: she was dark-haired, like Juan Villar, and didn't have her mother's long bones. She had inherited from her a kind of sexual aura and strong physical elegance. And of course her small upturned nose and those narrow almond-shaped eyes came from Marianne, but any likeness ended there.

For some months, the only thing we did was mess around. We would stroll along the streets of Madrid, talk for hours and then look for a hiding place (normally my house, which was empty in the afternoons) where we could lie down and undress and play around with our bodies. I was a little disappointed. Not only because our fondles didn't constitute a real sexual relationship, but also because Cristina – who had the beautiful body of a woman; so lovely, so rosy and sweet-smelling, so warm and inviting that it made me a slave to her shadow for life – was still, deep down, just a girl. And what I desired with all of my being was to be with a real, fully fledged woman.

Cristina loved flowers and all things colourful. She loved any object made of glass, little trinkets, figurines and purses. She also liked sweets: violet creams, wine gums and lollypops. She liked lollypops so much that often on our walks she would buy herself one and suck it as we strolled. Later, if she didn't finish it, she would wrap it back up in its wrapper and keep it for later, like children do. When she ate a peach she'd suck the pit dry then keep it in her mouth the whole afternoon, and I'd find it there, inside her mouth, when I kissed her. I told myself that my girlfriend wasn't a person but a fairy, a wild woodland creature. She didn't have any of the adult habits the rest of us were so keen to imitate. She didn't smoke. She didn't drink alcohol, not so much as a shandy, nor did she have any interest in drugs. She almost never wore a bra and her breasts moved about freely under her blouse, her nipples showing through her t-shirts. But this wasn't a sexual statement or gesture on her part. In fact, it was the opposite: a statement of Edenic innocence.

She kept all her baby teeth in a little ivory box which had a gentian flower carved into the lid. She had collectors' albums full of dried flowers and leaves. She kept pink, blue and yellow crystal vials where she collected the tears she'd shed on momentous occasions in her life, just like a general keeps the flags from pivotal battles. Her books were full of pressed flowers. She kept her childhood bear on her bed, a morose-looking teddy, one of whose ears had come away at the seam. She sang. Cristina was always singing. She sang real and made-up songs in a soft and high-pitched fairy voice that I cherished. I think my friends were surprised I was going out with such a girlish girl, although they all loved her: it was hard not to love Cristina. I think they all suspected it wouldn't last, and that I'd soon grow tired of her, or she of me. My friends' girlfriends were far more chic and sophisticated than Cristina, and when they got dolled up and put makeup and stockings and high heels on they looked like thirty-year-old women. Next to them, Cristina, who never dressed up, always looked like a child. Sometimes, when I'd see her with her two pigtails, licking a lollypop and looking at me with her bright smile, her cheeks full, I despaired that she was so childish and thought I should finish with her, that I should leave her as soon as possible. But when all's said and done, she was actually very young – only seventeen – and I told myself that with time she would turn into the fully fledged woman I so longed for.

33

Our life in Madrid

There's something tragic and wretched about youth. The echo of a lost battle. Our story, mine and Cristina's, is also the story of a battle lost. My parents were up in arms about my decision not to go to university but rather to study music and be a composer (back in those days, the Conservatory qualification wasn't a university degree and hardly served any purpose), and Cristina's parents felt the same when their daughter told them she wanted to be an opera singer. Our two families barely socialised with each other by then, their friendship having waned over time.

My parents thought it ridiculous that Cristina wanted to be an opera singer. Cristina with her lollypops and pigtails, with her fairy outfits. 'That girl,' my mum would say, 'has neither the temperament nor the personality to be an opera singer.' And anyway, what opera? Back then, practically the only opera in Spain went on at the Liceo de Barcelona. Madrid only put on zarzuelas.

My studies at the Conservatory were going well. During the summers I would take courses in Villafranca del Bierzo, in the mountains just north of Leon where the Halffters had a castle. Ignacio would also be there. In fact, almost all of us went: Macías, who was a few years older, José Manuel López López, Santiago Lanchares, Pistolesi, Jorge Fernández Guerra, Mauricio Sotelo, Jesús Rueda; all the young men who would go on to form the new generation of Spanish composers to which I myself would never belong. I remember Cristóbal Halffter reading one of my pieces for orchestra, his eyes moving up and down the enormous sheet of manuscript paper and then, every now and then, looking at me, unsure of the words to use. 'The only problem with this music,' he said at last, 'is that if César Franck had written it we'd all think it marvellous.' César Franck! The weakest, most limited, most inadequate of all the Romantic symphonists!

Otherwise, I did everything a young composer of my age should do. I met Luigi Nono in his 'Manuel de Falla' courses in Granada, and like everyone, was totally fascinated by his ascetic, magnetic persona. I read Massimo Cacciari's book *The Necessary Angel*. I read Theodor W. Adorno. I met Franco Donatoni in Siena, in classes at the Chigiana Academy, and also took a number of classes at the IRCAM in Paris, the musical research centre where, at the time, they were experimenting with machine-made music, data programming, and with the physical breaking down of sounds.

I tried. God knows I tried. I began to compose serial music, to work on 'blocks' and 'densities' under the tutelage of Francisco Guerrero (who never charged me a penny for the classes) and I grew interested in electronic music and microtonal music and the spectral breakdown of sound. I even considered the possibility of studying acoustics, physics and maths. I tried, but in the end it was no use, because none of that music moved me; it didn't satiate me.

Then I did some truly reckless things, like when, for example, I would come out in public saying that Adorno, the adored music critic and philosopher, was nothing more than an artful cretin. Adorno linked the notion of 'beauty' to capitalist dehumanisation, to the exploitation of man and to the 'human slaughterhouse', and he praised ugliness and unpleasantness as a form of consciousness-raising. According to Adorno, music should be rough and uncomfortable, because if it wasn't so, it became a weapon with which to exploit the individual. Have you ever heard such a load of crap?

Cristina and I finished our studies at more or less the same time. I began to teach music theory classes in the Conservatory. She auditioned for Spain's national radio choir and got in. Both of us now earned a salary. We rented a flat in the Chueca neighbourhood and moved in together, to the horror of our parents, who were disappointed by our choices not to marry, not to buy a property (paying rent was 'throwing money down the drain') and to sleep on a futon instead of on a bed with a metal spring base like everybody else. Not long afterwards, Cristina's family went back to England. Her parents never set foot inside our house, and mine didn't visit much either.

We masked our failures with relative prosperity and the modest accomplishment of a middle-class existence, which consists of a regular job, a monthly paycheque and a warm, welcoming home. I took the public exams at the Conservatory. I was a tenured professor now. Cristina sang almost every weekend in the RTVE orchestra's regular concerts, and we both slipped into a comfortable, perfectly insipid, typically Spanish life.

I wrote a symphony in D flat major which I called Symphony No. 1. I showed it to two of my old professors, Carmelo Bernaola and Luis de Pablo. They both told me my work showed craftsmanship and a good command of 'traditional language', but they advised me not to enter it for any competitions, because it would discredit me forever. But they gave me some sound advice. Bernaola told me that if this was the music I liked, I might think about becoming a film score composer. And Luis de Pablo told me the only place I'd ever have any kind of certain future as a composer was in the States.

All our plans fell apart. Cristina was given a part in a zarzuela, *La del Soto del Parral*, but she struggled to keep up with her regular choir rehearsals on top of those for the light opera, so in the end she had to abandon her role. I told her to send the choir to hell, but a minor role in a minor production wasn't promise enough for her to quit her permanent job with its monthly paycheques. I was drinking too much. In my later years I would more or less give up drinking, but back in those days I drank whisky and cognac, gin and tonics and vodka oranges, rum and Cokes and vermouth, sherry and port.

And then there were the women. I've never known anyone more naturally faithful than Cristina, or anyone as naturally unfaithful as me. In my defence, I'll say that it took years for me to give in to temptation and that I was faithful to Cristina for a long time. And then my slips (if you can call them that) were always brief and episodic. One-night stands when I was

away from Madrid or when Cristina went away with the choir. The reason
for my infidelities wasn't anything to do with her not being enough for me,
or me not loving her madly. Cristina and I had a passionate sex life, but in
spite of this, I desired other women. I desired all women, truth be told. I
think it's in the nature of lots of men to desire all women, and I really and
truly don't know if it's possible to go against your own nature. Walking
into a trap, like the fox from the fable?

My infidelities went unnoticed for a long time, and she might never
have found out a thing if it weren't for a gold-coloured bra that someone
left hidden behind the cistern in the bathroom, I guess with the intention
of Cristina finding it. I'm not sure who it was, because the week it happened, when Cristina was on tour in Latin America, I slept with at least
three women. If I had to guess, I'd say it was a Brazilian composition student who answered to the unusual name of Ontanna.

And that's how Cristina found out, in the worst possible way, what I
got up to when she wasn't there. She didn't scream. She didn't cry. I was
surprised by her reaction. Cristina could always surprise me. She told me
that if I wanted to be with other women I could, but that she didn't want
to know about it. It was, I imagine, her pragmatic, British stiff upper lip
speaking. She was very upset, and it was several weeks before she let me
touch her, or before she was composed enough to look me in the eye. But
despite everything, she told me to do whatever I wanted, that she neither
desired nor had the power to take my freedom from me. I think she believed that the motive for my infidelity was a desire for other experiences,
because we'd started out so young, before we'd had other sexual relationships. But the problem wasn't that I wanted to play the field before devoting myself to a monogamous relationship; rather, my soul just wasn't in any
way monogamous. The thought of her being with another man made me
sick to my stomach, but in spite of this I told her that she could also be
with other men if that's what she wanted, and that I didn't believe in being
faithful in a couple out of obligation (in truth, I didn't really know what I
believed), and nor did I agree with suppressing desires.

There was a bass in the RTVE choir who was in love with Cristina and spent the whole time trying to seduce her. She told him she had a boyfriend, and he told her that didn't matter, that he wasn't the jealous type. He was desperate to have her, and he smothered her with attention and surprise gifts, asked her repeatedly to spend the weekend with him in his house in Jávea. Cristina told me all of this herself, I suppose because she didn't want me finding out from anyone else.

I knew the bass in question, a tall guy (basses tend to be even taller than tenors) called Ígor. Ígor was a strong, well-built man in his forties, sophisticated, greying at the temples and single. He never concealed how much my presence displeased him, and even told me on a couple of occasions what a shame it was that a woman as beautiful as Cristina was with a kid like me. And I'd say: 'Settle down, Ígor. If you keep asking, you might get what you're after.' He was the type of guy who tells you he's had a vasectomy on first meeting, and is always looking for the most tasteful and good-natured way to bring up the size of his penis in front of women. I know that during one summer tour Ígor became entirely fixated on Cristina, and that his sole preoccupation was to get her into bed. 'Why don't you want to? I don't want you to be my wife; you needn't leave your husband. Why so prudish?' he would ask her in public, lavishing her with compliments.

On one occasion, when they were in Guadalajara in Mexico, he took his dick out in Cristina's hotel room. There were three or four other people present, all women. His idea was to show her what she was missing. I imagine the well-worn joke came out, the one about the best 'member of the choir'. These days his behaviour would be considered sexual harassment, but back then it was taken as a sign of his sophistication and liberal mindedness. Ígor had slept with plenty of the women in the choir, and they all knew he was hot on Cristina's heels. They waited impatiently for the day Cristina would fall into his trap.

She would tell me all of this herself, later on, when we were in bed, and I'd get so turned on that I'd make love to her for hours. The image of her in another man's arms, of her being pleasured by another man, made me

tremble with horror and jealousy, a jealousy that aroused me beyond belief. I was young, and didn't understand those feelings, which I took to be
a kind of sexual perversion. I told myself I must be seriously disturbed,
and that no one in their right mind could want their girlfriend to be with
another man, less still experience such pleasure from picturing it.

34

We begin to drift apart

One Easter we decided to go camping by the beach. We were somewhere in Alicante or Castellón on a half-empty campsite positioned on a hill covered in pine trees that stretched all the way to a cliff hanging over the sea.

We sat for hours reading under the pine trees. I was reading *The Alexandria Quartet* by Lawrence Durrell, and Cristina was dipping in and out of *Song of Immediate Satori*, a Japanese Zen classic, and *Out on a Limb*, Shirley MacLaine's 'spiritual autobiography'.

One afternoon, out of curiosity, I picked up *Song of Immediate Satori*, and began to read it. At that time I still felt a certain affinity with Eastern culture. And yet, the contents of that little book seemed hostile and inhumane. Zen, the old treatise said, is the same as death. What the Zen disciple looks for is death, and every time he or she lies down on their hard narrow bed it's as if they were climbing into their own tomb. Zen calls for total inactivity, the complete emptying of the mind. Zazen is a discipline that involves sitting absolutely still in front of a blank wall. Zazen is basically staring at a wall for hours, understanding that everything is empty, that everything is nothing, and that you too are empty, you too are nothing.

I told Cristina that the whole thing seemed morbid and sick to me. I didn't understand why she wanted to 'die' when she was young and beautiful and full of life, when she was in love and loved in return. She told me I didn't get it, and that I'd only read a few pages. I asked her why she wanted to sit still for hours looking at a blank wall, and she told me that

that was no more than a way to calm the mind and to stem the flow of thoughts. I told her she was falling into the clutches of religion, that the whole thing smelt to me of sin, penance, and isolation from the real world. She told me I was wrong.

From then on, Cristina tried less and less to find work as a singer. She suffered terribly during her encounters with the world and came back like a sparrow hawk returns after a ferocious battle in mid-air: covered in wounds. Anyone who isn't familiar with the art world can't possibly imagine how vicious and ruthless it can be. The formidable ego of most artists is really just the armour they need to withstand the brutal blows you have to face. Cristina possessed none of the ego, none of the necessary armour, and nor did she want to. But then she discovered the spiritual world. It was as if the Fairyland that lived inside her had, at last, found the way to manifest itself.

She began to attend yoga classes and meditate. She never tried to convince me to go with her. She told me how well she felt after yoga, but didn't expect me to go. She explained meditation to me. I was interested, in my own way, but every time I sat down to read one of the books she recommended, I put a barrier up.

She began to suffer from weird conditions; the kinds doctors don't consider real illnesses. Her skin began to itch, and it became so intense she couldn't sleep. She tried various creams. She went to several holistic doctors who recommended all kinds of treatments, one of which was quite simple: sea bathing. We didn't live by the sea, but one weekend we went to the beach anyway and the Mediterranean water worked wonders: the itching went away that second. But the moment we got back to Madrid's plateau, it returned. My mother told me that what we needed was to have a baby. The moment Cristina became pregnant, she insisted, all the imaginary problems that seemed so important to us now would disappear as if by magic.

Cristina got in contact with a therapist who was well regarded in the circles she moved in now. She was called Mónica, and was about forty or fifty, very pleasant, with deep blue eyes and an Asturian accent. Mónica practised all kinds of therapies using techniques I'd never heard of: reflexology and iridology and so on. She had studied Tibetan medicine and had a degree in bioenergetics from somewhere in Germany. Cristina told me that the moment she stepped foot in Mónica's house she felt like her life, which up until then had been lost and aimless, began to take direction.

In that first session with Mónica, the therapist took her pulse and looked at her irises. She told Cristina she was a very sensitive person who felt assailed by the outside world, who had, quite literally, 'thin' skin and felt the universe to be a dangerous place, which is why it irritated her when she came into contact with the hostile world. She explained to Cristina what the skin meant in esoteric terms, and about the need to grow 'thicker' skin to be able to face the relentless and brutally materialist world in the Kali Yuga age. Without ever having spoken to her before, she described Cristina's entire life. She told her she had problems with her mother, that she'd always felt her mother didn't love her and saw her as a threat or competitor, and that her mother's strong personality had always made her want to hide away and go by unnoticed. She told her she was experiencing an extremely intense sexual and romantic life, but that despite this, inside she was consumed by a great sadness. She told Cristina that her skin problems stemmed from her liver, that was her weak point, and if she wanted to harmonise her system and prevent future complications she had to change her diet. She forbade Cristina from eating white sugar, lactose products (especially cheese, an appalling Western custom), eggs, red meat, refined flours, all frozen and tinned foods, as well as anything containing preservatives or colourants of any kind. She must substitute chicory for coffee and instead of black tea drink the herbal kinds: lemon verbena, lime blossom or mint. White fish and seafood were also allowed, but only once a week, given that it was ideal to maintain a totally vegetarian diet, and the recommended sources of protein were soya beans, tempeh and seitan (virtually impossible to get hold of in those days in Madrid), and a mixture of pulses and cereals.

Cristina's new regime hit me like the onset of winter. It wasn't that she couldn't eat *anything*, but food had suddenly turned into an obsession for both of us, and a constant source of worry. We began to see herbalists, whose products were, on the whole, sad and monastic-looking. Insipid, tasteless biscuits. Brown sugar that lent coffee an unpleasant earthy flavour. Veggie burgers that tasted of cork. Cristina wasn't the fanatical type, and quickly tailored Mónica's strict diet to suit herself. She never stopped drinking black tea, for example, and she'd have a glass of wine on special occasions. From time to time she'd treat herself to a slice of tart or a pudding. But she adhered one hundred per cent to the ban on lactose, eggs and meat. Since neither of us could be bothered to spend all day in the kitchen, I ended up adopting more or less the same diet.

We had become slaves. It's true that it's hard not to be a slave to certain things. To meat, or to the absolute prohibition of meat. To alcohol, or to teetotalism. To sensuality, or to celibacy. We didn't know it then. One rarely notices one's become a slave. It usually happens for one's intended greater good, or as a result of a conversion to a faith. Faith makes slaves of us. That's why, in order not to become a slave to anything, you have to be faithless. Is it possible to live like that? Not believing in anything can lead to depression and a feeling of emptiness. Surely there must be a path between slavery and emptiness, albeit a path as narrow as a knife-edge. Those who walk this path are the only truly free beings, the only living beings. How many of them are there in the world?

A month into this new diet, Cristina's itching began to fade. It never disappeared entirely, but Cristina put this down to her not having followed Mónica's diet to a T. She felt better, slept better. But to me she seemed pale, even thinner and sad. We didn't make love as much as we used to. She said that this, too, was normal. That we couldn't spend all day on top of each other like rabbits.

Now Cristina saw Mónica regularly. She went to her consulting room at least once a month. And we spent a year like that, maybe two. In the summer, the itching almost disappeared altogether, but it came back as autumn began. It was Madrid's dry air, the central heating, the stress of the beginning of the new season. She carried on auditioning for zarzuelas, going for any role that might help propel her into a solo career, but they never picked her. I didn't understand why, when her voice was so beautiful.

Mónica advised her to fast and take clay baths for her liver and skin. She ran an alternative medicine centre in the Sierra de Gredos and invited Cristina there for a weekend fast (even if a full week-long fast were ideal, because that way the body overcomes the feeling of hunger and begins to use its energy reserves, and any initial weakness disappears).

I was becoming increasingly worried about Cristina. She was moving further and further out of my reach, seeming to drift ever further away from me, from the real world. She told me we'd been living a lie, that we'd been trying to convert art into a form of expression for our ego, and that true art should be an offering to the Spirit, an invocation and a service. She quickly began to believe that this was precisely the reason for her artistic failure: she'd entered into the art world looking for fame, glory, recognition, and for that very reason *they'd denied her those things.*

'Who?' I would ask her. 'Who's denied you those things?'

'The higher forces,' she'd say.

'What higher forces?'

'The higher forces that govern our lives.'

I said that was all well and good, but in that case how could she explain the fact that the world was full of artists hungry for fame and who get exactly what they wanted? How did she explain the fact that the higher forces didn't stop them from achieving success?

'The fact that other people can satisfy their egos' desires doesn't mean anything,' she told me. 'Everyone has a different karma and a different level of evolution. The issue here is that they don't allow *us* to function with *our* egos. What might work for other people doesn't work for *us*. Because we have the chance to evolve.'

'So, it doesn't matter that all those other people who are so behind in their spiritual evolution are successful, because even if they weren't they wouldn't understand anything anyway. Something like that? Since they're humans who haven't evolved, they are given all the gifts in the world, while we, who are superior to them, don't achieve anything.'

'Nobody's said anything about us being "superior",' Cristina said. 'I'm talking about each one of us having different experiences according to our own karma and level of spiritual evolution, that's all.'

By this time, these kinds of conversations were common between us. And I watched Cristina drift away. I watched her dark hair turn ashen. I watched her dressed in a brown tunic, walking barefoot along a mountain path edged with blackberries, drifting away from me, drifting away from the world. Because, when she talked about *us*, I no longer knew what *us* meant. Was it the two of us, or rather her and her fellow believers? What I actually think is that she used *us* out of courtesy to me, so as not to cast me aside, or perhaps to keep up the pretence that we were on that adventure of hers together.

In the end, she decided to go to Gredos to do a week-long fast.

She'd reverted to Fairyland. She told me that Mónica could *see*. That she saw beings in nature: fairies, *duendes*, ghosts, dead people, disembodied people. Mónica saw them with her eyes open. She saw the energy around people, and just by looking at you she knew what would happen to you, what you were thinking, what kind of life you'd had. The strangest thing about all of this was that I didn't doubt that all of that was true; that is, that Mónica was telling the truth, and that she really did see things. I've never been an aggressive atheist or a fanatical rationalist. I've always believed that art had a lot to do with what the ancients called magic. And yet, I was alarmed by the turn Cristina's life was taking.

35

Cristina in Rishikesh

I went to Gredos to visit her during her fast. Mónica's centre was in a re-mote spot in the sierra, between Candeleda and Arenas de San Pedro. On that occasion there must have been about fifteen people in the house, some living there on a permanent basis, others undergoing different kinds of therapies. The staff consisted of a cook, a woman in charge of the clean-ing and two women who helped Mónica with the treatments, one of whom was a doctor. It came as a surprise to me that anyone with a medical de-gree should be interested in those quack practices, and even more to hear her say that conventional and alternative medicines weren't contradictory but rather complementary, and that one day all the practices that went on up there would also be taught in universities.

The conversation continued in this crackpot vein for much of the eve-ning. Or at least that's how it felt to me. Only three or four other people were fasting like Cristina, so we came together in the canteen to have supper by the light of candles and gas lanterns. Those who were fasting just sipped at a watery vegetable broth, which they drank to avoid losing minerals. The rest of us ate a salad full of excessively green leaves (the greener and more bitter, the better, Mónica explained) and some 'roasted' vegetables that were, to my mind, raw. There wasn't any salt on the table. There was soy sauce, although to use it lavishly was frowned upon. There were some thin slices of wholegrain bread in baskets, but it was also frowned upon to eat too much of that. For pudding we ate cherries picked from local trees, so unripe they were light, almost yellowish pink, although

Mónica said they were perfectly edible and far better for you than those artificially red cherries you got in supermarkets.

All of them, without exception, had seen flying saucers and 'beings' in the woods, and had felt 'presences' in the house. Mónica claimed that up there in Gredos, extra-terrestrial visitations were common. After supper, we went out into the meadow in front of the house hoping to spot a UFO. It was a warm spring night, and the sky was bursting with stars. Mónica told us, in confidence, that she had been with Shirley MacLaine during one famous alien encounter, the encounter of the century, and she told us about the moment the mother ship positioned itself above them, and about the extra-terrestrial cities they took them to. And I could tell that Cristina had already heard this story. Nor did it escape my attention that she was completely entranced by Mónica. It was in that moment that I noticed a certain glint in Cristina's eyes. I don't think I'd ever seen it before. I'm sure there was some physical reason for it (like the fact that my little Cristina had gone for days without eating). But it shook me, because it gave me the feeling that her eyes were capable of seeing something that I couldn't.

Cristina and I broke away from the group to take a moonlit walk in the surrounding woods. She was walking very slowly. She had a bottle of natural spring water from which she'd occasionally take tiny sips. I found the glint in her eyes deeply unnerving. I told her I was worried about her, very worried in fact, and she pulled a face of disappointment and irritation.

'I've finally found something that makes me whole, that gives meaning to my life,' she said. 'I've finally met people I like, people who want something else from their existence. I don't know why you're so worried. It should be me worrying about you,' she said, 'because it seems to me you're completely lost. Lost in your drinking, in your bottles of malt whisky, in your little flings, in your growing frustration. Lost because you don't know where you're going and because you don't like yourself.'

'It's true,' I said, 'I don't like myself. But I thought you did.'

'Look,' she said, 'I've come here to focus on my recovery process, to find a bit of calm and silence.'

I took the hint that she wanted me to leave her in peace, and the next morning I went back to Madrid.

The moment I got back to the city, I went straight to the American International Institute, which in those days was close to the Villa Magna hotel, and I asked for a list of American universities. I hadn't forgotten about the seed Luis de Pablo had planted in my head a few years earlier. I spent that weekend writing letters to university music departments all over the States. To my great surprise, I received a reply from practically all of them. In most cases they told me there were no available places. Cristina and I were both surprised by their courteousness, accustomed as we were to Spanish bluntness and inefficiency. In other cases they sent me documents to fill in and asked me for more information about myself, letters of recommendation and some samples of my work.

That summer, my path diverged from Cristina's for the first time in many years. She went to India for two months to an ashram in Rishikesh, on the shore of the Ganges, and I went to the States for job interviews. I visited Rhode Island, Vermont, West Virginia, North Carolina and Hawaii. On my return, I had a firm offer to join the Department of Musicology at Rosley College, in Oakland, Rhode Island. The place – both the campus and the city of Oakland – seemed like paradise to me. The pay conditions were excellent, and we would live in one of those two-storey houses with porches and a big garden full of trees like the ones you saw in films, the kind that in Europe only a millionaire could dream of affording.

And then came our reunion in Madrid after a summer spent on different sides of the planet. I came back from the United States in very high spirits, thinking I was to be the bearer of great news. But in fact, my news didn't have the effect I thought it would. I told her about my job offer, about the oak trees in Rosley College, but it all seemed trifling and insignificant to her compared to the great Indian sun. I told her about the money I'd make and the house we would live in, and it all seemed mediocre and stupid to her. Money, a house, a job. Middle-class commodities, the values of empty people.

Cristina came back totally enamoured with India. The glint in her eyes, the special sparkle I'd noticed for the first time that evening in the Sierra de Gredos, had become more intense and concentrated, as if her eyes had acquired a capacity for seeing things that I couldn't see. They contained a glint of compassion and wonder, but also withdrawal and distance. And she wanted to go back to India. She suggested we go together for a year to the Swami Kailashananda ashram in Rishikesh.

'For a year?' I asked, taken aback. 'And what about the US?'

'We'll go to India for a year, and then to the US,' she said. 'We have a year, don't we?'

'Yes. My contract starts in a year.'

'So it's perfect.'

'And you'll want to come to the US afterwards?'

'I'll want to go wherever you go,' she said. 'Although there's always the chance that you won't want to leave India, and that we'll end up staying there.'

Her plan wasn't completely ludicrous. I'd give her India and she'd give me the States. And in both places we could be happy. And there was a possibility that we'd want to stay in India, just as it was also possible that we wouldn't last a whole year there and that we'd decide to come back after three months. We both had that horribly misleading feeling you get when you're young that everything is possible.

'But then, you don't want to be a singer any more?' I asked.

'In the ashram we sing non-stop,' she said. 'I'm learning another kind of singing. I've discovered the nectar of singing. I've learnt that song allows us to secrete a spiritual nectar inside of us. I've learnt that the human voice has magical properties.'

'But you've decided to give up on your professional career.'

'I've learnt something else, Juan Barbarín,' she said, looking at me with that extraordinary glint in her eyes. 'I've learnt that our life *is real*. That the things that happen to us really happen to us, and that everything is a matter of life or death, that there are no easy, or light or coincidental things. I've learnt that our life is a sacred gift that we've received and which we don't have the right to waste. Everything around us *is real*. It's truly happening. Life, death, love, our love – it's all real, but we don't live it as if it were real. We live it as if it were some kind of illusion, as if we were characters inside the pages of a book written hundreds of years ago.'

'I'm not following you.'

'I mean that we live in absolute oblivion. We're wasting our lives on nonsense. On fear, anxiety, jealousy, self-pity, selfishness. If we only realised that everything is real, that everything is here for us, because of us, then we would start to feel the need to *do something*.'

'That's what you learnt in India?'

'I think so, yes. I think it's what I learnt. Although it's not what they taught me.'

'What did they teach you?'

'Well, lots of things. To wash my clothes on a rock. To put out a candle with my fingers. To eat lentils without a fork. No, seriously, they taught me a lot. They wrung me out like a wet rope and squeezed out all the water and then they submerged me in water and then wrung me again and put me out in the sun and on like that, over and over, purifying, cleaning, purifying, vomiting, and screaming like a demon possessed. I became a demon for a month; I was a demon. My eyes were raw from crying. If you had seen me you would have been horrified. It was really ugly, really bad.'

'Sounds very interesting.'

'Don't be sarcastic. I mean they've shown me a lot of things, but one always learns things beyond what others teach you. There are things that no one ever tells you.'

'They hide them from you.'

'The best way to hide wisdom is to completely reveal it. No, no one hides anything. They just can't teach you some things. Not everything can be said. Some things you learn without ever having to be taught. They say the heart has its own ways of learning. They say you are already in the heart. You are the heart. Don't do a thing. Don't search for anything. Don't envision. Don't meditate. Don't try. Don't make any effort. You are already in the heart. The heart is everywhere. You are alive. All this is real. We don't have to do anything, because everything is the heart. That's what I learnt in India, Juan Barbarín, that India doesn't exist. That yoga doesn't exist. That Vedanta doesn't exist. That the only thing that exists is the heart.'

'So, you're not thinking about going back to India?'

'Haven't you realised that I'm still not back? I'm still in India, my love. Now I am India. Look, the palm of my hand is India. And here, in the centre of my hand, is my heart. You're here. And India is here.'

'Cristina, I get the feeling you're saying goodbye to me.'

'I love you, Juan Barbarín. I've always loved you. I'll always love you. And I know this love I have for you didn't begin in this life, but long ago, in another time, in another country.'

'So why are you saying goodbye to me?'

'No, Juan Barbarín, that's not what I'm saying,' Cristina said, a look of love in her eyes like I'd never seen before. 'I'm saying the opposite. That we will never be apart. One day, in Rishikesh, on one of the last days, I saw you next to the Ganges. I was sitting nearby, beneath a banyan tree.

'I knew I couldn't go up to you, because what I was seeing still hadn't happened. I knew that what I was seeing was the future. Because you didn't have much hair on the crown of your head, and what little you did have was grey.

'Then you got up, and smiled at me for the last time. And you walked off along the water's edge, along the rocks you get there on the banks of the river.

'I felt so sad I burst into tears.

'And I wept, and wept, and wept so hard that the sky began to weep too. The rain in Rishikesh is as natural and spontaneous as the wind. Out of nowhere it starts to rain and the whole city floods. I wept for a long time with the banyan protecting me, keeping me dry. Then its branches and leaves became drenched and began to drip on me.'

This is what Cristina told me, with her shining eyes.

This is what she told me, and for a space of time I had the feeling that the great Indian sun was passing gently above me too. I felt the warm

breeze among the banyans that grow along the Ganges. I had the feeling
of having been in India and having seen the pilgrims bathing in the Ganges, holding tight onto a rope to stop themselves from being dragged along
by the waters. I could smell the distinct scent of shit and Indian sandalwood and hear the calls of the street vendors and all those holy men as if
I had really been there.

Cristina wanted to spend at least six months in India, and we agreed
that I would meet up with her and that we'd spend some of the time together, perhaps half of it. But I never got to India. Cristina quit her job
with the RTVE choirs because she couldn't ask for that much leave, and
she went to Rishikesh for six months, and then she extended her stay for
another four months.

The months passed and time and again I put off my visit. We wrote
letters. Hers were passionate and spectacular, full of strange dreams and
visions, full of Sanskrit terms that I didn't completely understand. In one
of them she spoke about Lucy, a friend she'd made in the ashram, and
about Dave and Eberhard, more friends from the ashram. The name Eberhard turned up in subsequent letters, alongside weather reports for Ut-
tarakhand and other snippets of her life in Rishikesh. It was clear Cristina
was very happy, and that she was beginning to gain a certain status in the
ashram, where sometimes she was put in charge of leading Satsang. Eberhard was, as far as I could tell, one of the musicians, an Austrian who had
gone to India to study percussion and now played the tabla in a group of
players at the ashram, which also included a sitar, a tambura and a harmo-
nium. Cristina wrote to me that they'd even toyed with the idea of record-
ing an album together, with Cristina singing mantras and Eberhard
playing the tabla. For some inexplicable reason, I pictured him as a blond
fellow with a goatee, an idiot grin and a huge cock, and I tried to read
between the lines of Cristina's letters to work out if she felt something for
him, if they might even have slept together. In another letter, into which
she'd slipped some petals of a flower I didn't recognise, Cristina told me
she'd been initiated and that they'd given her the Sanskrit name Shakti.
She explained that initiation means you are reborn and now belong to the

spiritual family of the guru. She didn't sign off her letters as Cristina now, but rather as Shakti, the name of her new self. I asked myself if I could really claim to know this Shakti woman at all.

The idea of disappearing in the middle of my course was exhausting, so I decided to visit Cristina in the holidays. But Christmas came and I decided not to buy a ticket. I pictured myself sleeping on a straw mattress, in some dingy room in the ashram, freezing to death. I would go during the next vacation. But when Easter came, I never found the right moment to organise the trip. Finally, at the start of the summer, I went to a travel agency to buy a ticket for Delhi with the intention of spending June and July with Cristina. But after hours of dithering, during which I drove the girl in the agency half mad, I left not with a ticket to Delhi, but to Boston. I flew to the States at the end of June, and I didn't see Cristina again.

36

The guerrillas capture us

But *for now, let us* return to what happened after Gwen or Carmen, or whatever her name was, shot me in my left foot and left me writhing and squealing on the floor like an animal. On the surface, she'd done it *because I wouldn't keep quiet.* But of course another, entirely different reason was also plausible: she'd shot me because I'd revealed that she and I had slept together, letting the cat out of the bag in front of George.

As I lay there writhing in agony, Joseph asked George and Gwen for medical assistance. He told them that a wound like mine needed rest, and they answered that they had no intention of helping us in any way, and that what had happened was my own fault for disobeying orders. Then they told us to get up and, leading us back to the settlement's entrance at gunpoint, told us to go back to camp and explain to the others that under no circumstances were they to come into the island. The weirdest thing of all was that they handled us with a trepidation that bordered on disgust. It was almost as if we were the ones threatening them.

We set off. Wade and Joseph were supporting me. I was on the point of losing consciousness, and could feel warm blood pouring from my foot. Two or three hundred metres further along, once we'd lost sight of the 'savages' and their settlement, we stopped. They laid me on the floor and Joseph cleaned and bandaged my wound as best he could. We'd packed alcohol, bandages and antiseptic to prevent infection in any possible wounds, but the islanders had ransacked our bags and held onto all the food and medicines. Wade cut a couple of branches off some young trees, and, with the canvas we'd brought to protect us from the rain, he made a rudimentary stretcher to carry me. We were roughly two days from the village, maybe three given the cumbersome job of having to carry a man on a stretcher. And so the horror began.

It took us nearly an entire day to get to the valley where we'd seen the blue man, whose immense, transparent body we all looked for, I think in vague hope, or perhaps in fear – an unnamed and indistinct fear. Perhaps because blue is a hopeful colour, perhaps simply because that creature was like the invention of a dream. It rained almost unremittingly and we had no provisions, nor any protection from the rain now that we were using the canvas to carry my badly injured body. My suffering was indescribable. It felt like a ray of pure fire was scorching my left foot, knee and calf, and my less than comfortable transportation didn't help things. My head rolled from side to side, knocking against the canvas with almost every step. The constant jiggling put me in a daze. At times I didn't know if I was facing up or down, if they were moving me head or feet first. I had a fever and we didn't have anything to bring it down. In these circumstances, the rain was almost a blessing, soothing my scalding skin as it fell. Wade fashioned some straps out of strips of fabric, belts and reeds so that they could carry the stretcher on their shoulders instead of gripping it by the hands, and when we stopped to rest I saw my fellow explorers' raw, blistered and even bleeding shoulders, and the tears rolling down their grubby and defeated faces. At that moment, I wondered whether we were going to make it, whether we might in fact die in that sick, waterlogged, bug-filled garden possessed by a ghostly silence only broken by the sound of birds, the screeching of monkeys, the buzz of insects and the snap of weeds and canes as they fell under the machete's blade. Nobody said a word on those gruelling treks. Perhaps my companions wouldn't be able to hold out any longer, and would leave me there in the middle of the jungle.

The only sensible plan was to get to the river that crossed the valley, build a raft and let the river carry us all the way to the sea. With any luck, this river would lead into ours and take us directly home. In the event that we weren't so lucky (which, on current form, was perhaps to be expected), we'd be forced to cover miles of coast to reach the village. But anything was better than crossing that thick, humid and marshy jungle, dotted with swampy patches and pools of stagnant, mosquito-infested water. Every now and then we had to wade across lagoons plastered with duckweed and delicate white and pink floating flowers. The turbid, muddy water came up to the others' waists. We were generally lucky with the leeches, although in one of the lagoons Joseph and Sheila were both bitten, and had to take down their trousers, Sheila to remove one from her stomach, near her pubis, and Joseph to pull one off his penis; perhaps the only moment on the journey when I felt that someone was worse off than me. I still remember his yelps – 'Oh, shit, oh, shit. Son of a goddamn bitch' – his hysterical laughter when he saw the nasty thing clamped onto his penis, and his utter revulsion as he pulled it off, knowing that, not having any salt to sprinkle over it (that too had been robbed by the phony 'savages'), the parasite's teeth could remain stuck under the skin and cause an infection. When at last we arrived at the banks of the clean, sweet-smelling river, which flowed placidly northwards, we decided to spend the night there and build the raft the following morning. We didn't have anything to eat, nor did we have the energy to forage. But as normal on the island, things didn't turn out as we expected.

We had barely set up camp for the night when, to our surprise and horror, we were captured again a second time. It didn't take much for our assailants to surround us; they caught us completely unawares. At first we all assumed it was the same group as before – Gwen and George and the others – and that they'd followed us and decided not to let us go after all. But we soon realised that this was an entirely different group. They were dressed like typical South American guerrillas, in military camouflage, or at least in khaki and leaf-green garbs, many of them accessorised with sunglasses and caps.

There were some twelve men and six or seven women, all completely filthy and unkempt. Most of the men had long frizzy beards and some were smoking cigars, handmade out of leaves they called tobacco but which wasn't actually tobacco, since it stank of burnt leaves. The women were sunburnt on their faces and lips, and their skin was damaged from a life lived out in the open. They had yellow, broken teeth and foul-smelling breath. They all stank, and I have the impression (in fact, I'm quite certain) that they weren't used to washing too often. They were armed with old Kalashnikov AK-47s with Ingram Mac-10 automatic rifles – the preferred guns of terrorists – and several of them, most notably Zacarías, the group's leader, had M61 Vulcan ammunition belts slung across their chests. This meant they either had a machine gun somewhere, or those cartridges full of copper-tipped bullets were no more than part of the show of ferocity that's so characteristic of all guerrillas, and of fighting animals, I might add. Later on we learnt that in fact they had two M60 machine guns placed in camouflaged 'nests' inside the island, two Russian grenade launchers, and even a surface-to-air Mistral missile launcher capable of bringing down a helicopter from four kilometres away.

In our exhaustion we were forced to trek for almost an hour and a half more before getting to their hideout. The place was truly spectacular: a series of abandoned Hindu temples in the middle of the jungle, covered in statues of Hanuman, the monkey god, and carvings of copulating couples in every conceivable position, themselves covered in moss, creepers and vines, and even ficus plants which were growing up the walls and ornamental doors, or toranas. I stared, transfixed, at the vision of those golden monkeys climbing up the walls, lost in a limbo between wakefulness and sleep, unsure whether what I was seeing through the relentless curtain of rain I was seeing with my eyes, or was in fact a dream. I'm not sure exactly how many temples there were, perhaps six or seven. Some were completely hidden in the jungle, and others seemed to have succumbed to the gradual advance of the swampy land and collapsed and sunk into the mud (which was to be expected, given they were clearly over a thousand years old). They were built in the style of the temples of Orissa, in the Bay of Bengal, and had enormous stone towers with connecting curved faces called sikharas topped with bulbous cyclopean stone discs called amalakas, and I couldn't get my head around what those temples, characteristic of the most classic and serene Hindu art, were doing in an area so far from the influence of Hinduism. Years

earlier, as a young man, I'd been hugely interested in Indian art, becoming something of a small authority on styles and periods. I knew, for example, that there were no examples of classical Indian architecture east
of Bali. The latest architectural styles, those of Cambodia, Thailand or
Java, don't share many features with the Orissan style, so it was really
quite baffling to find such ancient temples so far east of Sulawesi. We
spent two weeks in that cluster of temples, and I think we had more than
enough opportunity to determine its age. They weren't comfortable constructions designed for human habitation, and our captors lived in them
like animals, sleeping on straw beds or directly on the floor. The rooms
in the temples and their elaborate pyramidal roofs or siliceous stone bul-
biforms only served one purpose: to protect them from the rain.

The guerrillas, as I'll call them from now on, seemed very happy. Their
excitement bordered on a hysteria which seemed completely inexplicable,
but which I decided was probably due to some natural psychotropic substance they foraged from the jungle. Zacarías, their leader, was Bolivian,
about forty years old and tall and strapping, with a rabid black beard.
There were also several Latin Americans among them, who must have
come from countries like Honduras, Peru, Nicaragua or El Salvador, and
whose accents I neither recognised nor differentiated. And then there
were North Americans and Europeans (Italians, Germans, an Icelander, a
Spaniard who called himself Pere and was always chewing on pale roots
and spitting out of one side of his mouth) and two Asians, who I'm pretty
sure were Korean.

Among the women there was a busty blonde, Zacarías's bedmate, who
everyone called 'Red Star' and who seemed to act as his deputy. I say 'bedmate' because they all shared the women, with the exception of Zacarías,
who slept only with Red Star. I admit I had the impression that he occasionally shared her with two of his comrades: an American called Charlie
and an Italian called Ventimiglia who was missing his right ear. I think
Red Star was Norwegian or German. The other women – whom you could
only distinguish from the men thanks to their lack of beards and the bulge
on their chests under their clothes – were common property; a way for the

guerrillas to display their rejection of the hypocrisy of bourgeois norms and their distaste for traditional institutions.

They called themselves The Popular Liberation Army, and the first thing they told us, the moment we got to the base and were ordered to get on our knees on the stone floor by the entrance of the largest of the temples, was not to expect any kind of special treatment, that all our 'privileges' were abolished, that we were 'enemies of class', and that the most important thing for the time being was our political re-education. Joseph spoke up saying that this wasn't the most important thing. The most important thing, he said, was seeing to the casualty among us. Red Star inspected my wound with patent disinterest, and declared – despite the grim appearance of the entry wound, which was the only side I could see – that it was a clean wound, that the bullet had gone in and out without hitting any bone, and that it didn't need any special treatment. Then they tied our ankles so we couldn't escape and gave us some of their frugal supper, which consisted of boiled roots and greyish pieces of roast meat covered in flies, and which made me feel so sick that, despite my ravenous hunger, I didn't even want to eat. I noticed that my friends were also looking at it suspiciously. Wade asked what kind of animal it'd come from, and the guerrillas replied cheerily and between sniggers that it was pork.

'But there aren't any pigs on the island,' Wade said.

'Oh, but there are,' Zacarías said. 'Dark pigs. Wild and dangerous pigs. We shoot them.'

They were laughing so hard I couldn't work out what they were saying, or if that meat really did come from an edible animal – that is, if it came from an animal at all.

After that surreal supper they forced us into the temple. The smell within those walls was indescribable: a dizzying stench of excrement and urine combined with the nauseating smells of blood, rotten meat and death. They led us directly to the end room, which was just beneath the sikhara, the huge stone tower that had seemed so impressive from outside. Inside there was a monstrous stone statue of Hanuman. At the monkey god's feet, squeezed in behind the candles, there were a host of black-and-white photos of all different sizes, featuring the faces of revolutionary leaders. Now, as I reflect on that temple, which often haunts me in my nightmares, I wonder whether perhaps we human beings are no more than monkeys and monsters ourselves, and whether the temple built in honour of the monkey god was actually dedicated to the monstrous side of humankind.

Our 'political re-education' began that very night. They asked us if we'd read *The Communist Manifesto.* I said I had, but when pushed I could only remember the opening line of the text, 'A spectre is haunting Europe,' and the last one, 'Working Men of All Countries, Unite!' Nor could I answer the other questions they asked me, all of them formed using recondite and esoteric Marxist jargon. They reeled off words like 'praxis' and 'dialectic', 'battle of the classes' and 'petite-bourgeois' and called each other 'comrade' and 'citizen'. Next, Zacarías asked us if we knew those faces in the photographs. Between us we couldn't even name a third of them, which of course only reinforced that we were 'enemies of the class'.

'All these men!' Zacarías bellowed, pointing to the photos glowing in the candlelight, and speaking in broken English that occasionally slipped into Spanish. 'All these heroes of the revolution have been slandered! They are the victims of campaigns designed to discredit them, paid for with Wall Street cash and supported by the bourgeois press. Capitalist propaganda has done its job! Lies paid for with the blood of the exploited! They call them murderers! They call them dictators! Look very carefully at the smile of our father, Stalin. Look at his shy, benevolent eyes, full of the patience of a Georgian peasant. Is that the smile of a murderer? Look at the expression on Lenin's face, equally intelligent and hopeful. Is that the face of a butcher? No, they weren't murderers or butchers. What happened was that they had the courage, the fucking balls, to dare to change the world! They did what they had to do. And if some bourgeois exploiter, some capitalist used to feeding off human blood got in their way, well, I'll be fucking damned if we were going to shed tears over them. How many centuries have they been exploiting us, treating us like animals, buying and selling us like goods? Murderers? They're the murderers!'

I told him, with the reckless courage instilled in me by a sky-rocketing fever, that I didn't understand why he called us 'enemies of the class'. He didn't know anything about us, I said. I was left wing and always had been. On hearing this, he guffawed. He asked what I did and I told him I was a music professor. He asked where I taught and I said in a university in the United States. Then he asked the others their profession. Joseph said he was a surgeon, Christian said he was a masseur and Sheila a student. Santiago said he worked as a waiter in a fast-food restaurant in Elizabeth, New Jersey, and Wade, much smarter than the rest of us, told him he was a car mechanic. This last one seemed to please Zacarías, given that, if Wade worked in a workshop, it meant he was part of the working class, even if he was a proletariat without any class conscience and totally ignorant of history's objective mechanisms. I was amazed he didn't clock that Wade was having him on.

'Oh, I know exactly what you mean by "left wing",' he said, pleased to have the chance to have a 'political chat' with me. 'What you mean is that, despite the fact that all your values are bourgeois and you live happily in the paradise of capitalism, you have a mildly guilty conscience, you know you're a parasite, and that your own comfort and wellbeing is all down to the pitiless exploitation of the Third World. And you also mean that you've got certain progressive "ideas", although really you've got zero intention of changing anything and you hope with all your heart that the revolution never happens. That "left" of yours is bullshit, brother,' he said in Spanish, clearly grasping that I spoke the language he felt most comfortable in. 'Democracy! Freedom! Let me guess, you're one of those people who stand up for freedom,' he said sarcastically, before moving back into his stilted English. 'Freedom! Bourgeois freedom is the freedom to buy and sell! What good is this freedom to the proletariat? Theory, for fuck's sake! That is what we need here! The-o-ry!'

He went on like that for hours, ranting. If we nodded off, the other guerrillas woke us up with a smack. 'No sleeping!' they barked. 'Sleep is for capitalists! Keep your eyes open!'

They all ogled Sheila rapaciously. Zacarías explained to us that in The Popular Liberation Army there was no such thing as private or human property. In other words, women were to be shared, and we could sleep with any of their women (except Red Star), and Sheila also had to offer herself to the comrades who wanted to lie with her. Seeing how furious this idea made us all, they desisted for the time being, but it was clear that if they wanted to enjoy Sheila, there was nothing we could do to stop them. Not only were we outnumbered, but we were tied and unarmed. Several women took off their camouflage shirts and showed us their dirty bodies, some of which were surprisingly beautiful. It goes without saying that none of us were in the mood to accept such a generous offer, so they retied our hands and locked the six of us up in that poky hole of a room. The temple echoed with the sounds of their orgy, which went on and on, lasting, as I recall, till dawn.

37

Are we ill without knowing it?

The following morning our captors barked at us to get up, and then untied our hands and led us out through the temple entrance and down the large stone steps which served as their lounging and eating area. In the light of the new day, my previous suspicions were confirmed. The cluster of temples was surrounded by a stone wall which was dotted with vast ornamental toranas. The wall had largely crumbled apart and I noticed the half-sunken carved stone toranas poking out here and there among the plants. The only wall still standing was the one just in front of us; the one we'd come in through the night before. In the bright light of the morning the temples seemed even more beautiful and mysterious than they had the night before, when my vision had been impaired by the rain, darkness and exhaustion. After a night spent in the suffocating and stinking temple, sitting outside in the fresh morning and looking at those enchanting towers emerging out of the mist was a pleasure unlike any I can remember having felt. They fed us boiled tubers and cassava cake for breakfast. It was hard and tough, and it was only by reminding ourselves that we had to eat something if we were to survive that we avoided spitting it out in disgust.

Ventimiglia, the Italian, appeared with a leather suitcase which, as far as I could see, contained hundreds of amber glass ampoules, the kind with rubber stoppers and an aluminium seal used for injections. He passed one to Red Star, who had a syringe in a metal autoclave. Then the vaccinations began. One by one, Red Star extracted a dose of something from the golden-yellow ampoules and injected the guerrillas. They presumed that we knew what it was, and were surprised when we refused to be injected. They thought we were members of the SIAR, a word we heard spoken for the first time then, and which we didn't recognise. It was only later that we remembered seeing the initials written on the motorway barriers. They jeered at us, calling us 'men of Abraham', and laughed when we asked who Abraham was.

'Abraham Lewellyn,' they said. 'Now you're going to tell us you don't know who Abraham Lewellyn is.'

They didn't believe that *the* Abraham Lewellyn was indeed unknown to us. They spoke about him with genuine hate and hostility, but also with palpable fear.

'It's the vaccine,' Red Star said when Joseph asked her what she was injecting.

'What kind of vaccine?' he asked. 'What does the vaccine immunise you against? It looks more like an antidote.'

'Call it what you want, doctor,' Red Star scoffed, 'but you know full well what will happen if you stop injecting yourselves.'

'No, I don't know. Tell me.'

Ventimiglia moved towards him, slowly descending the stairs until he was face to face with Joseph, and he stared into his eyes. He was heavily armed, like all of them, and seeing him in front of Joseph like that, with his hands on his hips, I thought for a moment that he was going to hit him. Joseph glared back, still chewing his cassava cake. In the end, Ventimiglia didn't hit him. Instead he began to explain, in English that was just as terrible as Zacarías's, that many years ago the island had been used as a testing ground for biological weapons, and that certain areas were perilously infected with a bacteria that produced a degenerative illness of the nervous system.

'You didn't know?' Ventimiglia asked. 'How the fuck did you not know that?'

Joseph went on chewing his cassava cake, staring wordlessly back at the Italian. We'd already explained to them several times that we were castaways, that we'd fallen out of the sky in a plane and crashed into the sea by the island, but they didn't believe us. Nor did they believe we weren't members of the SIAR and that we didn't know a thing about this Abraham Lewellyn they spoke of, or even what the SIAR was supposed to be.

'You've never taken the vaccine?' Ventimiglia asked, grabbing Joseph's arms and inspecting them for marks.

The other guerrillas did the same, scanning our arms and legs looking for needle marks. Two of them attempted to touch up Sheila, who elbowed them off and showered them with insults. They laughed, but left her in peace.

Ventimiglia wanted to know how long we'd been on the island, and on hearing that we'd been there over a month without having once vaccinated ourselves, he looked worried.

'They haven't told you about the illness?' he asked. 'If you've been here for more than a month unprotected then you must all have it. We're talking about biological warfare. We're talking about tests conducted twelve years ago, leaving the island crawling with bacteria even now. You contract the disease through the air, and it affects humans and large mammals. The first symptoms are aural and visual hallucinations. You start to hear things, voices in your head, voices speaking all around you. And then you start seeing strange things. People you haven't seen for ages, people who have died, fantastical beings, a blue elephant. So, for example, you might come across your long-dead grandfather and talk to him for hours. The hallucinations are very realistic. First the voices, then the visions, which become more and more lifelike. Then more and more terrifying. Giant, aggressive animals. Monstrous creatures.'

We avoided looking at each other. Ventimiglia fell silent. All of the guerrillas had turned to look up at the temple entrance. Zacarías, their leader, appeared at the top of the stairs and emerged from the temple with his shirt and trousers undone. Solveig, a very attractive Black woman, was standing next to him, completely naked apart from some boots. It was normal for them to be naked. Since they did everything as a community, they didn't even hide to take a shit or fornicate. They all greeted their leader in one way or another: either with a wave, or turning to face him and giving a little bow. It seemed to me that Solveig was proud to have been chosen that night, and that this was why she didn't bother to get dressed. She wanted to show off in front of the other women.

'The idea behind the illness is to shock and disorient the enemy,' Zacarías piped up, finishing his deputy's sentence for him as he buttoned up his shirt and pulled on his braces. 'The illness attacks the brain directly and begins to break down the nervous system. First there are the hallucinations. Then they become so vivid and so realistic that the victims become paranoid and start attacking and even killing one another. Once the illness spreads, you have to lock the victim in a cage, tie him to a bed and put a bit between his teeth to stop him from doing himself any damage. By this point the victim would be tearing pieces of his own flesh off with his teeth and shouting like a rabid animal. The only solution is to put him out of his misery by injecting a little air into his heart. If the bacteria isn't contained by the vaccine, there's no cure.'

My friends and I were still avoiding one another's eyes.

'Tell me,' Ventimiglia went on, inspecting us with a startling look of worry and fear on his face. 'Have any of you been having hallucinations? Have you seen anything unusual? Strange animals following you? An old relative appearing from nowhere? Have you heard voices? Voices that speak to you and call your name?'

A wave of terror came over me as I realised that Ventimiglia was describing exactly what had been happening to us since we'd arrived on the island. Everything suddenly made a brutal sort of sense. The packs of giant wolves, the enormous blue man shooting rays from his forehead, the flying saucer gliding through the palm trees, the capybara with the bow tie around its neck, and my childhood garden, the Meadow where I played as a boy and which I'd seen at the end of a tunnel cut into the mountainside, the floating stones.

The guerrillas weren't going to let us get away without injecting the 'vaccine', so we resigned ourselves to allowing Joseph to give us each a dose, the doctor demanding that we boil the needle after every injection.

They were amused by all our pussyfooting, but let it go. Joseph later told us that the liquid inside the ampoules wasn't a vaccine at all, but chlorpromazine, or rather Thorazine, an antipsychotic drug used to treat schizophrenia and other mental illnesses. I remembered years earlier having read in an article in the *New Yorker*, which I had a subscription to for a time, that in the Gulag's forced labour camps they'd used this substance to stop the inmates from dreaming, one of the drug's effects being to extinguish oneiric activity. Joseph told me he hadn't heard of such a thing.

Life in captivity is, above all, boring. Now we had time to talk and reflect. In the dead hours, when we weren't being submitted to interminable sessions of 'political re-education', we pondered our situation and tried to imagine what the hell that island and the SIAR were. Those more inclined to believe conspiracy theories – like Santiago and Christian – came up with all kinds of arguments: they wondered aloud if the SIAR was a terrorist organisation; whether it was, conversely, a quasi-governmental agency, a secret arm of the CIA that used the island to train terrorists; if perhaps the island was a kind of 'secret prison' or even a 'prison island' where they locked up the most dangerous and psychotic criminals, or a high-security psychiatric prison, or a chemical or biological arms-testing ground.

'It's obvious, man,' Santiago said. 'Now it all makes sense. They've got islands like this in the Pacific and Indian Oceans. We all know that. Places they do experiments, secret prisons.'

'Jack's right,' Christian said. 'We all know the gringos have detention and torture centres all over the place. They've got secret prisons on boats in international waters, and others on islands that don't belong to the States, where they can break all the rules they want.'

'It all makes sense, guys!' Santiago said. 'We've ended up in a place nobody knows about, a place nobody *is supposed* to know about. Weird shit's going down here. Illegal experiments, fucked-up things, the strangest fucking shit you can imagine, and that's why no one's coming for us. It's more likely they're just gonna leave us to die so we can't tell anyone what we've seen. We're fucked, guys, completely fucked. Nobody knows we're here because nobody knows this place exists, because officially, *this place doesn't exist*. No one can rescue us, and the only people who know the island exists and how to get here is the army, and they'll never let us off this island. What? So we can go tell everyone about it? We were done for the second we set foot on the island, because the bastards who live here infiltrated our group and the only reason they haven't finished us all off is because there are lots of us and because no one wants to slaughter kids and women and families and old people. That's not something you can just do like that in cold blood. Not even the bastards on this island are capable of doing something like that in cold blood. But we're done for, and that's the truth.'

38

Our political re-education

I recall those days with the guerrillas with a mixture of horror and disbelief. Try as we might, we couldn't fathom why they were so aggressive, and why they lived in such abject conditions. They told us that they had originally been part of the SIAR, that they'd gone to the island chasing an ideal, wanting to give meaning to their lives. But, they claimed, the SIAR had betrayed them and they'd had to break ranks from Abraham and the others and escape into the jungle to fulfil their own mission. Who was this Abraham they brought up so much? They didn't answer, but in their eyes you could see that they regarded him with a mixture of fear and loathing. What was their mission? we asked them. They looked at us as if we were complete imbeciles and replied that there was only one mission: global revolution.

I remember that the first political re-education 'class' Zacarías gave us in Marxism-Leninism focused on Lenin's ideas about 'freedom of criticism', which appear in his concise treatise *What Is to Be Done?* 'Critical Marxism,' Zacarías barked at us, 'is an aberration.' Lenin condemned this wish for 'freedom of criticism' as mere opportunism, a creation of the Social Democratic arm with their moderate, bourgeois tendencies. There I learnt that 'moderate', for Lenin (and of course for Zacarías too), was a derogatory term, just as 'extremist' or 'dogmatic' were used as a form of praise. 'Freedom of criticism' was, then, a contemptible principle that damaged those of the revolution. Scientists, Lenin argues, don't ask for 'freedom of criticism' for old discoveries with respect to new ones: they hope that the old ones are abandoned and the news ones embraced.

'And let's not forget,' Zacarías boomed, 'that Marxism is science. We practise scientific materialism based on history's objective laws; as objective as the laws of nature. "Freedom of criticism" for what? Lenin saw it for what it was!' he went on, still bellowing. '"Dogmatism", "doctrinairism", "ossification of the party – the inevitable retribution that follows the violent strait-lacing of thought". These are the criticisms of the counterrevolutionaries. Bah, "the violent strait-lacing of thought"! So what should we do? Allow anti-Soviet poison to be expressed however people like? Remove the obstacles that "oppress" the defenders of bourgeois democracy? In that case, the same thing would happen to us as happened to the Tsar, when the censors decided to permit the publication and sale of the works of revolutionary Marxism! It was an autocratic and reactionary government, but even so, it was still possible to read Marx and Engels unopposed, and that's how the theoretical bases of the revolution were formed. Because the Tsar was a bastard, but Vladimir Ilich was ten times worse. And in history it's always the biggest bastard who wins. "Without revolutionary theory, there can be no revolutionary movement," Vladimir Ilich writes. Theory, damn it! As Engels wrote in *The Peasant War in Germany*: "The German workers have two important advantages compared with the rest of Europe. First, they belong to the most theoretical people of Europe". That's what's missing around here, for fuck's sake, with these damn mosquitoes and all this shit! Theory!'

The guerrillas believed all classical Marxist assertions to the letter, and then added the manipulative simplification of Lenin and Stalin to them. Moreover, in a confusing ideological hodgepodge that no true Marxist in his right mind would swallow, they threw in the ideas of Mao, Trotsky and even a man as sick and evil as Pol Pot. The sinister leader of the Khmer Rouge was, in fact, their model and hero, because he was the only one – or so said Zacarías during his interminable rants – who had truly dared to apply communism in full; the only one who'd had the guts to really do what others merely said should be done. And he'd achieved all of this very nearby, he went on, in neighbouring Cambodia no less, even though Cambodia was thousands of kilometres from where we were by anyone's calculations. But the presence of the Hindu temples on the island, plus the general feeling of dreamlike unreality that our time there was taking on, made me doubt myself. Might we in fact be in Cambodia, on some island in Indonesia, maybe close to Sulawesi? This would explain a lot. The presence of monkeys in the forest, for one thing. But how could we have ended up there?

Strangely enough, it was the SIAR itself who had provided them with the information that had led to their 'awakening'. It was thanks to the SIAR's training courses, Zacarías told us, that they'd learnt to understand history and dialectics.

'Do you people understand dialectics, for Christ's sake?' he asked us threateningly one day, during another torturously long re-education session. We were sitting on the floor in front of the giant statue of Hanuman and the photos of the political leaders. 'If you don't understand dialectics, you don't understand a fucking thing! Dialectics is the intellectual formalisation of something we Latinos have always known! Dialectics is the science that allows us to discover that all things are the opposite of what they seem! For example: white isn't actually white – it's black. And black isn't really black – it's white. Got it? You see what dialectics is?'

We told him we did, that now we understood dialectics, but when Zacarías attempted to test us it soon became patently clear that we hadn't the slightest idea what dialectics were.

'Everything we see is a con,' Zacarías tried to explain, the glimmer of dozens of candles reflecting in the pupils of his shining eyes. 'Dialectics allows us to see beyond that con. We might see something so beautiful, a painting of Aphrodite emerging from the water, say. But in reality she isn't beautiful at all, and nor is the painting! The goddess isn't a goddess, but an old syphilitic prostitute put there for the brothel owners! I don't believe in God, but if we had to attribute creation to a God, there's no doubt it would be a bourgeois God, with his taste for flowers, colourful birds, the rippling waves of the sea and the wavy blonde locks of women who distract us with their ruddy breasts. A bourgeois God created the world to swindle us! A world of illusions that we can only destroy by means of violence!'

Another of Zacarías's obsessions was sleep and wakefulness. The world, he said, had been sleeping, and Marxism-Leninism had come to wake it up.

'We were asleep before they came along!' Zacarías yelled. He had a superhuman capacity to shout for hours on end. 'Before they came along, the bourgeois bacillus was rotting us to the core, keeping us asleep! We were asleep! But not any more. We're awake at last!'

And in fact, they really didn't sleep all that much. Hardly at all. They used every means they had to stay awake, and I think the drugs they took kept them in a constant state of agitation. The all-night orgies, too, served the primary function of preventing them from sleeping. According to Zacarías's philosophical politics (he argued that *everything was politics*, even sleep, health, your pulse, insects, the rain, the differentiation of the species, the gills on the fish, the colour of the flowers, reproduction through spores: 'all of it is po-li-tics, damn it'), human beings didn't need sleep. Their true destiny and vocation was lucidness, and a true revolutionary shouldn't ever sleep. Rest, yes, of course, perhaps even closing their eyes for a moment. But sleep? Never! This is what the guerrillas would say when exhaustion defeated them: that they were 'resting with their eyes closed'. But they never once admitted that they slept or, worse, that they dreamt. Dreaming, after all, was 'bourgeois territory', the 'territory of myth'.

When they dream, human beings give up their sense of sight, Zacarías would tell us whenever he realised one of us was asleep or trying to sleep. They lose their sense of touch: they go from being *subject* to *object*, from being a person to a thing. That is to say, that when human beings dream, they transform into merchandise. Dreaming dehumanises us and makes us unfit for the objective analysis of social relations and the system of production. Dreaming is essential to the capitalistic system, he would say. When the proletariat isn't working, the only thing he can do is sleep. But if he didn't sleep, if he stayed awake and held onto his analytical faculties, he could use those hours to reflect on his situation and develop class consciousness. And that is why – again, according to Zacarías's interpretation of events – capitalism was the great distributor, organiser, administrator, dispenser and promoter of sleep. Capitalism promoted soporifics among workers in the form of alcoholic drinks and different kinds of narcotics, like opium (with the help of which, they'd managed to subjugate millions), and also by means of different kinds of entertainment and spectacles, hobbies and distractions, games and colours, images and dance rhythms whose sole *raison d'être* was to hypnotise the masses. On top of that, capitalism brought figures from dreams to life in fairy tales, operas, fantasy novels, legends, magical thinking, spiritual teachings, crystal balls, fortune-telling, hand-reading, astral lights, spiritualism, theosophy, the eroticised presentation of ancient mysteries, the exposure of supposedly 'hidden' truths, pornography disguised as archaeology, titillating symbolic images, the surprising assimilation of symbolic chains that identify the vegetable with the animal and the human through artificial artistic representations, which attempt to erase the logical distinction between the rational and the symbolic, or between the different realms of nature, together with all kinds of techniques, characteristic of all the religious practices in the world, designed in order that the subject *closes his eyes*: prayers, meditation, yoga, incubation, spirituality exercises, orations, acts of repentance, contemplations, sacraments, devotional readings, Satsang, breathing exercises, pranayama, chanting, visualisations of internal images and scenes, isolation tanks, psychotropic drugs, the ritual ingestion of alkaloids, mystic dances, Sufi sama, sweat lodges, temazcals, vision quests, fasts, the Alpha State inducers, brain wave synchronisation glasses, experimentation in telepathy, telekinesis, trance, possession, channelling…

For this reason, when the guerrillas 'rested with their eyes closed' they tended to put themselves in uncomfortable positions, or lie down on a stone that dug in a little bit, so that they couldn't sink into deep sleep or lose all contact with reality. Sometimes one of them would 'rest' and another would budge him from time to time, or say things to him to stop him fully sleeping. Sometimes, when one of them was 'resting' the others shook them violently and asked them basic questions and didn't leave them in peace until they answered. I suspect that they developed the ability to answer in their sleep without fully waking up. But the spectacle could be riotously funny.

'Eh, Marcel,' Ossip, a Russian, would say to his fellow guerrilla from Des Moines who was snoring loudly next to him. 'Marcel, answer!'

When it became clear that Marcel was sleeping like a baby (and that he needed it), Ossip shook him violently by the shoulder.

'Marcel, tell me the number of Pi. Come on, Marcel. Pi, tell me the number.'

'Three point one four,' Marcel mumbled in his sleep.

'Three point one four, then what?' Ossip replied, shaking the shoulder of the poor slumbering man again. 'Come on, come on, what then? Marcel, what then?'

'Three point one four one six,' Marcel just about managed to get out.

This was a classic of theirs, asking what Pi, or even Archimedes' theorem was. Other typical questions were what year the Second World War ended, who was the first man to reach the South Pole, the name of the Irish activist who denounced colonialism in the Congo, Lumumba's date of birth, the first sentence of the Gettysburg Address, the epitaph on Karl Marx's gravestone, or the name of Trotsky's murderer. At other times they asked the sleeper to solve a simple sum like seven times five or eight times nine, or to come out with the square root of thirty-six. Or they'd ask him or her to define the right angle or hypotenuse, or to name the capital of a country (Estonia, Latvia, Lithuania were among their favourites), or to sing the first line of 'The Internationale', which can be understood exactly as a call to wake up and get out of bed: 'Stand up, damned of the Earth / Stand up, prisoners of starvation'.

Like I say, captivity is boring. During the two interminable weeks that followed, we took part in several of the terrorists' 'actions': these were practice exercises in defence, carried out in the jungle against imaginary enemies. We were also given courses in camouflage and survival, where my friends and I picked up some useful skills. But alongside this training, we had plenty of time to talk among ourselves. It was during this period of our captivity that I heard about Wade, Santiago and Joseph's lives before our time on the island.

39

Wade's story

These are the voices of a few tired, weary and starving wretches, cooped up in a stone room in a stone temple in total darkness. The stench is so overpowering it could only be coming from a dead body. But if there is a corpse somewhere, then where is it? The whole place stinks of death, not only of urine and faeces, but also decay. Animal corpses? Human corpses? The place itself is pitch black, but Christian continues to glow out of the darkness, shrouded in golden light. Thanks to him, we can just about make each other out. The guerrillas settle down, they stop yelling, singing, swearing and fornicating, and the forest's silence returns, broken only by the calling of a bird in the distance. It sounds like the cry of death. The cry of solitude. Then, in the distance, we hear explosions, or something like explosions, and I realise that I've heard these explosions before, perhaps in my dreams, but that only now, here inside this temple, have I stopped to reflect on what they are. All of us are chained at the feet and hands in the darkness. During the day, we're free to move around, but at night they tie us up with shackles and chains.

'There's something I've been wanting to ask you for a long time, Wade,' I said on our second night of captivity. We were petrified and none of us could sleep.

'Go ahead, John.'

'The minute… the very moment we arrived on the island… we were all in shock, crying, distraught, but you were smiling. On the plane, just before we crashed, everyone was screaming but you were calm. Calm, serene even… Why is that? And then, after we crashed, when we finished rowing the survivors over, when we were trying to see to the wounded... we were all frantic, but again you were perfectly calm. You seemed almost happy, Wade. Why? Did you know you'd be coming here? Did you already know this island existed? Is this where you were coming all along?'

'John, John, John,' Wade said, laughing. 'Press pause on your imagination, will you? Of course I didn't know about the island. Of course I wasn't coming here. How could you even think that?'

'We've been betrayed before,' I said. 'First George taking Lizzy's baby, the other children, then Gwen... Are you a traitor too? Are you one of them?'

'Fuck me, man,' I heard Santiago say. 'Wade isn't a traitor. Wade's a top guy.'

'Anything's possible, don't you think? Joseph, Christian, Sheila, Jack – think about it. He's always cheerful, moving around this island as if he owned the place. He knows exactly what to do in every situation, how to crack a coconut, follow a track, build a stretcher, lay traps. It was Wade who found fresh water. It was Wade who found the communication tower. It was Wade who found the mouth of the river where we set up camp. When we went into the jungle, we needed a machete and, hey presto, there's a machete right there in front of us lodged in a tree trunk. Doesn't that seem like a bit of a coincidence to you? It was Wade who spotted the "savages" walking through the valley with the children. What a stroke of luck! Tell me, how did he just magically spot them in the jungle with a pair of binoculars if he didn't know exactly where to look? All so that we'd see they had the children, which were probably fake children, and swallow the story about there being cannibals on the island.'

The others didn't say a word.

'I don't think any of this is just a coincidence,' I went on. 'I think you're one of them, Wade. I think you're probably their leader. I think your real name is Abraham Lewellyn. I think you have fun pulling the various strings of your little world, playing us all like marionettes. I think it surprised you, too, when Gwen shot me. Or was it all planned out? No, I don't think it was. I think it took you by surprise... but that must be one

of the biggest thrills of being a little god, right? The thrill of being surprised. Your creatures making their own decisions...'

'But he was on the plane, John,' Joseph said. 'You're talking nonsense.'

'What the fuck's going on here, Wade? What do you want from us?
Tell me. What's the big plan? Who are you? Are you Abraham Lewellyn?'

'Cool it, John,' Wade said. 'Don't shout or one of those wackos out
there will come in. You're wrong. I'm not "one of them", as you put it. I
wound up here the same way you did, and I'd never heard of this island
before. But I will tell you my story. In fact, I think it would be a good
idea if we all knew about each other's lives, because I've got the feeling
we're going to be stuck in this place a long time. And because maybe
then we can work out what we're all doing here, find the thread that
connects it all.'

'The reason is simple, Wade,' Joseph said. 'The reason is that we were
all on that flight and the engines failed and the plane crashed into the sea.'

'We've already talked about this,' Wade said, and although I couldn't
see his face in the dark, I could sense the smile in his voice and eyes. 'I was
born in Indiana. My father was Raymond Erickson, of Irish-Swedish descent. My mother was called Pearl and she was German, Irish and Native
American. She left me and my father when I was five, so I don't have any
memory of her as a boy. My father was a car mechanic – a good one at that.
He had an auto repair shop in Hammerstown, a real shithole down in
Gibson County, Indiana. Life was good: we lived on our own, had a couple
of wild dogs. My father was into all the things real men are supposed to be
into: hunting, guns, knives, a decent Kentucky bourbon, singing, fighting.
He liked getting into scraps with any man as dumb as him, usually on his
way out of the bar on a Friday night, while I waited for him at home. He
liked women, especially women of colour, which only ever brought him
trouble, because back then it wasn't looked upon too kind, a White man
stepping out with an African American woman.

'When he met Ogunde and brought her to live with us, life became
more normal for a while, and the fights and drinking calmed down, even
though a lot of his White supremacist buddies didn't understand how he

could let that woman in his house. They cut him off, and even threatened us now and then, and threw rocks through our windows. Their kids, who were just like their daddies, laughed at me in school and told me I had a "spook" for a mother now. It often came to blows, and even though I was tall and could put up a good fight, sometimes I lost. I couldn't understand why my father hung out with those racists in the first place. My mother, who I only knew from a couple of photos my father kept hidden away in a box in his office that I stumbled across one day by accident, was a quarter Native American after all.

'And then there was Ogunde. She was twenty, came from Georgia and had worked the kinds of jobs that meant she knew a thing or two about the world. She'd been a waitress and a stripper, and also worked for a while in one of those bars where the clients pay to talk to the girls. She had a sensational body, and for some reason I always assumed that my father had met her one night partying in a highway strip club called The Pink Crocodile on the outskirts of Hammerstown. People said all kinds of things about The Pink Crocodile and the women there, and the things you could do with the women there, but my friends and I weren't legal and they wouldn't let us in. To this day I'm not sure if Ogunde really was one of the strippers at The Pink Crocodile, but she certainly had the looks. She was an absolute knockout.

'I was a hot-blooded teenager and Ogunde had an unfortunate habit of walking around the house half-naked. Sometimes we would joke and mess around and fight like two kids. I was pretty innocent back then, and I think the games were all innocent too. One day my father had to go to Evanstown to buy a few parts and he called us from there and said he'd be staying the night. Ogunde and I decided to spend the day together and drive down to the Wabash River. We made a couple of sandwiches and took my father's Buick – a stunning 1953 Skylark – his prized possession which was driven only on special occasions. So we threw the sandwiches and a couple of sodas into the car and drove to Janycen Town, three miles downriver, where there was a deserted beach and an island in the middle of the river, an island covered in oak trees which, for some obscure reason, was known in the area as "Severed Head Is-land". We didn't have our swimsuits. Ogunde took off her clothes down to her underwear and got into the water like that. I followed her in and the water was icy, much colder that I could have imagined. We swam over to Severed Head Island and found ourselves caught in the full, magnificent force of the river. The current hadn't been as strong by the water's edge. Besides, who would've thought that a river that wide would have the force of a torrent? But in the middle of the water, the current dragged us downstream, and it took all our strength to reach the island. When we got there, we were both panting, and we threw ourselves down onto the grass to catch our breath. I remember feeling so happy to be on there, even if it was just a small spit of land in the middle of a river. A man feels like a king when he's on an island.

'I can't remember a happier day in my life. We lay there on the grass, feeling the warm caress of the sun on our frozen skin, watching the clouds go by above us. They were huge, those late-summer clouds in Indiana. Clouds like sailing ships. They reminded me of the ships the Spaniards used to cross the Atlantic. It was gloriously still that late summer in Indiana. Only the rushing waters of the Wabash, the oak leaves and the bird-song could be heard. My father's cherry red Buick was parked up on the shore, in the shade of an oak tree. I suppose I stared at it because I was embarrassed to look at Ogunde, still lying by my side on the grass. I could clearly make out the scent of her skin over the smell of the river or oaks, and that scent of a strong, wholesome adult woman pierced me like a knife. I was embarrassed to look at her, because her white underwear had gone see-through, revealing her black nipples and pubic area. It suddenly occurred to me that what we were doing was bad, and that if my father found us he'd give us both a good hiding with his belt. He'd never beaten me before, although he'd threatened to a couple of times and even gone as far as unbuckling his belt. But if he could see me now, Ogunde more or less naked at my side and giggling at how embarrassed this made me, I had the feeling my father would've whipped off his belt and beaten us both silly.

'Eventually we swam back to the shore, dried off, got dressed and tucked into our sandwiches and sodas. Then we found the fishing gear and threw out a line. We only caught one smallish bass, but it didn't matter to us – we were having fun. On our way home that afternoon Ogunde said we should go to the movies. I wasn't sure about the idea. What if one of the kids from school saw us out together? But Ogunde insisted. She said we could try the Rowland drive-in, about four miles away, and that's what we did. I figured we'd both be inside the car and no one would see us, which made me feel better. So we got to Rowland, parked up at the drive-in and watched some stupid science-fiction movie about green monsters and space ships. Instead of looking at the screen, I spent the whole time looking at Ogunde. Her lips were like the petals of a flower, lips made to kiss and be kissed. She had thick, black, curly eyelashes, and the most beautiful eyes I've ever seen. When she smiled, two little dimples appeared on either side of her mouth. I put my hand on her knee and she immediately brushed it off. I put my hand on her waist and she brushed it off. I put my hand on her breast and she brushed it off. Then I put my hand between her legs. She was wearing jeans, and neither of us could feel much through the thick fabric. She squeezed her thighs together, trapping my hand there to prevent me from moving it about, and we stayed like that for a long time. After a while I began to feel her pulse on the palm of my hand. It was as if her heart were there, between her thighs. That night we became lovers, and from then on we slept together at every opportunity.

'My father caught us in the act one afternoon coming home from the repair shop and beat the living daylight out of us. Or rather, he beat the living daylight out of Ogunde, and I took most of the blows trying to protect her. I was scared the old man would kill her and wind up in jail and that I'd be left alone in the world. The three of us ended up sitting around the kitchen table drinking bourbon, my father with a bloody nose, Ogunde with a split lip and two swollen eyes and me with two teeth missing. My father said we'd betrayed him, and that he had every right to retaliate. He said he wanted to kill us, and the only reason he didn't was because he didn't want to spend the rest of his days behind bars. I hoped he'd cool down. We went on drinking bourbon. I wasn't used to drinking back then, and I was already feeling woozy.

'In the end, my father said he was a magnanimous guy and that he was willing to forgive. But I would have to leave: he couldn't stand to see my face. I think he really was in love with Ogunde and that our betrayal hurt him deeply. He said he never wanted to see me again, that I was to clear out my room by the following morning, and that anything I left behind he'd burn so there was no reason for me to come back. I broke down in tears. I was really just a kid. And I was in love with Ogunde; so madly in love that I heard a buzzing in my ears and my knees went weak when I was around her. I tried to reason with my father. I got down on my knees and asked his forgiveness. I literally begged him on my knees, and I think seeing me like that disgusted him. He told me to stop acting like a fag. He said I'd acted like a man and now I'd better accept the consequences like a man. But his heart must have been breaking too. At the end of the day, I was his only son, and up until then he'd never laid a finger on me, nor had I given him any reason to. I think he was a good man, in his own way.

'And that's how my pilgrimage began. I could only take a few things with me. When I went to my room, I saw that my father had put his old military kitbag on my bed, the only gift he ever gave me in his life, and in it I packed what I considered to be the essentials. I didn't have many things, and the kitbag wasn't even full when I left that morning. I had some savings – about a hundred and thirty dollars – and Ogunde slipped me another hundred. She sneaked out of the house somehow and found me at the bus stop. I'm not sure how she knew I'd be there. Day was just breaking and the fields were shrouded in a blanket of violet mist. I saw her appear through the oak trees with her arms wrapped around her to keep her cardigan closed. It was cold. She stayed with me there on the bench at the bus stop for a few minutes and asked me what I thought I was going to do. I told her I was going to head east to look for my mother. We were both crying, and the world seemed a cold, miserable place, but also one full of tenderness and mystery, as thrilling as the start of a novel you've just opened, when the lives of the characters begin to unfold before your eyes and you still don't know what to expect. She told me to get set up somewhere else for a while, a year or so, long enough for my father to calm down, and then to come back. But she didn't know my father. She didn't know that when he said something was over, there was no going back. She told me not to forget that the Lord watches over us always (which took me by surprise, since I didn't know she was religious and I'd never seen her praying) and also told me to be respectful to women and not to get into any trouble. Then she kissed me on the lips and left. I haven't seen her since.

'I spent years looking for my mother, though not intensively by any means – I stopped off here and there along the way. I guess I wasn't in any hurry to find her, and I knew that if I did end up meeting her, it might be a let-down. It crossed my mind that it might be better to go on idealising her than to actually meet her in person. I told myself not to expect much from a lady who'd abandoned her five-year-old son. Anyhow, the point is that no one takes that long to find someone they really want to find.

'I became a drifter, which is how I learnt that I knew how to do a lot of things. My father had passed on a lot of practical knowledge I didn't even know I had. I could shoot, and track deer and bears in the forest. I knew how to drive, how to drink water balancing a ten-gallon carboy on my arm, how to shave with a straight razor and sharpen it on a leather strop, even on a rock. I could take a motor apart and put it back together again. I knew how to repair cars and how to ride motorcycles, cars and even buses. I could do electrical repairs and woodwork: make a stool that didn't wobble and fix up an old table so it looked like new. I knew how to play poker, and could shuffle a pack of cards with one hand. And I'd learnt all of this from my father. So I could be a bus driver, a woodworker, an electrician, a barber or a car mechanic, and all thanks to my old man. He taught me how to do other things too, things that aren't deemed so important these days, like spitting, swearing and telling a good joke. In other words, he taught me how to talk like a man, with that blend of macho arrogance and sentimental self-pity, humour and frustration, sarcasm and flattery that is common to men all over the world. This might sound stupid to you lot, college-educated types with your uncorrupted souls. But where I'm from, and in plenty of other places I've been, a man isn't respected or taken seriously, let alone liked or accepted, if he doesn't know how to carry himself – by which I mean, if he doesn't know how to talk right.

'I don't want to bore you all with every little thing I did. The seasons came and went, a whole lot of falls, which meant a lot of leaves to sweep. I lived all over. I came across a hippie commune in Vermont, close to Burlington, and I spent months there shovelling cow shit. And since my whole body stank of cow shit (my skin, my hair), and it was no use washing myself ten times because the stench of shit just hung right off me, none of the girls would go near me, so I left the commune and looked for another hippie commune where there'd be free love and drugs and no cow shit, and I ended up on another ranch, in Grand Island on the islands of Lake Champlain, a few miles from the Canadian border. It wasn't a real ranch, more like a kind of Buddhist monastery where a few nutjobs came together to meditate, eat raw beets and sing songs of praise in Sanskrit. They needed a handyman, someone who knew how to fix things, repair motors, saw wooden planks and hammer nails, so I stayed there a while. I never went to college, but in that ranch in the middle of Lake Champlain I learnt to read. It was a kind of college for me. The Fellers, the owners of the ranch, had an impressive library, and when I'd finished up my work for the day I would go there, kick back on the red leather sofa and read. The first book I read in my life was William Saroyan's *The Human Comedy*, which Iris Feller, my employers' eldest daughter, recommended to me. And that was where it all began. I didn't stay long, just long enough to realise – from speaking with the Fellers and with lots of the other folks who passed through the ranch – that I was a complete ignoramus, and a pretentious dumbass, and that I had to stop being ignorant and dumb as soon as possible. I kept on travelling, but now I read everything I could. I was a regular at the public libraries. I flitted from job to job, girl to girl and library to library.

'Officially speaking, I was still looking for my mother. Then I decided that enough was enough and if I really wanted to find her then it was high time I got on with it. Eventually, I tracked her down. She'd married an IRS agent from Saint Petersburg, Florida. She had two little girls and lived in a picturesque house with a little lake full of ducks and rushes and paper reeds. A truly beautiful place. She couldn't have imagined who I was when she saw me show up there.

'She told me she'd left "that part of her life" behind. She was alone in the house, which was, I guess, lucky for everyone involved. She showed me a photo of her with her new husband and their two girls. She didn't even ask after my father. We sat in the kitchen and she offered me a glass of lemonade. She asked if I needed money and I said no, but she opened the cookie jar anyway and handed me two hundred dollars. I was surprised that she had two hundred dollars just stashed there in a cookie jar. It was clear she wanted me to go. She was a tall, good-looking lady, but she'd aged prematurely, and something about her mouth made her look bitter. I stared at her, trying to find something of her in me, or maybe something of me in her, but she didn't want to look me in the eyes. I told her I'd like to meet my sisters. "They're not your sisters, Wade," she said, perfectly composed. I wanted to hit her. I wanted to hug her and beg her to love me, to show me some love, even a little. But you can't ask a person to love you; love is the one thing you can't ask for. You can ask for money or food or shelter, for your life and even death, but you can't ask a person to love you, no matter how much you need their love.

'After this I spent a few more years on the road. I was in the military for a while, but I didn't like it and I left. I knew what would happen if I stayed on in the army. I knew I'd fit in too well, that I'd move up the ranks too easily (of course, only ever as high as a redneck can go). I knew that one day I'd find myself looking up at a robin flying on the other side of some barbed wire fence and I'd know I was on the wrong side of the fence. I chose the robin. I always have. I chose the sound of the wind. I always have, and the wind has brought me here, and it's the wind that's making me talk now – the wind, and only the wind. I was a vice-captain on a barge that transported tar along the Potomac River. I worked in a tractor factory and then in a cattle feed packing plant. Whenever I could, I'd take my shotgun and go hunting in the woods, coming back mucky and happy, smelling of the earth and blood, with squirrels, partridges, a fox, maybe even a roebuck slung over my shoulder. I was the ranger at Shenandoah National Park and later a coal miner in West Virginia, the most beautiful place on earth. I worked as a logger in West Virginia for the simple pleasure of being able to watch that river all day, those dark waters, as dark as a mirror. But I always came back to machines, cars and motors. That's what I'm good at, car motors, or any kind of motor, truth be told. Doesn't matter if it's a motorcycle motor, an outboard motor or a harvester motor – I've seen them all, and if they could be fixed, I fixed them.

'The other thing I did was read, non-stop. I don't know why I had such a burning need to read. Always library books, or borrowed, dog-eared, yellowing pages, and sometimes I would hold them to my nose and sniff them; I was just intoxicated by the paper's perfume, even the cheap paper, because often it's the cheap editions that smell the best. I guess now I see that I read because I wanted to understand what life was like. Does that make sense? I read poetry and the odd history book because I knew I was an out-and-out philistine and I wanted to know something about the Romans, the Egyptians, Louis XVI... But novels were my real bag. And I would read them asking myself: is that what life is really like? Is that what *my* life is like? Do the stories in these novels in any way resemble my life? Some of the books completely captivated me and I would wonder if there really were people whose lives were like the ones in those books. Nightingale song and the blood of a wolf trapped in the poachers' trap. And the smell of monosodium glutamate from the can of mushroom soup that's just been heated up. And a Charlie Parker solo, and the special way Charlie Parker's solos sound when you hear them on the radio in the middle of the night: so intense, so assured, and so true they're almost scary, and which seem to finally reveal what's behind it all. Or Carmen McRae singing "The Sound of Silence": something as big and vast and magnificent and threatening as a sphinx in the middle of the desert.

'Where is all of this in novels? The feeling you get in your stomach, the feelings of desire and pain, vomit, nausea, the intense pleasure of peeing when you haven't been for hours, vertigo, exhaustion, the trembling that takes over our legs after any huge physical exertion, retching, desire, desiring a woman, wanting her to extreme and crazy levels until you lose all dignity and self-respect. Where is all this in novels?

'It fascinated me that novels rarely spoke of real life or the feeling produced by real life. But on the other hand, sometimes they would describe things more profound than life, or maybe it's that in novels life seems like something else. Something intense and melancholy that we rarely feel in a normal life. Something profoundly sad and meaningful. Something seemingly simple but which means lots of things and moves and fulfils us. A kind of symmetry. A drawing. And only rarely do both sensations – the sensation of life and the sensation of life as it appears in novels – come together in a personal experience. I mean, sometimes you read a book and you feel that this is like real life, but other times you read it and think this is how life should be.

'I'm not talking about phoney books, bad books, the ones that paint life in black ink or in rosy tones that have no connection to reality. I'm not talking about horror stories or fairy tales. I'm talking about real literature, the kind that wants to describe life as life really is. And I suppose what I'm trying to say is that really it's an impossible task because life is like a dog chasing after a bone: it's useless painting every last detail of the yellow corner of a house or the small red apples lying in the shade of Mr McGiver's apple tree, because the dog's already shot past that corner and run through the shadow and now it's chasing a cat along that dusty ditch full of dried-up carob pods. And if you linger on the dry carob pods you miss other things, you get lost in the details when in fact you should be pondering paths, dust, death. I know I'm not explaining myself too well. What I mean is that sometimes life is real beautiful and no book on earth can capture that beauty. But sometimes, or a lot of the time in fact, books are so much more beautiful than life.

'I decided I had to settle down. I'd been travelling for so long I barely had any friends. I probably don't have the right temperament for making friends. Too much of a loner. Too infatuated with the robin's song. Maybe all that shit about Indian blood is right, even though the proportion of Indian blood running through my veins is minimal. But it's also possible that it's the most potent. I wanted to put down some roots. I didn't know where, but I wasn't really fussed about the place itself as long as there was a forest nearby where I could get out from time to time to shoot and fish. And that's how I ended up in Farber, Connecticut. I had some money saved up, so I bought a car repair shop on a B road. The city was Farber, but the repair shop was practically in the middle of the forest. It was a big building on two floors. The living quarters were upstairs, and were big enough to house a decent-sized family. I had more than enough space, and the workshop itself was enormous too. I could have repaired train or helicopter engines in there. It had two pits from the fifties and I added two modern hydraulic pit jacks and left the pits as they were. I liked them being there. The space got a lot of light through big windows. I always had the sliding doors open. That's the good thing about working in a repair shop: you get to be out in the fresh air but protected from the rain and sun.

'I decided to specialise in gears and brakes, and I put up a great neon sign: ERICKSON'S. I was as proud as any property owner could be. It wasn't your average repair shop sign and lots of cars slowed down on seeing it thinking it was a restaurant. I sent a postcard to my father in Hammerstown telling him where I was. I didn't even know if he was dead or alive. Later I sent another one, to the same address. He didn't write back. I mean, I assumed he wasn't dead and hadn't moved on, that the old stubborn fool was still there, getting my postcards and not saying a word. Bitter, full of resentment. I decided to send him a postcard every Christmas in the hope that one day he might decide to reply.

'Before long I had four people working for me: an apprentice, Thomas; two mechanics, Lungren and Sapkowski (they were good mechanics, although Sapkowski was excessively proud and had a temper on him); and a girl, Dinah, who worked on reception and did the paperwork. She didn't seem at all daunted by working there with four tough guys all rough around the edges like Thomas, Lungren, Sapkowski and me. She lit up the shop, made it a happy place. Dinah called me Mr Erickson, but the truth is she ran the show. She told me off if I got food down me, wouldn't let me near her books with my greasy hands, and if I got dressed up to go out on the town, she'd redo my tie. She treated me like I was her father, or uncle, and I guess I enjoyed having someone like that in my life.

'I did enjoy being more settled, but I also had my doubts about that life. I'd never lived for so long in one place and I'd never owned anything. But the repair shop was going well because we did things properly: we didn't overcharge, we did what we said we'd do, and we didn't con the clients. Car repair shops are like any other business: your reputation is made right away, good or bad, and Erickson's gained a good reputation from the get-go.

'One day, Vinny, the driver of one of the local tow trucks, pulled a jeep up onto the shop forecourt. It was pretty old and the crankshaft had given up on a mountain road. It had New Hampshire plates, and out of it emerged a grey old fella and his wife, a lady much younger than him. The man was pretty tall and he had an unusually long face covered in vertical lines, and a powerful, broken nose; the nose of a boxer. There was something surly, or even hostile or obstinate about the man. Something hard and calcareous, which I liked. He seemed to be in a filthy mood, but then who enjoys breaking down on the road? He explained he lived in the mountains in New Hampshire and that he always rode his jeep across the roughest terrain, rattling over rocks and fallen tree trunks without a problem. I told him: well, it only takes that one time. I offered his wife a seat and a soda. She was wearing sunglasses and had red hair and the palest skin. Her legs were white like milk. And she really was a heck of a lot younger than him – maybe by thirty years. We looked over the car and discussed the problem. It was clear he liked cars. I put Sapkowski on the job and made a call to order in the parts. They had to bring them over from Stamford and it would take a day. I recommended the couple a motel in town, because they didn't seem like people with money to spare.

'The woman, who was very friendly and spoke with a Southern accent, told me that they'd come from New York and made a stop in

Cambridge to see his eldest daughter, Peggy, who was studying theology
and had serious health problems. Who knows how or why, but we ended
up in a long conversation, the three of us. I offered them a coffee and
we sat in the office. It's not something that tends to happen with cus-
tomers, but I enjoy chatting with strangers. It's an art, in fact, talking
with strangers, just like playing the harmonica or whittling wood is an
art. I noticed the man's young wife repeated whatever I said to the man.
He was hard of hearing, so I raised my voice so that she didn't have to
act as interpreter any more. There were two books lying around in my
office: a collection of stories by Nathaniel Hawthorne and Carson Mc-
Cullers' *The Ballad of the Sad Café*, which Dinah had been reading on
my recommendation. For this reason, maybe, we moved on to talking
about books, and I said, when he asked me, that I didn't think Hawthorne was a great writer, and that I didn't think he had a true "gift for
fiction", even though he was a great inventor of metaphors and, above
all, a great architect of situations. The man listened to my arguments
with interest and from one or two of the observations he put to me, I got
the impression that he was a man of letters, maybe even an author himself. It was lunchtime, and I proposed we head over to Larry's in my car
to eat something. They accepted. They also said they didn't want to
cause any bother, but the truth was they weren't bothering me in the
slightest. We introduced ourselves and shook hands. Wade Erickson.
Jerry Salinger. Colleen O'Neill.

'Even after all those years spent with my head buried in books, I think
this was the first time I ever really spoke about literature with anyone.

'"Are you a writer?" I asked him straight out.

'For some reason he looked at his hands, as if the shape of his hands
and fingers held the key to his occupation.

'"Yes," he answered. "A writer with a problem."

'"Yeah," I said, "your car's seen better days and those parts don't come
cheap." But he wasn't referring to his car. He was talking about a book he
was writing. "Would it seem strange to you if I told you about it?" he
asked. "Hearing you talk about Hawthorne I get the idea that you're a

well-read man, and I've been thinking that you might just have a good idea for me."

'The whole scenario seemed totally surreal. But I was intrigued.

'"Why do you think I could give you a good idea?" I asked. "What makes you think that?"

'"Because you understand stories," he said. "Because I think that you, unlike Nathaniel Hawthorne, have a 'gift for fiction'."

'He told me the plot of the book he was writing, and also the problem with it. He explained it in some detail, which took up most of lunch, but I was captivated listening to him because he spoke so well, so eloquently, choosing each word just so. His wife listened closely too, with obvious admiration, although something told me that it was the man she admired, and that she wasn't the slightest bit interested in what he was saying, and perhaps she didn't even understand all of it. And I realised she was even younger than I'd thought, not thirty but maybe even forty years his junior. But she wasn't remotely interested in literature, and she barely said a word throughout lunch. To me it seemed he looked down on her intellectually, and generally considered himself superior. They'd developed a strange relationship, those two, as tends to happen between an old man and a very young woman. He looked down on her and considered her inferior, but at the same time depended on her absolutely; and she, who obviously worshipped the man, treated him with the patience and detached admiration a mother might show to her spoilt, intolerable child.

'"Don't you think it's possible that Izabel is dead?" I asked him. "Maybe she's dead but she hasn't realised, and that's the whole problem. This would explain, for example, how she could get inside a closet and stay there for hours."

'"Absolutely not, no way," he said. "You want me to put a ghost in my book? I've never done anything like that."

'"Someone once said, and I'm afraid I can't remember who, that all books are about ghosts."

'"Jim Joyce," he said. "Yes, it was James Joyce who said that."

'He seemed to be thinking about what I'd said.

"'Dead, eh?" he said, while Colleen pulled several Saks receipts from her bag and smoothed them out on the table, profoundly disinterested in her husband's aesthetic dilemmas.

"'Then she discovers that even in death she's still awake," Jerry went on, talking to himself now. "And after that, that she can enter anyone's mind, that she can go anywhere."

"'And she can go back to the afternoon when Jim brought the black horse," I said, "and relive the scene and see what was really behind the rose bush, when the horse rode by with Rose on it."

"'My God," he said. "Who would have thought? A ghost!" He smiled, and it was the only time I ever saw him smile.

'He asked me if I'd studied literature and I told him I'd never so much as set foot inside a university, I hadn't even finished high school, and that seemed to please him.

"'You see? You see?" he said to his wife, who was busy concentrating on retouching her pale pink nails. "That's what I always say to my kids! It's what I've said a hundred times to my Peggy, that she shouldn't dream of taking a literature class! And I pray to God she never enrols at an Ivy League. Or ever sees a doctor. Although admittedly, that one takes some convincing. Illness, Mr Erickson, is but an illusion, *an idea*."

'I took them into Farber to get a room at Bruce Sonaris's motel, and they invited me for a drink after supper. I said I'd pick them up at eight. When I drove out of the motel forecourt, having left them at reception, I thought I saw them quarrelling. I couldn't see too clearly, because they were inside, but that's what it looked like. Driving back to the repair shop, I had a revelation. "That man," I said to myself, "that man is J.D. Salinger, the author of *The Catcher in the Rye!*" Suddenly it all made sense: Jerry, Jerome David Salinger, J.D. Salinger!

'When I got to the office, I asked Dinah for the paperwork of the owner of the jeep and there was his full name, Jerome David Salinger, and an address in Cornish, New Hampshire.

"'Do you know who that man who came in today was?" I asked. "It was J.D. Salinger! Salinger, the author of *The Catcher in the Rye*."

"'Oh dear, Wade," she said with mock pity, "have you forgotten to take your pills again?"

"'I'm serious," I said. "It's really him!"

"'I'm sorry, your Honour," Dinah joked, her tone full of sarcasm. "We had no choice. He started coming out with all kinds of crazy stuff, like how J.D. Salinger was a client at the workshop..."

"'But it's true!" I said. "Can't you see his name written here?"

"'Jesus, Wade," Dinah said, re-reading the forms and seeing the name written out before her eyes. "This guy's taken us for a ride. How much money did you give him?" I threw an eraser at her and walked out.

'That night I spoke with Salinger again, and then again the following day. I asked him if he was *the* Salinger and he told me he was. I told him I was happy to hear he was working on a new novel.

"'New?" he asked. "What do you mean?"

'I told him it would be a huge deal if he came out with a new novel, given that he hadn't published one since *Hapworth 16, 1924*, in 1965.

"'No, no, Mr Erickson," he said. "The fact that I'm writing a novel doesn't mean I'm going to publish it. I have no intention of publishing it. I don't write to publish; I write for myself."

"'Well," I said, "I don't think I've ever heard of a writer who 'writes for himself'."

"'Perhaps because barely any attention is paid to people who want to destroy their ego," Salinger replied. "And really that's the key to it all, the ego, and the way the ego gets a hold over us and everything we do."

'He told me he'd written several novels over the previous years, ten to be exact, but that the work he was wrapped up in at that time was truly vast, would end up being some nine hundred pages and was destined to be his magnum opus.

"'And it won't ever be published?" I asked.

"'Well," he said. "Maybe. If books still exist by then. If they still cut down trees to make paper and mix coal with rubber to make ink, and if there are still people who read then."

'I think in his will he'd written that the novels couldn't be published until a hundred years after his death. I couldn't stop thinking that the publication of these works could be a great help to his children, who'd be set up for life with the royalties. It turns out that in the battle against one's ego, people can be quite selfish.

'I didn't know then that my life was about to be turned on its head. I, who had never given much thought to the size of my own ego, was humbled to have met J.D. Salinger, the great recluse, and even more so to have been told I had "a gift for fiction". But I didn't think anything would come of it.

'Two or maybe three months passed. One day a man and a woman showed up at the repair shop in a Pontiac with New York plates looking for a mechanic by the name of Erickson. The man was tall, and wore scrappy jeans, a denim jacket, and a baseball cap pulled right down snug to his eyebrows. The woman was dressed more formally in a long skirt, expensive-looking caramel-coloured boots and a spotty cardigan. I asked what the problem was, and the man told me the car was fine; they hadn't come because of the car. "So?" I said. He asked if I was Wade Erickson and I told him I was. And he asked if he could steal an hour of my time and buy me beer. I guessed that he wanted to propose a business deal of some kind and I told him that neither the shop nor the land was up for sale, and that I had zero plans to expand the business. It was obvious the man was uncomfortable. The woman intervened.

'"Mr Erickson," she said. "Perhaps if my husband tells you his name you might have a better idea of the kind of business he'd like to discuss with you."

'"That's right," the man said. "I haven't introduced myself. My name's Thomas Pynchon."

'Well, you can imagine – my eyes just about popped out of their sockets. And you can probably also guess that I didn't altogether believe him.

'"You're Thomas Pynchon, the author of *Gravity's Rainbow*?"

'"That's right," he said, "that Thomas Pynchon."

'"Darling," his wife said, "perhaps you should show Mr Erickson your driving licence."

'He did, and his name was indeed Thomas Ruggles Pynchon Jr. We went to Larry's for a beer, and the man claiming to be Pynchon told me that he'd heard I might be able to help him with a problem.

'"Mr Erickson, do you know what's wrong with North American literature? Success. We gain a lot of success very quickly, and this has consequences. Suddenly, we receive a lot of money and a lot of glory. Look at what happened to Salinger: his first novel turned him into a legend and allowed him to give up working for the rest of his life. Look at Joseph Heller: he wrote one novel which was a major hit, and then went silent for years. It's a common literary fate in America. An author writes a book or two, is a huge hit and then never writes again, or takes twenty years to write the next work. Look at Bill Gaddis."

'I decided to cut my losses. I put on my best smile and told him I hadn't really read any of his work. This hit him hard, but he took it well.

'"Nothing?" he asked. "I thought you were meant to be a great reader."

'So I told him I'd read *V.*, and that I thought it was a great book, and also *The Crying of Lot 49*, which wasn't bad (worse for all the poor imitations it had inspired), but that I hadn't been able to finish *Gravity's Rainbow* (he hadn't published *Vineland* at that point, I don't think).

'"The problem is *Gravity's Rainbow*," he said. "What kind of book am I meant to write after that monstrosity? Mere copycat pieces. More of the same, don't you think? I reckon I'm probably out of ideas. The well's dried up."

'I didn't know what to say to him.

'"Your novels have convoluted plots," I said. What I was trying to say, politely, was that his books weren't my cup of tea, that I preferred Raymond Chandler or even William Saroyan. How could I tell him I preferred the smell of the grass and a black horse cantering through a meadow past a row of telegraph posts to a story about erections, banana trees or German rockets falling on London? How was I supposed to tell him that in my opinion his books contained too much artifice, like overly convoluted games? And not even fun games, because the only one playing was him, and a game only works if all the players know the rules. No. I couldn't go that far. I told him his novels were very obscure, that they were impossible to decipher. "It's as if they weren't narratives, but spheres," I told him. "A narrative is a line: first one thing happens, then another. In your novels there are no lines, or rather, they're curved lines, curving into themselves. Change. Write a novel that's a line."

'"A line?" he said.

'"A line, like you'd draw on a piece of paper. Like you'd draw on a map. Like the Mason-Dixon line."

'We didn't talk for much longer, and I'm not even sure what made me think about the Mason-Dixon line right in that moment. It's not something I tend to give much thought to, truth be told. I guess it was the whole idea of the line, the line drawn on a piece of paper, the line traced on a map. Years later, when he published *Mason & Dixon*, I received a signed copy from the author. On the flyleaf, there was a dedication. It simply said, "For Wade Erickson. He knows why. Thomas Pynchon".

'But that was just the beginning of it. The news spread, and from then on, I began getting visits from writers and writers' apprentices who came to my repair shop not to fix their cars, but to fix their stories, novels and storylines. I discovered I was good at it. Who knows why? I had good ideas, could see their errors, and I came up with possible solutions. Dinah, Lungren and Sapkowski didn't know what in the hell was going on. They thought I had problems with the IRS, that government bods were investigating my finances. But when you get investigated it's one inspector who comes, not a whole football team of them. I got letters, too, from writers living in far-flung places. I was forced to set some boundaries for my services as a literary assistant. Literary assistant, story advisor, narrative mechanic.

'Of course, it wasn't only published authors who wanted my advice, but also a lot of Creative Writing students, workshop directors... And it can take a long time to read a manuscript, especially if it's a novel. Otherwise, my "suggestions" or "ideas" tended to be brief. It might not seem this way, but I've never been a man of many words. Sometimes, the suggestion an author craved could be a single line. "Why not make Henry and Jenny uncle and niece instead of father and daughter?" for example. And I'd watch a light go on in their eyes right in front of me. "It's obvious his wife is dead," I'd say to another. "It's obvious that woman he's talking about no longer exists." Sometimes the creative spark doesn't need much to catch and set a whole forest ablaze.

'One of my most fertile creative genres was science fiction. I've never been particularly interested in it as a reader, but making up stories or finishing them or suggesting a mad plot twist in a conventional story became one of my specialties. One of the conditions in the contracts I signed, given that it didn't take long for authors to start appearing with their lawyers in tow, or even their lawyers on their behalf (I despised lawyers, but couldn't avoid them if I wanted to build my new business), was that my work remain anonymous. The author in question could include my name in their acknowledgements if they wanted to, but I wouldn't have the right to claim any royalties from any book or defend my authorship. I wasn't worried about any of those things because I didn't have literary ambitions, nor did I want to be famous. I did it for the sheer fun.

'My identity was shrouded in secrecy, but that didn't stop my reputation from growing. My ideas blossomed into other people's stories, novellas and even full-length novels. Harry Matthews came to see me with the idea of writing a book about me, but I forbade it. He told me about Oulipo, a group of French engineers, a bunch of wackos who spent their time playing word games, and he told me he'd love me to go with him to Paris to speak to them. But what was I going to do in Paris? Eat goose liver on baguettes? Buy myself a beret and a cigarette holder? Do my nails?

'Raymond Carver's wife came to see me and told me that Gordon Lish, a renowned writer and editor, had edited some of her husband's stories and had, to her mind, destroyed them. She asked me to read the originals against the edits. I only had to read a couple to give her my verdict. I told her that this Gordon Lish (whom I'd never heard of) was a cretin, and that what he'd done with her husband's stories was the equivalent of pruning a rose bush in spring, when the plant is in full bloom. I told her the originals were infinitely better than the edited versions, that what Gordon Lish had done was to create a kind of stream of dry, bitter, absurd telegrams that may well chime with his vision of the world but didn't respect the lyricism and complexity of the original, and I told her to tell her husband to go with his instinct, even if this meant getting it wrong sometimes. She told me she agreed with me, but then the stories appeared in Gordon Lish's version, and the whole world said Raymond Carver was a genius and that *What We Talk About When We Talk About Love* was his masterpiece. Lish had edited them in such a way that two characters might be talking about something but the reader didn't have a clue what that was. Everyone said that these kinds of things showed Carver's brilliance. You have to laugh at the critics sometimes.

'But soon after this I began to think about creating something myself. So much contact with creatives had awoken a desire in me to build something too, something beautiful and lasting. I thought about writing, as was only natural, but canned that idea almost immediately. First and foremost, I'm a man who's good with his hands. I tried to convince myself that writing was something you did with your hands, but I couldn't even look at a typewriter with a sheet of paper in it. We had two old typewriters in the office which we no longer used. I thought about taking one of them up to my apartment, but never went through with it. Without even trying, I knew I'd never be able to write a page.

'I had another idea. Back then I was full of ideas, really because ideas and stories were my job. I had the idea of building a temple, and pretty soon I couldn't think about anything else. The repair shop was still going well. Lungren and Sapkowski were still working for me, and then Dinah got married to the son of a hotel owner from Farber, Jimmy O'Connell, and she left us. She put on weight, had three kids, got a taste for cocktails, but she never stopped being the same delightful girl who teased me as if she were my own daughter. You know that poem by Frost that goes "Nothing gold can stay"? Well, it's just not true. Some gold never loses its glow. It might get a little faded, might tarnish a little, but it's still gold. I hired someone else to look after the office, Dorothy, and two more mechanics. I cut back my shop hours to mornings only, and would spend the rest of the day working on my temple.

'But a temple devoted to what? You could say it was a temple devoted to myself, since I've never been a religious man. Nor am I an atheist. I guess I've always believed in God, although in a kind of American God. I don't know, maybe for Americans the real God is America, and that's the source of all our problems. Our God isn't truly universal, omniscient and all that; God is the prairies, the mountains and the cities. And his "only Son made flesh" is the president. So I decided that the temple would be devoted to me and to the spirit of America. And to my mind, that spirit is revealed in the wind. The wind that blows on the great prairies and that never stops, the wind that makes us want to keep moving from one place to the next.

'The temple grew and grew and grew. I drew up an original plan, but then I began to add more towers and constructions, and then a second temple, and then a third. I didn't look up the model anywhere. I didn't consult books on architecture or Indian art. I just followed my intuition, kind of like visions in my head. They thrived at night: shadows in the middle of the forest, an enormous tower that looked like a corncob. That's how I thought of it, like a corncob, the spirit of the maize seed. That's right, a tower just like the one we're sitting under now. And not just similar, or a little bit like this tower; but identical, *exactly the same* as this one. What was I dreaming of? Was I dreaming of Indian temples, the temples of the Bay of Bengal? Or was I dreaming of this island and the very same temples that surround us now?

'I had a lot of land. The original temple was in the field behind the repair shop, perfectly visible from the highway, and it soon became famous. I built it with whatever materials I could lay my hands on, and used lots of old parts from cars, trucks, tractors and farming machinery. I spent my days with my head in a welding helmet, under an inferno of sparks. And I spent years like that. I don't think it was an "obsession". It was a pastime, entertainment, but it was also the desire to create something permanent, something that would stay standing even after I was gone. I spent a good few hours on my temples every day, but didn't work "day and night" as one journalist wrote. That's precisely why it took me so many years, because I took it easy.

'I became a celebrity. The temple and my picture were plastered all over the magazines, and all kinds of people came to see me. A couple of journalists from *Raw Magazine* came by and it was then that I heard the term *art brut* for the first time. They interviewed me, took hundreds of photos and put my temples on the front of their spring/summer issue. And that led to more articles in newspapers and magazines. They spoke about folkloric art, about popular architecture of "raw genius", about America's "rough and potent art". Others thought I was a freak and sneaked into my house looking for severed heads, girls locked up in the basement or I don't know what. They told me about some French postman, Ferdinand Cheval, who died in the twenties but had spent thirty-three years of his life building what he called the "Ideal Palace" and they showed me photos of it, and of his mausoleum, which had a vague resemblance to my temples, and also pictures of the real temples in India, especially the Orissa temples. I can't honestly say that I'd never seen pictures of Indian temples. Throughout your lifetime you see all kinds of things. But the truth is that I hadn't tried to follow any model, nor did I consult any art books. It's true that in Walt Disney's *The Jungle Book* you see temples pretty similar to the ones in Orissa, but I'd never seen that movie. Of course, no one believes you when you say you haven't seen this movie or read that book.

'Fame. I'd never planned to be famous, and now I wasn't just famous; I was rich too. My temples, of which there were now five, became a local tourist attraction. I had to find some way to organise all the visitors, and the franchise and logo of a "T" inside a circle just sort of emerged on their own. T-shirts, mugs, plates and key rings went on sale, all branded with the temple logo. They called them "Connecticut's Indian temples" or "Erickson's temples" and nobody knew, nor did they care, that they were dedicated to the wind, to the American spirit and to impermanence. I could have closed the auto repair shop and lived solely off the attention generated by my temples, but I didn't. In fact, by the time I finished the fifth temple I felt like the work was finished and that it was time to hang up my welding helmet and go back to my motors. I guess I was tired. Fame can be exhausting, and nine out of ten times it only brings trouble.

'I still sent a postcard home to my father every Christmas, and I never got any reply. Until one day I did get a response, just not in the form of a letter. It was the holidays, Christmas Eve. A car pulled up to the shop forecourt, and out of it stepped a Black man, about thirty years old. He asked if I was Wade Erickson.

'"That's me," I said.

'"I'm Raymond Erickson," he said, "your little brother."

'He had a big smile on his face.

'At first, I didn't know how to take the news. Raymond was my father and Ogunde's son. My little brother. My long-lost half-brother. He told me that my father and Ogunde got married and were still living in Hammerstown. They'd stayed there all those years. Raymond had brought a photo album with him. The whole thing was so strange and cruel and terrible. That photo album hurt me a lot. There was my father, and there was Ogunde, incredibly young, almost a girl. When I met her she'd seemed like a grown-up to me. But now, seeing photos from back then, I was amazed to see the watery innocence in her eyes and that look of inexperience and insecurity and tenderness that young people always wear. I flicked through the pages. There was my father with his work pants on and his corncob smoking pipe between his lips. And Ogunde, plump and smiling, a baby in her arms. And that baby was Raymond.

'The story doesn't end well. Raymond was looking for a fresh start. He said he'd been in some trouble and he asked me for a job in the repair shop.

'"What kind of trouble?" I asked. "Drugs?"

'"No, man," he said, acting offended. "I don't touch that shit."

'"Have you done time?" I asked.

'"Not really," he answered. "A few minor offences."

'I didn't want to probe him any further. If he'd been in prison it wasn't the end of the world; we all have the right to make mistakes and get a second chance. I told him to stay on for a while if he needed work. It was new to me, being a brother.

'Raymond didn't know a lot about cars, and he was a lousy worker. Too many mid-morning brewskis. Too many cigarette breaks. But he was the boss's brother. He moved into my house and soon everything made sense: the renovations I'd made, the spare rooms. The house was so big that even when he played music at full volume I could barely hear it. I was no longer alone. The robin hadn't just built a nest; he'd found someone to fill it too.

'Of course, Raymond wouldn't have been good company for anyone, but especially not for me. He quickly became the lord of the manor. No sooner had he moved in than his buddies showed up. I didn't like the look of them, but they were his friends: what could I do?

'Soon, his pals were coming over every night. They rarely came up to the apartment; instead they hung out in the workshop, turning on all the lights, drinking and listening to the radio. In winter it could get pretty cold, but they spent hours down there all the same, and the next day it would be covered in cigarette butts and empty beer cans and bottles. I wasn't so much annoyed; it was more that I felt invaded, or that I had lost my freedom. And I began to smell a rat. I began to suspect that Raymond wasn't really my brother. I imagined him reading about me in newspapers and magazines, learning all about my life and my roots in Hammerstown. I imagined him sneaking into my father's house and robbing the photo album and making up the story that he was that little Black boy in Ogunde's arms. So I took a couple of days off and said I was going fishing in Canada. But I didn't head north; I went west, to Indiana.

'I didn't recognise Hammerstown. Everything had changed. The city from my childhood had vanished. When I got to my father's house, I didn't know what I was going to find when I knocked on the door. No one answered. I peered through the windows. The house was clearly still lived in, but I didn't recognise the furniture. I sat on the porch and dozed off while I waited. I was woken by a fairly tall woman of colour. She jabbed my ribs with her umbrella and asked what I was doing there. I told her it was Wade, Wade Erickson. She told me she didn't know any Wade. I rubbed my eyes, looked at her and realised it wasn't Ogunde. "I'm Rose Mary," she told me curtly, "or Ms Latimer to you." She and her husband had bought the house seven years earlier, and she didn't know anything about the previous owners, nor had she ever heard of any Erickson or Ogunde. I told her I'd been sending postcards at Christmas for years. "Yeah," she said, "they got here all right." She told me to come inside, offered me a lemonade and took out a pile of my postcards, which she kept right there in a kitchen drawer. There were seven postcards signed Wade Erickson, with seven Happy Christmas messages. She told me she and her husband didn't know who this Wade Erickson was who wrote to them every year, and that they'd imagined it was a worshipper from the parish. Her husband was an Anabaptist pastor and had a lot of followers. Indiana has always been a land of Protestants.

'When I got back from Hammerstown, the first thing I noticed was that Raymond had been through my papers. Nothing was messed up, and nor am I a particularly neat and tidy guy. No, it was just a couple of details, but I knew for sure someone had been through my documents. And I mean my personal documents – the ones I kept in the house. I went to confront him straight away.

'"What were you looking for, Raymond?" I asked. "Money? A will? What were you looking for?"

'He looked at me with the eyes of a caged animal, and I was truly shaken. He said he needed money. That he was in debt. He told me he needed fifty thousand dollars.

'"What have you got yourself into?" I asked.

'He screamed that I was an idiot, spending all day there in my workshop and building my stupid temples. He said I didn't know the first thing about the real world. He said it wasn't easy being Black in such a messed-up world, that Black guys like him were used to people looking at him in fear every time he went into a store, and passers-by crossing to the other sidewalk. He told me it wasn't easy always being treated like a thug, having to put up with humiliation after humiliation from childhood. He said a lot of things. I told him I didn't have any money. And he made me a proposal. He told me he knew the repair shop and temples were insured. It was simple: all I needed was to start a fire and claim the insurance. He'd take the fifty thousand he needed and disappear from my life forever.

'It wasn't true I didn't have the fifty thousand. I had it. And I thought that if Raymond really was my half-brother I couldn't leave him to the mercy of whoever it was he owed. I told him I wanted to talk to those people, probably because I didn't believe they existed. But things quickly got out of control. One night he turned up at the shop with his buddies. They seemed pumped, their eyes shining and their pupils dilated, and it was clear they'd taken something. Crack, I guess. They parked the car inside the shop, which seemed odd to me, as they normally just parked up outside. They said they had a problem and walked me to the car. One of Raymond's friends, a kid called Lenny, opened the trunk. Inside was a man tied at the wrists and feet, with a black bag over his head. He was dead. They'd shot him several times in the heart and, by the looks of it, once in the head. At the sight of that dead body, or perhaps seeing the look of horror on my face, they started laughing like a bunch of lunatics. They laughed and laughed. They were crying, hysterical.

'I asked who he was, and Raymond said he was someone who didn't deserve to live. I'd completely lost control of the situation. This was serious, really serious. Cars kept speeding past on the road. Anyone could have seen us. Raymond's friends were so stupid and so high they hadn't even waited until nightfall to show up. Half the county must have seen them driving there and parking up in my forecourt. I told them I was calling the police.

'"What'd you mean, the police?" Raymond said. "You have to help us. You have to help me. I'm your brother."

'"I don't know if you're my brother or not, Raymond," I said. "What I do know is that there's a dead body in your car."

'He was all over the place and started telling me he had a plan, a fool-proof plan, and that they'd come to me precisely for that reason. He said everything was going to work out fine. The plan was to make the car and the body disappear. Without a car or a body, there was no case. Getting rid of the car was easy, Raymond said. I had a repair shop, so I could take the car apart and leave it in hundreds of parts. And I could use the parts later on other repair jobs, even sell them. It was a genius plan, and clearly they all thought as much.

"'And the dead body?" I asked. "You thinking of taking that apart too?"

'Raymond replied that they'd bury it in the woods and that no one would ever find it. And they'd burn the body first, he said, with gasoline, disfigure it, and they'd smash in his teeth so that no one would be able to identify the body.

'Things were going from bad to worse, and I was trying to stay calm. And yet now Raymond's buddies, Montgomery and Feliciano, had blocked my way. They weren't about to let me walk out of there.

"'You want me to be an accomplice to a murder?" I asked. "You're out of your mind, Raymond. Get out of here right now, and take your shit with you – that's the best deal I can offer. Get out, and I won't say a word. You weren't here. I didn't see anything. Or maybe I'll tell the police you were here, because half the state saw you drive here and park up in my shop; I'll say you came, we spoke for a while, and you went. I don't know anything. But I'm not helping you."

"'I thought you'd say something like that," he said, pulling a .45 automatic out of the waistband of his trousers. It was the first time I'd seen him with a handgun. "Look," he said, "I get you don't want to get involved. I get that. But I've got a plan. You don't have to actually *do* any of it if you don't want to. We'll tie you to a post here and tomorrow when Lungren and the Pole come you can tell them whatever you want."

"'No deal, Raymond," I said.

"'Okay," he said. "Okay, tough guy. We'll do it better, then. You want it to look real? You're right. The police won't just believe any old shit you tell them. I'll knock you about a bit and shoot you in the leg. I'll do it carefully, a clean shot. That way you'll stay well out of it all."

'So this was his plan. He'd hide out in my shop, burn and bury the body, and do me the courtesy of shooting me in the leg and leaving me tied up all night screaming in pain and bleeding – that was his way of leaving me well out of it. I was so mad I launched at him and snatched the gun. Now it was a stand-off. I was aiming at Raymond, his buddies were aiming at me. On top of the handgun, they had a pocket pistol. I didn't even get a good look at it. Lenny yelled that there was no way I was getting out of there alive and that they couldn't let me go because I'd head straight to the police. I went through my options. What could I do? I started to talk. I told them I'd help them, but that if they wanted to dismantle the car we'd have to begin right away.

'But everything happened too fast. I couldn't keep control of the situation, especially given that there was one of me and a whole group of them. Feliciano came up behind me and I heard a shot and fell to the floor. I felt the impact in the middle of my back. I tried to get up, but I couldn't. I was lying face down on the floor, writhing around like a lizard in the sun. Lenny walked over and kicked the gun out of my reach. They were shouting over each other. They pulled the corpse out of the truck and looked for a can of gasoline to burn it, but there was none in the shop. So they decided to burn the whole place down. That way they'd burn the body and the car at once. I screamed at them not to leave me there, and they dragged me outside.

'"Wait till you see these fireworks, bro," Raymond said.

'So, lying there on the floor, I watched as my business and my home burnt to the ground. The firemen took half an hour to get there from the moment the flames started rising, painting a huge orange stain onto the sky. But when they finally arrived, there wasn't much to save.

'And that's how my half-brother Raymond destroyed everything I'd built. But there was more. The bullet was still lodged in the middle of my spinal column. Mortifyingly, I'd shit myself. I thought it was from fear, but I soon found out I was wrong. The ambulance arrived and took me

straight to the Saint Francis Hospital in Stamford, where they operated
that same night. They explained later that the bullet had caused a me-
dulla lesion and had damaged my spinal cord. They'd performed a spinal
decompression on me, and managed to remove the bullet, but the me-
dulla lesion affected the nerves controlling the lower part of my body. I
lost movement in both legs and also my sphincters. Paraplegic. That's why
my bowels opened soon after I was shot. The bottom half of my body was
fine in theory, but it had become disconnected from my central nervous
system. All the organs were there, but they weren't receiving any orders
from my brain. After a while I regained some feeling, albeit in a different
way, which gave me hope. And thanks be to God, I also regained control
of my bowels.

'The robin's wings had been clipped. The flight had come to an end,
once and for all.

'Miraculously, though, the insurance company paid up. This was a
lucky escape, because I could no longer work. I took permanent medical
leave and tried to imagine a future for myself. The police caught Raymond and his buddies the day after the fire. It turned out that Lenny had
killed a mob boss. The death penalty still exists in Connecticut, but I
don't think they've applied it since 1976, so Lenny got sentenced to thirty
years. The others ten. Ten years for destroying my life and nearly killing
me. Cheap, eh? If he plays his cards right, Raymond will be out for good
behaviour in five.

'I found out a lot during the following weeks and months. I found out
that Raymond really was my brother. He was the son of my father and
Ogunde. She'd changed her name and was now Helen Erickson. I found
out that my father had died seven years earlier, and that Helen Erickson
lived in Wichita Falls, where she was the manager of an underwear workshop specialising in corsets and XL sizes. I wrote her, but she never replied. I don't know why, I guess she was ashamed: ashamed of her son and
what he'd done to me. But I would have liked to see her, I can't lie.

'I stayed put in Farber, close to the few friends I'd made in my life.
Dinah and her family were nearby, and they treated me like one of their

own. Yeah, I guess you could say that Dinah adopted me after the accident. I got on with everyone, with her husband and the kids, and with her
sister Lorna and her parents. I ate with them almost every day, and looked
after the kids, Francis and Juliet, who called me Uncle Wade. In life you
come across angels and devils. Dinah O'Connell was one of my angels.
Charming, smart, the life and soul. Jimmy and she adored each other.

'Eventually, Dinah got cancer. They gave her chemotherapy and she
lost all her hair. All that happened over barely two years. Yep, real fast.
When Dinah was sick I spent a lot of time with her. Sometimes I went
with her to the hospital when Jimmy couldn't. She wore a scarf on her
head to cover the hair loss, and she looked ill. She looked like she was
going to die. I would sit there cursing the universe and she'd say we were
"the odd couple" – her with her Amish headscarf and me in my wheelchair. The medicines they gave her burnt her insides and left her oesoph-
agus and stomach raw. But the chemotherapy worked. She made a complete
recovery, her hair grew again, and she went back to being the same old
Dinah. When the test results came back confirming the treatment had
worked and that the cancer had gone, the O'Connells threw a party. And
I sat crying with happiness in my room. I haven't cried many times in my
life, but that was one of them.

'Sometimes I think about cause and effect, about that row of dominoes
that land one on top of the other, and about whether it's possible to remove one of those tiles to stop the whole line from tumbling down. Where
did my line begin? I think the problem started with that ranch where I
was chief shit shoveller. If I'd had a better job, or smelt better at least, I
wouldn't have looked for a job on Grand Island in Lake Champlain, and I
wouldn't have fallen into the Fellers' ranch (or monastery) and I wouldn't
have discovered reading. I wouldn't have got interested in books, and
when Jerry Salinger showed up at my repair shop I wouldn't have had
anything to say to him, and I wouldn't have started selling stories to
blocked writers, and I wouldn't have had the desire to create something
myself, and I wouldn't have had the completely hare-brained idea of building Indian temples in the middle of the forest in Connecticut, and I

wouldn't have become famous, and Raymond wouldn't have heard about me or thought of coming to find me and doing his whole little brother act to scam all the money he could from me, and I wouldn't be in a wheel-chair. I feel like everything that's happened to me is so unlikely, so strange, and that it's linked by such a fragile logic, it must have happened to me for a reason, because it was fate. And you can't escape fate.

'I thought it might do me good to get out of Farber for a while, and I had the idea of travelling to India to look at the temples I'd unwittingly taken as inspiration for my own: the great Lingaraj Temple in Bhubaneswar – where they don't admit non-Hindus and you can only see it from the terrace of a nearby building – and other temples in the region. I had a real desire to be far, far away, in some remote place where nobody knew any-thing about me. And that's how I ended up on our plane. I suppose it was a bit reckless of me to take such a big trip on my own, but I think it was precisely the recklessness of the adventure I was setting out on that ap-pealed to me.

'I guess now you'll have your answers to a lot of things, including the reason why I've decided never to leave this island. I'm telling you, this is-land will be my final resting place. I'm staying. I'm going to live out how-ever many days I've got left here.

'You remember, John,' he added, directing himself just at me now, 'what happened after the accident. Everyone was screaming and hollering. There was a man on the floor in the aisle who was blocking the way. A big Black guy dressed in a blue suit. You were yelling at me to help you pick him up, saying you couldn't do it alone. I told you I couldn't help. You were screaming at me, and everyone was getting up and screaming, all the injured folks were screaming. And in the middle of it all, there I was – per-fectly still and silent. But what could I do without my wheelchair? What could I do with my dead legs? If I'd tried to get out of my seat I would have fallen on the floor and you'd have had to drag me off the plane with everyone clambering right over me and crushing me. But all the same, I put my hands on the armrest and tried to get up. And then the most amaz-ing feeling came over me. My legs were working again. My legs were responding. There they were, extended to their full length, heavy with their framework of muscles and bones; warm, alive. My bare feet were resting on the floor and I could feel my soles. A glorious feeling that I'd forgotten: feeling the earth's foundations. I stood up. I knew that what was happening to me was a miracle. For everyone else, this was a tragedy. Maybe a punishment. But for me, it was a miracle. And I smiled.'

40

The day of my ruin. We return

By the time Wade had finished telling us his story, I had a more immediate problem. My bullet wound had become infected and gangrene
had set in. Joseph asked the guerrillas for an axe or a saw to amputate the
lower part of my leg. If he didn't, the gangrene would spread through my
body, poisoning my blood and eventually killing me.

When he explained what he had to do, I told him I didn't want to go
through with it, that I'd prefer to let nature take its course, come what
may. 'Come what may?' he replied, flashing me a cold, cruel look. He
told me that if we did nothing I would die, and I could only respond that
I'd rather die quietly than go through the horrific alternative. If that
makes me a coward, I guess that's what I was. I told them – all of them,
given that we were always together in that temple – that I didn't have
anyone special in my life – no girlfriend, no parents, no kids. All I had
was a Labrador Retriever, and as fond as I was of Ballard, not even his
warm companionship was enough to make me want to cling to life at
that cost. Nobody depended on me, nobody was waiting for me, nobody
would cry over me. I think it was the first time in my life that it occurred
to me that if I disappeared off the face of the planet, nobody would so
much as shed a tear. Joseph shouted at me that I couldn't just give up
after everything we'd been through. He said I was a fool, a vain fool who
would rather die than lose one foot. But it wasn't the foot I was worried
about; it was having to have to go through the amputation with no anaesthetic. 'Don't you worry,' Joseph said. 'We'll get you something to numb
the pain.'

But in the end he couldn't keep that promise. The guerrillas didn't
have any medicine at all, just the vials of what they called their 'vaccine'.
For everything else, they used forest plants – presumably placebos for the
most part. We begged the guerrillas to let us go to our village where we
could perform the operation in more suitable conditions, but I've never
met less receptive or more stubborn people. They provided us with a bottle of gin, some cotton thread, a razor blade and an axe. That was it. So we
did it right there, inside the Hanuman temple, under the watchful eyes of
gods, celestial nymphs, serpent men and divine monkeys – some horrified,
others openly amused. Joseph explained again what they were going to do
to me. I told him I didn't want to know, but he told me anyway. He told me
that first I was to drink the entire bottle of gin, or at least half of it, and
then they'd put me face down and tie me up so I didn't struggle uncontrollably. I think by this point I was already crying like a little boy. He told me
that before cutting off my foot he would make an incision at the back of
my leg to tie the popliteal artery and vein and the great saphenous vein – a
simple procedure that would take a couple of minutes, and only required
the use of the cotton thread. This was all to help stem the bleeding and
was the most dangerous part. 'And what will the blood do when it reaches
the blocked veins and arteries?' I asked. 'It will divert along other veins,'
he said. 'There's no problem. Then we'll do the amputation and stitch you
up. You'll be so drunk you won't have a clue what's going on.'

It was only much later that he told me the truth: that he had been convinced I would die. He didn't have a scalpel, or a saw, or any gauze to
control blood flow. He didn't have forceps to clip the arteries or veins and
hold them in place while he tied them, and he had to cut the back of my
leg with the blade and probe around for the vein and artery with his fingers, then make Wade hold them while he tied them with the thread.
Asepsis was simply impossible in that place, and it was a genuine miracle
that the wound didn't get infected. The axe, on the other hand, splintered
the bone as it cut through. He told me all of this later down the line, when
I was out of any real danger and had started to recover. He told me that he
had been on the point of admitting I was right: that to do an amputation

like that, without the proper instruments, in completely unhygienic conditions, was madness, that it wasn't worth the risk. But by the look of things, the island didn't want to see the back of me just yet. No, the island wasn't quite finished with me.

But I can't describe the pain. Something inside of me won't allow me to describe it. I cried like a baby. I begged. I raved. I went through hell and back. I broke the chains of good and evil. I became an animal, a primate, a rock, metal, blood, air. I guess the gin helped, although drinking that much gin in one go made me vomit and retch, meaning I was less inebriated than planned. Together they pinned me down, and Joseph lodged something between my teeth – a thick piece of leather – so I didn't grind them to dust. I ceased to be human. I became a dog, then a monkey, skin, nerve, tendon, artery, then pain, only pain. I fell through different worlds. I'd taken on a consistency that allowed me to pass through lava and lead. I slipped beyond words. I came to a red mountain that was a living being, illuminated in shiny, flaming blood. I felt my entire past slip away, all my awareness draining out of me as I fell deeper and deeper towards the centre of the earth. I transformed into a knot of taut wires, each pulling me in a different direction. I dissolved into a pack of wild dogs, all snapping at each other. My eyes and ears and skin were like taut threads lit up in electric flashes of pain. Something inside of me burst, devastating everything – a black explosion of inverse luminosity that lay waste to all matter and broke the bonds that connected all the atoms of my body. Any awareness of the past, beliefs, good, fear, shame, honour, astuteness, intelligence, desire, civilisation itself – all of it was devastated, burnt to nothing. I lost my human form.

And then, somebody, somebody sitting at a table, heard me.

Somebody dressed in dark colours heard my cries. Perhaps at first they didn't know it was coming from me, but then they listened more carefully and realised that it was me crying out. And that someone was sitting at a stone table, a beautiful malachite table with semiprecious stones arranged in a mosaic of trees and birds, with lots of random, colourful pieces. Thousands of multicoloured pieces. Pieces of stone, ebony, glass, plastic, roots, metal and painted lead.

And this somebody opened their eyes. And now I could see with their eyes. I saw the malachite table and their hands and the thousands of pieces on the malachite table. And I had to remove some pieces to get to the right ones, and sometimes, when I removed one, another couple fell off the table. And these pieces then fell on the floor causing all sorts of problems. In fact, almost everything that happened, good or bad, was caused by the pieces falling off the malachite table and landing on the ground, getting lost there in the grass.

And that somebody who heard me decided then they needed to help me. Not because they didn't want to help sooner, but simply because they *didn't know of my existence* before then.

Next I saw a mountainside (this happened, I think, when I finally passed out), and from among the rocks appeared a huge goat. On further inspection it wasn't actually a goat, but a large, short-horned antelope with cinnamon-coloured flanks. It stared at me out of its left eye, then bent one leg.

To me it was obvious what was meant by that bent leg – 'you must follow me' – and the next thing I knew, the antelope leapt off up the mountain. I looked up to see that it was the highest mountain on the island, the original volcano whose summit was always shrouded in cloud.

'Climb the mountain,' the antelope said. 'Climb the mountain.'

I spent several days in a stupor, muddled by the combination of alcohol, blood loss and exhaustion. I could still feel my left foot where it should have been, and I would have to look down at my leg with my own eyes to confirm that my left foot and half of my calf were indeed no longer there. I complained that my foot hurt just as much as it had before the operation, and Joseph told me it was a phantom pain. The pain wasn't in my foot, but rather in my brain.

A few days after the amputation, we woke up one morning to discover that we were no longer chained. As far as we could tell, we were alone now in that forsaken temple in the middle of the jungle. We were convinced that our tormentors were hiding just the other side of the stone wall surrounding the complex of temples, or crouching in the vegetation, ready to jump out at us shouting triumphantly 'Surprise, traitors to the proletariat cause! We've got you again!' But that wasn't the case. A lyrebird flew over-head – the only one I ever saw on the island. It had dark blue, almost black feathers – possibly the most beautiful bird on the planet.

Slowing descending the stone steps of the temple, we walked towards the stone wall and under the arch covered in carved figures, the one re-maining torana. The second we crossed the threshold, we spotted one of the guerrillas. She was walking towards us, her right arm up in the air, the Kalashnikov slung over her right shoulder. It was Red Star. But she was in a terrible state. Awful. Something had sliced off a chunk of her body. Something like a giant axe or an iron blade had cut off the left side of her blonde head of hair, her left ear, cheek, shoulder, arm and body down to her waist. The left side of her face had been cleanly cut, leaving her teeth and skull exposed. Her eyes had come out of her sockets. I don't under-stand how she was still walking. We heard explosions in the distance be-tween the trees. Then there was a terrible shriek from somewhere deep in the jungle; the shriek of the blue man. You couldn't see that giant any-where, but the sound wasn't coming from very far away, perhaps only a couple of hundred metres. It was an ear-splitting sound, which seemed to rip through time and space. After that, a lightning bolt shot down, exactly like the ones that had fallen on Christian and Noboru. It shrouded Red Star in a blinding gold and white light, and then she burst into flames – furious red flames that looked as though they were being fanned by doz-ens of giant bellows. For a second, as the flames engulfed her, she looked beautiful. She wore a look of tender surprise, and her lips curved into a smile. It was as if she were very young again, as if she were the woman she'd once been, when she was a young mum with three kids on a ranch, and one night a ray hit them all during an electrical storm causing a fire in an adjoining barn and suffocating her three children to death. For a split second, we saw her as she really was, how she'd once been. Then she fell to the floor, wrapped in flames, and rolled around on the leaves. She didn't even scream. She was dead. Wade and Joseph looked like they might throw themselves on her to put out the flames, but it was no use. Red Star's body was now a charred black husk. I'd never seen anything burn so quickly or disintegrate so entirely. That singed, still smouldering body on the floor before us was exactly like the corpses we'd seen in the Valley of the Blue Man on our outward journey. The body didn't seem so much burnt as dissolved in the heat. Could the blue man have killed *all* the guerrillas? Was he the hazily defined enemy they fought against? Is that who they were trying to destroy from the safety of their machine-gun nests, with their grenade launchers and surface-to-air Mistral missile launcher?

It took us two days to get to the coast and walk as far as our beach, the lagoon and the mouth of the river, which we now thought of as home. The others were shocked to see us and many broke down in sobs. We were in a terrible state. We were gaunt, exhausted, filthy, eaten alive by insects and leeches, our skin covered in hives and scabies, which we'd caught from the guerrillas. I was delirious on a stretcher that had now all but fallen apart, my left leg wrapped in a bandage that had been dripping pus and blood for hours.

Despite everything, I was glad to be in that feverish, delirious state, because it meant I didn't have to face the parents: Lizzy, young Lizzy, Bruce and Gloria Griffin, Adele and Estelle's parents, who asked us if we'd seen their children, if we'd had word of them, if they were okay, if they were still alive. To our great shame, we'd returned defeated and duped, with no children, no guns – bearers of only bad news.

41

My recovery

After almost a week spent in the hospital, drifting in and out of feverish delirium, my wound finally began to heal. I can barely remember a thing about those days in the hospital hut. They gave me sedatives, morphine I suppose, and I lost myself in my reveries. I'm not entirely sure where that morphine came from. By the looks of things, Jimmy Bruëll had some, or he'd dug some up, perhaps in someone else's luggage. I'll never know if my experiences over those few days were real, or merely fever dreams. I saw all kinds of beings – some hideous, others bright and lovely. Some of them spoke; others simply stared at me and smiled. One day I saw Joseph and Sophie kissing and I guessed that too was a hallucination. They were right there, next to me, inside the hospital. She was dressed only in her underwear and Joseph had his arms around her. I guess they thought I was asleep. Next thing, they lay down on the other bed, drew the makeshift curtain and I had to listen to them make love. Half an hour later the curtain was drawn back again and I saw Sophie sitting on the edge of the bed, doing up her bra. Joseph was behind her, still lying on his back. Our eyes met and she grinned at me and put a finger to her lips. I turned around to let her put the rest of her clothes on unobserved, because I'd realised that what I was seeing definitely wasn't a hallucination.

I asked the doctor about it later, and he was as embarrassed as a schoolboy. He apologised a hundred times.

'Sophie and I...' he began. But he didn't have the words.

'For how long?'

'Basically from the start,' he said, to my surprise, given that I thought he'd been keen on Gwen. 'The situation is killing us. She's married with two kids. I'm married too, at least technically I am. My wife left me for a cardiologist. A heart specialist – who can compete with that? And Sophie... well, her husband doesn't pay her the slightest attention. Nor she him. They're not in love. And here we are, both of us on this fucking island. Both alone in our loneliness. We spotted each other on the day of the crash, and I think there was even something in that first look. She said: "What can I do?" and began helping me with the casualties.

'Nothing like that has ever happened to me,' he went on. 'In the middle of all the horror we were witnessing, when you'd think there's no room in your soul for anything other than the job at hand, bringing the wounded to the shore, helping them in some way, helping the dying, alleviating their pain as much as possible... In the middle of all that, she appeared, and we simply looked at each other. She said: "What can I do?" And she looked at me like no one has ever looked at me. She was always smiling, always full of spirit. And I knew it spelt trouble. "What's going on with you, Joe?" I thought to myself as I put bones in splints and stitched up open gashes. "Are you really going to fall in love with this woman you barely know?" At that point we were all convinced someone was coming to our rescue straight away, and that we wouldn't spend another night on the island. So what? We were both from Los Angeles. I thought about seeing her on our return. Days passed.

'I met her husband and the children. I realised she's totally wrapped up in her children, she's devoted her whole life to them. I was almost shocked to see how strong the bond is between those three. Her husband, on the other hand, came across as odd. He still does. Removed from the world, absorbed in his own problems.'

We were both in the hospital, me lying down and Joseph sitting at the foot of the bed. I felt a bit better. I was interested in what Joseph was telling me, relishing having a conversation. The sound of normal life. The vague memory of normal life.

'John, how do you know if what you're feeling is love?' he asked me then.

I thought for a moment.

'If you feel the overwhelming desire for the other person to be happy, even if you're not.'

Joseph sat thinking about this for a second. Rare for someone to ask me, the famous tomcat, what love is. But this cat knows. He knows exactly what it is, because he had it and let it go. He might have lost it, but he still knows.

42

I have hallucinations. Rosana pays me a visit

I *had a lot of visitors* over those days. My story became legendary. It's not hard to achieve legendary status in a society of ninety people.

My hallucinations hadn't gone away. I was no longer on painkillers, but I hadn't stopped seeing things. Every now and then I would see a black cat with a beautiful coat slinking into the hospital, where it would stay for a while, grooming its long whiskers, and then disappear again under the canvas door, just as it had arrived. I knew there were no cats on the island and that this one only existed in my imagination. I knew it couldn't possibly be a real cat. I hadn't seen it before or heard anyone mention the existence of a beautiful black cat. It wasn't feral, either. It was a well-fed, well-looked-after domesticated animal with a velvety coat. And I knew it wasn't real. I knew it was an invention of my delirium. I also dreamt about Rosana. I dreamt about her often.

One day a little fellow dressed in a blue smock and a pair of baggy trousers turned up. He was very tall and completely bald but for a blond moustache so thin it was almost indiscernible. He addressed me formally and told me his name was Anton Bruckner. Bruckner, the celebrated Austrian composer. He was identical to the photos I'd seen of him. We shook hands and I told him to take a seat, and although he appeared a little perplexed, he pulled up a wooden stool and sat down beside my bed.

'Herr Bruckner,' I said, 'I've always loved your music.'

'You're very kind,' he said. 'You're a musician yourself, if I'm not mistaken?'

'Yes. A composer,' I said. 'But not a successful one.'

'Do not concern yourself with success. Music has nothing to do with success or applause. Although we all like to receive both.'

'Of course that's not what music is,' I said. 'But how can one compose without receiving any recognition at all? How can one compose when one has lost all faith in oneself?'

'You, sir, are yet to understand what music really is,' Bruckner went on. 'Once you understand this, your desire for success will cease to be the driving force in your life.'

He spoke in strange English, with a thick Germanic accent. I didn't know Bruckner spoke English, but I did know that he had been well received in England, and that he'd always had great affection and admiration for that country. He'd also tried to emigrate to the United States several times. Of course, looking back I suppose that figure who'd just entered my hut wasn't really Bruckner, but a figment of my imagination.

'Tell me, Herr Bruckner, what is music really?'

'If I tell you, I will surely ruin any chance of you finding out for yourself,' he said. 'And that won't do at all. It's possible you have ended up here solely for that reason.'

'Are you really Anton Bruckner?'

From one of the pockets in his blue smock he pulled out a paper bag full of cherries and began eating them. He offered one to me. They were deep red and looked delicious. But I was afraid to eat food from the world of dreams, and politely declined.

'Music is a way of giving praise to God,' I said. 'Is that what you believe?'

He frowned slightly, spat a couple of cherry pits on the floor and then slipped the bag of cherries back into his peasant smock.

'We talk of "God" when talking to children,' Bruckner said, wiping his mouth with the back of his hand. 'We don't tend to use that word here.'

'You were always a good Catholic, a man of faith.'

'Indeed. But that did not spare me from hardship. I was always a wretched soul, Sr Barbarín. All my life, since I was a boy, I was a wretched loner. Nobody ever loved me. I never had a true friend. I never inspired the affections of a single woman. Does that seem like an easy way to live one's entire life?'

'But tell me, what is music really?'

'Music has a human side and a non-human side,' Bruckner said. 'Music represents the human being and also the cosmos in all its complexity, and it represents the link between the two. It represents what we know about human beings, as well as what we don't know. Reality in its entirety. The soul and the world in their entirety, and the bridge that links man's soul with the soul of the world.'

I said nothing. I was thinking that Bruckner would never have come out with anything like that.

'You're not really Herr Bruckner,' I said. 'You're a figment of my imagination, and you're saying things that I've thought or might think.'

When he left, I was pensive for a long time. Later I discovered three cherry pits on the floor in the hut. I picked them up, put them under my pillow and went to sleep. I was convinced that when I woke up the three cherry pits would have disappeared, but that wasn't the case. They were still there where I'd put them, and even today, as I write down these recollections, they remain in my possession.

I heard Rosana's voice outside the hut and I knew she'd come to see me. I think for the first time in a long while I really felt unpresentable and I wanted to comb my hair and take a look in the mirror. The colourful sheet that served as the door was drawn back and there she was.

'How are you doing, Juan Barbarín?' Rosana asked.

I raised the fingers on my right hand by means of a hello, as if I felt much weaker than I actually was. She sat herself down on the bed with pleasing familiarity. She was wearing white trousers and one of her semi-transparent shirts.

I thanked her for coming to see me and asked her why she hadn't come sooner, and she said that she had, a few times. Didn't I remember? I felt confused. A few times? But how long had I been in that hut?

'I don't know,' she said. 'How long do you think?'

'I think I've been confusing reality and dreams,' I said. 'Joseph told me I've had a sky-high fever for a long time, which can make a person have hallucinations. I guess I've been confusing real life for dreams. For the past few days I keep seeing a cat. A black cat.'

'A cat?' she said, with an amused smile.

'There are no cats on this island, are there?'

'None that I know of.'

'Nobody had a cat on the plane?'

'I haven't once seen a cat around here.'

'I don't think there really was a cat,' I said. 'I don't think there was a lost cat somewhere on the island and that it's suddenly shown up.'

'How can you be so sure?'

'Because if a cat really had appeared, someone would have eaten it, don't you think?'

Rosana looked away and began biting around her nails again.

'Geez, Juan Barbarín! The things you come out with!'

'I'm sorry. But please stop biting your nails.'

She took her fingers out of her mouth and let out a big sigh.

'Right, is that everything then?' she asked. 'Those are your terrible hallucinations? You've seen a cat that doesn't exist. It's not exactly the end of the world.'

'There are other things I've dreamt about too. I've seen…'

'What?'

'Nothing, it doesn't matter. They were just hallucinations.'

'You can tell me if you like.'

'You'd think I was completely mad. But I can tell you about some of the dreams I had about you. If you don't mind.'

'And I thought you'd forgotten about all that.'

'I had a really lovely dream about you. I want to tell you about it.'

'You're scaring me, Juan Barbarín.'

'Aren't you curious?'

'Yes. No.'

'Yes or no?'

'No.'

'No?'

'I'm curious, but you're being so mysterious about it all you're scaring me.'

'Trust me.'

'Okay, I suppose a dream's a dream,' Rosana said, chuckling again. 'Let's see, tell me what you've been doing with me in your dreams.'

'I'll tell you one I really like. It's my favourite. One of the most beautiful dreams I've ever had.

'In my dream you come in and sit down more or less where you're sitting right now. We talk and talk about all sorts of different things. You ask me about our expedition, and what we found out there in the jungle. And I tell you about the guerrillas. About how scared we were. And I tell you that I'd never in my life imagined that I'd go through the things I'm going through here; that I knew that horrific things and awful situations went on in the world, but that I was convinced that I'd never go through anything horrific or awful like that. I was convinced, to put it one way, *that I was safe.*'

'Poor Juan Barbarín,' she said.

'Then you asked if there was anything you could do for me. You said if there was anything you could do for me, I only had to ask, whatever it was. But what could you do for me? You were already doing a lot just coming to see me, talking to me. What could you do for me? Get me my leg back? Wipe that horrific night from my memory? Of course you couldn't. Then you told me I could count on you. "Even if you need to cry," you said. "Sometimes we all need to cry. And sometimes we need a shoulder to cry on."'

'I said that?'

'Yes. You said: "Sometimes we need to cry, and sometimes we need a shoulder to cry on." It's odd because I've always thought that crying is something you do on your own. It had never occurred to me that anyone would want to be with someone else to cry, or that you need the other in order to be able to cry. And you said: "If you need someone to listen to

you, if you need someone to hold you while you cry, I'm right here." You
said that you'd wept so much in your life that you were an expert in crying
and tears. You seemed so maternal, and I was deeply moved.'

'I've never been a mother,' Rosana said.

'I know.'

'I didn't say it to you as a mother, but as a friend.'

'There's something maternal about all women,' I said. 'Even nuns, lovers, wives, friends. Even in little girls. It's part of all women.'

'You like women,' Rosana said.

'You've noticed, then.'

'Okay, go on.'

'At that point the dream shifts. It shifts slightly in tone and we enter
into a world we might call Juan Barbarín's world. Although I was so moved
I really was on the verge of tears. So then I say to you: "Yes, sorry, but
there is something I'd like you to do for me. If you don't mind." You ask
me what it is I want. And I say: "I'd like to see you naked." You open your
eyes wide. An unexpected request. Perhaps a ridiculous request, in poor
taste. And I say: "No, not completely naked. Naked from the waist up."
"Now?" you ask. "Yes, why not?" I say. "Here?" you ask. "Yes, why not
here and now?" "But why?" you ask. "Why ask me to do that? How is it
going to help you seeing me naked?" "It's going to help me more than you
can imagine," I say. "But I don't want you to do anything that's going to
embarrass you." "I am embarrassed," you say, "really embarrassed to get
naked like that in front of you." I'm always surprised when someone says
they're embarrassed to do something. Aren't they embarrassed to admit
they're embarrassed? But, nonetheless, I tell you "Yes", that I understand.
"Forget it. I'm sorry."

'"But what I don't get," you say, "is why you want to see me naked.
Why is that so important for men? Seeing, just seeing. A little skin, a
body." "And listening to music?" I say. "Is that important? Or reading a
poem? A poem that talks about a rose or the shade of a tree? Why is that
so important? And yet, at any given moment it can be the most important
thing in the world. It can even save your life." "You just want me to take

my clothes off?" you ask. "You want me to take off my shirt and bra? That's all?" "Yes, that's all," I say.'

'Jesus,' Rosana said.

'Well, that's what my dreams are like,' I said. 'Then, in the dream, you suddenly begin to unbutton your shirt, and you take it off and place it at the foot of the bed. And then you bend your arms back and unhook your bra, slide it off each arm and leave it on top of your shirt. And you look me in the eye. Then I say: "Thank you." And I look into your eyes, and I look at your chest, and we stay like that for a while. Now we're both a little calmer. You move in closer to me, and lean your breasts into my face. You say: "You can touch them if you like. You can kiss them if you like." "Thank you,"' I say. "You should know," I say, "but you doubtless already do, that for a man, the most beautiful thing he can lay his eyes on is a woman's breasts. You asked me why it's important, and that's the answer: that there is no more beautiful a thing for the eyes to behold."'

'That's the explanation?' Rosana asks.

'Yes, that's the explanation.'

'There is nothing more beautiful than a woman's breasts.'

'For a man, that is.'

'Wow.'

'It's a nice dream, right?' I said. 'I hope it didn't bother you.'

'It's a lovely dream. Why would it bother me, Juan Barbarín? Don't be an idiot.'

'There's a scene just like it in *Elizabeth Costello* by Coetzee. Have you read it? I suppose my dream comes from that book. I was reading it before getting on the plane so it's fresh in my mind.'

'Okay, Juan Barbarín,' she said. 'I've really enjoyed you telling me your dream, but now I have to go.'

'I hope I haven't upset you.'

'If you ask me that one more time, I'm going to wallop you on the head,' she said, getting up.

'It was only a dream,' I said.

'But I hope you don't confuse dreams with reality again,' Rosana said.

She blew me a kiss and left the hut. It took me a while to put two and two together and realise what she meant. I hadn't been describing a dream at all. Everything I'd just recounted to Rosana had actually happened.

When this hit me, a big smile spread across the cat's face.

43

I befriend Noboru

Dharma, *my Brazilian fairy godfather,* carved me a pair of crutches, which I used to start walking again. He later measured me up and said he was going to make me an artificial leg and foot. I was a bit of an emotional wreck around this time, and Dharma's kindness made me well up.

I finally got up out of my reclining chair in front of the lagoon and began practising walking with my crutches. I hadn't imagined using crutches would be so hard. I was constantly falling over and it sapped my arms of all their strength. But soon enough I was moving about with relative ease. After all, I said to myself, humans get about on two legs, and now I had three.

We still took turns to keep guard from airplane beach, looking out on the plane's ruins. I was the perfect candidate to spend hours stretched out there in the shade of the palm trees, waiting for the help we all knew wasn't coming.

We'd made the rule that there must always be two people at the 'lookout post'. One day it was my turn to do a shift with Noboru, the young Japanese man who'd died in my arms and who we'd all watched be brought back to life by three lightning bolts. Since we both quite enjoyed doing our lookout shift we were now spending a lot of time together, and struck up a friendship. And, as new friends tend to do, we told each other our life stories.

Noboru was one of those young Japanese kids overwhelmed by social pressures. He reminded me that he had been a *hikikomori,* and had locked himself up in a room for most of his youth. By the sounds of things, before taking that trip to Los Angeles he'd gone almost three years without leaving a hotel room in Yokohama. The hotel was called the Science Hotel.

'Three years in the Science *Hotel*?' I asked, thinking I hadn't understood properly and that maybe the Science Hotel was a health spa, a resort up in the mountains, a monastery or a university. But no, it was a real hotel, a twenty-three-storey modern building in Yokohama with views overlooking the bay, the port, the futuristic Minato Mirai district and the Cosmo Clock 21 Ferris wheel, which also happens to be the biggest clock in the world. Noboru explained, however, that he kept his curtains permanently drawn: firstly because he wasn't interested in 'views', particularly when the view was of the biggest clock in the world; and secondly because, in general, he spent all night awake and his days asleep, which is what *hikikomori* tend to do. Given that he never left the room and the light in any hotel room with the curtains drawn is practically the same day or night, that decision to sleep during the day might come across as a little bit affected. But it wasn't a decision, he told me. He didn't have any reason in particular to spend all night awake and to sleep during the day. It just happened. He liked staying up late working at his computer. Working, playing, buying, chatting and doing the business that allowed him to maintain a healthy bank balance. He found that at night he felt hopeful, jubilant and full of energy, while the daylight only brought on anxiety.

'There's something that opens up at night,' Noboru said to me during one of our long conversations on the beach. 'Something that no one can quite grasp, but which remains closed to us during the day. There's a light in the darkness that only shines when everything is dark. Do you know what Thelonious Monk said about the light?'

'No idea.'

'He said: "It's always night, or else we wouldn't need light." Because, look, when there's no light, there's night. But what happens when there's no night, no darkness? When there's no darkness there's nothing. And that's why the world's reality is darkness. And in that darkness the light appears, piercing through it like a golden ray. That's when light has a purpose, just like a flower painted on a black background.

'Inside man's heart is a flower,' he said, putting his hand in the middle of his chest, 'that stays closed during the day. *Yoru no hana*. Night Flowers. When darkness falls, that flower unfurls and man starts to live.'

'You must really suffer here,' I said. 'After three years spent inside a room without once going out. But did you really never leave? Were you really inside that place for three whole years?'

'They call it agoraphobia,' he said. 'But couldn't you say that everyone else is claustrophobic? Every phobia has its opposite, which means either that there are no such things as phobias, or that everything we feel is a phobia of one kind or another. They call it "photophobia", a phobia of light, but the physical pain that the light produces, the dizziness, the nausea, the vertigo, all of those physical symptoms, they're not part of any "phobia". Yes,' he added, shrinking further into himself there on the ground, hugging his calves and almost burying his head in his knees, 'yes, I've been having a bad time since we got here, really bad, from too much light and because here I'm forced to be outside all the time, exposed to the sky and air. I think living without walls or a roof is monstrous. If there weren't so many mosquitoes in the jungle, I'd build myself a hut in there.'

'It's not safe,' I told him. 'It isn't safe to go inland.'

'I know,' he said. 'But it's torture for me being out in the open for days on end.'

We were both sitting on the sand. There were two seats positioned there for the lookout guards, under the shade of the trees. The long walk from the village did me good – a way of doing some exercise and practising with the crutches, which I now used with relative ease. The white wreckage of the other plane was directly ahead of us, sticking out of the sea just where the waves broke against the coral reefs.

'But didn't you have friends, family?'

'I did,' Noboru said. 'I had both, but I lost them a long time ago. I went mad. For many years I was mad. In a cult. In Aum Shinrikyo. Have you heard of Aum?'

'I think so,' I said, trying to cast my mind back to the newspaper head-lines from a few years before. 'But weren't the people who carried out the Tokyo subway sarin attack from Aum Shinrikyo?'

'Yes, exactly.'

'And you were part of that cult?'

'Yes.'

44

Santiago also finds it

round that time, Santiago had a truly bizarre experience. He'd decided to take a walk along the coast to collect eggs from the marine birds' nests we sometimes found on the beach. Who knows how he managed to trek for so long and so far from the village. I guess hunger can produce miracles. He left in the morning and came back at nightfall. He didn't find any eggs, but he did have a tale to tell.

The usual suspects were sitting around the campfire: Wade, Joseph, Rosana, Christian, Sheila, Joaquín, Xóchitl (the two of them were joined at the hip now), Sophie and Noboru, as well as some others who wanted to hear Santiago's story.

He explained that he'd set off along the coast looking for these eggs. He told us about the beaches that led on from our own. He told us about swamplands and a stretch of red rock formations that confirmed the island's volcanic origins, arches and columns of rock protruding from the sea, and sheltered coves with water so clear you could see the giant crabs on the sandy sea floor nine metres below. And beyond that... beyond that, he told us with wide eyes full of fear and wonder, there was a long sandy beach, and on the seafront a property. 'An estate,' he said.

We asked him what exactly he meant. A property surrounded by a stone wall, he said. Yes, it seemed too far-fetched to believe, but it was true. The wall was about eight feet high, with crescent-shaped alcoves cut out of it – sort of like stone benches where you could sit – every thirty feet or so.

'A stone wall in the middle of the beach?' I asked, trying to picture it.

'No, no, it wasn't *on* the beach,' Santiago explained. 'The wall was overlooking the beach, although that beach didn't back onto jungle like ours. Trees, yeah, but not the crazy-ass trees we have here, just oaks and poplars, like the ones you get in America... At first I thought the place must belong to an American who planted those trees there to remind him or her of home. But there weren't many trees on the other side of the wall. Just two. Two enormous trees.'

He had walked along the stone wall looking for an opening or a door. It seemed to surround quite a large property, but from the outside you couldn't see what was in there. I asked Santiago if he'd seen any kind of peculiar-shaped cloud in the sky, and he looked at me suspiciously, squinting his eyes.

'Yeah,' he said. 'Yeah, man, I did. The flying saucer was there overhead. I know some people still call it a cloud, but I know what a cloud is, and *that* was not a cloud. It was looking down on everything from above.'

Skirting the edge of the wall, which was covered in ivy, he had found a small, rusty metal door with no keyhole in it. And when he pushed it, he claimed, it had opened slowly, held back by all the brambles...

'Just a minute,' Wade interrupted, raising one hand. 'Ivy? Brambles? On this island?'

'Brambles, man. Yeah, I guess you're right – it was the first time I'd seen brambles on the island... Is that so crazy?'

'You don't get brambles on tropical islands,' Wade said. 'Brambles grow in cool climates.'

'What about Moses and the burning bush?' Santiago said, frowning. 'That bramble grew in the middle of the desert. You know the one I mean, right? The bush that wouldn't burn out, that just kept burning.'

'Okay, I'll give you that one,' Wade said, laughing. 'But, in any case, I've never seen bramble bushes on this island.'

Santiago carried on with his story, telling us how he'd pushed open the metal door and gone through. What he found inside was beyond belief...

'A green meadow,' he said, 'like the ones you get in American parks. You know? Or on golf courses. A field, a lawn. A big green lawn. But the strangest thing is that the grass looked as if it had been cut in the last few days. A week at most. But honestly it looked *freshly* cut.

'It wasn't hot in there,' Santiago went on, almost welling up. 'It was almost cold. There was a breeze, man, like a New Jersey fall kind of breeze. It was like I'd suddenly landed on the shores of the Hudson in October. I could almost smell the river. And it wasn't wild grass,' he repeated. 'That lawn had been mown in the last few days. It was like a park split on two levels, divided by a stone step.'

'And on the upper level there was a little house?' I asked, almost trembling.

'Yeah, man, a stone house,' Santiago said. 'Sort of medieval or something. Like really old... European or something, you know?'

'And it was abandoned and the windows were smashed,' I said. 'And it had a door in the middle and a window on each side of the door. And there was a tree on either side of the house, one dark and the other pale.'

'Exactly that,' he said, shaken up now. 'There were two trees. But the house had two floors. How do you know all this? Have you been there too?'

I asked him if he'd gone inside the house and he said he hadn't, that he'd freaked out all of a sudden.

'But why were you afraid?' I asked. 'There wasn't anyone there, was there? No threat. What were you afraid of?'

'I don't know, man. I was afraid that if I didn't get out of there right then, the door would close behind me and I wouldn't be able to leave. Know what I mean? Like an episode of *The Twilight Zone*, when you're trapped in a time zone or trapped inside a mirror... Like being trapped inside a house you can't escape from, but really that house is inside your head and you're actually in hospital...'

I asked Santiago what he was doing when he entered that place. He looked at me perplexed, and I asked him if he'd been singing.

'I was, man,' he said. 'How do you know that?'

'What were you singing?'

'"The Star-Spangled Banner", why? What difference does it make? How did you know I was singing?'

All eyes were on me. Joseph asked me if I'd been there before, if I knew about this 'estate' Santiago was talking about. I was reluctant to tell them the truth, but in the end I had no choice but to give them the whole story. I told them about my childhood Meadow. I told them, too, about the place I'd ended up when we were on the overhead highway inland. I told them I'd found a meadow there and that it was identical to the one Santiago described, apart from that it wasn't surrounded by a stone wall, but rather a hedge of cypresses.

Now everyone was giving me very funny looks. Joseph was staring at me, concerned. He knew I wasn't lying, and he knew Santiago wasn't lying either.

We planned an expedition to go back to that place and investigate further. But it proved impossible. We never found it.

45

Wade sees a ghost

Since all the remaining guns were now in the hands of Kunze and his cronies, who refused to share them, we had to fashion our own primitive weapons to hunt with: slingshots, bows and arrows, spears. One day around that time, Wade headed into the jungle to hunt with a bow and some arrows he'd made. He picked up the tracks of a large animal, maybe one of those wild boars the guerrillas had mentioned, and followed it for several kilometres.

That's how Wade ended up back in the hills with the aerial. He decided to return to those abandoned facilities to see if he could find anything that might be of use to us. The aerial and surrounding buildings were at the top of a bare, almost barren hill. When he was a couple of hundred metres away, Wade thought he saw something moving inside one of the buildings, darting from one window to another. He froze. It was probably an animal that had found its way inside. And if it was an animal, it might be edible. But what sort of beast could get inside a building and be visible through the windows? It had to be big, and the only big animals we'd seen on the island were the wolves. Wade was carrying a bow and ten arrows which, on a good day, could maybe help him kill a bird or a capuchin monkey. But they'd be all but useless against a beast as strong and big as a wolf, unless he was very, very lucky and his aim was on form. All the same, he positioned an arrow on the bow and crept slowly towards the building to try to see what was inside. Now he could see the figure clearly: it was a man, and he was carrying a double-barrel rifle.

At first he only saw the steel-blue barrel poking out of one of the windows. The man was crouching behind it, but you could make out his dark curly hair and sunglasses. He seemed petrified. He told Wade to stop right there if he didn't want to get shot. Wade froze, but kept a firm grip on his bow. The man shouted at him to drop it, and then asked Wade who he was.

'Just a fella out on a stroll,' Wade said. 'That's all. Just enjoying the fresh air.'

'One more smartass comment like that, asshole, and I'll blow your head off,' the man said from the window. 'Who the hell are you?'

Wade calmly placed his bow and arrows on the ground and told him he was one of the castaways, and that he'd come out looking for food. He assumed the man in the house was one of the Insiders, maybe even a kind of guard stationed there to watch our movements and make sure we didn't cross into the island's interior. Wade also assumed they were standing at the edge of some kind of boundary line, and that the guard would tell him to return to the coast and not come back inland. But that wasn't what happened. Instead the man asked Wade what he was called. Wade didn't have any intention of giving his name to some man hiding out aiming a shotgun at his head, so he said that didn't matter. And then the stranger said: 'You're Wade Erickson, right?' before climbing out of the building, still aiming his shotgun at Wade, passing one leg through the open window first, then the other. Wade immediately recognised the man, who was Black and had on a white shirt, cut-off jeans and a pair of filthy old trainers: it was Raymond, his half-brother.

'Raymond,' he said, quite stunned. 'What in God's name are you doing here?'

'Me? What are *you* doing here?' Raymond asked. 'Aren't you meant to be in a wheelchair?'

'You're right,' Wade said, 'I was. And it was all thanks to you.'

'Nah ah, brother, you can't put that on me. I didn't plan any of that. It was an accident. I was always wasted back in those days, and my buddies even more. We let a lot of shit get crazy, but what happened in the shop was an accident.'

'You wanted to burn the place down,' Wade spat. 'That was your master plan. And then one of your "buddies" shot me. Tell me, how is that "an accident"?'

'I know you're pissed, man,' Raymond said. 'But look, we're cool now, right, brother? Now you've got your legs back. I'm happy for you, man,' he said. 'I'm happy you can use your legs and that. We're cool, right, brother?'

'The whole situation was completely unbelievable,' Wade told us later on. 'I asked him to stop aiming at me and he put down his weapon, but he wouldn't come any closer to me. He seemed shocked.

'"Weren't you in jail?" I asked him. "Did you escape? How did a block-head like you manage to slip past the best penitentiary system in the world? What happened?"

'"Hasn't it occurred to you that I could be on probation? Hasn't it occurred to you that maybe they gave me probation for good behaviour?"

'"No," I said. "That would never occur to me. First, because I never think about you. And second, because they'd never put a lowlife like you on probation so soon."

'Raymond sat down watchfully on the ground, crossing his legs and resting the shotgun across his knees, and I sat down after him. We were about twenty-five feet apart, and neither of us, it seemed, wanted to get any closer. The thought crossed my mind that this was my moment to kill him. If I'd been close enough to launch myself at him, I could have easily snatched the gun and shot him right there and then, like a dog.

'Anyway, now that I had him in front of me, I realised my loathing wasn't so intense, and that I'd never have it in me to kill him. He was, at the end of the day, my half-brother, the son of Ogunde and my father.

'"You'd like to kill me, right?" Raymond said with a strange hint of melancholy. "I don't blame you, man. I really fucked you over. But I'm gonna tell you why you're not gonna kill me. I'm gonna tell you why you'll never lay a finger on me."

'"Why's that, Raymond?" I said, speaking softly. "What might be my reasons for not hurting you?"

'"Because I'm not your half-brother," Raymond said, shaking his head and smiling. "It's right there in front of you and you can't see it. You stupid old fool."

'"I made inquiries," I said. "I got letters from your mother. I know you're her son. Ogunde told me. For ages I thought you'd been lying to me, that you'd stolen that photo album and passed for that bastard child in the photos, and that you'd made it all up. But it turned out to be true. You're Ogunde's son."

'"Yeah, I'm Ogunde's son," Raymond said. "I'm Ogunde's son, you old fool. But you're not my half-brother. You're my father."

'This little bombshell knocked me for six,' Wade went on. 'Raymond told me he wasn't as young as he'd pretended to be. That he'd always had a baby face, but that in fact he'd just turned forty-three. He told me he'd come looking for me because he'd known for years that I was his father, that he'd found out by chance, reading one of his mom's letters, which she'd never sent and he'd found at the back of a drawer. So from Raymond I learnt that Ogunde was already pregnant when I left home. She didn't know at that time either, and once she did find out, she didn't know where the hell I was.

'The whole thing seemed too far-fetched. I told Raymond I didn't believe him, that it was all a pack of lies, and that I had no reason to trust him. But the truth is, I did believe him. Perhaps because I wanted nothing more than to believe him. I asked him what in hell's name he was doing there on that island, and if he was one of the Insiders.

'"What Insiders?" he asked. "You mean the savages?"

'"Yeah," I said. "But they're not 'savages', as you call them. They're in disguise."

'Raymond looked at me as if I'd lost my mind.

'"In disguise?" he said, and he repeated it several times.

'His eyes were crazed and he kept looking involuntarily behind him as if at any moment the so-called savages might emerge from behind the concrete buildings a little way up the hill. But he didn't want to take his eyes off me. He told me that they weren't "fake", they were a Polynesian tribe who didn't live permanently on the island, but came from an archipelago located about seventy miles south-east of there and made trips to the island at certain times of the year to practise sacred rituals.

'"To their minds," Raymond said, "this island is some kind of magical place; a land full of spirits. And they also believe that the volcano inland is the dwelling place of the gods. The ritual," he went on, "means hunting humans. They bring victims with them, let them loose on the island and then give chase. They slice them open, cook and eat them. But sometimes they come to hunt those who live here too. I still haven't quite got my head around the details," he said. "They might even leave a few victims here, members of an enemy tribe or something, and then they come a couple of times a year to hunt and eat them, as part of a ritual. They're not really cannibals. They don't eat human flesh to feed themselves. It's just a sacred act, a rite. I've seen them do it. And it's pretty disgusting, but there's also something kind of beautiful about it. Warriors come, and women too. The men do the hunting and skin the victim, and the women chop the bodies up and cook them. Those sluts go around butt naked," he went on, laughing. "They wear all kinds of shit in their hair and fangs stuck in their skin. They cut themselves to draw little tattoos, but the only clothes they wear are necklaces, earrings, bracelets, and a rope around their waist. Now why the hell would they wear a rope around their waists if their butts are left out for all to see? They're fucking savages," he went on, with a level of contempt that took even me by surprise. He told me he'd "fucked" a few and that they'd let him do whatever he wanted without putting up any resistance. He'd jump them from behind and they'd get on their knees without a word, then he'd fuck them, he told me, dump his load inside them and the women would just get up and carry on their way.

'"Fucking savages," he said again.

'And again I thought about killing the man.

'I asked if he was alone and he told me he was, that he'd ended up on his own. He said he'd landed on the island with a group of thirteen other men, and that the others had died, one by one, leaving him on his own. He began to tell me the story. The three men were on a small plane crossing the Gulf of Mexico en route to Bermuda. They were going to work, he told me, in a newly opened hotel complex. "To clean up after rich dicks," he said. The story sounded long and complicated, but I was willing to listen to it, because I just couldn't imagine how they'd ended up on our island if they'd been flying over the Gulf of Mexico.

'"We were headed to fucking Bermuda, man," Raymond explained, "and I was freaked out because I thought that if we entered the Bermuda Triangle the plane would be sucked into some other dimension and we might be captured by aliens or whatever. And pretty soon we did have technical problems. We had to do an emergency landing on a random island. The engines stopped running or some shit like that, and we had to land on a beach, in the first place we came across. And it was this island, see? We landed on this island."

'I explained to Raymond that the island where we were was thousands of miles from Bermuda. We were in the South Pacific, I told him, so his story made no sense at all.

'"I know that, man!" he shouted, looking at me with wild eyes. "We're in fucking Polynesia! Are you listening to a single word I'm telling you, man? We fell into the motherfucking Bermuda Triangle! We disappeared inside some space-time vortex."

'We both fell silent, still sitting on the grass a little distance apart from each other, me with my bow back in my hand and him with his shotgun. Neither of us were totally at ease, but we both pretended to be,' Wade told us. 'A father and son catching up on a hillside. A father and son. Raymond, my son. He was a little bit further up the slope than I was. And then something happened. A storm broke in the distance, up in the mountains. But it wasn't really a storm. It was the rays we'd seen more than once, those rays that seemed to fall like lightning bolts. Raymond jumped when he saw them. He said they were the rays that had killed most of his friends.

'"I thought you said the 'savages' had killed them?" I asked him calmly.

'"No, no, I'm not scared of that lot," Raymond said. "They killed two of my buddies with their blowpipes, but we taught them a good lesson, and now they're scared shitless of us. Know what we did?" he said, laughing. "We took two of their women, and we raped them. Then we tied them to some trees and slit them open. And we left them there, with their guts hanging out, *alive*. They squealed like pigs. After that, the savages haven't come near us."

"'Why are you telling me this, Raymond?" I asked, utterly sick to my stomach. "You're proud of what you did, are you?"

"'They're just savages," Raymond said. "They skinned one of ours. They skinned him alive! They didn't even take the trouble of killing him first. They're animals, and they got what they asked for."

'The rays were getting closer. We watched them move towards what I guessed to be the valley where we'd seen the blue giant. Rays of light, showering down to earth from above. Raymond looked terrified. He asked me if I'd seen the giant. He said it was the giant who'd finished off the rest of his friends.

"'Burnt them alive with his rays," he said.

"'What giant, Raymond?" I asked, pretending not to know what he was on about. "It's nothing but a little electrical storm."

"'Bullshit," he said. "How long have you been on this island? You must have seen the giant."

"'Calm down, Raymond," I said. "There is no giant."

'He stood up and stared into the distance, terror-stricken. Then he aimed the shotgun at me and told me not to follow him. He was backing away down the hill, aiming his gun at me to make sure I didn't follow him. When he was about five hundred feet away, he lowered the weapon, turned and ran.'

'But was it really Raymond?' Joseph asked. 'You got a good look at him, did you?'

'Are you really Joseph? Am I really Wade? Yes, it was Raymond.'

'Do you think he was telling the truth?' Christian asked. 'Do you think it's true he's not one of the Insiders?'

'I don't know what to believe,' Wade said. 'My brother Raymond is locked up in jail in Connecticut, where he'll be for some time. There's no way a cretin like him could escape jail, find his way out of the country and end up on this island. If by some miracle Raymond had escaped from jail, they would have picked him up in a matter of hours and locked him straight back up.'

'Maybe he got some kind of deal,' Joseph said. 'If he was mixed up in drugs on the outside he might have been able to cut a deal. He might have even been covered by the witness protection service.'

'You don't get it,' Wade said, staring at us with his big blue eyes wide open. 'That's not what's going on here. It was him, but it wasn't *really* him. That's what I'm trying to tell you. Everything he told me was a load of bull. My supposed paternity... No, no, no – it's just not possible. It's just what I desire, my imagination showing me what I wanted to see. It wasn't him. It can't be true.'

'You mean he was a kind of ghost?' Violeta asked.

'Yes, ma'am, something like that. That's what I think. A ghost. Some kind of ghost. I think he was a creation of the island. I think this island constructs things for us. I think this island is an intelligent being. It's probably not even an island. Isn't that what it said on that wall: "This is not an island"?'

'If it's not an island, what is it?' Joseph asked. 'I'm sorry, Wade, but I refuse to believe in ghosts and "intelligent islands". That's all well and good when you're reading poetry. But let's just apply Occam's razor here, shall we? Let's suppose Raymond isn't a ghost, but a real person. Let's suppose he really is one of the Insiders, which is the most logical assumption, because his story about the cannibals and the men burnt alive seems more like something out of a horror movie than something that would really happen. Everything he told you has one aim: to scare us. "The savages really are savages." "The savages are cannibals." "Those rays kill people." "Don't go into the island." "Stay on the coast." It's the same message we keep hearing.'

'It's not possible that what I saw was Raymond,' Wade said. 'What I saw can't be my son. What I saw was nothing less than a demon.'

Noboru proposed that what Wade had seen was, indeed, a spirit. He said the island was full of spirits, that it wasn't the first one we'd seen, and it wouldn't be the last.

46

Wade also finds it

In spite of everything, the next day Wade returned to the aerial hoping to find Raymond again. I couldn't stop thinking about what Raymond claimed to have done to those indigenous women. How long would it take a human to die in those conditions? It made me sick just thinking about it, and at the same time I couldn't stop thinking about it. If Raymond was the kind of person who did things like that and then boasted about them, who in their right mind would want to go near him? I'm not a father, but I imagine there are limits, even when it comes to blood.

Wade left at the crack of dawn and came back very late, when it was already night. The next day I saw him and asked him if he'd managed to find Raymond. 'Tonight,' he replied, and held his index finger to his lips.

Wade went the entire day without uttering a word. As the sun set he joined the circle of meditators, in which I was now also a regular. As always, Dharma conducted the session. I remember the meditation that night was centred around Nada, internal sounds. By concentrating on these sounds the mind begins to relax and it is possible to get close to the sphere of thoughtlessness, where clarity begins. They call this Nada Yoga or 'Internal Sound Yoga'.

When night fell, Wade started a small fire on the beach and one by one the regular group came together.

Then Wade opened his mouth to tell us what had happened.

He'd taken his machete, bow and arrows and rucksack, and set off towards the aerial station. He'd used five arrows trying to hunt the various birds who crossed his path on the way; two white, one black, another brown and finally a golden bird with a long heavy tail like a pheasant's. Perhaps because this last one was bigger and flew more slowly, he was able to hit it in the chest, but the bird didn't fall; it just carried on flying eastwards, disappearing into the trees with Wade's arrow in its chest. Wade had followed that bird, convinced it would come falling to earth any minute. No bird can fly with an arrow stuck in its thorax, piercing one of its lungs. He tore his way along the jungle floor, slashing through the undergrowth with swift swipes of his machete. But he soon lost sight of the bird, which was flying slowly under the forest canopy. Wade carried on in the same direction for a couple of kilometres, hoping that, sooner or later, the bird would fall. He didn't find it and guessed the bird had escaped for good, or perhaps even reached its nest, a refuge to die in peace. So Wade gave up his search and retraced his steps, heading south-east now, back in the direction of his original target: the hill with the aerial.

It didn't take him long to get there. The ground was pretty clear and his line of vision grew wider. Despite this, though, he couldn't find the aerial anywhere, and since it had always been Wade's point of reference around those parts, he felt disoriented and struggled to make out the hills in the dim light. He'd lost his bearings. Although he was a highly experienced hunter who'd spent many days now in that part of the island, Wade was lost. He began going up and down a set of low hills which reminded him of the so-called Knobs from his native Indiana, heading westward and retracing his steps in the hope that the aerial would appear. But instead, he eventually came across something else. High up in the sky, the flying saucer had appeared. The round shape hovered some eight hundred metres above, shining high in the sky as it moved slowly towards him.

'Okay, okay, stop right there,' Joseph spurted out. 'I think we're all in agreement that there was no flying saucer.'

'That's what I saw, doc!' Wade replied with a big grin on his face.

'Guys, I saw it too,' Santiago said. 'We've all seen it.'

When Wade saw that white apparition in the middle of the morning sky, he felt an inexplicable yet overwhelming happiness. But why happiness? He'd just lost a catch, then a trail, and now he'd lost his way among the hills – something that had never happened to him before on familiar terrain. A triple humiliation for a veteran hunter. And now that white thing had appeared in the sky and he was as happy as a schoolboy.

'I felt happy,' he told us. 'I sat down on the grass to rest for a while, and chewed on the little bit of smoked fish I had with me. The situation, stupid and embarrassing as it was, amused me. How could I have got lost? The only possible explanation was the flying saucer, which had appeared in the air and now seemed to be circling above my head. Clouds, doc,' he said, looking at Joseph with his big expressive eyes, 'don't spin around. I'm quite sure there are some funny-shaped clouds, but I draw the line at clouds spinning in circles. I thought about standing up on the hillside and making signs to whoever was up there – you know, like "Hey, folks, I'm here! Geez, what took you so long!" But why bother, if they already knew I was there? Whoever was inside the saucer knew I was there, that seemed pretty obvious to me. But if they knew my whereabouts, everyone's where-abouts, then why didn't they help us? What was the point in just watching us from above without intervening? Now that I had that thing right above my head, I could see it clearer than ever. It wasn't exactly a saucer, not like the ones you get in sci-fi magazines. Or maybe it was that it kept changing shape. By this point it looked more like a white rose, with petal-like shapes coming off the main body. They were made of some intensely white mater-ial – it didn't look like metal, more like porcelain.

'The saucer hovered off towards the west, and I put the rest of my measly lunch in my rucksack and headed in that direction, to the top of the hill. On the other side I spotted a valley with a wide, curving river running through it. Now I really was confused. What was that river doing there? It wasn't our river, of course, because our river runs miles west into the valley that reaches the mountains in the middle of the island; the valley where we saw the blue giant. So where had that river come from? It crossed my mind that we'd got it wrong and that the river we'd found in the mid-dle of the island wasn't our river, but another one, and that this one be-neath me was actually our river. Another possibility was that the river in front of me flowed into another one. But then it didn't make sense that it was so wide, given that if two rivers with such a large volume of water were to converge, the mouth of that river would be far, far wider than ours was. The two volumes of water add up, they don't cancel each other out.

'In the middle of the river there was a long strip of forested island, and on the island I saw a square shape, like a construction, a wall, maybe some ruins, I don't know. I couldn't make out that square too well, but it reminded me of a nineteenth-century painting I'd seen as a boy in school: a picture of the city of New Harmony, a model community founded on the Wabash River by a philanthropist called Robert Owen. Jesus, how many years had it been since I'd thought about all that – that anomalous episode in the history of the proud state of Indiana? As a boy I'd often imagined coming across New Harmony in the middle of the forest, crossing the city walls and finding myself in an ideal country where no one wore shoes, and everyone walked around with a smile on their face. I headed down to the shoreline and noted how the flora and fauna changed. Then I realised that the temperature had plummeted and the valley was very cool. There was a fresh breeze, like the one you get at the end of winter in Indiana, just as you feel spring setting in. That coolness felt like the most magical, the most unreal thing of all. I thought about naming that place the Cold Valley, and it occurred to me that if it was true that, for whatever reason, the temperature there was much more clement than on the rest of the island, then we might think about moving our camp there.

'I soon reached the banks of the river. The flying saucer was now very high up, and the clouds had shifted south-east, casting vast shadows over the valley. The saucer was above the clouds and shone so brightly that it looked like a bright dot, gleaming with an intense metallic sheen. I walked along the banks of the river where the vegetation wasn't so thick. Instead I found myself among large expanses of grass with trees and shrubs I'd never seen before on the island: oaks, sycamores, chestnuts, dogwood and junipers – plants suited to cooler climes. The air was fresh and it was less humid, and I recalled with nostalgia the mental clarity and alertness that cold, dry air affords.

'The river island was right in front of me, its trees swaying in the wind. I was curious to work out what that square I'd seen from up on the hill was. If they were buildings, or the ruins of buildings, they might serve us well as shelters. I was quaking with the sense I was discovering something. I felt like at last the island was opening its door to us, that it had tortured us enough and that now it had let us reach the Cold Valley where nature seemed gentler; better adapted to human life.

'I dived into the water to swim to the island, and was stunned by how cold it was; far colder than the rivers we'd been in so far. The current was strong and dragged me downstream and I struggled to make it across. I should have gone further upstream to take advantage of the current. Anyway, in the end I reached the sandy beach and realised that I was on an island within an island, which was strangely pleasing. What a feeling! There's always something special about reaching an island, it changes something inside you. I set off walking among the trees, and soon arrived at the construction I'd seen from the hills: a stone wall ten feet high with semicircular alcoves every thirty feet or so, exactly the same as the one Santiago had described. The silence was glorious; by which I mean that I couldn't hear the voices you hear when you're alone in the island forest. When I go hunting here, I tend to wrap a handkerchief around my head, covering my ears so I don't have to listen to those damn voices. They say the worst things; things I don't want to hear. I guess you all know what I'm talking about. But there, on the island within an island, the silence was complete. I could barely pick up the muffled hum of the insects and birdsong. Every now and then I purposefully stopped, expecting to hear the whispers return after a minute, but nothing. There were no voices or whispers on that river island.

'I skirted the wall looking for a way in. It was real long, maybe two hundred yards lengthwise. I got to one corner without having found a door or gate or any little gap, turned right and carried on about a hundred yards more before turning another corner and telling myself it was very strange to build a wall around such a large plot without a door. Finally, though, I did find a doorway. In the past it must have had a metal double-leaf door, but now the entrance was open. And it was bang in the middle of the north wall, that is, precisely the spot I'd set off from. Bad luck, I guess.

'On the inside of the wall I found a huge rectangular grassy enclosure, although this time it wasn't cut grass. But the strange thing was, despite the fact that it was quite long, it was just grass. Anywhere else on the island, all the parasitic plants would have invaded the place, but this huge rectangle was pretty clear. And it really was a big lawn, split on two levels by a stone step. I'd entered via the bottom level. And you know the rest: two sets of steps on either side of the central step to get up to the top, which was roughly five feet higher. And on that top level there was a small stone house, and a tree on either side of it. I don't remember what kind of trees they were, but one was dark and the other paler, exactly the same as the places John and Santiago described. The stone house was basically in ruins, its roof had fallen in and the windows were boarded up, although the stone walls were still standing. It had three storeys. Of that I'm sure. I know the house John saw was much smaller, with just one window either side of the front door. And the one Santiago saw had two storeys. Which means there are at least three meadows on this island, each one with the same design but different proportions: the one John saw, the one Santiago saw and the one I saw.

'I looked up. The flying saucer was still hovering above me, really high now, shining like a small sun. By then, I had more or less reached the middle of the lower meadow. The whole place was lovely: I hadn't felt so at ease for a long time. The feeling of being in a man-made, civilised place, even if there was no one there and the place had been abandoned for years. The feeling of the grass, of the wall protecting it from the outside, the sensation of being in a garden more than a jungle, even if it was completely neglected – the whole thing was delicious. And on top of it, the cold! The marvellous cold. The cool chill in the air. My God, I wanted to cry. The grass was swaying in the breeze.

'The Meadow. I know that's what John called it. I, too, had arrived at the Meadow. I stood totally still, fully aware that I was experiencing something sacred. I knew that Meadow didn't *exist* in the same way other places on the island, or in the world in general, exist. I knew that place wasn't easy to get to, and that the experience of being there was a gift. A kind of miracle. I knew the island was opening its doors to me, in the same way it had opened for John and Santiago, and I wanted the island to know that I was aware of the gift I was receiving. I said out loud: "Thank you." And then: "I'm Wade Erickson, from Hammerstown, Indiana."'

'Who were you talking to, dude?' Santiago asked, looking at Wade with a glum look on his face. 'I didn't say shit, man. I stood there quiet as a mouse.'

'Wade was talking to the island,' Joseph said, with frosty sarcasm.

'I don't know who I was talking to,' Wade said. 'But basic manners tells you that the first thing you do when you enter someone else's home is say hello and introduce yourself. Even if you don't know who lives there.

'I didn't know what to do. The first thing I thought of was to look around, to get a better idea of where I was. I was completely exposed, in the middle of a large patch of open land, in some unknown place deep inside the island, but despite this, I wasn't afraid. I had the feeling I'd been saved, and that neither the Insiders, the guerrillas, nor the islanders – and least of all Raymond with his gun and crazed glare – could reach me there, not even if they tried. I looked all around me. The stone walls, the step in the middle made of old stone that was green from lichen and humidity.

'And there was one more thing,' Wade continued. 'A stone statue of a bird perched at the top of a column. It was on my left, about a hundred feet away from where I was standing. I was surprised not to have noticed it from the start, because it was pretty big. The wide column was about ten feet tall, and it sat on a square plinth, about three feet tall. The statue seemed to be of a roosting falcon on the top of a branch, watching the world. Its eyes were unseeing – as tends to be the case with statues – but even so, the image of that bird was unsettling, terrifying even, and from it seemed to emanate an infinite capacity for evil. I didn't even want to get any closer.

'There was nothing to suggest why it might be there. I thought a statue observing the world from the heights of its imaginary tree should be paired alongside another statue representing peace and harmony, but there wasn't another one. In this, too, then, my Meadow, I mean, the Meadow I found, was slightly different from John's and Santiago's.

'What could I do in that place? I decided to go up onto the top level and enter the stone house, so I carried on towards the middle of the Meadow. I'd been edging towards the left to use the stairs on that side, but then I noticed that in the middle of the Meadow, at the foot of the stone step, there was a trap door in the ground. I walked towards it. It was a square hole covered by a rusty metal hatch that opened with a handle. In fact, it opened easily. The hatch led down into a square well, on one side of which there was a row of metal handgrips that formed a ladder.

'I tied my bow to my rucksack so it didn't get caught on the handles, tested the first two steps to make sure they were secure, and, without another thought, began to climb down.

'The well was deep. I never would have thought it could be so deep. I went down and down, but there was always one more step, never solid ground. The square of sky above my head was growing smaller. And then, suddenly, it disappeared altogether. It simply vanished, as if someone had shut the metal door from above.

'I was terrified. But what other explanation could there be? The metal hatch was pretty heavy and there was no way the wind could have blown it shut. Nor could night have fallen just like that. And there wasn't an animal big enough to block it by sitting or lying over it. Someone must have closed it. Or perhaps the clouds had covered that chink of blue sky, which might explain the mystery.

'My arms and fingers were stiff by the time I reached the bottom of the well. I flicked open the lighter I always carry. And there in front of me I saw a tunnel, three feet wide by eight feet tall. This small tunnel was barely thirty feet long, but it opened out into another one that was much taller and wider and stretched out in both directions. It was a spacious, well-built passageway; the floor dipped slightly in the middle and there were sump wells to collect the water. It must have been thirteen feet wide and ten feet tall, and running along the wall there were metal tubes with electric cables inside. Along the ceiling ran a row of lamps about sixty-five feet apart. It felt like a military edifice: solid and designed to last. Right there, on the wall, there was an old-fashioned knife switch; the kind with a wooden handle that you yank up and down. I don't think they've used switches like that since the fifties. It looked like something out of Dr Frankenstein's lab, in the old Hammer movie. I pushed it up without a moment's hesitation, more than anything to know what it feels like to use one of those things, because I didn't think for a second that it would work. Which is why I nearly jumped out of my skin when it cranked all the lights on.'

'Jesus, Wade,' Joseph said. 'You're telling us there are underground tunnels on this island? There's electricity on this island? What are you talking about?'

'I flicked shut my lighter,' Wade continued, 'and took a moment to just look around. It wasn't flooded with light, by any means. There weren't that many bulbs working, and they were really only bright enough for me to see where I was going without falling over. But the truly miraculous thing about that place was that it had electricity. I didn't expect the miracle to last long. I guessed that there was some electricity left in the old storage batteries, and that it'd run out in a matter of minutes. And that's why I decided to carry on along the tunnel. When the light went out, I'd just go back the way I'd come, feeling my way along the wall until I found the side tunnel which would lead me to the well. So I walked, and I walked, and I walked. I calculated that I must have crossed under the river some time ago, and I carried on walking in an easterly direction. I hadn't really kept my eye on which direction I was heading, but now it was too late to go back. It would have made more sense to head west; that is, in the direction of our camp, but we don't always think as quickly on our feet as we should. And anyway, I felt almost drunk with everything that had happened up until then. So I walked and walked, and every sixty-five feet a bulb hung from the ceiling, and it didn't seem to be getting any darker. Like I say, some of the bulbs were burnt out, and others flickered as if they were just about to. But most were working. I would have liked to unscrew one of the burnt-out ones to see if those bulbs could tell me anything else about that place and the people who'd built it, but the ceiling was too high and there was nothing to climb up on.

'I carried on walking until I came upon a wooden door to my right. It had a brass handle, and painted on it was the sign we'd seen before: a lion playing chess with a goat, and the initials "SIAR". I pressed my ear up against the door, but you couldn't hear anything on the other side. Then I pulled the handle and pushed the door as slowly as I could. It opened, more or less silently, onto a small chamber that looked like a control centre, or something like that. It was about thirteen feet by twenty and it was lit by a couple of lamps hanging from the ceiling, giving off a yellow, pasty light. The whole back wall was taken up with equipment covered in dials and metallic furniture holding piles of paper, files and also TV screens, some of them working. On an adjacent metal table there was more equipment, and more papers, and also two library-style green glass desk lamps. There was a chair at the table, facing away from me; one of those office chairs on casters with a tall back and leather arms. And someone was sitting in it. I could only see his arms on either side and his legs, dressed in khaki green pants, crossed at the ankle under the table. He must have been hunched over, because I couldn't see his head. I froze. The whole scene was totally surreal. The person sitting at the table must have heard me come in. Why hadn't he turned around to see who I was? I stood there, frozen to the spot, waiting. I also thought about tiptoeing back out before being discovered, and going back the way I'd come. At the same time, though, the whole thing was absurd. Why not talk to that man, whoever he was? Why not explain I was a castaway, that we'd had a plane crash and that we desperately needed a way to contact the outside world? That would've been the most logical thing, sure, but we know that kind of logic doesn't get you very far here.

'I didn't know what to do. The man in the chair seemed engrossed in something on his desk. I could hear little noises, small, sporadic clicks. The man's arms, which were the only part of him I could see clearly, moved slightly, as if he was doing something with his hands. I decided to go up to him, trusting that just maybe, on this occasion, instead of receiving shots or threats, I might have found someone willing to help us. But then my eyes fixed on the television screens covering the wall in front of me. On one of them, a group of women were washing clothes on the banks of a river. I realised I was watching several of the Indian women from our group, then Nicollette Sheridan, Matilde, Idoya and Rosana. On another screen you could see a cluster of huts from the village, but there was nobody in sight. On yet another, a few of the Chileans were sitting on the sand and playing that weird game of theirs, the one about the Second World War. On another you could see the women's bathing area. There were two or three women in the water, one of them standing with the water up to her waist, naked. On another, you could see inside one of the huts, where two bodies were stretched out on a palm leaf bed. I think they were two men, but I couldn't make them out properly. On another screen you could see a stretch of beach, the palm trees swaying gently in the breeze.

'All those cameras were watching *us*.

'So they didn't only know of our presence there, but they were watching us too. Observing us the whole time. They knew everything we did, 24/7. I don't know if they were able to hear our conversations, but if they'd managed to fit cameras that close, surely they must have been able to. Who knows, they might even have had lip-reading experts.

'All this seemed so far-fetched, so unbelievable, I thought I must be losing my mind. I felt dizzy. It was all too much. But now that I knew I was in danger, I grabbed my bow from behind my back, loaded an arrow and aimed.

'The man sitting at the table began to speak in a slow, detached voice; a voice as heavy as a rock.

'"Abe? Is that you?"

'I froze.

'"Abe?" the man repeated. "Lewellyn?"

'Faced with my silence, the man began to swivel his chair. First I saw his right hand: very pale and covered in a fine auburn down. Then I saw his face. The aquiline profile. The sharp, shining nose. It wasn't exactly a human face. It seemed to have been pieced together from an assortment of ill-fitting parts. His right eye was missing an eyelid and you could see the entire eyeball turning in its socket, the red muscles moving it from side to side. A piece of his jawbone was also exposed, again on the right-hand side, as if he were simply missing the corresponding bit of skin that should cover it. The rest of his face seemed to be made of patches of worn leather. His forehead was poorly cobbled together in four pieces. He looked like an old man. He had blond, almost white, thin hair on top of his head. But this couldn't be a man: I was certain he was no human being. This was a robot. A machine.

'"No, you are not Lewellyn," he said on seeing me.

'"Another word and I'll kill you," I said, still aiming at him.

'"You cannot kill one who is not alive," he said.

'He spoke slowly, and with apparent difficulty, pronouncing his s's with a horrible lisp, straining to pronounce his t's as the air escaped out of his exposed jawbone.

'"I can sure as hell leave you blind," I said. "I can do a lot of things you wouldn't like, I assure you. Turn around, let me see your hands."

'The man spun around fully in his swivel chair, shuffling his feet slowly. His long gnarled hands were resting on the armrests. He was thin, and seemed almost sunken in his seat as if he'd been there so long his body had begun to melt into the leather. He was wearing a white shirt missing its buttons on the cuffs and some khaki pants which were creased and worn at the knees. His body looked almost human, with wrinkles on his neck and veins on his hands, and hair on his calves and chest.

'"What do you want?" the robot asked.

'"I want to know what's going on," I said. "I want to know what goes on in this place, who you are, why you're watching us. I want to know what the fuck all this is!"

'"You want to *know*," the man said. "There is nothing to know."

'"Who are you all?" I asked. "What are you doing here?"

'He didn't answer, as if my question hadn't made sense to him. It was as if I hadn't spoken at all.

'"Are you alone down here?" I asked.

'"Yes."

"'Since when?"

"'Since 1972."

"'And what do you do down here?"

"'I keep watch."

"'On what? On us?"

'The artificial man didn't dignify my question with an answer. He seemed completely exhausted, and I soon began to share his fatigue. He didn't take his eyes off me – those grotesque eyes, that missing eyelid – but he seemed neither frightened nor curious. He just looked tired.

"'But why?" I asked. "Why are you watching us?"

"'Prevention. Vigilance is prevention."

"'We're castaways," I said. "There's nothing to see. Our plane crashed. None of us is here out of choice."

"'Actually, there is no such thing as an accident," was his reply.

'It suddenly dawned on me that I really was talking to a machine, that there wasn't real intelligence in the answers being given to me, that this creature merely mechanically regurgitated the phrases in his repertoire.

'I also realised that this bizarre machine was incapable of lying, and that it would answer all my questions candidly.

"'Don't you eat?" I asked. "You've been here forty years without eating?"

"'Yes, I eat," he said. "I leave once a week to eat."

"'What do you live on?"

"'Meat."

"'Animal meat?"

"'No," the man said.

"'Well, what kind of meat?"

"'Flesh. Flesh from animals like you."

"'And that's why you're watching us?" I asked. "Because you need us? To feed yourselves? We're here for you? We're fodder?"

'Then something truly horrible happened. Without a doubt the most terrifying thing I've ever experienced. The artificial man smiled at me.

'And that's it,' Wade said. 'After that, I remember nothing. I don't know what happened. I didn't feel a thing. My memory falls apart in that very moment, in the face of that horrendous smile – that eye with no eyelid and mouth with no lips.

'I woke up inside the main building of the aerial tower, I guess about four or five hours later. I was totally out of it, and my mouth was so numb I couldn't speak. They must have injected me with some drug. I was so dizzy it took me an hour before I could get my balance and walk again. By the time I was able to, it was already late afternoon. I got to the camp after dark.'

And that was Wade's story.

After hearing it, we spent several days searching keenly for video cameras hidden in the trees and huts, in particular the areas that corresponded to what Wade had seen on the monitors. We didn't find a thing. We also made a few trips to look for Wade's Cold Valley, where dogwood, chestnuts and oaks grew. Just as we anticipated, we didn't find it.

47

Kunze imposes his law

So now *we move on* to one of the most maddening and absurd epi-sodes of the whole story: the tale of Kunze's *coup d'état*. It happened while we were away from the village. Kunze had been left in charge of security and defence and was therefore in possession of all the weapons. The second he'd found himself in such an advantageous position, he'd jumped on the chance to exercise his power, to degrees none of us could have imagined.

The first thing he did was to create a 'Council' comprising himself, his wife and Bishop Tudelli. This triumvirate had clearly defined roles. Kunze was the supreme ruler, in charge of security and public order; Brigitta, his wife, was in charge of all the organisation, administration and contracts; and Tudelli was in charge of communal living, spiritual health and 'dia-logue with other religions'.

The second thing this Council did was to create a police force. For their sheriff they nominated Jung Fei Ye, ex-prison official within Singa-pore's penitentiary system, martial arts expert and retired police officer. The officials under his charge were Jimmy Bruëll, who doubled up as Kunze's bodyguard, and another man called Mr Kim. Now those three went around armed, Jimmy with a hunting rifle, Jung Fei Ye with a hand-gun and Mr Kim with a revolver. Kunze didn't let anyone touch his rifle, which he kept in his hut. This was, then, the distribution of weapons within our humble society. Kunze organised regular hunting drives, over the course of which they used the long guns. But they wouldn't lend them to anyone else, despite the fact that there were good hunters among the rest of us, like Wade and Joseph. Kunze declared that under no circumstances could a soldier lose his gun. As Wade and Joseph had practically gifted four perfectly good guns to the enemy, they had lost the right to bear arms.

The third thing Kunze did was establish a currency. He drafted some contracts in which he organised loans, to be paid back when we got off the island. He then prepared employment contracts, one for those who were salaried and had a fixed weekly wage; and another for those who were paid by the hour. There was soon a list of people on Kunze's payroll who were prepared do anything to protect their status. Kunze paid his salaried employees between one and two thousand tax-free US dollars a week. Not inconsiderable sums.

The fourth thing Kunze did was draft a constitution, which soon became known as the 'Kunze Constitution', although in actual fact it had been put together by the three members of the Council and the sheriff, with legal advice from Billy Higgins, the LA lawyer who'd lost his arm in the wolf attack. And it had Jung Fei Ye written all over it. Tudelli too, who had filled the Kunze Constitution with all kinds of holier-than-thou, sanctimonious concerns. Billy Higgins, who was the only one among them with a legal background, was named Justice. In fact, there was an actual judge among us: Dr Masoud, a seemingly respectable man who had been a judge in Delhi and Lucknow, his city of birth, and who was now retired. At first Kunze offered Billy Higgins the post of prosecutor and Dr Masoud that of judge, but when the latter saw the contents of the Kunze Constitution, Dr Masoud declared the whole thing a load of bull; bull he had no intention of being a part of. He told Kunze that what our small community needed was a Justice of the Peace who would settle conflicts peacefully and count on the backing of the majority of the castaways. He said he would be willing to put himself forward as a candidate for the role and to take it up if elected. But Kunze refused, and Dr Masoud had no further dealings with him or his so-called Council.

Kunze ordered his Constitution to be engraved on a series of wooden boards that were then hung, ceremoniously, in the middle of the village for all to see. It read like this:

We, the sovereign people of the Isle of Voices, establish the following laws to govern us in the absence of another legal body, invoking the help of Our Lord to enlighten our decisions and deliver us justice.

Punishable by law:

Murder and manslaughter. *Death penalty.*

Rape or sexual assault. *Death penalty, or 24 lashes and permanent banishment.*

Cannibalism. *12 to 24 lashes and permanent banishment.*

Abduction or sexual abuse of minors. *Death penalty, or 24 lashes and permanent exile.*

Drug dealing. *24 lashes and 3 months in exile.*

Drug abuse. *10 to 16 lashes and 1 month in exile.*

Stealing food. *3 to 12 lashes and 1 to 2 weeks' imprisonment without food (water only).*

Hiding food. *3 to 12 lashes and 1 to 2 weeks' imprisonment without food.*

Aiding an exile by giving him or her food. *10 lashes.*

Convening with an exile. *6 lashes.*

Causing public scandal. *3 to 10 lashes, 1 week's imprisonment and Rehabilitation Course in Moral Values under Mr Tudelli.*

Adultery. *10 lashes, 1 week's imprisonment and Rehabilitation Course in Moral Values.*

Abortion. *12 to 18 lashes and permanent banishment.*

Assisting abortion. *12 to 18 lashes and permanent banishment.*

Divorce. *Rehabilitation Course in Moral Values.*

Euthanasia. *Death penalty, or 16 to 24 lashes and permanent banishment.*

Pornography. *3 to 16 lashes, 3 days' to 2 weeks' imprisonment and Rehabilitation Course in Moral Values.*

Prostitution. *6 to 12 lashes and 2 weeks' imprisonment.*

Undignified behaviour. *3 to 16 lashes, 1 to 2 weeks' imprisonment and Rehabilitation Course in Moral Values.* [This 'Undignified behaviour' related mainly to sexual activities 'out of wedlock' and 'not intended for procreation', for example, masturbation, sodomy, oral sex, transvestism, 'obscene' dress, behaviour or 'attitude', dressing in the clothes of the opposite sex, etc.]

Public nudity except in designated bathing areas and always respecting the separation of sexes. *3 lashes and latrine cleaning duty.*

Making obscene gestures or blaspheming. *1 to 3 days' imprisonment.*

Tarnishing a good person's name. *2 to 7 days' imprisonment without food.*

Vandalism. Destruction of public or private property. *1 to 3 days' imprisonment and community service.*

Failure to comply with the dress code (to be covered from mid-thigh to shoulders except for designated bathing areas on the beach). *1 to 3 days' imprisonment and latrine cleaning duty.*

Making noise from 10 p.m. onwards. *Latrine cleaning duty and community service.*

Littering. *Latrine cleaning duty and community service.*

Resisting the authorities. Rebellion. Insurrection. *10 to 20 lashes for all participants in the insurrection, and 24 lashes and banishment for the ringleader.*

So you see, the Kunze Constitution didn't only punish theft, rape and murder; it also viciously persecuted 'public scandal' and offences against 'modesty' and 'morals'. It required us to be properly dressed at all times. It forbade us from being undressed in public unless we were in the designated bathing areas, separated by sex. It prohibited us from swimming naked or topless in the sea. The Constitution included the most ridiculous rules and prohibitions: no pornography, for example (where the hell were we going to find porn on the island?); no fornicating in public or drug trafficking; no littering, which seemed to hanker after the good old days when life was civilised. Other rules were frankly laughable: the idea that

we'd make no noise after 10 p.m., or that there would be completely separated bathing areas for a group of castaways.

All the sentences applied to both men and women, and the number
of lashes was the same in both cases, although for crimes regarding
'causing public scandal' and 'undignified behaviour' – terms vague
enough so as to embrace almost anything the authorities didn't like –
and 'adultery', the punishments were notoriously harsher for women
than for men. In fact, according to the Kunze Constitution, 'adultery'
could only be committed by a woman. The husband was accused of a
simple slip of 'infidelity', which wasn't a serious offence to warrant corporal punishment.

The lashings took place in public and attendance was obligatory for
everyone over the age of fourteen. They had erected the gallows in the
middle of the village, which were really just a simple X shape formed by
two young palm trunks tied together at the middle. Their main purpose
was to dissuade people from antisocial or criminal behaviour. I was incensed and horrified by the sight of that X there in the middle of the village. I had a good mind to tear that sinister gallows down, but my friends
warned me not to ask for trouble.

Kunze had also ordered two cells to be fashioned in separate caves
along the beach. Both caves were narrow and partially submerged in water
when the tide came in. One of them was ten metres deep and had a small
chamber you could stand up in. The other was smaller, about five metres
deep, and you couldn't stand up inside it anywhere. This one was considered the 'punishment cell' and was reserved for the most severe sentences.
When the tide came in, the water came up above the ankles, so whoever
was inside couldn't sit down or sleep. Doors made out of planks were built
and fastened to the rocks by chains attached with padlocks at the mouth
of each of the caves. Being locked up in there was a genuine torture, and
the poor souls who were forced to spend more than three days inside
would come out in a miserable state, stumbling about. They were forced to
do their business inside the foul-smelling cave, and were fed with leftover
scraps, fish bones, fruit peel and rinds.

Tudelli now celebrated Mass every day, and in his homilies he preached about human dignity and universal values. Wade and Joseph called a meeting with him to ask him to withdraw his support of Kunze and help them to put an end to the abuses. But Tudelli didn't see things the way Joseph and Wade did, and to him there was nothing abusive about Kunze's laws.

'The punishments are a little on the harsh side, it's true,' Tudelli said, placid as ever with his smarmy gestures and bird-like voice. 'But Mr Kunze is right when he says that we find ourselves in exceptional circumstances. The role of the Church is clear in this case: it consists, as always, in defending human dignity and universal human values. Values like private property, dignity, the integrity of the family... Nobody can contest such values. And if they do, anyone who wants to leave can do so. We're not holding anyone prisoner here!' he added with a smile, and flashing his gold teeth.

'But corporal punishments, Monsignor,' Joseph said. 'Public lashings. It's barbaric. And I suppose then you'll send them along to me to tend to their wounds?'

'We must listen to everyone,' Tudelli said. 'There are representatives here of countries that ascribe great value to corporal punishment. Sovereign countries, fully signed-up members of the United Nations.'

I saw the Kunze Constitution in action the very day I left hospital and was able to take my first steps. I was still clumsy on my crutches and struggled to get one foot in front of the other without falling over, but the exercise did me good. I was with my Spanish friends, Ignacio, Idoya, Julián and Matilde, who seemed to have taken it upon themselves to look after me. They treated me as if I were a little bird with a fractured wing. We went down to the beach, and they showed me one of the cave cells. Inside was one of the castaways, who'd been caught stealing food. Apparently they'd discovered that the man had a small store hidden in the jungle where he kept all the things he'd stolen. They'd sentenced him to a week in the cell, feeding him nothing but water and a handful of fish bones a day. The bones provided a source of calcium and protein. The only problem was eating them: you had to chew them down to a fine paste in order to stop them getting stuck in your throat. There this man was, trapped like an animal in a zoo. I asked him how he was doing, but my friends told me it was forbidden to talk to the 'convicts'. I said that no one could hope to have a functioning jail without a lock, and that it looked to me like those wooden boards wouldn't withstand more than a couple of kicks. But everyone was so afraid that they'd never dare attempt an escape.

We went to speak to the man's wife. She was upset, but not with Kunze. She told us her husband was a pig, and that they'd done the right thing locking him up. Apparently, she didn't know anything about his small food store in the jungle. It seemed the man had kept it all for himself. As is often the case among couples, especially those who've been living together for a long time, she was possessed by a thirst for revenge.

The whole thing seemed so outrageous to me I went to speak with Kunze myself.

He received me incredibly warmly in his hut, which had been extended to include some extra rooms and verandas. It had begun to look like a small mansion; a palace even. Brigitta Kunze poured me a glass of rosé wine then disappeared, leaving the two of us alone. I told him I didn't like his Constitution one bit, that he had no authority to impose such laws, nor the power to impose them, and that he must release that poor soul locked up in the cave at once. I told him the water entered the cell when the tide was in, and that he'd end up with strep throat or pneumonia. I said it was degrading to keep a human locked up and make him chew on fish bones all day just to keep from starving to death.

'My dear John,' Kunze said. 'You're a good man. You're an idealist. But you don't know human nature like I do.'

'I'm not talking about human nature,' I said. 'I'm talking about something far more essential. I'm talking about you not having the authority to do what you're doing. You don't have any right to impose laws on us. You're nobody. You're no different from the rest of us.'

'That's where you're wrong, John,' Kunze said. 'You say I don't have the "power". I have three "powers". I have all the guns. I have money. And I have another, which is even more important. I have God. My conscience is clean, because I know that what I'm doing is right. You think I'm shameless, but that's not the issue here. The issue is that you, sir, are a hypocrite, like all liberals. And like all liberals, you like to believe lies simply because they're pretty lies, or because to you they seem pretty.

'That man is locked up in there because of something he did. Because of something *he* did, not me. I didn't lock him up. He locked himself up. He was tried and found guilty. He was stealing food, taking food out of the mouths of children, of the sick and elderly. Does that seem like nothing to you? You don't think that merits punishment? His own wife agrees with his sentence. Do you know she spat on him in public? His own wife!

'Hold on,' he said, raising his hand when I went to speak. 'I already know what you're going to say. I know exactly what your arguments will be. I've heard them a million times. We're in an extreme situation. Think about it, John. Think about the fact that there are ninety of us, all forced to live indefinitely on an island with no food. Think about the fact that we're surrounded by a bunch of criminals who seem prepared to do anything – be it torture or mutilation – to keep us in line. We can't fight them because we're not organised, we don't know the terrain and we're not armed. And the situation is only going to get worse. We have to prevent problems before they present themselves. What's going to happen once we've eaten all the food from the plane, all those cans of food we've been feeding ourselves with up to now? We're exhausting all the natural resources of vegetables, and the fish are becoming more and more scarce. And there are ninety mouths to feed every single day.

'The Kunze Constitution might seem punitive. It may well *be* punitive. But I'm not going to allow our community to fall into disarray for your utopian, socialist ideals and belief in man's innate goodness. We have to defend civilisation and ensure the weak are protected. And civilisation is only possible when there are laws. And the law can only be imposed by means of one thing. Do you know what that is, John?'

'I'm guessing reason,' I said.

'No, John, reason doesn't have anything to do with it. The law can only be imposed by means of fear.

'If we begin going around naked and painting our faces different colours and having orgies, we'll end up as cannibals. Haven't you worked out that there are already women here sleeping with men for food? It's happening as we speak. They sell their bodies in exchange for a piece of smoked fish and some condensed milk. One of them is even married.'

'And how do you know?'

'I know,' Kunze said. 'Imagine if the husband found out. I've had words with her, but she denies it. She even made a pass at me. A stunning girl, by the way. We're all on tenterhooks. If the husband catches on to what his wife gets up to, he may well kill her. I wouldn't blame him if he did. He'd be charged with murder, that's a given, even in such extenuating circumstances. And the woman's body? Well, we'd dig another grave – what's one more among so many? – and we'd bury her. We're not that hungry yet. But what about in a month's time? Might it not occur to some of those among us that the most rational thing to do would be to eat her? Isn't that what those plane crash survivors in the Andes did – eat the dead?'

I was feeling woozy from the wine. I was weak and my stomach was empty, and after just a couple of sips I'd felt the sluggish effect of the alcohol. And now my head was completely foggy, and I couldn't even remember what I'd come to talk to Kunze about or what I'd hoped to get out of that meeting.

'And what about corporal punishment?' I asked. 'Is that civilised?'

'We have to respect other views,' he sneered. 'The Constitution we've established is based on the laws of nature, on universal human rights, the right to life, to physical and moral integrity, the right to private property… but the manner in which these universal laws are applied varies from culture to culture.'

The rosé had rendered me tongue-tied now. I couldn't reply or talk back at all.

'In many places,' Kunze went on, 'they tie you to the gallows and strike you with a rattan cane.' He smirked and blushed as he giggled to himself at this. 'Lashes, John. Cheap, easy and effective. Get caned, and you won't reoffend.'

Kunze showed us his three rattan canes one afternoon, proud as anything. They were each of varying thickness but all three were roughly a metre and a half long and had hemp rope wound around one end for a better grip.

Any offender would be stripped naked and tied to the wooden gallows so that their legs were fastened tightly together and couldn't move, thus protecting the sexual organs. Next their arms were pulled up above their heads with the torso slightly bent to ensure that the back was in the right position to receive the punishment. The X-shaped gallows they'd built ensured that the prisoner couldn't move out of the desired position: arms apart, waist tied to prevent any movement, and legs together.

In accordance with the Kunze Constitution, lashings could be given to anyone between the ages of fourteen and sixty-five, men and women alike. The buttocks were the only part of the body that should receive the lashes, although every now and then the cane would catch their thighs or lower back. The whipping was administered by a martial arts expert and followed a well-rehearsed, perfectly staged ritual that was the same every time. One day, Jung Fei Ye proudly gave us a demonstration. He grabbed the cane by the handle end and wielded it in the air, raising it to the left and then the right, his arm stretched out to achieve maximum thrust. Then he took a step forward and administered the blow, bringing the cane down with the full force of his arm, so that the tip of the cane cut the offender's skin like a blade. Before every lash, the tormentor would ask the offender if they were ready, to which they had to respond that they were. Afterwards, the offender had to thank his tormentor. Next, the doctor examined the convict, checking them over and testing their temperature with the thermometer. He would then decide whether the offender was in a fit condition to receive the rest of their punishment. If the doctor ruled that they weren't, they untied the offender and postponed the rest of the lashes until the following day, and so on like that until they'd received the full amount settled upon. The pain of the lashes was indescribable, and the scars left by the cane permanent. Three lashes would leave three horizontal stripes across the buttocks, a lifelong reminder of their humiliation. But this humiliation, Jung Fei Ye explained, the shame of having scarred buttocks, was precisely the most effective part of the punishment. I struggled even to imagine the effect of twelve lashes administered in a single session and on the same part of the body, not to mention the unspeakable punishment of sixteen or twenty-four, which must have sliced the flesh open right down to the bone. Jung Fei Ye told us that lashed offenders would have to receive medical treatment for the wounds and spend days or even weeks lying prostrate to recover. They provided antiseptic but no painkillers, since the pain was considered part of the punishment. But the rumour that they soaked the canes in saltwater to make the wounds hurt even more was, he told us, a myth.

'Those who feel the rattan cane don't ever go back to crime,' he said. 'They become submissive, obedient people. Respectful people. I've seen it countless times. The system works. It's cruel, certainly, but it works.'

48

Sophie, behind bars

Sebastian Leverkuhn, Sophie's son, had asthma, and his attacks were becoming more serious. His inhalers had run out some time ago, and now the boy spent whole nights awake. During the day he was better, but no sooner would he lie down to sleep than the shortness of breath and the wheezing chest would return. His bronchial tubes clammed up, stopping the air from getting in. Now Sebastian and Sophie went whole nights without sleep, and the boy was often so weak and tired that he would fall asleep sitting upright in the day. In fact, Joseph recommended he slept sitting half upright, but even so, the nights were hellish.

The island's climate, that muggy humidity, didn't agree with him.

Now Syra was always glued to Sebastian's side. She would plonk herself down next to him, take his hand in hers, and sit there quietly. Sometimes I would spot them together on the beach. Once I saw them sitting watching the sunset and I got the feeling I was witnessing the start of a love story. Sophie wasn't too fond of Syra, but she was nice to her because she could see her son enjoyed her company. The two children barely spoke to one another. I never saw them talking, in fact.

Dharma, my friends' yoga master, spoke to the Leverkuhns and told them that the boy's condition would improve if he kept a strictly vegetarian diet, and he taught him several breathing exercises which the Leverkuhns, with their empirical and incredulous mentality, didn't take seriously or bother to put into practice.

Sophie went to have a word with Jimmy Bruëll and asked him if she could have some medicine for her son's asthma. Jimmy told her that he might be able to help her, but that it was going to cost her more than a bunch of bananas or a dozen oysters.

'Where the hell do you even get all these things to sell?' Sophie asked, furious. 'You can't hide medicine. I don't have to pay you for medicine. If you have medicine, you should hand it over to Joseph and Roberta.'

'Well, I ain't no socialist, ma'am,' Jimmy sneered. 'I believe in the message of our founding fathers, in the quest for personal happiness, in the use of guns and private property.'

'We can force you to hand over the medicine,' Sophie said.

'No, you can't,' Jimmy said. 'Because I don't have any medicine. I don't have a thing, Mrs Architect. I'm a middleman. An entrepreneur. A hustler. I'm here, I'm there. I'm your friend who makes things happen. I don't own a mall. I don't have a stocked-up warehouse somewhere. I'm a kind of peddler, of the old-fashioned kind, ma'am. A poacher, if you will. Catch my drift?'

'Come on, Jimmy,' Sophie said. 'Don't give me that. Don't talk to me like someone off a TV show. We've got Wade for that.'

'I can try to get you your drugs,' Jimmy said.

'Good,' Sophie snapped. 'My son is suffocating. He can't breathe. I hope you get hold of them soon, Jimmy.'

'It's gonna cost you,' he said, winking at her.

'Come on, Jimmy, he's just a child.'

'Sweetie, my heart breaks for you, it really does, but have you ever tried that line with a doctor when he hands you the bill? Or in the drug store? Buying medical insurance? I'm running a business here. This is nothing but a business.'

'I don't have any money. I can pay you whatever you ask once we get out of here. If you want we can sign on it, in front of witnesses. I'll give you a grand in US dollars for the meds – will that cover it?'

'Money isn't worth anything here,' Jimmy said. 'Come on, Mrs Architect. Even you must understand that some things are worth more than money.'

After this episode, Sophie went to see Joseph and Wade. Joseph said he couldn't imagine how Jimmy managed to get hold of every medical item they ordered, and that the only possible answer was that he was getting things off the plane. But how? The raft had been deflated and unusable for ages. And anyway, there can't have been much left in the wreckage by now. It seemed more likely that during the first few days, when we went back and forth to the plane diving down to the hold, Jimmy had taken it upon himself to pilfer some of what he found and hide it away without telling anyone. At Sophie's request, a small group turned up at Jimmy's hut to search it for medication. He grumbled something about his 'constitutional' rights. In fact, he didn't actually need any constitution given that he had a gun and Kunze's backing, but anyway he let the men in with a smirk. They turned the place upside down looking for the secret hiding place where Jimmy kept all the items the rest of us coveted: tobacco, alcohol, medicines, contraceptives. But they didn't find a thing. Jimmy's secret store must have been in the jungle.

So when night fell, Sophie went to Jimmy's cabin, climbed into his bed and let him do what he wanted to her. I don't know, I guess she was convinced that things wouldn't get that far, and that at the last minute Jimmy would change his mind and give her the drugs without going through with the commercial transaction. I guess she thought that not even Jimmy would stoop so low. But Jimmy's moral standards were surprisingly loose. According to a few nosy islanders who'd crept up to the hut to see what was going on inside, Sophie had insisted Jimmy put on a condom. He didn't want to, and they'd argued over the issue for a while, until he finally gave in. Afterwards, he handed Sophie various asthma inhalers (terbutaline and salbutamol) and a few boxes of budesonide to be taken with corticosteroids in the long term. And for the first time in a long time, Sebastian was able to sleep through the night.

That morning Joseph went looking for Jimmy in his cabin. I happened to be hobbling by on my crutches with a towel thrown over my shoulder, on my way to the bathing area for my morning wash, when I was stopped in my tracks. Joseph was screaming Jimmy's name and ordering him to come out of his cabin. Jimmy emerged from behind the fabric door chewing on a slice of mango and holding a copy of *Little Dorrit*, with his finger marking the page. Joseph threw himself at him and knocked him to the floor with a single blow. Jimmy sat up looking pensive and touching his jaw in the place where Joseph's knuckles had made contact, spitting out chunks of unchewed mango. His finger was still keeping his page in *Little Dorrit*. Then he placed the book face down on the floor, wiped his mouth with the back of his hand and stood up.

'Have you got that out of your system now, doc?' he said. 'Can I go back to my book?'

Joseph launched at him again and the pair of them began rolling around on the ground. I don't think I'd ever seen a fight like it. Only in the movies had I seen two men really punching each other. Joseph had a really good arm, but even this paled in comparison to Jimmy's gargantuan muscly arms. He'd obviously learnt to box in prison. He knew all the dirty tricks, the hooks and illegal blows that leave your opponent breathless. To make matters worse, Joseph was incensed, while Jimmy was able to keep a cool head. Joseph got up again, but it was clear that Jimmy was the better fighter of the two. He was stronger, colder, crueller. Every time Joseph fell to the ground, Jimmy raised his two arms and told Joseph to leave it, that what had happened had nothing to do with him, he was blowing things out of proportion. Finally we were able to prise them apart. Wade went up to Joseph and told him that enough was enough. He told him that he'd defended a woman's honour but that he'd lost the fight, fair and square. That was enough. I couldn't believe Wade was saying all that. I felt like I was in the middle of a medieval duel, lost in a heraldic forest of blood and honour killings. A woman's *honour*? Then Leverkuhn showed up. He looked less than pleased. When we saw him approaching, a heavy silence fell. Leverkuhn was rarely seen in public, and he never spoke.

'I demand a general meeting tonight,' he said, and then he pointed awkwardly at Jimmy, but without making eye contact. 'This individual ought to be cast out of the community.'

'You need the whole group around to confront me?' Jimmy said, calmly picking up his book. 'Don't wanna resolve things like men?'

'I'm going to make them banish you,' Leverkuhn said. 'You're going to disappear off into the jungle, you son of a bitch. And you're going to starve to death in there, trying to eat monkey.'

The meeting took place that night, but things didn't go as he'd hoped. I remember it well, and I presume the capuchin monkeys and the giant wolves and the white cockatoos remember it too, because attacks and tirades like those we heard that night next to the river around the campfire don't happen every day on that remote coast. I remember how the flames of the fire made everyone's faces burn red and wild, and I remember the sparks crackling and rising up to the stars, and the glow of that amber fire reflected in the river water and on the leaves of the surrounding trees. I remember the sensation of the current, the fire, the sky, the trees enveloping our furious shouts, and the astonishment of the wild creatures who encircled us only to discover that of all nature's beasts, none is more savage than man.

Leverkuhn made a formal request for Jimmy Bruëll to be banished from our society, but not before revealing where he kept all the goods he peddled and which everybody needed. He declared that it was a disgrace that we had to 'pay' for the things we needed to survive, and that Bruëll – a criminal with a long career in petty and not so petty crimes, and who, according to Leverkuhn, had been in prison several times – didn't deserve the benefits of communal life. He called him a leech, abusive, a crook, a blackmailer, immoral, effectively a rapist who should be banned from coming anywhere near our village.

Kunze told Leverkuhn that he understood his frustration and agitation, but that the matters he was setting out were domestic ones. Kunze was as mild as ever, and at the same time indescribably ruthless. He added that he agreed with Leverkuhn that at the very least Jimmy should hand over all the medicine he was keeping, for use by the entire group. This all seemed so reasonable to me that I thought there'd be nothing more to discuss. Leverkuhn's motion to banish Jimmy from the community seemed to me a little excessive, but I was sure that if it came to a vote, Leverkuhn would lose, thus settling the matter. But Kunze didn't have the slightest intention of putting the issue to a vote. There was a legal system, a judicial power, an executive arm. There was no need for anything else.

Kunze said that if anyone deserved punishment, it was Mrs Leverkuhn. Mrs Leverkuhn, he said, stressing the 'Mrs', had committed adultery, which, according to the island's legal code, was a crime punishable by lashing. Sophie Leverkuhn had used her own body as currency in a commercial transaction, meaning this wasn't solely a case of adultery, but also prostitution. Two crimes. Kunze added that there was no doubt that Jimmy was far from a model of virtuous behaviour, but that he wasn't the guilty party in this matter, that he had every right to exploit his business as he saw fit, and that the woman had seduced him. This provoked an outcry of voices, shouts and even laughter, but Kunze fired his rifle twice in the air and said that under no circumstances would he tolerate a disturbance.

He then ordered the sheriff to arrest Sophie Leverkuhn and lock her up in one of the cells on the beach. Having consulted Tudelli and Billy Higgins, who nodded along to everything he said, Kunze spoke again, stating that, given the extenuating circumstances, the Council had decided that the penalty would be reduced to six lashes administered at noon the following day. They asked Sophie if she wished to add anything, to which she replied that she did not. Then Jung Fei Ye and Mr Kim approached her, tied her hands behind her back and took her away. Joseph threw himself at them to try to stop them, but they pointed the barrel of a gun at his chest, and Jimmy loaded the shotgun and pointed it at his head. Joseph raised his hands and stopped on the spot.

The night engulfed everything around us like a giant, merciless spider.

49

We're under attack

The next morning I woke to the sound of screaming all around me. I scrambled into my trousers, grabbed my crutches and shot out of my hut as quickly as I could. When I emerged outside, I found everyone pointing up at the clouds. A plane was flying over the island. We got a good look at it when it passed over the beach, its shape reflected fleetingly on the great mirror of damp sand. It was a kind of remote-controlled toy. Everyone ran down to the beach to look. Wade emerged from the jungle with a pair of wood pigeons slung around his neck. He would often catch them using snares and traps. Roberto B. and Sheila scuttled down from a palm tree. Swayla came out of the sea where she'd been taking her morning swim. Jimmy Bruëll arrived with his shotgun over his shoulder.

We watched as the plane made a wide turn over the jungle headland overlooking the village and then flew back towards the beach. On its way back it dipped much lower, and I think then we all got a better look. It had two propellers, one on each wing, and on the side the words 'Keep cool forever!', along with a drawing which looked to me like a red pig with a black mask and a pirate bandana on its head. The plane looked very old, with chipped paintwork and lots of raw-looking welds. Now it was flying over the river, and just as it came level with the village, it began to shoot out a kind of yellowish powder – like thousands of crystal marigolds falling slowly onto the black surface of the river. It was hard to tell if it was gas or powder. It was soon raining down onto the village. Then the plane turned in the direction of the lagoon, where dozens of castaways were jumping and dancing and shouting and waving at the plane, despite the fact that they probably all knew that the plane was unmanned and there was no one to wave to, and the yellow haze pouring forth from its belly was engulfing them, slipping among the tree trunks and huge palm leaves, which swayed gently in the breeze as if greeting the destruction and end of the world. Because that cloud was the yellow colour of death, of the world's destruction.

The plane now swung in the direction of the beach, releasing its cloud of yellow powder onto the groups of onlookers jumping up and down and chasing after its shadow on the sand. It nosedived to barely ten or twelve metres from the ground before ascending again off towards the sea, only to curve around again and come back over the beach heading back towards the lagoon and village. And then I noticed it: one by one, the people on the beach beginning to drop like flies. The kids and the women were the first to fall, then the elderly, and finally the taller, bigger men. We all inhaled that yellow smoke and passed out, almost instantly. All but a few unlucky ones. Sandy Pollock, a twenty-six-year-old chemical engineer, passed out on the shore of the river and drowned. Her sister, twenty-four-year-old Sibyll Pollock, who'd had drug problems in the past and modelled for art schools in the Valley, was up at the top of a palm tree when the plane appeared. She watched the scene unfold from above. Since the yellow haze fell to the ground, she attempted to stay in the tree as the dust storm descended and sent everyone to sleep. But she didn't have time to position herself securely in the branches and she fell from twelve metres, snapping her neck on impact. Others tried to dash into the jungle to hide in the vegetation, but they didn't have time either. Just two of all the castaways didn't fall asleep, and both had the good sense to drop to the floor and pretend to be asleep like everyone else.

I remained completely speechless as everyone around me fell to the ground – their eyes closed, heads floppy, knees buckled, and bodies collapsed into themselves as if they were made of paper. I'd been walking in the direction of the beach like everyone else, but had only reached the end of the village where the lagoon began. I watched as Omotola, dressed in one of his red and yellow African tunics, dropped to the ground, scattering a load of candlenuts he'd been carrying. And I watched as Gloria Griffin, dressed in a white swimsuit and up to her waist in the turquoise water of the lagoon, turned to me with a look of terror on her face. I watched her eyelids roll like those of a doll when you tilt it back, and her head flop to one side. She would have almost certainly died had it not been for me. I dived into the water, grabbed her by her hair, and pulled her to safety. A fresh cloud of yellow washed over the jungle and shore, shining like thousands of golden crystals on the lagoon's waters. I breathed in that foul mustard-coloured fog, disgusted. It had the bitter taste of castor oil, not unlike an insecticide, but it didn't sting the eyes or make it hard to breathe. Through the yellowy haze I spotted Jimmy Bruëll clutching his rifle. He looked at me and opened his mouth as if to say something, but then fell to his knees before his body collapsed face down in the sand, like a domino. But I had the distinct feeling that just before passing out, Jimmy had seen something.

I turned around and saw several figures approaching in the distance. It was hard to make them out through the thick clouds of yellow, but there were three of them, then four, then five... seven, eight. I wasn't even sure at first if they were people. They could have been monsters, or apes, or robots. The sea breeze swept the fog off into the jungle, revealing still more figures – armed men, advancing towards me. I didn't know what to do. Realising that everyone around me had collapsed, I dropped to the ground and pretended to be asleep.

The figures came marching through the trees, out from the dark leaves, towards the banks of the river. They'd emerged from the jungle. I remember I couldn't get my head around how they'd managed to reach us so quickly: a stupid thought really, given that I didn't know how long they'd been following us. As far as I could see there were fifteen or twenty of them (I'm not sure if there were other factions). They were heavily armed and wearing old-fashioned, black military masks. One of them was carrying a metal device with a long aerial. It was the remote control for the plane. I watched as the human insects – all of them bearing rifles, and in some cases K-52 assault rifles – began raiding the huts. It must have been the first time they'd been in our camp, and they were curious. They took our possessions and kicked our equipment and utensils, breaking whatever makeshift furniture they found, laughing and talking as they went, although it was hard to make out their words through the masks covering their mouths. I heard them kicking our bamboo furnishings to pieces; items we had built with our bare hands and infinite patience. I heard them snap and tear down palm-woven awnings and trample our clay pots to pieces. They were quite far away from me and I couldn't catch what they were saying, but I was overcome with fear just hearing their voices.

When at last they left the huts and came over towards the lagoon, they walked right by me. One of them, a woman I think, even stepped over my leg, and their horrible insect heads made me even more terrified. Their behaviour was utterly perplexing. They wandered among the fallen bodies, trampling on the faces and stomachs of those poor slumbering souls with their military boots, every now and then kicking one in the ribs or crotch out of some sadistic pleasure. I saw how they picked up Robert Frost, the dim Mormon (that's what I called him to distinguish him from Robert Kelly, 'the smart Mormon'), took down his trousers between fits of laughter leaving his pink, smooth arse bare, and positioned him on top of one of the women, who'd herself fallen face up with her legs spread. I pretended to be asleep, but kept my eyes half open. One of the women among them told the men off for what they did to Robert Frost, but it was the time-wasting that seemed to annoy her, and she seemed to have as little respect for the poor castaways as her friends, stepping on them without the least consideration. Up until that point, I still wasn't sure if our assailants belonged to the Insiders group or the guerrilla group, but when I got a look at their clothes and weapons it became clear they weren't guerrillas.

The one who appeared to be their leader said something out loud, and they all took off their old masks. Just as I had guessed, the woman who had told them off before was Gwen. She shook her head from one side to the other, and her wild, wavy hair tumbled over her shoulders. She was wearing military gear and armed with a Kalashnikov. She looked so fierce and terrifying that I shuddered at the thought that we'd kissed, that we'd

swum naked together, that we'd made love. I didn't recognise the other
members of the group, and noticed that George was conspicuous by his
absence, although given my limited line of vision, he might have been
there, out of sight.

They looked rough: unshaved and unkempt, with tattoos on their muscular, sunburnt arms. There was something pirate-like about them. They
looked like regular delinquents, mercenaries. The one who'd given the
order to take off their masks, however, was different. His hair was cut
short, he was squat and not particularly well built, and he had a small pale
face with enormous blue eyes – cold and intelligent, with small red lips
pressed thin. Without a shadow of a doubt, he was in charge. I heard the
man say something else and then from the forest appeared a swarm of men
armed with spears and bows and arrows. When I say a swarm, I don't just
mean the sheer number of them, but also the way they appeared out of
nowhere, so stealthily, and then seemed to fill the whole space. They were
barefoot and covered from head to toe in chokers, long grass and feathers,
their skin was almost entirely decorated in tattoos and adornments. I'd
never seen anything like it. I couldn't fail to notice that the White men
among them were the ones holding the firearms and clearly calling the
shots. The little fella with the bulging blue eyes strode back and forth
looking at the fallen bodies of those sleeping. I heard someone call him
Abe, and then Abraham. Abraham Lewellyn, the leader of the Insiders.
The group followed him, waiting patiently for their orders. He spoke in
their native language, but using the odd loose word in English, pronouncing them as they should. He spoke and also laughed a lot, and the other
White men and women laughed too. The strangers didn't laugh or say a
word; they stayed quiet, waiting. Finally, they began making their way
between the fallen bodies. I watched as two of them picked up Syra and
carried her off. We'd later learn that our strange torturers took Syra, Carl
and Sebastian. That is, all three of the children left in the village. They
abducted lots of young women too.

I tried to take in everything I could without moving a muscle, looking
from left to right and moving my face imperceptibly when nobody was

near. My main concern was to work out whether these people were who they claimed to be, or whether this was some kind of elaborate hoax. They seemed authentic, and not only because of the way they moved, or the special quality of their attentiveness, but because of the incredibly complicated detail of their headdresses, feather adornments and seashells, the tattoos and scorch marks all over their bodies. At the same time they were practically naked, with just one rope belt around their waist, which held a wooden sheath in place to protect their penis. They shaved the front part of their heads leaving the whole forehead bare and the rest of their hair became a tangled mess of thin plaits that reached all the way down to their shoulder blades, even their elbows, in some cases just tied at the end, and in others intricately woven with coloured beads, shells, teeth, feathers, coral or metal hoops, and then plaited again one into the other to form complex shapes.

Someone I *could* see from the floor, a broad-shouldered man with a pot belly who must have been one of the group's elders, maybe the shaman, was wearing a mask similar to those we might find in the Oceania section of anthropology museums, crowned with a kind of wig made from straw and feathers. He came so close to me that for one panic-stricken moment I thought he'd noticed I was awake. Maybe the mask he was wearing, whose holes were no more than tiny slits, meant he couldn't see clearly. The mask turned towards me for several seconds and I tried to stay completely still while my heart pounded inside my chest. Then something else caught his attention and he forgot all about me.

I watched as our captors moved among the bodies, choosing who they needed. I saw two of them pick up Swayla while a third tied her wrists with a rope. There were others who carried more limp, lifeless bodies over their shoulders, all of them young women. They took Xóchitl, Di Di – Brigitta Kunze's secretary-cum-maid – Pam Brunner, Hélène Dupont-Ardanzin, and two young women from the group of Indians, Leelavati and Vrajavala, this last woman being Dr Sutteesh's wife.

While the strangers went around cherry-picking women to take with them, the Insiders carried on destroying our most prized possessions and taking for themselves the few arms we had left. This, too, was incomprehensible, because they didn't raze the whole place, or take everything they could have. It was like they didn't want to destroy us altogether, just make our lives more miserable and difficult. They took the best part of the food we had stored: the smoked fish, the dried lizard and snake meat, as well as lots of the remaining cans of meat, fish, marmalade and fruit in syrup, which we had assiduously kept aside for a time when we could no longer rely on the island's natural resources.

Gwen had lived among us and knew all the hiding places. She directed them, working hand in hand with the leader, the small man with bulging eyes and red lips called Abraham Lewellyn. They also paid a visit to our hospital hut, where instead of going to the bother of robbing us of what little alcohol and analgesics we had left, they left us a suitcase full of doses of Thorazine and various syringes, clearly having some vested interest or motive for us to inject ourselves with that drug. And as for the rest, as I say, their destructive work was careless and arbitrary. They snapped all the bows and arrows, blowpipes, slings and spears they came across, and threw two razors and one of our axes into the river. Luckily they didn't find the rest of our carpentry tools, the other razors or remaining knives; or maybe Gwen had simply forgotten they existed. There was one other possibility: that they were toying with us, and that they knew that if they left us without tools or food at all they would be condemning us to death. Yes, I think they preferred to let us live than to kill us themselves. But their characteristic cruelty led them instead to make our lives as difficult as possible.

Joseph had already released Sophie from the cave cell where she'd spent the night. The two of them had headed straight to the village with Wade, Santiago and a few others, where they proceeded to tear down the gallows and smash the boards displaying the Kunze Constitution. There were plenty of us. I was there, as were my Spanish friends, Dharma and his wife, and several of the Indians, Dr Sutteesh and Dr Masoud included.

Kunze and his armed heavies came over, pointing their guns at us. They bellowed at us, saying we were committing a crime – insurrection.

Kunze ordered us to rebuild the gallows we'd just destroyed. Dharma Mittra asked him very sweetly if he planned to shoot and kill us all. I think it was the first time I'd heard him speak in public. Now the majority of the castaways were on our side. On Kunze's there was Jung Fei Ye, Pei Pei Je, Billy Higgins, Roberta, Bentley, Tudelli, Hansa, Jimmy Bruëll and all the others on his payroll. Then Dharma did something unexpected. He sat on the ground and put his arms together on his lap. Eva, who was by his side, did the same, and then all of us began to sit down calmly on the floor. We didn't do anything else; we just sat on the ground. But that was enough. That day marked the end of Kunze's rule, as well as his Constitution.

50

The night before leaving

W*e only waited one night* after the sleeping gas attack before setting off on our second expedition into the interior. Just long enough to get ourselves and our supplies ready, and to carve some thick, solid acacia canes to defend ourselves with in case of close combat. All of our existing arms, including the most rudimentary ones, had either been destroyed or taken by our assailants. So we opted for sticks – the poor man's weapon. The weapons of peasants who have nothing. That's what we were by then: outcasts, the scum of the earth. Which, at least in theory, meant we were also the salt of the earth. But we didn't feel like the salt of the earth.

I joined the terrified, poorly equipped group, who agreed to let me hobble behind them on the condition that I would head back if I couldn't keep up. How strong could an army like that be – one made up of fathers, mothers and boyfriends? Aside from the stalwart figures of Wade, Joseph and yours truly, this strange army also counted on the unexpected company of Jimmy Bruëll, who until that moment hadn't exactly stood out as a model of altruism.

We decided to follow our assailants' tracks and go all together. Any kind of strategy was beyond us, and nor could we use the element of surprise. Henry McCullough, Adele and Estelle's father, the Australian diplomat who'd been an ambassador in various countries (Bolivia, then Lebanon and then Sri Lanka), suggested that perhaps we could invoke our rights, reasoning with the kidnappers. He said the situation didn't make any sense; that those so-called Insiders didn't have any reason to fear or attack us, and that if we worked out what it was exactly that they wanted we might be able to come to an agreement.

'The ambassador still believes in the innate good of the individual,' Jimmy Bruëll said. 'You won't mind if I call you Pangloss?'

'I couldn't care less what you call me,' Henry answered, 'as long as you help me find my daughters.'

That Jimmy Bruëll was an odd sort. He asked me what my reasons were for joining the search party. Might the events of the last few days have had an effect on him? Had he, to a certain extent and in his own weird way, hit rock bottom too? He and Joseph avoided one another, but I think after their fisticuffs the previous day a kind of bond had formed between them; a primitive and atavistic connection which was beyond me but which I intuited despite my 'civilised man' rationalisations.

The night before we left I came across Wade sitting on the beach under the light of the stars, gazing out to sea, sitting apart from the fires dotted here and there, and, from what it seemed, and as they say in novels, 'lost in thought'. When he spotted me (or rather, when he heard me, because my new wooden leg made an unmistakable dull thud on the sand and announced my presence from many metres away) he asked me to sit and have a chat with him. He had that twinkle in his eyes again. That twinkle. That smile. I asked him what was on his mind.

'I'm thinking we might have got it wrong, John. That maybe we're not reacting the right way.

'There's a river, John. On the other side of the hills,' he went on, pointing off towards the dark form of the island rising up behind him. 'There's a great river, where it's mild and there's no jungle. There are meadows on the banks of the river. We could all go and move there. We could create New Harmony there, on the banks of the river.

'Tomorrow when we set off, I'm not going with you all. I have to go back to that island. I know what my mistake was now, John. I made a mistake. Maybe that's why I've been punished.'

He was holding some grains of white sand in the palm of his hand, as if that sand were proof of his sin. The powder of crushed prehistoric crustaceans, glowing in Orion's and the Pleiades' light.

'You haven't been punished, Wade,' I said, seeing my greatest hope fade before my eyes. Seeing how the island's insanity, the profound injustice and the absurd savagery we were being subjected to had begun to chip away at his dreamer's spirit, his desire for heroism.

'For there to be punishment, there must be blame,' I said. 'And there must be a justice system, even a perverse one. Even a cruel one. But here we've got neither of those things. No blame. No justice. And as such, no punishment.'

'I don't agree, John. I think I made a mistake. I was already in the Meadow. I should have gone up to the top level and I should have gone into that house,' Wade said, staring at me with his shining blue eyes. 'That's what I should have done. That's what you have to do in the Meadow. But then, there are distractions. There are snares. The Meadow is full of snares. It looks like there's nothing there, like it's empty. That's what's so amazing about the Meadow – that it's empty. *But it's not empty, John.* Now I see that.'

'It's not empty?'

'It's full. *Full of itself.* We always call a place with no people in it "empty". In the Meadow there aren't any people, but the Meadow itself is there. The Meadow itself. It's an intelligent being that takes pleasure in tricking us. It tests us, over and again, and we all fail, we never pass the tests. For example, the trap door right in the middle, at the foot of the step separating the two levels. You remember it?'

'Of course.'

'I should have paid no attention to it. I should have carried on up, gone up the steps to the next level and gone into the house. But I didn't do that. I got distracted. The Meadow tricked me, and I fell into its trap. I went down the hatch, down that ladder into the bowels of the earth. I had paradise right there, John, and I chose hell. Why?'

'When I went into the Meadow,' I said, choosing my words carefully to try to make Wade see sense, 'I mean, when I found it on this island, at the end of the motorway tunnel, I went up onto the upper level and into the house and nothing happened. I went through the whole house, room by room. The house isn't paradise, Wade. It's just a house. A dilapidated old house with no roof and the windows smashed in, just like you said.'

'No, no, no, John. No,' he said, gripping my hand suddenly and tensing his jaw in frustration and rage. 'It tricked you. It tricks us all the time. This whole island must be its biggest trick of all. It might even be possible that it's capable of tricking and deceiving across the whole planet. It's possible that the whole of Planet Earth is nothing but one of the Meadow's creations; a maze of guiles and ruses that draw us subtly towards it, and at the same time stop us actually finding it.'

'There wasn't anything there, Wade,' I said.

'There must have been something in the house, something you overlooked. Look, there are only three people on this island who have found the Meadow, and out of us three, only you have managed to get inside the house.'

'There was nothing there, Wade. I've already told you. There were four pieces of broken furniture. A blue man painted on the wall.'

'A blue man. Yes!'

'So tell me what that's supposed to mean.'

'And the flying saucer. It was there, right?'

'Yes, it was there.'

'The flying saucer flying over the Meadow.'

'It's a cloud, a small white cloud.'

'Call it a cloud if you like. That doesn't change a thing.'

'Wade, you know it's not possible to go back to that place, because it doesn't exist. None of it!'

'But you were there. You went through the tunnel on that motorway and you reached it.'

'Those places don't exist, Wade. They're dreams, projections. I don't know what they are. It's possible that the island is capable of seeing into our souls, and bringing what's inside there to life. I don't know.'

When I went back to the village, I bumped into Rosana by one of the campfires. She was sitting on the ground and staring into space. Maybe that night we were all that way. I sat down next to her and asked how she was doing.

'I'm scared to death,' she said, looking at me with an unbearably sad face, her eyes red from all the crying. 'I can't stop thinking, Juan Barbarín. I can't stop thinking about what might be happening to Syra. I don't know how I'm going to make it through tonight. I've never been this scared in my life.'

'We're going to look for her,' I said. 'And we're going to find her, and we're going to get her out of there.'

'I won't come back without her,' she said, obstinately. 'They'll have to kill me first, Juan Barbarín. I think I'm going to lose my mind.'

'I've spent all day thinking that if I get her back, I'll never shout at her again,' Rosana said, after a moment's pause. 'No matter what she does. No matter how much of a nightmare she is, or how badly she does at school. Even if she lies to me, or hides things, I'll never shout at her ever again.'

'We should get some rest. We've got a long hard day ahead of us.'

'I can't sleep. Could you really sleep now?'

'No.'

'Look,' she said, pointing at the fires on the beach. 'Nobody's sleeping tonight. I'm scared, Juan Barbarín. I'm really, really scared.'

'Come on,' I said. 'Let's go and sit with the others. Let's go and sit with the Latin Americans. They're always telling some tale or other. They'll distract us.'

51

The second expedition. We discover a silo

The following morning, the morning of our departure, Wade came and found me to say that he'd thought long and hard about it, and that maybe I was right. He was going to postpone his search for the Meadow and would lead our search party, given that he was the best forest tracker among us. He also said he thought I was probably right about not being able to find the Meadow at will, and that he didn't doubt for a moment that if it were his destiny to go back there then he would, regardless of the path he took.

I won't elaborate here on the details of our journey across the island. We'd only just left when we saw a capuchin monkey swinging towards us through the canopy of branches with a newborn baby clutching the thick hair of its belly. It was about ten metres above us, and someone raised their bow to shoot it, but Dr Sutteesh cried out, clear as a bell: 'Stop! You don't shoot breeding mothers.' And the monkey with her babe carried on its way through the branches, and both their lives were saved.

Dr Sutteesh must have been in his early thirties. He'd earned his doctorate in English Literature at the University of Calcutta and was a leading figure on the quite disparate works of Samuel Taylor Coleridge and William Wordsworth. He was also a cricket enthusiast and a good singer, mainly of traditional Indian songs and Irish ballads, which he sang in his soothing tenor. He had very dark skin, was rather short, and on his round face he sported a thin, well-groomed moustache. A cultured, refined man, and at the same time exceptionally kind and warm. He'd only been married to Vrajavala for four years, and on one of our short breaks during the expedition he told us that he was madly in love with his wife and would be willing to die, or even kill, for her. He told me he'd always been a pacifist, a scholar of the old poets, and that the smell of a book, the gum arabic and Indian ink, was to him lovelier than the smell of roses. But now he was so desperate he was willing to do anything. And he told me all this with his kind smile still on his face, his head cocked into a slight sideways tilt (characteristically Indian body language that always takes us Westerners aback in its apparently effeminate softness). But there was nothing effeminate about the short, exquisite Dr Sutteesh, devotee of the Lake Poets.

There are moments, small acts in a person's life, that seem to reveal who they really are. Dr Sutteesh's 'Stop!' as the capuchin monkey appeared with her baby, and the categorical 'You don't shoot breeding mothers', was one such moment.

Our captors' tracks led us to the plateau we already knew, an open region with a little tree cover leading to the rocky peak that opened out onto the Valley of the Blue Man. When we were just a few kilometres from the headland, Wade found that the trail we'd been following split into three different routes: one that carried on due south, another south-west and the last one south-east. It seemed we had to split up, so our small army was now divided into three factions.

On the third day of our trip – and the second day of being divided into smaller groups – we reached a lush paradise valley where the river extended into an archipelago of islands, around which the waters shone with particular intensity. And there, in that inundated valley, Wade well and truly lost the track we'd been following. Some people suggested we turn back, but Wade insisted we should keep going, convinced that once out of the swampy area we would pick up the abductors' tracks again.

We ended up in a rocky, barren region.

The terrain rolled up and down. Red rocks jutted out from the ground. The mountain range in the middle of the island was on our left. The peak of the volcano, as always, was cloaked in cloud. What was it that drew all those clouds to form around the mountain summits? I'm sure there must be a scientific explanation for it. Mountains, crests, even trifling ones, are often crowned by a cloud mass, even on the driest days or in the driest climates. It's as if the sheer volume of the mountain itself formed the cloud, or the clouds became caught on the rocky peak as they flew by and then wouldn't let go. I've seen this phenomenon lots of times all over the world, and I'm always enthralled watching craggy peaks and the sea of cloud that seems to accumulate over them, sometimes overwhelming them and spilling down the mountainside like a slow, rolling wave that never breaks. The same goes for watching a lone boulder in the middle of a landscape and the way in which, even on windy days, a cloud, sometimes but a misty wisp, will appear to stick to the highest part like a head of wavy hair, never fading away, or rather fading away only to be immediately replaced by a new head of hair which seems to appear out of nowhere. This same phenomenon could be seen at the summit of the volcano in the middle of the island, which I had never seen without cloud, and whose shape I could only guess at.

I was constantly glancing up at the sky, but the flying saucer, or the cloud formation which we'd grown accustomed to calling the 'flying saucer', didn't materialise.

The end of the fourth day had a big surprise in store for us. We were making our way through the valley full of red volcanic rocks – a place that, millions of years before, must have been a river of lava expelled by the volcano, opening up a path to the sea's waves – when we spotted it, perfectly visible among the rocks. It was an iron escape hatch, similar to one you might find on a submarine. It opened by means of a thick round handle and looked like it was in good condition. On one side of the block of cement where it opened up were the embossed initials 'SIAR'. It was very dirty. It was sealed shut with encrusted mud, its hinges covered in a thick layer of dust. It was clear that nobody had opened that door, which seemed to us like a portal into another world, for a long time. We thought it might be an air-raid shelter from the Second World War. But there? In the middle of nowhere, deep inside the island?

When, with superhuman effort, we finally managed to open the hatch, we poked our heads over into the dark well. We all peered over the edge, but not one of us thought about descending the metal staircase that ran down the side of it.

Wade shouted: 'Is there anybody down there? Can anybody hear me?'

Of course, there was no answer.

Wade said it was better not to risk it, that clearly no one had been down that hatch for years, which therefore meant that the people we were going after weren't down there. And yet, we all wanted to go in. How could we let a discovery like this pass? How could we *not* want to find out what was down there? We might discover a big silo, or an arsenal full of rifles and ammunition.

'It's a trap,' Wade said, an indecipherable look – of either fear or disgust – on his face. 'This island is full of traps. It doesn't want us to go any further. It wants to stop us, to distract us. We shouldn't go down there. The kids we're looking for aren't down there. Nor are the kidnapped women.'

And yet, despite Wade's warnings, we voted to go in. Just down the stairs, to see what was there. Then we'd move on.

What we found down that hatch would come to be known between us as 'the Silo'. It was an underground station roughly fifty metres deep, comprised of various rooms with stone walls, floors and ceilings. A group of twenty people could have lived down there for an entire year without having to return to the outside world. We asked ourselves why the people who'd built the Silo had dug down so deep. I doubt that even in wartime, in territories exposed to the worst bombing, they built bunkers that deep.

There were four sections connected by long stone corridors: the kitchen, the bedrooms and living area, the library and control room. To our surprise, the lights worked in all the rooms.

In the kitchen there was a store packed with food. All the tins and packets were past their use-by date, but the supplies we tried were perfectly edible. Suddenly, we had rice, oil, crackers, pasta, tomato sauce, biscuits, soup, lentils, chickpeas, guava jelly, condensed and powdered milk, ham, pickled quails, chicken fricassee, tuna, sardines in oil, mussels in brine, beans, oyster sauce, ketchup, tamarind sauce, couscous, peaches in syrup, pineapple in syrup, Dijon mustard, herring, strawberry, tropical, orange, grapefruit and peach juice, raisins, dried apricots, pork, ragu, meatballs in tomato sauce, meat ravioli, ricotta ravioli, mushroom ravioli, butternut squash ravioli in marinara sauce, pesto, four cheese and mushroom sauces, spam, gherkins, pickled onions, peppers, peas, clams, oysters, pork liver pâté, chocolate hazelnut spread, drinking chocolate, coffee, tea, camomile, as well as whisky, vodka, brandy, rum, Armagnac, Tokay, sherry, ruby port, Coca-Cola, soda water, sugar, salt, pepper, corn and wheat flour, ready mixes for waffles and pancakes, and much more besides.

The first thing we did that night, I have to admit, is make a slap-up meal at the enormous kitchen table, easily big enough to seat twenty-five people. I don't think I've ever eaten a more delicious meal than the one we prepared that night out of those expired tins we found in the Silo. We all overate. I felt a little queasy, but others got indigestion and some were even sick. I don't think it was that the tinned food was off, but rather the amount we consumed, and the richness, which our stomachs were no longer used to.

The other areas of the Silo weren't so immediately appealing, although once our food had settled we began to explore them with growing interest. The living quarters of the Silo, for example, afforded us almost as much pleasure as eating food that actually tasted of food. I'm referring to the showers, which, to our delight, had running hot water. In the cupboards we found loo roll, shampoo, shower gel, shaving foam and razors, deodorant and all kinds of gifts from civilisation, and we were soon all stark naked in the showers, whooping for joy as the hot water rushed over our skin and savouring the pleasure of sinking our hands into the unctuous scented shampoo on our heads.

After our banquet we all felt like new, and began exploring the rest of the rooms in the Silo. The library must have held at least twenty-five thousand volumes, all housed on two-metre-high oak shelves distributed along symmetrical grilles in a big circular room with a domed ceiling. In the middle of the room there was a rectangular table with six chairs and lamps with green glass lampshades, like the ones you get in American libraries. There were also several alcoves and nooks with sofas and armchairs to read in comfort.

The control room had a series of tables holding different kinds of devices whose function was lost on us. I guessed some were radio transmitters and receptors, and others signal boosters and sound boards. Yes, that's what we thought then: that the aim of all that equipment was to communicate with the outside world. Not such an easy task on that island. Some of the equipment had round glass screens like the ones I'd seen on radars in films from the seventies and eighties. Others looked like nothing I'd ever seen before. On the back wall of that rectangular room, which was raised higher than the others, were some forty television monitors. The SIAR insignia had been stamped all over the place: on the thick instruction manuals, the metal monitor stands, the backs of the plastic seats.

After various attempts, and having discovered a fuse panel with several three-way switches on it, we managed to turn on some of the equipment and a few TV monitors. Fuzzy black-and-white images – video camera footage taken in dingy places – appeared on some of the screens.

Roberto B. and Óscar had stayed behind in the library, spellbound by its bibliographical gems. Lizzy and a woman called Lily Whittfield were making an inventory of the supplies in the storeroom, which meant that in the control room it was Rosana, Joaquín, Wade, Dr Sutteesh and me.

Each of the monitors showed a different image: on the first you could see a children's playground next to the sea. There was a toboggan, a roundabout and a see-saw, as well as a group of children aged between four and ten playing, accompanied by mothers and minders. Lily said that the park was in San Francisco, and that the shadow we could see on the left over the water was the Golden Gate Bridge. On the second monitor you could see a rice paddy, clearly somewhere in South-East Asia, maybe an island in Indonesia. Half-naked men and women with wide straw hats on their heads, working the fields up to their knees in water. There was also a water buffalo with a boy of about nine on its back. On a third monitor we could make out our own village. You could just see the smoke from a campfire, and a few of our huts, some of them with their walls torn down. There wasn't a soul in sight.

A fourth monitor showed a room similar to the one in which we now found ourselves, with five or six women dressed in white overalls. They were all looking in the same direction, some standing, others sitting, perhaps watching something on the television. Next was the Oval Office in the White House, or at least, a replica of it. The presidential desk was empty, and a cleaning lady was vacuuming the rug. On another monitor was what looked like a summer camp. All the children were dressed in their swimsuits next to the river listening to their instructor, who was dressed in military uniform. Another monitor showed a woman undressing in a room. The woman removed her dress, and then began walking around the room in her bra and knickers, moving in and out of shot. She was smoking. On the following screen, a black-and-white Mickey Mouse cartoon was playing. Then it jumped to a series of movie scenes with Buster Keaton.

Next, we saw a field surrounded by a barbed wire fence and several armed men standing beside it. They were dressed in army camouflage gear, and one of them, too, was smoking. It could easily have been a scene from our island. There were palm trees in the background. On the following monitor I noticed a section of an underground stone tunnel, dimly lit by hanging lamps, and then, on the screen beside it, a bedroom with a huge double bed, a reading light on either side of it. Rosana let out a cry when she saw it and said that it was, without a shadow of a doubt, her bedroom in Madrid. Above the headboard, which she'd bought in an antiques shop in Brussels, hung an Indian textile depicting Krishna and the Gopis, which she herself had had framed.

On another monitor you could see a garden with a swimming pool. A forty-something woman was sunbathing on a lounger, and nearby several children were playing with the hose. On another a cell, or a room that appeared to be used as a cell. There was a metal table on one side and a camp bed on the other. At the back of the room you could make out a loo with no seat. A woman wearing a kind of pyjama set was lying on the bed, her long blonde hair tied in a bun at her neck. Another woman, wearing a similar uniform, was sitting at the table, eating a yoghurt directly from the tub with a teaspoon. We examined the image closely to see if either of them was one of our kidnapped women, but we didn't recognise them.

On the next screen we saw a living room; light and spacious with a carpeted floor, Queen Anne-style wooden furniture painted white, and floral curtains. Whose house could it be? And where? After that, another monitor showed an old white house with a wooden porch where two women dressed in saris were sitting on wicker chairs. Dr Sutteesh said it was his parents' house in Calcutta. One of the women was his mother; the other, his mother's sister, who had also lived in the house since her husband's death. I noticed Dr Sutteesh's amber eyes mist over. I really couldn't believe it. But Dr Sutteesh assured us it was true; that that was his house and the woman on the left his mother. What kind of man doesn't recognise his own mother?

Finally, on the last monitor was a bedroom that had a vaguely maritime look about it. Dark wooden panel walls, a painting of a brig leaning into the waves on the wall, a brass compass. Above the bed you could see a shelf lined with books, and also several bottles full of little white seashells from the beach. It was my bedroom in my house in Oakland. And someone was sleeping in the bed. In my bed. Two people, in fact, sleeping peacefully under the sheets.

'That's my room!' I shouted. 'That's my bed, in my room, in my house in Oakland!'

'There's someone in your bed,' Rosana said. 'Does anyone have the keys to your house?'

'Martha, the woman who comes to clean,' I said, completely riveted to the screen. 'Just her.'

The others, who had been in the library, came in when they heard our voices and stared at each of the TV monitors in turn.

On some of them, the images changed from minute to minute, and on the top right-hand corner the number of the corresponding camera appeared. My room switched to another room, and then another, and then the living room of a house, and then another bedroom, until finally my bedroom flashed up again, the two figures still lying there in the same position.

'It's a trap,' Wade muttered, looking from side to side suspiciously. 'We need to get out of here now. We need to load up the rucksacks with all the supplies we can, and get the hell out of here.'

'What makes you say it's a trap?' Rosana asked. 'I don't see any trap.'

'The trap is stopping us from advancing. Deterring us from going where we should be going.'

We were all mesmerised. Rosana watched her bedroom. I watched mine. Dr Sutteesh believed he'd spotted his wife on the monitor showing the image of a cell. In fact, the image flitted from one cell to another. It wasn't Vrajavala, but Leelavati. She was with Gloria Griffin in a cell. On another, we saw Di Di. On another monitor, the image jumped to the Indian temples in the middle of the jungle where the guerrillas had held us hostage. I couldn't even look at those images without shuddering. You could clearly see the stairway up to the main temple, where we'd been held prisoner.

'No, John,' Wade said. 'Those aren't the same temples.'

'I think they are,' I said.

'You're wrong,' Wade said. 'That isn't anywhere on this island. It's Farber, Connecticut. Those are the temples I built. But I don't want to look at them. I don't want to look at some sad black-and-white blurry screen and see my past all blurry and black and white.'

'Are you sure it's Connecticut?' I asked.

'One hundred per cent,' Wade said.

Óscar Panero let out a cry. On one of the monitors there was a room containing a bed and lots of shelves crammed with books. Above the bed, in the place where anyone else might have had a giant poster of Madonna or Prince or Silvio Rodríguez, there was a giant black-and-white photo of James Joyce.

'That's my old room in my parents' house,' Óscar said. 'But where the fuck is the video camera? Who put it there? Jesus, if Brenda found out about this...' Óscar was cradling his head in his hands. 'The things that have gone on in that bed.'

'Oh, man,' said Roberto B. 'Just imagine.'

Just then, on the screen, a woman entered the room, walked across it and closed the window and curtains.

'My mum,' Óscar said. 'She airs my room every day.'

'They've been watching us for years,' I said. 'They observe our every move, who we're sleeping with, the books we read, what we eat... Who are these people?'

'We don't know how long they've been watching us,' Óscar said. 'Why do you say years? We don't know that.'

'Imagine if they've been watching us from birth,' I said. 'Imagine if all our lives have been observed, analysed in every detail right from the start.'

Joaquín, who'd been rummaging around in cupboards and metal filing cabinets for a while, came over to us, his eyes gleaming. He'd found a number of VHS videos in their cases, which he waved at us with a mysterious air.

'They're SIAR instruction videos,' he said. 'Look, it says "Instruction Video" number one, two, three...'

'We should watch them,' Wade said, grabbing one of the tapes and staring at the SIAR sign on the sleeve: that now familiar lion playing chess with the goat. 'There might be some useful information on them.'

So now Wade too had fallen well and truly into the trap, I thought. He may have overcome the temptation of gawping at the video of his house, the temples he'd built with his own hands in Connecticut, but this one had got him.

'There are a few VHS players,' Joaquín said. 'And they look like they might work.'

We all went together to the back of the room, where there were several VHS players and copiers. Joaquín turned one on and inserted the tape marked 'Instruction Video No. 1'. After a couple of seconds of clunking from inside the old machine, the SIAR insignia appeared on the screen.

52

Memoir of Purgatory Island by The Count of Cammarano. The Eastern and Western Tables. A Skinner Institute Production

Instruction Video No. 1

'Hello there! My name is Rudiard Kipling McCoy, PhD. I earned my doctorate in physics at Harvard University and I am currently the Director of Communications for the Skinner Institute for Anthropological Research. I will be your host during this series of tapes, which we have filmed to help you gain a better understanding of this place in which we find ourselves.

'The story of this island dates back to the sixteenth century, when Prospero of Tesla, the Count of Cammarano, a noble from the Republic of Venice, was shipwrecked here with his daughter Angela. Sent off course by a heavy storm, Cammarano's ship crashed into the rocks jutting out of the water along the northern coastline. Everyone aboard died except for the Count and his daughter, who managed to tie themselves to some empty barrels and swim ashore. That was the winter of 1580.'

The video consists, simply, of a man speaking into the camera. He looks Asian, about forty years old and dressed in a tropical khaki-coloured shirt – the kind they call a *guayabera* in Central America. The man speaks the Queen's English, without a hint of an accent. He has dark skin. He could be Malay or Filipino.

'The Count of Cammarano was a magus, which was nothing out of the ordinary. Almost all men of science, the sages, philosophers, doctors, artists and even holy men were practising magi. "Magic" didn't have the negative or childlike connotations it holds today. Magic meant a belief in nature's elemental spirits and in the creative power of words, rather like the practice of rhetoric or singing. It was generally believed that Orpheus, creator of music and Plato's master, was the first magus.

'Finding himself stranded on this island without his books, instruments, library or laboratory, the Count of Cammarano decided to devote his life to his daughter's education, and he instructed her in all the subjects he knew. Since they didn't have any books or paper, he taught her using the Art of Memory so that her daughter remembered everything. He did, however, teach her how to write, marking the letters out in the wet sand on the beach. And that is how Angela grew up to believe that writing was an ephemeral art, and that everything that one writes lasts at most the time it takes for the tide to change.

'In 1592, when father and daughter had been on the island for twelve years, another ship ran aground on the reefs along the coast. Ten men and two women survived the wreck, among them Count Pomponazzi, Deaconess Isabella III, Queen of Istria, her aunt, and the English magus Richard Kelly.

'The new castaway, Count Pomponazzi, was young and passionate. On that island cut off from the world, far from the fineries of civilised life, but also far from its constraints, love between the Count and Angela soon blossomed. Angela was too athletic and dark-skinned to fit into any ideal of beauty from that time (according to the sixteenth-century preference for languor, and morbidly white skin). And yet, she'd grown into a beautiful woman who was not only enormously cultured, but also capable of the kinds of heroic feats usually attributed to mythological goddesses: soaring through trees on a vine, hunting wild boar with a bow and arrow, swimming on the backs of dolphins, holding onto their fins. Count Pomponazzi realised that in that synthesis of Diana, Aphrodite and Minerva he had found a rare gem and the only woman who could make him happy. He too was a magus, and he believed in the power of stones, music and song. His great-uncle was Pietro Pomponazzi, the famous Aristotelian philosopher who corrected the Thomistic doctrine on the immortality of souls and wrote a treatise on the influence of the celestial bodies on human life. The Count himself had received a very fine education and, despite not being a clergyman, spoke fluent Latin. The first amorous conversations between him and Angela were, in fact, held in Latin, a language of which she, too, had a perfect command. Both of them found that all their coyness melted away in that foreign tongue.

'After a few months on the island and several failed attempts, they finally managed to get their ship seaworthy again. As a result, Count Cammarano and young Angela Cammarano were able to return to civilisation. Count Pomponazzi married Angela di Tesla and they went to live in Pula, in Istria, where the Queen had a palace next to the sea. Angela di Tesla, Countess of Pomponazzi, Duchess of Cammarano and Princess of Istria, died at the age of thirty-four in labour with her fifth child, who was baptised Salvatore Sebastiano.

'As for the Count of Cammarano, after recuperating the estates and possessions that one of his father's bastard children had tried to appropriate in his absence, he remarried, this time his cousin, Adelina Teresa Mompiani, Duchess of Bertoldi, who was nineteen at the time, and, according to all the evidence, suffered from epilepsy. The Count wrote a book called *Memoir of the incidents that occurred on Purgatory Island between Saint Silvestro's Day and Saint Bucardo's Day, as recounted by Prospero Vincenzo Carlo Cosimo Enrico Edgardo Ludovico di Tesla, the Count of Cammarano*. The book was published in Venice in 1600, two years after the Count passed away, and there is no trace of any subsequent editions. Today, the book is a bibliographical collector's item, and no complete copy remains.

'Saint Silvestre's day is the 31st of December, and Saint Bucardo's is commemorated on the 2nd of February, which means that the "incidents" related by Count Cammarano must have taken place roughly within the space of a month. As for "Purgatory", the name they gave the island in the title, it doesn't appear anywhere else – not even in the book itself.

'Contrary to what one might imagine, the *Memoir* doesn't actually recount the life of the castaways on the island. It doesn't narrate "incidents" of any kind. And it couldn't be said to be a description of either a real or imagined island, like Gracián's *El Criticón* or Bacon's *New Atlantis*. *Memoir of the incidents that occurred on Purgatory Island* is, in fact, a collection of games, described in detail and arranged by types and categories following a taxonomy.

'Some three thousand games, of every kind imaginable, are described in the book. Cammarano's categorisation – a continuous assault on common sense – seems more like the product of the mind of a collector of curios than that of a philosopher. The author mixes up and combines categories on a whim, and once or twice assigns an entire category to a single game. Here are the outlines of the games compiled and described by the Count of Cammarano:

1. Games involving pieces, chips or boards.
2. Games involving balls or globes.
3. Games involving the use of a field, forest or waterfall.
4. Memory and logic games.
5. Dice games.
6. Games involving the use of one or more wardrobes. Games involving the use of one or more mirrors.
7. Games involving the appearance, disappearance or transformation of objects, animals or people. Games involving levitation, walking on water or through walls or other solid elements.
8. Filetto or Nine Men's Morris.
9. Chaturanga, Chinese Chess and Chess.
10. Games held in parks and cities, ports and bazaars, on porches and in halls, in corridors and attics, on stairs and in pantries, in abbeys and on pontoons, in lecture halls and libraries.
11. Games in which a glass sphere is used to invoke the spirits.
12. Musical games or games that use music, rhymes or dance. Danced games. Play dances.
13. Games involving strength and balance. Throwing and distance games. Jumping, games involving climbing up and down.

14 a. Memory games. Games for playing in the desert, in prison, after a shipwreck.

14 b. Games for recluses. Games for the melancholy. Games for solitary wanderers.

14 c. Games for abandoned courtesans, for nuns, abbesses, intelligent women, women well versed in philosophy. The Papal Game. The Double Game. The Triple Game. The Quadruple Game. The Quintuple Game.

15.   Games that take into account the position of the sun or the stars. Divination games or character description games using salamanders, hare hearts, astrological charts, bezoars, pendulums, *Caliris Oxyrhynchus*, golden tongues, panoply, arboretums, Venetian tapestries, falcon feathers, cibrastis, exhibitions of atrocities, mulascos, navigation charts, fibulas, tibias, the lines on one's palm, eldorados, Melusines, trophies, gambaras, vesperal illuminations, Theodicy, shadows, *hypnerotomachias*, echinoderms, jellyfish, luminae, mustard seeds, little egret eggs, duck feathers, star anise, sacred books, the flights of birds, cherry pits and artificial eyes.

16.   Wife-swapping games.

17.   Naming and word games.

18.   Games using batons, ribbons, ropes, spades, rackets, thread, chains, spears, bows and arrows, boxes, baskets or nets.

19.   Truth games. Games with humiliating punishments, special outfits, penalties and Ultramontane missions. Games involving persecution and punishment. Games involving humiliation and wisdom. Torture games. Games with whips and masks. Games based around fear, shame and embarrassment.

20.   Games based around courage and cowardice.

21.   Slave games. Games involving the buying and selling of people (both real or figurative).

22.   Games involving tricks and scenes, ongoing deceptions and fictitious realities. The Thirteenth Guest Game. The Ray that Does Not Come from God Game. The Enamoured Ass Game. The Day Without

Evening Game. The Game of the False Angel. The Game of San Ig-
nacio and the Queen of Sheba. The El Dorado Game. The Martín
Vázquez Calapeñas Game. The Rimburtín and Rimburtina Game.
The Golden Olive Tree Game. The Blue Tooth Game. The Crystal
Dog Game. The Oidor of Ravenna Game. The Mitridate, Re di
Ponto Game. Eudoxia's Game. The Blind Emperor of Byzantium
Game. The Shaved Beard Game. The Flying Horse Game. The
Sword and the Stone Game. The Execution games. Games involving
torment: gallows, decapitation, sambenitos, clamps, thralls, dun-
geons, laws, weightings, calls for bids, trials, military campaigns, de-
feats, disasters, banishments, victories and apotheosis.

23. Egyptian ladies games. *Ludus latrunculorum.*

24. Games using different kinds of beads. Games involving necklaces
    and rosaries. Games involving plates and glasses. Games involving
    dogs and cats, horses and hippos.

25. Games where novels come to life. Battle games, campaigns and con-
    quests. Playing God. Playing the Devil. Playing Christ. Playing the
    Prince of India. The Twelve Perfect Women Game. The White Rose
    Game. The One Hundred and Eight Secrets of the White Rose Soci-
    ety Game.

26. Games for fools and madmen. Games involving spirits and fairies.
    Games involving heavenly beings. Games involving angels and imag-
    inary friends. Games involving ladies of pleasure. Games involving
    floating casements. Games involving made-up days. Games involv-
    ing deities locked inside glass retorts, flasks, vials and hourglasses.

27. Theatre of the World Games.

28. Duchess of Amalfi Games. Princess of Navarra Games.

29. Giovanni Paolo Paolino's Thirty-Nine Games.

30. The Game of the Goose.

31. Prisoner's Dilemma. The Dictator Game. The Ultimatum Game.
    Stag Hunting Games.

32. Universal Games. Involving the lottery, machines, scales, pendulums,
    coils and springs, glass beads, effigies, amulets, coins, amphorae, bones.

'The Count's book was widely read among the intellectual circles and philosophers of Venice, Florence and Rome. They thought of it as a speculative philosophical treatise, or else a coded fantasy novel in the vein of *The Dream of Poliphilus*, or an esoteric book in the style of Horapollo's *Hieroglyphica*, given that the majority of the games described within its pages had never been played anywhere and many of them implied either logical problems or moral dilemmas.

'The book then falls into oblivion until 1651, when Caspar Tamerarius, an alchemist from Basel, finds it in a bookshop in Prague's Jewish quarter, buried among Hebrew volumes on numerology, and he makes it compulsory reading for the disciples following his Aurea Teachings. This is the moment the book of games, Cammarano's *Memoir of Purgatory Island*, begins to be read again, and this is the true beginning of its influence in the West.

'Tamerarius considered alchemy to be an activity concerning man in his totality, and he made his disciples study music, practise shooting arrows and equestrianism, and made them read the ancient poets, such as Dante, Virgil, Ovid, and even the moderns or contemporaries like Ludovico Ariosto and Torquato Tasso. And yet, his disciples began to spend more and more time discussing readings of Cammarano's book, to the extent that some of them ended up abandoning their search for the *lapis philosophorum* or Philosopher's Stone and instead devoted themselves to putting the games from Cammarano's book into practice.

'We should be clear that the idea of devoting oneself to "putting the games into practice" never occurred to Tamerarius. He also made his disciples read Homer, for example, but he didn't insist they journey to Turkey or go off navigating the Mediterranean. In one of Tamerarius's letters to the Bishop of Vézelay, François Tusselain, we read that "a group of my disciples, drunk on the Count of Cammarano's thousand and one games, have decided to go off to the city of Bordeaux to create a society devoted to the study of that peculiar book. How sorry I am to watch my boys abandon The Opus, which is also the supreme task a philosopher can undertake."

'And that is how the *Tabula*, or "The Table", appears in Bordeaux: a semi-religious society whose devotees not only dedicate their time to studying Cammarano's book, as Tamerarius specified, but also convince themselves that by putting the book's games into practice – that is, by playing them – they might gain some sort of spiritual illumination. And so, they systematically played *every game in the book*. In time, the *Tabula*, or "Table", would break up into a series of different Tables. After the emergence of the Eastern Table in Geneva, the Bordeaux Table began to be known as the Western Table. Later, the Northern Table would pop up in Stockholm and a Southern Table in Trieste. And slowly but surely each Table began taking on its own distinctive character: the Bordeaux Table was mystical, almost fanatical; the Geneva Table, intellectual and erudite; the Stockholm Table, libertine and unruly in the extreme. The Trieste Table would try to get involved in politics, law, business, the university, the Church, the literary academies, the chamber of commerce, in professional trades, national celebrations and nobility – *all without losing its secret nature*. In these four Tables we can isolate the origins of the society we call modern.

'Playing *all* the games that appear in Cammarano's book requires a lot of time, enormous economic resources, and, occasionally, even supernatural occurrences. To give just a few examples, it might variously require you to journey to Antioch, to spend hours at a time under the sea (something those who took up the challenge achieved with the help of diving bells attached to chains, although many died in the attempt), to communicate with immaterial beings, to invoke male and female demons, to be a prodigy in advanced mnemonics, have a comprehensive knowledge of music and mathematics, a broad vocabulary, physical dexterity, the kind of stamina achieved only after a long period of training, to be good with one's hands, brave, to be able to overcome vertigo, revulsion, fear, dizziness and any sense of ridiculousness, and finally, to have a very active imagination. Some of the games demand seemingly impossible tasks, like, for example, the Duchess of Amalfi concentration games, which consist in modifying the sound of a harp or flute, or the colours of candle flames, or the direction in which roses grow, or the path of a line of insects, all by means of concentration. Other games can only be completed by means of symbolic actions, like, for instance, the game of the Mausoleum at Halicarnassus, a building that no longer exists. Others just can't be played because their rules are incomprehensible. Some of the games require you to be married. One of the games requires the player to be dead.

'The different Tables interpreted the Rules of the Game in different ways. The Tables, in fact, began to call themselves "The Rules of the Game": "The Rule of the North", "The Rule of the East", etc. The Bordeaux Table, for example, tended towards an esoteric interpretation of the Wife-Swapping Games, understanding them as a fraternal exchange of gifts or even knowledge. You must bear in mind that many of the participants were clergymen and couldn't be formally married, or rather weren't prepared to go swapping their concubines. For their part, members of the Stockholm Table decided to take Wife-Swapping – without doubt one of the most extraordinary and surprising parts of Cammarano's book – to its logical conclusion. It may be that the stereotype of relaxed attitudes towards sexual partners among the Nordic people and the willingness with which they acknowledged marriage among priests and the institution of divorce are down to the influence of Count Cammarano's book.

'More and more Tables developed, and, paradoxically, the more Tables there were, the more secretive they became. They popped up in Mannheim, Ostia, London, La Rochelle, The Hague, Valencia, Syracuse, Valletta and Lisbon. But in their diversity the Tables now became less set in their ways. Since playing all three thousand games in Cammarano's book was nigh impossible, other Rules of the Game began to emerge.

'These New Rules, as they soon became known, got rid of the name *Tabula* – the proverbial table around which the players huddled with their cards, chips or dice – and began to adopt names that included words taken from Cammarano's many games, like "cross", "rose", "path", "mountain", "cloud", "hammer", "sun", "yoke", "spear", etc. On the whole, the New Rules weren't in any way new. The only novelty with respect to the *Tabulae* was that where before they attempted to play all the games, the New Rules focused on just a few; sometimes on the games from one particular category, and sometimes on a set number of games taken from the list at random.

'Meanwhile, the original book, a formidable volume written in an old-fashioned and excessively verbose style, which had been circulating for years, either in the form of hand-copied manuscripts, or orally communicated, or transcribed in letters, was eventually forgotten and replaced by countless replicas, summaries and analects where neither the original title nor its author's name appeared. But while it disappeared from sight and was erased from common knowledge, Cammarano's influence and his *Memoir of Purgatory Island* became universal. From the original four Tables in Bordeaux, Geneva, Stockholm and Trieste, the games became all-pervasive. They began to interfere in politics, art, social customs, philosophy, entertainment, law, science, religion, education and in public ceremonies.

'The game-playing became so widespread, so intricate, that today there's not a single aspect of our life that isn't ruled by some variation of the Count of Cammarano's games.

'On behalf of the Skinner Institute for Anthropological Research, thank you for your attention. Please now continue to Instruction Video No. 2.'

Instruction Video No. 2

'Hello there! My name is Rudiard Kipling McCoy, PhD. I earned my doctorate in physics at Harvard University and I am currently the Director of Communications for the Skinner Institute for Anthropological Research.

'The information contained in this Instruction Video is highly confidential, and only available to those who, like all of you in Bunker 122, have access level A2 or A3. Anyone not belonging to the SIAR or without the required access level A2 or A3 must stop viewing this tape immediately. Any failure to comply will result in legal action and is punishable by imprisonment for up to three years.

'The Skinner Institute for Anthropological Research was created at the end of the 1950s at Harvard University as an undergraduate dissertation research project for three Senior students: Paavo Pohjola, Emmerich Rickenbecker and Jukka Likkendala. The title of their project paid homage to Burrhus Frederic Skinner, the Edgar Pierce Professor of Psychology at Harvard, an early proponent of behavioural psychology, philosopher, social utopian and the author of the fêted novel *Walden Two*. In short, one of the most brilliant and lucid minds of the twentieth century.

'B.F. Skinner's theories claimed that psychology ought to be considered a science just like chemistry, physics or astronomy. Opposing the romantic idea that inside the human brain lies a "soul" or "mind" or "conscience", behavioural psychologists state that human behaviour is determined by environment, positive and negative circumstances and conditionings. As such, there is no "ghost in the machine", as classical philosophy would have it. There is no "inner man" as Saint Paul would have it; no "personality", "conscience" or "I". The "mind" doesn't exist. What exists is the behaviour of the individual, which is determined by, and depends entirely on, external factors. By modifying these external factors – which include positive and negative reinforcements, but also different kinds of "rewards" and "punishments" – it is possible to modify the behaviour of human beings. They call this "behavioural engineering" and it forms the basis of the utopian vision of the Skinner Institute, whose ultimate goal is the betterment of society and eradication of hurtful or negative behaviours. We are social utopians and we're not ashamed to show it. The world needs utopianism.

'The island on which you currently find yourselves is the biggest experiment in behavioural engineering ever conducted. The aim of the experiment is the study of human behaviour

a) in extreme conditions

b) in perfect conditions, that is, in artificial isolation, just as physical or chemical phenomena are studied in a laboratory.

'The SIAR's initial project consisted in setting up a detention centre in the basements of Building B at Harvard as part of the experimental component of Pohjola's, Rickenbecker's and Likkendala's Masters dissertations. They built realistic-looking cells sealed with ironclad or barred doors. They had prisoner and guard uniforms made. Then they recruited volunteers, again both prisoners and guards. It's important to note that the volunteers were subjected to psychological testing and that the three creators rejected any candidates with alcohol or drug problems or with a history of violence or vandalism. Each volunteer's role as either guard or prisoner was chosen at random (candidates were given a number and made to spin a tombola drum full of balls). The point is, no one decided that a particular person would become a guard or prisoner, and nor did the volunteers have any choice over their position in Centre B.

'The experiment was supposed to last two weeks. The prisoners agreed to remain "locked up" for this period and to behave however they liked, although failure to comply with the rules would carry the corresponding punishment (in fact, there was only one possible punishment: solitary confinement with no food for twenty-four hours). They were allowed to withdraw from the experiment at any time if they wished to do so, but their departure would be noted in their marks and academic records. As for the guards, they too would be penalised, but not for departing. They were free to leave at any time, with no consequences. Rather, they would be punished for any failure to follow the rules, or if they were caught committing certain prohibited acts, such as fraternising with the prisoners, allowing illicit objects into the cells, turning a blind eye to anyone not respecting the silent hours, etc.

'The experiment was surprisingly simple. The prisoners could do whatever they liked, apart from leave. The guards could leave whenever they wanted, but they had to abide by, and ensure that others abided by, certain rules. As you can see, it was about experimenting with different types of positive and negative conditioning and reinforcement.

'One of the other goals of that proto-SIAR experiment was to study the classic "master" and "slave" binary, starting from the dialectical notion that the slave is in fact more free than the master. The slave, after all, may not have freedom, but nor does he have any responsibilities. The master, meanwhile, has his freedom, but with that comes the burden of responsibilities.

'The experiment didn't go to plan. Despite the fact that all of the participants in Centre B (the name given to the experiment) were Harvard Psychology students, and despite everyone knowing they were participating in a scientific experiment with academic value as part of the curriculum, cases of maltreatment and abuse started from the very first days. In fact, they couldn't even see the experiment through. By the end of the first week, torture and even rape had become widespread inside Centre B, and the three directors of the SIAR were forced to shut it down and consider the experiment terminated. Two women were raped, one of them also beaten and submitted to electric shock torture. A man was raped by three of the guards, another two were similarly tortured and another beaten. And then there were the relentless insults, humiliations and mistreatment, both physical and verbal; in addition to all kinds of sexual and non-sexual harassment, such as forcing two prisoners to have sex in front of the guards, or making them defecate in front of the guards or other prisoners.

'As far as the results of the experiments go, there are differing opinions. Why did people of seemingly sound mind, cultured people from a good socio-economic background who were in an environment that was neither stressful, dangerous nor violent, begin to behave like wild animals? Why would an elite student from one of the best universities in the world turn into a torturer or rapist the second they were given the chance?

'Each of the members of the SIAR interpreted the outcome of the Centre B experiment differently.

'For Rickenbecker, the explanation was that the participants *knew* they were taking part in a game. The problem was that they became overly involved in that game, and perhaps torturing a person doesn't seem so heinous when you know that that other person can walk away at any time, that you aren't really a torturer, and the prisoner isn't really a prisoner.

'Out of the three of them, Rickenbecker's evaluation was the most pessimistic. His conclusions stated that the results of the experiment were invalid because they had failed to create a faithful replica of the environment they wished to study. He suggested that the best thing would be to analyse the behaviour of people who didn't know they were being studied, an idea that, as we'll see, would have serious repercussions.

'For Likkendala, the reason the guards acted as sadistically as they did wasn't because they were "playing" and it simply got out of hand. They acted with violence and cruelty *because they were given the opportunity to do so*. Likkendala proposed something called the "Likkendala Factor" which predicts that a person will do anything if given the opportunity, especially in the presence of the following three conditions: 1) Favourable Circumstances; 2) Authority to Act; 3) Impunity. The Likkendala Factor explains why a peaceful, civilised person turns into a killer when you put a gun in their hand, give them a military rank and stand them in front of an "enemy". For Likkendala, what happened in Centre B shows that the participant *desired* to have the chance to attack, rape and torture. Had they not found themselves in the circumstances provided by the experiment, those people would probably never have attacked anybody in their lives, or dreamt of doing so. In the presence of the Likkendala Factor, the true nature of human beings had thrived, and the suppressed desire to kill, rape and attack others had immediately revealed itself.

'"There is no such thing as 'good people'," Likkendala argued in the paper she wrote after the event. "There are merely people who don't have the opportunity to act in a violent way or who fear the consequences. That is all."

'For Likkendala, as opposed to Rickenbecker, the experiment had been successful precisely because the participants *knew* that what they were doing was a game. She argued that the fact that the violence, sadism and desire to dominate (as much as the inexplicable submission of the prisoners) had emerged as quickly as they did in a fictitious and artificial context told us a lot about human nature.

'Pohjola's assessment of the experiment was neither as negative as Rickenbecker's (who considered it a failed experiment), nor as positive as Likkendala's. For Pohjola, the events in Centre B could only be explained by the uniforms. His theory, put simply, claimed that if the guards hadn't been wearing a full prison guard's uniform, and if the prisoners hadn't been in their orange jumpsuits – the kind they wear in American prisons – nothing serious or even noteworthy would have happened. Of course, the concept of "uniform" also includes the scenography: the cells, the metal bunk beds, the bell that meant lights out, the communal showers, the plastic trays with separate food compartments, identical to those used in other detention centres, etc. For Pohjola, what happened didn't have anything to do with the participants knowing they were playing (Rickenbecker); nor did he believe that they acted with cruelty because they were given "the opportunity to do so" (Likkendala), but because they'd felt forced to act that way by a situation and scenography that had transformed them into something entirely unlike their normal selves. Pohjola used one key piece of information to back up his hypothesis: the distribution of roles between the guards and prisoners was random, and yet the individuals had identified one hundred per cent with those respective roles. In reality, Pohjola said, when a person puts on a prisoner uniform, they begin to feel and act like a prisoner.

'Despite the scandal caused by the Centre B experiment, and the harsh words written by B.F. Skinner in the *Wall Street Journal* denouncing the experiment as arbitrary, reckless and unscientific, the three founding members of the SIAR, Pohjola, Rickenbecker and Likkendala, managed to secure funding for a second project. The money didn't come out of Harvard's pocket, however, but from an anonymous patron. In the SIAR we tend to refer to this anonymous benefactor as either The Philanthropist or Mr X.

'For the next SIAR project, the budding psychologists tried something completely different. The participants of the original Centre B trial had all signed contracts and *knew full well* that they were participating in an experiment. The new project was about studying the behaviour of people who didn't know they were taking part in any kind of experiment.

'And so, a ghost department was created in the Faculty of Psychology at Harvard: "Music Psychology" was devised to attract a limited number of people who possessed a high level of psychological and emotional intelligence. Almost immediately, this fake department – where they made courses up as they went along, without any scientific basis – began to attract students from all over the country.

'As time went by, the SIAR started to become too conspicuous. We had to find a site where we could continue to carry out our anthropological investigations into behavioural engineering, and hence, in 1967, The Philanthropist bought the island on which you currently find yourself.

'You will be wondering who this mysterious "Mr X" is.

'The anonymous Philanthropist is in fact three people, three philanthropic millionaires: Mr Mikala Alto, Craig Lewellyn and Aarvo Pohjola, Paavo Pohjola's father. They are the ghost in the machine, the true inspiration behind the Skinner Institute for Anthropological Research.

'Of the three of them, only Craig Lewellyn, an Australian comms magnate, is known to the wider public. Mr Lewellyn now lives in London where he runs his vast corporation of newspapers, radio and TV channels from the L Enterprises HQ in Canary Wharf.

'Mikala Alto, the second of the millionaires financing the SIAR, is the owner of several air and shipping companies. He lives as a recluse in a hotel called the Garter, in Dallas, Texas, where legend has it that he occupies the entire top floor.

'And as for Aarvo Pohjola, the only graphic document on which his face appears is a fairly blurry film clip from 1961 lasting twenty seconds or so, in which he seems to be dressed in a Finnish Special Air Forces uniform, getting onto a fighter plane. Mr Pohjola participated in the Second World War as a member of the armed forces for his country, and was decorated several times, with the Finnish Order of the Lion and the Gentleman of the Order of the White Rose medal. An aloof, mysterious man, he is the owner of several mining developments (of uranium, plutonium, gold, diamonds, selenium, bauxite and tungsten), which has enabled him to become a leading player in the global energy market.

'The island was discovered by pure chance. Aarvo Pohjola, an aeronautics aficionado and amateur pilot, crash-landed on this very spot in a light aircraft when crossing the Pacific.

'Pohjola's plane ended up in pieces in the middle of the island, but Mr Pohjola and his co-pilot, Enno Kuiliammi, the only other crew member on board, managed to parachute their way to safety. They landed in the area known as quadrant 16, not far from the Black Column. The intense magnetism of this area not only has the effect of sending electrical devices haywire, but it is also harmful – potentially lethal – to the human body. Fortunately, Mr Pohjola and his co-pilot had the good sense to get away from there as quickly as they could, and they headed for the coast in the hope of finding help. Of course, none was forthcoming, because the island was, and indeed still is, uninhabited.

'Mr Pohjola was forced to spend three months on the island before he finally managed to escape. He wasn't found by the rescue services, so if he hadn't come up with his own way off it, he would have died here and the SIAR would have never got to the island. The island is like a trap, you see: it's practically impossible to get off it. It's impossible, too, to rescue anyone from it because it's impossible to find. If you manage to get off (which is extremely difficult), you don't ever get back. However, as I said, Mr Pohjola not only found a way to *leave* the island, but also to *return*.

'As he would come to explain, during his entire time on the island Mr Pohjola didn't sleep one wink. It wasn't a decision, of course. The fact is that his eyes never grew tired and he didn't feel the slightest fatigue. During the first couple of days he put his lack of tiredness down to worry, nerves and the general bizarreness of the situation. But after four days of insomnia, he began to think something out of the ordinary was going on. It's not physically possible to go that long without sleep without noting serious health side effects. But not only did Mr Pohjola not feel tired, he also noticed that in both mood and physical wellbeing, he was on top form. He soon came into contact with the Wamani – indigenous people of the region who have been visiting this island since time immemorial – who offered him food and shelter. It was the Wamani who revealed to him how to get on and off the island. Even today, Mr Pohjola and the Wamani are the only ones who hold that secret. For all other humans, the island can be a dream or a prison: either a longed-for, unattainable place you perceive, or a rock in the middle of the sea where no one can hear your cries for help.

'It doesn't take a genius to work out why the Wamani – who still practised rituals including cannibalism – wanted to help Mr Pohjola. There's no doubt that Mr Pohjola is a natural born leader, an intensely charismatic man used to pulling off feats that would prove too much for the average person. It's also possible that they were fascinated by this Unsleeping Man. But there was one thing about Mr Pohjola that impressed the Wamani above all: the fact that he'd been in quadrant 16, close to the Black Column, and had survived. In their eyes, this made him, if not quite a god, then a friend to the gods.

'The Wamani have been coming to this island for centuries. According to their traditions, this is Talu Na Monani, "The Island of Sound", or also Mana Na Monani, "The Island of Voices", on the basis that when you go into the woods, you hear voices whispering to you, a phenomenon produced by the elytra on certain insects. For the Wamani, the island is sacred territory, the place where Mani, Arani and Erere – their gods – dwell. They only come to the island to perform their Sacred Hunts and the sacred ritual of reappointing the King and Queen, ceremonies without which, at least according to their beliefs, the sun would stop rising and the moon plunge into the sea, creating a giant wave that would flood the world (by "the world", they mean the handful of islands they inhabit and which they call "dry land", since the Wamani are convinced that the islands they know make up the only land on the planet).

'For the Wamani, not practising the Sacred Hunt and the King and Queen ritual would mean the end of the world. The sea would flood "dry land", all humans would drown and water would rule the earth. The savagery of those rituals convinced Mr Pohjola that the Wamani had absolutely no contact with the outside world, and confirmed his idea that he'd touched down on the last paradisical terra incognita on earth.

'However, Mr Pohjola and his assistant weren't the first White men to come into contact with the Wamani, and the eldest among the tribe still remembered when other White men had visited, many years earlier, men whom they referred to as *doichu*. *Doichu* is probably an approximate pronunciation of the word *Deutsch*. Might the last visitors have been Germans, perhaps German members of the Third Reich? The Wamani claimed that the *doichu* came from the heavens, a belief that stemmed from their conviction that their islands were the only land on earth. If they didn't come from their islands, they must have come down from on high.

'The Wamani live on islands located about seventy nautical miles south-east of Mana Na Monani. That might seem quite a distance away, but for years the people of the Pacific have travelled far greater distances in their two-man canoes. It is thought, for example, that some of the agricultural varieties cultivated in Polynesia were brought to the region by Inca navigators, and, according to genetic studies, many Polynesian peoples have Melanesian ancestries. The unusual thing, therefore, is not that the Wamani managed to get to the island, but that they are the only ones who have been able to repeatedly do so.

'Thanks to the Wamani, Mr Pohjola was finally able to get off the island. They explained the "technique" or "secret" to him. Even more importantly, they also explained how to get back. Of course, they wanted that "friend to the gods" to come back and visit them in the future.

'And that's how Mr Pohjola became the most powerful man on earth.

'Up until that point he had simply been very wealthy. But on the island he became something greater.

'During his stay on the island, Mr Pohjola had the chance to learn more about the different phenomena that occur here. No doubt you will have all heard rumours about such things: tales of spirits, magical beings, the dead come back to life, extra-terrestrial sightings. Anticipating any questions or concerns you may have, we inform you now that there is *no* extra-terrestrial base on the island, and that you have *not* died and arrived in paradise... or hell, if you prefer. You may well have seen truly extraordinary things and places on the island. In most cases, those visions, similar to mirages in the desert, are due to stress and dehydration caused by the soaring temperatures.

'To name some of the phenomena that do occur on the island, and which you may have observed:

— the blue cloud
— the golden cloud
— the white cloud
— an intense magnetism that disrupts the functioning of electrical devices
— alterations in the gravitational field
— "whispering" sounds produced by *cucuro*, a small insect not unlike a grasshopper, which lives on the underside of the leaves on many of the island's trees.

'All these phenomena, strange as they may seem, can be explained in scientific terms. There is nothing "supernatural" on the island.

'I'm sure you've heard some mention of certain "zones" or areas on the island:

— the black monolith
— the sea of solid water
— the bay of jellyfish

'All of these areas are restricted for your own health and safety.

'The whole of the island's interior, especially the central mountains, are restricted zones that must be avoided at all costs. Mr Pohjola crash-landed in the interior zone and only survived thanks to his unusually hardy constitution. The insomnia was a side effect of his time in this hazardous region. Mr Pohjola's co-pilot, Enno Kuiliammi, was not so lucky, and he died here on the island. He went mad, and threw himself off a cliff into the sea.

'I repeat: the island's interior must be avoided at all costs. In general, the higher the altitude you are at, the greater the danger. Hence why the SIAR decided to build an underground system of bunkers, in whose facilities you currently find yourselves.

'The underground area is completely safe. Whenever you go out into the exterior, you must immunise yourselves beforehand with a dose of Xitofel. Xitofel isn't necessary in Central, down in the bunkers, or on the coast, but anything from ten metres above sea level begins to be risky.

'Thank you for your attention and interest. On Instruction Video No. 3 we will give you a detailed explanation of your mission in Bunker 122.

'On behalf of Mr Pohjola, Mr Alto, Mr Lewellyn and the Skinner Institute for Anthropological Research, thank you. And good luck.'

I was so tired I couldn't keep my eyes open. I was overwhelmed by the onslaught of information we'd just received, and wanted nothing more than to go to sleep. Without so much as a word, I walked off in the direction of the living quarters, where there were bunk beds with real mattresses and pillows. I lay down on one, and was asleep in seconds.

53

We reach Central

The following day we left the Silo with our rucksacks loaded up with supplies, and resumed our search. There are no words to describe the state of our spirits then. I remember we spoke non-stop about what we'd found in the Silo. Without a doubt the most shocking discovery was that the people living on the island had been spying on us and scrutinising our every move for some time.

It occurred to us that it couldn't have been a coincidence us all being on the same Global Orbit flight, and that we'd been brought to the island on purpose. But why? To then be ignored, tortured and abused? None of it made any sense.

We progressed walking parallel to the mountain range, which was on our left in the middle of the island, and made our way south through a rocky region of almost desert-like valleys covered in plant species one would expect to find in drier climes – woody plants, small gnarled trees like mesquites and huge spiky cacti. Sometimes the long violet bristly spines would get stuck in our skin. They could easily sink a couple of centimetres into your flesh, and retrieving them was hellish. We descended laboriously along a gorge of volcanic rock (we would have been grateful for a river), towards what looked like the green plains of the south of the island.

Wade, who was up in front, let out a cry, and then we saw a woman lying between the rocks some hundred metres below. She was dressed in shorts and a fuchsia t-shirt, which stood out among the ochres and purples of the rocks. A flock of black birds with vast wingspans were circling above, watching over their potential lunch. We climbed down to the woman, imagining we'd find her dead. But she wasn't dead. It was Swayla, young Swayla, exhausted and dehydrated.

Once she had recovered a little, she told us about her epic journey. She and the other women had been carried through the jungle dangling from long poles, and then, once they'd woken up, they'd trekked in a line tied with ropes, just like they used to tie up slaves to prevent them from escaping. They were all tied with gags, and not even when they were several days' walking distance from the village did their captors remove them. The islanders and Insiders never uttered a word to them and barely spoke among themselves. They ate, walked, climbed trees to scan the landscape in the distance, made fires – all in perfect silence. The Insiders communicated among themselves through gestures or with a few English words or words from their native language, which the main leader, this Abraham Lewellyn, seemed to speak pretty well. They only had their gags removed at meal times and having had prior warning that if they spoke or screamed they'd be gagged again straight away and left with no food. So all the women ate in silence and then submissively let their captors gag them again. This obsession among the Insiders with silence wasn't new, and some of us had learnt the hard way just how important silence was to them.

Swayla didn't know where they'd taken the rest of the women. They told her to retrace her steps, and not to enter further into the island under any circumstances.

'What terrible thing am I going to find if I do go further into the island then?' Swayla had plucked up the courage to ask them.

'Well, to give you a small idea,' the man named Abraham Lewellyn had replied, 'on this island, we and the Wamani are the good guys. That lot up in the mountains are real animals.'

That man had put the fear of god into her, she told us. He was small, it's true, a kind of puppet with big bulging eyes, but those bulging eyes shone with a force that sent shivers down your spine.

The others called him 'Abe' or 'Abraham', but they treated him with enormous respect and deference. The Wamani, too, treated him with respect. They all hung on his every word. But fundamentally, he didn't seem all that terrible. His voice was high-pitched, and when he spoke he was smooth talking and ironic. He clearly had a good sense of humour and seemed to be fiercely intelligent. Abnormally so, in fact. We asked Swayla why she thought that, and she couldn't explain.

'It's just a feeling,' she said. 'The feeling that he's not like anyone else. The feeling that he's capable of almost anything, with a mind that's always one step ahead and sees what other people can't, even when it's right in front of them.'

We asked her about the children. She told us she hadn't seen them, that her group had been made up of women and she hadn't heard anyone mention the children.

Dr Sutteesh asked after Vrajavala, and Roberto B. and Óscar after Xóchitl. Swayla told them that as far as she had seen, they were all fine, and that they'd all seemed like strong, resilient women.

We told Swayla we'd give her supplies to get back to the village, but the prospect of spending days crossing the island alone terrified her, so she joined our group.

By nightfall that day we reached an open plain. In the middle of a rolling landscape covered in grass and bracken, we spotted a strange copper-coloured metal column topped with a sphere about two metres in diameter which seemed to be made of tin. The column was square with bevelled edges and the entire length was covered in drawings like runes, which seemed to have been engraved with a chisel on the metal sheet covering it. It must have been ten metres tall, and its sides glimmered in the sunlight. The tin sphere at the top shone even brighter, and gave a reflection like a mirror. Unlike the other relics, ruins and edifices we'd come across on the island, this one appeared new and well looked after. We soon discovered more identical columns, one to the right and left, and then a long line of them, all crowned with those dazzling tin spheres and as far as the eye could see, rising and falling along the grassy hillsides.

In the distance, to the left, we could see the ocean. It was the southern coast, which meant we'd managed to cross from one side of the island to the other.

We approached the columns gingerly. According to Joaquín, that row of columns and spheres must have been some sort of protective blockade, and he suggested perhaps it wasn't safe to cross the line. We did a test, throwing things over the imaginary wall or energy shield that linked one column to the next. We even caught a few living creatures – a lizard, two frogs and a newt in a nearby stream – and threw them over, just to see if they came to any harm. We'd later learn that that line of columns did indeed create a wall of energy with the aim of keeping the blue giant out of that part of the island, a wide peninsula whose isthmus we were about to cross. The peninsula where the Insiders had their HQ.

I couldn't say why the energy shield wasn't activated just then. Might they have turned it off on purpose so that we could venture across?

A couple of kilometres further along, the bush grew thicker once more. We found out later that it was the energy shield created by the columns that stripped the land of all its dense vegetation. We crossed a deep hollow terrain, then climbed out again and found ourselves back among the trees, herbaceous giants and flowering scrubs. Behind us now were the island's rocky massif and the central volcano (which, now that it appeared before us so tall and imposing, turned out not to be located in the island's geographical centre, but slightly to the south). Its peak was, as ever, blanketed in clouds. I recalled the famous cloud of glory that covers Christ in the Ascension, and the resulting representation of Christ himself as a cloud. As a shadow.

Shadow of the cloud, shield me.

Shadow of the cloud, give me shelter.

Now that the peninsula was growing wider, the indistinct view of the sea in the distance had disappeared. About two hours after we had crossed the row of metal columns, we arrived at a wall about three metres high and wrapped from top to bottom in creepers, aerial roots and all manner of plants. We skirted it in a south-easterly direction, hoping to find a gap or door into the walled enclosure. I remember it like it was yesterday; we all walked in absolute silence. We'd been walking around the wall for about twenty minutes when we heard voices on the other side: some muted female shouts, accompanied by repetitive, rhythmic blows, like a piece of wood hitting something hollow, perhaps a bamboo cane, or a bamboo cane hitting a taut length of rope. We found a spot where a giant fig tree growing right next to the wall had let its liquid branches flow over the top of it, providing a kind of network of roots and branches that were easy enough to climb. Even I managed it, albeit aided by my companions. And so, one by one, we climbed over the wall.

There was quite a lot of space between the branches and roots, and lots of crannies and holds to grab onto. The banyan's canopy camou-flaged us so we weren't visible from the other side, but also afforded us a three-hundred-and-sixty-degree view three hundred metres into the distance.

On the other side of the wall there was a huge, gently sloping and well-kept lawn. Less than a hundred metres away we could see a tennis court where four women, all kitted out in white tennis outfits, were play-ing doubles. And they played very well; like semi-professionals. Tall wire fences surrounded the court to stop the balls flying off. Behind it we could see two more courts, both empty, and a thick row of shady trees, on the other side of which you could just about make out some buildings. We were stuck there for half an hour, watching the women play and un-able to move until they finished their game and began to retire, wiping the sweat from their faces and drinking from water bottles as they put their rackets back into their covers and the bright lime green balls into their plastic tubes.

You could hear their voices clearly. They were talking in English, one of them with an Australian accent.

'What's the time?' one woman asked.

'Five-thirty,' replied another.

'So we've got time for a dip,' replied the third woman.

When the four of them disappeared, chatting away and commenting on the game and someone called Jeffrey, we clambered down the roots onto the other side of the wall.

The place seemed like some sort of luxury holiday resort. Behind the courts there was a cluster of dark trees, on the other side of which we could now see a low brick building. The grassy knolls were the edge of a golf course, where little white flags marked holes here and there. In the distance I could see a ride-on lawnmower moving slowly down the other hillside, the distant hum of its engine cutting through the clear afternoon air.

Beyond the tennis courts there was a big swimming pool surrounded by a paved area with hammocks and sunshades. Some twenty or so men and women were in the pool, while others lounged on hammocks or sat under sunshades sipping from highball or cocktail glasses. Waiters carrying trays moved back and forth from inside the brick building to round aluminium tables. We approached them discreetly, but didn't attempt to hide ourselves; firstly because there was no way of doing so, and secondly because it seemed far-fetched that those fine-seeming people would want to do us any harm.

We were completely dumbstruck. I think we'd all assumed the Insiders lived in the jungle, perhaps in huts. We'd assumed they had guns and food, but I don't think any of us had imagined that while we were forced to live out in the open with no running water, food or medicine, there were others, just a few kilometres away, enjoying all the comforts of civilisation.

We were looking at Central. 'Central' they called it. Likkendala City, to give it its official name, had about sixty houses, several office buildings, a hospital, a college, warehouses where they kept vehicles and tools, an underground storehouse where they stockpiled supplies and guns, the circular building referred to as 'the temple', which took us by surprise the first time we saw it and served as a kind of meeting centre (for there were no churches or actual temples of any kind in Likkendala City). And then the hundred or so green barracks at the back where personnel were trained and the non-specialist workers lived. The total population was about four hundred, and the average age was thirty-five. I don't know why they hadn't built the city on the coast, which is always cooler. Whatever their reasons, the island's high temperatures weren't a problem for the people of Likkendala City, since almost all the houses boasted air-conditioning. A road connected the city to the port, which was located in a bay naturally protected from strong tides. The city also had an airport with a tarmac runway overrun with moss and grass, which had clearly been abandoned for years given that it wasn't possible to access or leave the island by air. Likkendala City's only connection to the outside world was via submarine. Of course, we would learn all these details later. Right then, the only thing we could do was gaze at the city laid out at our feet, and swivel our heads from side to side, unable to believe what we were seeing.

A waiter approached us and asked us graciously if we were members of the club. We gawped at him, with no answer. But this whole situation I've described lasted only a few minutes. Within seconds, several jeeps tore up the slope and surrounded us. A group of armed men jumped out and forced us into the vehicles at gunpoint. Then they drove us to the barracks we'd spotted at the far end of the city. Scenes of civilised life left us speechless as we drove past bungalows. A children's swing hanging from a tree. A man in a straw hat trimming a hedge. A group of men in blue work overalls leaning on what looked like the bar of a drinking joint that opened out onto the street. A group of women in leotards doing yoga on a lawn. When we reached the barracks, they pulled us out of the jeeps, still without a word, and shut us up in those buildings, two to a room. And that's how we fell captive to the Insiders.

They put me in a very basic room – more of a cell, really – with Wade. The ceiling and walls were white but for a khaki green strip, about a metre high from the floor, that ran around the room. On either side there was a bed with a cotton quilt on it, and in the middle of the room a Formica table with two metal seats. The room had a barred window with a blind, a fan on the ceiling, and a small bathroom with a mirror, a sink and a toilet – spartan comforts for most people, but to us it was like being in a five-star hotel. You opened the tap and water came out. You flicked the switch and the light came on. With just a push of a button on the wall, the fan whirred into motion. The bed was a real bed, and the sheets were clean, and we had a roof over our heads, a real roof, and real walls, even if they were the walls of a cell. I remember feeling happy to be in there, and I remember Wade looking at me less than kindly.

'Happy hostage, are you, John?'

'Don't be so negative,' I said. 'These people can't be so bad. Look how they live. They've got pools, tennis courts, electricity... There are families living here. Didn't you see the swings and kids' toys? This could be the end of our troubles.'

When night fell they served us dinner: salad, cassava, rice, black beans in sauce and boiled fish, and a green jelly for dessert. Delicious, every last morsel.

Half an hour after they'd taken away our plates, the lights went out.

54

We meet Abraham Lewellyn

We *couldn't believe that the* inhabitants of that city really were the same people who'd been hounding and harassing us for months, the same people who had gassed us like animals and kidnapped our children and women. But any doubts faded the following morning.

They woke us up at six-thirty and led us to some showers located at the back of the barracks where they gave us bars of soap and towels and let us have a wash before handing us new clothes to replace our rags. They made us shower all together, men and women alike. We kept our backs turned. Next, two armed men told Wade and me to follow them. They handcuffed us from behind, led us out of the barracks and into town. We were walking at a steady pace, which allowed me to take a better look around.

I still had a good feeling about the place. The prefab houses were neat, nestled among beautifully tended gardens. Tables, chairs and benches sat in the shade of the trees, generally banyans and acacias with giant canopies, where groups of friends or families would sit chatting come evening. On the verandas hung hammocks, and crystal, mother-of-pearl and bamboo mobiles, which chimed in the breeze. Beethoven's Sixth Symphony was playing out of the speakers mounted on the posts. We passed some vans carrying workers wearing blue or grey overalls, and jeeps with men and women in hard hats and white coats. Nothing could surprise us any more, not even the sight of armed men carrying long rifles. We saw a group of children trudging their way into school in double file, some of them dressed in hats with feathers, and green and red capes. We didn't spot any of ours among them. We also saw a kind of storage building with its doors open and two lorries inside; it resembled the lorries they used after the Second World War. The people we crossed paths with looked at us inquisitively, but they didn't seem particularly surprised to see us walking along with our hands cuffed behind our backs being escorted by two men with guns.

They took us to the office building we'd seen the day before. It had two floors and was painted that yellow squash colour. We went down a long corridor with doors on either side, then up a floor where our two guards ushered us into a spacious office with two leather sofas and a coffee table on one side, a large desk on the other. The walls were panelled with dark, cheap wood (stained plywood, probably, although the effect was welcoming and cosy), and there were several tropical plants in pots on the floor and along the window ledges. The window blinds were half open, pleasantly filtering the intense morning light. On the back wall, behind the desk, hung a large oil portrait of a tall man with a gaunt, pale face dressed in a navy blue suit. On the brass plate at the bottom of the picture frame I read the name: Aarvo Pohjola. The men who had escorted us placed two chairs in front of the desk and told us to sit and wait.

We did what we were told and were then left on our own in the office. Wade glanced at me and I noticed his pupils shifting up and then left and right. I followed the direction of his gaze and saw two cameras in the top back corners of the room. They were watching us. Listening to us. We stayed silent. I studied the face of the man in the portrait carefully. He looked to be about sixty, was tall, well built and handsome, with grey hair and intense dark eyes. I tried to work out who he was, or rather who he'd been, that mysterious Aarvo Pohjola, but the portrait's brushstrokes gave nothing away.

Just then, a side door opened and through it walked the same man who I'd seen directing operations during the gassing in the village. He introduced himself as Abraham Lewellyn, a name now etched in all of our minds in one way or another, and for a second it looked like he was going to come up and shake our hands, which would have been impossible given we were both handcuffed from behind. Instead, he sat down behind his desk, let out a heavy sigh and looked at us with a strange smile. He was a small, insignificant-looking fellow, and at the same time, and I can't pinpoint why, extremely charismatic.

'At last we meet – isn't that right?' he said nervously, as if he wasn't sure where to begin.

'Where are the women?' Wade asked with extraordinary composure. 'Where are the children?'

'You're not here to ask questions,' the man said, opening a cardboard folder on the desk and studying the documents inside.

'Why are you treating us like criminals?' I asked. 'Our plane came down on your island. We're stranded here. Why are you treating us like this?'

He didn't pay me the slightest attention. The desk was covered in pieces of paper and files and he busied himself opening orange folders and leafing through their contents: photocopies of documents and typed-up sheets of paper. I suppose he was trying to gain time, or to provoke us into losing our tempers. At first, I thought it was all theatrics. Later I learnt that the files contained detailed reports on each and every one of us.

'John Barbarin,' he said, looking at me. 'Born in Madrid, Spain. Tenure in Rosley College, Lecturer in Composition, Oakland, Rhode Island. Composer recognised for his neoromantic and tonal affinities. Author of one opera, one chamber opera, three string quartets, five symphonies, none of which have been performed... Is that right?'

'One of the quartets was performed,' I said. 'By the Emerson Quartet, I think you'll find.'

'Wade Erickson,' the man went on, moving on to Wade's file. 'Car mechanic. Owner of a repair shop in Farber, Connecticut. Now retired as a result of a hold-up in which he was left injured. The assailant was his half-brother, Raymond Erickson, currently in prison. The bullet entered his spinal column, leaving him paraplegic and confined to a wheelchair.'

Wade glared at him, not saying a word.

'Things have gone well for you on the island, haven't they, Wade?'

Wade didn't answer. I admired his self-control.

'Don't you have anything to say? I said things have gone well for you on the island. The island has been good to you. More so than to anyone I've ever met. With one exception, of course.'

'I can't complain,' Wade said.

'Good,' Lewellyn said. 'Now let's get down to business.'

He fell silent and looked around him. I looked around the room, scouring it for clues, for possible answers. On one wall, there was a poster with instructions in case of choking, like the ones you get in American restaurants. There were also signed photos of Aldrin, the astronaut, Ronald Reagan, Art Pepper, Bobby Kennedy, Nancy Sinatra and some other people I didn't recognise.

'Suppose,' Wade began, 'suppose you tell us what it is we're doing here.'

'Why don't you tell me?' Lewellyn answered. 'You're the ones who turned up here uninvited. Nobody asked you to come. What the hell are you doing here?'

'We've told you a thousand times,' I said. 'It was an accident.'

Lewellyn gave another deep sigh and leant back in his leather chair. All of a sudden, the image seemed quite comical to me. The seat was too big, too imposing for that man.

'Carmen and George told me you don't know a thing,' he said at last, 'and I didn't believe them. I can't believe you've survived so long under these conditions. The island is normally merciless. That's what we can't get our heads around.

'Mr Pohjola seems to hold you in high esteem. To be frank, personally I can't understand why. A car mechanic from Connecticut and a third-rate composer and ladies' man... Yes, it is very odd indeed, but for some reason, each in your own way, you two have reached some kind of... some kind of understanding with the island...'

Wade and I said nothing.

'On this island...' Lewellyn said, now staring out towards the light streaming in through the plastic slats of the blinds. 'How can I put it so you understand? Let's say that on this island, in one particular spot, there's a box… no, let's call it a room… A room. Do you follow? And inside that room lies EVERYTHING.

'Let's say, too, that three of your lot, God only knows how, have managed to find this room. Let's say that three of you, for who knows what reason, have managed to come to a kind of agreement with this island, so the island has allowed you to find the room. Those three people are you two, Wade Erickson, John Barbarin, and a third, Santiago Reina.'

'Oh,' Wade said.

'I hope that answers your question, Mr Erickson,' Lewellyn said. 'That's why you've been brought here.'

'Brought?' I interjected. 'We weren't "brought" here. We came of our own volition. And anyway, if you wanted to bring us here, why didn't you just take us when you ambushed the village? You took plenty of others.'

Abraham Lewellyn stared at me, his big, bloodshot eyes gleaming.

'You had to come of your own volition,' he said. 'On the island there are things that have to be done a certain way. If you don't do them as they ought to be done, the outcome is unpredictable. Mr Pohjola told us that you must get here on your own. Mr Pohjola has his particular way of doing things. He alone truly knows and understands the island.'

'You never quit talking about this Mr Pohjola,' Wade said. 'It's Aarvo Pohjola we're talking about, right?'

'That's right.'

'From the way you speak,' Wade went on, 'it sounds as if it isn't you calling the shots, but Mr Pohjola.'

'That's correct.'

'Come on, Lewellyn,' Wade said. 'You can't pull the wool over my eyes. You're in charge of this whole circus.'

'Me?' he almost shrieked, as if the very idea were absurd. 'No, no, you're quite mistaken. I just follow orders…'

'You mean to tell me that it's not you who gives the orders around here?'

'Is that what you think?' Lewellyn asked, seemingly amused. 'That I'm in charge of all these people? Some kind of King of the Island?'

'Everyone talks about you as if you were the boss.'

'I'm just the go-between,' Lewellyn said. 'I don't give the orders. It's Mr Pohjola who does that.'

'So, this famous Mr Pohjola, is he by any chance on the island?' I asked.

'Yes,' he answered curtly. 'Mr Pohjola is on the island.'

'Come on, Lewellyn,' Wade said. 'What the hell are you talking about? Pohjola was already an old man in the seventies. He can't be on the island. Aarvo Pohjola must have died... twenty, thirty years ago.'

'So Mr Pohjola is on the island,' I said, fascinated. 'And you speak with him?'

'Well, of course I speak with him. He is our leader. He is our guide. He is the one who tells us what we must do.'

'So, all those dumbass things you lot do; those crazy, ridiculous things – attacking the village, kidnapping the children, the set-ups, the costumes, all that stuff... you do it on Pohjola's orders?'

Lewellyn sighed and sat back in his seat once again. He seemed bored and tired, as if the same questions had floated there, over that desk, many, many times before.

Wade and I glanced at each other.

The Wizard of Oz came to my mind.

'Let's see,' I said. 'I'm not sure I quite follow. As I understand it, somewhere on this island there's a room you lot are looking for. And the three of us, for some unknown reason, have managed to get to this room.'

'Exactly,' Lewellyn said.

'And you want us to tell you how you get there, correct? But this can all be resolved quite easily. I'll tell you how to get there. I'll tell you right now. I've got no interest in hiding it from you. You just have to find one of the tunnels in the abandoned motorway. You'll know which one to take because one of the tunnels is completely blocked by a pile of rubble and weeds. The other is almost completely obstructed, but you can get through to the other side.'

Abraham Lewellyn looked at me with a faint smile, as if what I was telling him held some hidden meaning that I wasn't aware of.

'What exactly is this place you call "the abandoned motorway"?' he asked.

'Well,' I said, 'it's hard to describe it any other way, because it's just an abandoned motorway. A two-lane viaduct that crosses one of the valleys, held up by concrete columns. I don't think there's more than one construction like the one I'm describing.'

'There is no abandoned motorway on the island,' Lewellyn said, looking at me amused. 'What on earth are you talking about?'

'We all saw it,' I said. 'All of us on that trip. We spent the night there.'

'That's something Mr Pohjola put there for you,' Lewellyn said, looking at me now with something close to envy. 'Yes, it's one of Mr Pohjola's sets. Thorough down to the last detail, completely realistic, rusty, old, dotted with lichen, rock solid as if it had been there for fifty, a hundred, a thousand years. You touched its columns, and walked up the old abandoned motorway, and went into one of the tunnels cutting through the mountain, I'm guessing...'

'More or less.'

'And yet, *none of this existed*. They are spectacles put on by Mr Pohjola. Spectacles. That's all. Mr Pohjola makes them with the materials he has at his disposal, which are virtually infinite and inexhaustible. He can use your memories, or his own memories, or create memories out of things that never existed. For him all the earth's materials are the stuff of dreams.'

'You say that Mr Pohjola "puts on spectacles"?' I asked, completely riveted by what Lewellyn was telling us. 'But how the hell can anyone just produce a motorway out of nothing?'

Abraham Lewellyn took a deep breath and let it out before answering, as if looking for a way to explain himself.

'There are three powerful men behind the SIAR,' he said at last. 'One of them was the man who found the island. In time the three men clashed, but Mr Aarvo Pohjola, the man who discovered the island, trounced the others and took control over everything. All this is water under the bridge. The SIAR disappeared a while ago. Their games were nothing to the island. The island destroyed the SIAR, split it up, reduced it to nothing. But Mr Pohjola was close to the Black Column. When he landed on the island, he spent weeks living near it. He didn't die, he didn't go mad, as seems to happen to other people. "Black Column" is the name the natives give to one of the mountains on the island's interior, a basaltic peak really, which looks like a column shooting out of the earth. The magnetism is so intense in that area that all electrical devices go haywire. Not even gravity works normally near the Black Column. Rocks float in the air...'

Wade and I glanced at one another.

'In reality, the Black Column is a tremendous source of energy. It seems to contain within it some unknown energy or mineral.

'In any case, Mr Pohjola was transformed when he arrived on the island. Some say he's no longer human. Others believe he lost his mind. His power surpasses all of us. His abilities are inconceivable.'

'He turned into a blue giant,' Wade said.

Abraham looked at him pensively for a moment. Then he lowered his gaze and took a deep breath.

'You lot really don't know anything, do you?' he said again, as if confirming a truth so unthinkable that he refused to accept it. 'How have you managed to survive so long? This island is ruthless... How have you not all been killed?'

'Is he in this building?' Wade asked. 'Is he listening to us right now?'

Abraham Lewellyn looked to either side anxiously, as if Wade's words filled him with terror.

'Mr Pohjola isn't *here*,' he said, looking at Wade furiously. 'Nobody can speak to him.'

'But *you* can.'

'Yes.'

'Do you speak telepathically?' Wade asked.

'When I have a query, I go and see him.'

'Only you?'

'Yes, of course,' Lewellyn said.

'Where does he live?'

'That's of no concern to you.'

'And the others?'

'What do you mean?'

'Why can't the others go to speak to Pohjola if he really exists? Why does he only let you go? Why are you the only one who's allowed to enjoy this special privilege?'

'Speaking with Pohjola truly is a privilege,' he said. 'But it's a privilege that comes at a great price. If I didn't go to speak to him, no one else would.'

'Why not?'

'Because they'd be too afraid,' Lewellyn replied.

'Pohjola!' Wade called out suddenly. 'Where are you hiding, Pohjola? I want a word with you! Are you listening?'

'Shh!' Lewellyn said. 'Be quiet! Shut up right now!'

That instant, the door opened and the armed men who'd escorted us there entered the room. And it was no more Mr Nice Guy. They gagged us roughly, shoving a piece of wood in our mouths, and they marched us out of there, aiming their rifles at us and occasionally thrusting the barrels into our ribs. From there, we were led straight back to our cell.

55

Bruckner in the Meadow

That night, after lights out, I tried to practise the meditation tech-niques I'd learnt from Dharma. I sat on one of the chairs, rested my hands on my knees and closed my eyes. I followed the steps he'd given us, paying attention to my breathing and relaxing my entire body, ob-serving the motions of my mind, and then concentrating all my attention on a single point.

Images, thoughts and memories flooded my mind. Worries. Voices.

Patiently, I put all my attention on my breathing and tried to make those unpleasant, intrusive thoughts dissolve and leave me in peace. Then I focused again on the space between my eyebrows. I saw the image of a dark room, in the middle of which was Dharma. He was dressed as I'd seen him so many times in the village: barefoot, wearing simple light trou-sers and a black t-shirt. Around his neck hung a rudraksha seed rosary with a red tassel on the end.

'Dharma,' I said, 'How can I get out of here?'

'Keep meditating,' he told me. 'Keep meditating.'

Then he sat on the floor in front of me, crossed his legs and put his hands on his knees in the classic mudra position, index finger and thumb touching, the other three fingers extended, palms facing up. Then he said: 'Copy me. Pretend you are me.'

I did as instructed.

Almost immediately I noticed a change: in how I felt, in my body. Be-cause now I'd entered Dharma's state. I thought I could feel a gentle breeze, a force lifting me up above myself. I felt my body physically transform into thousands and then millions of light particles that instantly started to move, dissolved in space. For a few seconds, I had a vision, or perhaps the feeling, of being one of those Escher drawings where a castle turns into hundreds of swallows that dissolve into the air. At the same time, my consciousness was suddenly luminous. I lost all awareness of my physical body, which vanished around me, and became aware of a much subtler body that seemed to be made up of light or energy, without clearly defined limits.

Soon the whole room disappeared, and I saw myself walking through the countryside along a grassy hillside. Rosana was there, a little further up. She held out her hand to me.

'Juan Barbarín,' she said. 'I'm happy to see you here. Mr Pohjola would like to speak with you.'

'You know Mr Pohjola?'

I followed her, and together we walked up the hillside through the shady thick trees and branches and shrubs with big dark leaves, and then we emerged and found ourselves walking along the streets of Pozuelo.

'We're in Pozuelo,' I said. 'These are the streets of Pozuelo.'

'That's what it looks like,' she said.

We were, in fact, on Calle de los Olmos in the Pozuelo of my childhood. Rosana opened the gate to Cristina's house and we went in and walked across the lawn. She was ahead of me and when she reached the wall of cypresses that separated the Villars' garden from the next one, she stopped.

'You have to go in,' she said. 'Mr Pohjola is waiting for you.'

I carried on in the direction of the row of cypresses and slipped through it without any trouble.

And that's how, for the second time since arriving on the island, I entered the Meadow. I slipped through the cypresses and there I was, in the old garden where I'd played as a boy. On the upper level there were two trees, one dark and one light, probably a carob and a willow, and between the two trees there was a little stone house with a broken roof and windows, some partially boarded up.

I went up and saw that in front of the house was a table and two benches like the ones you get in beer gardens in Germany and Austria. And, in fact, on the table there were two pitchers of golden beer sparkling in the sunlight. All of a sudden I felt incredibly, unbearably thirsty. Next to the table stood a tall, balding man dressed in nineteenth-century peasant garb: a sky-blue smock with long shirt tails, baggy, beige trousers and sturdy rambling shoes. On seeing me he smiled timidly, and held out his hand in a courteous gesture. I had already recognised who he was. His hair – both the cropped, thin bristles on his head and the almost non-existent moustache on his top lip – was so pale it was almost invisible. He was tall, thickset but not quite fat, and had a bony little head with a nose like the beak of a parrot or cockatoo. His eyes were small, shiny and deeply expressive. I shook his hand.

'Please, take a seat,' he said in a high-pitched, cheery voice. 'Come have a bock with me.'

We each sat down on a bench, then he took one of the pitchers and raised it in the air. I was scared to eat or drink the foodstuff from my dreams, so I took the pitcher and raised it to his, then put it to my mouth fully intending to pretend to take a sip. But when the cool liquid hit my lips I couldn't resist and I drank from the pitcher. A long, long swig of golden, tangy, delicious ice-cold beer.

'Who are you?' I asked. 'Are you Mr Pohjola?'

'Pardon me?' the man asked.

I repeated the question.

'My name is Bruckner,' he told me, 'at your service.'

His thick accent and outmoded way of speaking made it hard to understand what he was saying.

'When will you finish your ninth symphony, Mr Bruckner?' I asked.

'Oh, we're working on it, we're working on it,' he said. 'At present I'm busy with a cantata about the island of Helgoland...'

I wasn't convinced. This was information anyone could get hold of.

'Mr Bruckner, this garden here... this Meadow, this house, these trees – what is it all?'

'I'm sorry?' he asked. 'Pardon me, dear sir. I fear I haven't understood your question.'

'Where we are right now?' I said. 'It's not a real place, is it?'

'We are in Toblach,' he said. 'Toblach, close to Herr Mahler's abode.'

'Herr Mahler is around too?' I asked. 'Herr Gustav Mahler?'

'A quite brilliant young man,' he said. 'He wanted to take instruction from me, but I only had to listen to him play for five minutes to realise I had nothing to teach him. He used to visit me regularly in Vienna, and when he left I would always accompany him right to the door down on the street. A quite remarkable young man. He could show a little more interest in counterpoint, it's true. But counterpoint only seems to interest the older ones...'

'Toblach,' I said. 'So we're in Austria?'

'Indeed we are, my dear friend,' he said, chuckling. 'Where else?'

'We can't be in Toblach,' I said. 'We can't be in Austria. We can't be close to Herr Mahler's house. We can't be talking here, you and I, because I live in the twenty-first century and you and Mahler died a hundred years ago.'

Bruckner nodded gently then took a long swig of beer and wiped his mouth with the back of his hand, discreetly stifling a burp.

'This is the Garden of Resurrection,' he told me. 'This place is everywhere and nowhere. For me it is in Toblach. It may be somewhere else for you. That doesn't matter. Nor does time matter much here.'

'Tell me more,' I said. 'I want to know about the Garden of Resurrection.'

'Oh, words, words,' Bruckner said with a heavy sigh. 'I've never been a man of many words. Speaking... that is surely what music is for? I mean, to let music itself speak.'

'This garden we're sitting in... is it the Adagio from the Eighth Symphony?' I asked.

Bruckner looked around, but I got the impression that the idea didn't come as much of a surprise. He was still holding the glass handle of his pitcher and slowly, unconsciously, rubbing it with his thumb.

Then he sank his hand into one of his pockets and pulled out a paper bag full of cherries, which he began to eat, lost in thought, leaving the golden stones on the table, next to his bock.

'Yes, it's possible,' he said at last. 'It might well be the Adagio. Or the Finale, I don't know. No, probably the Adagio. In any case, it's clearly the Eighth Symphony.'

We both fell silent.

I've always felt that the Adagio from the Eighth Symphony describes a garden, one that takes the now well-known form of the Meadow, which I've come across in several places in my life. Certain elements might differ slightly, as might the dimensions. The Meadow might be surrounded by a tall stone wall or a simple wall of plants, it might be divided by a single step or an entire retaining wall, which you climb via a staircase. The trees might be small or very big, and between them there might be a wooden hut or a two-storey stone house. In front of the step, on the lower level, there is a trap door or hatch, which opens up into the ground. The Meadow always matches these descriptions, and the Meadow where I found myself just then was no different.

'Mr Bruckner,' I asked, 'why are we here? What does this place mean? Does it represent the mystery of music? Is it a map of Reality? A representation of the Soul?'

Bruckner went on gazing around him. It seemed to me that he was looking at the countryside and plants as peasants are wont to do: directly, rationally, free from pastoral idealism. And that surprised me, because I'd always thought that Bruckner, like Beethoven or Mahler, was one of the great idealisers of nature. He left the stone of the last cherry he'd eaten on the table, crumpled shut the paper bag and put it back in the pocket of his smock. Then he stood up from his chair, leaning on his knees as an elderly person might do, and walked off in the direction of the house. He took a few steps then stopped.

'When I began writing the Eighth Symphony,' he said, 'I was thinking of the duet between the lovers from the second act of *Tristan und Isolde*...

A man, a woman, a woman, a man… That syncopated figure from the start, which in Wagner is in A flat major and in my Adagio in D flat. That is the music of the Meadow, Herr Barbarin; of what you call "the Meadow", the music of the two lovers… The battle between two forces… One that descends – a descending scale in D flat major – and the other ascending… and the sinuous, chromatic motif of the snake… The music from the Adagio represents paradise, perhaps… The air blowing in the Meadow where a man and woman lie in one another's arms… Hasn't it ever occurred to you that the two trees, one light and the other dark, one strong and the other soft, represent a man and woman?'

'A man and woman?' I said. 'No, the truth is I hadn't. I've always understood them as something more mystical…'

'What could be more mystical!' Bruckner exclaimed. 'I've always thought that *Tristan und Isolde* contained the most mystical music ever written… I said it, and they laughed at me… Yes, I think you can still make out their cackles in the distance… "*Tristan* is the representation of sexual love!" they said. "Passion! Not mysticism! Old Bruckner doesn't know what he's talking about! Poor old fool! He's as naïve as a child!" And I say that they're the ones who haven't understood *Tristan*…

'A male tree and a female tree. Both separated, but their roots entwined under the ground. And their leaves and their branches also meet up above, perhaps. But where they definitely both meet is in their shade, when evening falls. Their shades grow and unite across the Meadow. Do you see, Herr Barbarin?

'I have always loved the shade of trees. The shade of the trees lining the streets of Linz. The shade of the limes along the avenues of the imperial city of Vienna. The shade of the elders on a cherished walk through the countryside. The shade of the trees is our shelter from the sun and rain. And out of the shade of the trees – do you see? – emerges a house…

'We could say that the house represents the son. Christ, who is the Son and also the shade, the cloud's shadow on the surface of the earth. You have seen the cloud a few times. But you have never searched out the cloud's shadow. What are we – we poor sheep led to the slaughterhouse –

but part of the cloud's shade, that which the cloud leaves on the earth's surface? A trace. A shadow. And from the trees' shade emerged a house...

'Music is Christ because Christ is "sound made flesh". Do you see?'

I stood up from my seat, but he gestured at me to wait.

'You aren't really Anton Bruckner,' I said. 'You are a philosopher. A mystic. Are you Aarvo Pohjola?'

'Look at your feet,' he told me, firmly.

I looked down in a daze, unsure of what I was supposed to be seeing. I looked at my feet and what I saw was nothing out of the ordinary, though for me it was quite extraordinary.

'My God!' I shouted. 'I've got both of my feet!'

'You cannot be in this place and not be complete,' Bruckner said. 'You say you don't understand, that you don't know what you're doing here. The answer is quite simple. You have come here to create. That's what music is for, to create. You must create a house, and enter the house and live there in it. You must create shade and live in that shade, and let others live in it too. What is music for? To open a flower in your brain. And out of that flower grows a tree. Out of the tree a creature. And that creature will set off walking. You are a feather of God's great bird. When all its feathers are alive, the great bird will open its eyes and take flight. Until that moment, the great bird is nothing but a dream, a collection, a list, a library, a museum, an ossuary...

'Do you understand that I'm talking to you of a transformation, of an inner transformation? Do you understand that I'm telling you that you are here because you desire this transformation?'

'A transformation,' I said. 'What should I transform into?'

'Into a star,' Bruckner said. 'What else?'

He pointed to the crisp blue sky, which held no stars at all. And I looked up to this vast expanse of bright blue, imagining all the invisible stars, and imagining my star among them, the one that had always been waiting for me, the one that always *knew about me*.

'But why?' I asked. 'What for?'

'What for?' said Bruckner, or whoever it was talking to me. 'That is the question. Many have searched for that "star within man" but they don't know why, or to what end. They desired to ascend the great chain of being, but they still didn't know why.'

'To help others, perhaps,' I said. 'To help those who suffer.'

'That is the answer,' Bruckner said. 'To undertake the great duty of love. To help others. To help those suffering.'

I tried to stand up again, but couldn't. I saw the man who wasn't Bruckner and who might have been Pohjola walking slowly towards the house, and how, the closer he got to it, the bigger that house became. It was like the house was coming back to life as the climbing plants flowered and panes of glass and net curtains appeared now in the windows. I watched as the man finally reached the front door, took the handle and opened it. And then he disappeared inside, closing the door behind him.

56

A message from Mr Pohjola

Now *my fellow trekkers were* taken every day to a stone quarry about twelve kilometres from Central, where they were made to work like slaves. They would physically carry Wade to work there each morning and then carry him back last thing in the evening to the cell, completely exhausted, his lips chapped with thirst and his arms sunburnt. He told me it was clear that the quarry had been out of use for years, and that the work they were made to do served no practical purpose. Five days after we arrived in the city, Jimmy Bruëll's group were also captured, locked up in the barracks, and forced to work the quarry all day. I never caught sight of any of them – owing to my physical condition, I didn't go to the quarry – but Wade would come back every day and recount the dreadful brutalities they'd been subjected to.

He told me the work was exhausting even for a young, strong man, and that they gave them all the same tasks: stone breaking with huge metal-headed hammers whose handles wore the skin from their hands after a couple of hours; and then loading wheelbarrows which they had to push along the rocky, slippery paths that ran around the edge of the quarry before falling away down the open mountainside; and then they were made to come back pushing the wheelbarrows back up the hill to the path, open wounds and all. Anyone who refused to work was whipped. The guards had installed a horizontal wooden crossbar to which they'd attached two handcuffs: they would cuff the prisoner with his arms raised, strip his clothes from his back and lash him with a leather whip. I asked if they'd given the same treatment to the women, and he told me that up until that point they'd only lashed Jimmy and Jung Fei Ye, both times because of a woman.

It appeared that the first of these incidents arose when Rosana simply refused to work any more. She threw her hammer to the ground and sat down on a rock. It was an act of bravery, certainly. Wade didn't know what Rosana was thinking. Maybe she thought that if they all refused to work, the guards wouldn't be able to make them. Three or four of the guards approached her and told her to get straight back to work or they'd lash her. Rosana told them calmly that she was a citizen of the European Union and that what they were doing was completely illegal. She said they were all castaways, survivors of a plane crash, and that their obligation was to lend them humanitarian aid and help them get in contact with the nearest consulate from our countries of origin so that we could be repatriated as soon as possible. My God, I guess she had it pretty well planned out. I think the guards were confused. The big boss, a rough-looking fellow called Brady, had to come over and confront her.

'Let's put it this way,' Wade explained, 'you wouldn't want to meet Brady down a dark alleyway. A giant man, strong, and with a big beer belly. He's got the beard of an Australian miner and rancid, stinking breath from chain-smoking cigars. Brady flashes her the whip he always carried in his belt and says, "Lady, if you don't get up right now you're going to have to have words with my mate Jiminy Cricket." He calls it Jiminy Cricket, his whip. Next thing Jimmy turns up and starts insulting the guards in that smooth, slow, smiling style of his. Credit where credit's due: Jimmy is the master of the insult. He's never crude, and always smiles. He's smooth, intelligent, surprising and erudite. He hits you where you least expect, and always hits you right where it hurts.

'So the guards turned their backs on Rosana, and directed all their wrath at him, giving him a good beating. First with their rifle butts, then their feet. Then the rest of us moved in shouting at them, but the guards surrounded Jimmy and aimed their guns at us. I think Jimmy was almost unconscious when they tied him to the post to beat him. They gave him ten lashes and by the end of it his back was covered in bloody lines. He's in hospital now. And as for Jung Fei Ye, he offered to take Lizzy's lashes for her. Her hands were red raw and she too had refused to go on working. Such a noble act coming from that Singaporean ex-cop, who I'd considered a cold-hearted torturer, blew me away. In a sign of respect, Jung Fei Ye had bent his head and asked for the honour of receiving the lashes in Lizzy's place. Brady said he'd rather see Lizzy naked than Jung Fei Ye, who then pointed out that Brady didn't need to beat Lizzy to see her breasts; he didn't have to hurt her, just order her to take her top off. Brady thought that Jung Fei Ye was mocking him, so he tied him to the horizontal bar and gave him ten lashes. That's a lot of lashes, John. Think about it. One lash. The man writhes, all the muscles in his body clench involuntarily, and a red band appears on his back. The tormentor raises the whip, prepares himself, gathers momentum and delivers another blow. The man writhes again. And like that, ten times. Jung Fei Ye didn't make a single sound, but by the end of it his back was dripping blood. Not the faintest moan. That guy's as hard as nails. They went to take him to the hospital too, but he refused to go. He said he'd carry on working. How's about that, John? He carried on working, but he couldn't hack it. His shirt was drenched in blood. He collapsed and they took him to hospital.'

Nothing Wade told me seemed to make any sense. Why had two of the worst members of our group, a criminal and a torturer, now suddenly become defenders of the weak? Why had Jimmy Bruëll, who I considered the most selfish one among us, offered himself up to be punished in place of another, and in particular in the place of a woman – he who'd spent his life feeding off women, deceiving them and stealing from them? Could it be guilt that drove him to do it? Might Jimmy feel guilty about what happened with Sophie Leverkuhn? And Jung Fei Ye, who'd spent his life dishing out lashings with the rod? What had moved him to take Lizzy's lashings? A sense of justice? In his case might it have been his beliefs that led him to behave so selflessly, and so nobly; the same beliefs that had led him, on many other occasions, to be the tormentor? Were our beliefs all we had, for better or for worse? Of course, a belief system couldn't explain Jimmy's. Jimmy didn't believe in anything. Could it be, then, that compassion surpasses beliefs, and that those who don't believe in anything either turn into mere predatory creatures lying in wait for their next meal, or find themselves – when they least expect it – on the side of the law of compassion? But how does one discover that law? By enduring pain? By happy accident? Is it a mysterious ray of light? Is it something that was always in our nature finally spilling out? Is it the result of inner growth? I had always believed that pain desensitises, and I railed against the idea that suffering is some sort of life 'test' containing profound lessons. I'd always believed it's better to enjoy pleasure and beauty as master than to suffer pain and misfortune. But I no longer knew what I believed. I no longer knew what I knew. I no longer knew or understood anything.

What I know is that man cannot live without laws. Nobody deliberately does wrong, given that the whole world behaves according to a system of beliefs. We all hope that the world responds, in some way, to our wishes and needs. There isn't a human on earth who doesn't believe they deserve some dark kind of justice and retribution for the vile degradation that is living. All humans believe in a kind of God. The short humans have a short God, and the wide ones a wide God. The green ones have a green God, and the cold ones a cold God. Only those who really ask themselves the true nature of things, only those who really desire to know themselves, are willing to risk living without beliefs. To live without beliefs means going beyond laws to truly study oneself. It means questioning all those learnt laws. It means putting your trust in the world's love, feeling the warmth of a distant star in your heart. But it's surely not possible to do such a thing if you don't feel this love in some way or know how to trust it, even a little.

I'm not sure how many days I'd spent locked up in my cell when, one morning, two unarmed men showed up at the door telling me that Abraham wanted to see me. They led me slowly across town, which allowed me to take a better look at the place. It surprised me to see that the people living in Central seemed completely run-of-the-mill. Families were eating their breakfast, or perhaps lunch, on verandas. Children were playing in gardens. I spotted what looked like a Japanese bridge – half painted – over a pond complete with ducks and reeds. There were blue dragonflies everywhere I looked, maybe because there were ponds all over the place. I spotted an Indian elephant being herded by two men as if it were a cow. I asked the men escorting me what the hell an elephant was doing there, but they didn't answer. The workers wore full-length grey overalls. I have no idea how they could stand wearing such heavy togs in that weather. The tropical sun bore down into the ground. Likkendala City had something of a frontier town about it – the atmosphere was what I imagined a lawless saloon town in the American Wild West might have felt like. Despite its best efforts, Central still felt more like a camp than a real city.

Lewellyn was waiting for me in his home, a quaint bungalow surrounded by a well-tended garden full of flowers. That was the first of a series of meetings with Lewellyn which, rather than help me understand him and get a better grasp of the place we found ourselves, only left me more mystified. Lewellyn was on the veranda reading a Nancy Mitford novel and drinking iced tea, which he served himself from a tall crystal jug covered with a cloth to stop insects flying in. He invited me to sit down and have a glass with him. Now he was the obliging host, a civilised, cultured man receiving another civilised, cultured man in his home.

I sat down in the chair he offered me and asked him what he was up to, treating me so well while my friends were out being forced to work like slaves.

'Slaves!' Lewellyn said, his eyes widening. 'Slaves, you say. That's like saying that I am a slave to my stomach because I have to work to feed it. Or that my stomach is a slave to me because it swallows whatever I put into it unquestioningly. We're slaves to time. We can't stop it, or reverse it. We're slaves to our need to breathe. We can't free ourselves of it. My eyes are slaves to the light. My fingernails are my slaves. What does it really mean to be a slave? This is a world of slaves. Because there are laws; laws that cannot be evaded. We all serve something. We're all slaves to something, or someone, don't you think?'

'And you, sir, are a slave to Mr Pohjola?'

'It's not called slavery when one is serving a higher being; something far, far bigger than oneself.'

He made a face to indicate that we were getting up to go. At times he reminded me of a bird – those bulging eyes, that big head, his prominent, beaky nose and harried movements.

On that occasion, he took me to the round building they'd called 'the temple' to watch an orchestra rehearsing. Yes, to my great surprise there was a full symphonic orchestra in Likkendala City, which, if my rough calculations were anything to go by, meant that a quarter of its inhabitants must have been professional musicians. According to Lewellyn, the Likkendala Philharmonic was rehearsing the pieces they'd perform in a concert scheduled for the following fortnight. A special concert to celebrate Mr Pohjola's birthday – unsurprisingly, an important date on the island.

At most there were a dozen people in the hall listening to the rehearsal. Lewellyn introduced me to one of them: a tall, blonde woman, about forty years old and very attractive. Jill Dunhill was a doctor. We shook hands and she said how pleased she was to meet me, one of those lines that in the civilised world we toss out every day without much thought, and which on that occasion seemed a mark of exquisite graciousness and moving warmth. More than once I caught her looking at me, then quickly turning away as soon as our eyes met, which surprised and confused me still further. I was even more shocked to learn that the conductor of the orchestra was none other than George – professional kiddy-thief and apparent chief villain – and that the concertmaster was Gwen Heller, otherwise known as Carmen Aoristadis – adventurer, fake biologist and the person responsible for the loss of my left leg. I think Lewellyn took great pleasure in seeing my surprise when first George, then Carmen, walked out onto the stage and took up their places. He explained to me that they were husband and wife and had met in London during a masterclass series given by Sir Georg Solti, back when they were both promising youngsters. Then Lewellyn added, a little cryptically, that many of the island's inhabitants had shown promise in their youth.

But the biggest surprise of all was the music they were playing. I think when I heard the opening phrase – that long melody written for viola and Appalachian dulcimer – I literally jumped out of my seat. It was my Third

Symphony, dedicated to the memory of Anton Bruckner, an immensely ambitious work that had never been played in public and which slept peacefully in a drawer of my studio desk in manuscript form. How in God's name had they got hold of that score? I asked Lewellyn a thousand times, but he just smiled, raised his bushy elfin eyebrows and held his forefinger to his lips, signalling for me to be quiet.

On another occasion, he took me to the port, a small natural cove which, as he explained in painstaking detail, they had to keep completely free of aquatic plants and in which they'd erected a long wooden pier. The cove was unguarded since, as far as I could tell, there was no possibility it could be reached by sea. The Insiders had, of course, safeguarded their peninsula from the rest of the island with the towers and their energy shield. There were just a few vessels in the port: two small boats, a yacht that could hold up to fifteen people and a three-masted schooner which, according to Lewellyn, they had found abandoned on the island's coastline three years earlier. They also had a submarine moored at the end of the pier, and this appeared to be their main means of communication with the outside world. It didn't seem very big, but it's a well-known fact that boats are deceptive, and that they all seem smaller from the outside than they really are. I asked myself why Lewellyn was showing me all these things and if he hadn't clocked that he was, in effect, showing me the main escape route off the island.

A few days later I saw Jill Dunhill again on one of my strolls with Lewellyn. This time he was giving me a tour of the row of columns that separated Central and its peninsula from the rest of the island. He explained to me that when the columns were turned on, they created an energy shield which helped protect them all from dangers lurking elsewhere on the island. I asked him what kind of energy it was and he said it was a new source, discovered some years back in the mountains in the interior. He didn't share any more detail, nor did I need to know any more, but I inferred that it was the anti-gravitational force that grew stronger the closer you got to the so-called Black Column. Lewellyn went on and on to me about how that energy would revolutionise the world, adding that atomic energy was child's play in comparison.

'Why are you showing me all of this, Lewellyn?' I asked him. 'Why are you telling me all this? Are you trying to convince us we'll never get out of here? Are you trying to show me just how solid the walls of your prison are?'

'You are full of suspicions and prejudices, aren't you?' he replied. 'You see hidden intentions in everything.'

Just then, we noticed a van coming towards us along the same road we'd driven up in our jeep. It was one of the pale blue vans they used on their trips around the island. It pulled up next to us and we saw Jill Dunhill inside, sitting next to a young man in the driver's seat.

'The alarm sounded,' she told us. 'By the looks of it, a group of men ran into Omé. Three are burnt, two dead.'

'Jesus,' Lewellyn said. 'Well, be careful. Have you told Burt to collect the bodies?'

'Yes,' the driver said. 'He's behind us with two others.'

I saw the driver speak into his walkie-talkie and then tell Dr Dunhill that it was safe to go on. A moment later they set off and followed the road until they reached in line with one of the columns. Once on the other side of the imaginary line which linked that column to the others, the driver accelerated and we watched the van disappear behind the hill.

'Back at Central they will have told him over radio that they cut the power in that sector,' Lewellyn said, referring to the caution with which the driver had cleared the column. 'But even so, you have to go carefully. They'll reconnect it now.'

'What's Omé?' I asked.

'You call him "the blue man". Omé is the name the Wamani give him.'

The penny was beginning to drop.

'So, the real purpose of the energy shield is to protect you from Omé,' I said.

'Mainly from Omé, but from other things too.'

'Tell me, Lewellyn, what the hell goes on on this island?' I asked him over and over during our conversations. 'You don't seem like a criminal. You're an educated man, you run this place, though I can't for the life of me fathom its purpose, even if it is full of families and workers and all kinds of professionals. I mean, you've even got an orchestra! And yet despite all this you treat us as if we were criminals. You hound us, beat us, shoot us. Not only do you not help us, you abuse us!'

'And why should we help you?' he asked.

'If you tripped and fell over, I would automatically help you up again. Helping the person next to us is a human instinct. It's in our nature.'

'An instinct, yes,' he said, smirking. 'So it's a reflex. It's not an innate part of our moral nature.'

At night I would tell Wade everything I'd found out about the island and recount my conversations with Lewellyn. He asked me if I could imagine why he was giving me special treatment. But my powers of imagination had long since been overshadowed by the facts.

We had already devised a more or less comprehensive escape plan which involved stealing one of the vessels at the port when, one morning, two men came looking for me and Wade and took us to Lewellyn's office. They weren't carrying guns this time, and nor did they handcuff us.

Little Lewellyn seemed very excited about something. He knew how to control himself and keep a cool exterior, but I had begun to get to know him – or at least that was my impression – and he seemed elated about something to me. Wade glowered at him murderously. I knew he was having to use all his willpower not to go for the jugular of that man who was responsible for almost all our misfortune. Lewellyn offered us some water, filling two glasses from a yellow plastic jug full of ice, and we both accepted. On the island, you never refused an invitation to drink. There were several fans on in his office, but the heat was still insufferable.

'As of tomorrow, you will no longer work in the quarry,' Lewellyn told us, fanning himself absent-mindedly with an oriental-style fan. 'I suppose you'll be happy to hear that.'

Wade and I didn't move or react at all. Lewellyn observed us intently, like a scientist studying an exotic insect.

'What's wrong?' he asked. 'Aren't you pleased?'

'What's the next torture you've got in store for us?' Wade asked. 'Where are the women you abducted? Where are the children?'

'Oh, you really are like a broken record,' Lewellyn snapped. 'The children... what do the children matter? They're not yours. In no way are they yours. How have you managed to convince yourselves that they really matter to you? Why do you keep going on like this? Why not just let it go?'

'Well, you know how it works,' Wade said, taking a deep breath and forcing himself to calm down, and even smile. 'People form bonds and then begin to care about each other.'

'That's how it works, is it?' Lewellyn said.

'Yes, I believe so.'

'Oh, how sorry I am not to be up to your moral expectations,' Lewellyn said.

'I'm sorry too.'

'I'm sorry I'm not a warm-hearted saint,' Lewellyn said.

'What you consider being a saint, I consider being normal. A normal, decent person, like the millions of them who exist.'

'Maybe *you're* a saint,' Lewellyn said.

'No, buddy, I know full well I ain't no saint. I'm a guy just like any other. But if I see a lost kid then I take him by the hand and get him home. You lot would empty out his pockets and steal his shoes.'

'You must think me a deeply flawed person.'

'You're pretty nasty, yeah, buddy,' Wade said, looking daggers at Lewellyn now. 'If that's what you mean, then, yeah, that's what I think. You're far from perfect.'

'Far from perfect,' Lewellyn drawled. '*Far from Perfect.* That can be the title of my autobiography when I write it.'

Wade turned to me and I shrugged.

'You two just don't get it,' Lewellyn said. 'You don't seem to understand that you've landed on private property. This place has proprietors, owners who have controlled this land for a very long time. Since forever, the very beginning. It's not some public garden open to all, where you can just run around freely.'

'We get that much,' Wade said. 'We get that the island is private property.'

'I'm not talking about the island,' Lewellyn said. 'I'm talking about the world.'

I glanced at Wade but he didn't take his eyes off the little man sitting on the other side of the table.

'I'm talking about the world,' Lewellyn repeated evenly. 'You lot, you liberals and lefties, revolutionaries, hippies, mincing ecologists, spoilt little brats, defenders of losers, slackers, good-for-nothings and cowards – who told you the world was your childhood garden and that that's how it should be and that anything else was unfair and intolerable? The world has masters, and those who aren't masters must be servants and serve. How could it be any other way?'

'In plenty of places it's not like that,' I said.

'That's momentary. The masters of the world might lose the odd battle, or lose a country or region for a few decades. That doesn't matter, because their power is absolute and they're the ones with a full hand. They've got technology and mass media. They control medicine production, grain and foodstuffs, energy sources. They've even begun controlling the weather. They've found new ways to control the mind, to deflect the attention of entire populations, to create whole societies made up of submissive, obedient beings. Hence their interest in this island. Hence the vital role this island plays in their plans.

'But we're digressing. I haven't called you here to talk about ethics or political philosophy. I called you here because I have received a message from Mr Pohjola that concerns you. It appears,' he added, with a sigh, 'that Mr Pohjola has taken a special shine to you two. God knows why.'

'He wants to talk to us?' I asked.

'Yes, with both of you.'

'Holy cow,' Wade said.

'Mr Pohjola wishes to speak to you both face to face. He wants me to take you to his house.'

'So he does have a house,' I said, astonished.

'Everybody has a house, Mr Barbarín,' Lewellyn said.

I looked at Wade, who was laughing and stroking his chin with his thumb and forefinger. He shot Lewellyn a look of admiration; the kind a card sharp feels in the presence of an even slicker card sharp.

'We're going to his house?' my friend asked. 'We're going to meet the great man himself?'

'That's right.'

Wade laughed.

'It's far away,' Lewellyn added. 'In the interior. It is a great honour that he is granting you. I hope you're aware of that. I hope you give this event its due import... George, for example, would kill to go with me to see Mr Pohjola. He's been here for years and has never had the chance.'

'So no one else is coming with us?' Wade asked. 'No armed men this time?'

'We won't go armed.'

'You mean we're going *just us three*?' I said then. 'Wade, you and I?'

'Yes,' Abraham said, looking at me. 'Us three. It'll take us a couple of days to get there. It's up in the mountains. Two days up and another two down. Maybe three and three, given your condition. But,' he said, still staring at us with his bulging red eyes, 'don't get any ideas about this being your big chance to "escape". I hope you understand that it is absolutely not in your interest to harm me once we're alone out there. We've got a lot of hostages. If something happens to me, I trust you understand that your friends will suffer the consequences. No, don't look at me like that. I'm simply protecting my safety, perhaps even my life. If you think I get anything out of going up to the mountains with your two, you can think again. But an order is an order, and you don't disobey Mr Pohjola. You don't dream of disobeying him. The three of us will go, and you two will behave like civilised human beings.'

The idea of leaving that city just the three of us seemed like a great opportunity not only to escape, but to take Lewellyn prisoner and trade him in exchange for our friends. But I wanted to squeeze as much out of the negotiations as possible.

'Very well,' I said. 'But I want one other person to come with us.'

'Yes,' he said, 'I know.'

'You know?'

'It's my job to know,' he said. 'And Mr Pohjola's job, of course.'

'You don't know anything,' I retorted.

'Mr Pohjola warned me. He told me you would ask for another person to accompany us. It's okay. There's no problem. We saw this coming.'

'So which person are you talking about?' I asked, confused.

'The same one as you.'

'You can't possibly know whom I'm talking about,' I said.

Abraham Lewellyn looked at me with his wide eyes and sneered. Then he placed his fan on the table, opened one of the drawers in his desk and pulled out a piece of paper, folded in two. He handed it to me and asked me to read it. This is what was written on the piece of paper, in a blue pen and in that typical American handwriting that doggedly imitates typed letters:

I want one other person to come with us.

Yes, I know.

You know?

It's my job to know.

You don't know anything.

It's okay. There's no problem. We saw this coming.

So which person are you talking about?

The same one as you.

You can't possibly know whom I'm talking about.

You're talking about Rosana. You want Rosana to come with us.

'You're talking about Rosana. You want Rosana to come with us.'

57

Count Balasz's dreams. Salomé, Games Mistress

The *White Rose Society, also* known as the Brotherhood of Sky Gazers, appears in Vienna at the end of the eighteenth century with the emergence across Europe of more and more Tables or *Tabulae*, those essentially secret societies devoted to playing the games from the Count of Cammarano's book, and often associated with Freemasonry or the Rosicrucian movement.

The White Rose Society was dedicated to the compulsive and incessant practice of three of the games included in the book: the Island Game (a Higher Mathematics numbers game); the White Rose Game; and number XVII of the 'Silence Games' included among the 108 Secret Games. In doing so they were merely following the general tendency of the times, since the games' devotees had long since retracted the original requirement to play *all* the games from the book.

In fact, some of the members devoted themselves entirely to Game XVII of the 'Silence Games', otherwise simply called 'Sky Gazing' (despite its straightforward instructions, there was nothing simple about it), which is where the society's nickname comes from. At the end of the nineteenth century the White Rose Society, or Brotherhood of Sky Gazers, was overseen by Count Balasz, a Hungarian nobleman with an immense fortune, a zoologist and Ancient Egypt aficionado who came to the conclusion, after a lifetime of study and contemplation, that the White Rose Game, the Island Game and number XVII of the Silence Games were really one and the same, and that they all referred to a place that physically existed somewhere in the world.

And so, after years of oblivion, the island reappeared on the horizon of the modern imagination.

The name 'the White Rose Society' came from one of the games in the book, which involved a supposed 'White Rose Society' whose members would practise 108 games, the strangest and more esoteric counting among them. But Count Balasz began to believe that the White Rose and the Island really did exist somewhere in the world. And he dedicated the rest of his life to finding them.

'The White Rose, if it exists,' he writes in one of his diaries, 'must be on Purgatory Island, otherwise known as Cammarano Island or the Island of Voices. I have become convinced that this island, which for many is as symbolic as the Grail, Nibelheim or Avalon, really exists in some part of the Indian or Pacific Ocean.'

The Count's diaries allow us to reconstruct the epic story of his quest for that island named Purgatory Island, Cammarano Island or the Island of Voices, as well as the extraordinary circumstance of his eventual 'encounter' with it.

This encounter took place at night, over many nights.

In October 1877, Count Balasz had a series of dreams in which members of a society of monks who lived up on a remote mountain instructed him on all manner of esoteric matters. In his dreams, the monks explained to him the true significance of the games – the Island Game, the White Rose Game and the Sky Gazing Game – and assured him that the Garden of Eden described in the Bible, and which is named and evoked in so many ancient traditions, wasn't a myth, nor a symbol of an 'interior state', but in fact a real place. The Garden of Eden or Garden of Paradise, also known as the Garden of Resurrection, they told him, *really existed* on earth.

In the first dream, Count Balasz saw himself in a rocky wilderness, surrounded by mountains. He set off walking along a path that led up through the trees and lush plants, and soon reached the monastery doors.

A group of monks were there waiting for him and they greeted him by name and warmly invited him to go in. His voice had been heard, they told him. The highest authorities of the University had decided to accept him as an auditing student *in somnii* – that is, a dreaming student.

A university? Count Balasz said to himself. Not a monastery? Not a convent? Then he remembered that in the Middle Ages the figures of the scholar and clergyman were interchangeable, and he imagined that those friars called the place where they lived 'University' for the simple reason that they'd decided to dedicate their lives to learning.

During his first dreams, Count Balasz spoke to monks both young and old who asked him questions and told him about the different subjects. They called one another 'brother', like they do in religious orders, but he couldn't work out their hierarchy, nor did he manage to meet with the Prior who oversaw the institution.

On other occasions he had conversations with women, although the Count learnt that they weren't nuns, but deaconesses, with the same powers and capacities within the order as their male counterparts. The women wore long brown tunics under which they were naked, and whenever they removed their tunics (something they regularly did) they simultaneously put on big masks covered in bison or lion hair and adorned with pheasant feathers and buffalo horns. This meant that whenever they were naked their faces were covered by those hairy, imposing masks, and whenever they took the masks off, their bodies were covered by their brown tunics.

It was clear that this dual order of men and women bore little relation to the regular Church. Its rituals and customs often left the Count profoundly bemused. For example, there were the mixed gender bathing rituals, which they performed in great big thermal pools; on such occasions the deaconesses didn't wear their monstrous masks, and young couples often paired off to copulate in the flowerbeds.

Count Balasz looked on mortified at these scenes, asking himself if he might not be the butt of some kind of joke. But who's ever been the butt of an elaborate joke *in their dreams*?

There was a monk called Philemon, an elderly, very learned man with a mild face and faintly ironic eyes, and he taught the Count astonishing things about numbers he'd never come across in any book. Philemon told him: 'God has spoken to men in three languages.'

'What's the third language?' the Count would ask tirelessly.

But Philemon never answered.

When he woke up, Count Balasz tried to write down the solution to the great mathematical enigmas he'd been shown in his dream, but he couldn't. It's not that he didn't remember the numbers he'd seen in his dream, but now that he was awake, those numbers no longer made any sense.

In one of his dreams, a woman with large eyes and long brown wavy hair told him that the three games did, in fact (as with all the games in Count Cammarano's book), reveal the key to finding a place that really existed. She said that Count Cammarano had written the book as a kind of conundrum: anyone who read it properly then gained access to the place they were in that very moment, and to which he had been admitted strictly as an *in somnii* student. This place was located on a remote island.

The island had several names. Purgatory was the name given to it by Count Cammarano. Others called it the Island of Voices.

The woman also told him that playing around with numbers alone could never get him to the island containing the Garden of Paradise. She was called Salomé, and she was slim, beautiful, gentle and imposing, very feminine and at the same time had a look at once inscrutable and maternal about her. Her abundant wavy air enveloped her face like a rich, warm hazel halo. She must have been about forty, and was wearing a fine brown woollen tunic like a Grecian peplos that emphasised her chest and then draped down to the ground in heavy pleats. She always appeared to him alone at a table with different symbolic objects laid out upon it: a red rose, a white Madonna lily, a clepsydra, a sword, a skull, a bronze rooster, a pomegranate split open, a pile of salt, a book...

Count Balasz understood this table to be one of the ancient games Tables or *Tabulae*, which would make Salomé the Games Mistress. It was hard to tell what exactly the role of this woman in the monastery was, but he began to suspect that Salomé might well be the Abbess: in charge of not only the deaconesses, but of the University's entire population of men and women. As for the icons on the table (which changed from dream to dream, or perhaps were always the same and just appeared different), they remained indecipherable to the Brotherhood of Sky Gazers, no matter how many times they tried. The red rose and Madonna lily could be interpreted as love and wisdom (that is, *philosophy*), but what did a pile of salt have to do with a book? And the rooster? An old gnostic symbol?

Count Balasz became obsessed with the idea of finding the Garden of Paradise (or the Garden of Resurrection as he'd begun to call it) in the waking world, but he wasn't getting anywhere. The members of the White Rose Society had gained a perfect command of the three games – the Island Game, the White Rose Game and the Sky Gazing Game – but still no door had opened, no path revealed itself to them. And yet, night after night Philemon and Salomé assured the Count that the Garden really did exist and, what's more, that it was possible to reach it.

By now he dreamt of the woman called Salomé every night, but she, who always appeared sitting at her table, looking at him seriously with her beautiful eyes, no longer spoke to him. She didn't speak; she sang. Salomé only communicated with him through song. Her melodies were intriguing and had an oriental, faraway feel to them. Every now and then he was able to hear the song lyrics clearly. Other times he understood the words but didn't get their meaning. Sometimes he understood nothing at all.

He dreamt of Salomé sitting at her table with a row of deaconesses in their brown tunics to one side, and on the other a row of monks wearing off-white robes. Now, instead of speaking to him, the two choruses sang. First the deaconesses. Then the monks. Then different voices interwove into a sound completely unlike the polyphony the Count knew so well. Then Salomé herself began to sing. Her voice was unforgettable, and yet, the moment he woke from his dream, the Count couldn't say whether her vocal type was a natural contralto, a mezzo, a dramatic soprano, a soubrette, or a coloratura soprano. Salomé sang and the Count strained to hear the lyrics. Sometimes she sang in Latin, which the Count had a good grasp of. Sometimes in Greek, a language of which he knew just a few words. Sometimes she sang in Egyptian. In his dream, the Count knew it was Egyptian without anyone having to explain it to him. She also sang in Hebrew and Sanskrit, which had been a fashionable language in Germany since the end of the eighteenth century and of which the Count knew a hundred or so expressions. But on the whole, he was at a loss to decipher the meaning of her lyrics. Wordlessly, speaking straight to his heart, Salomé explained that concentrating on words and their meanings wouldn't help him reach the island. So the Count was obliged to listen to the *sound* of the music, and Salomé's voice in particular. When she sang, the icons on the table began to float and dance in the air. Then they began to transform.

Afterwards, all of the monks and deaconesses undressed, their movements swift and efficient as they let their brown and off-white tunics fall to the floor. They were almost all young and svelte, although there were also a few older, plumper people among them. The women donned their ferocious animal masks, with their lion hair and buffalo horns, and the men wore garlands of flowers in their hair. And they began to dance with one another. A woman and a man approached Salomé and removed her tunic, letting it fall from her shoulders to the floor and leaving her completely nude. And they carried on singing as they danced in couples, man and woman, twirling around the room, and Salomé went on singing. Out of all the naked women, she was the only one who didn't cover her face.

The Count understood that Salomé's voice was hiding the most profound, mysterious message he'd ever been given. But he simply couldn't decipher it. He tried and tried, he tried until he wept, until, at last, he realised that really there was nothing to decipher. The message was not the words, the notes or numbers. No, the message was the *voice itself.* And so, at last, the Count understood, and that night he woke up in the middle of his dream and cried with happiness because at last he'd discovered the key to the mystery.

He felt such great respect for that magnificent woman that when the two assistants removed her tunic, the Count lowered his gaze. Now this ritual was repeated night after night, and whenever the moment came for the acolytes to take down Salomé's tunic, the Count lowered his eyes out of a mixture of respect and shame. One day he caught a glimpse of Salomé's breasts before bowing his head: nurturing, perfect breasts, and the vision of them haunted him even during his waking hours, as if he'd witnessed a forbidden secret. The following night, again speaking directly to his heart, Salomé told him not to look away, not to be embarrassed to look at her. When the two helpers removed her tunic, the Count forced himself to look at her despite the violence of his feelings. And he saw Salomé's naked body for the first time.

He thought then that he had been wrong before: the message was not the voice. The message was not the notes. Or the numbers, or words. *The message was the body.*

Then the symbolic objects floating in the air transformed again and landed gently on the table. Salomé finished her song. The dancers finished their song too, stood still, kissed one another on the lips and returned to their places to put their tunics back on. A monk and a deaconess pulled up Salomé's tunic from her feet and slipped it over her arms and onto her shoulders.

Then Salomé spoke again. She thanked him for his efforts and called him 'spiritual brother', which profoundly moved Count Balasz.

Next, Salomé told him that she was going to ask him to do something in the conscious world. The following 18th of December he must attend the first performance of Herr Anton Bruckner's last symphony. It would be played by the Vienna Philharmonic under the direction of Hans Richter. The Count asked her to repeat this several times to make absolutely sure he'd heard correctly. But Salomé's instructions were precise and left no room for doubt.

It was the first time Salomé had made reference to the conscious world. Intrigued, Count Balasz got hold of a ticket, and when the day came he headed off to the Musikverein. The concert was Anton Bruckner's Eighth

Symphony, whose premiere had been delayed by several years, for various reasons: in some cases because the conductors had considered it a pointless, absurd work, and in others because the orchestra hadn't been able to master its technical complexities. Bruckner himself had revised it several times to try to fix its supposed errors. Of course, the Count didn't know any of these details. He was a music lover, but didn't follow the inner workings of the contemporary music scene. Nor had he ever heard Bruckner's work.

And listening to that music – boundless, passionate, fabulously simple and at the same time boasting extraordinary psychological complexity; sublime like the stone architecture of a basilica and tender like flowers growing along a stream; almost excessively majestic and at the same time heavy with enigmatic nostalgia – the Count felt that at last he'd found the way. Once home, with Bruckner's music still resounding in his head, he felt exultant and also lifted on a marvellous surge, as if on a broad rising spiral inside of him. After the concert, he didn't want to talk to anybody or partake in any social gatherings, which might destroy the impression Bruckner's music had left on him. So he rushed straight home and shut himself away in his bedchamber, insisting that no one disturb him. He played the three games – the Island Game, the White Rose Game and the Sky Gazing Game – and then went to bed.

That night he had his final dream about the mountain, the monastery, the monks, the priestesses and Salomé. And it was the strangest of all the dreams he'd had until then.

In it, the monks received him at the entrance to the sacred mountain, led him up to the monastery and through the temple's living quarters, which was adorned all over with wreaths of flowers and candles as if it were a great celebration. Finally, they reached Salomé's table. She asked him if he had listened to what she'd asked him to listen to. He replied that he had, and asked if the answer to his questions lay in that music, and if he should try to make sense of it by means of numbers, because he was convinced, in spite of everything, that the solution to the enigma lay in numbers.

'The solution to the enigma is this,' Salomé told him. 'There is no enigma. Everything is exactly as it appears.'

'Madam,' the Count said, lowering his gaze respectfully, 'the other day I watched you all, quite naked, and inside my heart I heard a voice that told me that the message is the body. But I cannot fathom the notion that the body is superior to music or numbers.'

'The body is the vehicle,' Salomé replied. 'It is what makes us human. It is what allows us to evolve and understand. It is the centre of our spiritual work. Hating or fearing the body leads us to hell. The beauty and dignity of the body are a reflection of the beauty and dignity of the invisible part of us. To honour the body is to honour our soul. To work on the body is to work on the invisible part. There are three things we must work on: the body, our emotions and our concentration. But it all begins with the body.'

Count Balasz bowed his head, trying to take in Salomé's words.

'Very good,' she said. 'Now watch this theatrical performance we've prepared on your behalf.'

Salomé made a sign and everyone moved to the sides of the great hall, leaving the central area free.

The theatrical performance was lifelike and cruel in the extreme. It included three scenes: the first was called 'Isolde's Youth'. The second, 'Aphrodite's Birth'. The third, 'The Annunciation of Mary'. There was a very tall and heavyset blonde young lady who played all three main female parts: Isolde, Aphrodite and Mary. There was something so tender and graceful about her, in the flushed softness of her skin and the roundness of her feminine attributes. He was sure her shoulders and neck would smell of milk, like a young fawn.

Two choruses, one male and the other female, took turns to comment on and describe the action in Latin.

In 'Isolde's Youth', the Princess of Ireland appeared as a wise woman devoted to healing with herbal medicines. The actress appeared dressed in a long white wig that disguised her natural long blonde hair, and with a druid cloak covered in different tree twigs, dried flowers, bird feathers and seashells. She should have been representing a young Isolde, but instead, with her long white hair she looked like an old lady. Two big performing dogs, or two wolves, one with dark fur and the other albino, walked over to the young actress and stood on either side of her. Then the dark wolf began to sing in the voice of a young man, and the white wolf in the voice of a woman, and finally Isolde herself began to howl like a wolf. The male wolf sang in Latin, the female wolf in Old High German and Isolde sang in the language of the animals. Next came the sound of a voice that said: 'Isolde had never forgotten her savage side.' The Count couldn't work out where exactly this voice was coming from. Was he the only one hearing it? Was it playing in the air? Was Salomé speaking those words?

Next came the scene from 'Aphrodite's Birth'. The choirs sang beautiful alternating melodies celebrating the emergence of Aphrodite from the foaming sea. The young actress removed her cloak and white wig revealing her naked body underneath, and came towards us now from the back of the hall perched on an enormous seashell being pulled along by two children seemingly without the slightest difficulty. The young woman covered her breasts and sex demurely, although a triangle of fine brown hair, of pinkish splendour, was still visible behind her hand. Arriving at the centre of the hall, she flung her hands wide, at which point the female choir, followed by the male one, sang: 'Glory to you, Aphrodite, goddess of love.' Then several figures dressed as Silenus appeared from either side armed with long whips, and proceeded to lash the young woman. They lashed her with such viciousness that she was soon completely covered in blood, and yet her aggressors kept going. The whip cut the actress's delicate, tender skin, and yet the girl stood frozen to the spot and made no attempt to shield herself as the lashes rained down on her back, stomach and thighs. The vision of such a young and beautiful body being lacerated in that way was almost unbearable, but Count Balasz made himself watch despite his horror and concern. Then the voice said: 'Look at what you've done to Aphrodite!'

The actress, on the point of fainting, then prepared herself to act out the final scene: the 'Annunciation of Mary'. Two women approached her, sat her down on a wooden bench which they'd moved to the middle of the stage, and covered her head with a veil that reached down to her shoulders but didn't hide her naked body, now dripping with blood. The woman's suffering was palpable. Her wounds and the blood were real, and Count Balasz was moved to tears. The angel appeared and the choir sang the well-known words: 'Mary, I come in the name of the Lord; I have come to tell you are going to have a child.'

Then something tremendously strange happened. The woman, who now represented the Virgin Mary, stood up on her bench and her stomach began to grow and swell. In a matter of seconds, her waters had broken, she'd begun having contractions and had sat back down on the bench. She spread her legs wide and everyone present watched as the young woman's vagina began to dilate, revealing a ball-like object emerging from inside her body. The woman was now screaming in pain. Her vulva stretched to twice, three times, four times its normal size and went on growing, and soon the baby's full head was visible, followed by its shoulders, arms, torso and the umbilical cord. The woman was still groaning like an animal as she took hold of the shining, wet baby covered in blood and amniotic fluid emerging from inside of her. Once the whole body was out, she held it in her arms and clutched it to her chest, the twisted white and violet cord still uncut. Then the two children reappeared from the back of the room pulling the enormous shell, while handfuls of golden dust and geranium and cyclamen petals rained down from the upper galleries onto the bloody mother and child, sticking to their skin. The bench moved backwards, somebody removed the veil from the woman's head and she, still attached to the child by the thick umbilical cord emerging glistening and twisted from between her vulva, staggered towards Aphrodite's shell and then mounted it. A kind of fine rain began to fall from above, drenching the mother and child and washing away all of the blood from the flagellation and birth, leaving both figures almost spotlessly clean. And the voice said: 'You haven't understood that Aphrodite and Mary are one and the same.'

At that moment, the Count woke in his bed, sweating as if he were running a burning fever. Those final words continued to ring in his head.

'You haven't understood that Aphrodite and Mary are one and the same.' The Count was alone in his room. Through the window, the light of the moon shone over the Viennese skyline. He wanted to go back to sleep to see the end of the performance, if indeed there was any more to see. But he couldn't.

'What have I just witnessed?' the poor man wondered, confused and disoriented. 'What could it mean: "You haven't understood that Aphrodite and Mary are one and the same"? Everything I've just seen is an offence to the real religion. It's scandalous, and if I dared share it in public I'd be excommunicated. How could a simple game of Higher Mathematics have carried me to that dreamland?'

He wondered if perhaps he had fallen in love with that woman from his dreams. He couldn't put his finger on what he felt for her, nor whether she was a kind of saint, or merely a common harlot. What was Salomé? Was she the hieratical abbess of a convent or the Whore of Babylon? To what did she devote her life? To the love or God or carnal desire? Was she a messenger of love or a devil?

He was a man of science, a rigorous thinker and devoted scholar. He was married to Princess Wilarda Philarda, a pious woman who came from a respected Prussian family and had given him a daughter he adored. But until then, he'd never imagined a woman could have such a powerful effect on him as Salomé did.

And that's as far as the notes in Count Balasz's diaries go. We know that soon after, his daughter had a nervous breakdown and was admitted to the Bad Kreuzen psychiatric sanatorium, precisely where Herr Bruckner was spending a period of rest and repose after the depression that followed the premiere of his Eighth Symphony. We know that Count Balasz came across Anton Bruckner in Bad Kreuzen several times, and spoke to him on several occasions. Much more than that, we don't know.

58

Lewellyn leads us to Pohjola's house

W*e left the next day* at sunrise in a small van driven by a young red-head called Burt. When we reached the wall of energy we all got out; everyone, including Burt, who stood there staring at it with his arms crossed, looking quite comical in his pistachio-green overalls and red hat. Everyone who worked in the vicinity of that energy shield wore loud colours so that the cameras could pick them up. Lewellyn approached one of the columns, opened a small door with a key he took from his pocket and deactivated that section of the invisible wall. He told us we had exactly one minute to cross over to the other side.

We darted across and turned round to watch Burt stride back to the van, start the engine and drive off back in the direction of Central.

Wade, Rosana and I looked at one another. We were free. We were out of the Insiders' reach. It was just us and the island again!

I remember the feeling of joy and relief on finding myself in open and wild territory again. Joy at being on the island! As we set off walking, Wade suddenly came out with a poem:

Out of the night that covers me,
Black as the pit from pole to pole,
I thank whatever gods may be
For my unconquerable soul…

It was 'Invictus' by William Ernest Henley.

We hiked for two days, moving further into the mountains and climbing increasingly chilly valleys where the vegetation changed, becoming more like alpine forests. The aerial palm gave way to the dark murmuring oak. Conifers laden with greenish-blue needles appeared now. The flowers grew smaller and more delicate. The bushes thrummed with the buzz of bees. The world's mysteries revealed themselves to us again after our tedious captivity and all of the toil the others had endured as slaves. I wondered how my fellow travelling mates, Rosana and Wade, were going to react once we were alone with Abraham Lewellyn, out there in the middle of the mountains. Would they turn vengeful and violent? But the world's mystery, the possibility of the mountains with their unspoilt, endless paths seemed to have had an effect on us. Now we'd fallen in step with the logic of the insects, crags and spectacular views of Purgatory Island. We barely spoke. We barely looked at one another. We crossed cool streams where we drank and splashed our faces and necks, and to me it seemed that that pure water, flowing down from up above, blessed us and cleansed us of our sins. A breeze blew in the valleys and as it filtered through the trees it seemed to pluck notes from the leaves and branches, rocks and brush. There were no strange voices, no pervasive choir of forest murmurs up at that altitude, even when you found yourself alone. I mentioned it to Lewellyn, who merely repeated that, indeed, there were no voices up in the mountains.

I tried to get more answers out of Lewellyn on our breaks. He was unusually communicative, and told me many things about the island and its history. He told me about Count Cammarano and the Germans and their experiments during the Second World War. It seemed the Nazis had found the island on their search for rubber, which they needed in vast quantities for tyres. In the end the German engineers managed to resolve the problem by creating a synthetic rubber, and they no longer needed to import the material from Malaysia or other countries in the Pacific. He even told me about the SIAR and their behavioural experiments, and revealed his utmost disdain for utopian ideals.

'What are you talking about?' I asked him. 'All of you are the product of a utopian ideal.'

'Oh no, no, no,' he said, almost annoyed. 'You're mistaken. Our work on the island has absolutely nothing to do with creating any kind of social utopia or conducting psychological experiments. Our role here is to take advantage of the island's energy resources. That place you people call "our city", Central, is really a base for a mining development in the middle of the island. Most of the people living in Central are engineers, physicists, chemists. Either that or machine operators, cleaners, miners, labourers, foremen, guards, office workers, cooks. We don't work with unobservable phenomena here. We're practical men. We work with energy, forces, metals.'

'I thought you were looking for a "room",' I said. 'A room that contains "EVERYTHING".'

'That is merely a metaphor,' Lewellyn said.

'A metaphor? I don't believe you,' I said.

'You can believe or disbelieve what you like.'

'I'd also like to know what the hell you need physicists for in a mining development... But leaving the physicists to one side for a second. What about the musicians? You have a superb orchestra with first-class musicians here. Here, in the middle of the Pacific Ocean! So tell me, what could you possibly need an orchestra for in a mining development?'

The others were listening to our conversation somewhat astonished. But Lewellyn didn't want to answer my question, and fell silent.

'A mining development,' Wade said. 'A mining development, right. And the children – what are they? The canaries? Do you use them to check there aren't any dangerous gases? Or maybe you send them down the narrowest tunnels?'

Lewellyn shot him a terrible look with his bulging red eyes. I'd been dreading that moment; all the hate and resentment that had been building up in us for months had to come out at some point. Up until then, all four of us had remained civil. But I knew it couldn't last, and Lewellyn knew it too. And there I was, Juan Barbarín, chatting away to our chief torturer

Abraham Lewellyn, sitting on a cliff edge overlooking a glorious view of a valley. Wade had stood up and was making his way towards Lewellyn with hands stretched open, as if he were preparing to strangle him.

'Erickson,' Abraham said, without moving a millimetre, 'you'd do well to keep all of your friends back in Central in mind. Keep in mind that we're also holding a group of young women and a handful of children hostage up in the mountains. You may not quite understand this, but if I disappeared, all hell would break loose in Central. What I mean is that I'm on your side, and I've done more for you than you can imagine. I know you don't believe me, but it's true. And if you so much as touch me, the first thing that will happen is that the others down there will retaliate against your lot. I think you know what I mean. I am aware that this is my lifeline and the sole reason none of you will try to do me harm during these days we spend together.'

Wade stopped in his tracks, folded his arms and stroked his beard. He was smiling, trying to calm himself down, to act wisely rather than impulsively.

'You know, I've been thinking, Lewellyn,' Wade said. 'Now that it's just the four of us here, we could easily tie you at the wrists and ankles and take you as our prisoner. One of us can head back to Central and negotiate. Release our lot, and in exchange we'll release you. If you're really as valuable and important as you say, I think they'll agree to it.'

'Don't be a fool, Erickson,' Lewellyn replied. 'You don't have it in you to pull off a stunt like that. You don't have the discipline or the nerve.'

'Don't have it in me?' Wade said, and I noticed that something inside of him grew dark, as if a great light had gone off in the world and everything began to fill with night. 'Don't have it in me? You mean if your lot down there didn't play ball, we wouldn't have it in us to slice off one of your fingers, or an ear, take it to them and say "We're going to keep bringing you pieces of this bastard until you cooperate"?'

'And who's going to cut off my finger?' Lewellyn scoffed. 'You, Wade? Have you even pulled a knife on someone? I don't doubt you know how to use your fists, and I know you're a hunter and that you know how to butcher a boar or flay a fox. But cut another person's finger off? A person isn't a fox, Wade. You couldn't go through with it. None of you would ever go through with it. You could make me your prisoner, it's true. And do you know what would happen? A group of armed men would simply come along and rescue me, and flog the lot of you.'

'You might be right,' Wade said. 'Getting them to negotiate would be tough, and given that you lot are a bunch of wild animals, if I took one of your ears to them, they would probably come at mine. You've done it before. We know what scum you are, and you might be right – maybe we can't sink to your level.'

'We've done it before?' Lewellyn said, clearly taken aback. 'I don't follow, Erickson. What are you talking about?'

'Eileen,' Wade said. 'She was the first. Mutilated, tortured, her lips sewn shut. The poor woman still hasn't got her speech back.'

'Eileen got lost in the middle of the island,' Lewellyn said firmly, perhaps beginning to feel alarmed and thinking that he'd underestimated the depths of our wrath. 'She was lost, and she would have died if we hadn't come to her rescue. We brought her to Central. She was in a terrible state. She hadn't eaten or drunk for days, and she'd fallen and cut herself. She had wounds, some infected, and insect bites, and leech marks... The island showed her no mercy at all. In the hospital the doctor looked her over and it was then that they found the tumour in her left breast. She needed the operation. We operated. What do you think would have happened if we hadn't intervened? It was malignant. It would have spread all through her body. After that, she was obsessed with escaping. She asked us question after question after question, incessantly. She didn't even wait to recover. She could only think about escaping. And she did. She escaped. She was lucky to get through the energy shield while it was under maintenance and the current was weak. You can get through the wall when it's at that level, but not without sustaining internal wounds. My guess is that she ran through it, meaning that her injuries were less serious. But she was never "tortured". Why would we torture her? Because we wanted something from her? We only ever helped her. We told her not to leave Central, that it was dangerous, but she wouldn't listen. And as she stumbled through the island fleeing us and trying to get back to your beach, she was captured by the Wamani. The Wamani are a backward people. It's true we have come to a sort of tacit agreement with them. They respect us because of our superior technologies and weapons, and we don't interfere in their rites or traditions.

'Am I getting through to you, Wade? We don't interfere because we're not here on some great humanitarian mission. Anyway, you're a cultured sort of fellow, I suppose you've read Montaigne? His essay on cannibals. Now there's a text to get the cogs turning! How can we be sure that we're the civilised ones, and that the cannibals are the real savages? Might not they think just the same thing themselves, that we're the savages and they the truly civilised people in this world? It's all relative, my friend! There are no absolute truths. She was taken by the Wamani who I guess fooled around and had a bit of fun with her. No, I don't mean they abused her sexually. That's not their style. The Wamani's style is ripping off a piece of their victim, a piece of thigh, for example, and cooking it. Or killing and flaying her. They make capes and garments out of human skin. They are savage in the true sense of the word. I'm not sure exactly what they did to her. Marks on her skin, I'm guessing. Those silly doodles they draw on one another, marking their skin with red-hot coal and piercing themselves with harpoons and sharks' teeth. I'm not a hundred per cent sure. They might have been honouring her; showing her their admiration. They all go through the same rituals themselves. They inflict pain on themselves voluntarily to abolish the involuntary pains the world inflicts on them. It's a magic act. A strange compensatory psychological mechanism. If I mutilate myself as part of a ritual, I annul the possibility of the world mutilating me in the brutal randomness of accidents and illness. I control life by controlling death. I kill in order to live. Haven't you read Joseph Campbell? And they sewed up her lips. Yes, that's common practice among the Wamani. They do dreadful things to their victims, but they don't sew everyone's lips. I'm sure they sewed Eileen's mouth closed in order to shut her up; I'd bet there was no way of getting her to pipe down. She must have talked, screamed, sobbed, moaned and begged, insulted them. But she had to shut up. They had to shut her up. And the most drastic and efficient way to shut someone up is to sew their lips together. So that's what they did.'

We were all silent. I sighed and only then became aware of the tension that had been building up throughout Lewellyn's long monologue.

'So you're saying you lot aren't guilty of anything,' Wade said. 'You just found Eileen wounded and dehydrated and sick in the jungle. You looked after her. You operated on her in hygienic conditions and, of course, with anaesthetics, and you saved her life.'

'That's correct.'

'And then she escaped. She got injured crossing the energy shield and then was captured by the Wamani, who tattooed her skin and sewed up her mouth so that no one could hear her cries.'

'More or less, yes.'

'So you guys aren't the villains. In fact, you're the good guys in this story.'

Lewellyn looked at Wade frostily. He seemed genuinely offended by Wade's pig-headedness, and with the obstinacy we all showed towards him.

'Tell me something,' I said then. 'What's this obsession with silence all about? Why have you got such a thing about keeping quiet? They shot me because I spoke out. Because I wouldn't shut up. George repeated over and over: "I don't want to hear your voice. I don't want to hear your voice." Why?'

'You don't know?' Lewellyn asked, with that smirk of his that I so detested. 'You really still have to ask?'

Wade walked slowly towards him. Lewellyn instinctively stood up and took a few steps back.

'Let's simplify things a little, shall we?' Wade said. 'I think this miserable worm is probably right. Even if we make him our prisoner, the others will never play ball with us. But I'm sick of his worm face with those bulging eyes. I'm sick of hearing his little elementary school teacher voice with all his airs. His know-it-all tone. His sarcasm. He thinks he's so damn smart! I'm sick of him never answering our questions. John has asked you a simple question, scumbag, and you're going to answer it.'

'I merely meant that he should know the answer,' Lewellyn said, lowering his eyes as if the conversation were deadly boring.

'What are you going to do?' Rosana asked Wade.

'I'm going to beat the crap out of this scumbag,' Wade said. 'For the kids, for Eileen, for John, for you, for all of us. For treating us like dogs when you could have helped us. I'm going to beat the hell out of you.'

'Oh, right, very manly,' Rosana said. 'Sort it out with your fists. Let's see some blood and broken teeth. Really sensible. At last, we might get somewhere...'

She was clearly irritated, but she didn't raise her voice or move. I was amazed by how she controlled her emotions, and also by the tremendous clarity words can take on when spoken quietly and calmly in a heated situation.

'So you don't think he deserves it?' Wade asked.

'Of course he deserves it,' Rosana said. 'He deserves it and some. But I think we can make better use of him. Let's talk seriously. Let's focus on what's important. We're not near the city now, which means we can have a serious discussion about what we're going to do,' she added, getting up from the rock she'd been sitting on and squaring up to Lewellyn. 'Lewellyn is going to tell us where the children are. No, better still, he's going to take us to where they are. We'll rescue the children and let Lewellyn go back to Central without having laid a finger on him. That's what's going to happen.'

'Miss,' Lewellyn said, completely unfazed, 'our objective here is reaching Mr Pohjola's house. That's where we're going, nowhere else. And besides,' he sneered, 'you can't force me to take you somewhere if you yourselves have no idea where that place is. You didn't think of that, did you?'

Rosana stared at him intensely. I knew she was incredibly wound up, on the point of exploding, and again I admired her self-control.

'The truth is, I'm a little disappointed in you all,' Lewellyn said. 'You're absolutely nothing like I'd imagined. Being with you now, one gets the feeling of being on a trip with a bunch of overgrown, well-intentioned, very well-behaved schoolchildren. I can't for the life of me fathom how you've survived this long on the island.'

The next thing we knew, Rosana had gone up to Lewellyn and slapped him in the face. A real slap, the sound of which echoed through the valley and even scared away a few crows in the distant trees beneath us. Lewellyn hadn't expected it, and was left open-mouthed, holding his chin, speechless. Wade laughed. He'd crouched down, pulled an apple from his rucksack and began eating it. He was one of those people who always had to be working his jaw. He munched his apple and laughed away.

'You bitch,' Lewellyn said in disbelief.

Wade said Rosana's plan seemed like a good one to him, but that first they should pay their visit, as planned, to the mysterious Mr Pohjola and see what they could get out of him.

'If he really does exist and he really is the one who controls the island, then it's in our interests to meet him. After we've seen Pohjola, we'll make Lewellyn lead us to the kids, just as Rosana says. Once we've got them we'll head back to the village.'

It seemed like a sensible enough plan. But Rosana didn't like it. She said it would be stupid to walk straight into the dragon's lair now that we were free and could go wherever we liked.

In the end, though, we voted to go with Lewellyn to Pohjola's house; to talk to the mysterious King of the Island and then, depending on how our meeting with him went, to make a decision about what to do next. Of course, it never crossed any of our minds to go back with Lewellyn to Central. Now free from our shackles, why would we willingly go back there? I suppose this is something Lewellyn knew all along. How did he think he was going to get us back to Central then? What could possibly convince us to go back across the energy shield? How did he plan to convince us to return? By using the argument that if we didn't he'd hurt our friends? Of course, there was one other possibility: that Mr Pohjola did really exist and that Lewellyn merely followed his orders.

And in fact, a couple of days into our trek through the mountains, the feeling of Pohjola, of Pohjola's existence, the conviction that Pohjola was awaiting us began to grow in all three of us, until it became almost physical, like a distant murmur or muffled vibration. Now we all looked upwards as we walked. We looked up at the mountaintops and valleys around us, scanning them, longing for some sign of Pohjola's property: a stone wall, a house, a tower peeping out from the treetops.

59

A cabin in the woods

Lewellyn *told us one morning* that we would reach Pohjola's area by early afternoon. From that point on we should follow instructions closely, and ask no questions. He told us we couldn't go directly to the house, because it was forbidden and might result in all of our deaths. I was deeply intrigued. We asked him if the house was big or small, made of stone or wood. We asked him how Pohjola stocked up on provisions living all this way from Central, and also why he'd chosen to live so far off the beaten track. But Lewellyn didn't answer any of our questions.

We reached an area where stones and clumps of earth and grass and flowers were suspended in the air, and Lewellyn seemed particularly uneasy on seeing those gravitational blips, which actually filled us with childish glee. He took out a bottle of blue pills and popped several into his mouth. When we asked him what they were, he told us it was just melatonin, to help combat the effects of the high altitude. We walked along crags and rocky valleys, we skirted precipices along paths that curved left and right overlooking the abyss. I thought that Lewellyn was trying to disorient us so that we wouldn't memorise the way. It seemed unlikely ours was the only route to get to the place someone had decided to build a house. How would they have got all the materials up there? It might be a wooden house; they could have felled the trees up there. At around midday we reached a mysterious, sublime spot with a fountain: a simple metal pipe protruding from a stone basin, spouting a heavy stream of water. Two cypresses stood next to the fountain. They were the only real cypresses I'd seen up until then on the island, and I guessed they'd been planted there deliberately. The three of us headed towards the fountain to have a drink of fresh, clean water and refill our bottles, but Lewellyn shouted at us not to go near it, let alone drink from it.

'What's wrong with the water?' Rosana asked.

'That fountain's not real,' Lewellyn said. 'Don't drink from it. If you drink from it, you won't be able to return.'

'What do you mean it's not real?' Wade asked.

'It's part of Mr Pohjola's dream,' Lewellyn said.

We spent all day walking, delving deeper and deeper inside Mr Pohjola's dream. It occurred to me that if this were a Joseph Conrad novel, 'Mr Pohjola's Dream' would turn out to be the name of a house or property, the name of an old, wealthy man, shrouded in mystery, whom I imagined dressed in work trousers and a blue shirt with a straw hat on his head and a rifle in his hand, walking among the rocks looking for deer or goats.

We moved deeper and deeper into Mr Pohjola's Dream. How long had we really been walking inside that reverie; feeding it, or perhaps feeding off it?

Pohjola. Ever since I'd first heard that name, I hadn't been able to stop thinking about the character from *The Kalevala*, the nineteenth-century Finnish epic poem compiled by Elias Lönnrott, and about the tone poem by Jean Sibelius, *Pohjola's Daughter*, one of his greatest masterpieces: profound, grand, sober music like the land where it was conceived. Perhaps that was the reason Mr Pohjola had chosen those remote heights to build his house: because he couldn't bear the tropical heat down on the coast. Because he wanted to live in a climate that reminded him of his own frosty birthplace.

The palm trees from the valley were now a distant memory. Now we could see birches, laurels, wild rose bushes, apple trees, blackthorns. We noticed a blue waterfall. It's not common to see a waterfall with crystalline water; usually the water turns white in the fall as it is pumped with air. But those falls were a beautiful turquoise. Lewellyn didn't let us near that either. We came across a wooden bench on the grass, a bench like the ones you find in Europe on avenues under linden trees, but we were forced to pass by this too. We stumbled across a rusty traffic light, still upright in the middle of the grass and with a wild creeper wound around the lower half. We found a stone sculpture of a naked nymph covering her pubis and breasts. Then, for a long time, we didn't come across anything. We climbed up and down hillsides, walked across rocky terrains and along cliff edges until we found some clumps of earth dotted with pine cones floating in mid-air, and a squirrel, also floating, nibbling on one. For some reason, that image of a living creature suspended in the air gave me a strange feeling of revulsion and horror. The fog was beginning to descend from the mountains. I noticed we were moving deeper and deeper into it; it reached up to our knees, then our waists. The fog brought with it the damp and the night. Lewellyn began to curse under his breath.

For a couple of hours we made our way across a high mountain valley that stretched out in a radius of five or so kilometres between two vertical grey rock faces. When night fell we had to switch on our torches, which turned out to be of little use against the fog. In the end, Lewellyn slumped to the ground, exhausted, and confessed that he couldn't find the house.

'You mean to say you're lost,' Wade said. 'We got lost in the fog.'

'No, we're not lost,' Lewellyn said. 'The house should be here, but it's not.'

'Just explain that one for me, would you?' Wade said. 'How can it not be here?'

'I can't explain it any more clearly,' Lewellyn said. 'The house should be right here,' he added, pointing with both hands to the spot where we stood. 'Here, behind these rocks, there's a stream. The house should be here, more or less where we are now.'

We all sat on the ground. We were exhausted, and the grass was wet from the fog. Lewellyn opened his rucksack with a sigh and, after rummaging around for a while, pulled out a small clay ocarina, which he began to play. The ocarina only produced five notes, which he repeated in a meandering, mournful tune. He played for ten minutes, and we just listened. Then the fog began to lift. Lewellyn went on playing and playing, until finally the starry sky began to reveal itself above our heads. Fifteen minutes

later, the sky was completely clear. Above us we could see the dark outline
of the fir trees and the dazzling sea of stars. An owl hooted in the distance
and another owl seemed to answer it from the other side of the forest. I
wondered in that moment – to this day I still wonder – if Lewellyn really
did clear the fog by playing his ocarina, or if both things happened at
once, like one of those coincidences or 'superstitions' that drove Skinner's
pigeons mad in that well-known experiment in behaviourism. It was probably a coincidence. Or perhaps Lewellyn knew that that fog would clear at
nightfall. And yet, the sense that it had been he who controlled the weather
with that music was too strong to ignore. I asked myself, for example, why
George also carried an ocarina. And why an ocarina – such a simple and
limited instrument? I began to think that the ocarina must have been the
Wamani's instrument of choice; used since time immemorial to defend
themselves against the island's menaces, and that perhaps it was they who
had discovered, who knows how long ago, that the only way of getting
about the island or controlling its spectres and apparitions was through
music.

Lewellyn said we'd have to find the house another way, and told us to
form a line and that from then on we'd walk in single file. I was to go first,
then Rosana, then Wade and finally Lewellyn. I said I didn't understand
why I should go first when I didn't know the way, and he answered that it
was clear that he couldn't find the house, so I should try. We did as he said
and set off. Lewellyn told me not to think about anything, and to walk
'wherever my feet took me'. It was madness, yes, but we obeyed him anyway. And we walked like that for thirty minutes. I tried to walk 'wherever
my feet took me' and my feet took us uphill, through the trees and then
back into an open area. Lewellyn ordered us to stop and Wade to lead.
Where I'd been going around in circles from here to there, doing my best
to walk 'wherever my feet took me', Wade, conversely, walked in a straight
line, leading us further and further into the firs. And we walked like that
for another half an hour, with Wade up front, lighting the way with his
torch. On Lewellyn's instructions, I held the other torch, which wasn't as
bright. Then Wade stopped so abruptly that we almost bumped into one

another. He said there was something up ahead. A wall built from planks
of wood. A house.

We all peered our heads out from the file to look. And indeed, at the
end of the very long ray of light coming from Wade's torch you could see
something, although what exactly I couldn't tell. The vegetation was thick
in the forest. Big ferns and blackberry bushes and all kinds of brush.
Lewellyn seemed more tense now and told Wade to carry on very slowly,
and to stop at the first sign. 'At the first sign of what?' I thought to ask, but
I held myself back, knowing that I wouldn't get an answer.

'Pohjola!' Wade yelled, scaring the rest of us to death. 'Here we are!
Hey, Pohjola! Aarvo Pohjola!'

'Quiet, you idiot!' Lewellyn said. 'You're going to get us killed!'

'It's just an old cabin,' Wade said. 'Is this the great Aarvo Pohjola's
house? Is this really where the great man lives?'

It was a small, deserted cabin among the trees, perched on an enormous granite rock. An old hut in the forest where an elderly hermit,
maybe a little gone in the head, might have lived twenty or thirty years
ago drinking cranberry wine and eating roasted squirrel. The structure
was slightly crooked, perhaps because over the years the beams had
begun to give way. It was covered in dust and cobwebs, and wild creepers
were growing up its walls. Ash-grey mushrooms sprouted from the bottom of the wooden planks, sprawling over each other. The old hut was
being slowly devoured by nature; all of the materials that made it were
returning, little by little, to the place they'd come from. The wooden roof
was made of dry palm leaves, held in place by stones. The cabin had a
door and one square window with the glass still intact, a strange detail
for a structure that had presumably been uninhabited for years. The window was also so dirty you couldn't see through it. With a degree of desperate irony, we asked Lewellyn if this really was Mr Pohjola's 'house', but
he didn't answer. I got the impression it was the first time he'd seen that
old cabin.

'No one go near it,' he ordered, spreading his arms wide and standing
in Wade's way. 'Nobody knock on the door.'

He asked Wade for the torch and began edging towards the cabin door, step by step, moving exquisitely slowly. What was Lewellyn afraid of? He seemed to cower instinctively, like a startled animal, as he crept closer to the door. By the end he was so hunched it was almost as if he were kneeling before the house, the way you kneel before an idol or a benevolent but imperious father.

Creatures of silence emerged from the woods
On fresh-cut paths, abandoning nests and lairs.

Wade had begun to recite a poem in a gentle but confident voice. I thought Lewellyn was going to turn around and make signs at him to be quiet, but he didn't, and Wade went on:

And one could tell it wasn't out of stealth
Or out of fear they kept so to themselves

Lewellyn sat down by the hut door in an almost fetal position, leaning slightly to the left and with his legs crossed. He turned off the torch and sat there completely still. And we watched him, lighting the scene with the other torch. He closed his eyes. His lips were slightly parted, and although he wasn't moving them, I imagined that inside he was repeating some words over and over. A prayer, perhaps. A plea. An invocation. Perhaps he was asking for forgiveness. I don't know. Now he was lying flat on the grass in front of the hut, his head just brushing against the wooden planks of the door. He looked like a child, or maybe a moribund old man, or maybe both things, a moribund old man transforming into a pure, innocent child. I got the impression that Lewellyn was happy for the duration of those minutes. He wasn't smiling, it's true, but there are states of happiness that transcend contentment and laughter, transcend even tears. He was lying in front of the door exactly like a dog waits at its owner's door even when its owner is dead, because the dog doesn't understand death, and as such, will never lose hope.

Creatures of silence emerged from the woods
On fresh-cut paths, abandoning nests and lairs.
And one could tell it wasn't out of stealth
Or out of fear they kept so to themselves,

But out of listening. Bellow, shriek, and roar
Shrank back inside them. Where before there'd stood
A makeshift hut or two to shelter them,

A refuge now, dug out of dark, drear longing,
Its entrance framed with trembling, creaking timbers.
You built them temples in their sense of hearing.

Wade fell silent. Then Lewellyn opened his eyes, slowly sat up and knocked on the door with his knuckles. A few seconds passed. We all stood in complete silence, waiting. *Where before there'd stood / A makeshift hut or two to shelter them, / A refuge now, dug out of dark, drear longing, / Its entrance framed with trembling, creaking timbers. / You built them temples in their sense of hearing...* It was the first of Rilke's *Sonnets to Orpheus,* poems I'd read obsessively as a young man until I'd committed many of them to memory in German, when I still didn't know a word of German. *Its entrance framed with trembling, creaking timbers.* I had always wondered, reading this poem, why the timbers of the doorframe trembled so. I'd always felt that that doorframe was alive, that the house trembled with the vehement, monstrous throb of life. And that inside the house there was something marvellous and awful at once, the greatest gift that a man can receive, and also, the worst punishment.

Oh, Towering tree in the ear!

Then something truly extraordinary happened. A light went on inside the hut. Rosana, who was by my side, stifled a scream and grabbed hold of my arm. Lewellyn had raised his knuckles to knock on the door again, but his hand had frozen suspended in the air. He too had spotted the light that had gone on inside the hut and which was now shining a square of soft golden light on the grass. But the light's sudden appearance seemed to petrify him. He drew away from the door, moving very slowly and still bent over, almost like a creeping cat, and joined us again.

I asked him what was happening and he said, his voice trembling, that it was very strange.

'Dear God, have mercy on us,' Lewellyn said, shaking like a leaf. 'Oh, Lord, have mercy on me,' he said, speaking in a low voice, as if he were afraid whoever was inside the hut might hear him, that we were all in danger, and had to get away from there. Wade and I glanced at one another.

'Lewellyn,' I said, and I couldn't help whispering, 'we've been trekking for three whole days just to get here, and now you want us to turn around without going in?'

'This has never happened before,' Lewellyn said. 'We're in danger.'

'You're one hell of an actor,' Wade said. 'This stunt with the hut is pretty impressive. The abandoned hut, full of cobwebs, half in ruins, and the light that switches on from the inside. Real impressive.'

'Fools,' Lewellyn said. 'Is that what you all think – that this is some kind of stunt?'

'Mr Pohjola doesn't exist,' I said. 'That's what I think. There's no one in there. Just a light bulb that you switched on when you were down there by the door.'

'Fools,' Lewellyn repeated. 'Cretinous fools... That's who they send me: trusting fools who turn into incredulous fools. Is this really the best the world has to offer... Is there really no hope for humanity... Enslaved fools turned tyrannical fools. Clueless fools... who ruin everything... that's what they send me...

'You and Wade led *me* here, not the other way around. I've never seen this place in my life. I wasn't the one leading the way. I wasn't up ahead. How can it be a "stunt" if I didn't even know where we were going?'

Wade looked at me with that half-smile he always wore on his handsome face, an almost concerned smile full of self-doubt and uncertainty, and I could see he was thinking something along the lines of 'this guy has a point'. And I also noticed in him the irrepressible desire to believe, his undying hope, that irresistible draw to abandon oneself to the possibility of the moment, as fresh as a fruit, as fresh as the early morning dew or the pulsating guts of a trout just pulled from its stream. Abandoning oneself to possibility: the stuff of the young, the brave, the ignorant, the wretched and content.

I watched Wade staring at the cabin, and I knew right away what he was going to do, and I knew he shouldn't do it and that I should stop him and that I wouldn't be able to stop him even if I tried. I grabbed him by the arm and said: 'No, Wade.' But he pulled away from me gently and strode towards the hut. Lewellyn turned to me.

'Tell him to come back,' he said. 'He won't listen to me, but he will to you. You're his friend. Tell him to come back. Tell him that if he doesn't, he'll die.'

We watched Wade slowly approach the cabin, like a giant morphing into a child. His perfectly bald head, his wide shoulders, his dark back. He got to the door and without even knocking first took the handle and turned it. He pushed the door open, then turned back to us, still holding the handle. I think that was the last time I saw him. That was the last time I felt his blue eyes on me. The light inside lit up his arm and face and made his eyes shine. Lewellyn begged him not to go in, but for some reason he didn't move an inch from where we were standing, and he spoke in such a quiet voice it's possible Wade didn't even hear him. Wade looked at me, and in that second transmitted something to me. Something, I can't explain exactly what, passed from him to me. I think it had to do with those blue eyes, a colour that had never really come from his irises, but rather inside of him. He passed his blue colour on to me so that I could keep it inside, and since then that blue has never deserted me, just as I'll never neglect the memory of my friend. I know that part of him will live on in me forever. My friend from the mountains, Wade, the god of dew, the giant who knew the secrets of the dell and smiled at the clouds.

Wade walked into the hut and closed the door behind him. And then the light we could see through the window went out. Several minutes passed. Lewellyn was shaking and kept saying: 'God, have mercy on me.'

Lord, have mercy on me.' He was as white as a ghost. I asked him what was going on and why he was so terrified. Several more minutes passed and we couldn't hear a sound from inside the hut, and Wade didn't appear. In the end I said I was going in after him. Lewellyn snatched my arm, but then let go again.

I approached the hut, placed my ear against the door and tried to make out what was going on inside. Then I called Wade's name out loud. 'Wade! Wade!' Finally I turned the handle and pushed the door open. Inside there was a table, and on the table a tin plate and cup. There was a chair in front of the table, another to the right, and a third on its side on the floor, covered in cobwebs. At the back of the room I saw a camp bed and a corner cupboard with some pots and pans on the shelves. To the right, just beneath the window, there was a small coal stove also covered in cobwebs. On the table there was an unlit candle in a candlestick. The hut was empty. There was no one in there. I called out Wade's name a couple more times. Then I turned around and walked out the way I'd gone in.

60

Farewell, brother of the wind

I *can't really remember how the* night ended. We walked away from the hut until we reached the edge of the forest. Once we found some shelter from the rain between the rocks, we made our bed there. I was so exhausted I fell asleep the moment my head touched the ground. I hadn't even taken off my right shoe.

When I woke up the next morning, I noticed that the sky was overcast – not from clouds, but mist. It was so thick I couldn't see ten metres ahead of me. Rosana was still beside me, sleeping curled up in a ball. She'd fallen asleep with her lips shut tight in a childish pout. Her head was resting on my rucksack, and her mouth, its expression, seemed to be asking for, or offering, a kiss.

Lewellyn and his things had gone. He'd disappeared during the night and I knew we wouldn't see him again. I guessed he was already on his way back to Central, scrambling over rocks as fast as his legs would take him to get out of that perilous region of the floating rocks. So Rosana and I were free. We were lost in the middle of the mountains, but we were free.

I needed to relieve myself, so I went off down the hillside. I could still just about see Rosana sleeping under the rock ledge where we'd set up camp for the night. I squatted among the fragrant rhododendrons and opened my bowels, and there I stayed for a moment, soaking up the marvellous morning silence. Somewhere off in the distance, the birds were cawing away. But there weren't any voices. The voices of the Island of Voices had fallen silent forever.

Just as I had finished and was about to return to our overnight camp I spotted something down the hill that took me by surprise. It was a stone wall peeping out between the hazy swirls of mist. I thought that it must have been a trick of the eye, but in any case, I decided to get closer. Yes, to my great surprise, there was a stone wall there. Old stones, now dark from the damp and lichen. A well-built wall, the handiwork of a decent mason, about three metres tall. Could this be Pohjola's actual house? The property we'd spent days trying to find to no avail? I walked along the outside of the wall. There were still a lot of tall, thick ferns in that region, which were hard to move through. Then I saw brambles laden with blackberries. Delicious dark blackberries, glistening in their juicy ripeness. Along I went, through the russet leaves of the ferns and dodging the prickly brambles. It was a long wall, and I hobbled alongside it hoping to come across a door. I turned a corner and carried on advancing through the thickening fog, through the ferns, trudging along that wet, invisible ground, wading across the thick sea of bracken that reached as far up as my chest, and sometimes tripping on the bumpy ground, which I couldn't see. The terrain was swampy now, and I felt the cold water soak into my shoe. Then the wall simply disappeared. I found myself alone in the middle of a coppery, fern-covered patch of land, in the middle of a sea of humidity, drenched from tip to toe in the fog and dew, lost, defenceless. I waited for the fog to clear a little; sure that the wall would reappear, but I couldn't see it anywhere. I waited a couple of minutes and began to think I'd lost my bearings and the wall had never been there at all. Blanketed in fog and surrounded by ferns, I didn't have any point of reference. And then it occurred to me to start to sing.

I sang the Adagio from Bruckner's Eighth Symphony.

The morning mist began to lift. The sunlight fell now like beacons of rain, like faded cascades of yellowy light. The mist turned yellow, golden and pink. In the forest a cuckoo, then a nightingale began to sing. I thought about how the scene was only missing a quail, and just then a quail began to sound. Of course, none of that came from Bruckner's Eighth, but from an earlier one, a symphony of such glorious beauty written by a composer from Brabant whose name also began with B, in which the birds' voices had been carefully noted in the score: nightingale: flute; cuckoo: clarinet; quail: oboe.

I went on singing, and the mist around me lifted. My line of vision grew longer and wider and new ferns appeared on all sides. Finally, I was able to see the wall again. There it was in front of me, where it had always been, where it was always supposed to be, a doorway crowned on both sides with stone spheres. I hobbled over to it. It was an old wooden double doorway, completely dilapidated. The doors, which once upon a time must have been painted sky blue, were no longer on their hinges, making it easy to enter. And so in I went, still singing.

But once inside the enclosure my desire, or my need to sing, vanished. A blue sky appeared above me. The mist drew back and I found myself, once again, in the Meadow. It was very big, bigger than the Meadow from my childhood, bigger than the Meadow I'd reached on the other side of the motorway tunnel, bigger even than the Meadow from my dream. A wide expanse of grass split on two levels, although no longer divided by a limestone step but a retaining wall, about two metres tall; a wall made of dark stone like the one around this Meadow, and capped with a balustrade of stone not unlike the kind you see on Baroque English palaces. There were two staircases, one on each side, also with stone banisters supported on balustrades, which provided access to the upper level. On this higher section there was a Tudor-style stone house, and on one side, an enormous cedar tree. On the other side stood an oak, clearly hundreds of years old, with a trunk so thick you could have carved a door wide enough to fit a cart pulled by two oxen. The grass was trim, as if several gardeners tended that Meadow. A cloud the shape of a flying saucer had appeared in the morning sky. It was brilliant white and suspended frozen in the middle of the sky, although I could have sworn it wasn't there a few moments earlier. But we knew by now how crafty the clouds are.

I was standing in the Meadow on the lower level, unsure what to do, overwhelmed with joy. The morning sun was warming me up and starting to dry my hair and sodden clothes. I stopped shivering and was filled with a delicious warm glow. I had a great sense of clarity all of a sudden. I took a deep breath, and the rush of clean air in my lungs also seemed to help me hear and see better. Everything around me shone: the outlines of objects, the astonishing sharpness of the thousands of oak leaves. Despite being some distance away, I felt like I could make out the delicate pattern of veins on their surface. The alignment of the house, the lichen stains on the old stone, the parallel lines of the cornices, the erect outline of the tiles and chimneys, the stone window frames and sills supported by fluted corbels. My God, what splendid clarity! What magical precision!

I hobbled towards the steps to the left and climbed onto the upper level of the Meadow. The cloud cast its shadow over it. Once in front of the house, I moved a few steps into the shade.

And then I turned to look at the house. It occurred to me that I should go in, that everything I'd done in my life up until that moment had been but a journey towards this house. And now, at last, I'd reached it, that same house Wade and Lewellyn had been searching for. The house we'd all been searching for, perhaps, in one way or another. Now that I was there, I had to go inside. And yet, I didn't have any desire to do so, because I couldn't imagine what I might find within its walls, and because the sun in that garden was glorious. It filled me with a sensation of warmth that I didn't, under any circumstances, want to lose. I walked towards the front door, out of the shadow of the clouds, although something told me that now I'd stood in the shadow cast by the house, I was protected from anything that might happen to me. And it was then that I saw Wade appear. There he was in the doorway, smiling at me. He seemed very tall. Taller than usual.

'John.'

'Wade. What happened to you? What happened in that hut?'

'It's not your time yet, John,' he told me. 'First you must go up the mountain. You can't come in here yet.'

'What mountain?'

'When you leave here you'll see it. Head up the mountain. You'll have to do it alone. Head up the mountain.'

I couldn't work out what Wade was doing in that house. He seemed
very at home there, as if he'd known it forever. As if, in some way, it were
his home. He was leaning on the doorframe and looking out into the
morning sun with a faint smile on his face, which creased the corners of
his eyes. His knife was in its rubber sheath in his belt and he seemed like
the Wade from before, back when we still had hope. He was wearing the
khaki trousers he'd worn at the start of all this, and the perfectly fitting
army boots that he'd found among the wreckage of the plane.

'Wade,' I said. 'Is that you? Is that really my friend Wade Erickson?'

'All of us,' Wade answered, 'are but the shadow of Mr Pohjola. Different forms and personalities that are really masks, covers, impersonations
of Mr Pohjola. Do you see?'

'You mean that Mr Pohjola uses your form to speak to me? You mean
he transforms into you to get in contact with me?'

'He doesn't just "use my form",' Wade said, crossing his arms and looking at me as he used to, lifting his chin slightly like he was straining to see,
although I know that Wade had eyes like a hawk. 'He doesn't only "transform into me" to speak to you. All of us are Mr Pohjola's forms and characters. I am Wade, your friend, but I am also Pohjola. You could see me
here in another guise: as your father, for example, or some old friend, or
your mother, or someone from your past, woman, man, it makes no difference – I would still be Pohjola. Do you see?'

'I think so,' I said. 'I think I understand.'

'No, no, you don't understand. I am Mr Pohjola. But you are too. We
are figures from his dream. We're his characterisations. Figments of his
imagination. Mere forms.'

'You and me? Both of us?'

'Yes.'

'I'm just a form, one of Mr Pohjola's characters?'

'I'm afraid so.'

'So when you and I talk, Mr Pohjola is really talking to himself.'

'Correct again,' he said.

'And the Meadow? The island?'

Wade fell silent. The lines on his forehead looked like rolling waves when he raised his eyes to look up to the sky, to look around him as if wanting to soak it all in: the light, the cool freshness of the grass, the stone balustrade with its yellowish stains of ancient lichen, the shade of the two giant trees on either side of the house, a bird's call in the distance.

'The Meadow and the island too? They're Pohjola?' I asked. 'Mr Pohjola isn't a human being, right? He's the island.'

'That's right, yes,' Wade said. 'But an island can only be a being. An island is a being, just as every being is an island. This is your island, brother,' he added with a wink. 'This island is you.'

'What?'

'You heard. I'm handing it over to you, my friend. It's your island. It's for you.'

'I'd always thought that this island was yours, brother,' I said. 'Your island, brother Wade. Your island, brother of the wind. The island of the brother of the wind.'

'Yes,' Wade said, still smiling and uncrossing his arms before stretching them deliciously up in the air. 'It's true. I am the brother of the wind. You got that right, Johnny boy.'

'Of course you are. You always have been.'

'Always on the move. Chasing the robin. Always checking you're on the right side of the wire fence. Being the curious one looking in from the outside, not the cooped-up chicken inside. Yes, brother of the rain, you're right. How could I have forgotten?'

'Brother of the rain?' I tittered. 'That's me?'

'Yes. I've never had a brother, John Barbarin. But you've been like a brother to me.'

'I've never had a brother either, Wade Erickson. You've been like my brother too.'

'Brother of the rain,' Wade said, as if only just finding a name by which to call me. 'You fall from the sky and are lost on the earth, brother of the rain. You come from on high and turn to clay. You will weep over my grave, brother of the rain, and I, brother of the wind, will blow over yours.

You will wash away the old bones and I will toss them about, so that they mix with the forest leaves.'

'There's still time for that,' I said. 'There are still plenty more hunts to come, brother of the wind, plenty of trips through the forest, plenty of walks along the stream. Many days of fishing and sleeping out in the open.'

'Yes,' Wade said, shielding his eyes with one hand and looking up to the sky to check the time. 'It'll rain this afternoon, but who cares? We can go out anyway. The important thing is not to build any temples, you see, brother of the rain? The important thing is not to build temples.'

'Not to build temples, eh?'

'You should watch out for that,' Wade said, winking again.

'Watch out for that, yes.'

'You can't be too careful.'

'You can take a gamble.'

'Sure you can.'

'But not build temples,' I repeated.

'That's right.'

'You built temples,' I said. 'I've built some too.'

'We all do it. We do it out of a desire to die. That's why we build temples, because we've grown tired of living and we want to be slaves, so we look for a master when really we should be looking for paths and scents and new songs to sing.'

'Scents,' I said. 'I've never gone looking for any scents or paths. I've only sought out women.'

'Women.' Wade sighed. 'You're right. Women. Women, sisters, lovers. I spent years looking for my mother.'

'I remember. And when you found her in Florida, she didn't want anything to do with you.'

'Slipped me two hundred dollars,' Wade said, smiling. 'Took out two hundred dollars from the cookie jar. For a moment I thought she was going to offer me a cookie. But those dollars were the sweetest candy she was prepared to give me. John, that's the saddest thing that ever happened to me. It's what broke my heart.'

'Do you still think about her?'

'Yeah. I think maybe that's the reason I didn't want a family of my own – so I couldn't break anyone else's heart.'

'But not all...' I began. 'I mean it doesn't always... Not all parents...'

'We all end up breaking each other's hearts. I've learnt that now. It can't be avoided. Parents break their children's hearts. Children break their parents' hearts. Parents break each other's hearts... lovers, brothers, friends... It can't be helped...'

'But a heart can heal. Don't you think it's possible for a heart to heal?'

'I don't think so,' Wade said. 'I think once it's broken it can't be healed.'

'Don't you think the wind can heal your heart?' I asked.

'The wind...' Wade said, pensively. 'The wind has no notion of these things. The wind heals, that's true, but on its own terms. The wind writes stories. That's how it heals. That's the wind's job. It is the great storyteller. It's what moves men across lands.'

'It moves us all, I guess.'

'Some more than others. The wind isn't everyone's friend. Not everyone heeds its call to travel, to take flight. But everyone needs its stories.'

'And you think that's what stories are for? To heal broken hearts?'

'Hell, what do I know?' Wade said, good-humouredly. 'I couldn't tell you. I'm no professor. I don't know nothing. I'm just thinking out loud.'

'Like the wind.'

'Exactly, like the wind.'

'Telling stories.'

'Yeah,' Wade said. 'I guess that's what the wind does. Tell stories. Stories and poems. And in the end they're the same thing, stories and poems. They're all stories, don't you think?'

We both fell silent. Wade pulled a walnut out of his pocket. I don't know where he'd got it from, but I'd often been amazed by his capacity to find something to chew in almost any situation. He sat on the stoop and pulled out his knife. Next he placed the point of the knife in the tiny hole between the two shell halves, extracted the pieces of nutty flesh and brought them to his mouth. He tossed the shells away on the grass. It occurred to me that I'd seen him a dozen times in that same position, sitting on the floor with his arms resting on his knees and splitting some fruit or other in half and eating it as he looked around him. Or crouching, or with one knee on the ground, eating a kola nut, or a noni, or a piece of coconut.

'You don't eat cherries any more?' I asked him.

'Cherries?'

'I saw you eating cherries once.'

'Cherries?'

'Yes.'

'That wasn't me,' Wade said, shaking his head.

He pulled out another walnut and offered it to me, holding it between two fingers. I said no with a shake of my head.

'Do you think I could come with you?' I asked. 'Do you think I could go in there too?'

He turned around and looked inside the house. I could only make out a white wall, a polished reddish wooden floor.

'Nah,' he said, shaking his head again. 'I've already told you you can't, Johnny boy. You're not ready yet. You have to go up the mountain. You've got one serious mountain to climb!'

'Why?'

'Why...' he echoed, as if my reaction were extremely amusing.

'Yes, why?'

'If there were a why, it'd make sense.'

'If it doesn't make sense, there's no reason to do it.'

'That's true,' he said.

He cracked another walnut, popped it in his mouth and threw the shell on the grass again.

'Just do it, okay?' he said.

'Okay,' I said.

I watched as he cracked and ate a third nut.

'Different brothers and sisters do different things,' Wade said then, waving his knife in the air, as if it helped him in his reasoning, and still munching away. 'The brother of the wind follows in the birds' wake. The brother of the rain connects the sky with the earth. The brother of the fire burns things. And the sister of the stones supports the world.

'And they all have a voice. But each one is a different voice. The brother of the rain makes other sounds ring out. The brother of the wind speaks with words. The sister of the stones sings. The brother of the fire listens. Those are the four voices.

'Then the four brothers and sisters must learn what doesn't come naturally to them. You see? One day I might learn to sing. One day the earth might shift and the water listen. One day the wind might cease to blow.'

'I'm never going to see you again, am I, Wade Erickson?' I asked.

'Sure, we'll see each other. We'll be seeing each other again. That I can guarantee.'

'When?' I asked.

'In the spring,' he said, distracted now by a walnut that wouldn't open, 'when spring returns to the banks of the Wabash. Go see Hammerstown. Head a few miles upriver. Look for a robin's nest among the elms. That's where I'll be.'

I could feel my eyes welling up.

'Don't be sad, Johnny boy,' he told me. 'The world is full of tears. Don't be sad.'

'I lost my old friends forever,' I said. 'And now I've found them all again. They were all on the island. My childhood friends! How is that possible? Where did they all come from? They were all there, and I can't even talk to them. I've become strange to them, and they strange to me. I've broken all the links to my past, and I don't even know why. My parents are both dead, but before they died I went years without speaking to my father, and then spent years being angry at my mother, and I'm not even sure why. I don't have siblings. I've only loved one woman in my life, and I left her. I left her, Wade. Without a word. I slipped out like a thief. She was waiting for me and I guess she waited for a while until she realised that I wasn't coming back. And she got on with her life and forgot about me. Everyone forgets about me, slips away from me. I've lost everything, abandoned everything, and in return for what? Nothing. I've sold myself for nothing. Tell me, what meaning does my life have?'

'Its meaning lies in the moment your heart broke,' Wade said, and then he added, pointing to the broken nutshells on the grass: 'But look at these nutshells, could you make a nut of them again?'

'I don't know, my friend. Could I?'

Wade stared at the walnut between his fingers. Then he stood up and shook the leftover shells from his trousers and shirt.

'Here, take this,' he said. 'Keep it safe, and be whole again.'

I moved towards him, put out my hand and took the walnut. It was warm.

'Thank you,' I said.

'So long, brother of the rain.'

'So long, brother of the wind. I'll never forget you.'

'If you ever get out of this place... If you ever find yourself in South Indiana...'

Wade fell silent.

'What is it?'

'Nah, no matter. It's not important. Just remember what I told you, okay?'

'You've told me a lot of things.'

'That's true,' he said, laughing, but I also thought I glimpsed tears in his eyes.

It looked like he was about to turn around to go back into the house and disappear forever, but right in that moment a breeze began to blow and Wade paused and turned around to feel the wind's caress.

I'll never forget the sensation of the wind moving through the lawn in the Meadow and the way it seemed to make every blade stand on end, as if thousands of hands were plucking the green strings of a harp, drawing them out from a dream, the sadness and feeling of desolation of it all, and also the beauty, as if that breeze were actually blowing through an island of oak trees on the Wabash River in Indiana, where a red Buick Skylark watches from the banks as love blossoms on Severed Head Island; the wind whipping through a city in ruins, the scene of a battle, or Rishikesh, on the banks of the Ganges, between the pagoda-shaped temples and the blue statues of monkey gods; or through the elms in Oakland, Rhode Island, there by the jutting clock tower of the Faculty of Sciences, by the yellowy flagstone path that I took every morning ogling the legs of the young women as they passed...

The breeze blew through the Meadow and brought with it the memory of all the sad things in the world. It brought, too, the memory of all the dead, because the Meadow was really a cemetery, a vast ossuary at the very end of the world. And then I finally understood why I was in the Meadow, and why it was empty and lonely and surrounded by a big stone wall, and why that grass grew there: green grass made up of millions and millions of green blades, one for every man and every woman who had ever lived. I hesitated to ask Wade about this in case he told me it was true, that at last I'd discovered the truth and that marvellous garden covered in green grass and that what I'd spent my whole life searching for was really a graveyard, that the Meadow was really a cemetery. And that deep down that is what life is: a pilgrimage that ends among the cypresses, a walk that ends at dusk in front of a door that says: 'Many enter, none shall leave.' I turned around to look at the Meadow, telling myself that the dead must have been accumulating for centuries underneath that well-kept lawn, and probably now that I had discovered what the place really was, I would at last see the headstones and crosses. But there was nothing. Only grass. And the wind had begun to blow.

That breeze changed everything and led me to the true meaning of the Meadow. Because that breeze was in fact the life of the Meadow, the Meadow's own awareness of itself. The Meadow came back to life, and it wasn't really a cemetery, but a garden holding the sweet sleep of the dead, the place of miracles, the Garden of Resurrection that the White Rose Society had searched for. And the cloud wasn't a cloud or a flying saucer, but the White Rose hovering above us which opens our mind to the mind of the cosmos. All of this became intelligible to me the very second that breeze began to blow, the breeze which was the Meadow's conscience, its intelligence, its memory. That breeze is still blowing now, in this very second, somewhere in the world, keeping hope alive.

'The wind,' Wade said, holding out his open hand to feel the breeze on his palm. 'Look, John, it came to say goodbye to me.'

'Really?' I said. 'Don't you think, rather, that it's blowing in from somewhere?'

'From where? What do you mean?'

'I feel like it's blowing in from other Meadows. I feel like this wind is coming from another world.'

'What do I know?' Wade said. 'Dying doesn't make you no smarter. It's been good knowing you, John.'

I realised he was going to go, that he couldn't stay there any longer with me, and I knew, too, that this was the last time I would see him.

'So long, brother of the wind,' I said, raising my right hand.

'So long, brother,' he said. 'I won't forget you.'

He slowly turned away from me, stepped into the house and closed the door behind him.

61

We find the wolves

Rosana *and I were alone* in the middle of the mountains now. Of course, we didn't see Abraham Lewellyn again. We went looking for the cabin where Wade had disappeared, but we couldn't find it. It was ridiculous, because we both remembered exactly where it had been and we weren't that far away. I went over what I'd seen in the cabin several times, and how old and grimy and derelict it all was, but she kept asking me over and over again, desperate for a rational explanation for what had happened. Could there be a back door? Or a trap door in the floor that Wade might have gone down? We called out to Wade in the forest, but I already knew it was no use, and I think she did too. The hut had disappeared and Wade had gone with it. I didn't tell her anything about the Meadow or my conversation with Wade – if indeed it was Wade I'd spoken to – not out of any desire to keep the secret to myself, nor out of fear that she'd take me for a madman, but because there are some things that just can't be explained.

We decided to carry on heading into the mountains towards the Black Column in the hopes of finding the children. And it was from that point onwards that we no longer slept. We lost any feeling of sleepiness or need to sleep. We fashioned two long walking sticks and now we walked side by side, along the winding mountain paths, like two pilgrims. Rosana convinced me of the usefulness of those sticks both to help us take on any steep climbs and to protect us from any hostile animals, especially wolves. She told me that when she used to go climbing in the mountains in the north of Spain she'd always used a stick, and that back home she wouldn't dream of going out into the countryside without one. So we walked together for three solid days, feeling the rain on our heads and resting side by side at night, and occasionally holding each other for warmth, but never sleeping. We carried on like that until the day we found Syra.

The next day, we woke shivering with cold and soaked in the morning dew. I set about making a fire, and the next thing we knew we were surrounded by wolves. I don't know where they came from, or when or how they'd appeared. We were on the edge of a forest of very tall firs, and the wolves seemed to have materialised from its shadows. There must have been fifty of them, and they were so enormous they didn't seem like real animals. Even with their forelegs on the ground, their pointed snouts reached significantly above our heads. I tried to catch Rosana's attention. She was still lying down, and upon sitting up and seeing the wolves she let out a scream. We were surrounded on all sides, trapped in a twenty-metre circle. They didn't seem hostile or threatening. Some of them were sitting on their haunches. Others had their tongues hanging out, which, according to Rosana, was a sign that they weren't aggressive. They seemed to be keeping an eye on us, as if waiting for a signal.

Rosana and I stood up slowly, back to back. Other than our walking sticks, we had absolutely no weapons. In any case, who could bring down a pack of giant wolves?

'Wolves don't attack people,' Rosana whispered. 'Don't be afraid. If they come any closer, don't make any sudden movements. They'll just sniff us a bit then leave. They don't seem aggressive or hungry.'

'And what makes you the wolf expert?' I asked, trembling with fear.

'I've spent my whole life walking in the mountains and have come across wolves more than once. The really dangerous animals are dogs. Dogs do attack and bite, but not wolves.'

She said it as if it were something she'd repeated a lot and that she went on repeating because of the pleasure she'd experienced when she said it for the very first time. But I wasn't sure she still believed that what she was saying was true.

An enormous wolf, maybe the dominant male, the king of the pack, emerged from the forest gloom. Although later we discovered that it wasn't a king, but rather a queen. Her coat was very pale; a chalky off-white. She was absolutely immense, with a great mane of hair growing from her neck and ribs, and those beautiful piercing and intelligent eyes that wolves have. Eyes that seem to smile, but that hold cold, ruthless thoughts. The wolf had a little girl riding on her back. She was about twelve, slim, and had dark skin. Her long black hair fell over her shoulders and topless chest. I recognised the thick violet frames of her glasses. Around her waist she was wearing a typical Wamani garment made of patches of leather sewn together, with seashells covering her groin and bottom. I also noticed she had a few Wamani chokers hanging around her neck.

'Syra!' Rosana cried.

The huge white wolf stopped about five metres from us. Her jaws were half open and you could see her long pink tongue. The sight of her yellowish fangs sent chills through me. Syra covered her breasts with her forearms and let out a little giggle. That coy gesture surprised me. There was no doubt in my mind that she was covering herself because of me.

'Syra,' I said. 'What happened? Where are the other children?'

She giggled again and pushed her glasses up onto the bridge of her nose. Since she was covering her small breasts with her forearms – with her wrists really, not her hands – she had to tilt her head down to nudge those glasses up.

'Syra, darling, are you okay?' Rosana asked.

Syra coughed hard. It was her usual cough, dry and hoarse. Then she let out another laugh.

'Syra, answer me!' Rosana said, losing her patience.

The wolves in the ring began to growl. The ones with their tongues out now shut their jaws, and those that had been sitting on their haunches stood up.

'Get off that dog!' Rosana said, authoritatively.

'You'd better calm down,' I said. 'You're putting them on edge. Besides, they're hardly dogs.'

'Well, they don't scare me,' Rosana said with gritted teeth, and she bent down to pick up her walking stick, which she then brandished in the air with two hands. 'Come on then, who wants it, eh?'

'Have you lost your mind?' I said. 'Don't move!'

I was amazed by her bravery, or rather her nerve, her temerity.

'Mum, put the stick down,' Syra said. 'You're frightening the wolves!'

The big white wolf was also growling and baring her fangs.

'I said put the stick down!' Syra repeated. 'Jeez, you just don't listen!'

'Rosana, put the stick on the ground,' I said.

I noticed that the girl was stroking the neck and head of the big white wolf, and then did the same to her ears, and I noticed too that the wolf responded well to her petting and calmed down.

'You have to put the stick down on the ground and say that the rule of the rod is over,' Syra said. 'We wolves don't like the rule of the rod. We like the rule of the wolves, not the rule of the rod.'

Rosana slowly lowered the stick and rested it on the ground.

'You have to say that the rule of the rod is over,' Syra repeated. 'We wolves don't like the rule of the rod. Didn't you hear what I said? You have to say it, aloud.'

'Say what?'

'You have to say that the rule of the rod is over. If you don't, they won't let me come with you.'

'The rule of the rod is over,' Rosana said. 'There you go. I've said it.'

'Juan Barbarín has to say it too,' Syra said, and she let out another of her giggles. She looked at us highly amused atop her wolf, and nudging her glasses up onto the bridge of her nose every now and then. 'Have you been in bed together? Are you girlfriend and boyfriend now? I bet you have been in bed together!'

'Syra!' Rosana said.

'You can't shout at me,' Syra replied. 'You've said now that the rule of the rod is over. Now Juan Barbarín has to say it too.'

'The rule of the rod is over,' I said.

'You don't mean it,' Syra said, now chewing on the skin around her nails. 'We don't believe you. Or rather, the wolves don't believe you. You have to mean it, Juan Barbarín.'

I said it again. I'm not sure what the difference was between the first and second time, but the moment I repeated it, Syra dismounted the big white wolf, sliding down the right-hand side of her mane, and walked towards us. She was still covering her breasts with her wrists, and she coughed again, several times. Rosana hugged her tightly.

'Where have you been?' she said, burying her face in the girl's dark hair. 'Where have you been, my darling?'

And over her mother's shoulder, Syra looked at me. Her face was deadly serious, and I could see her eyes were brimming with tears. But I couldn't work out if she was crying from happiness because at last we'd found her or from sadness now that she had to leave the wolves.

62

We find Joseph and his group

I think it was the following day that we were reunited with Joseph and his group. Syra told us that all the children had been taken to a camp at the top of the mountains, and that there were also a load of children on the run. She told us the children had been put to work in some kind of mine where they extracted a mineral that was like dark stones. She informed us that adults couldn't go up that high because their heads started to hurt straight away. By the end of the working day the children also had headaches, and many of them went mad and escaped and then spent their time fighting against each other. There were two armies, she told us: one was led by a boy who insisted on being called Red Fang; and the other by a girl called Taylor the Witch, and they were terrible. They went around killing each other, stabbing other kids with spears and arrows and knives, crucifying their prisoners. That's right, she told us, they put them on crosses they made themselves with planks of wood and branches. They tied the victims' feet to the bottom of the cross and hammered their hands to the crosspiece with nails.

Syra also told us that the ones who got up as far as the Black Column were able to fly, and they would hurl themselves off something I understood to be a huge bowl-shaped depression in the middle of the mountains, and from there they flew over the valleys like birds. All the wars between the children were fought in the hope of taking over the Black Column in order to fly. That's why the children were at war and why, up in the mountains, the great cycle of the Wars of the Children had been declared: to control and rule over the rock from which it is possible to fly.

She hadn't seen any of this with her own eyes. She'd merely heard about it, because on the first day, as they made their way back to camp after a day's work down in the mines, she'd lost the others, hence how she came across the wolves. Rosana seemed disappointed to hear that Syra hadn't escaped, but had merely wandered off and got lost, and I got the impression she was about to tell her off for being so ditzy; always in her own world. Syra told us that the wolves had found her straight away, that they'd appeared in the forest and approached her and that she'd stroked their bellies and ears thinking it was a pack of large dogs.

She had always liked dogs and wanted one, but her mum wouldn't let her have one. Rosana claimed their house was too small for a dog and that if they did get one she would just end up looking after it. We asked Syra how long she'd been with the wolves and she answered that it had been a long time, a long long time. She'd spent many days with them and was able to communicate with them; they understood her and she them. She said wolves were no different from people. I don't think I'd ever heard Syra talk about any topic at such length, and you could tell how hard it was for her to put her experience into words. We had to reconstruct much of her story, piecing together loose, faltering words. I thought that perhaps the trouble Syra had with words in general, and her inability to understand human ways, probably helped her to better understand the wolves' language and to live with them. Always roving around mounted on the great white wolf. Flying across hillsides astride the enormous creature, jumping with her over cliffs and crags. Learning to howl, feed and drink like them.

When we found Joseph and the others they confirmed much of what Syra had told us. They had reached the Black Column and witnessed first-hand the children flying like crows up in the sky. Dozens of children flying in circles around the valley from which the Black Column rose. The Black Column, which was no more than a dark rock jutting out of the rock face. They'd also witnessed the War of the Children and even seen Taylor the Witch, a thirteen-year-old girl who ate only metal – extracted from the area surrounding the Black Column – and who had acquired special powers. And they'd saved countless children nailed to crosses, exhausted and on the brink of death from starvation and dehydration. As soon as they recovered from their wounds and gathered their strength they all fled back up the mountain to Taylor the Witch or Red Fang, the leaders of the two armies fighting for control of the Black Column, which for years had been under the control of a third army whose members went by the name of the 'Birds of Infinity', a group of feral children who hadn't eaten human food for a long time and who were led by another being, of indeterminate sex, called Tremal Naik. Joseph's group hadn't seen any of these flying children up close, but the ones who still spoke English (most of the infant soldiers in the War of the Children had forgotten their mother tongue and now spoke a language that the island taught them; a language similar to Wamani) had told them that those flying children were barely human, that their ability to fly made them first euphoric, then mad. They said that seen from up close, those children were hideous. They had eyes like cats or reptiles, and thin, excessively long bony arms, and fingers like claws, and apparently many of them had begun to sprout feathers.

In turn, Rosana and I filled the others in on what had happened with the Insiders in Likkendala City, or Central, as they called it. We told them about the energy shield that kept the peninsula safe from attacks by the blue giant, whom they called 'Omé', and we described life in Central, the home comforts: the electricity, the running water, the bungalows with gardens, the school, the hospital, the swimming pools and golf courses. We also told them about Abraham Lewellyn, the stone quarries and forced labour, and Joseph, Sophie Leverkuhn and the others looked at us as if we were insane, as if they couldn't believe what we were telling them. Joseph said we ought to go back to Central to rescue the rest of our group still imprisoned there, and we went over the difficulties involved in pulling off such a trip. They wanted to know how we'd managed to escape, and Rosana and I looked at one another in dismay, since explaining everything that had happened would be no mean feat and implied, above all for me, bringing up Aarvo Pohjola, the story of the island, boats crossing the sea in the sixteenth century, everything we'd found in the underground bunker, and then describing, however vaguely, what had happened to us when we went looking for Pohjola's house. Somehow, we managed to bring them up to date. Joseph asked us what we meant by Wade having 'disappeared', and then, when he listened to the story of our search for Pohjola's house up in the mountains, he became tetchy and told us that Lewellyn had pulled the wool over our eyes, fooled us as if we were little children, that houses don't just disappear, and that he didn't believe in lights that simply came on in the middle of the forest. He said nobody just vanishes into thin air the way Wade supposedly did. He insinuated that Wade had come to some kind of agreement with Lewellyn, and that the whole story smelt of an elaborate set-up.

'So even after everything we've experienced,' I said, humiliated by Joseph's comments and feeling my cheeks burning, 'you still won't accept that inexplicable things do happen on this island.'

'No, John, I haven't accepted it, nor will I, because there is no such thing as something "inexplicable": not on this island, not anywhere. There is always an explanation.'

'If it's any consolation,' I said, 'Lewellyn assured me several times that the white cloud isn't a flying saucer and that there are absolutely no extra-terrestrials on this island.'

'Oh good, yes, that makes me feel so much better,' Joseph snapped.

'A few months ago, I would have agreed with you. I would have said, for example, that Lewellyn's story about Pohjola was a classic case of paranoid delirium and that Freud had described similar clinical cases...'

'Well, I'm a surgeon,' Joseph sneered. 'I haven't read Freud. But I don't think this Pohjola character is the figment of a paranoid mind. It's clear this Lewellyn is no more paranoid than you or I. No, it's not paranoia; it's manipulation, a set-up. How can you be so blind, John?'

'Well, you weren't there,' I said.

'God, John, a house that changes location? A house that is different every time you look for it? An abandoned hut with a light that suddenly goes on? Walking in single file "wherever your feet lead you"?'

'Inexplicable things happen on this island. You've seen plenty of them with your own eyes.'

'So Wade got to you in the end,' Joseph said with a weary smile. 'That crackpot mystic from Indiana...'

'I don't think you understood Wade,' I said. 'He wasn't a mystic. He was a wanderer, a nature lover, a man of action.'

'Why are you speaking about him in the past? You really believe he's disappeared? From what you've told me, I get the feeling Wade must have struck some kind of deal with Lewellyn. Part of the deal, I suppose, was to let you two go. No, John, don't you worry about Wade. I'm sure he's there in that town you mentioned with his feet up on a wicker chair sipping a nice cold beer.'

'You don't know what you're talking about,' I said. 'Why would Wade want to come to an agreement with Lewellyn?'

'We don't know that, John. Maybe it'll benefit us all. Maybe he thought he had the chance to do something for the rest of us. I'm not judging him.'

I didn't reply.

So long, brother of the wind.

'Do you know,' Joseph went on, 'one of the biggest sources of frustration for scientists is humankind's obsession with believing in fantasies and pipe dreams. Science isn't easy. Understanding even the simplest thing requires years of study, and even then there are always thousands of things that escape us, because reality is incredibly complex. And yet, science is the most reliable tool we have.'

He breathed a heavy sigh. I could tell he was tired. I knew that tiredness; the kind that comes from trying to explain things, trying to defend your position.

We both fell silent for a moment.

'Joseph,' I said. 'Wade is dead.'

'Are you sure about that?'

'Yes, I'm sure.'

'You can't be certain. Did you see his body?'

'No.'

'So you can't be certain.'

'It's true, I can't be certain.'

'And yet you are.'

'I'm not one hundred per cent certain of anything any more. But I'm almost certain of this.'

'Jesus,' Joseph said. 'When will it end?'

'What?'

'I don't know. This. All of this.'

We were sitting on some rocks, alone, looking out onto the valley that stretched out beneath us. Like two old friends who hadn't seen one another in a long time. Like two old soldiers telling one another about the battles they'd fought.

'Must be quite a tense situation, the three of you together, no?' I said.

'What do you mean?'

'Sophie, Leverkuhn and you.'

'Oh, yes, well,' he said with a muted laugh. 'You can't imagine. There have been some pretty awful confrontations in the last three days.'

'And are you two all right?'

Joseph sighed. 'I don't know, John. I don't know.'

'Come on, doc. You can get through this.'

'She slept with me. She was married to Arno, but she slept with me. And then she slept with that man, John. It makes you think, something like that.'

'They were pretty exceptional circumstances,' I said. 'You know why she did it. Don't think about that any more. Forget about what happened.'

'I can't stop thinking about it.'

'You have to erase it from your mind. Now. Right now. Once and for all.'

'That's easy for you to say.'

'Man up. Move on! And don't tell me it's easy for me to say,' I said, pointing at my left leg. 'If you're capable of doing this, of cutting off a man's leg and for that man to go on walking and talking, then you can do the same yourself.'

Joseph fell silent.

'A sick kid, Joe. A twelve-year-old kid who can't breathe. Imagine that as a mother, night after night.'

'There were other ways around it,' Joseph said.

'Maybe there weren't.'

That evening I spotted the two of them talking, sitting slightly apart from each other on the rocks with their backs to me. I watched as Joseph slipped his arm around Sophie's waist and she rested her head upon his shoulder.

63

I decide to climb the mountains

cting on the information Syra had given us, the next morning the group decided to go back up to the region surrounding the Black Column and find the camp where they were holding the children. Syra said she would go up with the wolves, which she claimed were friends of the children. They weren't afraid of the mines, the mineral or the Black Column. The pack would protect the children on the way down, as nobody would dare attack them. It was a hare-brained plan, for sure, but that made it perfectly fitting.

The idea was to rescue the children, take them back to the village, and from there form a new army with the remaining castaways to go and rescue the others who were still imprisoned in Central.

I think it both surprised and hurt Rosana that I'd decided not to go with them. Joseph advised me it was better if I went back and stayed on the coast, that I'd already done so much more than anyone could ask of me. But I had no intention of doing so.

The truth is that up until that morning I still hadn't decided on a plan of action. I guess my initial idea was simply to follow the others in their search for the kids. But something happened that morning to make me change my mind. When I awoke and looked up at the sky, I saw that the bank of cloud that normally covered the volcano hadn't appeared, and that for the first time since arriving on the island, I could see the peak of the mountain.

Normally, mountains, or at least tall and significant mountains, *living* mountains, are hidden from view by the clouds. We don't get to see much from down in the valley. But then, one day, the veil lifts and we can see their full height.

I sat on a rock to look at the peak, and all of a sudden I had a familiar and powerful feeling come over me, as if I were looking at myself in the mirror, and, at the same time, as if I were an eagle capable of seeing the world from above. I've never held a great passion for the mountain; not like my friends who ski or climb or partake in that other activity which would later become known as 'hiking'. Having been born in a city located in the middle of a vast *meseta*, it's the sea that I've always yearned for. I've always thought of myself as 'a man of the valley, not of the peak'. I'm not one for the cold, the snow, rocky slopes, chilblains, thick coats, walking boots, rucksacks, heavy loads, all the sweating and exhaustion that turn mountaineers into panting rams and poor conversationalists. I've always preferred shores, meadows and esplanades. Nothing in my life or character has ever called me to the mountains, and before that day, I'd certainly never felt the need to climb one.

'You have to go up the mountain, John.'

I remembered Wade's words from the Meadow, of course, but I also recalled that small gazelle which had pointed up the mountain with its paws on the day of my ruin (in my head, that is what I called the day they amputated my leg).

You have to go up the mountain.

Not long afterwards, Rosana joined me. 'Impressive, isn't it?' she said. 'One day we'll have to climb it. It doesn't look too tricky.' I knew that she'd climbed plenty of mountains in her time and I asked her how we'd get up there without any ropes or pegs or any of those other things mountaineers used.

'Oh, no,' she said, 'I'm not a mountaineer. I've never used ropes. I go up on foot. There are plenty of mountains with peaks you can reach that way. Mountaineers look for the trickiest rock faces, while we hikers choose the easy routes.'

I asked her how long she thought it would take to get up and down that mountain. 'Two days up and another two down. Maybe three. Hard to say.

Probably three days to get right up to the top, although you never know what kinds of roundabout routes you'll have to take. There might be gorges, chimneys, rock faces you have to skirt around to find an accessible route. You might come up against storms, rain, gale-force winds. They can all slow you down.'

And then I said to her: 'I am that mountain.'

She thought I was speaking metaphorically. But the island didn't tolerate metaphors. 'Yes,' she said. 'I've often had that sensation up in the mountains. The thing is that I don't like myself, so when I think "I am that mountain", I'm thinking that I'm going to climb to the very top and conquer it forever.'

'I don't like myself either,' I said. 'I don't know if I like that mountain, either. The truth is I'm afraid of it, but I feel as if it's calling me. I feel as if it *is* me. I don't know it, I'm afraid of it, but it's me. That's why I'm going to climb to the top.'

Rosana said the idea of going up alone was completely reckless. I would need supplies and water and then all that weight would make the climb even harder. She asked me to wait for a few days to get better prepared for the trip, and to let her go with me. But I didn't want anyone to go with me. I told her it was something I had to do by myself. We hugged as I said goodbye, and we both cried. She told me one more time not to spend more than three days ascending, because if I did I'd run out of supplies on the return. I thanked her for her concern but told her I'd be all right. I also told her that if I didn't come back, it wouldn't be such a great loss either. A third-rate composer popping his clogs up in the mountains on a desert island in the middle of the ocean. In fact, I said this last part in my head, but it was what I felt.

As if to compensate for the lack of clouds up on the mountaintop, that morning, it was the valleys that were choked with fog. Peaks covered in pine trees peeped out of those foamy waves of pale motionless sea flooding the valley. After I said goodbye to my friends, who were themselves setting off to find the children, I watched as they descended the green hillside and vanished inside that misty blanket. It was a strange scene, watching them disappear one after the other. Rosana didn't turn around to look at me. Syra did, and gave me a smile and a wave. Once they had all disappeared into the mist, I took my walking stick and set off up the hill.

64

My ascent to the volcano

I had enough food with me to last six days, enough water for two, having assumed that along the way I'd come across bountiful streams from which to fill up my bottles. Sophie had lent me a white woollen throw, which I wore over my shoulders and the straps of my rucksack. Leverkuhn had given me a penknife and Rosana a pair of clean socks and a box of plasters, one of the most sought-after articles among hikers, whose feet naturally end up covered in blisters and sores.

At no point during the first morning did I get the feeling that I was heading upwards. Instead, it seemed I was constantly coming up against obstacles. Rivers, ravines, mires, tarns, precipices. I was amazed by how many intensely green tarns I came across, all swarming with mosquitoes, water beetles and grey dragonflies. The vegetation and the air quality also changed the higher I went. The ground became rockier. The path – or rather the channel carved out from the rain, which in that godforsaken place passed for a path – ran between two huge flat-top slabs of russet rock, and as I walked between them, I had the feeling of having crossed a threshold into another world (a world of canyons, ancient lava riverbeds and volcanic avalanches full of tephra). The flora changed too. Now I was surrounded by gnarled, woody bushes covered in a kind of grey lichen which I hadn't seen before on the island, and a strange tree that reminded me of a baobab with its monstrously swollen trunk. The first one appeared at the top of a steep rocky slope, like an extraordinary sentinel. It didn't have branches like a baobab. Instead, that tree was crowned with what I can only describe as tentacles, at the end of which blossomed beautiful pink flowers. Those flowers caught the sunlight and smelt (once I got close enough to smell them) of mandarin and rose. It was an adenium, a plant you can find in most American florists and which are often cultivated as bonsai. The ones I saw reached as high as three metres.

Now I was heading along a dry riverbed beneath high rock faces that formed shaded caves down below. Thick-trunked adenium grew here and there, always with their crown of pink flowers. Sand-coloured lizards scurried between the pale rocks. The sun was harsh, but the breeze was cool and the air cleaner than on the coast and in the jungles in the interior. I kept one eye on the caves on either side of me, filled with the unnerving sense that they were inhabited.

The gorge gradually disappeared on both sides and eventually I found myself at the bottom of a rocky, gravelly scree that led up to the volcano and was constantly battered by strong winds. I sat down on a round rock to rest and eat something. An enormous black centipede crawled out from between the pumice rocks at my feet. Instinctively, I moved back, fearing it might bite me with its venomous forcipules, but the creature scuttled away and hid. I knew that centipedes are predators, and inject venom when they bite. I began flipping all the rocks around me with my staff, trembling with fear and disgust, but no more myriapoda appeared.

The terrain kept on changing, descending and then sloping up again. I came to a plateau of pinkish, white and ochre rocks and stones, and the volcano's peak was still there before me, showing me the way. Then I descended a little further and the volcano disappeared. I went up another crag and there was the volcano again, but when I went down the next slope I found another mountain in front of me, and the volcano, once again, was nowhere to be seen. I began to despair. I was going up and down a seemingly never-ending mountain range. That afternoon, exhausted and ready to find a spot in which to spend the night, I came to a lovely valley flanked on either side by concave rock faces, a stream running through it. The sunlight bounced off the water onto the cliffs, producing green and blue reflections that swam in waves like mirages or flights of fancy. In the deepest parts of the stream, under the water, you could see rolling roe and algae and cress. Faces that spoke, laughed, wept. Suddenly, looking into those waters, I thought I saw a nymph swimming beneath the shining layer of budding cress. On closer inspection I saw it was a giant salamander, over one metre long, whose flecked flesh-coloured skin looked like weatherworn leather. The animal was floating among the underwater stems and exploring the undulating algae on the base of the stream, looking, I suppose, for insect eggs, amphibian larvae and small crustaceans. It had a disproportionately large head and a long thick tail, and it was floating perpendicular to its shadow below, suspended in its world of blue light and emerald sand, completely unaware of the big questions troubling humanity. I envied it. I also wondered whether it might be edible and if I were capable of catching it, but when I tried, it flicked its tail and disappeared off into the shadows of the aquatic plants as if it were a spirit.

It was in that winding valley that the little erect trees with greenish-yellowy leaves – the ones that looked like poplars – grew, at the top of the cornices of rock. I also spotted several aloes and more blooming adenium. Those aloes reminded me of the south of Spain, although they were a smaller variety and with thinner leaves and white spines. It was a delicious spot; one in which another time I might have taken a female friend for a picnic, with a bottle of wine and a book of poems. The water ran wide across the white stones and looked like a black mirror festooned with gems. The tender-leaved poplars lent the spot the charm of a secluded idyll. It brought to mind knights and virgins, dragons and unicorns. The soft lapping of the water reflected on the concave walls, creating a pattern of mysterious flickers.

At sundown, I looked for a cave in which to spend the night. The region's intense diastrophism and its collapsing rock faces made for plenty of shelters, alcoves, nooks and crannies, many of them with a fine sandy bed, which in that calcareous world seemed to me as soft and cosy as a feather pillow. I set up my camp in an alcove in the cliff face, made a small fire to warm myself up and ward off any animals and, having eaten, lay down to rest. To my surprise and delight, my eyes began to droop. I don't know how many days I'd gone without sleeping. The moment I shut my eyes I saw three white unicorns riding along one after the other among tall yellow flowers and knew, a second before fully losing consciousness, that I was already asleep.

I woke up a little before dawn to the sound of a bird squawking. I spotted it straight away, perched upright on a rock at the bottom of an adenium, pecking at the ground. It was a starling, a species common to those parts. Then I noticed more of them. They were average-sized birds with golden-yellow beaks and black plumage specked with white dots and flashes of a colour that seemed both purple and green at once. I thought about trying to catch the bird to eat it, but I didn't know how.

When I left my cubbyhole, I looked up and saw that the summit was once again shrouded in cloud. I didn't feel much closer to it than when I'd begun my ascent, and asked myself if that mountain might not be another of the island's strange games, the kind where one climbs higher and higher without ever getting anywhere.

The ascent, I told myself, is like our memory.

One doesn't climb towards the future, but towards the past.

The ascent is like a descent.

To ascend is to let go. To ascend is to give in.

That was day two of my trip, but it was clear I wasn't going to reach the volcano's summit either that day or the next. The valley was shut off in a U shape at one end by a sheer rock face with a river tumbling over it both in tiered waterfalls and as run-off eroding the rocks. The very thought of turning back and retracing my steps was unbearable, so I began to climb the rock face with the crashing waterfall. In the damp lichen-filled alcoves I found puddles of green water, as warm as broth, teeming with tadpoles. Then I came across a ledge I could follow. It rose obliquely among the fragrant aloes and narrowed to an opening some two hundred metres up, which allowed me, not without some difficulty, to get over the crest.

From then on, the terrain was terribly rocky, and sometimes I didn't know the best route to take. Often, the most feasible paths between the rocks seemed to lead me too far from my ultimate goal, forcing me to take winding routes.

I came to a dry, barren area whipped by rough winds and devoid of any signs of life except a few centipedes and lizards. The only thing around me were dusky red mountains bunched in rippling folds and deep rocky canyons. They seemed to stretch all the way to the horizon, and in all directions, with sheer drops and thin strips of water shining down below in the basins. There were a lot of crows circling the canyons. Or it's possible they weren't crows, but much larger birds – vultures or buzzards.

I came to a valley flanked by limestone rocks that had been moulded and punctured by the rains and which had a few aloes dotted here and there, as well as adenium and a strange tree with a wiry trunk and a thick crown of lush green leaves which I recognised as a dragon tree, the dragon's blood tree. The appearance of that species at such a high altitude surprised me. I thought it must be an anomaly (I related dragon trees with the Canary Islands, and also, of course, with the magical varnish that Stradivarius used on his violins), but then I saw another, and then another, and soon I found myself surrounded by a whole forest of dragon trees.

I was constantly surprised by the different species of trees in those parts. Just when I thought I'd left the real vegetation behind me, the ground became awash with some new and unexpected flower. As well as dragon trees and aloe, I saw myrrh trees, with their bitter-sweet leaves, and strange, twisted trees with prickly branches that stuck out in all directions. The bark of those trees, which reminded me of the skin of an onion, tasted intensely of incense. And in fact it was Boswellia, from which frankincense is extracted.

Incense, myrrh, dragon trees, aloe. The air was thick with Sabaean perfumes.

I came to an area with some high hills, where I was given an expansive view of the island, the muddled and labyrinthine world of mountains into which I'd spent days getting deeper and deeper. I also had a view of the green of the jungles, which began much further down. In the distance you could clearly see the outline of the island's east coast – an area we knew nothing about – and beyond that, the immense sea.

To my left a spectacular mauve and magenta canyon unfurled before me. A pea-green river, fine and snaking like a blood vessel, ran along the bottom of the canyon. Its delicate curves followed the line of the immense headlands. The vertical folds and skirt pleats of the canyon walls created beguiling tricks with superimposed shadows to the east, and to the west were flooded with golden light. The odd cloud floating slowly to the east would cast oval or vertical shadows over the landscape. In the abyss that opened up before me to my left there were some isolated rock heads that formed something akin to floating plateaus, a little like the 'table tops' in Monument Valley or the tepuis in the Venezuelan jungle, but far more slender. And on top of some of them, little dells of dragon trees grew and overlooked the void. The vultures liked to build their nests there. Looking at those aerial islands held up on long needles of rock I felt a wave of vertigo, a sensation that felt at once pleasant and nauseating. I imagined what it would be like to live there on one of those plateaus, some of which were the size of a room, others the size of a tennis court. I imagined what it would be like to lean over the edge and let yourself fall into that landscape there, at the edge of the world, to keep falling and falling until eventually crashing into the rocks. I imagined the faint, barely distinguishable sound my body would make as it smashed to the ground, and the way the world, with its majestic indifference, would accept that great anonymous fall as just another episode in its existence of rock, light and strength. The birds would swoop down to feed on my corpse, and in that way I would return, in flesh and blood, to the tepuis, to the high crests, to the skies.

Evening fell. I entered an area protected from the wind where more dragon trees and Boswellia were growing. Looking up I saw a rocky boulder, behind which I found a small cave, its ground and walls worn smooth; a welcoming shelter between the rocks, ideal for the night. I lit a fire in the entrance of my new home and ate my assigned food ration, and then another, because I was ravenous.

65

I have an accident

On the morning of day three, I witnessed the most amazing sight. I woke up as day was dawning and saw that the blanket of cloud that usually covered the mountain had disappeared again. Now you could see the perfect outline of the summit and I realised that it was indeed a volcano, almost certainly one with a huge crater in the middle.

My suicidal thoughts from the previous day, my fantasies about letting myself fall thousands of metres to the ground, had vanished. I was in excellent spirits and full of energy. It's true, my body ached. My left leg was hurting badly, as was my lower back. My right foot was covered in blisters and sores, and I tried to treat the wounds by dabbing dragon's blood sap on them. I remembered having read somewhere that the Arabs and Romans used that liquid for its curative properties. It barely stung at all, and five minutes after having applied it, I began to feel better. I told myself it would be useful to take some of that medicine with me, and I spent the first part of the morning extracting sap from dragon trees with the penknife Leverkuhn had given me. I wanted to collect as much of that sticky stuff as possible.

I was absorbed in this odd little task, scraping the bark with my penknife, extracting the red sap from the tree trunks and collecting it in one of the coconut shells I used to drink stream water, when suddenly I felt a stabbing pain in my right foot. I screamed and dropped the coconut. When I turned around I saw a centipede slinking along among the rocks. It had just dug its forcipules into my heel, injecting me with a double dose of venom. I ranted and raved at the creature for having attacked my remaining foot. The pain was intense and would only get worse in the following hours. I applied dragon's blood to the wounds and tried to convince myself that the balm helped, although half an hour later both bites were swollen, making it both more difficult and painful to apply.

I hobbled back to the cave where I'd spent the night, grabbed my things and set off. I thought I saw beings darting between the dragon trees; little boys or girls dressed in garments made of flowers. Their faces were painted black and their lips all different colours. My God, I thought, is the venom making me hallucinate? Whenever I looked harder, the children disappeared.

The swellings were burning now, but I had a hunch that the summit was close; with one last push for a couple of hours I was sure I could reach the crater. Now I was seeing human faces and forms all over the place: in the rocks, the dragon tree trunks, the brittle bark of the myrrh trees, even in the clouds. Big, melancholy faces loomed over me in the clouds, smiling or crying. Others seemed to be frowning or opening their mouths to tell me something. Some of them cursed me. A woman shouted at me. A young man blew on me, his cheeks puffed out, as if pushing a cloud-caravel over a vast golden expanse. Once or twice I found myself staring at my own right hand, as if the lines on my palm were a map. Sometimes I thought I could see through my hand, as if my palm were actually a lens.

There was no longer any mistaking that I was heading up a long, unremitting slope. The breeze was cool, even under the midday sun, but I was sweating like a beast from the effort. The walking stick turned out to be invaluable, and I realised that I wouldn't have got all that way without it. Now I was putting my weight on it zealously, almost furiously. I began to get the feeling that I wouldn't make it to the top of the volcano that day – the third – as planned, and just the thought of my failure made me rage. But the pain in my right foot was worsening, and every step was torturous. I was getting muscle spasms in my right leg now. I stopped every so often to apply the dragon's blood but I could see the bites were turning red and I was worried that if I went on I'd end up with necrosis. What would I do then, with one amputated foot and the other gangrenous? Didn't it make more sense to turn around and head back before it was too late? But I was determined to get to the top. Unbending and suicidal, you might say. Unbending and idiotic, perhaps. Man doesn't get a say in who he loves or who he dreams about, but sometimes he gets to choose his own death.

Up on the mountain, as in life, a man is the victim of his own choices. His decision to take the path to the left or right, the shortcut or the long way around, determines the dangers he will face. Especially when the hiker in question lacks any experience at all, as was my case.

I carried on for several hours along a very tight ledge that ran alongside the abyss. I'm not sure how I ended up there. I'm not sure why, on finding myself on that narrowest of paths, I didn't turn around and try to take a less treacherous route up. The ledge was wide and easy enough to navigate at the start, but gradually the incline became more marked and the path narrower, until it ended up as a ledge less than half a metre wide, with an almost sheer drop down into a gorge. And your friend here hobbled pitifully along that ledge with his wooden leg, his walking stick and his swollen venom-filled foot. I think I spent the whole way thinking that if the path became too narrow and risky I would go back – the path grew narrower, there were a lot of loose rocks, and sometimes I had to feel them out with my stick before taking my next step, to be sure they wouldn't come away under my weight. The rocks sometimes tumbled down into the abyss, but despite this I went on, as if I couldn't actually stop. It was as if, instead of paralysing me, the vertigo and fear of dying spurred me on.

I've since asked myself how a path like that could have existed. It couldn't have been man-made – cut into the rock years earlier – because that whole area, on an uninhabited mountain, was almost inaccessible. I couldn't imagine it had ever been a through road. It couldn't have been a manufactured path, or one gradually worn into the rock by passing people and animals. It had to be a natural formation, a ledge running along the mountain's almost vertical skirt, probably the upper edge of an immense slab of rock.

I wondered what would happen if the ledge grew even narrower, or if eventually it was cut off by a steep incline or decline that I wasn't able to tackle. A voice inside told me to turn around, that if I carried on walking along that ledge poised over the void I'd end up killing myself. But the force that had got me that far kept on pushing me forward. Eventually the ledge became so narrow that I was forced to do what I'd feared: I had to back my body right up against the rock face and edge along sideways, moving one leg, then the other. There simply wasn't room to walk facing ahead. The ledge was now so narrow that the tips of my feet stuck out over the void.

I did my best not to look down, but at the same time it was impossible not to. It was the most beautiful place on earth. Not even my terror or vertigo could diminish its beauty. I was above the clouds, one of which was floating over the ravines, canyons and gullies all around me, drifting slowly north-east.

You could see the best part of the island from up there, although the mountain I was climbing blocked my view to the west. I was amazed to have reached a point from which I could see from one tip to the other, amazed to be able to take in the whole island at once. I also saw vultures flying beneath me with their huge brown wings outstretched, looking down on their potential prey in the valleys and on the canyon floor, and I said to myself that if those enormous birds decided to attack me, I'd lose my footing and go tumbling into the void at the mere brush of one of their wings. Up above, as if emerging from the invisible summit, I saw the white cloud moving slowly like a water lily adrift on the immense pond of the sky. It wasn't moving in the same direction as the other clouds, perhaps because it was much higher than them. It was far above me and seemed to be doing a recce of the island. It turned, following the line of the cliff, and then passed directly over me and I lost sight of it behind the sheer mountain face.

The motion of that cloud above me, the motion of the vultures soaring over the valley with their great outstretched wings, the motion of the clouds' shadows over the landscape, the motion of the rivers out towards the plains, towards the sea, the planet's steady rotation. Movements happening simultaneously, and yet, totally independent of each other. A concert for voice but no composition. Heterophony: voices that sound at the same time, but with no real relation between them. There was a desolate beauty to it all. A strange beauty that we don't usually dare observe. The beauty of what is here without us understanding why. The beauty of the vastness as well as the indifference of things. The beauty of the world's nameless immensity.

I don't think I'd ever felt such wild and uninhibited solitude. I recalled Robinson Crusoe's feeling when he climbs up somewhere and contemplates his island for the first time. I was overcome with the kind of frenzy that must afflict both the suicidal and the sainted. The feeling of having reached a limit; a feeling we never get in life yet for which we're always vaguely searching. The feeling of truth, of living truly, and being truly there, wherever we are, and truly *being*, and experiencing our existence as one ought to; as we had occasionally suspected it ought to be. A feeling of eagles and time, of celebration and emptiness.

Splendour, the feeling of being alive. Finally experiencing existence, finally being able to say: 'It's me. I am Juan Barbarín, and I'm here, and I'm alive.'

I bellowed into the void that I was alive, and I bellowed my name, and nothing in that vast landscape stirred. The world accepted my cries of plenitude with serene acquiescence.

I carried on walking along the ledge for a long time. I'm not exactly sure for how long, but it felt to me like hours. It's perfectly possible that it was just thirty or forty minutes, because peril and fear tend to distort our sense of time. There came a point where the path became wider and I could go back to walking head on, and I realised the worst was behind me. The almost vertical ledge that I'd spent who knows how long skirting came to an end and I was able to rejoin a scalable slope. Now out of danger, I fell to my knees and gave thanks to the powers that be for having got me that far. I don't know who I thanked. I can't remember.

I came across a scree with a daunting incline, but given the ledge I'd had to take to get to that point, to me it seemed as unchallenging as a city avenue.

The steep slope of purplish earth was flecked with tephra – lava tear-drops petrified in the air millions of years earlier. They would have formed in a single day during a violent explosion of lava and rocks, and then remained in place for millions of years. They would remain there, too, for millions more.

I reached the other slope and could begin to see the valleys and ravines on the island's western side. The island was small on this side, and to the south I saw a wide peninsula which I figured was where Central and the Insiders were. I noticed a white dot close to the coast and guessed that was Likkendala City.

The almost sheer slope led towards a cluster of those rocks generally known as 'fairy chimneys', and which are formed by wind erosion. And that's when it happened.

I'd had other falls, but not like this one. I guess I must have tripped on a stone not looking where I was going, or perhaps I put too much weight on a loose slab of rock. In any case, my legs gave way and I went flying through the air before landing painfully on my backside and tumbling down the mountain. I rolled further and further down what seemed to me an almost vertical slope, kicking up clouds of purple dust. There was nothing to grab hold of to stop myself. Even in my confusion, I knew I was approaching a cliff edge, so I did everything I could to stay upright long enough to find something to hold onto before being tossed into the void. Down at the bottom of the slope I could see the vertical fairy chimneys I'd just admired from above, each one crowned with its loose stone. Beyond that, after a drop of two thousand metres, was the valley. I thought I was going to die as I grappled for anything to hold onto, but to no avail. Finally, I approached the rocks. I didn't know how to protect myself from the impact. I was falling feet first with my legs slightly bent, which meant these lower limbs received the full force of the blow. I felt a violent yank on my left side and saw that the straps tying my wooden leg to my stump had come loose, sending my prosthetic flying. It felt as if one of my limbs really had been yanked off, although there was no pain. I watched my false leg fly through the air between two of the fairy chimneys and land among the rocks. In the ensuing silence I heard it bounce down the slope once or twice more. I'm not sure exactly where it ended up. For all I knew it could have landed just a couple of dozen metres below me, but getting down there with one leg and not so much as a safety rope would have been tantamount to suicide. It was also more than likely that it had broken in the fall. So my left leg was no more, and now I was hobbling, lost up a mountain.

I quickly took stock of my situation. My rucksack was still on my back and had cushioned the blows to my skull and spine. I'd taken one hell of a hit to my coccyx, my hands were in bloody shreds from my efforts to stop, and my right leg was covered in cuts. But there were no broken bones. The skin on the swelling from the centipede bites hadn't torn, as I feared it might have. I sat up slowly to see where I was, leaning on my hands and raising my torso until I could put my right foot on the floor and push myself up with it. And from that position I saw that just beyond the rocks and fairy chimneys that had broken my fall, there was an almost sheer drop into the abyss. My left leg was lost.

Next I turned to look at the slope I'd tumbled down. I'd fallen easily a hundred metres, and I asked myself how the hell I was going to get back up. It was all gravel and earth; there was nothing to hold onto.

I screamed and swore; all the worst swearwords I knew in Spanish, then in English, and then in Spanish again. I screamed at the island. I screamed at Pohjola. I called out for Wade. Nothing. The vultures were circling above me looking for carrion. The air whistled. I called out to the cloud. I called out to Omé, the blue giant. I raged at God. I said awful things to him. I've never even believed in God, but I screamed at him, as if God really existed and could hear me.

Then, trembling and breathless, my voice hoarse from so much screaming, I made up my mind to get out of there. It was either that, or being stuck out there all night. I turned around and faced the long shingly incline. Strangely enough, getting up there didn't prove too difficult after all. I crawled on all fours, leaning on my forearms, right knee and left stump, and slumping down onto my abdomen whenever I felt myself sliding backwards, counteracting gravity by putting as much of my body surface on the ground as possible. The whole way I carried on swearing and inventing new insults. Sometimes I wept in sheer despair.

I reached the top of the ridge by nightfall. My walking stick was up there, in the place where I'd slipped and fallen. I embraced it as if it were an old friend. I crawled along on all fours a couple more metres to move away from the dangerous edge, and then just about managed to get up, leaning on my stick and throbbing right foot. The agony of standing on it made my whole body shake.

I was exhausted and aching, but I had to find somewhere to sleep for the night. I hobbled pitifully between the rocks, still heading upwards. It smelt of water, of grass and frankincense trees. It was almost completely dark when I spotted the shimmer of water from a small pool between the rocks. I was amazed to find a natural spring at such a high altitude, and so close to what I presumed to be the volcano's summit. For a moment I thought it might be a mephitic well full of stagnant rainwater, but it smelt clean. The pond was surrounded by large flat rocks which were still warm from the sun. I knelt down at the water's edge, filled my bottles and drank thirstily. The cold water had a slightly mineral tang to it. I looked for a grassy area close to the rocks then lay down on the ground and applied some more dragon's blood sap to the centipede bites on my foot. The resin was gradually thickening and I calculated that by the following day it would be solid and useless to me. The pain wasn't easing, and the swelling had grown. I could feel the venom circulating through my bloodstream, entering my heart, rising up to my brain, pumping through my veins and nervous system. I was quite sure that centipede venom couldn't kill me, and it seemed highly unlikely that it would paralyse me so many hours after I was bitten, but I was convulsing now, and felt truly awful with a shivering fever. I was in shock, and even thought about praying. But to whom?

I curled up on the floor, covered myself as best I could with my shawl and, in spite of the pain and cold and fear, soon fell asleep. I spent the entire night dreaming of Cristina and white horses and deer entering and exiting a big house with no doors.

66

Priestesses

The next morning I was awoken by the hum of voices in the distance. They were female voices, singing a melody that sounded like Gregorian chant. I think I spent a while listening to those voices without being fully awake or understanding quite how strange it was to be hearing voices there, and in the predicament in which I found myself. When I opened my eyes, now completely awake, those distant voices were still there.

I was surrounded on all sides by coppery, dewy ferns. Above me, the sky was blue. To my left there was a round rock. I was cold. My bones ached and my cuts from the previous night were sore. Instinctively I looked for my wooden leg to put it on, and then I remembered that I no longer had it. My right ankle was still swollen and didn't look good. The red marks around the bite itself had grown. They reminded me of gangrene, although I assumed that my leg couldn't become gangrenous from a mere bite. I sat down on the ground and took some deep breaths to try to combat the terror washing over me. Then I sat up against the rock and finally got to my feet. The pool from which I'd drunk the night before was thirty metres below and the sky was reflected in it. To my left, where the mountainside continued further below, I had a better view, but everything was shrouded in mist. And then it dawned on me that it wasn't mist, but rather the cloud I always saw at the peak.

Those voices were clearer now. They were indeed singing a Gregorian melody, or a medieval sequence that made me think of those in Hildegard of Bingen's *Ordo Virtutum*. The voices seemed to be coming from beyond a cluster of rocks above the pool of water. I stayed deadly still, merely peeping my head out above the ferns. And I waited. After a minute or so, I saw another head appear from behind the rocks, and then another, and another. A line of women ambling among the rocks and singing. They approached me in single file, dressed in dark brown tunics tied at the waist with ropes or leather belts. Some of the women had blonde hair, some brown and others very dark hair, and all but two or three of them looked Western. Some wore their hair short, but others had long manes that tumbled over their shoulders. They had something hanging down their backs half hidden under their hair and the hoods of their religious garbs. At first I didn't recognise what they were, or I assumed they were small leather rucksacks. I counted the women as they emerged from behind those rocks and filed towards the pool. There were twelve of them.

They went down as far as the water's edge, and once there stopped singing and began to take off their clothes. Almost all of them were wearing leather moccasins or sandals, although some were in trainers. They slipped off their footwear and then whatever those things hanging on their backs were, undid their belts and cords at the waist and pulled them over their heads. They were completely naked under their tunics, and now I could see that they were all different ages, between twenty and fifty perhaps, although the majority looked about thirty. I could barely get a look at their faces because the moment they were undressed the women all took the objects they'd been carrying on their backs and placed them over their heads. They turned out to be big wooden Wamani masks decorated with shells, horns, fur and feathers, all representing monstrous animals. Once they'd tied their masks securely behind their heads, the first woman, whose slim, rosy body I had noted admiringly, began to sing again. They all slipped into the pool up to their waists. Now only the first woman, who was clearly their leader, sang as the others sank their hands into the water and then washed their faces, necks, the centre of their chests and waists, in what seemed to be a ritual bath.

Salomé.

I understood that what I was seeing was one of the island's many spectacles.

Count Balasz's dream.

Mr Pohjola's dream.

'We are figures from his dream,' Abraham Lewellyn had said.

'They are shows put on by Mr Pohjola,' Abraham had said.

The whole world is the stuff of his dreams.

I felt tricked again. Am I, I wondered, the only real person on this island of ghosts and phantasmagorias? Was I really part of Pohjola's dream as Wade had suggested in our last meeting? I wondered if perhaps it was true after all that whoever climbs up the mountains goes mad, and it occurred to me that all of the visions there in front of me, those naked women with their faces hidden behind tribal masks, marked the onset of madness.

I wanted to scream in desperation and rage. Perhaps I did scream, I don't know. Suddenly, the woman singing fell silent, and all the masks on the other women in the water turned in my direction. They'd heard me. Perhaps they'd even seen me. It made no sense to stay hidden, so I decided to confront those figments of my own imagination. I stood up painfully using my stick and hobbled towards the pool. Then I stopped, and we stared at each other, the women and me. For a few seconds, none of us did or said anything. Some of the women covered their breasts with their arms, like nymphs in statues do. Others had their arms down at their sides. Salomé looked at me without covering herself.

I started walking again. It wasn't easy with only one stick, and when I was ten metres from the edge of the pool I lost my balance and fell down onto the hard, dry grass. And I stayed there on the ground, propping myself up and staring at the women. It was extraordinarily strange that they were naked but at the same time had their faces covered with those masks covered in feathers and hair and antlers. The effect was terrifying, ferocious. Humans don't seem human unless we can see their faces.

'Who are you?' I asked. 'What do you want from me? I know perfectly well you're just a dream. Can you give me food in dreams? Can I turn into a dream like you? Is that why I've come to this island, to turn into a dream and live out this unreal existence until the world comes to an end?'

They were still frozen to the spot, staring at me in shock. Then, to my horror, it dawned on me that I had been terribly impudent, and that no doubt those women were real, very real, probably another of the many groups of raving lunatics that inhabited the island; like the guerrillas, a group belonging to the original SIAR, the product of one of their bizarre behavioural experiments. I thought about a group of wild nuns, viragos from the rocks who hated men. I thought they would take me prisoner. I thought that, once again, I'd be made a scapegoat for the fixations and delusional laws they'd imposed on themselves. But it was too late to escape; there were twelve of them, and I was just one man at the very limit of his strength.

The woman who had been singing, the one I had identified as Salomé from Count Balasz's dreams, began to walk towards the edge of the pool, wading slowly through the water. She emerged without making the slightest attempt to cover her modesty and carried on walking towards me, gaping at me in total fascination through the slits of the wild mask. She came over to where I was, and knelt down in front of me on the grass.

'Juan Barbarín,' she said in Spanish. 'Look at you, so slim!'

Then she removed her mask and I saw her face. Her face as immense as the sun. Her face that turned transparent, allowing me to see scenes from other lives. She looked at me with an intense expression of compassion in her brown eyes. She looked at me, her mouth grimacing in such intense pain I thought she was going to burst into tears. And then, indeed, I watched as her eyes did fill with tears.

'Is it really you?' I asked, my voice cracking. 'You're not a dream?'

'No, I'm not a dream,' she said, laughing and crying at the same time.

'It's not possible,' I said. 'It can't really be you.'

'I'm not a dream. Look,' she said, and she took my right hand and held it close to her left breast. 'Feel my heart?'

'Yes.'

Then she drew my hand to her lips and kissed it. I looked at her hands. They weren't the same hands. Or rather they were, but they didn't seem so to me. The years had slipped through those hands as they had slipped through the rest of her body and now, for the first time, she didn't look like a girl to me. Her girlish appearance hadn't altogether disappeared, but now it gave her face and eyes a gentle youthful glow, which I found profoundly moving.

'Cristina,' I said. 'Is that really you?'

'Yes, it's me.'

'Cristina Villar, my Cristina, what are you doing here?'

'It's me, Juan Barbarín, it's me.'

'You're not an illusion? You're not a dream?'

'No, I'm not a dream,' she said, laughing. 'I'm flesh and blood. I'm real.'

She was staring at me with such sadness and compassion I was almost worried. Her eyes were shining as if brimming with tears.

'But what are you doing here?' she asked. 'How did you get here?'

'It's a long story,' I said, my voice trembling.

'Are you alone?' she asked. The other women had begun to gather around and they were looking at me, and also about them, in dread, as if they feared an attack or ambush.

'Yes, I'm alone,' I said. 'I came up here alone.'

'Oh my God, Juan Barbarín!' Cristina said, seeing the stump of my left leg. 'Oh my God!'

'I had a wooden leg. I lost it on the way up. Help me, Cristina, help me. I need help.'

There were tears streaming down my face, and I was shaking so violently that I couldn't steady myself on my good leg and stick to get up. Putting on her tunic first, Cristina then knelt down beside me, took my head and rested it on her chest. In a voice as sweet as water running under the willows, she told me it was all right and to calm down. She spoke to me, and her voice sounded like water running under the willows, outside of time. Like naked boys rollicking through the indifferent bushes. Like young girls and adolescents with birds in their hands and garlands of yucca flowers in their hair. Like apples reflected in the water. Like raindrops falling in a puddle in some remote, silent place.

Madrid's ancient rain on the grey flagstones.

A patch of grass.

A car, burning.

Marigolds. Poppies. The smell of the wet earth after the spring rain.

Trixie, come on, Trixie!

Where has your puppy gone?

What puppy?

Your puppy. Where's it got to?

Trixie isn't a puppy. She's a capybara.

The sound of old voices talking as you drift into sleep.

The rain in Madrid.

A childhood in Madrid.

You must take your time. You mustn't run before you can walk.

Juan Barbarín, will you keep still!

Come on, come down. Supper is on the table.

You shouldn't go in those caves. There might be animals. It's dangerous.

He's dead! He's dead!

Mum!

Mum!

Cristina!

It's just a dream. You were dreaming.

My God, my God, my God.

You were dreaming.

There are loads, too many. Nobody can manage that many.

Slow down now, slow down. First one, then another. One at a time. We'll take it step by step.

I'm never going to do it. I can't. I'm never going to do it.

Down again, and now from above. Everyone, everyone together, with all our strength. Now! Now!

Juan Barbarín!

Don't leave things outside. Can't you see that anyone could come and pinch them?

Can I kiss you there?

Kiss me wherever you like.

I want to kiss you all over.

You can kiss me wherever you like.

It rained all weekend, and when Monday arrived the sun came out again.

Just a Coca-Cola?

All right then, a beer.

One beer easily turns into two.

Are you cold?

I'm always cold. Look at my hands. Look at my feet. They're always cold. Why?

Juan Barbarín, you're doing it again.

Always the same. Always the same, time and again!

It's insane. It's truly insane. I don't have a clue what it's about.

Me neither. It's absurd.

It's completely absurd.

But they don't care.

Be careful. Look before crossing.

Look both ways.

Yes, Mum.

Look both ways.

I know, I know.

It's April.

April already? I can't believe it.

Time flies, doesn't it?

Back then, we thought Valencia was far away. Valencia was exotic, with its unfamiliar climate, unfamiliar smells, unfamiliar food. Going to Valencia was almost like going to another country.

The smell of the orange blossom!

And the jasmine! At night, the jasmine.

It's impossible to sleep here.

Mum, a mosquito bit me.

Is it itchy?

Yeah, really itchy. I need some Phenergan.

Sometimes it was like that, all very strange and angry, but then we packed our bags, took off to another city and we seemed to start afresh.

It's full of water! It rained through the night!

Get out of there. There'll be rats. Get out.

That woman is mad. She's in the middle of the street screaming. Someone should go out there and move her. She's going to get hit by a bus. It's dangerous.

They came at night. They caught us unawares.

Again, but now with the glissandos where they're written.

Watch that G sharp. With the third, not the second.

Mozart is my favourite composer.

Mine's Brahms.

Brahms was German.

She's mad. She's going to get run over. She's had a drink. She's pissed.

This will never happen again.

Come, come to bed with me.

I want you. I want you so much I could die.

G sharp. You always hit G natural.

Legato, legato. Focus. You're not paying attention.

Can I kiss you?

You don't ask a girl permission to kiss her.

No?

No, you kiss her and that's it.

And if she doesn't want to?

If she doesn't want to, she gives you a good box on the nose.

Isn't it better to ask her first?

No.

It's raining.

Raining already?

Yes.

Oh, the washing!

Is it outside?

Yes, it's all outside.

Goodnight, ladies, goodnight to you all.

Goodnight, good night.

Come back soon.

Goodbye, goodbye.

Open the umbrella.

I'm coming, I'm coming.

So impatient!

67

The University

Her face over me. *Her* immense face, immense thoughts. Immense eyes and lips.

Juan Barbarín. Our memory creates everything. Our memory destroys everything. We are the product of our memories' inventions and destructions. We are all survivors of the shipwrecks of our imaginations. Products of the gods' imaginations.

Salomé, tell me what the mystery is.

Yes, I'll tell you. The mystery is the cloud and what's hidden beneath the cloud.

I understand. I am the mountain...

Yes, you are the mountain, and the cloud...

I am the mountain and you are the cloud.

You and I are the same, fragments...

Fragments of the gods' imaginations.

Then, one day, we began to see ourselves as an altered reflection of the other. We no longer saw the other person, but rather we saw ourselves in them. It was not our own image that we saw reflected back at us; as we looked upon this other person it didn't feel like we were looking at someone else, but at ourselves. That was the beginning of love's peak season. The very pinnacle of love.

Salomé, Salomé...

I'm here.

Where?

Here, behind you.

I can't see you.

Here, beneath you. Above you. All around you.

Why can't I see you?

Can't you see that glimmer? A glimmer above you?

In the glass?

Yes, in the glass. A glimmer sliding down.

Yes, yes, I can see it. Glimmering drops. Water sliding down. It's the rain.

No, it isn't the rain.

It isn't the rain? So what is it?

It's me.

You're the rain?

I'm scared to open my eyes.

I open them a little. I'm alone on the mountain, alone among the rocks. I'm dying of weakness, starvation and thirst. I flicker in and out of consciousness. It comes, it goes. I am like a fading ember.

An ember in the gods' imaginations.

Don't worry, I'm with you.

Who are you? Are you Cristina?

Cristina died.

I don't believe you.

Yes, she died three years ago.

That can't be, I've only just seen her. She's here. I've just seen her.

Cristina is dead. She died because of you. She died thinking about you.

No, it's not true. She forgot all about me, left me in her past. She put her life back together, met another man.

We are but fragments, fragments of dreams, shadows of fragments of dreams.

I open my eyes. I'm lying on a bed in a small, whitewashed room with a Peruvian-style multicoloured blanket over me. The daylight is pouring in through a small window on one of the walls. It feels like dusk, but if that's the case, where did the rest of the day go? How did it simply vanish into thin air? And, the biggest mystery of all – at what point did I fall asleep? Then it comes flooding back to me, how Cristina – if this woman really is Cristina – and the other women brought me here, the long tunnel cutting through the mountain face, the tunnel exit, the vision of the crater, the men coming down with stretchers, the white building among the pine trees, conifers all over the sides of the crater. I think I remember they gave me something to drink, a hot tea. I suppose it must have contained some kind of soothing herb, maybe even a soporific.

I'm dressed in cotton pyjamas. My right ankle is bandaged and I smell good, of lavender soap and lavender seeds. They've bathed me, treated my wound, dressed me in a pair of pyjamas and put me in bed to rest. I don't know what the time is, or for how long I've been asleep.

The room is very basic. The floor is paved in crooked ceramic tiles. There are rows of parallel wooden beams on the ceiling. Next to the bed I see a small wooden table painted pale green, and on top of it a vase hold-ing some pinkish adenium flowers in water. At the end of the room there is a pine chest. It's sanded and polished, but not varnished. On the wall, close to the window opening out onto the evening light, a small round mirror with a brass frame. My walking stick is on the floor, next to the bed. It's surrounded by three intricate patterns of beautiful flower petals, as if it were a holy object.

When I sit up in the bed and try to support myself on the stick, I real-ise how tired and aching I really am. I go over to the chest, lower myself to the floor and lift the lid. Inside it, there is a pile of clean, pressed clothes – cotton underwear that looks handmade, some Ibiza-style cream cotton trousers with a tie at the waist in the same material, a long blue silk shirt with small mother-of-pearl buttons, and my white shawl, washed and folded. Next to the chest is a pair of leather sandals. I try the clothes for size and they all fit. I can't find the rest of my clothes. Given that they were all old, dirty and wrecked, I assume they must have thrown them away.

I take my stick and hobble out of the room. There is a hallway with clay floor tiles and several wooden doors identical to the one to my room. Where am I? In a monastery? A lamasery? To my left, the hallway leads down to an archway that opens out into the daylight. I walk with difficulty towards it and see a wide flagstone paved area, a stone balustrade, yellowish from the humidity, and a big ceramic plant pot with a bougainvillea plant in it, its magnificent fuchsia flowers and branches creeping up the balustrade. Behind this there's nothing but sky, and in the sky two clouds as big as whales, and above the balustrade a date palm tree and the top of two giant cypresses. When at last I reach outside, I see that it's a long, wide terrace covering the entire façade of the building. From there, I can admire the paradise of the crater that spreads out before me. It is a serene, green landscape, but not tropical like on the coast. It looks southern to me, Mediterranean.

The crater is very wide, completely green and surrounded by an immense rocky valley. I can't get my head around how big it is. It looks like a world of its own with different areas and countries, its own clouds, its own cloud shadows. I wonder how big it must be: ten, maybe fifteen kilometres in diameter? It can't be that big. But nor can my eyes deceive me.

The vegetation climbs up the sides of the crater in imposing forests of conifers and sloping mountain meadows where I can see some tiny white animals grazing. They are so far away it's impossible to tell if they are cows or sheep. Higher up there is a strip of purplish rock about four hundred metres tall with no vegetation on it. These almost sheer rock faces make the valley virtually inaccessible. On top of this, the cave we came through to get here could easily flood or become blocked. I wonder if those who live on the island's lowlands even know about this bountiful idyll.

The basin floor is a vast plain divided into plots and cultivated fields that stretch as far as the eye can see, with the odd fallow patch or copse. There are several clouds floating in the sky casting patches of shadow over the fields. Among the many-hued tessellation of cropland, I spy the intense green of corn, the gold of wheat and the gilt copper colour of rye. On some rolling hillocks I think I can make out rows of vineyards. The odd palm tree appears here and there, by the edge of a path or in the middle of a wheat field – out of place, isolated and magnificent. There are also wooded areas and, I think, swampy regions, and then, unless my eyes are deceiving me, a river that zigzags through the fields, flanked by huge trees with bristling crowns that look like breadfruit trees. In the middle of the inverted cone of the crater there is a wide, irregular-shaped lake that gleams as if it were a looking glass. Beyond it, in the distance, everything appears abstract, blurred.

The building where I find myself is located in an elevated area on the north side of the crater, and it's surrounded by pines and firs, between which I glimpse other buildings of different heights. They remind me of Tibetan temples, which are built one on top of the other on hillsides and connected by terraces, ramps and stairways forming something akin to a little citadel, a city-cum-building. And yet, in this case, none of the buildings are of the same style. The engraved wooden corbels and windows covered in imaginative latticework look Tibetan, but other buildings I spot seem more Grecian. White sculptures poke out among the flowering rhododendron bushes, abandoned paranymphs, an Ionic column lit up in the sunlight that filters through the trees, balustrades with the balusters entwined with wild rose bushes.

'Brother,' says a voice behind me.

It is a young, tall and very blonde woman dressed in a cream tunic.

'Salomé would like to see you,' she says in English, but with a faint hint of a Swedish or Norwegian accent. 'Please, follow me.'

'I'm Juan Barbarín,' I say, so that she doesn't even think about calling me 'brother' again.

'I'm Tulla Sjöstrom.'

'Tulla? You're Norwegian?'

'Yes.'

'What is this place?'

'Pardon me?' the woman asks, perplexed.

'Where are we? What is this? A monastery?'

'This is the University. The White University.'

'The White University? That's the name of this place?'

'Yes.'

'But it isn't actually a university,' I say.

'Yes, it is,' Tulla says.

'I'd like to see Cristina.'

'I don't know anyone with that name.'

'It's the woman who found me.'

'It was Salomé who found you and brought you here.'

'Salomé?'

'Come with me and you can ask her all the questions you want. Salomé is expecting you.'

We go down some stairs, across terraces, walking in and out of buildings. I feel weak and exhausted. I haven't had any practice walking with just one foot and one stick. Some of the buildings seem abandoned. There are little roundabouts and terraces overcome with weeds. On some steps – bright yellow from the humidity and covered in parasitic plants – I see a pregnant goat with a small bell around her neck gnawing away furiously at the white flowers growing in the joins between the stones. I ask Tulla what flowers they are and she says they are white asphodels, and that goat, whose name is Amaltea, only eats those funeral flowers.

From up on one of the terraces I spy a rectangular swimming pool in the middle of a well-kept lawn with yuccas in bloom and flowerbeds bursting with white and pink hydrangeas. There are a lot of men and women either swimming in the pool or sunbathing on the grass. A girl in a sporty, navy blue swimsuit is diving off a diving board.

We enter another building of many rooms, some very big, all with wooden floors and almost all with huge round windows. Together, Tulla and I walk along the galleries. The occasional door is left open, allowing me to sneak a peek at what lies inside. In one of the rooms I see a group of women of all different ages dressed in tunics. They're dancing to some very faint, delicate music coming from a dulcimer. In another room I see a group of about forty men and women all sitting on the wooden floor with their right arms raised. A translucent, shimmering bubble floats above their heads in mid-air, and they are all following its movement slowly with their arms. In another room, a group of men dance and copy the motions of a series of lines and geometric shapes painted on the floor. In the next room, I see men and women dressed in tunics huddled around tables covered in yellow sheets of paper with numbers and geometric shapes on them. The men and women are chatting affably with a man with a white beard who's wandering from table to table. In another room, this time decorated with orange calendula, people are learning Sanskrit. In another there is a grand piano and lots of other instruments, and a group of musicians playing Schubert's Trout Quintet as another group of five young people in loose tunics dance hand in hand on a big Persian rug. In another room, a circle of men and women sitting on the floor with their legs crossed meditate around a candle. The flame changes from green to pink and then from pink to blue. In another room a woman with her hands across her waist sings accompanied by a pianist with long red hair, under the watchful eye of her teacher. I'm surprised to hear they're performing 'Vilja Song' from *The Merry Widow*. What on earth goes on in this place? Where am I? Who are all these people?

Salomé is waiting for me in a small room with a wooden floor and tall rectangular windows. In the rooms I'd passed to get here, there was hardly any furniture; some tables or chairs in one or two, and in others small school desks, long and low to the ground. In most of the rooms the people had been sitting on floor cushions or little stools or lounging in Japanese-style easy chairs. Now, in this room, there are rugs on the floor, shelves full of antique volumes and comfy-looking built-in seats in the bay windows made out of a smooth, polished wood stained the colour of strong tea. Salomé is waiting for me on one of those seats. She is dressed in a long cornflower-blue cotton tunic, which clings discreetly to the curves of her body. One of her feet, tense – arched and bare – is poking out from the hem of the tunic. Her nails are painted pale pink. It doesn't escape my notice that she has made herself up for the occasion. Eyes, lips, lashes.

But Salomé is Cristina. Salomé is Cristina and Cristina is Salomé. She places her hand on the window seat to indicate that I should sit down next to her. She has a ring with a red stone on her ring finger and I wonder if it might be a wedding ring. I sit down clumsily, supporting myself as best I can on my stick, and I assume the same posture as her: my knee bent and arm leaning against the windowsill.

We talk. She explains that in the University traditionally everyone calls her Salomé, and many of the people there don't even know her real name. I take it to mean that Salomé is a kind of title. I ask her if she runs the University and she replies that she does, and it has fallen to her to be the rector; or really, she says, *primus inter pares.* She's been in this place for seven years, she explains, four of which she has spent as Mistress of the Game, her official title. Next I ask her what this White University place really is and what they're all doing there. She explains that the University is a science research centre. I'm surprised to hear the word 'science' used in connection with the activities I've seen on my way here. Salomé says that their work here in the University is empirical; human beings, consciousness and evolution are the subject of their investigations. She repeats that it is an empirical study, unrelated to philosophy, ideology or religion; hence why they consider it a science.

My sweet Cristina is all grown up. My sweet Cristina with her childlike beauty has transformed into the majestic Salomé, the radiant culmination of that young girl from the fairy kingdom who I once loved. I'm surprised to see both how much and how little she has changed. Do I still find her beautiful? The truth is she seems more beautiful now than she did before, because now she is a total mystery to me. I wonder if she has had children. I tell myself she must belong to someone else now, and that over the years she must have been with others, given herself to others, and I feel a stab of pain and jealousy. She hasn't lost the luminous, juvenile air that she had then, but nor is she a little girl. She is a woman in her prime. The thing I so longed for has at last come to pass. But she is no longer mine.

And for her? Does it hurt her seeing me? She seems very calm, mildly excited by this unexpected encounter, but calm. Everything about her exudes serenity, just like this place, just like this room, just like these window seats where we're sitting, just like the aroma of honeysuckle and musk, jasmine and mint that wafts in through the open window. There's something at once calm and profoundly tender about her that I can't help but be moved by. Something clean. A clean person. A clean gaze, brimming with intelligence and tenderness. But is there really such a thing as a clean person, or a clean gaze? Is it possible to exist in this world and be clean?

Then she asks me a question that takes me completely by surprise. She asks me if it's really me. I tell her it is, that it's really me, and I try to make a joke, but she asks me if I remember how I got to the island and she tells me I should know that this is all truly strange; beyond the realm of what's possible. How can you have ended up here, she asks, in this remote corner of the planet, by pure chance?

I tell her my story. I tell her about the accident, our plane that crashed into the sea three months ago. She is shocked to learn that there were more people with me; no fewer than ninety survivors. She asks me where the others are and I explain that we built a settlement on the beach and most of them are still there, and no one has come to rescue us in all this time. She tells me that this last point doesn't surprise her and was to be expected, since the island is practically untraceable. She says they will have searched for us for a few weeks before eventually concluding that the plane had sunk. She asks what our living conditions as castaways are like, how we've been surviving, and I recount a short version of all our struggles and woes. I ask her if they could help my friends in some way and she says she'll take care of it right away. She asks me to tell her more about the castaways and to describe the settlement's location in more detail so they can find it quicker.

And despite everything, the whole time I have the sneaking suspicion that she only half believes me, that she is less than convinced about the existence of Castaway Village and our many trials and tribulations.

'But tell me,' she says, lowering her gaze, and as if telling herself to cut to the chase and ask her most burning question, 'what made you come up here? And why did you come alone? If you're with a big group and you wanted, for whatever reason, to explore the volcano's summit, why didn't you come together?'

'We didn't want to explore the volcano's summit. Coming up here was my idea.'

'But how did it occur to you?'

'That's an entirely logical question,' I say, looking her in the eyes, 'but I'm afraid there's little logic to my answer. I came up here because they told me to.'

'They told you to? Who told you to?'

'Well, in the first place, I think *you* did.'

'Me?'

'Yes. You came to me in a dream.'

'A dream. Tell me about it.'

'It wasn't a normal dream. It was more like a vision, a hallucination. I called you asking for help. I don't know why I called you. I don't know how, I saw you. I saw you dressed in a brown tunic, sitting at a table covered in different objects. Then you sent me a message, an image: a deer, or a goat, which was signalling up to the mountaintop with its bent leg.'

'A goat!' Cristina cried, laughing. 'It was Amaltea. It was Amaltea the goat.'

'I think I've seen her.'

'It was Amaltea who led you here.'

'Both of you, I guess.'

Cristina looks at me intrigued. Then she closes her eyes and stays like that for a few seconds. When she opens them again she tells me that she too saw me in a dream, a couple of weeks ago.

In her dream, she saw me inside a dark cave, a poorly lit cave with monstrous carvings on the wall. I was lying face down on a table and there was a group of men holding me, including a man with a black beard and shining eyes who had an axe in his hand. I was screaming and crying and begging them not to hurt me, and the man hacked my leg off. Then she entered the cave and pulled me out of there, pulled me into the light, took me up the mountain, far from that terrible place. And on the mountain-side, Amaltea appeared, pointing the way to me, pointing up the mountain, and she sent me her image to guide me.

I tell her that that's exactly how it went and she doesn't understand. I explain that the cave she saw in her dream was in fact the inside of an old deserted Indian temple, with the monstrous sculptures of Hanuman, the monkey god. I tell her that the dream she just described was exactly how Joseph amputated my leg. On hearing this, Cristina looks at me in horror, and I notice her eyes well up.

'You're telling me they cut off your leg *with an axe*?'

'Yes. Joseph, my friend Joseph, didn't have a better alternative. We didn't have anaesthetic either. We were being held prisoner. It was lucky they gave us the axe to do the operation. If they hadn't, I would be dead.'

'Jesus, Juan Barbarín. They cut off your leg without any anaesthetic?'

'That's right.'

'So you mean, you only lost it recently? A few weeks ago? Here, on the island?'

'Yes.'

'But that's barbaric! What you're telling me is completely barbaric!'

Heaving sobs rise up in my chest and I find myself unable to contain them. Cristina shuffles over and embraces me, and I cry into her chest. I'm ashamed to cry like that, but I can't help it.

'I'm sorry.'

'Cry as much as you like,' she whispers. 'It's okay.'

A minute goes by. An hour goes by. A year goes by.

There's a path between the elder trees, in Carinthia, and inside one of those trunks lives a very old woman who dreams the world.

That woman is Cristina. But she isn't old. She's young. She's young like a lavender plant bursting with flowers.

The grass in the Meadow sways in the wind.

'How could you have dreamt what was really happening to me?' I ask. 'How can we have both seen the same thing? What you're telling me isn't possible.'

'Why not?'

'Because dreams happen inside our head. They can't be shared. You can't see someone else's dream, enter someone else's dream.'

'Well,' she said, 'now you've seen it is possible.'

We pull apart. She's smiling at me. She says it's time for her to leave me, that she has classes to give and some matters to resolve. I can't hide my disappointment.

'I'll see you tonight, at dinner,' she says. 'I'd like to stay and talk more with you, Juan Barbarín, but there are some things I have to attend to now.'

'Okay.'

'They'll come by later to take your measurements and make you another artificial leg. Is that okay? We have excellent carpenters here. I'm sure they can make a good leg for you.'

'I'd be very grateful.'

'Do you know how to ride a horse?'

'I've never been on one.'

'Okay, in that case we'll look for a trained horse for you. A very calm one, okay? That way you can take walks along the paths, or head down the valley if you like.'

'A horse! I can't say it would have occurred to me.'

'We have one called Aurelianus, who I think will be just right.'

'Thank you.'

'My God, Juan Barbarín. All those years...'

'Yes, so many.'

'I'm going to tell Philemon to look after you,' she says.

'Philemon? That's his real name? Is Mort around here somewhere too?' I asked, remembering the popular Spanish comic strip.

'They're names from the University!' she laughs. 'I'm going to tell him to show you around and explain everything. I think you'll get on with Philemon. Wait here, I'll send him along right away.'

She leans in and kisses me on the cheek. Then she leaves me there alone.

68

I write about silence

Life at the University is astonishingly calm. The silence here feels miraculous, especially after living out in the open listening to the sounds of nature for months – the sea, the birds, the rain. But the silence up here is something else altogether.

Whenever we talk about silence, really we are talking about some kind of sound. We talk about silence but we're thinking of the sea, the wind or the birds. When we talk about silence, really we are talking about space.

Space is possibility. Things happen according to how much space is available – physical space, and temporal space. Space in our attention, in our will, in our life. When we talk about space and silence, really we are talking about our life. About the silence and space necessary for things to happen.

One has to fight hard to conquer that space and to deserve it. Building or owning a house is one of life's most onerous tasks. But possessing a house is really just to possess space. Possessing a house is also to possess silence.

It's the same with music. Music, true music, always emerges from silence. Music is only possible once silence has been achieved. Then there is a distinguishing factor, something that springs up. That something that springs up is music.

Music is nothing if, when you listen to it, you don't perceive that it is but a mask or symbol of silence, that beneath each and every one of its sounds lies silence, just like the stalk submerged in dark water lies beneath the flower of an Indian water lily.

When we say 'Oh, what silence!' we are usually prompted by birdsong or the whistling wind. We call the sound of the wind 'silence'. In ancient times, humans wanted to imitate birdsong. Perhaps that's how they began to speak. Yes, it's possible that this was the mission that fell to the birds in the animal kingdom, in the natural world, and that this is the remote explanation for the legend of Adam and Eve. A snake awoke Eve's consciousness, elevating her above the animal condition. But let's consider that the snake was in fact a bird. Only at the end does Yahweh condemn the snake to drag itself around the earth's surface. Only at the end is the snake as we know it now. Yahweh's condemnation is doubly painful because, before, the serpent had wings. A talking animal that lives up a tree can only be a bird.

Different cultures recall this legend in the figure of the dragon – the combination of a snake and a bird – or with the symbol of the feathered bird.

It was humans imitating birdsong that helped us to develop the voice box. Word, and song. No, I don't agree with those eighteenth-century philosophers who say that humans sang before they could speak, although this myth would be a lovely justification for the art of opera. What is true is that the voice and music have always been connected, and that people who speak also sing. *This* explains the art of opera, where singers pretend to be speaking.

The music starts up. What do we do? We fall silent. We have to. Without that silence, music isn't possible. We have to silence those voices in our head in order to listen to the music and also to perform it. We tell them: shush, shush a moment, I need to listen. Music invites us to be silent. Music creates silence.

When the music stops, the silence is even more intense. But something remains in the air, because it's not possible to have a completely empty silence: the memory of the music lives on. The memory of the music in the air particles. And in the body's cells.

We enter into silence every night, and at dawn we return from it. Silence nourishes us. Silence is our father. Sound, on the other hand, is our mother. The mother's voice quivers in her whole body and gently reaches the fetus in its amniotic dream. Each time we sing, we sing to the earth and to the mother. We sing so our mother can hear us. We sing when we are afraid. The earth protects us. The mother shields us from harm.

All human life is a combination of this presence and absence. A rich, luminous and full absence, in the same way that sound, in the most mysterious way, always fills the silence.

We are the owners both of what we have and the emptiness between the things we have. But the gaps, the silence, are the most important part. When we breathe, the most important moment is the one after exhalation. For an instant, breathing stops and, for the space of barely a second, we live without the need to breathe. During that instant, we are immortal. During that instant we aren't animals. We're free from nature's cycles. The mind also stops in that instant, and suddenly we are able to *see*. We are awash with clarity. Our consciousness becomes limitless. Then the mechanism, the body, begins to breathe again.

If we could go three minutes without breathing, our consciousness would become boundless. We would see and feel and understand things we haven't ever seen, felt or understood.

In the silence of the mind, the door to memory opens.

Our most important possession is that which we don't have and never will. The gap between things. The void. Silence. Our thoughts happen inside us involuntarily, but the silence inside our thoughts… that is truly ours. It is in the silence between the expression of one thought and another where the true sensation of 'I' can emerge.

Because the true 'I' lives in silence and can only emerge when there is total silence.

69

Lessons from the University

The silence of the University isn't just the silence of the mountains, the silence of the wind, the silence of the music, the silence that creates the music around it when it begins to play. It is also the silence of love. When two people love each other, they cease to speak. Sometimes, on the terraces of the University, I come across a couple holding hands and looking out onto the landscape of the valley. Sometimes I see two people holding hands as they stroll. Or a pair swimming together in the nude or walking naked among the blooming yucca plants.

I get the feeling that this is the University of lovers. I say as much to Cristina and she can't stop laughing.

But I hardly ever see her. She's always busy. She has to be in a hundred different places, sort out a hundred different things. She gives singing classes. And then there are dances; dances every day. The days in the University often end with a dance after dinner, especially Fridays and Saturdays. There are musicians here, lots of them, and they play dances, Indian music, Brazilian music, Latin American music, even disco music, almost every night after dinner, and everyone dances for hours. I tell Cristina I've never seen such party animals in my life. 'It's the Science of Happiness,' she replies.

The Science of Happiness. Is that what they teach here at the University?

Philemon is about sixty, quite tall, bony and strong-looking. He has thick grey hair and goes around dressed in a long off-white tunic and leather sandals. He has a Roman nose and a powerful chin. His face is strong, serious, wind-beaten. He looks like a medieval monk. He's jumpy and tough, hard as nails, but light. Since our first conversation I've felt an instinctive fondness for him.

'I'm Philemon,' he said the day we met. 'Salomé has asked me to look after you and show you the University.'

'Pleased to meet you,' I said. 'I'm assuming Philemon isn't your real name.'

'My name is Ciran,' he said, smiling. 'Philemon and Salomé are traditional names of the University. Symbolic titles, if you like.'

'You're Irish,' I say.

'From Sligo, like William Butler Yeats.'

'I've never been to Ireland.'

'*This land of Saints,*' he recites in a theatrical actor's voice, '*of plaster Saints!*'

'What do you specialise in?' I ask, imagining that he's going to tell me he's an actor and spent years working in the Abbey Theatre.

'I'm a theoretical physicist. I studied at Trinity College in Dublin, and then at Oxford and Harvard, and then I taught at Harvard for a few years. Make no mistake: I'm no namby-pamby mystic, one of those New Age "enlightened" types,' he said, good-humouredly. 'I'm a scientist with a soul as tough as old boots. I can fill a great big blackboard with formulae. I'm one of those weirdos who believe in string theory and M-theory.'

'I'm very interested in all of that,' I said.

Ciran shows me around the many University rooms and explains some of the activities that go on there. The University, he tells me, is based on seven premises. The first is that human beings cannot evolve beyond themselves without help. The second, that consciousness doesn't exist 'inside' our head, but rather that the whole of a human is a map and expression of consciousness, which comes from outside of the physical body. The third states that everything we know about ourselves and the world is a creation of the mind, and that in order to evolve we have to go beyond the mind and the world of categories that the mind creates. The fourth premise is that it isn't possible to understand with the mind, since the mind only understands sequences and therefore only understands by means of elimination. The fifth states that the main vehicle for understanding reality is the body and the expression of the body through the senses, dance, music and singing. The sixth is that the search must be empirical, which is to say based on personal verification. The seventh is that through meditation, entering inside oneself, you can find all of the internal or external reality, present, past and future, and that you must practise meditation constantly. And that the distinction between 'subjective' and 'objective' is inexact, since once we enter our interior, we can also access objective realities and objective reality in general.

The teachings at the University, Ciran tells me, are divided into three main groups: the Preliminary Teachings (the arts), the Parallel Teachings (sciences and humanities) and the Central Teachings (focused on self-awareness and the development of consciousness).

Let's begin with the Preliminary Teachings.

The first is Dance, which they consider to be the most important subject of all, the one that everyone, without exception, must practise, and to the very best of their abilities. Morwen, one of the teachers, explains to me that the Sacred Dances, which are the ones everyone practises (unlike the specialist studies in ballet, contemporary, Graham, Dalcroze, etc.), are very simple and based on circle and spiral forms. They are, she explains, ways of putting yourself in contact with the earth and opening certain 'centres of consciousness' inside us. I ask Morwen how it's possible to open a 'centre of awareness' inside my head merely by dancing around in a circle. In response, she asks me genially why I thought those 'centres of consciousness' were in my head. I ask her where, if not there, my consciousness could be. She rests her hands over the place where her ovaries are and talks to me completely naturally about the uterus, the hips and female energy. 'Moving your hips in circles releases sexual energy, directs it up along the spine, makes us dynamic, optimistic and creative,' she explains, staring at me provocatively. Oh, divine body language. I ask her if it is some kind of Celtic ritual, something to do with Stonehenge and the druids, and she laughs at me brazenly, flirts with me, touches my arm.

Morwen leads us to a meadow a little further away, where a group of naked women are dancing with yellow garlands on their heads. Despite the fact that nudity is a relatively common sight in the University, we keep a respectful distance from them. Morwen explains that they do different dances according to the goddess influencing them in any given moment, and that there are female dances, male dances and also mixed dances, in which everyone takes part. The seven goddesses are Aphrodite, Hera, Artemis, Hestia, Athena, Persephone and Demeter. The gods are Zeus, Poseidon, Hades, Hermes, Apollo, Dionysus, Ares and Hephaestus.

I ask her which they're dancing right then, and Morwen tells me that it's a basic training dance called Dance of the Inner Being. The movements of this dance are determined by an internal urge generated in the solar plexus region. I watch those naked women dancing on the grass and it feels like I'm watching a scene from Greece three thousand years ago. In all that time, what's changed? Not even the female form or the form of wild flowers or the light or the breeze has changed. I don't think I've ever seen anything as beautiful as those women dancing naked in the middle of nature. I ask myself why we don't do things like that all the time in normal life.

The Inner Being is something they bring up a lot. For them it is something well defined and specific, like a hand or a tooth. I imagine it as a kind of magical animal who lives inside each of us, tucked inside the womb, solar plexus, the right side of our heart, and inside our head. The inner god, a free and luminous creature who awakens and sets off walking, they tell me, and who, on being roused or evoked, spreads its arms and begins its own dance inside us.

Voice and Song are also important at the White University. They study vocal technique, opera and lied, and also orthodox and oriental song, and improvisation. The singing of lieder from the German traditions (mainly Schubert, but also Brahms, Hugo Wolf, Strauss, etc.) is considered one of the main routes away from the Path of Melancholy, but opera and operetta are also important to them, even the most sentimental operas, since the main purpose of singing – of any singing, they tell me – is to open the heart.

Every Thursday, in the University's main building they do Satsang, or the ritualistic singing of mantras, in sessions that can last several hours. They are convinced that the sound of those mantras (the sound, that is, not its meaning) affects the vibration of your cells and has curative effects, on both the physical and the subtle body. Morwen and Ciran take me along to one of their sessions, and over the space of an hour and a half we sing in the call and response style the mantra 'Oṃ bhūr bhuvaḥ svaḥ tát savitúr váreṇyaṃ bhárgo devásya dhīmahi dhíyo yó naḥ pracodáyāt'. When we leave the room I feel a happiness I can't comprehend. It's as if a grey veil has been lifted from my eyes. I look at the crows on the grass and a tall oleander, its flowers blowing gently in the breeze, and I feel an incomprehensible sensation of love and peace.

But I feel something else too. A fracture. A pain.

Good God, my heart is broken. I can feel it's broken, wounded; I can feel it cracked inside my thorax and barely held together by the bones and tissue surrounding it. And then I begin to cry. Why am I crying? I move away from Morwen and Ciran, hobbling clumsily with my stick.

Sunlight falls over the earth and envelops me. Happiness lies here. Happiness and its enigma are suddenly revealed to me. Happiness, warmth, life, existence, the mere fact of being alive, of being here, in this place, now, in this moment. Morwen and Ciran watch me from a distance. But how to explain this to them?

I held happiness in my hands, and I threw it up into the air, and my happiness spread its wings and flew far, far away. That's how I lost it.

Music is central to the White University. They study different styles and traditions: for example, Indian Dravidian music, but they place a special emphasis on European tonal music, which they call the 'Path of Melancholy'. They also refer to this as the music of the Great Masters of the Past. Then they study atonal, microtonal and spectral music, which they call the 'Path of Sonorous Totality'. It is this music which they believe heralds a new opening in the consciousness. Could it be that here in the

University I might learn to love the music I've always feared and loathed? They study Nono, Stockhausen, Morton Feldman, Saariaho and Haas avidly. Philemon professes his fondness for the music of Georg Friedrich Haas, which surprises me. He talks to me about *In Vain* and *Natures mortes*. I am no less surprised.

They're Pythagoreans, and for them music infiltrates and explains everything. They use music to heal, to alleviate pain, to answer cosmological problems, to relax the mind and enter into the realm of emotion, since the world of emotions, which they call 'Lucidity', has a precise and almost physical reality for them.

Lucidity has three levels: inferior emotions, based on affinities; the superior emotions, based on the unconditional love of the earth and living beings; and multidimensional emotions, which prove completely incomprehensible (at least for me).

The multidimensional level responds to the curious laws of their anatomy, which at times also seems like a map of the psyche or hierophany of the earth. To give an example, I would say that we consider human beings to be like a flower, while for them human beings are the flower, the tree, the root, and also the forest, the cloud and the sun, and also the past and future of the sun, and the relationship between our sun and other suns.

Ciran is very chummy with Giovanni the librarian, a friendly green-eyed Italian with black-rimmed glasses and impish eyes. He is a specialist in medieval and Renaissance Romance poetry and has a vineyard, which he tends in his spare time. He makes a rosé wine that isn't half bad, and tastes a little bit like the Portuguese Mateus Rosé. The three of us eat lunch on the library terrace. Giovanni places a bookstand in front of the library door, letting everyone know that it's lunchtime, and we eat nettle salad, braised lentils and grilled courgette in tomato sauce, all washed down with Giovanni's rosé.

They tell me all sorts of things about the University, including the three blue monks, whose job is to grow and pick medicinal plants, and who we will see that very evening, dressed in their typical attire, arguing over varieties of privet in one of the deserted gardens.

Then there are the three golden monks, whose job is to collect flower essences and dew. With these essences they make filters to work on ailments of the spirit. Ciran and Giovanni explain that the three golden monks play an important role in the University, and that when they are working nobody should go near them so as not to make them lose their concentration or break their communication with the world of Lucidity, through which the filters will acquire the spiritual vibration necessary for them to work.

The floral filters, they tell me, contain light. And that light is a fairy. They show me vials with fairies inside. I tell them I don't think it's right that they keep fairies in glass vials and they assure me, deadly serious, that nobody can trap a fairy in a vial unless the fairy wants to be caught, and that I shouldn't think of fairies as psychological beings subject to time and space, but elemental and immortal beings.

I'm not sure if it's just the wine, but all of a sudden the things they are telling me begin to make sense in my head. Not only do they make sense, but the whole thing makes me so happy I start laughing. I laugh hearing about the kingdom of Lucidity and thinking about the plants and trees and the women there. And then they ask me a very strange question: they ask if I've ever been there.

We go to see the theatres. In the University there are a lot of celebrations and shows. They have two theatres, one of which is an open-air perfect replica of the Epidaurus theatre, and the other a beautiful white building with a blue dome, which reminds me of the Secession style. There they put on plays, operas and ballets. It seems to me that not all of these works serve a solely artistic purpose.

The theatre also forms part of their learning, because they see it as both a way to access one's emotions and an important vehicle of self-awareness. 'No one comes to this University to study a particular subject,' Bianca, one of the teachers, tells me. 'They come to study themselves.' Part of their theatre studies consist in discovering their own mechanisms, in learning to see themselves, in discovering the way in which the body, memory and emotions interact.

They study Acting Technique, Sensory Memory and Emotional Memory, and then something called Family Constellations, through which they re-enact the past and present family of one specific person for that person to then understand not only their position within their own family saga, but also the web of symbolic and narrative relationships that exist within that saga, including the influence of deceased relatives. And in that way all manner of cruelties, wrongdoings and abuses are revealed, alongside the many beautiful things, which quite often ends up transforming the person's understanding of life.

We enter the main building, a kind of palace made up of different architectural elements, one on top of another, almost like a miniature city, and they show me the different routes: the Path of Melancholy, the Path of the Desert, the Poem of the Magpie, the Path of the Fish, the Dream of Saint Eustatius, the Sisterhood of the White Rose.

They're convinced that works of art have the ability to awaken our Inner Being's memory and intuition and, what's more, that they are curative and regenerative. Sordid art and the deliberate cultivation of horror is pointless to them, since for them art is about beauty. They're not oblivious, however, to the different faces of beauty, which for them are Venusian (the beauty of all that is sensual and luminous), Cyclopsian (the beauty of all that is giant and huge), Convulsive (the beauty of all that is rhythmic, broken, fragmented, ironic or modern), Medusian (the beauty of all that is horrible), Nyctimenian (the beauty of all things nocturnal, solitary, isolated and remote), Apollonian (the beauty of clarity, proportion and order), Nefertitian (the beauty of the face, the gaze and the personality), Dionysian (the beauty of ecstasy, speed, vertigo and inebriation) and Vertumnus (the beauty of natural forms, of all things tender and mundane). They do sculpture, drawing, portraiture, surrealist or *Art informel* painting, epic and lyric poetry, the novel, the world novel, the river and island novel, the desert novel, short stories and other literary genres, often as part of vast and convoluted projects combining Dance, Music and Theatre.

They also practise the Art of Looking, which has strange curative effects. Some of them spend entire afternoons looking at the roses or some ash trees swaying in the breeze. According to them, we go through most of our life without seeing the majority of the things in front of us.

I barely see Cristina. She's always snowed under with something or another. But one afternoon I find her in the middle of the important task of hanging a swing in the Gardalis woods.

Gardalis is an area located above the University's buildings, where enormous blue firs – the biggest trees in the valley – grow, some of them as tall as eighty metres. I find her there with a group of women, some dressed in floral tunics, others in jeans and t-shirts, two or three in bikinis. The swing hangs from two thick golden ropes that are tied up above. Looking up, I discover several young men high in the fir's branches, some forty metres from the ground. They are fastening the swing to a thick branch and fooling about throwing pine cones at the women down below. One of the bikini-clad women is the first to try out the swing. Since the ropes are so long, she hardly has to push herself off at all before it looks like she's flying. The swing's trajectory is long and very slow. I watch as a pair of naked straight legs soar past me, pointing up to the sky, and then back again, bent under the swing.

Cristina and the others giggle like girls and take turns on the swing. She greets me when she sees me there and invites me to have a go. But I don't want a go on anything, and she looks at me perplexed before realising that I'm in a bad mood.

Let's move on next to the Parallel Teachings.

Science is far from neglected at the University, although given that the objective of the White Students (as I've begun to call them) is inner knowledge, they don't study it for its own sake, but always in relation to something else. They take classes in Physics, Mathematics, Geometry, Fractals and Chaos Theory, which they relate in the most astounding ways to psychology and something they call the Sea of Consciousness.

They also study Biology; something called General Living Systems Studies, which includes anything from protozoa to the biosphere. Gaia theory is as important to them as ecosystem analyses. They study several different types of ecosystem, and consider the notion of a natural ecosystem to be antiquated, since for them the distinction between natural and artificial is outdated. I ask Ciran if they follow Vladimir Ivanovich Vernadsky and his 'noosphere', but he tells me that the concepts of noosphere or Pierre Teilhard de Chardin's 'christosphere' are too simplistic and limited for them. They consider culture and machines, and also flowers, gases, ideas, systems, customs, laws and art to be part of the ecosystem. They also study the theories of Humberto Maturana and Francisco Varela, Autopoiesis and Self-organisation of Living Systems.

Anatomy and physiology are also subjects to which they devote a lot of time, given that the human body, in its broadest sense, is at the very heart of their field of investigation.

Another subject I was surprised to see studied at the White University is Linguistics, which some of the professors (all of them belonging to the Department of Linguistics) consider central to the University's Parallel Teachings. They study General Linguistics, Principles of Structuralism, Applications of Structuralism to Human Sciences, Post-structuralism and Deconstruction. They relate Deconstruction to oriental philosophy, and try to explain Deconstruction in terms of tantric, Vedic and Buddhist philosophy, thus interweaving both cultures and relocating philosophical nihilism (or simply postmodern philosophical visions) to the empirical realm of meditation. In their eyes, the 'destruction of the subject', which caused so much fuss in the West a few years ago, is merely one of the first states of meditation, and has none of the tragic or destructive implications that some philosophers see. The disappearance of the subject is, for them, an intermediary state between the fiction of the subject, in which we've been living, and the apparition of the 'Real I'.

On top of all this, they take classes on things that, to tell the truth, seem incredibly dull to me, all to do with the so-called Human Sciences. Among them, they lend particular importance to Systems Theory and Semiotics, and those who study these subjects consider them to be the most important lessons of all.

And so we come to the Central Teachings.

The White Students study something called the Science of Breathing. They believe that human attention moves certain energies, and that breathing can move various invisible energies that affect one's psychic state, as well as having a regulating effect on the organs, blood pressure and, above all, the glands. The Science of Breathing activates the body's energetic centres, cleans the subtle energy channels, regulates the functioning of the organs and stimulates the production of serotonin and dopamine. It also serves as an effective preparation for meditation. Through pranayama, they also bring about something called 'pranic healing', which they sometimes practise holding out their hands.

I ask them if they really believe in these things, and they always have the same answer: that they don't believe in anything.

They also practise Self-Observation, which comprises Knowledge of the mind's functions, Knowledge of mechanisms and the study of the mind-body-emotion relationship. Knowledge of mechanisms involves a practical investigation into one's behavioural patterns, thought patterns and mechanical actions. This is the Fourth Path, they tell me, and it can be practised anywhere, anytime. It doesn't require either silence or special poses or attire. This is also what makes it the most difficult and demanding of all the Paths.

They can cultivate their Attention by several different means. They are convinced that Attention has a decisive effect on what they call the Creative Capacity of Consciousness. Concentration, or conscious cultivation of one's Attention, allows them to extend their periods of consciousness. Since it exhausts the lower mind, it is an effective way to silence what they call the 'interior dialogue', the product of the automatic functioning of the mind. Ciran and Cristina tell me that Attention is the tool that allows you to control your mind and also to be able to direct at will the energy of the consciousness. Attention gathers these dispersed rays into one single light beam, and that way the power of thought can act on solid material.

The Non Doings or Habit Breaking are both techniques used in the University to break the habits of perception that keep human beings locked into a set vision or solid form, preventing them from feeling life and making them lose all memory of themselves. The Non Doings are habit-breaking actions. For example, eating with your left hand if you're right-handed, carrying a chickpea around in your mouth, changing the way you dress, focusing your attention on the gap between breaths, etc. In this way you can discover the mechanisms, biases, system of beliefs and assumptions by which you live.

Siloé, a delightful young Mexican woman, explains to me in Spanish that the term 'desacostumbrarse' or 'habit-breaking' is taken from a book by the Argentinian writer Julio Cortázar. She writes poetry, and she tells me that even though she has since discovered meditation, visualisation and in particular dance at the White University, it was writing that brought her here. Now dancing is the most important thing in her life. I tell her that when I was her age love was the most important thing in my life, and she replies that she's also found love at the University, with a Spanish guy called José Luis Olmedo. 'That's right,' I say, 'I'd forgotten this is a university of lovers.'

They do a lot of work on Hatha Yoga poses, and are extremely flexible as a result. They work especially hard on stretching and flexibility and strengthening their joints (which, they assure me, is where the past accumulates). Hatha Yoga calms the mind, opens the body's energy centres (which they call 'chakras', a word that in Sanskrit means 'wheel') and accesses other states of consciousness (they believe that each pose automatically carries a certain state of consciousness with it). What's more, the asanas help to clean the subtle channels, reverse the ageing process, stimulate blood flow and harmonise the work of the body's organs and glands.

I go up to the Gardalis garden again, obsessed with the memory of its singular beauty. It's not really a garden, because no gardener tends it. But it looks like a garden. The grass is springy and thick with patches of lush green clover. The trunks of the firs burst out of the grass like columns. A red squirrel with an S-shaped tail looks at me, caught unawares in the middle of the lawn, and then darts up one of the tree trunks. The swing remains in the same place, hanging from its long golden chains. I sit down on it, leaving my walking stick on the ground, and rock back and forth gently. The lightest of thrusts sets it off. I glide over the grass and my own shadow, and I begin to come away from the ground, and the swing climbs up and up. It feels as if I might carry on flying up beyond the tops of the firs, but instead I begin to descend again. And I swing back and forth over the grass. My shadow is down there, running across the grass, the daisies, the barbed edges of the dandelion leaves, the clover, the wild white asphodels, and then I swing backwards, as if sucked in by the green immateriality of the forest, and when I reach as far back as I can go, I begin to rush forward again, swinging my legs even more to get even higher. A voice whispers in my ear: 'Let go when you are as high as you can go.' But I cling hard to the chains. Letting go isn't an option.

As part of their Attention practices, they work on Visualisation and Active Imagination, techniques to control and reprogramme the mind by creating mental images and colours. The colours, in whatever form they come, are important to them, and they attribute particular powers and properties to each one. They take immense pleasure in the colours of the flowers, of fruit, leaves and animals, especially birds' plumage. They also enjoy the colours found in works of art, whether in Indian frescos, gothic stained-glass windows or David Hockney's landscapes. But most of all they are interested in psychic colours. They claim they affect your physical state and mood and that they can stimulate and awaken the dormant areas of the psyche that give us access to the Great Mind and also higher spiritual levels.

'Great Mind' is the name they give to a kind of Transpersonal Mind that contains an almost unlimited reserve of information on a diverse range of subjects, the future, the past and each and every human being. The Transpersonal Mind isn't the 'Real I', who, according to them, can only begin to reveal itself when one's inner dialogue has been put on pause and the 'little I' or 'lower mind' disappears, given that the Transpersonal Mind is transpersonal and the 'Real I' is still individual and I still experience it as my true and real me, the most real thing I've ever felt and the source and reason behind all reality. Supposedly, the Great Mind is a level of consciousness that can be reached through meditation. Inside the Great Mind one can delve into any kind of subject, resolve any kind of problem – be it technical, scientific, emotional, psychic, practical or artistic – contact spiritual entities, see into the future or the past, contact people who are far away, assess the state of another person's health and energy, however far away they are, do energy healings remotely, get ideas and inspiration in the form of stories, symbols, voices, words, conversations with beings of light, images, etc.

Almost all of the practices that go on at the University, like Dance, Singing, Hatha Yoga, the Science of Breathing, etc., are used as meditation preparation. Meditation is considered the most important and definitive practice of all. The state of meditation is produced when you achieve perfect concentration, a total silence of the mind and uninterrupted state of attention. It's not something that can be 'done' or 'made', they tell me, because the state of meditation comes when you abandon all action, all intention, all tension, all desire, all efforts, all hopes, and concentrate only on being. In the state of meditation you access the next state of consciousness, which is when the 'Real I' makes its appearance. That is the beginning of what they call 'Real Life'. For them all human life as we know it is nothing more than a vague memory, a hazy shadow of Real Life. Only on very rare occasions throughout our lives, they assure me, do we have Real Life experiences. And yet, if the 'Real I' does reveal itself, even if only once and for a very short time, the experience can be enough to completely transform our lives.

And if all that weren't enough, they also work on dreams. They try to remain lucid during their dreams, to wake up inside their dreams (they call this 'dreamings') and to use their dreams to have 'objective' experiences like coming into contact with energy entities or visiting different places, planes or dimensions. In this they also include astral travel, out-of-body experiences and so-called near-death experiences or NDE. For them NDE are relatively common and aren't necessarily connected to death, to states of brain death or cardiac arrests or shock or asphyxia as we often hear described. They also happen, they explain to me, during meditation, during strolls through the countryside and by means of artistic experiences.

I find the Dreaming activities extremely intriguing. They teach me various techniques to wake up inside my dreams and leave my body, even though, they tell me, it can take years of practice to have an experience like that. Dreamings are 'easier', so to speak, and begin to happen in a more or less regular manner when one practises Carlos Castaneda's techniques to handle energies, like Tensegrity or Recapitulation.

I am amazed at the things they tell me about out-of-body experiences. It seems some of the teachers at the University are able to fly consciously to far-off planets, which they describe to me in minute detail.

They also study something called Sacred Sexuality, which is basically the study of energy: reality as energy and human beings as energy. For them everything is energy; even your thoughts, mind and emotions. They study 'sexual energy' which they pinpoint in their second chakra. They celebrate the essential dignity of the human body (that's why, at least this is what I think, some of them are set the assignment of being naked for up to three whole days in a row) and they study sexuality as central to life, since it is the only thing truly universal to all human beings. In sexuality they see pleasure, fun, play, communication with another human, an expression of love, its generative capacity and a vehicle to comprehending the connection with life, nature, the species and divinity. They study different ways of stimulating and prolonging pleasure without reaching orgasm, and ways to make orgasms more intense, and they see sexual pleasure as an expression of love and a way to discover the other's Being of Light, a vehicle towards gaining mystic understanding and transpersonal experiences. To understand human sexuality as a simple method of procreation makes no sense at all, they say. To do that is to reduce humankind to the level of animals. For them a good proportion of our problems as humans stems from the inexplicable hatred towards the body that pervades many cultures: the prohibition of sexual pleasure in Christianity; female castration in many African cultures; the repression of the feminine component in Islam; Vedanta's celebration of celibacy; Jainism's prohibition of sensual pleasures (food, drink, sex) that were later passed on to Buddhism and then Christianity; the ban on inebriation or certain foods in several cultures (the prohibition of pork or alcohol, vegetarianism, 'impure' foods on certain days); the forbidding of baring one's skin as a woman in Islam or Orthodox Judaism; the universal laws that exist against homosexuality; the proscription of dance, or singing, or even music in some extreme versions of Islam; the identification of female dancers, singers or actors as prostitutes; the contempt for Enlightenment in art, dance, opera, the novel, poetry, the lyric, emotion; the defence, to the death, of a masculine and strictly Intellectual model to the exclusion of feminine models, focused on the body, movement, expression, feelings... 'Yes, it feels like the entire history of humanity,' Cristina says in one of our rare conversations, 'is a battle fought not only against women and their role in society, but against something much more profound, which encompasses the whole female archetype – the body, dance, sexuality, pleasure, beauty – in favour of power, order, intelligence, classifications, war, punishment, control.'

I'll just say, lastly, that for them Sacred Sexuality gives them experiences we would call 'mystical' – they barely use that word, which they deem to be woolly – and helps them to see their lover's Being of Light, which in instances of intense amorous surrender are revealed as a creature out of time and space; a creature that exists beyond its present form and incarnation.

And there are more subjects still. Anatomy, for example, which they consider very important for comprehensive understanding. They study a peculiar anatomy where the physical body is just one part of the picture. It includes subtle bodies, energy centres inside and outside of the body (six inside the body and two more above the head). They represent humans' different pranic or energy levels or casings: the human being as an auric egg, the human being as part of the Complete Being, which in diagrams takes the form of a pyramid, a bird or a sphere, depending on the approach.

They also practise Energetic Healing through song, dance, music, meditation, painting, visualisation, pranayama, etc. It's remarkable how many different practices they relate to medicine and healing. I might have said that the main purpose of the University's teachings is healing. I've since learnt that healing is but one independent branch of the teachings here.

There are, in reality, three main branches of knowledge studied at the University: Healing, the Art of Happiness and Realisation. Healing, symbolically ascribed to Asclepius, god of medicine and dreams, engages in numerous shamanic techniques, such as cave confinement, symbolic confinements, journeys of power, vision quests, and all manner of physical tests designed to take your powers of perception beyond their limits. Also they ingest sacred plants that bring on visions. This takes place during carefully planned ceremonies that usually last the whole night and are preceded by at least three days of purification. I have little idea about which plants you can grow or forage here, but they've told me about some: a vine they found in the jungle, a flower, and some fungi that could be *Psilocybe cubensis* (I wonder if the vine is perhaps ayahuasca), although all these hallucinogenic plants generally grow in America, not in other continents. The students who are most interested in healing apply all the University's teachings – from music to Hatha Yoga – to just that. They also study how to use, grow and forage medicinal herbs with the blue monks, and with the golden monks how to fabricate filters and floral elixirs, for which they have to delve extraordinarily deep, both in their work on themselves and in meditation.

All of the teachings at the University intersect. They all overlap.

In all seriousness, they study and practise something that they call Magic, or 'Working with Form', since for them 'magic' is 'working with energy by way of the form'; a strange and elusive concept for me, which implies one accepting a curiously harmonious vision of reality based on something like mutually resonant states. So, for example, if I paint a red flower – Philemon explains for me – I'm activating within me everything I relate with the colour red, like love or success, or happiness. For magic to happen, then, one must believe in an objective relation between the psychic and the physical, which I simply can't accept or fully understand. They talk about 'morphogenetic fields' and study the Science of Links, and they claim that form has an influence on things, so plants won't grow the same way in a round or triangular garden, nor will a person dream the same dream under a dome as they would in a room with a pyramid-shaped ceiling.

And then from all this they get magic theatre, magic music, magic painting and magic psychotherapy.

But 'working with energy by way of the form' has other aspects that are even more mysterious and which, speaking for myself at least, are pretty hard to swallow. Working directly with energy means understanding everything that exists and everything that happens as mere energy. Those who work directly with energy learn to see energy directly. They see beings surrounded by their aura. They see the different subtle bodies with their different forms and colours. They see the form of feelings and thoughts, the spiritual masters and spiritual parasites, the shadows and the beings of light. They see the shining egg – which is really the human form – and the thousands of light beams coming from every corner of the cosmos to converge in every shining egg.

Through all of these practices – yoga, Non Doing, Self-Observation, their practice with dreams and the cultivation of one's attention, powers of listening, dance, singing, etc. – they develop parts of the brain that are normally inactive. As such, the White Students gain psychic powers like thought transmission, telekinesis, premonition and direct vision of energy. In general, the University doesn't give much importance to these 'powers' and the students are advised to understand them as signs that their progress is real, but neither to work on nor try to use them.

They also gain something else, something even more important: inner peace, a state of constant wonder and happiness, and the desire to help others.

There comes a moment during the teachings, Philemon tells me, when you see yourself. Another, in which you see the world. Another, in which the 'Real I' reveals itself to you. Once you have lived for a second, even just one second, in Reality, he says, everything changes. Nothing will ever be the same, and at last the teachings begin to make sense. Reality begins. Freedom begins.

This is the moment when something new has formed inside of us; a kind of centre, a magnet, a stone, a flame. From this moment on we can go back into the world, because we have gained something permanent inside of us. We can also stay here, he says, to continue this undertaking of transformation.

But what happens after that, he says, cannot be discussed.

70

My meanderings through the valley

O*n Cristina's suggestion, I'm learning* to ride. The horse helps me get around while the carpenters finish my false leg.

Just as she promised, my grey horse is very docile and walks everywhere, never breaking into a trot. I head down the paths leading to the valley with my fine beast Aurelianus. That's what everyone here calls it: the valley, although really it's the base of a volcanic crater. The valley, as I've already explained, is very big, and a large part of it is used for agriculture. Here they farm corn, coffee, tomatoes, rice, onions, potatoes, oats, lentils, melons, cabbage, borage and hops, and there are also apple, almond, walnut, pear, fig, papaya, avocado, cherry and plum trees. I would never have imagined that all those things could grow alongside one another. They also have beehives to collect honey and wax for candles, and a fair amount of livestock, including a small herd of cows and several of goats. Lots of people here are vegetarian, but even those who aren't avoid sacrificing the animals, only eating them when they die of natural causes. They use their milk to produce all different kinds of cheese and butter. They also keep turkeys and hens. So they have lactose products as well as eggs for protein. Since hops grow well on the land here, they make two kinds of beer, a blonde and an ale. They also have coffee, which they roast very lightly and has a smooth flavour. Rarely do they drink fresh milk. Instead, they use it to produce butter and cheese, and also some fresh products like yoghurt, cottage and fresh cheese, and sour cream. They have two bulls and twenty cows, all seemingly fit and strong. They also use them as working animals to drag the carts, the chief heavy vehicle here, and to plough the fields. They're Charolais cattle with white coats and stumpy horns, and absolutely enormous. They tell me that the oldest bull, Zeus, weighs one thousand four hundred kilos, while the younger one weighs about nine hundred kilos. The Charolais are strong, working animals and they grow quickly, produce a lot of milk and are also very generative, as they tend to give birth to twins. It's not breading season and there aren't many calves about, but I do spot some quite young cows. I'm awestruck by the beauty of those resplendent, perfect creatures and their noble form. No one ever thinks of a cow when they're looking for an effigy of nobility, but those Charolais seem as noble and majestic to me as any lion, horse or stag. They have big square heads with a narrow tuft of wavy hair between their short horns. The bulls are immensely strong, and their bulging, taut muscles stick out shamelessly from beneath their hair. Of course, the breeders don't refer to their 'hair', but their 'coat'. Their coat, then, is fuzzy and blindingly white. In my strolls through the valley I never grow tired of looking at those formidable, serene animals. I realise I've never noticed the majestic beauty of cows before. Perhaps no one does, so that they can enjoy eating them guilt-free. Humans have a habit of venerating the animals that scare us and denigrating those we terrorise.

I don't know the exact number of goats they have: I think there are three or four flocks that roam the woods and hillside pastures. The goat's cheese they make is delicious. Nothing beats an afternoon snack of goat's cheese, dried figs and oatmeal bread washed down with blonde ale.

The valley is divided into terraces and meadows separated by low stone walls like the ones you often get in Spain. The walls here are expertly made and strewn with lichen, revealing their age. The valley abounds with waterways, and they've also created a course of canals to cut off and redirect the water with wooden sluices that open and close. Their other big water resource comes from reservoirs. It often rains up here, but the rains aren't as heavy as they are down at sea level, and they say sometimes they can go weeks without a drop of rain.

The temperature is very agreeable. During the day, when the sun is out, it's hot, but in the evening it cools right down; the nights are mild and the dawns cool. Often at night you're grateful for a light blanket. And it isn't as humid here as on the rest of the island.

These days I go around in new, clean clothes; I eat every day, and have a bed and a roof over my head. I'm free from the awful jungle heat, from the suffocating humidity and the insects. Aurelianus and I have become good buddies. Together we slowly explore this place. And yet, I'm not happy. There's a shadow tailing me day and night. She's called Cristina. She's called Salomé.

I think about going further down into the valley, reaching that lake dotted with green islands that I've seen from above at the very centre of the crater, but I can't seem to find any paths that lead me beyond a certain point. I occasionally come across someone in huts and sheds. If he or she is meditating or sleeping, I don't bother them. But if they're working in the field or milking a cow, I stop and ask them which way to go from there. The answer is always vague and unsatisfactory.

There are pomegranate trees that haven't been picked, wild roses and apple trees. I ask them why they let the pomegranates go off, and they say they have too much food, and that if they collected everything that grows on all the fruit trees they wouldn't get through it all and it would end up going bad anyway. They do make a lot of jams, chutneys and preserves, as well as raisins, prunes and dried figs, which they store in larders, but the agricultural resources in the valley could feed a population ten times the size of its current one.

I ask what lies beyond, in the distance, and no one can explain it to me. 'Beyond where?' they ask. I tell them: 'Beyond the lake.' 'Ah, the lake. There are lots of lakes,' they say. 'Yes, but there's one that's bigger than the others.' I can't work out if they genuinely don't know what I'm talking about or if they merely pretend not to.

One day, meandering through the valley on my trusty steed, I enter a wooded area and come across what looks like the dry bed of a stream. I come off the path I was following and convince my faithful Aurelianus to keep following the new one, which isn't really a path but rather a riverbed, now dry because they've presumably redirected its flow along canals to water the crops. The trees are very tall in these parts; a dense glade of alders like the ones you get in Europe along riverbanks. I continue along this path for a couple of kilometres, and finally I come out into an open clearing: large meadows sectioned off by rows of trees. There are no cattle or farmland in sight here, but there are paths along the meadows and signs of old canals that might have controlled the watering or grazing. But it's clear that this area, these pastures, have been abandoned. Blackberries grow all around the stone walls, some of which have begun to fall apart, and no one has repaired them. The channels that should direct the water are dry and full of weeds, their sluices broken.

I seek out the old paths, but everywhere is covered in weeds. The feeling of solitude and of being far away is quite pleasant. I plod through groves. There are elms, oaks, ash, alders; trees suited to mild maritime climates, and under which old shady corridors emerge, now invaded by weeds from lack of use. Almost immediately I am aware of the smell of water and the squawk of aquatic birds.

The lake shimmers in the sunlight as I go down the hill. At last, I've found it! The sheet of water seems to span different regions and climates, each one endowed with its own colour and temperature: scintillating silver for the area where the sun shines, ultramarine blue in the deeper parts, silty green on dark purple shores in the distance. There are several forested islets on the lake, which impede my view of the other shore.

I tell myself that a sealed lake that has been receiving minerals and sediments from different streams for centuries must be rotten and poisonous, but that's not the case.

The water seems clean, and on the shores reeds and papyrus grow and sway in step with the blowing breeze. The shoreline is pleasingly irregular, with small coves, white sandy half-moon beaches, and green peninsulas that jut out into the water. I guide my horse to the water's edge and the animal drinks thirstily. There are swans and ducks in the lake, as well as egrets and cranes. If the water isn't poisonous, there must be fish, maybe trout or bass, although I've never seen the valley's inhabitants eating fish.

We head along the grassy shore of large pastures specked with spring flowers: dandelions, daisies, tiny white and yellow daffodils, small leopard orchids, their white petals flecked with fuchsia, and mayflowers. Beyond this, the trees. I spy a wooden cabin, dark and vaguely threatening. It peeps out from behind two big cypresses with low-slung, thick crowns. Around it, dotted randomly about the pasture, I spot oaks, elms, ash, some mild climate shady trees – but don't cypresses grow in the south? I don't know much about trees, and the variety of species I find in that place reminds me of the almost insane fantasy of English gardens, since only in a garden that has been designed would you get a traveller's palm next to a cypress next to an elm. But this isn't what most alarms me. What most alarms me is the cabin.

I make Aurelianus stop. Before me stands an old, dusty cabin that must have been abandoned there years ago. But I feel sheer terror at the sight of it, because it looks identical to Pohjola's hut, the one we found that night up in the mountains. The one where my friend disappeared.

I approach it slowly. Is it the same one or not? On that other occasion it was dark, and we saw the cabin in flashes of torchlight. We were all exhausted after a long journey and under immense emotional strain. I can't be sure that this cabin I'm looking at now and that one are identical. That is, that they're one and the same cabin. But, just like the other one, this cabin has a door with a wooden stoop, and a window on the right with its glass intact albeit obscured with a layer of dust and spiders' webs.

I walk around the cabin without getting too close, and I hear voices. My heart begins to pound. To the rear there is a clearing of grass with no trees on it, and I find several little girls playing there. They're playing those typical little-girl games, dancing along to a ditty. I don't catch the lyrics. They must be about ten years old. Some are blonde and others brunette or redheads. One of them has black hair. They're wearing old-fashioned knee-length dresses with embroidered floral patterns and long socks in different colours.

'Hello!' I say so as not to startle them. 'What are you all doing here?'

The girls stop and look at me, indeed startled. One of them has something in her hands. She's holding it carefully in her cupped palms.

'What are you all up to?' I ask. 'Do you live here?'

The girl then opens her hands releasing whatever was inside. It's a big, brown moth, which flaps its wings hard and disappears clumsily off towards the cabin. Another of the girls, the one with the red hair, picks a flower from the grassy ground and walks towards me.

'Oh, a flower,' I say, trying to seem friendly.

I've never known how to talk to children. I don't understand them, and as is often the case with bachelors, I have to confess I'm a bit scared of them.

The girl comes closer and hands me the flower. It's a poppy, but a strange poppy, because it has two red petals and two white ones. I don't think I've ever seen one like it.

'Thank you,' I say, leaning down from my horse to take the flower.

'Keep it,' the girl says, gesturing for me to put it in my shirt pocket. 'Keep it safe.'

She speaks strangely, almost singing. I can't make out her accent.

'Okay, I'll do that.'

'Keep it,' the girl says, 'for a hundred years.'

'For a hundred years?'

'Yes, for a hundred years.'

'Very well,' I say.

The girl backs away without taking her serious eyes off me. Then they all run off into the woods.

I tug on Aurelianus's reins to make him walk on in the direction of the cabin, but the animal doesn't want to move and stays put, his hoofs rooted to the spot.

'Hello?' I shout. 'Is anyone there?'

I think the window is about to open and that Wade will appear, smiling and munching on something – a walnut, an apple, a wild pear.

'Wade Erickson!' I shout. 'Are you there?'

My words are echoed by nature's silence, the chorus of insects, the distant caws of the birds, the whisper of the breeze between the trees.

'Pohjola!' I shout with a trembling voice. 'Aarvo Pohjola!'

Nobody answers. Nobody moves inside the cabin.

I ride away from there slowly. With every step, I can feel the cabin and its influence leaving me. I feel the powerful allure of the cabin, its attraction, like a dark heart beating at the earth's core, or perhaps at the corner of the earth, the bleak, murky corner of the earth. The poppy is still in my hand. I put it away carefully in my shirt pocket and tell myself that when I get back to the University, I'll press it inside a book to preserve it.

71

Cristina's life

'*After a year in the* ashram in Rishikesh, I went to New York,' Cristina tells me. 'Every now and then students of a disciple of Swami Kailas-hananda would show up at the ashram. This disciple had run a small yoga studio in New York for years. The students were almost always disappointed and confused by their experience in Rishikesh. The Swami seemed self-important and cold to them. They found life in the ashram hard. It was all karma yoga, karma yoga, karma yoga, you know? Service to the guru, service to the ashram, selfless service, non-stop work, always down at the guru's feet, always a mere speck of dust or mosquito next to the guru's luminous magnificence.

'And yet, when they spoke about Dharma, their master in New York, their eyes lit up. They told me that Dharma was the complete opposite of their teacher. He rarely insisted on the theoretical aspects that formed such a big part of the teachings at the ashram: all those Sanskrit terms, all those notes about stones, planets and numbers that we took, filling notebook after notebook. Dharma, they told me, spoke very little, and when he did he said very simple things, and with a sense of humour. They said he was a humble man, and even though he had a lot of followers and was beginning to become well known, he claimed he wasn't a teacher at all. "I'm not a guru," he would say, "just an instructor." And I felt a strong attraction to that voice calling me from afar, to that man who swore he wasn't a teacher – in a world in which everyone thinks they're a teacher and goes around like one.

'I was tired of India. It was a gruelling experience. Everything about it was hard: the weather, the diet, the solitude, the filth, the insects, the animals all over the place, the scorching summer and freezing winter, when the whole place was covered in snow. All the inner experiences were incredibly intense, but after a few months there I no longer felt any joy. I had to go back to the West. I wanted to meet Dharma. So I went to New York, I met him, and he became my yoga instructor for three years.'

'Dharma is a common name in yoga circles, is it?' I ask.

'Yes, I guess so,' Cristina says. 'It's a Sanskrit name meaning "law". Why do you ask?'

'When you talk about Dharma, the yoga teacher in New York, I don't suppose you mean Dharma Mittra...'

'Dharma Mittra, yes.'

'Dharma Mittra, who has a yoga centre in New York and is married to a Jewish woman called Eva who also practises yoga... A Brazilian man, strong, dark skin, wavy hair...'

'But you know Dharma?' Cristina asks, laughing.

'I met him here, on the island. He was on the plane with his wife.'

'That's impossible. You're pulling my leg.'

'He's here, on the island. He's here right now, back at the beach. It was he who made me the wooden leg I lost climbing the volcano.'

'That's impossible,' Cristina says.

'Yes, another astonishing coincidence.'

'He made you your wooden leg?'

'Yes. A perfect leg with a joint at the knee.'

'Dharma has always been very handy with wood. Back at the centre in New York he was always building furniture, wall partitions, wardrobes, counters...'

'It was him, too, who helped me build my hut a few days after we arrived. At first I thought he was a woodworker.'

'I can't believe he's here on the island,' she says, bringing her hands to her face.

And that's how I learn that a year after going back to Rishikesh, Cristina went to America and settled in Manhattan, just 170 miles from where I was at that time, and where I lived for no less than three years. For three years I lived in Oakland, Rhode Island, while she was living in New York's East Village. For three years, the window of her apartment on Saint Mark's Place in Lower Manhattan was just a couple of hundred kilometres as the crow flies from the window of my study in Oakland. Three and a half hours by car. Maybe five taking the train from Penn Station and then the Greyhound from Midmay.

My life suddenly feels like a farce.

We are sitting on one of the terraces overlooking the valley. This has become one of my favourite spots in the White University. The terrace railing is a white stone bench built in a wavy line. The stone is so polished it has the oily lustre of silk. A fig tree grows in an open circle in the flagstones. On the nearest wall to us a luxuriant bougainvillea with intense pink and purple flowers (it is, in fact, two bougainvillea entwined) are visited by all kinds of wasps and butterflies. Some dry bougainvillea flowers lie scattered on the ground. They look like fake paper flowers. The forested sides of the crater run in a long, majestic loop. The clouds, perched motionless at different heights in the blue sky, look like flowers floating on a pond. As usual, the swallows are circling overhead.

It took her a long time to get over me, she says. A lot of journeys, a lot of tears. Eventually she met someone else and fell in love with him. And it was then that she truly began the long, difficult business of forgetting. This happened five years after we split up. She met him in Mexico, she says, on a course. During those years she was experimenting a lot with shamanism. Years of trips to Peru and Mexico. In the latter country, short trips would gradually become longer. In Mexico City, in San Miguel de Allende, in Real de Catorce, in Oaxaca. This fellow was a friend of a Mexican lady who was in turn a friend of the people Cristina was working with. This lady lived in Mexico City, in Polanco, in the Colonia Irrigación, and organised all kinds of esoteric gatherings in her house.

Cristina tells me that she met the man who would become her husband one evening during an informal gathering between friends. They left together, and walking down the street towards a larger avenue to take a taxi ('one of those electric green Mexico nights,' she says, although I don't understand why Mexican nights are green and not blue or pink) they struck up a conversation. So they spent the entire night walking and talking their way around Mexico City, through the solitary streets lined with gardens with huge sleeping mimosa and coral trees, and past the all-night cafés and the restaurants that haven't changed since the seventies. And that's how, having dodged the dangers lurking in the Mexican night, they ended up in the Alameda Central, still talking, sitting on a bench and watching as the dawn rose above the blue windows of the Torre Latinoamericana. He was quite a bit older than her, a mature man, she said, funny and with many a story to tell; strong, mild-mannered, an avid walker and with a lot of life behind him: grown-up children, a couple of wives and some tragedy. There wasn't a hint of ambiguity about his soul, no hazy parts or resentments, and he had a direct, cool gaze. He was both a realist and a dreamer. And six months later, they were married. The wedding was in Baltimore, she tells me, where he was living at the time, at Saint Stephen's Church, on the 29th of March. I'm surprised that the marriage detail and the date and place of the wedding itself are important to her. When we were together the topic of marriage never came up, and I don't think it was important to either of us to seal our relationship with a legal document. I ask her if she wore white and she tells me she did, but not a traditional wedding dress. I ask her if she wore something old, new, borrowed and blue, and she says yes, yes, of course she did. So Cristina had got married by the Church, dressed in white, and with a bouquet of orange blossom in her hand.

'It wasn't orange blossom, actually,' she says. 'They were beautiful, tiny white blackthorn flowers.'

I ask her if she's still married to him and she says yes. I know I don't have any right to be hurt, but I am. Pain never asks permission. It hurts, and I look down at her hands, and at the ring on her finger that I noticed the other day.

'I've never forgotten you,' I tell her.

'No?'

'I don't think there's been a single day, in all these years, that I haven't thought about you.'

'But there was another woman,' Cristina says.

'What do you mean?'

'Back then. When I was in Rishikesh.'

'No, there wasn't another woman.'

'No?'

'There was never any other woman.'

'Really?'

'No.'

'I was convinced you'd met someone. I always thought us separating was my fault for having left you on your own in Madrid for so long. I just disappeared and I stayed away for almost a year. And I know you don't know how to be on your own. I knew you wouldn't be able to handle being alone for that long. It was careless on my part. What happened was my fault.'

'Well, there you're wrong. It turns out I'm the master of being on my own.'

'Oh, really?'

'I've lived on my own since then.'

'Really?'

'Yes.'

'So you didn't meet anybody when I was in India?'

'No.'

'Gosh. That really is a surprise.'

'What made you think I met someone?'

'I just always assumed that's what happened.'

'There was never anyone else – not then, and not since.'

'But you've had things with other people.'

'A lot. Which is to say none.'

'I mean you must have fallen in love.'

'No, I've never fallen in love again.'

'But you must have lived with someone else, even for a short period.'

'Well, no, the truth is I haven't.'

'You haven't lived with anyone else?'

'Not for more than a week.'

'A week!' she says, bringing her hands up to her cheeks in shock.

'I've always been a solitary tomcat,' I say. 'A tomcat on the prowl for sensations.'

'So you never married, and you don't have any children.'

'No.'

'I always thought you'd be married with kids, happy as a lark somewhere in the States. I've always imagined that.'

'No, Cristina. I don't have a wife. I don't have any children. I don't have anything. I just have Ballard, my dog. He's the only one waiting for me back at home.'

'You have a dog?' She giggles. 'I never would have imagined you with a dog. You never liked animals...'

'No.'

'So? How did you end up with Ballard? Was he a gift?'

'Let's just say I inherited him. But I liked having a dog from the start. Another soul – one who depends on me, who seeks me out, waits for me, needs me. I like hearing him bark when I get home.'

She falls silent and stares out across the valley. We're under the shade of the fig tree, swimming in its sweet perfume. I think about how easy it would be to climb up onto the ledge and jump into the void, to end it all.

'Cristina,' I say. 'Your husband... This man you met in Mexico and then married...'

'Yes?'

'It's Ciran, isn't it?'

'Yes,' she says. 'It's Ciran.'

Now it's me who falls silent.

'I really like him,' I say eventually, feeling my lips and hands shake. 'We've become good friends.'

'Yes, I know.'

Ciran is her husband. I knew it all along. I intuited it. I knew without anyone having to tell me. But things don't truly hurt us until they're out in the open and we can articulate them in words. It is not things themselves that cause the most damage, but the names we give to those things. Ciran is her husband. Cristina is his wife. She isn't my wife; she is with another man.

So why did I come all the way up here? Why did I have to climb to the top of the mountain?

72

Two friends talk

Philemon tells me one morning that they found the village a few days ago. It didn't prove too difficult with my directions. It turns out there's only one big river that leads north. Goran and Matvei, teachers of Indian dance and cosmology respectively, have gone down to the coast with tools and two of the University's carpenters and they've shown my fellow castaways how to build large vessels that will allow them, if they follow a certain course, to reach the cargo liners' passage in a couple of days. Goran and Matvei also took the letter that Salomé asked me to write; without it, they would never have trusted those two strangers. Philemon tells me that the carpenters' work will be easier than we'd first thought, because when they got to the village my friends already had a sailing boat big enough for roughly half of the castaways.

'A sailing boat?' I ask. 'I don't know where they could have got their hands on a sailing boat.'

'Well, anyway,' Philemon says, 'with that boat they could leave the island. If they follow the instructions we gave them to a T, they'll find an extremely narrow maritime passage through which it's possible to escape the island's magnetic force and reach the open sea.'

But the excessive elation with which Philemon relates all this tells me that there's more.

'Not all of them wanted to leave,' he says. 'Some of your friends have decided to come here.'

'What?' I say.

'Quite,' he says. 'It came as a surprise to us too. You would have thought that after three months stranded on the island, and going through all they've been through, they would be desperate to go home.'

'But you mean, some of them wanted to come here, to the University?'

'That's right, yes.'

Ciran points down at the ground, clearly entertained.

'They're here now?' I ask, completely incredulous.

'Yes,' he says. 'We brought them. They got here a couple of hours ago.'

'But who? Which of them came?'

He tells me to go and see for myself. They arrived this morning and have already had a chance to wash – 'priorities', Ciran says with a grin – and to put on fresh clothes. 'They should be eating lunch in the garden of palms,' he tells me.

I walk there as fast as my good leg will take me. There are many, many more of them than I'd imagined. Who would choose to come here given the chance to go home to their loved ones? Perhaps those who didn't have loved ones or a home? Or the incurably curious among us, maybe. They're all dressed in the University's distinctive pale garments. There they are – my friends, my family. Joseph, Sophie, Sebastian, Carl, Rosana, Syra, Dharma Mittra, Eva, Julián and Matilde, Joaquín, Xóchitl and two more from Dharma's group, Mike Garson and Lily Whittfield, as well as Jimmy Bruëll, to my surprise. I greet them all effusively and squeeze Joseph, Sophie and the children, before hugging Rosana, and then Syra, who resists my embrace as much as she possibly can. They already knew I was up here, but in any case they seem relieved to see me. Joseph inspects my centipede bite, which is still causing me some pain, and he says it doesn't look good, that it would be better if I left it uncovered. They've served them tea, grapefruit juice, milk, fruit, goat's cheese, dried figs, candied chestnuts, bread, sautéed peppers and scrambled egg with mushrooms – a breakfast of kings that my friends wolf down with almost religious zeal. They eat like beggars, staring at their plates and devouring every last morsel.

I notice Joaquín and Xóchitl sitting together, giggling, holding hands and staring into each other's eyes. 'When did this happen?' I ask them, intrigued. I'm not entirely sure if they make a good couple or not. Joaquín seems too fragile, too delicate next to that svelte, striking Mexican woman. Xóchitl is stunning, with intense eyes and long hair that tumbles over her shoulders, but there's something tragic about her too, something dark and terrible that I always sense. Perhaps it is that sadness, that tremendous darkness, that attracts him to her, and perhaps it's Joaquín's kindness, that puckish aura of his, the combination of a man both extremely virile and delicate in character, that makes him attractive to her. Who knows, maybe they've found their perfect balance in one another: Xóchitl, a dose of reality for Joaquín; and Joaquín, calm waters for Xóchitl.

'From the start,' Joaquín replies. 'Since day dot. For me, at least.'

'We made friends straight away,' Xóchitl adds, facing Joaquín. 'Love came later.'

I ask Joaquín if he's already said hello to Salomé, the woman who runs this place, and he tells me he hasn't, that they've mentioned Salomé but that no one has seen her.

'Well,' I say, 'there's a nice surprise waiting for you when you do.'

I also ask him if it's been a long time since he saw his cousin Cristina.

'Years,' he replies. 'It's been years since any of us had word from her, really.' But he doesn't know why I'm bringing up Cristina.

'At last, you've decided to talk about her,' he says. 'I was nervous to mention her in conversation. I know things didn't end well between you two. But it seemed unnatural that in all this time you hadn't once mentioned her name; that you hadn't asked me anything about her.'

'You're right,' I say. 'But from now on we'll talk about her regularly. You'll see.'

'I've always really loved Cristina,' Joaquín says. 'My English cousin, daughter of her gorgeous English mother.'

I tell him it's hard not to love Cristina. I also tell him how happy I am to have him, Julián and Matilde there. My old friends. My old friends and my new ones.

But what made them decide to come up here? Dharma takes an interest in my new wooden leg. I tell him how I lost the one he'd made and so they'd had to make me this new one.

'Well,' he said, holding his chin, as he always does when he's thinking hard, 'there's room for a little improvement. Do they have tools here?'

'An entire workshop,' I say.

I notice Rosana and Jimmy Bruëll sitting next to each other joking about. She's tiny, and he's very tall, almost a giant next to her. She must be ten years his senior, but it's obvious they've become lovers. They're wrapped in that warm glow that surrounds two people who share a bed (even if there is no actual bed). I guess Rosana must see the look of disbelief on my face.

'Surprised, Johnny boy?' Jimmy says, winking at me.

'To tell the truth, I am a little,' I say.

Rosana is blushing.

'Jimmy took my mum's lashes to save her,' Syra says laughing and chewing the skin around her nails.

'Syra!' Rosana cries. She's not telling her off for biting her nails, but for telling tales about her.

'He's still got the marks on his back,' Syra says.

Then she coughs violently.

Wade, Joseph, Rosana. I don't think there have ever been people to whom I feel more connected. My best friends. The three people with whom I've gone through the most intense experiences of my life, for whom I've risked my life, and who have risked their lives for me. But now the fellowship of the ring has disbanded. Or maybe it hasn't, after all. Maybe Wade is still on the island, somewhere, in some way.

'Lots has happened since we last saw each other,' I tell Joseph later that day, talking in private. 'Like, for example, Rosana and Jimmy.'

'Yes, they're a couple now. Almost nothing surprises me any more, but this... well, this surprises me. She's an attractive woman, I'm not doubting that, but you'd imagine Jimmy with some model out of *Sports Illustrated* with her lips pumped full of Botox.'

'Maybe he's tired of those *Sports Illustrated* models,' I say.

'And Rosana? What can she possibly see in Jimmy?'

'Ah, that doesn't come as so much of a surprise to me,' I lie. 'He's a handsome guy. A ladies' man.'

'A passing fling, you mean?'

'I don't know.'

'You seem jealous,' he says, laughing.

'Jealous? Me?'

'I thought Rosana was into you.'

'She's a friend. We're friends, nothing more. Anyway, Jimmy might change. I know the island has changed me. He can change too.'

'Come off it, John. Nobody ever changes.'

'Some people do. It's possible to start off bad and become good. Don't you think?'

'I suppose it's possible,' Joseph says, clearly wanting to change the subject.

A few days have passed since my friends arrived. Joseph and I are sitting on a bench at a wooden table under a fig tree, looking out over the valley and drinking glasses of blonde ale, like two old friends. The bumblebees buzz, moving from flower to flower. The starlings sing above our heads. We are cloaked in the heady shade of the fig tree, staring out at the sun-drenched landscape. The University buildings, the great stone wall with its rows of windows and terraces and staircases, begin a little further up. And I remember a conversation we had some time ago, about the likelihood of us finding civilisation again one day, and sharing a beer on a terrace or in some café. But everything is like that: remote and impossible, or easy and palpable. Things are either dreams or habits. There is no middle ground.

We sit there in silence. The beer they make in this place is never as cold as I'd like it to be, but it's good all the same. The feeling of being here drinking out in the open, the bitter taste of the beer, the sun's warmth and my slight drowsiness is all completely delicious.

'What is this place, John?' Joseph asks me. 'Have we made a mistake coming here?'

'I don't know what it is,' I say. 'There are a lot of mysteries still to be solved. A lot of things I don't understand. But I like it.'

'But what do they do here?'

'I think they're trying to live in a different way. They're convinced an alternative humanity is possible.'

'And they don't have a doctor,' he says.

'Oh, yes, plenty. But none who really cure people,' I say with a wink.

'I don't understand where we are,' he says, pointing out onto the landscape surrounding us. 'Are we on another island? What is this?'

'We're in the volcano's crater.'

'What volcano?'

'In the crater of our island's volcano.'

'So we're still on our island.'

'Yes, of course. How did they bring you here? Couldn't you tell you didn't leave the island?'

'I don't know,' Joseph said. 'I fell asleep and woke up here. It was the same for all of us. I don't know how they put us to sleep. They didn't say anything.'

'And Jimmy? How did they get him out of Central?'

'They didn't. Jimmy and the others were already back at the village.'

'Really? They escaped?'

'As far as I know that fellow Abraham Lewellyn went back to Central and released them all. After Wade, Rosana and your adventure in the mountains...'

'Oh, really?'

'When he came back down, the first thing he did was release our lot.'

'I'll be damned.'

'Quite. He gave them supplies and a sailing boat and they sailed to the village along the coast.'

'He gave them the sailing boat? He let them all go, just like that?'

'Just like that. Nobody gave any explanations.'

'But why would he do that?'

'My friend, you knew Lewellyn better than all of us; if you can't answer that question… You're the only one he spoke to, isn't that right?'

'Yes.'

'You spoke on an almost daily basis, while the others cut stone in a mine.'

'No, not every day, but on several occasions, yes. I don't know why. He took me to places, showed me things, told me about Central. I don't know why.'

'And you have no idea why he decided to let the others go and hand them a boat?'

'No.'

We fall silent and drink our beer slowly.

'The strangest things happened up there in the mountains,' I say.

'Yes, you told me.'

'Maybe Mr Pohjola told him to free them and give them the sailing boat,' I say innocently, and glancing at him to see his reaction.

'Mr Pohjola,' Joseph says, letting out a long sigh.

'What other explanation is there? If Lewellyn decided to let them go the moment he came down from the mountains, it must be because of something that happened up in the mountains.'

'Well, you know what went on up in the mountains.'

'Yes, very strange things happened.'

'But you didn't find this Pohjola fellow.'

'No.'

'You searched for his house and it didn't show up anywhere, and you found an old abandoned cabin in the woods and the next day Lewellyn had disappeared.'

'Basically.'

'So Pohjola doesn't exist, and if he does exist then he can't have said anything to Lewellyn because he wasn't there.'

'That's what it looks like.'

'Wade hasn't come back,' Joseph says.

'You expected him to?'

'I don't know.'

'Joe, Wade is dead.'

'You don't know that. You can't be sure. You didn't see him die. No-body saw him die. You can't just die from going into a hut.'

'He vanished.'

'Nobody just vanishes into thin air.'

'You still think he's back at Central with Lewellyn?'

'I don't think anything any more, John. I've stopped thinking.'

We fall silent again. Both of us take another sip of our beer. Joseph looks at me and gives a little nod as if to say: not too bad.

'I see you found the children,' I say.

'Yes, we got them all back.'

'Were they okay?'

'Yes, they were fine. At first they had trouble sleeping, but they're back to themselves now. Sebastian had been getting a lot of headaches, but they stopped when he got back down to the coast. The only odd thing is that Seymour has begun to talk.'

'And that's a bad thing?'

'He's too young. It's possible for a baby that small to start to say some words, but Seymour had two major brain injuries at birth. The doctors told Lizzy he'd probably never talk.'

'Well, well,' I respond.

'I know what you're going to say. That miracles happen in this place.'

'You said it, not me.'

'Do you believe it? You really think miracles happen here?'

'I don't know,' I say. 'Maybe miracles happen everywhere without us noticing them.'

'You know I don't believe in miracles.'

'Nobody can believe in miracles. A miracle is an impossible thing to believe in. What I think is that maybe they're not miracles.'

'No? In that case what are they? Anomalies?'

'I don't know. Inexplicable occurrences.'

'Yes, inexplicable occurrences.'

Joseph falls silent. He's not interested in these things, and I suspect he never will be.

'But what did Goran and Matvei tell you?' I ask. 'What was it that made you want to come here?'

'They showed us your letter, of course. Otherwise we wouldn't have believed them. And there were plenty who didn't believe the letter had really come from you. They thought it was another trap from the Insiders. But they told us things... they told us about this place. You told us about it, too, in your letter. Goran and Matvei told me that they had a community of five hundred people up here and that they didn't have a surgeon or allopathic doctor. "Allopathic doctor". It makes me laugh, that expression. It seemed their last one left two years ago. They offered for me to come here and see the place, and to be their doctor if I liked the idea. I talked it over with Sophie and she said it couldn't hurt to try.'

'I'm surprised she didn't want to go back to LA.'

'Yes, me too. She's a woman with a great sense of adventure, John. She likes challenges, new things.'

'And there was me thinking we'd all had enough adventures for one lifetime.'

'Yes, I thought so too.'

'And Leverkuhn? How did he take being separated from his kids?'

'We don't know where Leverkuhn is.' Joseph sighed. 'He disappeared. That's another reason Sophie didn't want to leave the island.'

'Disappeared?'

'Disappeared.'

'Maybe the Insiders are going for the architects now?'

Joseph starts chuckling, then I join in.

'We shouldn't laugh,' he says.

'No, we shouldn't.'

73

My last shot

But there's something that doesn't make sense, and hasn't since I arrived here. I know that Cristina and Ciran don't live together. She has her lodgings in a building in the uppermost part of the University, which is a kind of residence for the teachers. I know where she lives because I've followed her on more than one occasion. I don't know why she doesn't invite me to see the place, why she doesn't ask me to join her for tea, perhaps even dinner. Is she worried I'll misinterpret her invitation? Does she want to keep her distance? Is she scared I want to rekindle a romantic relationship with her? Yes, there's no doubt she's scared, that she doesn't want to lead me on. That must be why she's lied. Not literally, since she and Ciran are legally husband and wife, but the reality is that it's been years since they've lived as a couple. So English, this desire to cling to the literal truth! Those scruples – the result of mere, unreasoned habit – that produce such tense gestures, such forced smiles!

Ciran tells me about it when I ask him. He says they rushed into marriage too quickly. He tells me that six, or maybe eight months into living together they realised they weren't really a couple and that the fondness they felt for one another was more friendly than passionate. A brotherly, sisterly love, an intense spiritual bond, but not being in love. After Mexico they went to live in Baltimore, and then to Taos in New Mexico. By that point they'd already discovered they weren't really in love. But they got along well, and liked being together. They liked talking at the end of the day. They enjoyed travelling together. They had a lot of interests and friends in common. So they decided to carry on cohabiting, just not sleeping together. No, that's not quite true: in fact, they carried on sleeping together, in the same bed. They never saw a reason to stop. But they no longer lived as husband and wife. They shared the bed as two friends or siblings would do.

I ask Ciran if it is an open relationship and he says no, not as such, although there was a mutual understanding that jealousy had no place in their marriage. He had decided to take a personal vow of celibacy. It wasn't a definitive decision, so he didn't take it in front of anyone or even tell anyone. Not even Cristina knew about it at first. They carried on sleeping in the same bed because it worked for them, but they assumed that at some point someone else would appear on the horizon, another woman for Ciran, another man for Cristina, at which point they'd have to make a decision about their shared life.

The years rolled on. Cristina had several encounters with other men during that time. I don't know how many or how intense they were, although I'd like to. I'm not sure exactly why I want to know. I'm not sure what I stand to gain from such information, or what I stand to lose, or what I might save myself from, but I would like to know exactly how many men she has been with over the years and what she felt for them and what she did in bed with them. Ciran mentions this period in passing, and immediately regrets it – he feels like he's sharing things that are private to Cristina. He says they weren't in an 'open relationship', but given that they weren't a real couple, they both accepted that the other was free to start romantic or sexual relationships with other people. Not even Ciran entirely ruled out the possibility of meeting someone and falling in love, in which case he'd renounce his celibacy. But it never happened. Ciran reminded me several times that he was fifteen years older than Cristina, and too old now for great, passionate love affairs. So his monastic life continued, and weighed lighter on him as time went on, producing a strange feeling of freedom and relief, as if giving up sex had really freed him from an invisible burden. I quiz Ciran more about Cristina's relationships with other men and he says that they didn't talk about it much, that sometimes Cristina mentioned she was going out with someone or had met someone, and that he thinks that she fell in love on a trip to San Francisco once. But then Ciran tells me that these aren't topics for gentlemanly conversation and that if I want to know more about Cristina's life I should ask her myself.

The idea that Cristina has 'gone out' and slept with other men deeply bothers me, but this thing about her having 'fallen in love' with someone in San Francisco seems much more serious.

'Tell me about this man from San Francisco,' I say to Cristina one day on a walk to the Gardalis gardens.

Around us, blackbirds soar down to the grass, while red squirrels climb the cedar trunks. Ripe blackberries glisten on the brambles.

'Which man?' she asks. 'What are you talking about?'

'Cristina, why did you lie to me?'

'Lie to you?

'Okay, I accept that technically you didn't lie...'

'If technically I didn't lie, then I didn't lie. Don't tell me I've lied if I haven't lied.'

'Sometimes you are so British. Life doesn't always divide neatly into truths and untruths, correct or incorrect. This isn't a driving test. There are untrue things that are really true; and there are truths that don't speak to anything anyone feels to be true; and there are truths people say in such a way that they appear to be lies, and that is a form of lying; and there are truths that people say in the knowledge that the other won't understand them or will understand by them something untrue, and that is also a convoluted form of lying. You made me believe you were with Ciran, didn't you?'

'And what if I did? What has that got to do with anything?'

'You told me you were married to Ciran.'

'I *am* married to Ciran. It's one hundred per cent true.'

'I know that, but you haven't lived together for a long time.'

'What has that got to do with anything?'

'I've been talking to Ciran, but he doesn't want to tell me anything. He won't talk about you.'

'And he's right not to,' she says. 'Other people's lives shouldn't be fodder for gossip.'

'So tell me yourself.'

'Why, Juan Barbarín? What right do you have to ask anything about me? Why this sudden interest in my life?'

I fall silent. I know she's right.

'I'd like to stay here,' I say.

'Here, at the University?'

'Yes.'

'Don't you want to go back to your life, back home?'

'Nobody's waiting for me there. The truth is, I don't have a life. I don't have a home.'

'You have both. You have a lovely, comfortable home, you told me yourself. You have the house you always dreamt of owning. And you do have a life, of course you do. The problem is you don't like it.'

'Don't be mean.'

'You can't complain, Juan Barbarín.'

'Why not?'

Now we're strolling through Gardalis's high alpine meadows dotted with gentians that look out over the entire valley. There are some tiny metal robots moving along the grass collecting the purple grey pine cones that have fallen from the cedars. Without realising, we've been climbing steadily higher, and now we've come to the sacred garden, or what I consider to be a sacred garden, since it's really an open mountainside.

'Nothing is going to happen between us,' Cristina says after a few moments of silence. 'We're not going to go back to being lovers. We're not getting back together, Juan. That's not going to happen.'

'I never... I never thought...'

'I know what you're like,' she interrupts. 'You're like a spoilt child who wants what's in front of him, and when what you have in front of you disappears, you forget about it in a flash. Now you see me, I'm right here, and all of a sudden you want me for yourself. You fill your head with romantic dreams, you think that after this magical encounter we're going to fall head over heels back in love. That's you, a typical only child, a tiny little king. You want it all, and you want it now... You're selfish, Juan Barbarín, and tremendously immature, and the years haven't changed you. Not even this island has changed you.'

'Jesus,' I say, overcome with pain. 'You haven't forgiven me. You've never forgiven me.'

'I have forgiven you. The truth is I never thought I had anything to forgive. I already told you I thought that what happened was my fault.'

'No, that's not true. You haven't forgiven me.'

'Maybe not.'

We've reached the spot with the swing hanging from a tall branch. It looks like a pointless object now. She's riled up, upset, overcome with newfound emotions. I haven't seen her like this since I got here. All of a sudden she no longer looks like Salomé, the Mistress of the Game, but like a woman brimming with pain, on the verge of tears.

'I always thought that it was me who caused us to split up; my going to Rishikesh and abandoning you. But the truth was that going to Rishikesh was the first thing I'd done for myself since meeting you.'

'What do you mean?'

'I always put our relationship first, ahead of everything else. I came back from England for you. Made my parents livid. They wanted me to study there.'

'But you told me...'

'Yes, I said that, and maybe I even believed it, or tried to make myself believe it. But look at life as a musician in England compared to Spain. Look at all the possibilities to make a career out of singing in England, with all its festivals and opera houses and concert halls, compared to Spain.'

'But back then...'

'It soon became clear to me that if I wanted a singing career, I'd have to go back to England. But I didn't want to leave you, and you had no plans to move anywhere. You took a couple of courses in Venice and

Berlin, came home shocked to the core and then never wanted to go anywhere else again.'

'I came back shocked to the core, as you put it, because I didn't like the
music they were making on those courses everyone was taking. Sciarrino,
Nono, Donatoni, Berio, Boulez – they weren't my idols!'

'It doesn't matter. Whatever your problem was, I suggested we go together to England and you didn't want to. And that was fine, because our
relationship was the most important thing to me, and if you'd decided to
go to Saudi Arabia, where singing is practically banned, I'd have gone
with you.'

'I know.'

'I always put you and our relationship before myself. I always came
second. Always.'

'I know.'

'No, you don't know. You don't know because it's never occurred to
you. You jumped into bed with every woman you met, first behind my
back and then, after I'd caught you out a couple of times, without even
bothering to try to hide it. I told myself that it was a phase you were going
through. I told myself you must have things you needed to prove to yourself, complexes, what do I know. A woman in love is the very definition of
a stupid woman. I always let you do whatever you wanted.'

'I don't know why you did,' I say weakly. 'I behaved like an animal. I
was so disrespectful.'

'I let you do whatever you wanted because I've always believed that
people must be free in this life, free to decide what they want and free to
decide what they do not. And anyway, what could I do? Forbid you to
sleep with other women?'

'But it must have been so humiliating for you.'

'Yes, it was humiliating. But we're free, Juan Barbarín. I only loved you;
I didn't own you. Nobody can own another person. I was free to leave you,
but I didn't want to because I knew you loved me, and I hoped that in time
you'd recognise the value of our love.'

'What could I do? I knew that if you wanted to be with other women then you'd find them no matter what I said or did, and no matter how many promises you made me. And I didn't want to be weighed down by lies, and I preferred for things to be in the open, do you see? You say you were disrespectful, but what would showing me respect have meant in practice? Being unfaithful in secret? Making sure I didn't find out?'

'Well, yes, even that would have been more respectful.'

'I thought the only thing left for me to do was to leave and cut my ties with you forever, but I didn't want to because I loved you. I loved you so much, Juan Barbarín. I loved you so much. I've never loved anyone like that. I would have died for you. I would have walked over hot coals for you.'

'And I for you.'

'I don't doubt it. I know you loved me. I know you truly loved me, and that's why I stayed. But I put our relationship before everything, and you put yourself before anything or anyone else. Our relationship worked so long as I accepted coming second and going along with all your decisions. When I finally took the initiative, when I did something that wasn't primarily for us, but for me, you disappeared. And worse, you knew I had agreed to come and be with you in America after a year in Rishikesh. I just asked you for one year for me, Juan Barbarín. I asked you for one year to then give it all up and come and be with you, but that was too much. It didn't work.'

Neither of us says anything for a minute.

'Cristina, I love you.'

'You love me?'

'Yes.'

'What does that mean?'

'It means I love you. I love you like I loved you back then. I've never stopped loving you. I've never loved anyone more than I love you.'

She slumps down onto the swing and holds the ropes, as if she is exhausted all of a sudden.

'There's something I've been wanting to say to you,' she says, staring into the distance. 'In a few days the carpenters down in the village with your friends will have finished the boats. Together with the sailing boat you already have, and the instructions we gave you, you'll be able to get far enough away from the island to reach the cargo route in a couple of days. It's sort of like a motorway crossing the sea. Sooner or later, a boat will spot you and you'll be rescued. We're going to take whoever wants to leave back to the coast, and I think you should go with them.'

'You think I should, or you're ordering me to?'

'I can't order you to do anything,' she said. 'There are no orders here. It's more like a plea, a request. I'm pleading with you to go with the others.'

'Why?'

'Because there's no point in you staying here. Because if you stay, we'll both end up hurting one another. Because you'll soon work out that you want to leave, that you can't handle the isolation and silence. Because nothing we do here interests you.'

'You're wrong, I am interested.'

She stares mulishly into the distance, her jaw clenched.

74

The final hut

Cristina is wrong; the work of the University does interest me. I realise that the teaching of the White University truly began for me soon after we arrived on the island. I start to think that the whole island is part of the University. When did it all begin? It's hard to say. Maybe when I met Rosana. Maybe everything always starts with a woman in my case; a woman I'm attracted to and try to make attracted to me. I approached what I called 'the circle of meditators' to get closer to Rosana. Then I became intrigued by the whole experience and carried on participating. Could those words, my presence and that briefest of practices have really had some kind of influence on me?

As for all the other impossible things that have happened on the island, to me and to the others, I'd rather not think about it. What does it all mean? How can it be explained? It seems there's something about this island that has to do with sound, music and also voice. Singing, talking. 'Singing and dancing are the two most important things you can do in life,' Wade said to me in the Meadow, if indeed it was Wade I was talking to. But even if it wasn't, even if it was Pohjola, in that moment it was Wade who spoke to me about a nightingale's nest on the edge of the River Wabash. A devil, a god. A conference of devils and gods. Mice and dust. And a path to free oneself from the gods: the White University.

My hallucination phase. A little fellow (in real life he was very tall, almost imposing) claiming to be Anton Bruckner. My dream about Rosana, Dharma, Bruckner. The time I was locked up in a cell in Central. Was it just a dream? But there are dreams you know aren't just dreams. I'll never forget the things Bruckner told me. Where did they come from? Whose voice was that? Who, or what, was speaking to me inside that dream?

I want to go up to Gardalis, but I can't find the path. The higher I go, the steeper the slope becomes. I find some stone steps where Amaltea, the pregnant goat, is chewing on flowers. 'Was it you?' I ask her. 'Was it you who led me to the mountain? Are you the goat I saw in my vision?' I walk past her and keep heading on up. Amaltea's bell tinkles dreamily behind me. I move into the sun. The wildlife is green, lush and cheerful again. Clouds race across the sky.

My cloud!

There it is, high above me.

Resplendent.

It's heading north-west, and I follow it.

I walk among the cedars. I see a man in the distance, standing between two trunks. And then another. And a third. Is this Gardalis? I look for the swing as a point of reference. I look for a cedar with a horizontal branch high above me. Then I tell myself that maybe they've taken the swing down. There are five or six men standing between the tree trunks. One of them looks like Wade. I walk towards him. He's standing stock-still under the shade of the trees, and as I get closer I realise it really is Wade. There he is, with his hands on his hips, legs apart, leaning his weight on his left leg. He's wearing a rucksack, a thick belt with a dagger in its leather case and another knife strapped to his right ankle.

'Wade… What are you doing here?'

He smiles at me and puts his finger to his lips.

'But, Wade, you're alive?'

He points to his left, and gestures at me to keep walking.

Just up ahead there's an open clearing. Other men, women and children smile at me, greet me and signal that I should keep walking. I leave the shade of the cedars and find myself in a rectangular meadow split into two levels by a stone step. On the upper part, at the back, there's a wooden hut with a two-pitched roof.

It reminds me of Gustav Mahler's hut in Toblach, in South Tyrol, the small cabin where he wrote *The Song of the Earth* and the Ninth Symphony. Like that one it has a door with a little window between two big windows on the south-facing wall, and two other little windows on the side walls.

And this is how I end up, perhaps for the last time, back in the Meadow.

But there's something different about this Meadow. It's full of graves. Tombstones and tawny stone crosses are strewn all over the lower level. It's the cemetery where for centuries they've buried those who die while attending the White University. I walk among the tombstones, most of which are very old. I read names and dates, melodious, old-fashioned names that don't tell me anything. I half-heartedly search for Wade's grave. I look for one with my name on it. But I don't recognise any of these names. I don't know who all these dead people are. I suppose it's not important. What are the dead once they are dead? The dead are nothing. Words inscribed in stone aspire to last, but they are nothing. Amaltea has been following me from a distance. I can hear the sad tinkling of her bell. At first I think it's a church bell. I turn around and see the animal coming out from under the shade of the trees. She wanders into the Meadow and begins munching on the white asphodels growing between the tombstones.

The dead watch me from the edges of the Meadow not daring to enter.

'Wade. What does all of this mean?'

He shrugs his shoulders.

I go up to the higher level. To my surprise the door to the hut opens easily, and I step inside. It's very cosy, and also clean – not a trace of dust or cobwebs. Inside, at the back, there's an upright piano with its stool, and facing the double window that overlooks the valley, a polished but unvarnished wooden desk and a seat. I open the piano and play a few chords. It's tuned, and sounds good considering it's inside a hut, exposed to the damp and changing temperatures. It's a Bösendorfer, about forty years old. I take a seat and start playing. Oh, if only I'd had a piano during all this time on the island. But that time has come to an end. I'll soon be gone from here, back to my life and my Labrador and my own piano.

I play the second movement of Beethoven's Sonata No. 27. Next I play Chopin's Ballade No. 1. Next, the opening of Bach's Italian Concerto. And lastly, I begin to play the Adagio from Bruckner's Eighth Symphony. Someone bangs loudly on the door, and I get such a fright that I stop playing. The banging comes back. I get up from the piano stool and walk towards the door. There's no one to be seen through the little window. Did whoever was banging duck down? Is he there somewhere, lurking? But who could have knocked? Wade? Anton Bruckner? I take the simple wooden doorknob in my hand and open it. But there's no one there. I step out to have a look. Nobody, anywhere. I walk around the hut and look among the trees and grassy hillsides all around. There's no one to be found.

I tell myself that at last I've reached the Meadow. At last I've truly entered it. At last I've been let in. On the lower level the golden tombstones disappear behind the tall grass and white asphodel flowers. The vision of the crosses and tombstones feels more peaceful and soothing than solemn – an invitation to be silent and meditate. At last I've been let in. The battle is done. The tension that got me all the way here – pitching me here and there as if between a giant's fists or at the edge of an abyss – has disappeared, and now I'm in the Meadow, in the restful expanse of green pasture that exists at the deepest part of our thoughts. This is the deepest part of the world. This is the world, because the world is all depth, repose, existence. Now I am at peace with myself. I have come to the end of all those battles. I accept who I am. I accept my life, my punishment, my enlightenment, my limits, my blessings. The war is over. I am at peace.

75

I offer up a poppy

Some of the people who came up here have decided to go back to Cast-away Village after all, and regroup with the others who are leaving the island. Among those who have decided to stay here in the University are Rosana and Jimmy Bruëll. Now Jimmy spends his days either in the library swatting up on meditation or practising martial arts. Rosana has decided to work the fields. Everyone at the University is supposed to do different jobs on rotation, although you can, if you wish, do one specific job of your choosing. She tells me she's always liked having a vegetable plot and working the land, and that she's decided to stay for at least one year, before heading back to the real world. She seems happy, very serene. Syra is less happy, because there are very few children and teenagers at the University. In total, maybe thirty kids aged between eight and four-teen. She and Sebastian aren't speaking, but it doesn't seem too serious, and I'm sure they'll make up. Joseph and Sophie have also decided to stay for at least a year. The one who struggles most to fit in here, I think, is Sophie. The world of fashion, art, magazines and architecture in which she used to move couldn't be further from this monastery in the moun-tains. But she finds things to keep herself occupied. She also says that she doesn't want to leave the island until they find her husband, but what's she likely to find up here? If she really wanted to find Leverkuhn she wouldn't stay in the University; she'd organise a search party. I have a feeling Leverkuhn is dead.

For their part, Xóchitl and Joaquín have chosen civilisation. Xóchitl wants to return to Los Angeles and Joaquín plans to follow her. Julián and

Matilde will go back to Madrid. Julián says that for them these months on the island have just been a continuation of the long journey they had already embarked upon when the plane crashed here, and that they just want to go home. Lily Whittfield and Mike Garson are also going home, as are Dharma and Eva. I would have thought that they'd fit in here better than anyone, but Philemon tells me I'm wrong, that Dharma has already been in his own White University, which he left a long time ago. And on top of that, it turns out they have two children waiting for them back in New York.

I don't know how they communicate with the coast from up here, but Philemon says that within a couple of days the boats will be ready and that those leaving will be taken to the coast the following day to board them. And all of a sudden, a distance opens up between those who are staying and those of us who are leaving. The others all seem blissfully happy, swathed in the mountain light, while we are anxious about the journey ahead. They seem taller, bigger. We should be happy; at last we'll be leaving this infernal island. And it's possible that the others *are* happy, but not me. I feel like I'm being driven out. I feel like I haven't managed to convince the island. Or I couldn't get the better of it. Instead, I feel it's got the better of me.

Those of us leaving are very nervous. There's still one more adventure to come: getting out to sea, being spotted by a boat before running out of water and supplies, being repatriated from who knows where. But however the adventure ends, we're all going back to our homes, families, pets, old habits, to that glorious life we all had without realising it. I try to imagine all the colours of the civilised world: concerts, restaurants, social events, my studio, my piano, books and bed.

And so, at last, we come to our final day at the White University. In the morning it pours with rain. It sounds like furious chords in F-sharp major thundering down. The raindrops splash against the windowsills and flagstone paths. I don't know what to do with myself. I head out to the library and bump into Xóchitl and Joaquín sitting on a stone bench, sheltered from the rain. They're so wrapped up in their happiness they don't even stop smooching or whispering into each other's ears as they tell me I should visit them in Los Angeles. I tell them I will, and that I hope they'll come and visit me in Rhode Island, and then I hurry on, fleeing from their happiness.

I pay a visit to the library, but Giovanni isn't there, so I head back out ready for a soaking, but instead the rain stops and shafts of light begin to appear here and there through the branches of the cedars. The world beyond the dark leafy crowns lights up, the clouds clear in the wind, and everything is flooded. The wind continues to blow, sending the delicate raindrops still clinging to the pine needles rippling off into the air. Wind and sun. I walk beneath the cedars, there at the edge of the world. The damp earth soaks my feet. And nothing matters any more. It's over now. I had it all and I lost it. What is the meaning of life? I don't know. What do we live for? I don't know.

I walk up to Gardalis, to the old cemetery and I take another stroll among the tombstones. There, hidden in a corner, covered with jars of fresh roses and other flowers, I find a grave that has no cross; it has only a round stone with the inscription 'Prinz Mayerling Von Thymus' and the dates 1823–1899. I wonder who this long-forgotten nineteenth-century prince who died on the Island of Voices could have been.

I enter the hut and feel like I've come home, to my final home. This isn't the case, of course, firstly because the cabin is more of a workshop than a home, and secondly because I'm leaving for good tomorrow. My studio in Oakland is just as peaceful, far cosier, and the piano is infinitely better. Why, then, do I have the feeling that this is where I could really get some composing done, write some worthwhile music? I sit down at the piano and start to play, and end up improvising for about an hour. Then I play the first movement from Beethoven's Sonata No. 31, one of my favourites. There's a passage towards the recapitulation – for nothing is conventional in this movement, which is full of surprises and things that appear and disappear all of a sudden – in which an ascending passage of semiquavers that initially appears to be a mere adornment begins to unbraid itself into one of those melismatic and never-ending melodies typical of Beethoven's final period, a rush of very delicate, mysterious notes that flip and turn on top of one another before suddenly coming to a stop in a suspended chord. D flat, B flat, G, F, a dominant ninth. You have to play it ever so slightly independently from what comes before: quieter, intensely sweetly. Whenever I play this sonata I'm always longing to get to the long melisma and suspended chord. The sweetness, the mystery and the surprise of this chord never fail to enchant me. Something opens up here: a possibility, a window. It's like the window in that story by Lord Dunsany, through which you can glimpse another world. It's like the 'magic casement' from Keats' 'Ode to a Nightingale', which looks out over the foam of perilous seas in faery lands forlorn. The chord seems to come from another concept of time, which doesn't seem to belong to the arc that runs from past to future. It seems to suggest other eyes that see other things. It seems to suggest a fourth dimension we can't explain but in which, out of nowhere, we find ourselves. Time hangs suspended in an orb of light and marvel. The sonata stops and, as such, the world stops with it. It's a dominant chord, which quickly resolves to the tonic, but time continues to float suspended. And then the mediant, becoming the dominant, leads into the relative minor and everything goes darker and we enter a world of delicate sadness and shadow. Finally another dominant chord sounds, like a sign that the timeless ecstasy has come to an end, and suddenly the sonata picks up busily again. Time has returned. The heart starts beating again. The lungs breathe. The vision fades. The window vanishes into thin air. The roses from the other world that we'd glimpsed now only exist as memories.

The sonata movement continues on its course, but not for very long at all. Suddenly, we're into a coda. The left hand is playing the main theme, and then it's all over. Everything falls silent.

I listen to the silence of the island. The breeze is blowing between the branches of the firs. A distant nightingale is singing among the leaves, and, very close by, a starling calls out. The two voices are completely unrelated.

I leave the hut and go and sit on the stone step that splits the Meadow into two levels. Below, the light floods the great expanse of the valley in such a way that I feel like I'm looking at a huge lake, a sea of golden sunlight.

I close my eyes and begin to feel a glow. It's the glow of the valley through the firs, the glow of the sea through the palm trees. It's the glow of the sea during our months on the coast, the astonishing beauty of the world around us, but which we are incapable of seeing. They hand us paradise, but we, with our meanness and our demons, turn it into hell.

Keep shining, sea of the world, remind me, with this glow, of the astonishing reality, the never-ending adventure. Shine, sea of Eden! Humankind's journey has only just begun!

And then it happens. Right there and then, it starts to happen.

I start to grow, to rise up above myself. I grow and grow towards the clouds. I'm a blue giant, so huge I could navigate myself. I am a sea.

I rise up above myself to the very peaks of thought, to the limits of the human form.

I feel a lightness, an elation, a completeness I've never felt before. Something starts to breathe inside of me. Something opens up, something is set free. Something is beginning.

And I carry on growing, becoming more and more immense.

Afterwards, when it's all over, I spend the day in a blissful daze. Could such a thing really happen, I wonder? Could it be possible?

I spend the rest of the day looking for Cristina, but I can't find her anywhere. I know she's avoiding me, but I also know that we have to say goodbye sooner or later.

When evening falls, she comes looking for me. I'm on the terrace, a book in hand, when I feel her shadow fall across me. I didn't hear her coming, and now she's just here, in front of me, like some sort of round-hipped genie. She sits down on the stone seat beside me. I'm dying to put my arms around her, to kiss her arms and neck, but I know I'm not allowed.

'The other day we said some horrible things to each other,' she says in a formal, impersonal tone. 'I said some very harsh things to you. I'm sorry.'

'I deserve it.'

'No, you don't, all that's in the past now. I'm not sure why I was so keen to dredge all of that up. Again, I'm sorry. I don't hold any grudge against you, Juan Barbarín. All is forgotten. Everything's okay.'

'You don't hold any grudge against me?'

'If I did once, I cleaned and burnt it a long time ago. But clearly there was a part of me that still wanted to tell you all those things.'

'I'm leaving tomorrow, Cristina.'

'So I hear.'

'Are we really going to say goodbye to each other again?'

'We didn't say goodbye the first time around.'

'Are you happy I'm leaving?'

'No.'

'So you want me to stay?'

'No.'

'This morning I discovered a new place,' I say. 'The Meadow.'

'Which meadow?'

'Our Meadow.'

'From Calle de los Olmos?'

'Yes.'

'That's the place you discovered?'

'Yes. Have you been there too?'

'Yes, I have.'

'What's it doing here?'

'I don't know.'

'It's a cemetery.'

'Yes. That's where Mayerling's grave is. Have you seen it?'

'Yes.'

'We don't know if it's really his grave or just a cenotaph.'

'And there's a cabin on the upper level.'

'There's always a cabin on the upper level.'

'I could stay here and work in that cabin, don't you think?' I ask.

'You're leaving tomorrow, Juan Barbarín.'

'Let me stay.'

'I can't stop you from staying.'

'So I'll stay.'

'No, tomorrow you go.'

'I don't want to go.'

'And I don't want you to stay.'

'My God, you really hate me. You've never stopped hating me.'

'If you stay, if you insist on staying, I'll do everything in my power not to see you. I'll arrange things so we don't run into each other. There are a lot of people here, a lot of things to be done.'

'You won't even talk to me?'

'We've already spoken, Juan Barbarín. We've gone over the old days, we've lost our tempers and we've made up. What else is there to say?'

'You really hate me.'

'I don't hate you, Juan Barbarín.'

'Yes, you hate me, and I deserve it. I deserve everything I've been through. All of it.'

Neither of us speaks for a moment.

'Cristina, this morning I had an experience in that Meadow, in that cemetery.'

'An experience?'

'I saw myself as I've never seen myself before.'

'Oh.'

'I saw a vast blue sea, a shining sea.'

'Ah.'

'So you're not interested? You don't want to hear about it?'

'You know that we can close our eyes but not our ears.'

'You think I'm lying? You think this is a ruse to convince you? Jesus, you really do have a terrible idea of me.'

'Tell me about your experience. I've spent years listening to other people's experiences. One more won't kill me.'

'I realise now that since I arrived on the island I've had lots of other "experiences". Not just that dream you and I shared, which is pretty unbelievable in itself. There have been other inexplicable experiences, but what took place this morning was different. Far more intense. I've understood who I am. I've understood what I can come to be. Do you understand what I'm talking about?'

'Yes.'

'I've finally understood that I've spent my entire life inside one very small room. Do you know what I'm talking about?'

'Yes.'

'Holed up in a very small room, without noticing that the door is open, and that it's possible to get out of there and go wherever I want. Do you know what I'm talking about?'

'Yes.'

'I want to go back to that cabin.'

'You've been given a gift,' she said with a sigh.

'Yes, I have.'

'But the gift doesn't tend to repeat itself. Once or maybe two or three times in a lifetime, and it's usually the hidden consequence of a process we're not altogether aware of. If you go back to the cabin tomorrow, nothing will happen. Now what you have to do is start working.'

'That's what I want to do.'

She lets out another deep breath, and for a few seconds I get the feeling she's doing something. I don't know exactly what. Counting in her head? Repeating a mantra? Doing some kind of exercise? She closes her eyes and her breathing becomes even more measured. Then she opens them again.

'Look, Juan,' she said. 'I'm not always Salomé. Sometimes I'm just Cristina, and I'm very stupid and stubborn. But sometimes I have to be Salomé, and it's as Salomé that I'm speaking to you now. If you want to stay, stay. Nobody has any right to stop you. Everyone who comes to our door is allowed in – that's one of the University's rules, a rule of knowledge. Stay and be one more among us. Study, search, meditate. You are welcome here.'

'You're saying I can stay.'

'Yes. You've got this far. You've found the way, and for that reason we received you with open arms. But you must understand that this love we offer you isn't personal, it's not based in kinship or rejection. It's a kind of cold, unconditional and also impersonal love.'

'I understand. You mean that it's Salomé who welcomes me, but Cristina won't ever see me again.'

'That Cristina doesn't exist any more, Juan. She rose to the surface the other day, *samskaras* that are still buried hidden there. But she won't be coming back.'

'You want me to stay because I want to stay and not because I want to be near you.'

'Yes.'

'I want to stay for both reasons.'

'Then you'll suffer, and you'll make me suffer too.'

'And there's no chance at all that Cristina will change her mind?' I ask.

But she's said her piece, and is silent now. I know that look well, that Anglo-Saxon stance, the satisfaction of cutting off any wistful grumbling and showing, with that unbending attitude, that there's no point whatsoever in insisting. Her eyes like swords, her mouth clamped shut with that stern Lady Justice expression.

I don't know what to do. I close the book in my hands and spot something pressed between its pages. It's the flower that I put there a few days ago to dry. I remove it with clumsy, trembling fingers. I'm not even sure why I put it in the book. It's dry and pressed, but its colours are undimmed. It's the poppy that the girl in the valley gave to me a few days ago. An unusual poppy with two red petals and two white ones.

'Here,' I say to Cristina. 'A parting gift. Keep it for a hundred years.'

'What?' she says.

She looks at the flower I hand to her and places it delicately in the palm of her hand, studying it carefully. I notice her hands are trembling.

'Is it a poppy?' she asks.

'Yes.'

'A poppy with two white petals and two red ones!'

'Yes,' I say, surprised by her evident surprise.

'What did you say before?' she asks. 'What did you just say to me?'

'I said you should keep it for a hundred years.'

She closes her eyes, then brings the white and red poppy to her heart. Her eyes are closed and it looks like she's smiling. It looks like the fuchsia light of the bougainvillea growing on the wall beside us is reflected in her rosy eyelids and smiling lips. And then her smile no longer resembles a smile, but a grimace, one of intense suffering. And then tears start spilling from her thick, dark eyelashes, rolling down her cheeks like before, back when we were twenty and I was always amazed at how easily she cried, the way her eyes would overflow with tears like raindrops in a soft, warm spring shower...

76

Paths beneath the willow trees

A *young woman, almost a girl,* is sitting on a *ghat* on the shore of the Ganges. That great river the colour of milky tea rushes between the two verges, dotted with sturdy dark trees and ornate white temples. The pagoda-like temples seem to float among the tropical green clouds covering the hillsides. The yellowy steps of the ghat lead down into the water. They have tied several ropes to secure iron rings to prevent those who go into the water to perform ritual baths from being dragged away by the current. She knows she has to bathe in her clothes. That's Indian custom. The men remove their shirts and leave on just their dhoti, but the women are not permitted to remove their shirts. Maybe she could bathe in a swimsuit, being a Western woman, but it would be seen as disrespectful. She too would consider it disrespectful.

Despite the stuffy heat, the water is freezing. It flows down from the glaciers in the Himalayas, and has barely had any time to warm up on its way to the foothills. It still carries that wild, early energy of mountain torrents, even though by this point the Ganges is already a very wide river. A young, lively river preparing itself for its long journey across the Indian plains. The girl walks down the steps and towards one of the ropes. She takes hold of the thick hemp and steps into the water. The steps go on, invisible now under the opaque surface, and she keeps going, feeling the icy water surround her ankles, her calves, her hips. When the water reaches her waist, she takes a deep breath and submerges her whole body, but without taking her hands off the rope. Then she brings her head up out of the water. She repeats this immersion three times while she chants a mantra. 'Mother Ganges,' she says in her head, 'clean my past. Mother Ganges, carry my karma with you, leave me clean and renewed. I don't want to hold onto anything. I don't want to be tied to anything. I don't want to defend anything. I'm breaking all ties, all connections, all that limits and enslaves me.'

She knows how hard she has worked to say those words.

'I don't want to be tied to anything. I'm breaking all ties.'

He must have got here a week ago and he still hasn't showed up. She knows it's just a day's journey in the car from Delhi to Rishikesh: ten to twelve hours (and barely two hundred kilometres separating them). He should have been able to get there by now. The days go by and he doesn't show up, and she has a terrible feeling. All of a sudden, she knows: he's not coming. She's lost him forever. She calls Madrid just in case. She calls their house, the house where the pair of them have been living together for the last few years, but nobody picks up. Eventually she calls his parents. She speaks to his mother, who's never been particularly fond of her. The woman seems taken aback, almost moved that she would call her from so far. She tells her that he hasn't gone to India, and that he's not going to go to India. She tells her he's left for the US and she answers the mother saying that that's not possible, that there must be some mistake.

'No,' his mother says, perhaps only now beginning to understand that there's no mistake. 'What's happened is that he doesn't have the guts to tell you to your face. He hasn't dared tell you to your face.'

'Tell me what?' she asks. 'Tell me that he's not coming to India?'

'No,' his mother says patiently, perhaps relishing the moment. 'He doesn't have the guts to tell you he wants to leave you. That he's left you.'

'I don't believe it,' she says. 'It's not possible. Nothing's happened. We haven't even spoken about splitting up. We haven't argued. Why would he just split up with me out of the blue like that, without any explanation?'

'Nothing's happened?' his mother says. Her voice sounds even more shrill and piercing through the earpiece of this Indian phone, a human voice jumping from repeater to repeater and from there to a satellite in orbit and then from the satellite back down to the earth's surface. 'You don't think anything has happened? You abandoned him. You walked out of your home together. How long have you been in India? Almost a year you've been there. You've abandoned Juan. You expected him to come running along after you like a lapdog. You expected him to drop every-thing just like you did, to leave his work and career and follow you there to... to that place, wherever it is. You had a good job, Cristina. You were in a privileged position, the two of you. And then you go and throw it all away and disappear, leaving him on his own for months on end. What did you expect? What did you think was going to happen? Did you think he was going to drop everything and follow you? If you thought that then you really don't know men at all.'

She is lost for words. She's no longer used to hearing such aggressive voices, so full of recriminations and spite. Even his mother's Madrilen-ian accent seems strange. That aggressive, brusque Spanish manner which, with an absolute lack of consideration, almost physically pene-trates the other.

'You've joined a cult,' his mother goes on. 'You should come back right away. I can't understand why your parents don't go and get you out of there.'

'I'm not in a cult,' she says meekly.

'If I were your father, I'd be on the next plane to get you out of there and bring you back to Spain,' his mother says.

'I'm not in a cult,' she repeats, on the verge of tears. 'Why are you say-ing these things to me? Why are you talking to me like this? What have I done to you to make you speak to me this way?'

'You've made my son unhappy,' the woman replies. 'Cristina, how do you expect me to speak to you? You abandoned my son. You had a perfect life in Madrid. You had a house that you could have been paying off in-stead of throwing your money away on rent, but that's a whole other issue. You both had wonderful jobs. Your lives were sorted. And so young! Why did you have to run off to some cult?'

Conversations this long cost a fortune. Cristina has to pay a shedload of rupees for these international calls. She calls him, but he doesn't ever

pick up. Grudgingly, his mother gives her his telephone number and address in the States, and she calls and calls repeatedly. The line isn't good.
There's white noise, and sometimes she can hear herself as an echo as she
speaks. This happens when she gets through to her father and brother. She
never manages to speak to Juan Barbarín. Just once he picks up and says
in English 'Hello?' She says her name, and then there's the sound of muttering and he hangs up. So she writes him a letter, two or three letters, and
sends them to his address in Oakland, Rhode Island. But she never receives any reply.

She goes to the edge of the Ganges hoping that the great river, the
great Mother, has an answer for her. She slips into the freezing water and
does her ablutions. Then she returns to the top of the steps, shivering with
cold. Shivering with fear, with desolation. And she starts to cry. Despite
how cold she is, she goes back into the river and repeats the ritual bath.
And she asks Mother Ganges to help her, to show her the light, not to take
her love from her. Please, Mother Ganges, the girl weeps, mixing her tears
with the tears of the river of the dead. Please, don't take that from me. Just
that, Mother Ganges, just leave me that. I'll give you everything else. I
don't want any of the other stuff. But don't take that from me.

But the ties… Didn't you say you wanted to be set free of all ties?

All but this tie. This one tie. Please, don't take it from me. Take everything else… Please, Mother Ganges…

She gets out of the water still shivering with cold. She sits a little higher
up the ghat, unable to contain her tears.

And then she sees him, walking along the edge of the river, in the middle of a group of pilgrims. It's him. He's dressed all in white: white trousers and a white summer shirt, a white wrap over his shoulders and he's
using a long walking stick. There's no doubting it's him. He's wearing
sandals and is limping. Why is he limping so much? She's shaking on the
steps in her soaking clothes and with her arms wrapped around her knees
to warm up. She watches as this man, Juan Barbarín, walks among a group
of Indian pilgrims. Then the others leave and he is left alone at the water's
edge. She watches as he stares into the water. It can hardly be possible, but

it is him. She runs over, but it's not him; just an Indian man who vaguely resembles him. A man with the Shaiva symbol on his forehead. A brown, slim man with dark almond eyes that remind her of Juan Barbarín's. And a beautiful smile. She looks at him. He looks at her and smiles. Since she doesn't stop staring at him, he holds his hands up to his heart and says 'Namaste'. She does the same. She's still shaking and now the breeze has picked up and it's very unpleasant being there with her sopping sari sticking to her body.

'What's your name?' she asks the man.

'What?' he says. 'Don't you recognise me? It's me!'

'Me?' She chuckles through her tears. 'What do you mean "me"?'

She doubts herself. Could it really be him? Because this man looks a lot like Juan Barbarín, even though it's not Juan Barbarín because he's years older than Juan. And besides, this man is Indian and has a limp and what looks like an artificial leg. She's spotted him once or twice before along the river's edge. And on those other occasions it occurred to her that this man reminded her of her boyfriend, and most likely their eyes crossed before and they smiled at each other, or at least he smiled at her over from the opposite shore during the evening aarti, when everyone gives offerings of flowers and candles to the water of the Ganges and the river carries the floating lights to Varanasi. And she has smiled at him too, so he must have got the wrong idea and come back to look for her. Or is it really a chance encounter?

'Don't you remember me from another life?' the man asks, smiling. He has a lovely delicate Indian accent: melodic, with r's that are vaguely reminiscent of the Spanish r.

'No, I don't remember you.'

'Then why are you looking at me like that and smiling? Why did you greet me if you don't know me?'

'Do you remember me from another life?' she asks.

'Of course,' he says. 'Not just from one, from many. We've spent many lives together.'

'How many?'

'Very many.'

'Were we husband and wife?'

'Yes. Respectfully, we have been husband and wife in many other lives.'

The man limps painfully and has to lean on his walking stick. He is svelte, strong and athletic, but his limp makes him look frail. A frail Shaiva pilgrim who has travelled up to Rishikesh to spend a few nights on the patio of an ashram, bathe in the river, eat whatever alms they give him and then carry on his journey to the next ashram, the next sacred festival and the next Shaiva celebration.

She cannot make up her mind about him. He does not seem like the usual filthy old beggar, doing his best to get close to her. In fact, beneath his weariness and ragged clothes she perceives an old-fashioned refinement; the refinement of dusty rose gardens in sunny climes. She asks him if he's a beggar. He tells her he was a lawyer for many years in New Delhi, and that in the end he decided to leave his career to become a sadhu, an ascetic. She asks him if he's married or has children. He says he did have a wife but that she died, and that they didn't have children because she couldn't.

'I'm sorry,' she says.

'But you,' he says, 'why are you so sad? Why such sad eyes, Deepali? Where is your husband?'

'I don't have a husband.'

He seems taken back, and asks her why not. He doesn't understand how she could have travelled so far on her own. He can't get his head around a woman being in a foreign country completely on her own. She is used to people finding this strange.

'I am on my own,' she says. 'I am on my own.'

'You're very beautiful,' he says. 'I don't understand. Are you very poor?'

'No, I'm not poor.'

'So you're sick?'

'No, I'm not sick,' Cristina says, half laughing despite herself.

'Forgive me, Deepali,' he says. When he smiles, she notices the tip of one of his incisors is chipped.

'Deepali?'

'This was your name before. When we were husband and wife.'

'You're having me on.'

'It's the truth. Now you have another name because you're Christian. But that's the only reason why.'

'I'm not Christian.'

'Of course you are.'

She's in no mood to argue.

'You really don't remember me?' the man goes on. 'We've seen each other a few times before along the river. And you smiled at me. I thought you remembered me, as I did you. I thought that was the reason you smiled at me.'

'No. You remind me of a friend.'

'See? I knew you remembered me.'

'No, no,' she says. 'I mean your face is familiar. You look like a man I know.'

'That's how remembering happens. If you take a proper look at the people you come across, you always think you recognise them. Almost all faces are familiar, even those we've never seen before. That's because you know them from other lives.'

'Nothing like that has ever happened to me before,' she says.

'No? Look. Look around you. Choose a person, woman or man, it doesn't matter, and look at them carefully. You'll soon see you recognise them. You'll soon get the feeling of having seen them before. If you dig a little deeper, you'll see that it is your daughter, your mother, your sister, your father, your uncle, or the person who killed you, or the person you killed. The person you deceived, or the person who deceived you...'

'And isn't that because we're all human beings?'

'That I couldn't say,' he says, shrugging his shoulders comically. 'I couldn't say!'

'Or maybe it's that we're all from the same family. Maybe we are all really the same person, multiplied millions of times under different guises.'

'That's it, Deepali. *Achha, achha.* That's it.'

They both fall silent.

'Dear Deepali,' the man says, now very serious. 'I'm a sadhu now and I practise *brahmacharya*. I've renounced earthly pleasures and family. I don't have any belongings. I don't even have a house. I'd like to be able to help you in your sadness, but I can't.'

'I understand.'

'But I'm going to propose something. Right now I cannot be with a woman or even think about marrying you. But in the future I will look for you.'

'In another life?' she asks.

'I hope it won't be in another, because you will forget me, Deepali. You always forget me.'

'I'm sorry.'

'But you never completely forget, Deepali.'

'Like now,' she says.

'I'll bring you a sign so you know it's me. I'll bring you a red and white poppy. Will you remember?'

'Yes. A red and white poppy.'

'I'll put it in your hands and I'll say: "Keep it for a hundred years." That way, you'll know it's me.'

She begins to weep. He tells her not to cry, that she shouldn't cry. And she tells him that she's not crying because of what he's just said, but for another, very different reason. She tells him about her boyfriend, about how he has left her, about her unanswered calls and letters. He doesn't ask any questions. He listens to her attentively, but doesn't say anything. Perhaps because he doesn't know the whole story, or perhaps because the things she tells him have a different meaning for him than for her.

'Sometimes one must wait, Deepali,' he says eventually, looking at her with deep tenderness. 'Dear wife. Sometimes one must wait many years. I will come back for you, and then you will remember me. But you must remember the flower, Deepali.'

'The flower?'

'A white and red poppy. Will you remember?'

'I will.'

Just another lunatic on the shore of the Ganges, she tells herself on her way back to the ashram. Just another head case. The river is awash with them. The shores, the ghats, the neighbouring streets, the patios to the ashrams; they've heaving with sadhus, all of them either half mad or stark raving mad. Fakirs with bulging eyes. Old men with white beards and moustaches so long they have to tie them around their heads. All sleeping on the floor, surrounded by cow dung and pesky rats. Sacred lunatics who walk around with a bronze trident and tin bowl. Some are genuine ascetics looking for enlightenment; others are simply beggars in elaborate disguise; some are just poor madmen ranting to themselves. It's often hard to tell one from the other.

The next day she goes down to the river to look for the stranger and continue their conversation. She can't see him anywhere. And she doesn't see him again. She doesn't even know his name.

'Why are you crying?' I ask her. 'Cristina, why are you crying?'

She sighs heavily, dries her eyes and looks at me, but she can't stop crying. She stares at me and carries on crying, and her eyes contract in such an intense gesture of pain that she reminds me of old Pietàs. Her lips screw up in an expression of such heart-rending anguish I feel as if I've been stabbed in the stomach. She tries to speak but can't. Then I move in towards her and wrap my arms around her. All I want is to hold her, to have her close to me, to clutch her to my chest and let all the love that I can no longer hold in spill out of me. We stay like that for a while, until she stops crying and I can feel her breathing becoming regular again. I take her tear-stained, warm face in my hands and kiss her on the lips, and she kisses me.

'My love,' she says. 'My love, my love.'

'So you do love me too.'

'I always have. Always, my love.'

We kiss passionately for a long time. Anyone could see us on the terrace, but it's clear that she no longer cares. A woman, a man. Isolde,

Tristan. A mouth, another mouth. A face, another face. Time passes, and time dissolves. The smells of the evening and the swallows' song swirl and dance above us. The clouds float over the sea. The forest creatures are getting ready for night. A new star announces its arrival in the firmament. We speak in whispers, kiss and talk, using our mouths and tongues to kiss and talk, talk and kiss in turn. We talk of love. We kiss as we repeat over and again that we love each other, that we'll never part again. And we breathe, and sometimes we breathe through the other's mouth.

She's calmer now and her burning, wet cheek is resting on my shoulder. I stroke her shoulder. I stroke her chest. I stroke her stomach. Everything in her swells and shrinks to the rhythm of her breathing: her stomach, her chest, her arm. Then she tells me the story of what happened to her in Rishikesh when, in a moment of absolute desolation, when she felt alone and abandoned and so removed from everything, lost and drowning in darkness, she met a pilgrim on the edge of the Ganges who looked like me. A pilgrim she'd seen the year before and whom, in fact, she'd mentioned to me.

'He was exactly like you,' she says, 'exactly as you were when I found you among the ferns, at the spring beyond the crater, when we found you. Do you remember? The white shawl over your shoulders, the long walking stick, the missing leg... you even have his chipped tooth. How can so many coincidences be possible?'

She asks me where I got the white and red poppy from, and I tell her that a little girl in the valley gave it to me a few days ago. This seems to fluster her. She asks me lots of questions about the girl, about her appearance, her clothes, her hair, if she had been wearing rings, bracelets or any other signs, and she also asks me if the girl told me to give the poppy away and say that phrase, the one about the hundred years.

'She told me to keep it,' I say. 'She told me to keep it for a hundred years.'

'That's what she said?'

'Yes. Her speech was odd, as if she were using a language she was uncomfortable with.'

'She appeared, gave you the flower, told you to keep it for a hundred years, then disappeared?'

'Yes.'

'Were there others with her?'

'Yes, some other little girls. They were playing, and then they ran off.'

'Have you seen children in the valley before or since?' she asks, staring at me fixedly, alarmed maybe, as I stay there with my arms wrapped around her shoulders, kissing her forehead, her dark hair, her pounding temple, and running my hand over the curves of her body, as if to convince myself that she's real.

'Of course I've seen other children in the valley,' I say. 'The valley is full of children, especially in the area around the lake. Why does that surprise you so much?'

'Because there are no children in the valley. Those figures you saw weren't children.'

'So what were they?'

'Gods.'

'Gods?' I say incredulously.

'Gods, devils, daemons, spirits, *aos sí*... thoughts, complexes, impulses... each one has a name... here, thanks to the work of the University, it's possible to *see them*...

'They exist in the in-between world. They are part of us, unknown dimensions of us. At the same time, they connect us to each other. They live in parallel dimensions, jump through time and space, make connections, create visions, synchronicities, coincidences. Sometimes they help us, sometimes they attack us. Most of them feed off our attention... But tell me, what does the sentence "keep it for a hundred years" mean to you?'

'Perhaps that we've spent our lives moving apart and then finding each other again, but that the next time we find each other it'll be too late and we'll both be dead. Or maybe that within a hundred years, when we're both dead, we'll be able to find each other in another life, and this time everything will go right and we won't ever be apart again.'

We watch the herons soaring above the valley. The clouds and the herons move in the same direction, and this detail, for some reason, makes me happy.

'It hasn't been easy for you to find me,' Cristina says.

'But I've found you.'

'We're not going to part this time,' she says, clutching my hand and bringing it to her lips. 'This time you're mine forever.'

'But what if I hadn't given you that flower...?'

'I needed a symbol,' she says. 'A sign.'

'A sign? And if the sign hadn't come?'

'The sign comes when it has to.'

'And that's how you live your life? Waiting for signs?'

'Not always. Not if I'm deciding whether to have the soup or not. But in the important moments...'

'You're mad,' I say. 'You've always been completely mad!'

'Quiet, you.'

Our mouths meet again, and they're so familiar it feels like it's only been a few hours or a few days since we kissed. I feel like no time has passed at all, that I'm the same as I ever was and she is too, and we're kissing in the garden of the house in Pozuelo, on the other side of the wall of cypresses, amidst the splendour of the mullein, daisies and flowering wild fennel in the abandoned garden. I breathe in the perfume of the honeysuckle from Madrid's spring, and I'm surrounded by big mock-orange bushes in bloom and the distant hum of the traffic on the La Coruña motorway. I recognise her tongue and the tempestuous way it enters my mouth like an uncontainable invasion, and how delicious it is to fight her warm tongue – her big, imperious, smooth, round tongue – with mine. Why are kisses so sweet? Why don't we ever tire of them? What is it about a kiss? Now she enters me and I her, and our bodies come together in their warmest, most intimate parts. But these sensations express something eternal and moving. Something mysterious, grave and profound. They are the expression of love. Her tongue slips into my mouth and I feel my soul move through hers. Why?

'But tell me,' I ask, 'who was that sadhu on the shore of the Ganges? Was it me?'

'Who knows,' she says. 'Who knows who or what you are. Who knows who or what any of us are.'

We're naked now, side by side, and looking at each other with faint smiles on our faces. A year has passed since the episode with the red and white poppy. Her elbow is propped up on the bed and her face rests in her hand. Her long dark hair is falling in line with her forearm. Her breasts are plump with blue and purplish veins running across them. Her nipples are swollen and dark brown. Her enormous belly moves towards me. It's so enormous it's almost comical. In just a few weeks our child will be born. There are no ultrasounds in this place, and we don't know if it's a boy or a girl. What we do know is that if it's a girl she'll be called Amapola, Poppy. If it's a boy, Erick, in memory of Wade. That's what we've decided. Joseph will be there at the birth. He regrets not having any anaesthetic, but births are rare at the University, and the few women who do become pregnant wouldn't want an epidural anyway; they'd opt for a natural birth, like Cristina. I think she is a little frightened. The new frightens us all. But it also amazes and rejuvenates us.

I run my mouth all over her body. I kiss her breasts and her immense, taut tummy, curved like a temple dome. I kiss the inside of her groin, her thighs, her dark pubis as warm and smooth as the most inviting corner of the warmest, happiest room of the warmest, cosiest, happiest house. Her whole body is swollen, blushing – as ripe as a plump cherry. Her lips, her cheeks, her arms, her hips. Her eyes are shining. Her hair is shining. There is something intensely red about her. Her dainty nose is also slightly rosy and swollen, as are her eyelids, as if she'd drunk a little wine. Something intensely red that gives me the most boundless delight. An adventure, the chapters of which never cease to amaze me. A gesture that never fails to move and intrigue me. A path beneath the willow trees. A love story in the middle of the world. In among the noise and dust of the world.

Andrés Ibáñez is a Spanish novelist and poet. He trained at the Conservatorio de Madrid and worked as a jazz pianist for ten years. He has lived in New York and Mexico and writes regularly about books and classical music for Spanish cultural publications. He published his first novel in 1995 and in 2014 was awarded the prestigious Premio Nacional de la Crítica for *Sea of Eden*, originally published in Spanish as *Brilla, mar del Edén*.